15/6

Blitz

It is the convention in publishing to encourage the author to reveal something of his life and background for the readers of his book, but David Fraser writes: 'My own background and life are not important. The subject of this book is, and I hope I have managed to convey something of those times as a mark of respect for those who lived through them and as a record of how it was then for later generations.'

Blitz

David Fraser

Pan Books
in association with
Macmillan London

First published 1979 by Macmillan London Ltd
This edition published 1980 by Pan Books Ltd,
Cavaye Place, London SW10 9PG
in association with Macmillan London Ltd
© Literary Holdings (Gibraltar) Ltd 1979
ISBN 0 330 26168 1
Printed and bound in Great Britain by
Hazell Watson & Viney Ltd,
Aylesbury, Bucks

Author's Note

No writer can hope to deal fictionally with a period in British life as meticulously recorded – and remembered – as the London Blitz of September 1940 without conforming to the text of history and, in that sense, this book can perhaps best be characterised as documentary-fiction.

The task of researching place, period and events was a sobering one and made possible only by the co-operation and generosity of a wide range of advisers. For written and verbal material, maps and documents, I am indebted particularly to the staff of the Public Record Office at Kew, the Chief Archivist of the Port of London Authority, the archivist-historian of the Churchill War Rooms, the Chief Librarians of the *Daily Express* and the *Daily Telegraph*, Mr George Moonie of D. C. Thomson & Co Ltd, Dundee, the assistant librarian of the London Fire Brigade, the Luftwaffe archive, the staffs of the City, Westminster and Southwark public libraries, the British Museum and the many private individuals who allowed me to record their personal memories of the events of this period.

One final word of gratitude: the idea of undertaking a novel based on the events of the Blitz was not mine. It was originated by Mrs Susan Watt, at that time the London representative of the American publishers Doubleday & Company Inc of New York. I hope I have managed to fulfil some of the hopes she nourished for it.

Blitz

SATURDAY
7 September

Two hundred feet beneath the summer-green countryside, the duty control team of R.A.F. Fighter Command brooded uneasily over a blank table map of the English Channel. From a balcony encircling the room fifteen feet above the plotting table, the Controller stared fixedly at the clock on the wall as if it held the key to an unfathomable conundrum.

The Controller's unease was discreetly veiled; in moments of tension he resorted to an excessive nonchalance that verged on sleepiness, but below him his junior officers strode about with the earnest efficiency of young men anxious to prove there was a war on. Clip-boards and message sheaves in their hands, they moved from one end of the bare map to the other, stopping by each of the W.A.A.F. girl plotters, responding to repeated shakes of the head with scowls of irritation.

Flying Officer Tom Russell leaned on the balcony rail a judicious ten yards away from his preoccupied Controller and sympathised with all of them. They had more than routine to contend with today. In an anteroom behind the control desk the brass hats were huddled around a table with Air Chief Marshal Hugh Dowding – sifting written reports, juggling strengths, arguing tactics. Their arrival had been unannounced, unscheduled, and its effect on the team was salutary. Before Dowding and his group commanders had been in session for an hour the word was all over the Filter Room : the Germans were massing their invasion barges along the French and Belgian coasts and Hitler's threatened *Seeloewe* – Operation Sealion – was primed for launching. There was no doubt left in the minds of the men and women in the Command bunker at Bentley Priory :

1

Fighter Command was to be confronted yet again with a battle against overwhelming odds. It was not prepared.

Since mid-August Hermann Goering had pitched his Luftwaffe at south-east England in a once-and-for-all bid to destroy the guardian airfields of Fighter Command. His success rate was remarkable. The Battle of Britain, as Churchill had described it, had become a battle for survival; the survival of airfield runways, aircraft, exhausted pilots. The thin blue line of Number Eleven Group had been stretched to breaking point day after endless day; no one knew better than the staff at Bentley Priory what the outcome would be if those attacks continued unabated for another two weeks; Goering would pound the stuffing out of England's first line of defence, leaving the Channel clear for the landing barges of Operation Sealion.

The foundations of unease had been laid early today, long before the arrival of the group commanders. It was mid-afternoon and still there was no sign of the now-predictable German bomber force. The map table was blank. The 'seeing eye' electronics of the Chain Home stations reported no build-up over France, no skein of fighter escorts streaming in to meet and umbrella the Luftwaffe bombers over the Thames Estuary, no diversionary feints along the French coast to draw R.A.F. fighters into open sky. Today there was only routine; the correlation of fighter strengths at sector airfields, the monitoring of bored Hurricane and Spitfire pilots crossing empty skies on uninterrupted patrol.

Today there was a blank map table and an emergency meeting of senior officers. Unease was an understatement of the cast of mind at Bentley Priory Control. Unease was a politician's emotion.

Tom Russell let his eye fall to the wooden-framed hymn-guide nailed to the wall behind the map table. It displayed a single word: Sunny. It had read that way for six weeks now but the information was academic. The first full year of war had brought with it one of the brightest, hottest summers in living memory: a bumper harvest year, a green and gold and blue year, a year for optimism, a year for scoffing at the perils of war. In the towns, men too old for call-up had heeded the

Ministry of Food's call to 'Dig for Victory' and their allotments were burgeoning with prize vegetables. In the countryside, flower gardens rioted with colour. It would never end, said the weather prophets over their thin beer in the pubs.

Russell smiled ruefully. Tell that to the Marines — or, more practically, to these human moles in the Filter Room. Some of the pale-faced girls who glanced each day at that sign on the wall could actually vouch for its accuracy; if they were lucky, their shifts occasionally ended while the sun still shone. But more often than not they were as impervious to weather conditions as they were to the passage of night and day. Time and weather were abnormalities: they had no place in a world of permanent twilight, of suppressed nervousness and riveting concentration. 'Up there' meant bed and they retreated to it mechanically, heads numbed from the whispering embrace of earphones, bodies stiff and drained by nervous fatigue and that heart-in-mouth tension peculiar to people who map the fortunes of a bloody war they never see.

The Duty Controller shifted impatiently in his chair. The twenty-four-hour clock hit fifteen fifty-six. He heard the clunk of a door and the clack of cleated heels on concrete and leaned forward again hopefully as a sergeant marched quickly to a flight lieutenant bent over one corner of the table. The officer took a yellow tearsheet, studied it for a moment and said something to the girl plotter at his side. She shifted her headphones to catch what he said, nodded and took a counter from the trough fronting the map table. She settled it on the end of her croupier's rake and shoved it into place. The Pas de Calais.

As the Controller bent to read, spectacles low on his nose, Russell looked back to the map. A second counter now sat by the first and a third was on its way to join it. The Controller jerked to his feet and leaned out over the balcony rail. He muttered something under his breath and looked at the clock again. Three more counters skated across the table under the push of the plotter's rake and came to rest on the crowded white space around the Pas de Calais.

The Controller hooked a finger at Russell but his telephone rang and he snatched it up as the flying officer came to his side.

3

The initial ten bombers plotted on the table had grown to seventy when he replaced the instrument. Another chip was added as Group Sector Headquarters were placed on standby.

The Controller turned at last to Russell.

'The old man'll have to know about this, Tom. Tell him. . . .'

Tom Russell knew the guard on the door but he was not permitted to escape the formal process of identification. He showed his card, got a nod of acceptance, and knocked once. From inside came a curt, 'Come.'

The men hunched along two sides of the long table had the red-rimmed eyes of late-night poker players. All of them were formally dressed, not a button undone to relieve their sedentary discomfort and compensate for the lack of air in the hot, confined space; but then, Dowding himself was as stiffly proper as he always was and no inferior would have dared challenge his obdurate sense of military correctness. Many of the senior officers had flown to the Priory under their own hand, exercising a rare privilege these days to squeeze into a Spitfire cockpit and do what they had been trained to do. Air Vice Marshal Keith Park, the Number Eleven Group chief, was one of them. He seemed relieved that someone had, if only temporarily, broken up the discussion.

Dowding's saturnine face angled up at Russell.

'The Controller apologises for disturbing you, sir.' Russell took in the rest of them in a single courtesy: 'Gentlemen. He thinks you should be made aware of some developments in the last few minutes.' He paused. 'We're getting a very big build-up over the Pas de Calais, sir.'

Dowding looked around the table. 'Well?'

Chairs scraped back and Tom Russell held open the door as they filed out, rippling their hands over crumpled uniforms, stretching aching backs. He followed them out to the balcony and stood discreetly in the rear as they ringed it, gazing down at the table like Regency bucks at a cockfight. The Duty Controller did not acknowledge them; his eyes were locked on the map and he was speaking quietly into the microphone in front of him.

Park was the first to break the silence. 'They should be break-
ng up,' he said to the Controller. 'Has anything been sent?'

'Squadrons are up to meet them, sir. The usual strength. I
uestioned the wisdom of sending more until—'

'Yes, yes,' said Dowding. He looked across at Park as if ex-
ecting a comment, but got none.

The opposing R.A.F. counters spilled across the table to greet
he massive force, now numbering well over 400 aircraft. An
fficer at Dowding's shoulder, hoping to make a name for him-
elf, barked over the balcony to a grim-faced young flight lieu-
enant holding a clip-board, 'Have you checked this?'

The man looked up at him with the briefest flicker of distaste.
ir? Yes, sir. There's no mistake.'

Dowding bent over the Controller. 'Caution. I don't want
ver-reaction. See how it develops and play it accordingly.
o ... I shall be here, anyway.'

He looked down at the map table. Park was right; the Luft-
affe should be splitting up in the face of the approaching
.A.F. Hurricanes. They should be. But they weren't.

aturday, 1600

he fat man slapped his stomach with gourmet satisfaction and
eamed with pleasure. The thin mist had begun to shred over the
istant cliffs and they lay now like a white ribbon strung along
he far edge of the sea. He stared, shading his eyes, then lifted
is face to the sky, jowls trembling with unsuppressed excite-
ent. A swarm of aircraft, massed in perfect formation, curled
nd wheeled to attach themselves to the stream of aircraft
lready making for the white ribbon of cliffs.

In less than a quarter of an hour the whirling fighter escort
nd their bombers, pregnant with high explosive, would cross
he coast over Beachy Head. Twenty minutes later they would
e over London, tier upon tier of them, an armada more than a
ile high; eight hundred square miles of devastation moving
ke a locust plague upon the English capital.

Reichsmarschall Hermann Wilhelm Goering whirled buoyantly and slapped his stomach again. He was a born performer. His pale-blue and gold uniform with its glittering rows of decorations like oversize sequins was an actor's garb. He struck a pose and the photographers, who accompanied him everywhere, clicked obediently. The retinue of officers around him at the forward observation post on the cliffs of Cap Gris-Nez stood well out of range. The porcine warlord allowed his face to settle into a suitably intimidating frown; then, waving the cameramen away, he burst into laughter. From the safety of ten yards' distance his staff stamped and clapped in approval. Fists met gloved palms, peaked caps trembled on craned heads as the second wave of the armada streamed out over the sea. This time there would be no mistake. One hammer blow and . . . conquest.

The Reichsmarschall waved a hand at the departing bombers. *Der Aldertag* – the Day of the Eagles – in August had been a disaster from which he still smarted. He had lost face; there was no point in pretending it hadn't happened. But the First World War fighter pilot who had shot down twenty-two Allied planes and earned Germany's highest decoration for valour was no stranger to the tribulations of battle.

He had heard the jokes in Berlin about the spare set of rubber medals he was supposed to have had made so that he could wear them in the bath. The whispered nickname *Der Dicke* – Fatty – occasioned neither anger nor bitterness. President of the Reichstag, Reichs Master of the Hunt, Master of the Forest and overlord of the most destructive armoury the world had ever seen – he was big enough to take the envious mockery of fools.

After today, there would be no more jokes. After today, there would be no London.

Saturday, 1630

Melvyn J. Shaffer hung his coat in the wall closet and made a mental note to leave it home next time. The English weather myth, dear to every American in London, was no longer working to schedule. Flaming June in September.

He dropped his jacket on a chair on his way through to the

6

kitchen and filled the antique whistling kettle with water. He applied a match to the gas ring and for fifteen seconds nothing happened; then it combusted with a *whoof* of exploding gas. The charms of English life. He turned the low-pressure flame to its highest point and settled the kettle over it. If the gas didn't cut out it might boil in five or ten minutes. He went back to the living-room, collapsed on the overstuffed couch, feet up, and lit a cigarette.

He had been waiting for this day, this moment of this day, since he stepped off the plane from New York two weeks back. As of one hour fifteen minutes ago, London was his. Official. He was in sole command. The voice of the American Broadcasting Network Inc. from London was his voice; what happened here would exist for tens of millions in the United States only as he saw it, felt and believed it. For two weeks he had been free of apprehension. Today? God damn Vincent Hirschfield.

He glared moodily at the typewriter that squatted accusingly on the desk beneath the window. Hirschfield's typewriter – the servant of Hirschfield's conscience-stricken beliefs. Tonight he would have to sit in front of it and wring words from it. His own. At the moment he was uncertain if there was a word in his head – one primary thought – that wouldn't be influenced in some way by the man he had just put on the plane to New York.

Vincent Hirschfield, face it, had put him here. Without the old man's say-so he would still be on the home affairs desk in New York, praying for a war that was not being covered by someone with more seniority or better connections. Without Vince, come to think of it, he might still be a C.B.S. stringer waiting for the big chance in some outpost of oblivion. Hirschfield had spotted him, nursed him, pushed him when he had neither the nerve nor the muscle to push himself and, finally, persuaded the A.B.N. board in New York to accept Shaffer as his replacement in London. That called for a lot of faith. You repaid faith with loyalty. Melvyn J. Shaffer would not be meeting that payment. A.B.N. wouldn't allow him that privilege.

Hirschfield had worked London from the summit of thirty-

7

two years of unparalleled experience as a foreign correspondent. He had watched the Bore War build high, watched Hitler set the torch to Europe. Since early in 1939 his files to A.B.N. had become a series of doomsday forecasts of Hitler's intentions of world domination. He had prophesied the manipulation of Britain's naïve Prime Minister, attacked the sour diplomacy of U.S. ambassador Joseph Kennedy, ridiculed the concept that America could stay out of the German war. And he had known precisely where his principles would lead him. A.B.N. was officially anti-war. The repeated editorial motto was 'Keep America out of it.' Two weeks ago the axe had fallen. Hirschfield had been recalled by the Board. They had wrapped it up in embroidered diplomacy but everyone had known the real score.

Clarence O'Keefe, the senior editor, News, had handed it to Shaffer straight. 'They're taking him off the job. He wants you as his replacement and I said I'd go along with that. So make your choice here and now. You go in there and play it their way or I send somebody else.'

He hadn't told Vince about 'the choice'; he knew — would have guessed — anyway. In the car this morning, when Shaffer drove the old man to Croydon airport for the New York flight, they had circled each other like alleycats.

'They won't listen to you, Mel. You'll know, you'll see, you'll accept the facts — but they won't listen. That goddamn Board isn't too distant a cousin, in some ways, to our friend Adolf. No — wait a minute. Hear me out. It's a matter of momentum. The Nazis have it. They started out believing they were invincible; the heroes of a Wagnerian opera. Now they *know* they are. When a guy outstrips his own propaganda he becomes unstable. Norway fell in a day, France in a couple of weeks. What'll you give me? England in a month? Russia in two? America in three? You can't reason with a charging rhino and it can't reason with itself. Over in New York, same state of mind; different logistics. Repeat after me — "This is strictly a European war." Ignore the dissident voices, the liberal punks and the soothsayers. Isolation is the name of the game and God'll strike you down if you forget it. And ignore the facts, too. Facts are lousy and they spell trouble. Keep it stuck firmly in the front of your head: if America doesn't go to the war, the war won't come to America.'

Shaffer had remembered a pre-war quote of Chamberlain, then the British Prime Minister. 'Englishmen are trying on gas-masks because of a quarrel in a faraway country between people of whom we know little or nothing.' He didn't articulate it; Hirschfield was in no need of ammunition.

Instead, he raised Joe Kennedy's favourite accusation.

Hirschfield took it well. 'Right. We're back to politics. Who's ready to promise the voters a few hundred thousand dead American sons in election year? Sure, Roosevelt's thinking elections. That's why he's stalling over the fifty moth-eaten destroyers the Brits asked him for. F.D.R. has his own christ-crazy war, too. Kent nearly nailed him for good.'

Shaffer had known nothing of the Kent story up to his arrival in London when Hirschfield had briefed him in the strictest confidence. Hirschfield was one of the few U.S. newsmen to have breached the secrecy surrounding it but had been refused permission to file the story. It was that kind of story. Less than four months earlier, British detectives playing with diplomatic fire had broken into the technically immune London apartment of a U.S. Embassy clerk, Tyler Gatewood Kent, and discovered fifteen hundred pieces of secret correspondence between POTUS – the codeword for the President Of The United States – and 'Naval Person' – Prime Minister Winston Churchill. It was a leak of such devastating potential that the only solution to the affair was an immediate diplomatic cover-up. The clerk had admitted channelling all fifteen hundred messages to the German Embassy and, he'd added defiantly, had done it to sabotage Roosevelt's efforts to drag America into the war. Whatever his status in law, there was no doubt in Shaffer's mind that the man would have emerged as a patriot in the eyes of many Americans had the affair been disclosed.

When they had checked in at the Croydon desk, they smoked a farewell cigarette and Hirschfield tried to make it easier. 'Go back to that padded cell in Brook Street, put your feet up and

have some of that lousy English coffee, Mel. And forget what
I said, O.K.? It's heresy. You'll make out.'

'If I hold on to my sanity.'

Vince had doubled over at that. Very funny. 'You want sanity
in a bomber's war? Listen, kid. Coupla weeks ago, a German
Heinkel flew over here and dropped a few thousand leaflets
headed "Hitler's last appeal to the British people". Every last
damn one came floating down in the same place. You know
where? The grounds of a hospital for the mentally deficient.
The locals raffled 'em to help buy a Spitfire. And you want
sanity?'

The farewell had deteriorated into a wake. The loudspeaker
announcement of the New York flight just saved it from total
self-immolation. At the gate a girl in airline uniform was tugging at a white silk blouse; the material clung to her breasts and
Hirschfield had caught Shaffer's fleeting appraisal.

'Get it before they ration it,' he drawled. Famous last words.

The kettle gave out a hesitant whistle and he went into the
kitchen to make coffee. The stuff came out of a bottle and was
as English as its label. He came back to the living-room and
opened the windows to the makings of an early evening breeze.
In an hour or so the blackout would fall and the city would
die on its feet. Thank God he had no commitments for the
night—leaving aside a phone call to Rita and the kids and the
small matter of his first London broadcast. He had been trying
to discount the broadcast for the past three hours.

Hirschfield had warned him about that. Bombs will fall, he'd
said. Men will fight blazing fires, dig up unexploded bombs,
burrow into a thousand tons of precariously balanced rubble as
if they were born to it. Tragedy and blind bravery will be a
commonplace. Children will be maimed or made orphans or
both in the space of a second. Bank clerks and housewives will
be roasted alive in shelters where they sleep; grilled like hedge-
hogs in clay ovens.

'You'll write it once in the white heat of discovery and next
day it'll be there again. Same heroes, same tragedies. It goes on
repeating itself till the heroes become caricatures and the
tragedies sound like clichés.'

Then what the hell do you tell the folks back home?

They had been through that, too. You work the beat; ministry to ministry, night-club to bomb site, drawing-room to restaurant. Making trades, oiling palms, clinching connections, exacting promises: sifting the dead wood from the ripe fruit, the propaganda opinion slaves from the knowledgeable vendors of news. The government information ministries were there to be officially used, of course, but they had lips buttoned tighter than Trappist monks. The country was beside itself at the moment with the government's self-generated Fifth Column scare — every foreigner around every corner was a potential German spy — and nowhere was the phobia more evident than at the Ministry of Information (currently universally referred to by the Press Corps as the Ministry of Disinformation).

'This isn't Abyssinia, Mel,' Hirschfield had said. 'And it isn't Berlin or Paris either. This is a standstill war. No advancing frontline, no salients, no strategic withdrawals; nothing you can plot on a map. Ask what's happening and they'll hand you a line that'll make O'Keefe throw up over his tuna-on-rye back there in New York. When you run out of superlatives for burned bodies and crushed real estate, you're going to be left with only your nose to tell you what's happening. Don't worry about it — you'll take it in through the pores, provided you're around the right people at the right time.'

Thanks, Vince. You're a real comfort. All that had to be remembered was that Ed Murrow had been breaking ground for C.B.S. since the war began and he and Fred Bate of N.B.C. had London carved up between them. They also had their networks one hundred per cent behind them to report the war the way they saw it, not as a two-bit street fight that would never come to anything by American standards. All Shaffer had to do was beat them at a game they had practically invented. With an arm tied behind his back.

Rita. Call Rita first. He dialled the overseas operator. Sorry, sir, the delay on private calls to the United States was six hours. Perhaps the caller would prefer to book in advance for tomorrow — if he could wait until after 10.30 a.m. He said No thanks. He wasn't about to tie himself down that firmly on his first full day at the helm. Even for Rita. No sweat; Rita would understand. She'd understood in Rome, Berlin and Paris, and Westchester was infinitely more comforting a place to understand in. She had her mother on hand a half-mile away, the boys in school and a nice house she was intent on furnishing the way she had dreamed of for years. Ten years, to be exact. Jerry had been born in Rome, Petey in Paris and both of them had been conceived between months-long assignments in temporary beds. Rita had built her own world in her head and now she was giving it physical shape.

They had had the usual fight when he told her two weeks ago to pack their bags for London, and he couldn't blame her; but it hadn't ended as it usually did. She went through the scenario of how he was her rod and staff and she couldn't breathe without him but this time she said No. Categorically, immovably, irrevocably No. Jerry had chalked up seven months in grade school and he was shaping up well after the peripatetic agonies of digesting his education through a three-way sieve of hastily learned Italian, German and French. Petey was beginning to look and sound like any normal three-year-old. At last. And Rita? Rita had a house and a cat and a dog and a P.T.A. committee and fallen arches from running too hard for too long. She'd put down some roots and she wasn't about to dig them up for A.B.N. and the dubious privileges of the European air war. No snarling and scratching; no locked bedroom door to prove her point. A kiss and a sigh and a drive to the station to catch the morning commuter train to New York. A wave and a few tears.

He'd had it coming. Well, that was par for the course. The bright ones married their typewriters and took comfort in occasional beds wherever the action took them. He sipped the terrible coffee and made a face, only partly triggered by the taste. How much time did Rita give over to thinking about the beds her promising husband inhabited on his continuous forays for A.B.N.? Not much, he guessed. Rita had the extrovert's outlook: grab it while it's going and think about groceries when it's gone.

He slopped down some more of the evil liquid. The first time

ad been right here in London, eight years ago; two years after
erry was born. He had been switched from Rome to play
oliday relief for the C.B.S. resident; too short a time to develop
ny kind of professional reputation but too long to make do
ithout human comfort. C.B.S. refused his request to bring over
ita and Jerry, so he had looked around. He didn't have far to
ok. She was a typist in an accountant's office along the block
om the C.B.S. shingle in Hereford Street and they'd met at
hat passed in London for a lunch counter. Cockney girl; very
ungry. He'd felt guilty as hell when he got back to Rome and
ven guiltier when Rita came to meet him at the airport with
erry wrapped in a shawl. It got easier after that.

The great thing was to survive, Hirschfield said as he walked
the executioner's axe. Well, physical comfort was part of
rviving and if the marriage survived, too, in spite of it. . . .

The thin, tremulous wail of an air-raid siren sounded plain-
vely from somewhere east of the city. Probably over the
hames Estuary, he thought idly; they never got much farther
an the Kent airfields. Midway through, the wail was inter-
ipted much nearer to home by the crash of breaking glass, a
gh-pitched giggle and the click-clack of heels. More voices,
other shattering of glass and a man's voice raised in protest.
e got up and opened the door.

A crouched figure at his feet was mopping ineffectually at
spreading pool of red wine with a polka-dot handkerchief.
ne man peered up at him. 'Sorry, old chap. Here, steady with
e old feet. This stuff's lethal.' He dabbed at Shaffer's toecaps.
woman's face darted around the stairwell leading up to the
ext floor, emitted a squeak of mirth and disappeared.

'Said it was bloody ridiculous,' spat the kneeling man in
sgust. He struggled to his feet. 'For Christ's sake, Vera, get a
oth or something, instead of standing there like a bloody spare
rt!' There was no response. 'Silly cow,' he added thickly.

Shaffer fetched a cloth and mopped up the wine. The tubby
an kicked shards of broken glass into a corner of the corridor.
'Awfully good of you, old chap.' The arm was short and the
ck of the outstretched hand covered in fine black hairs. 'Fisk.
rchie Fisk.'

Shaffer shook it. 'Mel Shaffer. You having some kind of party?'

'Sort of. More like an extended hangover, know what I mean Not much else we can do, really. The wife'll be going cracker at home. Carshalton.'

Voices were still bubbling down from the floor above. Archi Fisk followed Shaffer's glance. 'Vera, Tommy Rogers' wife Know Tommy, do you?'

Shaffer shook his head doubtfully. 'Tommy . . . ?'

'Neighbour of yours. Just down the corridor. Pots of money Used to be in fish but sold out at the right time. Does bugge all now except give parties. I've got a little *pied-à-terre* jus above yours.'

'I haven't had much time to get to meet people,' said Shaffer 'You know how it is.'

'Must meet our Vera. Bit of a cracker on the side, I don' mind telling you. Not that I . . . nothing like that. Good chum Tommy. But. . . .' He leered.

'Archie!' A man's voice bellowed from above. 'You got a woman down there?' There was a shrill scream of laughter.

'I think your friends need you,' said Shaffer, unable to sup press a grin as the wavering figure in front of him blew a prolonged raspberry.

'Bloody right they do,' said Fisk. 'They'll all be over the edge of the roof, state they're in.' He wobbled unsteadily.

'What are they doing on the roof, or is that a silly question?'

Archie Fisk looked at him without comprehending, then linked thumbs and swung his arms in a diving curve 'Wrrrrmmmnnn. Wizard prang! Tallyho!' He slapped two fingers below his nose. 'Achtung Spitfeuer!' He removed the 'moustache', regained equilibrium, turned unsteadily and walked into the wall. He blinked. 'Jerry,' he said. 'Jerry.' He took Shaffer by the arm and led him to the stairs. 'You're a Yank. Could tell that. Come and see the sights.'

Shaffer allowed himself to be led up the stairs to a small cupboard-like room, from which ran a flight of wooden steps. Archie Fisk put a finger to his lips. 'Caretaker!' he hissed. 'The girls come up here for a bit of the old sunbathing when he's not here. Starkers, some of them. Doesn't know how close he is to paradise.' With Shaffer's help he made the roof.

The revellers stood in the sunshine dotted about the roof in twos and threes — eight of them in all. Fisk brushed at a stain on his lapel and managed to crush the carnation hanging for-lornly from his buttonhole. Its petals fell around his feet. 'Not my day, old boy,' he said.

Shaffer nodded at the celebrants. 'They all come up here to. . . ?'

'Watch the raids, old son. Best view for miles up here. Quite safe. Jerry never comes this way.' A look of alarm crossed his face. His eyes glinted over Shaffer's shoulder.

'Jesus,' he muttered under his breath. 'Fasten your safety belts. Dot's on the prowl.'

Shaffer turned to find the woman almost on top of him; a three-dimensional animated Beardsley print, dripping pearls and enveloped in what appeared to be a full-length toga.

'Dorothy Saundersby.' The limp wrist hung under Shaffer's nose. 'You can call me Dot.'

Shaffer gave the hand a tentative shake and she looked dis-appointed.

'Mr . . . er . . . ,' said Fisk, tapping his forehead

'Shaffer. Mel Shaffer.'

'An American!'

Dorothy Saundersby had the look of a lepidopterist chancing on some rare species of butterfly. She took a sip of her drink, looked slyly over the rim of her glass at the others, then, reassured that they were not about to steal her prize, slipped her arm through Shaffer's and hauled him to the farthest point of the roof. 'You stay with Dot,' she said protectively.

The city was bathed in late sunshine. Windows shone like mirrors, roofs glistened with bronze fire; red brick punctuated grey stone and green space, and black ribbons of tarmacadam stitched the whole into one badly made patchwork quilt. Shaffer shaded his eyes with his free hand and stared at the grid of vapour trails high above to the south-east.

'They're heading away from the city,' he said.

Dot nodded. 'Our boys meet them over the coast. They'll

stop them there.' She made no attempt to hide her disappointment.

'You're an expert,' Shaffer said.

'You get to learn things.' She held the remains of her drink to his lips. 'Don't you find that?'

'I'm a whisky man,' said Shaffer, pushing the glass aside. He tried to disengage his arm but it was locked in a tourniquet.

'And what's a nice young Yank doing in a place like this?'

Shaffer told her. She was unimpressed. 'Had a cousin who worked in the papers once,' she said. 'Spent most of his time at funerals and weddings. Funny way to earn a living.'

'I wouldn't argue with that.'

Another siren began to crank up from a long way east.

'Miles away,' said a disappointed voice from the far side of the roof. 'Gravesend, I reckon.' There was a loud debate as to the precise location of the sound.

'If that's Gravesend, I'm a Chinaman,' said a man Shaffer assumed to be the ubiquitous Vera's husband, Tommy. Behind his back Vera pulled the corners of her eyes into slits.

'Margate, I'd say,' said Archie Fisk.

'Gravesend! Couldn't be anywhere else. Look at the direction of those trails. Straight as a die.'

'Or Thameshaven,' suggested Archie, hedging his bet.

'Same thing.'

A compromise having been reached, they stood in silence. Then: 'Well, that's it then,' said Vera. She up-ended her empty glass pointedly. The dying siren was picked up by another. The group began to file from the roof; disconsolate punters at a rained-off race meeting.

Fisk ambled over to Shaffer. 'Fancy a snifter, old chap? Sun's nearly over the yard-arm. Tiffin time. I've got a bottle of that American whisky stuff downstairs.'

'Bourbon,' said Dot with a sniff of contempt.

Archie smiled icily. 'There's not much Dot doesn't know about drink,' he said. He ruined the barb by belching loudly.

'Charming,' said Dot.

Shaffer felt the grip around his arm ease minutely.

'Real kind,' he said, 'but you know how it is: I've got work to do. Got to get down to it some time.' He tried once more to extricate himself, but Dot reapplied a grip that would have done credit to a money-lender.

'Some other time, then,' said Fisk. He walked to the stairwell and clumped down it until only his head showed above the level of the roof. He sank lower and rested his nose on the rough concrete. He rolled his eyes across at them. 'Wot, no knickers?' he giggled. He began to choke, missed his footing and with a howl slid out of sight.

'Dirty devil,' said Dot. 'He gets like that when he's had too many. Take no notice.' Then, as an after-thought: 'Hope he broke something valuable.'

'I've really got to....,' began Shaffer. He had a dread that at any moment she would lean her head on his shoulder. She leaned her head on his shoulder.

'Somehow war makes things different, doesn't it...Mel? Can I call you Mel? I mean, it seems as if we've known each other for years. That's really what I mean. Any other time and, well, maybe we'd pass the time of day, but now things seem so speeded up, don't you feel that? I do. Eat, drink and be merry....' She stopped suddenly as if she had blundered into the wrong conversation. A faint shudder ran through her. 'You know what I mean.'

'Sure.' Shaffer searched for an exit. Twisting his arm awkwardly, he glanced at his watch. 'It *can't* be that time!' The emphasis was heavy. Dorothy Saundersby chose not to hear him. She had lifted her head from his shoulder and her hand released his arm. She was staring into the distance, frowning.

'Here,' she said. 'That can't be right.'

Shaffer, granted his freedom, glanced over the rooftops. The vapour trails had curved into a pincer shape, high in the sky, but that wasn't what had caught her eye. Hundreds of feet below the trails was what looked like a swarm of insects. Unlike insects, they held to a slow-moving, deliberate pattern. It was growing bigger.

He shaded his eyes with both hands and tried to count them. Impossible. From very near a siren whined hurriedly. Then another.

Dorothy Saundersby threw a glance behind her at the stairwell. 'Tommy,' she said, almost conversationally. Then louder: 'Tommy!' The steady drone, more a feeling in the air than a noise, had taken on the threatening drum of faraway thunder.

'Tommy!' No reply. She looked up once more at the growing swarm.

Shaffer touched her elbow. 'Maybe we'd better . . . ,' he began.

She pulled away, turned to the stairs and began to take the steps. The glass fell from her hand and exploded on the empty roof.

Saturday, 1640

If there was anything guaranteed to set Derek Scully's teeth on edge it was referees, but, apart from a few good-natured shouts about where they had left their white sticks and occasional references to their pedigree, the crowd never seemed to pay them much attention. People didn't seem to realise it was referees who won or lost games. Derek knew different. He made it his business to know their names, their quirks – like how much they relied on the support of the linesmen when they were in doubt – and which town they came from. The last was a crucial factor. Taking a rough calculation of the referee's home town in relation to the challenging team and West Ham, it wasn't difficult to see where his bias lay.

If Wolves came to play and the ref. came from Stoke, in Derek Scully's eyes he might just as well have worn Wolves' colours and played twelfth man. He kept a notebook listing such facts and, before any game, knew whether the ref. would cause trouble. O'Ryan was this one's name and he came from Luton. Derek wasn't exactly sure where Luton was, but he would have taken bets it was a damn sight nearer Tottenham than West Ham. On top of that O'Ryan seemed to have a gammy leg. The last Tottenham goal – their fourth to West Ham's one – followed a cut-and-dried blatant foul; anyone could see that. Except O'Ryan, who had been limping along at the far end of the field like a cripple.

'He oughta be in a bloody wheelchair,' Derek fumed venomously.

'He's got holes in his hands,' said Paul Warrender.

'Eh?'

'Our goalie. Useless. Ought to be in a wheelchair, you're right.'

'Not him, twerp. The referee. Goalie didn't stand a chance, did he, against twelve players?'

'He's not as good as he was,' said Paul Warrender defensively.

'What's *good* got to do with it? I tell you, somebody's shoved the ref. a fiver. That goal!' Derek snorted derisively. 'Cut-and-bloody-dried.'

'Tottenham aren't bad,' said Paul. Then quickly, 'I mean, for Tottenham.'

Derek Scully looked loftily around the ground.

'Your dad's Tottenham, isn't he?' he said with exaggerated lightness, as if excusing an incurable disease.

Paul Warrender tugged at the corners of his West Ham scarf like a security blanket. 'Don't make no difference to me,' he said unconvincingly.

Derek nodded, still craning his neck over the crowd.

Sometimes he worried about Paul Warrender.

The heat, scooped into the bowl of the stadium, lay still and stale, muffling the roars, stifling the electricity of the match. Derek flicked the back of the newspaper hat worn by the man standing in front of him until, by degrees, it slid over his eyes. He waited until the man re-positioned it then repeated the trick, grinning at Paul.

At the third attempt the man turned and glared at Paul. 'You being bleedin' funny, son?' Paul stared at him and pulled a face.

'Cheeky young sod!' said the man.

Derek Scully tapped him on the shoulder, intercepting the annoyance. 'In the wrong stable, mate,' he said, fingering the man's Tottenham scarf.

'Leave off,' said the man. 'It's a game, ain't it?'

Derek pursed his lips and blew a kiss, squashing the paper hat gently over the man's eyes. He watched him squeeze away through the crowd. At a respectable distance the man turned and threw back: 'Ought to be in the army. Little bastards.'

The man next to Paul muttered, 'Come to cause trouble, have you?' Paul froze. Derek tugged his arm, still smiling. 'Got a fag, Pole?' It was a nickname Paul Warrender hated. Like most nicknames, it traded on vulnerability. As a young child his father had called him 'Twig'. It had been their own shared affection. The dawning realisation over the years that it referred to his thinness came as a betrayal. For five years he had been waiting to 'fatten out' as his mother promised he would. It never happened. He saw other children 'thicken' into manhood and waited for it with a fierce hunger, the flapping arms of his jacket and the seat of his baggy shorts hanging round him like a penance for some unexplained transgression, imprisoning him in perpetual adolescence.

He fumbled in his pocket and drew out a crumpled packet of Craven A. Derek Scully took one and lit it, blowing the smoke backwards with a toss of his head. The two boys were almost exactly the same age — Derek Scully's fifteenth birthday had been two months ago — but that was the only thing they even vaguely shared, even though they had spent their lives as neighbours and gone to the same school. If either of them had been asked to explain their friendship it would, in all probability, have been answered with a shrug. You didn't question things like that, they just happened. But familiarity breeds strange bedfellows and the Scullys and the Warrenders had been one family long before the two boys were born.

Nonetheless, everyone agreed, it was a strange partnership. The thick-set, swarthy young Scully who refused to wear a coat even in the middle of winter and always sported an open-necked shirt and a smile of easy-going defiance, and the frail, diffident Paul, who looked as if he needed a good meal and an injection of self-confidence.

'West Ham, WHAM, WHAM!' began Derek Scully, jerking his head at Paul, who took up the refrain: 'West Ham, WHAM, WHAM!'

'TOTTENHAM, Wham, Wham!' roared the man at Paul's shoulder. Someone alongside him, sensing a new sport, joined in.

Derek glared at them both. He raised his voice : 'West Ham!
WHAM! WHAM! TOTTENHAM!'

A small group near the rails took it up : 'WHAM, WHAM!'
The crowd began to split into confused chants : 'WHAM HAM,
TottenWham!' The local supporters waved their scarfs, obscur-
ing the view of those behind.

'WE WON FOUR ONE!' yelled the Tottenham contingent
from behind. The burly man next to Paul waved a hand in the
air synchronising their challenge.

Derek Scully looked round with black hatred. The initiative
was slipping from his hands.

'WHAM, WHAM!' bellowed the man, waving two fingers of
contemptuous dismissal. The gesture, as he had anticipated, was
returned. He elbowed Paul out of the way and reached across
for Derek's shirt-front, gripping it in docker's hands. Derek
stared at him wildly, gasping for breath as his collar began to
tighten on his neck.

'Give over,' he croaked hoarsely.

Someone began to laugh and the crowd, regardless of rivalry,
watched with amused indifference as, spluttering, Derek was
hoisted on tiptoe, his face burning.

'Totten-Ham,' said Scully's tormentor as if teaching the alpha-
bet. At his elbow Paul shivered with impotence. There was
nothing he could do. Derek's eyes raked him with silent accusation. Paul shook his head. What *could* he do?

Warming to the crowd's attention, the man began to drag
Derek towards him. There was a sudden clatter of coins.

'You've dropped something,' Paul burst out, a hand on the
bulging shoulder.

'Eh?'

More coins clattered at his feet. His grip eased and he looked
down at the coins rolling between the forest of legs. He dropped
his grip and shoved at the spectators round him. He went down
on one knee and began to grope for the money.

Breathing heavily, Paul dropped the last of his coins and
wormed his way through the crowd to safety. Derek joined
him.

'Bastard!' said Scully, tugging at his torn shirt. 'Bloody

bastard!' Then, glaring at Paul Warrender: 'Fat lot of bloody use you were, standing there!'

Paul began to explain. Before he had got two words out the ground was howled into silence. The referee had a hand in the air and the players trickled to a halt staring for guidance. One of them tapped the ball out of play and a linesman, picking it up, ran on to the field.

'Just what we needed!' said Scully. 'Just what we bloody needed!'

The siren built to a howl and then began to fade. The crowd remained silent, unsure. On the far terrace a tentative surge towards the exits was checked with ragged jeers.

'Watch him,' said Derek Scully. His self-assurance had returned. He nodded to himself. 'There, what did I tell you!'

The referee had called on the linesmen and one of them ran to the players' entrance. He waved his flag from the line. The referee beckoned the players from the field.

'They've called it off!' cried Paul.

'Of course they've bloody-well called it off!' said Derek.

'Doesn't that mean a draw? It's fair squares if a warning goes. Must be,' said Paul.

Derek was silent. The thought hadn't occurred to him. Maybe it was a draw. Even so, he'd paid his money, hadn't he? Paid it for a full game and they were getting half of one. What kind of fair was that? Parts of the crowd began to boo. Derek joined in, then winced, clutching his throat.

'Sod it!' he said. He looked across at Paul, pushed tight against his shoulder, and spoke from the corner of his mouth. 'Fancy the docks?' Then, as an afterthought, answering his own question: 'Naaah!'

'Docks?'

Derek raised his eyes in despair and flapped a hand to silence him. 'Forget it.'

The ground began to empty and they found themselves drawn along in the press towards the exit. Suddenly Derek stopped. 'Hang about. Look over there.' Paul looked but could see nothing over the sea of bobbing heads.

'There! It's him.'

'Who? Somebody we know?'

'Could say that,' growled Derek. He forged through the crowd, ignoring the curses. They were less than five feet away, distanced by the crush, when Paul saw the man; the burly docker stood half a head over the rest, his flat hat cutting through the press of bodies.

'It's him,' said Derek, breathing heavily.

'Come on!' said Paul. 'Leave it!' He had seen what happened when strange, unreasoning rages gripped his friend and it always meant trouble.

Another siren began to sound, even closer this time, and he lost Scully's reply. Derek had a grip on his arm and he was propelled forward until they fetched up immediately behind the immense figure of the man who had humiliated Derek.

'Ready?' said Derek. With a lurch, he barged through the crowd and, leaping high, grasped the man's scarf. He jerked down on it with all his strength and the man wavered like a wrestler caught off balance. He collapsed headlong into the crowd.

'Come on!' yelled Derek.

Paul stumbled over the spread-eagled figure and raced for the exit. When they met up outside the ground both of them were laughing.

Behind, in the mêlée, the hapless giant swore and raged as he tried to regain his feet.

'So perish all enemies!' shouted Paul. They sprinted away from the ground and Derek waved his scarf triumphantly: 'West Ham. WHAM, WHAM!'

They came to rest in an alleyway. Derek leaned against the wall and let his shoulders sag, catching his breath.

'The docks!' he panted. Then, as if taking Paul reluctantly into his confidence: 'No All Clear.' He winked. 'Not that that means anything. Half an hour, everyone'll be running home, down the shelters, leaving work.'

Paul stared at him, still not seeing the point.

'The docks,' said Derek Scully. 'They all clear out, right?'

'If it's a real raid,' agreed Paul.

'So, it's a real one. The docks are empty.' Derek's eyes sparkled. 'Tea, sugar, coffee. Right?'

Paul shrugged.

'Look, do you want to go home or what?'

'Tea, sugar, coffee ... what you talking...?' It dawned on Paul at last and sent a chill shiver of excitement down his spine. Derek read the sign before it had time to run its course.

'Right. Now, do you want to go home?'

'No,' said Paul, 'course not.'

Derek punched his arm.

'Come on then!'

They ran off down the alley towards the docks.

Saturday, 1645

Jack Warrender was working late. The day shift at the docks had signed off and had either gone home for a quick meal or straight to the pub. Day shift and night shift had become indistinguishable with increasing overtime. Work went on by floodlight, sometimes even flashlight. Men passing the dock gates after a twelve-hour shift didn't know whether to say 'Good morning' or 'Good night' to their incoming mates. It was all the same. The Surrey Commercial Docks had become the nearest thing to perpetual motion.

For Jack Warrender it had meant not twice as much work but ten times. His normal job of invoicing deliveries and despatches for Quebec Dock had, with the departure of younger men into the armed forces, expanded to include personnel filing, wages monitoring and, if the occasion demanded, compensation payments to the wives whose menfolk never went home again after their twelve hours. Apart from the last he enjoyed the extra work. His day was filled to the brim and there was no time for reflection. It also meant he had more chance to get out, down on the dockside among the men.

Most of the office blokes — white collars — avoided that; wolf whistles and catcalls followed them along the quays until the starch in their cuffs weighed on them like shackles. Jack Warrender had passed through that particular stage himself ten years and more ago. He'd never tried, like some of the others, to make an effort and drink at the same pubs; the barrier between ink and oil would never be overcome that way. He had seen too many make fools of themselves by trying to patronise the dockers who could slice pretentiousness into strips so fine it fell apart at the touch.

Jack Warrender had walked the docks for years; he knew the men and they knew him. Not as an equal — no white collar was ever quite that — but as a respected emissary from an effete and sheltered world who had at least made the effort.

Over centuries, the traditions of the waterfront had melded dockers into a tight, closed community. Men who lived and worked among bales of copra and jute, Canadian timber, Indian tea and Brazilian coffee that flooded in daily to the biggest port in the world were a race apart, even from the East Enders who worked more conventionally on the other side of Mile End Road. Like the steelworkers of Sheffield or the miners of Durham, they saw themselves as an élite workforce, and, like any community fostered within a community, it bred, along with fierce pride, a volatile sensitivity to anything that infringed it.

Jack Warrender had seen what happened when that innate dignity — arrogance was a more common word — was abused. Strikes, lockouts, appalling hardship; eventual capitulation and simmering hatreds.

It was hard for even the toughest of men to face an unheated home and hollow-eyed children in the middle of winter, particularly when he couldn't find money for the price of a pint that might have strengthened his resolve. Not that it was that bad anymore. There was more than enough work to go round nowadays, but the dockers were keenly aware that, no matter how they chose to see themselves, in the eyes of their employers they were 'casuals' who not very long ago had been singled out like slaves for a day's work, knowing that it might be their last for a week.

In a way, Jack thought, the war was the best thing that could have happened to them, not only because of the work but because three months ago the government had ordered the registration of *all* dock labour. Overnight the evil of the casual with its attendant insecurity had gone. The dockers had at last been welcomed into the fold — if only in a spirit of national emergency. There was talk in the air, too, of negotiations for a guaranteed minimum wage; the ultimate security. Nobody quite believed that it would ever happen, of course, but it was a mark of the strength of the dockers' belief in their worth that it had finally taken root in the heads of the bureaucrats.

Jack Warrender had been responsible for labour registration at the Quebec Dock. If he had known the men before, he knew them even better now. Though only a servant of the Act, he had in the men's minds come to represent a beginning and an end. In short, Jack Warrender was liked. In turn, his work had become his life. Maybe it wasn't much; endless yellow forms, filing cabinets, index cards tabulating the men, index cards tabulating their hours, cross-indexing to their wages. Yet through those cards, which he had grown to treasure, he knew every man in the dock. Stored in cabinets around him in the tiny, airless room in which he worked they became his own security. Fixed and stable, his life ran on routine; it was something his father had worked all his life for, knowing it was a dream. He had died still dreaming; a poor man, his last years spent as a hired hand on a totter's cart.

Jack had been thinking about his father. It was one of those thoughts that nag at the back of the mind all day, refusing to go away, like a name caught on the tip of the tongue. He had submerged himself in the problem of Jacey Turner and, for an hour, the work had sublimated the thought. Jacey Turner was a docker — or, at least, that was how he liked to describe himself. The problem was: *was* Jacey Turner a docker or wasn't he? True, he worked at the docks, had his card. Even truer, he was playing, and had played, a noisy part in the militant movement that had begun to swell as the government began to recognise the muscle of the union movement. The man had an innate sense of knowing when he was pushing at an open door; and the war had opened the door wide. If the docks stopped, the country stopped; even the government had realised that. It wasn't only the Luftwaffe who could do that.

But, according to Jack's file, Jacey Turner had done less than thirty-five days' solid work in the docks. Real work. Back-bending work. He'd bent his tongue often enough, but that was a different matter. Illness was Jacey's trouble. But not illness that kept him from his drinking down at the Crown. Then there was his wife. It was all down on the records. Hetty Turner had children at a rate that would bemuse the Irish. Three times, according to the files, Jacey had taken a fortnight off to look after the other children during his wife's confinements. Three times in a year! For some reason, Jacey Turner's problem brought thoughts of his father closer.

Then the sirens sounded.

Jack Warrender dropped the pencil on the table and rubbed his eyes. Through the small window he could see the roofs of the sheds above Quebec Dock, men moving like matchstick figures beneath them. A South African freighter lay abaft a Canadian wheat ship. Around them was a gang of lighters; worker ants clustered around the queens. On the other side of the dock he could make out the white and blue funnel of an Argentinian trader. He could read the name on its stern: *Laranaga*.

'Probably a scare,' said the boy.

Jack sharpened his pencil. 'Hope so, Charlie. Lots of work to do.'

Charlie was the dock superintendent's idea of a substitute for a secretary. There was no shortage of secretaries, but that kind of appointment was calculated carefully. A secretary automatically presumed the need for an assistant; a deputy; a whole department. Jack Warrender's position did not justify such ambitious moves. So: Charlie. Charlie the compromise. A young lad, fresh out of school, whose father worked over at Millwall and, presumably, swung enough disturbance weight to win his son a white-collar job. Not that Jack really minded. Charlie was a fair-minded lad. One of the few. He made no grumble about fetching and carrying and had an almost embarrassing loyalty. He had as much understanding of Jack's

27

filing system as he would of a Chinese newspaper, and his knowledge of figures seemed to peter out once he had reached the thumb of his right hand, but he was willing. Willing.

'Call it a day, Charlie,' said Jack.

'Not if you're going to stay, Mr Warrender.'

'You know I *always* stay, Charlie. Things to work out.'

'Can't I give you a hand? Got nothing to do at 'ome.'

The sirens wailed again downriver.

'Off you go, son,' said Jack sternly.

'Sounds like they're going, Mr Warrender.'

'That was the preliminary, son; not the All Clear.' Jack patted him on the arm. 'Off you go.'

The sheet of yellow paper in front of him blurred as the boy blocked the light from the window. Jack had calculated he could work until at least seven by daylight, thus saving electricity.

'You're in the light, Charlie.'

The boy shuffled the pencils on Jack's desk. 'Sorry, Mr Warrender. I've seen to the files.'

Jack nodded his thanks.

'Right then,' said Charlie. 'See you tomorrow. Or down the shelters.' He walked to the metal catwalk that led down to the warehouse, paused and looked back. 'Can you see, Mr Warrender? Turn them on, eh?' He flicked on the lights. 'Bad for your eyes.'

'Ta, Charlie. Goodnight.'

''Night, Mr Warrender.'

'Jack.'

'Sorry, Mr Warrender?' the boy was puzzled.

'Jack. Call me Jack, eh Charlie?'

'Oh. Yes, Mr Warrender. Jack.' The boy grinned hugely. 'Jack. Yes. Right, Mr Warrender.' He thumped away happily down the steps.

Jack Warrender switched the lights off again and settled in front of his desk. The docks were emptying. The sirens had picked up from Silvertown across the river. Jack bent over a yellow card. The name on it was Dennis Williams. He tried to concentrate.

The overtime hadn't been added to the week's list. The pay

ffice had blundered again. How often had he had to complain
o them? He rubbed out the total and wrote in his own figure.
No, there was more; it wasn't just the overtime. In the distance
here was a low rumble. It had been too good to last. He only
needed a few minutes. The buggers were determined to spoil it!

He juggled at high speed with the Williams's livelihood,
ound the error, corrected it and initialled it with a flourish.

He bit on a sandwich, stored since dinner-time in his desk,
nd gave a shudder. The thin smear of scrambled egg was garn-
shed with carrot. 'Good for the eyes,' Elsie always said.

'Don't like carrots,' he always replied.

'No. But your *eyes* like carrots,' she always retorted.

He smiled and swallowed. It wasn't *that* bad. Better than
am. And there was real butter. He settled into his chair and
ocked back on its legs.

Flowers. That was what he was trying to think about.
lowers. For his father's grave. It had been over three weeks
ow and with this weather the old ones would be yellow.
omorrow, he would. . . .

He crunched the carrot and egg happily. Tomorrow was
unday. A day off. He would go to. . . .

Along the river a plume of smoke blew from a factory
himney. High that. Too high!

A burst of flame leapt over Deptford.

He bent back over the yellow form, trying to concentrate.
Vhy didn't they let him get on with the job?

aturday, 1645

haffer stayed on the roof long enough to confirm Dorothy
aundersby's worst fears. The stormcloud of bombers unrolled
cross the clear, bright sky as though trying to blot out the sun,
ave on wave of them stacked in varying altitude formations.
here was something odd about their muffled boom as they
pproached; a gnawing, broken sound not unlike the unco-
rdinated marching feet of a vast army breaking step. Vince
irschfield had mentioned it; the Luftwaffe desynchronised

their engines, changed pitch to confuse the English sound-locators.

The immensity of the spectacle rooted him to the spot. It *was* a spectacle, the supreme air circus homing in on the field to astound the craning rubbernecks below, sneering at earth-bound impotence, flaunting power that gave man dominance over Nature. The first wave settled in a perfect arrowhead and hugged the serpentine bends of the Thames to the unmistakable loop at Greenwich and the Isle of Dogs. The pilots counted the bridges, Hirschfield said, all the way to the heartland; step by step down the throat of England.

The first wave sprinkled a rain of grey flecks and wheeled northwards and the first smoke towers rose behind them. Then came the sound, a distant clatter of kettledrums, muted by the city's roar. The second wave was already making its approach, guided to its target, if guidance were needed, by the mushrooming black smoke. This time the explosions were louder; interlocked rumbles of manmade thunder. Shaffer came down to earth with a start.

The elevator had stopped working; he took the service stairs three at a time and sprinted to the lock-up behind the block. He revved the old Morris hard, peeled rubber from its tyres as he reversed into the yard and jolted into Brook Street. Without thinking he pulled hard right past Claridges and cursed when he saw the build-up of cars, buses and cabs around Grosvenor Square. He wrenched the wheel right again and roared up to Oxford Street. Right again. Had to be. He screeched over the cobbles of Oxford Circus and swept right into Regent Street. Just ahead of him the traffic stood nose-to-tail all the way to Piccadilly Circus. Regent Street was in chaos.

Flooding north along the wide pavements, threading impatiently through the stationary traffic, moved hundreds of civilians — mostly women towing children, carrying babes-in-arms. As Shaffer brought the Morris to a standstill beside the impressive corner site of Dickens & Jones's department store he was able to see where the ragged army was heading. A line-up seven or eight deep curled across the front of the store and around the corner, all of them laden like Tibetan porters with carrier bags, baskets, satchels, rucksacks and string-tied paper parcels. A taxi squeezed between the Morris and the kerb.

The cabbie switched off his engine and winked across at him. 'That's your lot, guv,' he said with a resigned shrug.

'What's the goddamn hold-up?' Shaffer seethed.

The cabbie hooked a thumb at the line-up. 'Whatsa time?'

'Four fifty-five. Why?'

'Early. Gets earlier every day. They're queueing up for the shelters under the store, see. Down in the basements. S'posed to be the safest in London, they say. People come from all over to get a place. Look at 'em! Stop the traffic every time. Ask me, there'll be a bloody riot here soon. They was fighting with the law coupla nights ago. Buggers, they are.'

The burbling of idling engines now blotted out the rippling boom of distant explosions but the smoke towers were visible above the rooftops. Late afternoon shoppers hurried by, seemingly unmoved by the momentous assault being made on their city only a few miles away.

'What were they fighting about?'

The cabbie aimed a thumb again at the waiting shelterers. 'Only the first seven hundred gets in, don't they? That's where your trouble starts. Quart into a pint pot, mate. The rest gets sent home and – well, they turn nasty, don't they?'

The man settled his flat cap squarely on his head. 'Dead loss this, guv. Which way you going?'

'Across the river. East End.'

The cabbie eyed the drifting smoke clouds to the south-east. 'Your bleeding funeral. Come on then. Follow me.'

He reversed three feet, bringing the boot of the cab within an inch of a snorting double-decker bus behind. The bus hooted loudly and the driver stuck his head out the window.

'Hey, you, cabbie,' he snarled. ''Aven't you got a bleeding horn?'

The cabbie leaned round and grinned horribly. 'What? Looking at you?'

He bumped his cab on to the pavement and Shaffer backed up to follow, spinning the wheel back and forth to lever the Morris through the impossible gap. He glued the car to the cab's rear bumper and they bumped diagonally across the pavement corner into a side-street. The cabbie waved and accelerated away through the streaming crowds hastening towards the end of the line forty yards along the street. Before Shaffer could follow suit, a mounted policeman spurred his black mare across the traffic lane and signalled him to halt.

He smashed his hands on the wheel-rim in frustration. If the fire tenders had the same problems the whole damn town could burn down in half an hour.

He switched off and lit a cigarette to settle his nerves. The queue — the English, said Hirschfield, had invented the queue — was lengthening by the minute. From behind him came a shriek and he turned to watch an old woman shuffling round the corner. She was small and fat and was chewing agitatedly on the dead butt of a cigar. She wore a pinafore stabbed with holes and a white mongrel skidded reluctantly at her heels, dragged along by a piece of string tied round her waist. She was screeching at nobody in particular, occasionally turning back to bellow insults at an unseen enemy. The mounted policeman trotted forward to the end of the line and began to bring to it some semblance of order.

The old woman stopped at the corner and regarded the waiting shelterers.

'Bleedin' liberty,' she shouted. A few faces turned to look at her, averting their faces quickly in fine English embarrassment when they met her accusing eye. 'Cissy Higgins,' she expanded. 'Turned away!'

From the expressions on the faces of her audience, the fact that Cissy Higgins had been turned away registered as a positive act of public benefaction, but, like the warm-up comedian who knows that the first sixty seconds of patter hold the balance of victory or defeat, she pressed on.

'You lot don't stand a cat-in-hell's,' she yelled. 'The rozzers blocked off the place hours ago. They're turning everyone away.'

The mounted policeman clattered up on his black charger and leaned down to her.

The woman reacted as if she had been stung. She cupped her hands to her mouth.

'Telling me to shut up, he is!' she bawled. 'Trying to keep me quiet. You've all 'ad it!'

From very near a siren's wail cleaved the air and the crowd involuntarily moved closer to the protective wall. One or two of them were looking decidedly apprehensive. The policeman was the first to recognise it.

'Everyone gets a chance,' he said quickly, raising his voice. 'Keep an orderly file, please.'

'She says they're blocking the street,' a man objected loudly. 'Come a bloody long way.'

'He's right! Bleedin' carve-up,' screeched the harridan.

'Will you shut up!' roared the policeman.

'Got our rights! Got our rights!' chanted the old woman, sensing her moment had come. A group of small children had begun to cry and the wailing had a marked effect on the crowd.

The policeman, thought Shaffer, was a natural psychologist. He saw his dilemma, came up with a solution and put it into action in a matter of seconds. A slight touch of the spurs and the black horse arched its gleaming neck and nudged the old woman in the small of the back.

"Ere—what you doing? 'Ere. . . .' She turned for support to the crowd. 'You all saw that. He set that bleedin' horse on me deliberate. He—'

Nudge. She bounded forward with a squeak, turned to repel the attack and the animal's nose butted her gently on one shoulder. Butt, butt. Butt, butt. The mongrel made off, came to the end of its tether and pulled her off balance. She turned to swear at it and the horse advanced again. Nudge, nudge.

The crowd's apprehension turned to amusement. Titters at first, then open guffaws. The mood changed again; there were cheers as Cissy Higgins began to run, the dog yelping and whining at her feet.

'Bloody little Hitlers!' she hurled at Shaffer as she hobbled past the Morris in full flight. 'I'll have my bloody M.P. on him, you wait!'

The policeman reined in beside Shaffer's open window and

lifted his cap one-handed to scratch his hair. 'The things we have to do,' he growled. 'Pantomime and point duty.' He settled the cap on his head and eyed the long stream of cars behind the Morris. 'O.K., sir. Let you go, now. Sorry about the hold up.' He waved him on.

In Tottenham Court Road Shaffer pulled in behind an ambulance, bell ringing wildly, and clung to its tail, jumping traffic lights, forging an insistent path through Holborn and Cheapside to London Bridge. It led him into Tooley Street and headed east.

Saturday, 1700

'Jack?' Bernie Plomer called up the stairs. 'You there, Jack?'

Bernie worked in the dock office and had formed the first contingent of Air Raid Precautions wardens specifically for Lavender Dock. Nobody had taken much notice. Bernie was always organising something; if it wasn't the darts team it was a raffle. But, gradually, he had bullied and bored enough men to form a sizeable unit. They drilled every Tuesday and Friday night; two hours of stirrup-pumping, Dealing with an Incendiary Bomb, Strapping a Broken Leg, and then off to the pub to discuss The Defence of the Realm.

For the past year Jack Warrender had fought off Bernie's attempts to get him to join the Mild and Bitter Brigade. He'd had enough of that kind of thing in a war Bernie couldn't even remember. Besides, there was too much work to be done to play soldiers.

'I'm all right, Bernie,' he called down the open-frame iron stairs. 'Be finished in half an hour.'

Bernie's feet clattered up the stairs. He was wearing his black helmet and struggling with his haversack. 'Forget the half hour, Jack. The buggers are coming upriver, right at us. Just got a call.' Under stress, Bernie had the habit of talking in a form of military shorthand.

'Be with you in a minute!' protested Jack. He had lost a piece of paper to which ten minutes of calculation had been committed.

'Five. No more. Give you five. No, three.' The voice echoed back as Bernie clattered downstairs again. 'Three, hear me?'

'Who couldn't?' muttered Jack.

He had found the missing sheet of paper beneath his sandwich wrapping. It was damp and the figures had begun to run. He cursed softly and began to translate them on to a fresh piece of paper.

There was a familiar rush of pressured air and he craned forward to look out. He saw nothing. That puzzled him. There didn't seem to be much air to breathe all of a sudden. His head felt dizzy. A red blur filled the corners of his eyes and they ached badly. Been overdoing it, he was thinking when he heard Bernie Plomer's voice raised. It sounded a long way away. He stared at the paper with the calculations on it; a single ragged line of ink scratched across it from corner to corner.

He wasn't conscious that his hand had moved. He was still staring at it when his body gave up the struggle and fell sprawling.

Saturday, 1715

Ex-Marine sergeant Arthur Scully rapped on the last of the three watertight steel doors at Windy Corner; two long, three short.

'Password!' snapped a muted voice on the far side.

'Juno!' Arthur snapped back, sharp as the creases in his darkblue uniform trousers.

The door swung back and the Marine guard lowered his .303 Enfield. 'Wotcher, Arthur.'

He held back the heavy door, cannibalised from an old First World War Dreadnought, and Arthur's crew of four Marines hefted the two-wheeled water-barrel over the raised sill and trundled it into the corridor. The guard pretended a close examination of his fellow Marines as Standing Orders dictated he should, and there was an exchange of good-natured banter.

'That's enough!' Arthur growled warningly. He had spent six years in irksome retirement before the corps recalled him to the colours as an active pensioner, but that terrible stretch of enforced idleness had in no way blunted his appetite for good order and military discipline. The way things stood, these youngsters were more 'soldier' than he was, but like most civvies-in-uniform they hadn't got it into their heads yet that their souls belonged to the nation.

The corridor echoed with noise. Down below, in the rabbit's warren of damp passages running under Horse Guards and St James's Park, teams of men were pouring concrete and hammering supports into place to reinforce the foundations. Like everything else at the Annexe, it was an exercise shrouded in the utmost secrecy.

It had been that way since Sir Maurice Hankey, then Secretary to the Cabinet, received the order in March 1936 to find a secure place in which the Cabinet could meet in time of war. Hankey, an ex-Marine, had given the job to Leslie Hollis, a serving Marine officer who finally settled on a strongly built grey stone block of government offices on the corner of Horse Guards and Great George Street. Its virtue was that it gave access three floors below ground level to a weblike maze of accommodation, once the wine cellars of late-Victorian houses.

In October 1937 Hollis instructed an elderly Civil Service messenger, George Rance, to move into the building, the Annexe, and begin the near-impossible task of furnishing and equipping it for wartime occupation without allowing anyone in the services, the government or the ministries to even guess at what he was doing. Old George was now a day or two short of his sixty-sixth birthday but he had been a perfect choice for the job. He was not a friendly man; he had no close relationships and was studiously avoided by fellow workers who had run foul of his temper. George had 'acquired' mountains of material: concrete and timber, £18 for a job lot, to shore up the foundations; hundreds of desks and tables and chairs, beds and blankets, crockery, portable lavatories, stationery, even watertight ships' doors. It had been a classic exercise in fraudulent conversion. George never presented himself in person; he merely wrote requisitions and passed them through channels. But, as an old hand at the Civil Service game, he knew precisely how far he could go in requesting supplies without exciting uriosity. His 'indents' were always modest but, once they had ·een signed by an unsuspecting department head, he carefully dded to them his real requirements. No one ever checked back.

In late 1937 the Cabinet had come down to try out the make-hift War Room – long trestle tables formed up in a square to eat twenty-five ministers and service chiefs – and in 1938 it ame into official, though infrequent, use. The Prime Minister, Neville Chamberlain, never liked the place and was late for the only three meetings held there when he was in office. He was not well and the War Room was very stuffy. On the other and, he found the corridors outside intensely draughty; they vere supplied with treated air through huge ducts from the Admiralty and it emerged like an express train from a tunnel. Windy Corner had earned its name because it stood at a meet-ng point of three badly angled outflows of cold air.

Chamberlain made his wireless broadcast announcing war vith Germany from the Annexe, sitting before the microphone gainst the backdrop of an old army blanket. It was to be his ast visit. When Winston Churchill became Prime Minister in May 1940 the Annexe really came into its own. It now boasted 80 rooms and a staff of 300 men and women. There would be nore. Recently, there had been an acceleration of activity to trengthen the 'bombshield' and down below, in those four-feet-ix high passageways, tram-lines removed from the tarmacadam ·f Whitehall only weeks earlier were being neatly sliced into andy lengths and immured in concrete as pit props.

Next week, according to the gossip, the complex had to be eady for Winston's full-time use, although he'd made it known hat he was damned if he'd be turned out of Number Ten after ne'd spent forty years of politicking to get there. Still, he'd been lown once or twice to look round and so had Mrs Churchill. His bedroom was Room 65a/b and Clementine's 65b/b, but the ood lady had already decided it might be wiser to look for a ·edroom a little farther away from her husband's centre of ·perations. Winston, it seemed, planned to hold his War Cabinet meetings between midnight and three in the morning. He maintained an almost Continental working day: up at 8.30, ·reakfast in bed and then maybe two or three hours between

37

the sheets reading Cabinet papers. Out of bed and dressed by eleven, down to business in his office at Number 10 or at Chequers, where he liked to spend his weekends, then a long lunch and, at three o'clock sharp, he'd get his head down again for a three-hour sleep. At six he'd be wakened and his real day would begin. They said he often went on to three in the morning, calling his advisers to him, sometimes from their beds, at all hours. Mrs Churchill had spotted a half way reasonable little room behind the kitchens outside Windy Corner and it seemed likely she would take it over.

Arthur's squad began the evening water duty. The Annexe — or Rance's House as it was known to the initiated — was still a primitive place; it had no piped water supply of its own. Every drop had to be carried in by hand and waste was pumped into the Thames manually. Arthur Scully had won the right to furnish fresh-water supplies in the V.I.P. rooms and offices on the War Room floor and he guarded the privilege jealously. Penetration to this level was granted only to the guard, essential staff, the War Cabinet and a handful of generals, admirals and air marshals. Of the 300 human moles crammed into the draughty miles of Annexe corridors, fewer than twenty ever set foot over the threshold at Windy Corner, the main sentry post.

He brought the men to a halt by the archway leading to the Churchill rooms. Just beyond it old George Rance had stuck a piece of cardboard on the yellow brick wall. On it, scrawled in his own spidery hand, was The Message. It came from an address by Queen Victoria to the House of Lords in 1900, but George had seen it on a war poster and copied it out. It read:

'Please understand there is no depression in *this* House and we are not interested in the possibilities of defeat. They do not exist.'

'Right you are then,' Arthur growled at his men. 'Let's see you in a line. Backs to the wall. Smartly now.' He stood in front of them. 'Squad. Squad — 'shun! Stand at ... ease!'

He preferred them to be out of the way when he dealt with Winston's water can. He always handled it himself. He knew they made Smart Alec remarks about his 'boot-licking' behind his back but he didn't care. There were some things a senior N.C.O. had to be partial about. He drew himself to attention at the door of 65a/b, adjusted his red duty sash and settled his cap squarely. He knocked. He was about to turn the handle when the door opened. He breathed in sharply, hands at his sides in preparation for the salute.

It wasn't necessary.

'Hallo, Arthur. Laying in the old water, are we?'

Frank Sawyers, Winston's butler, stepped to one side to allow Arthur entrance. The Prime Minister's private quarters were tiny; a three-quarter bed, made up with grey army blankets, ran to the centre of the room immediately in front of the door. At the foot of the bed was a small table on which stood the hallowed water-can, a jug and two glasses and the humidor for his cigars. Facing the bed from the far wall was Winston's desk and above it was suspended a B.B.C. microphone and a little sign that lit up: 'Silence. On the air.' Winston made all his broadcasts from down here now and rehearsed them here, too, while Mrs Churchill and Michel Saint-Denis, the B.B.C. producer in charge of overseas broadcasting, sat and listened. His portable washbasin and loo stood in a corner. It was no fit place for the nation's leader, Arthur reflected, but it was a credit to the old man that he was prepared to put up with it at his age. The only thing he'd insisted on was that George Rance got a carpenter to box in the pipes over his bed; he didn't intend to have water dripping on him in his sleep.

'Sorry, Frank. Interrupting you, am I?'

'Course not. Nip in a sec.' Sawyers closed the door on the mounting curiosity of the squad along the corridor. 'Fag?' He offered an opened Woodbine packet.

Arthur shook his head. 'Thought you'd be over Chequers way, Frank.'

'Would be, normally. His Nibs had to be at Number Ten today, though. Got him off to sleep just after three. Thought I'd come down here and take a gander at the quarters.' He looked around him. 'I know old George had his work cut out getting stuff down here but, bloody hell, you'd've thought he could've done a bit better'n this for the Prime bloody Minister, wouldn't you?'

'Bit grim, all right,' returned Arthur guardedly. He was chummy with Frank but he also valued George Rance's grudging acquaintance. 'Old George did his best, you can bet your life.'

'Suppose so.'

Sawyers dragged deeply on his cigarette and a segment of ash dropped to the floor. He fell to his haunches with a snap of distress, scraped the dead tobacco from the coconut matting and slipped it into a matchbox. 'Going to be a right swine to keep clean, this place is,' he muttered.

He beckoned Arthur with a crooked finger to a point as far as possible from the door leading through to the Map Room. 'Something in the wind, old mate,' he whispered. 'You see Rance's weatherboard out there?'

'No.'

The weatherboard had started life simply enough as a guide to the state of the weather above ground. Personnel manning the War Rooms complex worked a four-day shift without a break and rarely knew what was happening in the world outside. Since the air-raids started, however, George Rance had given new meanings to the small wooden slats that fitted the weatherboard frame. Rain, Snow, Fog, Sunny now had a coded significance all their own.

'Says Windy,' said Sawyers.

Windy meant there was an air-raid on overhead.

'In daylight?' If it was true, Jerry was getting bloody cocky, flying over London at this time of day.

'Probably got it wrong.' Sawyers tapped the side of his bony nose.

'Kent again, eh? The aerodromes.'

That was more like it. They all knew what was happening to the fighter stations in Kent. Goering had started sending his bombers over on 13 August. The Battle of Britain, Winston called it in one of his speeches to the Commons, although at the time no one knew how bad it was really going to be. Even the Air Staff failed to recognise it as a decisive change of tactics because Jerry had been stepping up his attacks on ships and Channel coast towns for several weeks before. But by the end of that second week in August, by Gawd, they knew it was a battle all right. Wave after wave of Heinkels and Dorniers had raked the aerodromes of south-east England with their bombs, destroying British aircraft on the ground, pounding installations, cratering runways. The high blue skies of summer became a cockpit of weaving vapour trails and the word 'dogfight' entered the vocabulary of every child in Britain. The fighter pilots, no more than kids themselves most of them, had become the new knights of Old England, their exploits as legendary as their lives were brief. The talk was that Dowding had lost a quarter of his pilots in the first four weeks; that the survivors were at their wits' ends, poor young devils; exhausted, out-numbered, out-gunned. They were living on their nerves and the promise that tomorrow would bring more planes and more pilots to back them up; but Winston had called them The Few and he knew the worst of it. The only new pilots were un-blooded trainees and dozens of them had been blown to pieces in the air, sometimes in the first few seconds of their first dog-fights.

Sawyers drew nearer, his mouth on Arthur's ear. 'Not Kent, the way I hear it. Bigger'n that. Chiefs of Staff are meeting up-stairs. Something's up. I saw Mr Hollis just now and he said they were thinking about waking His Nibs up. Must be—'

'Not the invasion?' Arthur fidgeted impatiently.

'I dunno, do I? But if they want to wake him up it stands to reason it's pretty big. I don't know what's worse, myself — the bloody invasion or waking him up in the middle of his nap.'

Arthur's military composure buckled. 'Christ almighty, Frank — you're not saying Jerry's landed!'

'Don't ask me. I just work here. There's messages coming in from every which way. I don't think they even know for sure what's happening in *there*.' He indicated the Map Room with a thumb over his shoulder. 'Can't even find half the air force bods, they tell me. They went to some meeting or other.'

Arthur pulled himself together. 'Well. Can't stand around talking, Frank. Leave them young buggers out there much longer,

41

they'll think something funny's going on.' He took Winston's water-can and marched down the corridor to the water-barrel. The squad stiffened to the 'Eyes front' position. 'Watch it!' he snarled. He filled the can and returned with it to 65a/b, wiping the bottom of it with his clean handkerchief to make sure it left no unsightly rings on the polished wood table.

Sawyers was flicking a duster over the desk. He turned. 'If this is what I think it is, Arthur, I'd say we'll be moving in here permanent next week. Everything ready, is it?'

Arthur shook his head. 'Still working downstairs. George was telling me he'd like another month but I know he's pushing 'em hard.'

'Can't see His Nibs getting any joy out of them cooking arrangements up there.' Sawyers angled his hand disdainfully in the direction of the kitchen. 'Can't see the staff leaving Number Ten for *this*, either. You know what I can see happening? Me going up and down that bloody spiral staircase through the Number Ten annexe every time he wants a bite to eat or a decent bottle of wine. Be on my bloody knees before I'm finished, I'm telling you.'

'War, Frank, innit?' Arthur pronounced sternly.

'Well, I'll tell you this Arthur, I—'

The door from the Map Room swung open without warning and Arthur click-heeled to attention.

'Ah — Sar'nt Scully. Mr Sawyers?' The newcomer looked about him keenly. 'Is the P.M. still sleeping, do you know?'

Sawyers nodded. 'Was when I saw him last, Mr Hollis. Never comes to before six o'clock unless I wake him. Regular as clockwork.'

Brigadier Leslie Hollis, commandant of the War Room complex and its founding architect, raised his index finger to the concrete ceiling. 'Then go and wake him now, Mr Sawyers. There'll never be a better time for creating a precedent.' He swung on Arthur. 'You finished here?'

'Just the Hospitality Room to do, *sah*!'

'Then do it and get those men off this floor, sar'nt,' said Hollis. 'And on your way out, pass the word for Ives, will you?'

Arthur saluted stiffly and stalked into the corridor. He shepherded his crew down to the Hospitality Room, next door to the locked Cabinet Room, and refreshed the two water jars and the glass carafes Mrs Churchill had installed there as a gesture to high-ranking visitors of sensitivity. He hustled his crew back along the corridor to Windy Corner. The Marine guard, ramrod-stiff at his post, swung the Enfield up and across his chest.

'Password!' There was no smile on his face this time.

Outside, at the door of the Churchill's kitchen, where the tunnel swung right to the V.I.P. rooms and the staff accommodation, Arthur looked in. A trio of army chefs in white jackets and blue check ducks stiffened guiltily.

'One of you,' commanded Arthur. 'Pass the word for the P.M.'s valet, Mr Ives.' The three men relaxed when they recognised the old soldier.

Arthur dropped his voice to a low growl. 'And be bloody snappy about it, you idle so-and-sos. Don't you know there's a war on?'

Saturday, 1720

The journey from London Bridge to the Surrey Docks — discounting burst water-mains, fractured gas pipes, rubble, craters, fallen trolley-bus wires, gutted lorries and broken traffic lights — took a good car ten minutes. Thanks to the ambulance in front, which ploughed heedlessly through every hazard at a steady forty miles an hour, Shaffer reckoned he might make it in five.

Over the bridge, left along Tooley Street, past the police station, Dockhead, Jamaica Road and on to the Lower Road heading for Deptford. The dock entrance lay half way up, opposite the incongruous green space of Redriff Park.

Immediately beyond Tower Bridge, marking the limits of the Upper Pool, the warehouses and wharves ran along the river for ten miles like stained and splintered teeth. Among those black alleyways Dickens had found his darkest inspiration. Fagin held imaginary court in the top storey of a warehouse here, with his army of ragged urchins, but the reality of it had been bleaker than even Dickens could conjure; children had slept on beds of soot and a Russian named Engels had found there the perfect catalyst for his rage.

Upper Odessa Wharf, Apollinaris Wharf, Cherry Garden Pier, Talbot's Yard, Hope Sufferance Wharf, St Saviour's Flour Mill. A pinched, mean dampness had found its resting place here, long before Dickens or Engels saw light; it was born of the swamp, a reluctant landlord. But landlord it had become. Perched on stilts, the warehouse loading bays jutted into the river forming catwalks that stretched from yard to yard. Paint, wood, coal, oil and grain were siphoned from lighters into the bowels of the buildings that jostled for priority along the river bank. That was dockland's life-blood.

And, in between, houses, slipped in as afterthoughts. The newspapers called them 'cottages' as if otherwise at a loss to describe a dwelling that consisted of three tiny rooms, a communal lavatory and a water pump. Built in a week, the walls were held together by a mix of dust and water passing for concrete, no thicker than a single brick. A neighbour's bad cough could keep six families awake. An argument between husband and wife played to rapt audiences; the sudden punctuation of silence served only to make the most intimate moments more public. A child could grow to manhood here known, not from the day of his birth, but the hour of his conception.

Primitive. Squalid. A running sore. The do-gooders came to stare and left for their Acacia Avenues in their cosy suburbs, their consciences sated on moral outrage, compassion or whatever spiritual opiate they sought. Something, everyone agreed, should be done about conditions in the docks. The people who lived there agreed — something like decent sanitation, decent housing, decent roads would do for a start. As for the rest: well, if it was squalid, then the streets of Venice were squalid, but of course, *they* were also picturesque. If it was primitive, then what were the hovels of Paris and Rome that graced the picture postcards? And if it was a slur on the city of London, wasn't it also its heart? Did they want to cut out the heart? Perhaps it was fear, not charity, that prompted the questions in

Parliament, the grandiose plans for modernisation that never left the drawing-board. No one ever bothered to explain.

The war had come to London with malice towards only some. Since August bombs had rained on the south and the East End while the West End moaned about the inconvenience of the blackout in easy safety. The realisation bred an atmosphere of simmering resentment in dockland. The label 'Bolshevism' had been tagged to it — a portmanteau word that did not take account of how war had exposed the city's centuries-old neglect like an open wound.

No shelters had been built, medical and social services were creaking along under the misguidance of ancient machinery; homeless families were shunted from one office to another; all incapable of dealing with a mother and a father and eight children who suddenly had nowhere to live. Evacuation to safer areas had been minimal in the opening months of the Phoney War. People sat and waited for somebody to do something. Nobody did.

'Wonder them buggers up West don't ask us to switch our bloody lights on when Jerry come over, just so *they* don't get bombed by mistake!' one gnarled stevedore had said to Shaffer when Hirschfield had taken him to a working pub downriver. It was the first indication he had had of the undercurrent that was growing a little more each day. Shaffer had suggested Hirschfield file it. Vince told him to write it off to experience; it wouldn't last five minutes with the censor. Write about tough, jolly dockers with wide leather belts holding in their beer bellies, scarves about their necks and a twinkle in their eyes and you might be in business, he had added.

A sudden squeal of brakes and the ambulance skidded to a halt, then crept forward gingerly around a huge crater in the road. As he passed it, Shaffer looked down on the twisted metal fin of an unexploded bomb nestling in the spaghetti-twist of a telephone cable. They picked up speed and at the beginning of Lower Road the ambulance turned off. A vast pall of smoke was blowing upriver; the beat of engines and the thunderclaps of bombs filled the air.

A tremendous whistling rush of air came out of nowhere and

Shaffer hurled himself flat across the passenger seat as the bomb exploded. He felt the car lift, the steering-wheel shudder against his hip. When he looked up again a fountain of flame was boiling from a ruptured gas main two or three streets away, flailing and spitting above the roofs of nearby houses.

The sky filled with aircraft. Thousands! He swung the Morris into a side-street, got out and began to run. The blasts were merging into one; a gathering avalanche of rage. A flash like summer lightning from beyond the dock gates. Another.

Later he would try to rationalise the exact sequence of events, but he never got nearer than recalling that first blinding flash. The rest, like overlapping nightmares, was lost in noise and filth and flame.

There was a scream. Shaffer stumbled to a run towards the dock entrance gate and someone collided with him in a Stygian cloud of burning rubber. He reached out blindly, the smoke burning his eyes and nose, closing his throat. It was a little girl. Her hair was soot-blackened, her dress filthy. She screamed again as he tried to hold her and ran on past him. He couldn't call out without swallowing burning rubber. Another rush of air. He recognised it sooner this time and threw himself at the ground. A clatter of tin cans. He got to his feet and staggered forward past a fireman who was kicking nine-inch-long incendiary tubes into the gutter, oblivious of the spitting flame.

'Hey, you!' A man waved a piece of paper idiotically from the window of the main dock office; Shaffer ignored him. The man shouted again and Shaffer turned in time to see the small wooden window-frame catch fire. Still clutching his piece of paper, the man catapulted through it, his hair ablaze. He bounced to his feet as soon as he hit the ground, screaming hysterically. Then he fainted. Two other men scrambled from the blazing office and dragged him away, feet first, in the direction of a fire-engine, scuffing his blackening scalp on the paving.

Shaffer pressed himself hard against the dock wall and began to move along it, his ears pounding with pressure. He tasted blood in his throat and sank back into a doorway feeling for the wound. It was sweat. He laughed out loud. Easy! Take it easy. He was shaking. Not trembling; shaking. His body wouldn't keep still. He wanted to laugh again. Or cry. Shout. Anything.

'Hallooo!' he shouted.

The word was engulfed by the greater roar of burning. But then, an answering echo: 'Halloo-oo-oo!' A bunch of men came at the double around a concrete air vent. The leader skidded to a halt when he saw Shaffer, raised a hand and shouted, 'Stay there, mister! Don't move! Get your se—'

The rest was lost. A sheet of rattling stone crashed from the roof of the building above Shaffer's head. When the dust cleared the man gave a congratulatory thumbs-up sign, and they raced on.

Shaffer became aware of a light-headed feeling of absolute freedom, the sensation that comes with the knowledge that life is totally out of control and events taking a predestined course. He swayed across a small dock bridge. The shaking had stopped. He experienced dramatic well-being, like an athlete who reaches the peak of his form on the last lap of a punishing marathon. Almost idly, he watched a ripple of bombs, spaced as neatly as a tailor's tack, stitch themselves across the roof of a warehouse complex. He counted them as they punched neat holes in the roof. Five. The sixth hit the water. Spray rose and settled and a miniature rainbow grew and faded in the mist. Then the smoke. The small holes disappeared as the whole roof disintegrated. Voices punched the flames' roar and he saw someone waving desperately from the stern of a blazing ship. Men were throwing themselves over the side into the water; others swung down on ropes to the quay.

A sign read 'Quebec Docks. Admittance only to authorised personnel.' He raced through the gates, aware of something brushing against his feet. Tall grass? He slipped on the cobbles of a lane that led to the water's edge.

'God in heaven!'

The voice was so close Shaffer spun round as if he had been attacked. An elderly man stood clutching his cap staring back at his ship, his donkey jacket smouldering. 'Leave it be! Mother of God! Leave the bugger be!' He tugged at Shaffer's arm, hauled him a few yards. The thunderclap picked up both of them and tossed them like leaves across the yard. When they dared look behind them the ship had gone.

'Hail, Mary, Mother of. . . .' The man scrambled to his feet and kicked out. A rat flew through the air from his boot. Shaffer knew then with bristling horror what had been brushing his ankles. The long grass. Rats. There were thousands of them, hump-backed with fear, racing away from the quays, flushed from warehouses and ships' holds by the heat. He leaped to his feet, terrified, arms pinned to his chest.

'Follow them! Follow them!' shrieked the man. 'They know!'

He shoved at Shaffer then and with a snarl of impatience pushed him aside. He was a good six feet in front when Shaffer saw the massive wound opening up at the back of his head, neat as a sliced apple. Before he could shout, a sheet of incendiaries descended like a curtain ahead of them and the man turned, impossibly alive. He began to run back to the quay.

Shaffer called after him. 'Come back, you damned fool!' But the old man stumbled on into the smoke and the steam like a demented marionette.

He watched him disappear and the urge to follow, primitive as fear itself, overwhelmed him. He lunged into the black smoke but covered only a few yards. An explosion scooped a hole in the black cloud and through it hurtled a jet of gravel and dirt and loose stones and . . . rats. Something hit him very hard high on one side of his head and catapulted him sideways. The ground gave way and he fell head first into the pit. Momentarily, he saw a mêlée of burning fur racing in circles to a piping chorus of pain, then his head struck something hard and he lost consciousness.

Saturday, 1820

Elsie Warrender heard the engines as she prepared her husband's tea. But she had other things on her mind. She was boiling cod and carrots — he would learn to like carrots — and had every reason to be anxious. Twice before she had prepared the meal and each time he had been an hour late. The cod resembled rice pudding when he arrived; it broke down into the water until she had to strain it to search for white meat. The carrots had been soft as lard and tasteless. He had eaten both without complaint, but it had annoyed her. Elsie Warrender couldn't countenance failure in the kitchen.

She had it on a low gas. She prodded the cod with a fork. Another fifteen minutes and it would be the same old story. She glanced through at the alarm clock on the living-room mantelpiece. He was already half an hour late. He was supposed to work a twelve-hour shift but he never left on time. There was a limit, she'd told him; a body can only take so much. She had omitted to mention that, apart from running the household, looking after Jack and their son Paul and their daughter Gladys, Elsie did a full week's work as a daily at a house in Chelsea. Nine in the morning to six at night and home in time to start work again preparing high tea. It was getting harder to snatch a few hours' sleep between the sirens.

'Pot calling the kettle black,' is how Jack put it, so they went on working all the hours God sent. He wouldn't change. The only thing capable of forcing change on them was the war and even that was too small to notice.

Nelson's Green was a thin strip of tenement houses, transport cafés and one-man businesses pinched between the Lower Pool and the Lavender and Albion Docks. Of all areas of dockland, it had had more than its share of hardship since war began. A lot of the younger men — even the married ones — had taken perhaps the one chance life would give them to break away from dock work to breathe some outside air by joining up in the forces. It meant, in turn, that the older men had had to make up for lost numbers. Wives found themselves trying to exist on a pittance, deprived of the material and moral support of a man about the house.

Coupled with that was the sheer strain. Shopping nowadays could take hours. A journey half way across the city to follow up a rumour that a stall in Paddington was selling eatable offal — still unrationed — at a fair price would end in despair at finding the stall closed or wrecked. Hours on the buses and the Tube

49

each way. And somehow a day's work had to be crammed in around that. And then, when the kids had been gathered in for the day, there came the battle to get them to sleep. When the bombing first began, there were regular trips down to the Anderson shelter, hooped sheets of galvanised iron bolted to a supporting frame, planted in six-feet-deep pits and covered with earth. The Home Secretary, Sir John Anderson, had given birth to the idea and had issued them free to anyone who wanted them.

Not that so many bothered now. The backyard Andersons were slowly filling with water through neglect.

They were tough in the docks, always had been, but everyone had their limit and Elsie knew Jack was reaching his. It had begun to show in little things; the way he could talk only about his work when he wasn't sitting for hours on end saying nothing. Twice he had asked her if she wanted to leave the Green, although they'd both known it was pie-in-the-sky. They were trapped here. Everything they had in the world was tied up in the docks; their home, their possessions, their friends, their children, their income. One night could see it all gone, that was the truth of it. Sink or swim. But they hadn't sunk yet.

The gas flickered and died.

'Elsie?'

The door scraped open and Florence Scully ran in from the yard. Florence and her husband Arthur, their boy Geoff and younger son Derek, had been the Warrenders' neighbours for twenty-six years. The two women had a deep-rooted respect for the sanctity of each other's home and the privacy that went with it, but they had shared their loneliness and their fears and their private worries for so long that their relationship was more binding now than the ties of blood and kin. Florence, thin and sparrow-like and a bundle of nervous energy, was the antithesis of Elsie's stolid, unemotional efficiency, but they complemented each other. Perhaps more than anyone, even Arthur, Elsie knew the real strength of the little woman.

'Elsie!' Flo scampered in and slammed the door. 'What *are* you doing?' She stared at the cooker.

'Doing, love? Now, nothing. Gas has just gone.' She jabbed the cod in disgust. 'Told him to be on time. His own fault.'

'But didn't you hear... ? Haven't you... ?'

Florence was, as ever, lost for words in the face of Elsie's imperturbability. 'Outdoors, Elsie! It's terrible!'

'Sounds bad,' admitted Elsie. 'Still, they all sound like that when they start.'

'It's been going on for half an hour! More! I was so frightened I daren't even come round. The street's full of smoke. I've never seen anything like it! And the boys. Derek hasn't come home. Is Paul... ?'

Elsie wiped her hands briskly on her apron. It was true: her mind had been so full of other things she had scarcely heard anything. Flo was right. There was a good old racket going on, and something *did* smell.

'Them boys'll never find their way home in this, Elsie. Ooooh —that Derek!' Flo was beside herself.

'Nothing much we can do, love. They know their way around, don't worry.' But she had difficulty keeping a frown from her face. How could she have been so thoughtless? Paul had been gone for hours and it never crossed her mind. 'They've most likely gone down a shelter,' she said soothingly. 'Must have. At a football match, weren't they? Well, they'd follow the crowds down the shelter. They're not daft. Yourself you ought to be worrying about. Arthur's at work, I suppose.'

'He went on at four.' Flo was calmer now but her body tensed at each explosion. 'I think they've hit something down the end of the road, Elsie. Over in the Surrey. Heard it ever so close. It was—'

She spun round, clutching at her throat, as the door crashed open behind her. Alfred Dunn glared in at them, a whistle in his mouth. He let it fall on its cord.

'You deaf?' he snarled.

Alfred Dunn was the local warden in Nelson's Green. He lived two streets away in a house his father had bought. For forty years and more, Alf had been a fixture in the Green; a quiet, solitary man who was disliked by most of his neighbours although no one would admit to being sure of exactly why. He was just *different*, Alf Dunn.

'Listen to it!' he snapped. Smoke seeped from the yard into the house and he pushed the door to, his hand on the latch. 'What you two trying to do then—catch one?'

'I've been living with it for weeks, Alfie Dunn,' said Elsie. 'If I took notice every time a bomb went off I'd be out of me mind.'

'Every time a—' He jerked a finger behind him. 'You ain't heard nothing like this, girl. Nor has anybody else. This ain't workers' bloody playtime. Where's Jack?'

'Work,' said Elsie. 'Look, Alf, the boys aren't back.'

'Paul and Derek,' said Flo, so that there should be no mistake. 'They went to some football match and they haven't come back.'

Dunn clapped a hand to his forehead in exasperation.

'Will you look for them, Alf?' pleaded Flo. 'We'd be ever so—'

'Look for them? In that lot!' Dunn mellowed. 'Yes, course. Can't be far. Down a shelter, probably. I'll tell them to stay there till this is over. As long as you two get out of here. Like now. No messing!' He stood stiffly by the open door, choking on the smoke.

'Have you seen Jack?' Elsie took the cod off the gas ring and put it in the oven. 'Didn't go through his office by any chance, Alf? He's late again.'

'If he's staying on in that lot it's his own bloody look out,' growled Dunn. 'It's up to you two to look after yourselves. Told Jack a hundred times: the sirens aren't there for fun. Takes no notice of me.'

The house trembled fitfully.

'Look, I can't stay here all day. Are you two coming or aren't you?'

'Don't seem right somehow,' Elsie was saying when Dunn's arm was hurled from the door and he lurched against the kitchen wall. The explosion followed, rattling saucepans on the shelf.

Florence Scully fell to her knees. A cup leapt from the table and shattered before Elsie could grab it. She felt the foundations move.

Alfred Dunn was shouting at them. 'Look at it! Just look at it!'

A wall of flame had risen over Lavender Dock. Elsie bent and lifted Flo to her feet. She could feel her trembling.

'Here, Alfie. Take her down the shelter. I'll just lock up here and be down.' Elsie pushed Flo into his arms.

'What about the boys?' said the little woman. 'I'm not going anywhere until the boys. . . .'

'Do you want to get killed? 'Cause if you do, just stay here! Never mind the boys, I'll find them.' Dunn crouched in the doorway and peered out into the yard. Smoke and dust were everywhere. From somewhere came the jangle of firebells and a jabber of raised voices.

Flo brushed his arm from hers. 'I'm not going,' she said flatly, looking across at Elsie. Elsie was taking crockery down from the shelf and laying it on the floor. She looked up. 'If it gets any worse we'll go down our shelter,' she said to Dunn. The Warrenders, by the grace of good luck and bad planning, had inherited a strip of no-man's-land, once marked down for development. It stretched beyond the tiny paved yard for no more than thirty feet but it had been an ideal site for an Anderson. No one had questioned their right to use the plot and it afforded the ultimate luxury of not having to use the communal shelters or trek to the Tube. Elsie had used it only once and then under protest. It was more comfortable under the table, she'd found, and anyway she didn't have much faith in a couple of pieces of tin covered with soil.

A stick of bombs rained to earth nearby, their explosions becoming one, a prolonged cacophony of shrieking steel. Elsie's hands clutched at her ears. She had never heard that before. The glass of the alarm clock was vibrating fit to bust.

'Wash my hands of you,' said Dunn threateningly. Both women ignored him. 'Orright then.' He dodged outside, slamming the door behind him.

'I can't even make a pot of tea,' said Elsie.

Flo didn't seem to hear. She sat, eyes closed, hands clenched in her pinny. Her eyelids flickered at each new explosion. 'They're right over the top of us, Elsie,' she stuttered. 'They've never come in the afternoon like this before.'

'At least we can see what they're up to,' retorted Elsie. She felt in need of a little reassurance herself. 'Best way is to just ignore it. Do no good brooding.' She made a play of scanning the kitchen cabinet. 'The boys'll be hungry when they get home.'

'They shouldn't be out in—'

'So we'll have some, let me see—'

'And what about Jack? Your Jack?'

'Well, there's some spam. And I've got—'

'They could be anywhere, Elsie. Out th—'

'Flo?'

'Yes?'

'Cut some bread.'

Elsie Warrender shoved the half-loaf into her lap and hoped Flo hadn't noticed the trembling of her hand.

The street was in turmoil. As Alfred Dunn stepped out from the alley behind the Warrenders' house a lorry slewed across the pavement. The cab door opened and the driver legged it for shelter. A woman was standing in the middle of the street, shouting at someone, but he couldn't make out who; the din from downriver now blanketed everything. A boy chased in wild circles trying to catch a half-crazed dog; a baby was crying in its pram across the street; its mother emerged from a house, stilled it with an oath and hustled away, a shopping bag bulging on her arm.

Dunn plunged into it, despairing. Nobody took any notice, that was the trouble. They all thought they were fireproof but when it happened to them they were as stupid and unreasoning as chickens. Order, that's what was needed. Old-fashioned discipline. Well, maybe *now* they would listen. Maybe now they wouldn't take the mickey out of the wardens like they had for the past two years. Sarcastic buggers needed a lesson and, by God, they were getting it.

Somebody called his name. A man he didn't recognise

through the smoke was waving his arms from an upstairs window. At first Dunn thought he was in distress.

'I'll get a ladder,' he yelled. 'Don't move!'

'Don't want your bloody ladder.' Bert bloody Mason. Bert was the street's tough. Hard drinking, argumentative even when sober, his rages were legendary; more often than not their passage was marked upon his wife's body. Now the ham fists were shaking at Dunn.

'Where was your bloody sirens this time, mate? Walking around like bleedin' Mosley, with your bloody armband and bucket of sand. Fat lot of sodding good you are. Didn't have time to put me trousers on before the bleeding bombs come. I'll bloody well be seeing someone about this, you just—' He broke off to snarl an obscenity back into the room.

Dunn turned away. He saw a small red-brick chimney, one he had known from childhood as a local landmark out beyond Island Yard, crumble and fall.

The thought struck him as he saw it vanish: what *had* happened to the sirens?

Come to that: where were the bloody anti-aircraft guns?

Saturday, 2007

At his official post at the top of the flight of marble steps from the main entrance to the Annexe, Arthur Scully bunched his fists tight along the broad red seam of his trousers, chest out, head back, chin tucked deep into his collar. His salute quivered under tension for ten seconds as General Sir John Dill, Chief of the Imperial General Staff, led his brood of aides and advisers clattering down to their cars. The Marine in full battledress who squatted over the gleaming barrel of a machine-gun at the top of the steps ignored the general and kept his eyes glued to the inner double doors, through which, one day very soon, the Hun might come.

Arthur sliced down his right hand and stamped his left foot to the 'At ease' position, hands clamped behind his back. Like he'd always told his lads when the fighting began — whether against the wogs at Basrah or the Pathans on the Frontier or the old Hun at Wipers in the last lot—it was pride in what you were and how you behaved that counted. Firing a rifle, for instance, wasn't to be thought of as putting red-hot lead into mortal flesh; it was drill. Up, *two three*, aim, *two three*, squeeze, *two three*, fire. Reload—hand on bolt, *two three*, cock, *two three*, back and forward and down, *two three*. You may be down on your guts and your luck and up to here in shit and derision, but the more you worried about the state of your equipment the less you worried about your neck—or, worse, the enemy's. Discipline never let you down; as long as he remembered that his mind wouldn't wander and make a fool of him.

The guards on the main door closed in on the latest arrival, then parted again. Jimmy Cole came grunting up the steep steps, gas cape over his shoulder, tin hat awry, gas mask pouch drab and sorrowfully out of character with his Marine uniform.

Arthur and Jimmy were, as Hollis put it, the outer skin of the onion; not guards, not soldiers, not life-on-the-line men, but their roles as messengers, attendants and general functionaries were no less important. Jimmy Cole was a fire-watcher, a Jim Crow in Winston's slang, and he spent his nights on the Annexe roof, equipped with sand bucket and spade and the unpatriotic hope that Fate might deal him at least one little incendiary bomb before the war was over and won.

'You been out, Arthur?' he wheezed as he paused beside the machine-gun emplacement.

'No.' Arthur knew what was coming and he didn't want to hear it.

'He's gone and done it this time,' said Cole. He took off his shiny black tin hat and mopped the inside band with a large red handkerchief. 'Nothing up our way, yet.' Jimmy lived in Lambeth. 'But he's caning the East End something rotten. I come out of the house when I hears the old crump-crump-crump and I runs down the bottom of the garden where I can see and in that time—can't be more'n ten seconds—there's a cloud of smoke over the river and for miles on both sides. Every bloody fire-engine in London must be down there. We heard ten and more going past our house while we was having tea. I'm telling you, Arthur, he's bloody done it this time.'

The 'he' in all such conversations never required identification; Adolf Hitler, the German Chancellor, had become the focal point of British militancy—encouraged by a well-judged propaganda campaign which promoted the idea that he was not quite right in the head. Hitler was not just shorthand for Germany—the old First World War phrase 'the only good German is a dead 'un' was only just returning to common usage—he was the devil personified. He sat at the controls of every Messerschmitt, operated the bomb release in every Heinkel, was at the wheel of every tank that rumbled across Poland, Czechoslovakia, France, Holland and Belgium. 'He' was to blame.

'Better get on up there, Jimmy,' Arthur rumbled, cocking his head upwards.

'I bet you're worried sick about the wife and kids.'

'We all takes our chances best we can. We're in the front line here, you and me. Can't afford to think about anything else.' He directed a cold stare into Cole's flop-jowled face. 'Right, my lad?'

Cole turned away, head shaking wearily, and walked to the staircase that took him to his high perch over the river. Arthur turned face front. Silly old sod, he thought sadly, going about troubling people like that; worrying them. No tact. Too old and too tired to be tactful.

He stiffened as he heard laboured steps echoing up from the wide spiralling staircase below. There was no mistaking it, once you'd heard it a couple of times; that was the sound of Winston climbing up from Floor B. The stairs were too much for him really, down or up. He'd told Frank Sawyers once: 'The last thing I shall be able to do in this war is run away. I don't have the stomach for it or the legs.'

Arthur stamped to attention, turned right to face the head of the stairs and came to the salute. The heads of two patient Marines appeared first, then Winston's. He was wearing his long black coat and a polka-dot silk scarf. General Ismay and Sir Edward Bridges walked behind and Winston's Parliamentary Private Secretary, Brendan Bracken, brought up the rear with

Brigadier Hollis. Arthur's salute shivered with respect as the Marines stood aside on the mezzanine corridor. Bracken handed Winston his black derby. The Prime Minister looked about him searchingly, first at the machine gunner in his nest of sandbags, then at Arthur. He stepped forward a couple of paces and inspected Arthur's perfect presence.

'Hmmmm,' grunted the great man. 'First-class turn out.'

Arthur felt his ears tingle, sensed the blush rising from his neck to his cheeks. Winston turned to Hollis.

'Another of your Marines, Hollis.'

'Yes, sir.'

'Has he been on duty long?'

Hollis raised an eyebrow at Arthur and they telegraphed silently. 'Mid-afternoon, sir. Four o'clock.'

'And his tour ends. . . ?'

'Four a.m., sir.'

Churchill turned on Arthur and eyed his poker-straight stance. 'A long time for a man who may have interests' — he laid emphasis on the word — 'out there. What's your name, sergeant?'

'Eight-nine-five Sergeant Scully, sah. Corps of Royal Marines.'

'We're taking a turn on the roof, Sergeant Scully. I think we deserve a personal guard. By the time they get to the top, I don't think these chaps here will have strength enough to guard themselves. Hmmmmph?' The two Marine bearers made twitching movements with their mouths implying that the idea was incongruous. 'You have an N.C.O. who could replace Sergeant Scully at his post, Hollis?'

Hollis made swift beckoning motions with his hands to the sergeant-major of the guard below on the main door. 'Yes, sir,' said Hollis.

'Then' — the Prime Minister looked about him at his escort — 'if you gentlemen are ready, pray let's continue to the summit, shall we?'

It was Jimmy Cole's misfortune not only that he had chosen to break the rules by smoking a crafty Woodbine but that he should be caught doing so by the Prime Minister and three members of the War Cabinet. He saw them too late and stubbed

58

the pinpoint of burning tobacco against the rough stone of the cupola; a wedge of sparks fled over the balustrade on to the sloping roof. Winston turned his face from it sternly but Arthur emerged into the night in time to see it. For a moment his indignation blinded him to everything else; then, as he glanced guiltily at the officers, he realised that their faces and Cole's were suffused with a curious stuttering bronze light. He swung to the east and for a moment his control deserted him.

London was burning! Not with the flickering, ground-creeping glow that marks the effects of artillery bombardment in the field, but hungrily, monstrously, insanely. Tower Bridge stood black and whole against a mushroom of flame that straddled the river and engulfed it; flame licked at the sky from invisible sources, reaching heights of a hundred and fifty, maybe two hundred, feet. He tried to order it in his mind. Southwark and Bermondsey were in there somewhere; burning. All of dockland south of the river. There were flames on the north bank, too; St Katherine's Dock had probably been hit. Perhaps the Tower of London. But they hadn't got St Paul's; Wren's heavenly dome and its golden cross swam triumphantly above raging pillows of smoke, the sky behind it brighter than eternal day.

He came to his senses and resumed his stiff-backed pose. Churchill and Ismay were at his left shoulder, Bracken and Hollis on his right. For good or ill, he was encircled by them, made part of them. They stood in silence for several minutes, then the Prime Minister rasped, 'That man will live to rue this day, Ismay.'

'It's senseless. They must know—'

'Herr Hitler knows what he's doing, don't ever doubt that. He's tried to break our first line and he's failed. Now he intends to break our spirit. Well, he's doomed to failure there, too.'

'I think this substantiates our Intelligence reports on Sealion, sir,' said Bridges quietly. 'He thinks he's destroyed the fighter squadrons. We know he regarded that as an essential preliminary to an invasion. Our forecast of the timing looks pretty good. I assume this is their idea of a softening-up exercise before they send in the invasion barges.'

'Poppycock!' Churchill exploded. 'The man's a fool. Forget

your Intelligence, Bridges. Know thine enemy. I can see what goes on in Herr Hitler's mind. He wanted Poland. He took Poland. He set his eyes on the Czechs. He consumed them like *hors d'oeuvres*. He bettered us in Norway, at Dunkirk. He lusted for France, Holland and Belgium and he chose his time and they fell to him. Then' — he raised a pudgy finger demonstratively in the bronze glow — 'then he turned to *us*. The might of the entire German war machine was hurled at our heads. The R.A.F. held him. Believe me, Bridges, Herr Hitler is an impatient man. Unstable. He has failed for the first time in this war. For twenty-five days he's used everything in his arsenal to bring us to our knees. Pray to your stars, Bridges, that this is what I think it is.'

'The last throw, sir?'

'Oh no. He has more in his armoury than this. But if we're very lucky, this day marks Herr Hitler's decision to switch his strategy. Blasting our aerodromes, he may be thinking, is an expensive and embarrassing waste of time and effort. Perhaps, he may also be thinking, it would be less expensive to switch the attack to the people of London.'

'Every convention of war rules against that, with respect, sir,' interjected Hollis. His eyes were fixed on the rioting flames. 'The destruction of civilian life for the sheer sake of it—'

'Put your conventions in cold storage, Hollis,' the Prime Minister growled sonorously. 'Herr Hitler has.'

'I think, nevertheless, we should give some consideration to bolstering the Cromwell warning, sir,' insisted Bridges. 'If your reading of the situation is correct, and nothing comes of it, we can order a general stand-down in forty-eight hours. At least, we'll have the benefit of a breathing space for civil organisation.'

Churchill produced a wallet case from his coat and withdrew a ten-inch Havana cigar. He chewed introspectively on it, unlighted. 'Very well. I can't argue with the sense of that. We'll go downstairs. You'd better call John Dill, Bracken. He's gone back to the War House.'

The Prime Minister flashed a glance at Arthur Scully, as if he had forgotten he was there. 'You must forgive us our indiscretions, sergeant,' he said meaningfully. 'Heat of the moment. Something a soldier learns to deal with, hmmmmph?'

'*Sah!*' snapped Arthur, polished heels tight together.

'Now I know your name, I shall make a point of looking for you, sergeant. We shall see a great deal of each other this autumn, I fancy.'

'Privilege, sah,' stuttered Arthur. 'Great honour.' He was grateful for discipline, for the right of the soldier to stare straight ahead and spit unemotional words like chewing tobacco.

Winston looked out over the flames of the East End. 'Perhaps that means more to you than you care to say.'

'Sah!'

'You live in the East End?'

'Yes, sah.'

'Where?'

'Nelson's Green, sah. Rotherhithe, sah.'

Churchill looked over his shoulder at Ismay who made a little bunching motion with his face. The Prime Minister laid a hand on Arthur's shoulder. 'We don't know exactly how bad it is, sergeant, but you must be prepared to find great desolation there.' He looked sharply at Hollis. 'Any reason, Hollis, why the sergeant shouldn't be permitted – er – compassionate leave now? This moment?'

'No, sah. Please, sah.' Arthur astounded himself by this flouting of a senior officer's presence, but it had to be said. 'Begging your pardon, sah, and thanking you for your interest, sah, but no, sah. Respectfully, sah, I never stood down from my post in my life, sah, and I don't aim to start now, sah.' He raised his eyes to the out-dazzled stars. 'Not with Jerry up there, sah.'

'You have a wife? Children?'

'Wife, yes, sah. One boy at home, one with the colours in North Africa, sah.'

'Then pray God they're safe and sound. They should be proud of you, Sergeant Scully. May we all approach our duty with as much courage.'

'My job, sah. Privilege to serve under you, sah.' He had to get that in. It was what he felt, what motivated him, what had now transformed his life in these unthinkable few minutes. The Almighty would take his Flo or leave her be for him to find when he got home tomorrow morning; nothing could change that and nothing he could do would alter the course of providence. Flo was where she'd always been — at the farthest extremity of his thoughts, beyond the pale of war. They had spent a lifetime apart, worrying about each other at first, then worrying less and, finally, barely wondering at all. War had always been his job, the job that paid the rent. A wife had to respect a man's job.

The group turned away and trooped through the door on to the stairs. Arthur stood alone for several minutes after they had gone, no thoughts in his mind to speak of but his eyes round with wonder in the glare.

Jimmy Cole's voice roused him. 'Bloody hell's flames, Arthur They gone, have they?'

Cole poked his head through the entry door, nervous as a recruit poised to go over the top for the first time.

'Come on out here. Course they've gone,' Arthur snapped. 'What kind of a lummock do you think you looked, then, I'd like to know? Sneaking a snout like you was wet behind the ears and didn't know no better. On *duty*. With *that* going on.' He waved an arm at the flaming sky.

'How was I supposed to know they was—?'

'You're supposed to be trustworthy, my old son, entcha? That's your duty, and don't you never forget it. 'Cause if you do, I'm going to come up behind you when you're not looking and bloody well remind you, good and proper. Right, lad?'

'Well, if you put it like that—' began Cole lamely.

'I do, my lad. I bloody well do.'

He was blazing like the fires of London. He was taller than the flames. He was Sergeant Arthur Scully of His Majesty's Corps of Royal Marines and Winston Churchill had noted his name and commended his courage.

By God, he would be worthy of that.

Saturday, 2110

As daylight faded over Rotherhithe and Wapping and a mock sunset of blazing homes and warehouses rivalled nature's own, dockland became an ant's nest doused with scalding water. There was nowhere to run, but they ran.

Shaffer ran.

He ran without at first knowing he was running at all, gathering himself up from the crater where he had lain for ... how long? An hour? Two? He would learn much later that it had been over two hours since the burning, stinking bundle of fur had knocked him off balance into the comparative safety of the pit. He had some vague memory of a bridge he had crossed on his way in. He spotted it and staggered over it, not knowing which way it led. There was no point in travelling back the way he had come; in that direction lay the very heart of the firestorm.

Through a swirling cloud of brick dust ahead he could see the river. Against its far bank a small tug flinched past licking flames, towing a clutch of lighters. Its paintwork was cracked and blistered in the reflected heat. Around it, other barges, loosed from their moorings, blazed dangerously downriver like Hindu funeral pyres. They struck landing jetties and ignited them before careering on, aimless pyromaniacs leaving their marks all the way down to the estuary. By nightfall they would be back, still blazing, on the rising tide.

Shaffer clambered through a web of shattered steel; once a crane, maybe. He was on a wharf, or was it the edge of a dock? A group of firemen, faces blackened, were leaning back on the branches of their hoses, directing spitting jets into the flames. The blazing timber steamed, hissed, sizzled and, as the jets moved elsewhere, dried and ignited again. The heat was overpowering and the firemen took it in turns to put their mouths to the rims of the nozzles to draw in cool air collecting around the surging water. Others, lungs scorched, sat racked like bronchitics until they were dragged to their feet and ordered back to the fire. There was no room for passengers. Only the dead could rest.

A roof collapsed on Shaffer's right. A cloud of burning dust gushed from it and began to fall in a stinging rain. Pepper. Tons of it. He ran, half-blinded, as it scourged his eyes and skin with savage needlepoints, groped through the open door of a workmen's brick shelter and blinked through his tears. All around him warehouses were tumbling like cardboard boxes. Some of them didn't even fall, they just seemed to evaporate. Disembowelled, they spilled their contents across the quays; barrels of bonded liquor exploded like artillery shells; molten rubber, thick as lava, slopped down to congeal in the water; rivers of blazing varnish mingled with tributaries of flaming molasses. Out beyond the dock the Thames itself was on fire. Sugar, liquified in the heat, had pooled across its surface and ignited, its flames leaping around trapped ships until the steel plates of their hulls bent and spat staccato bursts of rivets, white hot, across the water.

And now the wind.

The superheated air rose, funnelled by the pillar of fire, giving birth to a towering vacuum which sucked hungrily for oxygen. The stifled giant inhaled a storm that whipped the core to a fireball. Nothing could withstand it. And yet, under its umbrella, scrabbling like men possessed, the rescue workers dug with torn hands at mountains of rubble, dragging the dead aside, seeking the spark of life in the barely living.

'Over there!' A handful of men had broken away from the twisted heap of rubble through which they had been sifting and were running towards him. He turned his head. Behind him a direct hit had sliced through part of a single-storey block of offices. He hadn't even heard the explosion. The men clambered into the wreckage, seemingly without considering their own safety, their clothes ripped to tatters.

Shaffer shook away the pain in his head and lumbered across to meet them. He joined the human chain handing bricks and masonry through the shattered window, spurred on by groans and screams from inside. A man was dragged out, eyes bulging in a blackened, bruised face.

'Under, under, under,' he chanted. They carried him away. Two others, more dead than alive, were pulled from under a cat's-cradle of twisted girders. The rescue team worked for fifteen minutes and then pulled back.

'Quiet!' yelled their leader. He perched himself atop a heap of glass and stone. The men stood silent, straining to grasp at any human sound through the deafening devastation around them. The leader pressed his ear to the mound. He stood up, shook his head.

'Sid, c'm here!'

A thin, middle-aged man in a uniform three sizes too big for him clambered up to join him. He bent double and stared fixedly at the ground, then began to move across the site sniffing like a dog. Shaffer watched with a mixture of fascination and repugnance. They called them 'body sniffers', men who could locate blood by smell, sometimes even under a ton of rubble. If it was fresh they could pinpoint the location of a body to a square foot. If it was old, they ignored it. For all the creeping horror their unlikely talent occasioned, the body sniffers had saved lives when all hope had gone. The thin man shook his head.

'Right, then, this way!'

The leader waved an arm and the team moved on as suddenly as it had arrived. Shaffer was left alone. He stared at the brick in his hand, weighed it and threw it from him in a fit of helpless rage.

'Jesus Christ!' He bellowed out loud, but the wind swallowed his curse. A stick of bombs flashed and roared from a distant tenement block as if in answer.

He gravitated aimlessly towards the explosion.

'All right, son?'

Two old men barred his way; they were all so old, these men. They wore Home Guard arm-bands and helmets. One carried a rifle.

'I'm all right.'

The rifleman peered at him quizzically. 'You sure? You look—' He broke off in mid-sentence, askance at Shaffer's accent. 'What you doing here, son?' Shaffer told him. The rifle jerked in the direction the rescue men had taken.

'The road's back there. It's not so bad. There's a shelter there. You know your way?'

Shaffer nodded. 'I'll find it.' He stared into the blaze. 'You don't mean to go into that?'

'Don't you worry 'bout us. Just get on out of here. Blind Jack'll see you right.' Again the old Lee Enfield rifle pointed.

'Who?' A pounding began again at the base of Shaffer's skull.

'Blind Jack,' repeated the old man. 'See? There he is.'

Through the oily grey smoke Shaffer made out what looked like a weathervane, jutting from a still relatively intact building near the river. It was in the form of an old-style mariner looking down over to the estuary, hand shading his eyes.

'Should've been like this,' said the man with the rifle, miming it, flattened palm fringing his brow. 'Wood of his arm warped.' He let his hand drop down over his eyes. 'Blind Jack, see?'

Shaffer nodded numbly. 'Blind Jack,' he said, still not understanding.

'All right, let's be havin' yer.' The other old man terminated the banter.

'On my way. Thanks,' said Shaffer.

He made for the sanctuary of the dock wall, reached it and found an exit. He turned to look back but the two old stagers had gone. He looked for Blind Jack but that too had gone or was invisible in the smoke. He pushed out on to the street and began to walk back to the car.

The sign bolted to the corner of the half-fallen wall read 'Keeton's Road'. At the far end of it a crowd had gathered. They stood silent and still as in a fresco, mesmerised by the savaged remains of a small building. Even the rescue workers who dug among the stones were strangely subdued, as if steeling themselves against something they knew was there to be found.

He slipped in among them, meeting no resistance. A burly man, a docker in overalls with a sweat-band tied around his neck, tried to move forward but was restrained by two policemen. He sank to his haunches, fists clenched in his eyes, his body shaking with grief. A woman alongside him was gently led away.

'What. . . ?' whispered Shaffer to a youth next to him.

The boy shook his head. An ambulance had drawn up, the doors were flung open and bundles of linen were dumped unceremoniously on the shattered pavement.

Small bodies, incredibly frail in death, were handed down from the hill of rubble. One by one they were slipped into oversize canvas shrouds.

'Direct,' said the boy next to Shaffer. He was talking to no one in particular.

'The children were at school?' Shaffer asked.

'Na. They took the kids out of it and sent them home when it started, didn't they?' Shaffer took 'it' to mean the bombing.

'I don't see. . . .'

The boy turned a narrow yellow face to stare at him. 'When the bombin' got bad they decided to use the school as an evac. centre. So all the kids they'd sent home came back with their muvvers. Clever, ain't it?'

'How . . . how many?' Shaffer tasted the obscenity of the question.

'Four hundred.' The youth looked back at the scene, then spun back to Shaffer. 'You askin' a lot of questions, ain't ya? Ain't English, are ya? What's your game then?' He tugged at the sleeve of a man alongside him. ' 'Ere! This geezer's a foreigner asking questions.'

Shaffer felt the crowd's eyes on him. He began to reach for his Press Card but a hand pinned his arm.

'Wotcha up to then, mate, eh?' The men glared at him with uncompromising hostility.

'He's a foreign,' parroted a woman.

'Makin' notes, was ya?' Shaffer pulled his arm free, aware that he had slipped his notebook from his pocket; an instinctive gesture.

'I'm an American,' he said quickly.

'Bloody foreigner!' said the youth. 'Watch out for 'em, the wireless said.'

'Buggers come to see what they done,' said another.

The crowd tightened around Shaffer and he couldn't turn.

'My boy's in that,' said the same voice tightly.

'For God's sake, I'm as appalled as you. Can't you—'

'Turn him in! Fifth bloody columnist.'

He had seen it so many times before; grief seeking release in blind rage. If there wasn't a scapegoat they would create one; there was no room for reason. A hand plucked at his shoulder, dragging him backwards. He jerked away, managing to keep his balance, using the momentum to push forward.

"Ere, stop him!'

'Call the rozzers.'

'Bloody Jerry, he is!'

'Askin', he was. *Askin'!*'

'Bloody vulture!'

He forced a path to the edge of the crowd and glanced back. Five men were trying to follow him. He fought the urge to run; instead he walked quickly at an angle from the crowd, weaving between the jam of fire-engines and ambulances.

'What'd I tell you? He's bloody runnin' for it.'

'Stop the bugger! 'Ere, you at the front. . . .'

Shaffer broke into a trot. He turned into a narrow alleyway, out into a courtyard and across to an identical alley. He could no longer hear voices. His throat was dry, his body layered with sweat. Couldn't blame them. If it had been Jerry or Petey under that awful mound he would have reacted just as blindly.

Above the docks the fireball lit the sky with an eerie saffron glow. Around it, confused by night turned to day, wheeled a phalanx of birds blown like moths by the heat. And still the bombs fell. He found the inner dock wall again and tried to remember the location of the bridge he had crossed. The brickwork was hot to the touch; radiation surged from every structure he passed. His left shoe began to smoulder and he stamped it out in a shower of sparks. Shelter. He knew that without rest it was only a matter of time before his body capitulated.

He leaned in a doorway. The warehouse was still intact, it's roof peppered with small holes shining like blood-red stars. He gasped air. Cooler. But for how long? Illuminated by the hellish glow, he could see another door on the far side of the warehouse floor.

A scream echoed round the walls.

'Bleedin' hell!' hissed a voice. 'Can't you shut it!'

'I'm burnt!'

'Hold on to the bloody thing, you soddin' great ape!'

The two boys skidded to a halt beside a bale of evil-smelling jute and stared at Shaffer wide-eyed. They both clutched blankets slung over their shoulders like sacks.

'O.K., mister, we ain't done nuffin.'

The larger of the two waved back his companion and began to retreat warily. The other gave a groan and dropped his blanket, clutching at his hand.

'It caught fire,' he gasped. 'Look at me hand.'

'Sod your hand.'

'I told you we should've—'

'I said shut up, will ya!'

The bigger boy clutched his blanket tighter. His eyes were brimming with tears and hostility.

'We're goin to get killed!' shrilled his companion.

'Nobody's going to get killed,' said Shaffer. He took a step forward. The boys backed away.

'We didn't mean it, honestly, mister,' said the one with the burned hand.

'What have you got there? Mean what?'

'Nuffin!'

Shaffer lunged and tore the blanket. Tea flooded at his feet. The boy turned to run.

'No!' Shaffer yelled. He gestured to the other. 'Tell him to stop!'

'Derek!'

The boy screamed the name at the top of his voice. His friend stopped. Turned.

'If you run out there you'll be roasted alive. I'm lost too, but if we stay calm, maybe. . . . You know the docks?'

The big boy nodded. 'You don't work here?'

'Do I sound as if I work here? Look, I don't care a damn if

69

you were stealing the Crown Jewels, understand? Right now I'm more interested in staying alive. You want to stay alive?'

'I don't wanna stay here.'

'Right. Now both of you, listen. There's a dock bridge somewhere out by this warehouse. If we can find it, it's a straight road back.'

'Over the Basin,' said the big boy. 'Our house is along there. Baltic Street, Nelson's Green.'

They walked to the far exit and peered out. The bridge lay some forty yards ahead of them. A tangle of hoses led from the dock and the way was partly blocked by a pump. They could make it.

'Straight on, turn right. There's an opening,' sobbed the boy with the burn. He was nursing his hand in the cool hollow of his throat.

The three of them pounded over the bridge, ignoring shouts from behind, ignoring everything. Twice Shaffer slipped in pools of oil, once teetering on the edge of a dock twelve feet above burning water. Then they were out in the street.

'You know your way from here?'

They nodded in unison. 'Good, then lead on, because I don't. Let's get you home.'

'You ain't going to tell. . . ?'

'Like I said. None of my business.'

A plane screamed low over their heads and they ducked into an arched tunnel between houses; when there was no punctuating crash in its wake they emerged again and raced on. The streets were beyond identification; flat-faced, blank-eyed boxes of drab grey brick fronted by narrow footways and separated by no more than fifteen feet of stone-block road. Anti-blast paper criss-crossed the windows that were still intact and cardboard-box tops filled the gaps where panes had been sucked out by blast. Each street was the same, a sullen stretch of terracing of uniform colour, shape and size with only an occasional corner grocery shop to break the pattern.

'Strewth! We're all right,' the bigger boy gasped as they rounded a corner into another row of small, gaunt houses. He dodged across the smoke-filled road and hammered on a door.

Number 12. There was no answer and he ran to the next door, Number 14.

The door jerked wide as Shaffer and the sobbing youngster gained the pavement and a short, capable-looking little woman bobbed her head outside and 'Ooohed!' with relief. She dragged both boys inside and appeared again to beckon Shaffer over the threshold. He looked up at the sky as he turned to shut the door. There was no sky, just an open umbrella of fire.

'Oh, mister, thank Gawd you found 'em. Will you come through, then?' She waved her hand behind her shyly.

He stepped three good paces from the front door and reached the door into the living-room. It was barely wide enough to accommodate the scrubbed-top table which claimed most of the floor area. A primitive radio perched on a shelf wedged into one corner and a plain wooden armchair sat in front of the coal fire. There didn't seem to be much else. The elder boy had perched himself on the table, back to the wall; the younger one was being doctored in the kitchen by a weedy little woman who twittered like a bird over the ugly skin burn.

'Got some butter, 'ave you, Elsie?' the sparrow called out. 'Marge won't be no good for this. Proper burn he's got here.' She clutched the whimpering boy to her. 'Silly little devil. Teach you to go where you shouldn't be, worrying your mum and me sick.'

Elsie produced butter from a kitchen wall-cupboard and bound the wound in a square of clean white cotton. They led the boy to the table and pulled out a chair. He sat down. The elder boy, Derek, leered.

'Is de li'le boofuls better den, is he? Poorly li'le fella burn hisself, diddums.'

'Bloody 'ave you!' the younger boy erupted. 'If it wasn't for you and your sodding—'

'That's enough, Paul!' The boy's mother dropped a hand on his shoulder and bunched a roll of his flesh in her fist.

'You, too, Derek,' snapped the sparrow. 'Another word outa you and I'll ding your lug so hard you'll hear bells all night.'

The big boy smirked.

'I don't know what I'm thinking about,' said Elsie, wiping

71

her fingers on her apron. She extended a boiled red hand and Shaffer shook it. 'I'm Elsie Warrender and this' — she patted the shoulder of the boy in the chair — 'this is my Paul. My youngest. That's Flo Scully. She's my neighbour. And that's her boy Derek.' The long introduction robbed her of inspiration. She dropped her eyes.

'Mel Shaffer.'

'Wherever did you find 'em?' Elsie said worriedly.

Both boys flashed startled looks at him. He said, 'We kind of found each other. In the docks. I was lost and so were they.'

'Was that the way it was, Paul?' Elsie Warrender shook her son's shoulders with gentle insistence.

The boy's eyes met hers briefly. 'We coulda been killed, mum. They was bombing us. Everything. This fire started and—'

'All right. Calm down. Tell us later when you've had a lie down. Go on, up them stairs and stretch out on the bed. Derek, you get yourself next door and do the same.'

The big boy slouched off the table and strolled out through the kitchen door, hands in pockets. His departure drew Shaffer's eyes to the window overlooking a narrow paved yard and an open stretch of garden beyond, lit eerily by flames towering over a high wall.

'Isn't there a shelter you can get to nearby?' he urged. 'If one of those bombs. . . .' They appeared to be completely unaware of the danger around them; impervious to blast, deaf to the roars and crackles of disintegrating buildings and the steady crump-crump of the bombs. What in hell's name was wrong with them?

'The gent's right, Flo,' mused Elsie. 'Paul! *Paul!*' The bandaged warrior clumped down the stairs he had just ascended. 'Out there, down that shelter with you, my lad. Flo — go send that Derek down, too. And Flo?' The little woman turned at the kitchen door. 'See if your gas is on, will you? I reckon we could do with a nice cuppa rosie just now. Don't you?'

Shaffer began to relax and as the tension ebbed exhaustion flowed in to take its place. According to his watch he had been out there for nearly five hours but for the life of him he

72

couldn't account for three-quarters of the time. He allowed the women to pamper him, boil him water to wash in and pour him a cup of thin, tasteless tea. He honoured his word to the two kids and kept his description of the rescue down to bare essentials. It wasn't difficult; the women appeared to be hypnotised by the sound of his voice rather than what he had to say and Elsie, anticipating his discomfort, admitted they had never met an American before and never seen one off a cinema screen. Their praise for his gallantry, his selfless heroism, was made up, he decided, of five per cent gratitude and ninety-five per cent awe. He was up there with John Barrymore and Cary Grant and they weren't about to let him down. After an hour, though, Elsie Warrender began to look at the alarm clock perched on the mantel over the fire with increasing concern.

'Jack should be here any minute,' she said, willing it to come true. He assumed Jack was the man of the house and flinched inwardly at the prospect of another round of hero-worship.

'He's probably helping out, eh Elsie?' Flo said comfortingly.

As she finished, the house shook with an intensified burst of bombing so close that Shaffer came half out of his chair. They heard the whistling passage of a 'screamer' – a bomb with special fins made to scream like a demon as it fell, Elsie explained equably – but its explosion merely added to the general din and neither woman seemed disposed to consider it important. Their plain, hard-worked faces were fixed with homely smiles of vacuous confidence and they sipped their tea as though it were their elixir of life.

'Glad'll be back soon, too,' said Flo, switching anxieties. 'Better if she stayed up West, though. Put up for the night somewhere, eh?'

'Not my Glad. Never spent a night away from home yet.'

The subject opened up a whole store of retailable memories and Elsie fished a scrapbook from the front parlour. Gladys Warrender, her daughter, was the pride of the family and Shaffer was regaled with her life story from nappies to leotards. Gladys worked as a dancer at the Café de Paris. The snapshots of her as a child showed promise; the glossy publicity still of

73

her in spangled skimpy one-piece with a feather head-dress and a plunging *décolletage* confirmed it.

'Perhaps you could go to her show,' said Elsie, inspired.

'I'd like that.'

It wasn't a lie but it *was* an excuse, the one he had been groping for for the past seventy-five minutes. He was feeling better, stronger, and he had to get out of this place and back on the beat where he belonged.

'Look, Mrs Warrender; what do you say I look in on your daughter at the club? Bring her home or see to it she gets a hotel room for the night?'

'Oh, no. You've done enough,' said Elsie Warrender uncertainly.

'No trouble. At least you'll know she's safe.'

'She's very independent-minded, our Glad. I wouldn't want her getting on her high horse because she thought we were interfering.'

'Leave it to me. Besides. I really must get back. I want—'

The kitchen door slammed back and struck one corner of the sink. The old man was short, round-shouldered, bald; his face was a mess of blood, sweat and soot. He leaned for support in the doorway.

'Jack!' Elsie ran to him, clung to him. He did nothing; just stood there.

Shaffer got to his feet as the man staggered unsteadily to a chair and flopped down. A pile of ledgers under his arm clattered to the floor. He didn't seem to have noticed.

'Jack?' Elsie Warrender's eyes flickered nervously over Shaffer. 'Jack, this is Mr Shaffer. He's been ever so good to young Paul and. . . .'

Shaffer touched her arm and shook his head. The old guy was clearly in an advanced state of shock; his eyes were wide, staring, glazed; his body lifeless.

She persisted. 'Jack? Look, love. . . .' She straightened and tried to make light of it. 'Not hisself tonight,' she said brightly. 'Not hisself. Works too hard, his trouble. Tired out.'

Shaffer edged to the open door. 'I'll let myself out,' he hissed. She trapped her upper lip in her teeth and nodded.

He was closing the door when the voice came out of the crumpled figure like a lost soul from a catacomb.

'All gone, Elsie. Everything. Nothing left.'

'There, pet. Don't you worry. Everything'll be all right. You'll see.'

"S'all gone,' gulped Jack Warrender. 'Better off dead.'

Saturday, 2230

The drive back to Brook Street took an hour. Elsie Warrender had scribbled a rough street map that led him to where he'd parked the Morris — still intact but immured in several inches of brickdust — but the roads between dockland and London Bridge were jammed solid. Fire-engines and ambulances accounted for much of the chaos; dozens of them racing helter-skelter from fire to fire, rubble heap to crater, ignoring red lights and traffic concentrations alike. Moving through them, against the tide, were ragged armies of dazed refugees clutching bundles of clothing, pets, children; automatons wrung dry of fear. Taxi-cabs had been commandeered to haul small fire pumps, and trucks and pantechnicons to ship the less seriously wounded to hospitals.

But what brought the traffic to a standstill and made the work of the rescue services very nearly impossible were the mighty lines of cars streaming in from the West End and the north bringing crowds of sightseers who had come to stare in wonder at the holocaust. They thronged the eastbound side of Tooley Street nose to tail.

When he gained London Bridge Shaffer saw from the car the whole awesome panorama for the first time. A vast umbrella of light hung over the Surrey Docks; Silvertown glowed like a blown ember; Millwall, Poplar, Deptford, West Ham, Woolwich were reduced to little more than fuel for the inferno. And yet, with only occasional breaks, the German bombers still rolled in from the Channel, their target visible even before they crossed the Kent coast.

By contrast the City of London was virtually unscathed. Here and there an office block wore a fluttering pennant of flame where an incendiary had been swept off target by the rising wind, and in Cannon Street a couple of side-streets were roped off to isolate a U.X.B. — current argot for an unexploded bomb — but without the sirens and the clanging bells and the drifting human detritus it could have been just another summer's night there.

Shaffer reached his apartment in a curiously uplifted frame of mind; the farther the physical elements of the disaster receded the more buoyant he felt. It was a revealing insight into the human capacity for mental self-healing but he didn't recognise that until much later. For the moment he was safe and whole. He stripped off the filthy clothing, luxuriated in a five-inch hot bath, put on fresh clothes and drove to Piccadilly Circus.

The Café de Paris was already a favourite haunt of his; he'd checked in twice since he arrived on the strength of its being *the* after-dark outpost of the society set and, more indulgently, because Ken 'Snakehips' Johnson's Caribbean band was fêted as London's best. Shaffer had blown alto sax at Princeton, enshrined his art form once by tooting in a 42nd Street basement with Charlie Bird Parker and Tex Beneke, and was a fevered disciple of the Hot Club de Paris. He had also discovered a closer tie on his first visit with Vince Hirschfield; the artist behind the bar turned out to be his Paris soul-buddy from Harry's New York Bar in the Rue Daunou, Harry McElhone.

For a club renowned as a hang-out of the former Prince of Wales and Mrs Simpson, the café's entrance was inconspicuous; it was sandwiched between Lyons' Corner House and the Rialto cinema in Coventry Street. He took the long flight of stairs down to the foyer and crossed to the balcony overlooking the restaurant.

For a moment he felt as if he was in a time warp. It was mind-crippling; ludicrous. An hour separating carnage from sybaritic self-indulgence. In the long long-ago the café had been a bear-pit and the natural geography was unchanged. From the balcony encircling the lower room a double staircase descended on either side of the bandstand where Ken was into a carioca designed as a backing for a squawky trumpet solo by Les Hutchinson. The floor was crowded with musical-comedy dress uniforms and elegant evening gowns; there were a lot of Canadian officers, too, a few uniformed nurses and the usual blue-blood civilians. The swirling, gyrating kaleidoscope of colour was caught and reflected and multiplied by the mirrored walls, turning the whole into a crazy ballroom scene out of a modern *War and Peace*. The Café de Paris was one gigantic hall of mirrors, a hand-me-down from the restaurant it had once been before the First World War – the Elysée – which had been modelled on the first-class dining-room and ballroom of the ill-fated liner *Titanic*.

Shaffer ordered a heavy-duty Scotch and ran a lightning sketch of the bombing for Harry McElhone's benefit and they shook their heads over it as they might have done at the news that the Yankees had gone down to an upstate Saturday afternoon ball club.

The band hit a closing chord, the lights dimmed and the show started. Shaffer perched on the balcony rail to get a good view of the floor and the dancers came in high-kicking to 'Oh, Johnny'. He had no difficulty in identifying Gladys Warrender; he recognised her at once from Elsie's publicity still. Her stage name, Harry had told him, was Carole Davis after her two favourite stars, Carole Landis and Bette Davis. She was a beautiful girl, no doubt about that; dark, electrifying, sinuous.

He watched the faces of the customers and the taste of the Scotch turned sour in his mouth. Laughter, good food, good taste. Sassoon's lines ran like an oil-slick over his own relaxed mind.

> I'd like to see a tank come lurching down the stalls. . . ,
> To mock the shattered heroes of Bapaume.

Five miles away the world was coming to an end and here they played in bright, sequestered luxury. Safety. The Café de Paris was celebrated as the safest club in London. Bombproof. Eat, drink and be merry for tonight we survive. No – it wasn't like that. The roles of East End and West could so easily have been reversed. And would the dockers have laid aside their pints in remorse if they had been?

The dancers swept out with a final bump and grind and a stand-up comedian took over. The laughter rose from the bear-pit and echoed around the upper balcony. Shaffer swallowed the last of the Scotch, said goodnight to Harry and went down the stairs to find Charles, the head waiter. He was an imperious man, innocent of condescension; a royal equerry who had missed his vocation. He led Shaffer into the yellow-painted brick corridor down from the girls' dressing-rooms, and withdrew.

They came out in a clucking stream, some in evening gowns on their way to attendant stage-door Johnnies, others in street clothes that stripped them of that old high-kicking glamour. Gladys Warrender was just another girl on the street, still beautiful but smaller than he'd imagined and not exactly dressed for Sardi's.

'Miss Warrender?'

She levelled a frosty stare and walked on.

'Just give me a second, huh?' He wanted to separate her from her friends. She didn't look the type to appreciate emotional scenes in public.

'All right, Carole?' one of the girls called out.

'Yes, fine.' She stopped irritably. 'Look, why don't you go find yourself a nice girl somewhere?'

'Your mother — Elsie — asked me to look in on you.'

That got her. 'Mum? What's wrong? Who are you?'

'Nothing's happened. Calm down.' He told her briefly. She listened without interruption, her teeth gnawing on her lower lip. When he finished she drew a quick, decisive breath.

'I must get home. Now. Look, thanks for what you did, but—'

'You think it makes sense to go home? Your folks'd be happier if they knew you were safe. In a hotel, say.'

'No. I'm going home.' She turned away at once and he followed her along the corridor and up several flights of stone steps. They emerged in Coventry Street and she made for the corner of Piccadilly Circus. He couldn't spare her the first shock of that towering red glow across the eastern sky and she slapped a hand to her cheek.

'My car's over there in the square,' he said quietly. 'No —

don't argue, please. You won't get a cab to take you east and I guess the Underground isn't running just now. Come on.'

He avoided the main roads and kept north of the river, aiming at the rose-flame outline of the Tower of London. He turned into the bridge approach and found the way barred by striped poles balanced on upended oil drums. 'No vehicles beyond this point. By order,' read the black-on-white sign. He was about to reverse but she clamped a hand on his arm.

'No. Don't. I'll get out here.' She opened the door and swung her feet to the ground.

'That's crazy! You're miles from home and. . . .'

She got out and bent in to look at him. 'I'll manage. I know my way.'

'But for crying out loud, Gladys.' He controlled himself. 'One more time. I want to take you home. It's no trouble.'

'You go home to bed. You've done enough already. I'll be all right.' She straightened as if to move away and he remembered something.

He dug a business card from his wallet. 'Hey, just a second.' He scribbled on the back of it and handed the card out to her. 'My card.' She put it in her handbag without looking at it. He said ruefully, 'Are you always so stubborn?'

She made a little smile and moved away.

He leaned out of the window. 'Next time I'll bring roses.'

She didn't turn her head. He watched her walk away, a diminutive, vulnerable figure dwarfed between the towers and girderwork of the huge bridge and the infernal sky. She became a moving blur, a fudged speck, then the writhing fire patterns swallowed her altogether.

He sighed, swung the Morris in a U-turn and headed for home.

The words poured out in a torrent of emotional release. All consideration of sleep had gone. His mind raced ahead of his typing fingers, feeding off the adrenalin of recollection: the blazing docks, the waiting wives, the broken bodies of the Keeton's Road schoolchildren; the pride of the girl who walked home alone. When he finished he read it through and saw Vince Hirschfield's prophecy running through every line. The white heat of first baptism. Then he remembered Clarence O'Keefe and the 'choice'. It was wrong. Purple prose; heart-wringing, how-will-it-all-end, where-are-you-now-that-we-need-you propagandist makeweight. They had ditched Hirschfield for just that. The cool appraisal; that's what the A.B.N. board were in business for. The long eye gazing down a corridor of perspective. No more goddamn bombs on goddamn real estate. We played that one.

It took less than thirty minutes to manufacture a clinical assessment of the Luftwaffe's switch of strategy, its implications and the long-term effect of blanket bombing. He drove over to Broadcasting House and filed it.

He arrived back in Brook Street at two-twenty. Undressed. Worried. Thought.

And finally slept.

SUNDAY
8 September

Sunday, 0700

The final 'All Clear' had sounded over Nelson's Green at half past four in the morning. At first it brought no sense of relief; the fires still burned, the rescue workers continued their digging. Then, gradually, an unearthly silence settled over the streets. The unbroken drone that had filled the skies for the past twelve hours left a hollow pocket in its wake. Like a punch-drunk boxer reeling against the ropes, the East End grasped the blessed respite with only one thought in mind: sleep. They slept in shelters, beneath beds, on the doorsteps of ruined houses. They slept sitting up, packed along wooden benches in crowded reception centres like convicts awaiting transportation. They slept single-mindedly, as if they might never have the chance to sleep again.

Dead to the world.

Alfred Dunn savoured the irony of it.

'Dead to the world.'

He repeated the phrase to himself. He had passed through exhaustion and emerged light-headed and detached on its farthest shore. At 5.30 something had uncoiled, like a badly wound spring, inside him. His legs had refused to move; to breathe was a gross imposition on the muscles of his chest. His mates had taken him from the A.R.P. hut near Deptford Road Station and driven him home on a milk-float, but twenty minutes of lying stiffly between the bedcovers had brought neither sleep nor peace of mind. The house was a fun-fair ghost-train passing through a landscape of flashing lights, screams and vague tremblings. He got up and dressed. The street, by comparison, was a familiar torture.

For an hour he had patrolled it and the area around. Now,

as morning broke with a sickly grin on its face, he had little recollection of how he had filled the time. There had been something about a baby injured by flying glass; a family trapped in their shelter by sandbags blown across the doorway; a horse.

Horse? A dim memory of thrashing hooves beating a frenzied tattoo across the cobblestones, until someone had the merciful sense to end its misery. He wiped a hand across his eyes. And, of course, there had been young Derek Scully.

Alfred Dunn had never been quite sure why he chose the thankless task of being A.R.P. warden for the Green. At its best it relegated him to the role of a bumbling do-gooder; a misfit in a world of professionals. A.R.P. — Air Raid Precautions; it even sounded amateurish. The firemen, demolition workers, ambulance drivers, even the Local Defence Volunteers, now renamed by Churchill the Home Guard, had achieved some kind of status. But the warden, equipped with his authority to reprimand and report those who failed to comply with the rules of war — forgot to carry gas masks, lit a sly cigarette in the blackout, shone a stealthy guiding flashlight or twitched the corner of a blackout blind — had, inevitably, become the butt of public resentment. There was even a nickname: 'Little Hitlers'. Would they ever be able to call the A.R.P. that again after the past twelve hours? If there was any justice in this world they wouldn't. The wardens had earned their spurs in their baptism of fire.

All he knew now, standing before the back door of Number 12, Baltic Street, was that the worst part was to come.

Arthur Scully was shirtless, soaping his body with the calculated deliberation of a surgeon preparing for a major operation. His torso shone pink under the carbolic. He turned his head from the sink as Dunn edged open the kitchen door and blew a bubble of lather from his chin.

'Alf?'

'I knocked, but. . . .'

'Soap in me ears,' whoofed Arthur, shaking his head to unblock them. 'Come in. Won't be half a tick.'

Dunn sat on the edge of the copper.

'Nightanaarf,' burbled Arthur, swilling cold water over his face. He flapped a hand behind his back. ''s a towel. Hanging up.'

Dunn passed it to him.

'Ta. That's better.' He dried himself vigorously, buffing torso and shoulders and arms. Regulation spit and polish. 'Night and a half,' he repeated, intelligible now. 'Flo said you'd called in. Thanks for keepin' an eye on 'em.'

'They ought to use the shelter. I told them. You ought to have a word, Arthur.'

Arthur flipped the towel back over the kitchen drying line and slipped on a shirt.

'It was the kids what did it. The women wouldn't leave the house until they turned up. You know what women are. Tell 'em till you're blue in the face but when it comes to the crunch you might just as well talk to a wall. Still, you're right. No place to be last night.' He gestured Dunn to follow him to the living-room and they sat down at the table. 'I didn't get much chance to see what happened. Came straight home. Flo's in bed. Don't want to wake her. Still a hell of a lot of fires about. You been out in it?'

'Off and on,' said Dunn evenly.

Arthur nodded. 'Bad business, Alf. Being here, you wouldn't get the picture, like, but I was up on the roof up West. I could see the whole lot from there.' He added, with an air of studied casualness: 'The Governor was there. Had a few words.' And, as if to leave no room for doubt: 'With me.' He shrugged airily. 'Asked me a few things about the docks. Not that there was much time for chit-chat, mind you.'

'The Governor?' yawned Dunn, cupping a hand to his mouth. 'Who's he?'

Arthur Scully glared in mortification. 'The *Governor*. His Nibs. Who else?'

'Oh, you mean Churchill. Up there was he? I'm with you now.' Dunn seemed singularly unimpressed.

Arthur stared at him; a courtier recording an act of blatant *lèse-majesté*. 'The Prime Minister.' He bore heavily on the title. 'The Prime Minister, Mr Churchill, made it quite clear, imminently' — he corrected himself with a flush of irritation — 'eminently clear, *eminently* clear, that he wasn't going to sit back and let this kind of thing go on. Oh, no. Our bloody Adolf has been and gorn and done it this time. You'll see.'

He sat back in the chair with the look of a man who has personally orchestrated a military reprisal.

If he was conscious of his *faux pas* Alfred Dunn was careful to hide it. 'He'd better hurry up then, is all I can say. This rate, he's got about three days. After that there won't be enough left of the Green to build a car-park.'

Arthur stiffened.

'Normally, I'd say that was defeatist talk. Not like you, though, I know that. Got to make allowances for last night, but there's no good being defeatist. Don't win wars that way. Just what Hitler wants, that is.'

He was sitting to attention. 'Backbone, Alf. That's what this is all about. Jerry's never had it. Not real backbone. Robots, that's what they are. Give 'em some little village full of old women and kids and they're kings, but stick 'em up against real soldiers, mate, and you won't see 'em for dust. Run away from a Jerry and he's the happiest bugger in the world. Stick your fingers up and' — he pursed his lips — 'phhht!'

'Funny that,' said Alfred Dunn. He wasn't smiling.

'Funny? What you mean, funny?' Arthur frowned. Alf Dunn had always been a bit funny himself. Understandable after his wife Maud got taken queer, but even before that there'd been an awkward side to him. Probably something to do with him missing the First World War. That sort of thing could affect a man. Alf had failed the army medical. While the rest trooped off to Verdun and Passchendaele and the Somme, he'd kicked his heels in his dad's shop until it went bust and then he took on as a postman. Not much of a job for a man. Maybe it was that. Alf had been at school with Arthur and he'd seemed all right then, just like the rest of them; a bit moody but nothing queer, like. When Arthur and the rest came home, Alf Dunn was a different man. Solitary; *really* moody. An edge to him that put people's backs up straight away. You'd have thought he'd been through the war himself.

On the charitable side, though, there were wars and wars. Alf Dunn might have been fighting his own.

'... not like that,' Dunn was saying. 'What you just said, about sticking your fingers up. I saw somebody do that. Last night. Old bloke ran out in the street, covered in water he was from a main gone under his house. A bomb, we reckoned, got buried right underneath. He was going daft, looking up at the Jerry planes, shoutin' and swearin', sticking his fingers up so they could see him.' He looked blandly across the table at Arthur Scully. 'Didn't do him much good. Couple of minutes later his house came down like a pack of cards. Lucky he was outside. His old woman wasn't. We brought her out an hour later. Dead, o' course.'

Arthur swallowed. There was no point trying to reason with Alf when he was in one of his moods. 'I said it was a bad business. Don't think I don't realise that. All I'm trying to say is, we've got to pull together and that means taking it on the chin for a while.' He changed the subject in the face of Alfred Dunn's baleful unbelieving stare. 'Winston's coming down the East End today, I heard last night. That'll buck 'em up. Bound to.'

'No wonder he made today a day of National Prayer, then,' said Dunn bleakly.

'What do you mean by that?' Arthur was now distinctly fed up with the warden's attitude.

'Nothing.' Dunn waved a hand. 'Maybe you're right. At least it might help pull people together.'

'Course it will, course it will. That's the spirit,' Arthur beamed. Better; much better.

'Anyway, don't make much difference what we think. We got enough problems.' Dunn hesitated awkwardly.

'How's Maud?'

He was knocked off his stride by that and tried to cover his agitation with a burst of coughing.

'Dust. Can't move for it out there,' he grunted. 'Maudie's all right. Some days worse than others; you know how it is. She'll be all right.' He sliced that topic of conversation abruptly. 'How are the kids? Paul? Derek?'

'None the worse for being daft as brushes. You know the silly little buggers left the West Ham match and got caught in the

85

docks? Strolling around the bloody docks, I ask you! They'd heard the siren but they thought it was a false alarm. Kids!'

'You'll have to watch 'em, Arthur. In the docks.' Dunn chose his words carefully. The fact wasn't lost on Arthur.

'Watch 'em? How d'you mean, watch? You can't watch kids every hour of the day.'

'It's not just the bombing. There's something else.'

'Eh? Like what?'

'Looting.' Dunn formed the word with exaggerated precision. 'It's been going on for months now, always during the raids. That way they reckon the police will be too busy to care—have their hands full. 'Cept, what the looters don't know is the army's been called in. They've been told to shoot on sight. Nobody's copped it yet but it's bound to happen. Couple of kids like Paul and Derek wandering around there during a raid ... people could get the wrong idea. You know nobody's allowed in without authority.'

'Hadn't thought of it like—' began Arthur Scully.

Dunn cut him short. 'Paul and Derek were spotted by the police last night. Docks police. They tried to ... er ... stop 'em but they run off. ...'

'I'm not surprised. They knew they shouldn't have been there. Hope it shook some sense into them.'

'There was some talk; misunderstanding. The police had a word with me afterwards. Y'see, Ronnie Hayes recognised Derek. Air was full of smoke and God knows what, nobody knew what was going on, but they sort of got the impression the lads were. ... Well, they said they were carrying something over their shoulders. Blankets, they thought. Maybe their coats. It was getting dark; easy to make a mistake. But you have a word with 'em, and get Jack Warrender to do the same.' He stood up, pressing his knuckles into his back with a grimace of pain. 'Before there's an accident, Arthur. We wouldn't forgive ourselves.' He paused at the door. 'And the women, Arthur. Talk to them about the shelter. For their own good.'

'Can't argue with that, Alf.' Arthur was subdued. He didn't want to understand at all. Not about Derek.

'If you want I'll have a word with Derek, too. Might come more official, like, from me.'

'Leave him to me. I'll talk to Jack as well. Time and a place for high spirits. War ain't either.'

'Even so, if you want . . . if you feel. . . . Anyway, I'll be on hand. I used to get on well with Der . . . your lad. There's no tellin', he might listen.' Dunn brushed the thought away with a self-deprecating click of the tongue. 'Be one of the first, though.'

'You're doing a good job, Alf. Don't you forget that. We've all got our jobs and we should be proud of 'em. Mr Churchill said as much.'

'Ah, Mr Churchill. Course.' Alfred Dunn nodded a little too enthusiastically. 'Well, here's hoping we catch a glimpse of him . . . down here.'

He glanced out into the yard. A fine drizzle was falling, a grainy mixture of concrete-dust and grit. 'I'll be off.'

He looked up at the sky, or that part of it still unobscured by the smoke wafting in a horizontal cloud from the old Surrey. 'Bloody hot yesterday. Funny the kids took their coats to the match. They must have known something we didn't, eh, Arthur?'

He trudged out into the yard without waiting for an answer.

The boy was still asleep, curled tight as a caterpillar in an untidy swirl of sheets. Arthur debated whether to wake him; decided against it.

Only when Alf Dunn had left had the real implication of what he'd been saying come home. As near as dammit he'd been hinting – no, it was stronger than just a hint, he'd been accusing – Derek and Paul of lifting things from the docks. All that stuff about coats over their shoulders, the police trying to stop them, it was an out-and-out accusation. All right, they shouldn't have been there in the first place, he was willing to grant that, but thieving was another kettle of fish. Who the hell was Alf Dunn to tell him his boy was a thief?

Arthur allowed the first indignant stirrings of resentment to rise and expand. Derek had always been high-spirited, yes. At times a bloody handful – he wouldn't argue with that. But kids his age attracted trouble like other people caught colds, especi-

87

ally in the Green. There'd been the fights at school; the time he'd been caught playing truant; all that rubbish about the bike he'd borrowed from somebody and forgotten to take back. But everything had always been cleared up. Derek was no angel, but how many sons were? And who would want them to be?

Skipping school and getting into scraps was still a long way short of out-and-out pinching things. Maybe it was Alf Dunn he should be having a few words with; not young Derek. There was a law against mud-slinging. If Alf Dunn was going around the Green telling every Tom, Dick and Harry Derek Scully was a crook, it was high time he was reminded where to draw the line.

Dunn's whole attitude had needled Arthur right from the beginning. Now it fuelled his anger. For a start, there'd been the way he'd gone on about the docks being flattened by the end of the week. The way he sneered at the Prime Minister, Mr Churchill. He'd better watch hisself!

There was a law against that, too. Less than a month ago the P.M. had let it be known that he'd sent a telegram to civil servants and military commanders urging them to 'check and rebuke expressions of loose and ill-digested opinion in their circle, or by subordinates' and report or remove anyone who was found to be 'consciously exercising a disturbing or depressing influence'. Arthur remembered the exact words because he'd had them typed up and stuck on the notice board at the Annexe.

'Mr Glumpot The Defeatist' was on posters all along the Tube and all over the buses, but people just laughed. To Arthur's way of thinking laughing was just the way the defeatists wanted it. Morale was where it all began and ended. An army without morale was an army beaten before it set foot on the field. They were all part of the army now, every man Jack of them. Even Alf Dunn. That's why it mattered.

Arthur looked down again at his sleeping son. Poor young rip. Flaked out proper he was. Couldn't have got a wink of sleep down that shelter and he'd only got his head down when the 'All Clear' sounded at half-past five.

Alf Dunn could go bugger himself with his lies.

He was about to close the door when something made him

88

pause. He sniffed. Scent? Or was it something in the smoke out-side? No, definitely some kind of scent. He sniffed again. The room reeked of it. He'd been too full of his own thoughts to notice it before, but now there was no escaping it. He tiptoed across the room, sniffing for the source.

Derek's jacket and trousers lay draped over the foot of the iron bedstead. He picked them up, puzzled. The smell was stronger now; in the cloth. He felt in the pockets and his hand touched something that felt like dried herbs. He plucked out a little and held it to his nose. Tea. Scented tea. The fine leaves permeated the boy's clothes; in the pockets, under the lapels, in the turn-ups. Where could he have...? The half-formed question answered itself. He froze. Then, careful not to wake the boy, he raised the corner of the sheet and felt for the single blanket. It wasn't there. Derek was lying on the uncovered mattress. His blanket was missing.

Elsie Warrender, Florence Scully and Janice, Florence's daughter-in-law, sat around the table in the Scully's living-room. The gas had been re-connected an hour earlier and they'd made cups of cocoa. None of them had had more than two hours' sleep but somehow they were too tired to feel tired, as Flo put it. The truth was, the events of last night had made it well-nigh im-possible to switch off. Elsie had got up first to find that Jack had beaten her to it. He was sitting in the kitchen and didn't hear her come down until she touched his shoulder. Even then he'd only grunted. She made him tea but it stood beside him on the table until it got cold. He didn't want breakfast and she felt increasingly that her presence was wearing on him. 'I'll just pop next door,' she'd said. 'See if everybody's all right.'

He gave no indication he'd heard her.

'Gladys and Paul are asleep upstairs,' she added. The faintest of nods. 'If you want anything ... well, I'll only be half a mo, all right?'

There were some things that could only be worried through, she thought, and it was best done alone. She'd felt that way herself sometimes; snatched a minute to go upstairs and lie on the bed and chew on her problems. Like the time Gladys had come to her with the pain in her chest, just over her right breast. They waited a week before the doctors told them it was mastitis but it was a week when she'd found it difficult to listen to anyone. Course, they hadn't told Jack because he'd had enough on his plate. And anyway, it worked out all right in the end. Things usually did.

Now, with the Scullys, she made herself believe it.

'So who was this Gary Cooper then?' Janice Scully was saying in that irritating way she had. 'You two sound like you've got a crush on him yourselves. Dad better watch it.'

Florence Scully twittered with embarrassment. 'Don't be so silly, Jan. He was a young man.'

'Best kind.' Janice pouted mischievously. 'Pity I missed him.' She was a boldly pretty girl in a common sort of way and her face went all funny as though she meant it.

'I don't think Geoff would like to hear you say that,' said Elsie reprovingly. Janice's husband was a company sergeant-major serving in North Africa. He'd last been home on leave over a year ago.

'It was a joke, Elsie. No need to get all Holy Mary. Anyway, the last thing I want to know is what Geoff is up to among all them orientals. When the cat's away....

'Geoff's a good lad, Janice. You don't know how lucky you are,' snapped Florence Scully. She changed the subject quickly. 'Do you think we ought to write or something, Elsie?'

'Write?'

'To that Mr . . . you know, the American gentleman.'

'Mr Shaffer it was,' said Elsie. 'You mean a sort of "thank-you" note? That'd be nice. I was never one with words, though. Not on paper.'

Janice shifted impatiently on her perch at one corner of the table. She studied her long, shapely legs. 'Well, what did Gladys have to say about him? He brought her home, didn't he?'

'Oh, she *mentioned* him. Like what a nice chap he was and that.'

Janice rolled her eyes at the ceiling in a gesture of despair. 'Sometimes I give up on your Glad, Elsie. How old's she now? Twenty? Twenty-one?'

'Twenty-one,' said Elsie. 'In May.'

'Twenty-one, coming up twenty-two. How old were you when you had her? And mum. Twenty-four when you had Geoff, weren't you? I got married at twenty-one and that was late starting for around here. You ought to have a word with your Glad, Elsie. Passing up a chance like that!'

'Jan!' Florence Scully slapped her daughter-in-law's hand disapprovingly. 'Honest, I don't know where you get some of your ideas from. Talking like that. You take no notice, Elsie, it's just her way.'

'You know something, mum? You're a prude, that's what you are.' Janice softened the rebuke with a grin. 'Elsie knows what I mean.' She cocked her head. 'Let's face it, Glad's been working up West for – what? – more than a year now. She's never mentioned one chap, not all the time she's been there.'

'She's had . . . young men,' said Elsie uncertainly. 'There was that young lad Brian, I think that was his name. Brought him home for tea.'

'Brian Carter! Exactly! You know what he did? He worked the lights at the place where she was dancing. Know where he lives? Wapping! Wapping, I ask you. Thick as two short planks he is. She's not still. . . ?'

'Oh, no, she hasn't seen him for months. She works very hard, Jan,' said Elsie, making the best of an impossible defensive situation.

There was a brisk rat-a-tat-tat at the front door and a cheery voice bellowed, 'Anyone home?'

Elsie opened the living-room door without moving from her chair and shouted, 'Barry, love. Come and have a cup of cocoa.'

Barry Warrender clumped through the front parlour, bent over his mother and dropped a kiss on top of her head. His Auxiliary Fire Service uniform and thigh-high rubber leggings were caked with mud and oil and his big round face was scratched and singed and blue with morning beard growth.

'No thanks. Just going home. Thought I'd see how you were.'

Barry was well over six feet and as broad as a trolley-bus, particularly around the front where his wide black leather belt swelled over a growing paunch.

'Your Edie all right, love?' asked Elsie. Her question was tinged with involuntary guilt. How could she! All last night, with hell breaking loose, and she'd never once given thought to Barry's pregnant wife in their little house across Southwark Park.

'Popped in around midnight. Had a fire in Castle Street round the corner. She's O.K. Her mum's the one who was scared.'

Edie's mother, Mrs Wilcox, had moved in two weeks ago to be with her daughter in the last stages of her confinement. She wasn't handy, Mrs Wilcox; a grumbling, sour-faced woman who thought Edie had married beneath her. When Edie's time came, Flo and Elsie would be called in to deal with the necessities; meanwhile it was better for all concerned that Mrs Wilcox be left to queen it over her daughter's home alone.

'She's due any day now,' said Flo Scully thoughtfully. Flo was better than any district nurse, better than any doctor, even. Flo had been bringing kids into the world for thirty years – and laying out the dead. 'I've got everything ready, dear,' she added. 'Tell your Edie she's not to worry. Just send her neighbour round when she feels the pains coming on, like we said.'

Barry blew her a kiss. 'Thanks, Auntie Flo.' He breathed mightily through his nose and the air ignited a deep rumbling cough in his barrel chest. Elsie got up and stared him in the face.

'Don't you go getting bad with that asthma, love. Not while you're out with them fires.' She touched his face. 'You look tired, boy. You go and get yourself to bed.'

He kissed her lightly on the cheek. 'No time for sleep, mum. Just got an hour to wash and brush up and have a bite of breakfast, then I'm back on call.'

'Oh, Barry.'

'Can't be helped. I'd better be sliding off, then. Say hullo to Glad and tell young Paul to keep his nose clean. One of the lads saw him and Derek up the Lavender last night, silly young buggers. Tell him, O.K? I don't fancy digging them two out from under.'

He kissed his mother again, wiggled his fingers at Janice and clumped out. As he reached the front door Arthur Scully's voice echoed down the stairs. 'All right, young Barry?'

'Fine, Uncle Arthur. Can't stop. See you later.'

Arthur came into the living-room. There was a frown on his face and he despatched it with an effort.

'Something up, love?' Flo half rose from her chair.

'No, nothing. Sit yourself down, Flo. Done enough.'

'We was just talking about you, dad,' said Janice, looking triumphantly at the others. 'Weren't we?'

'Talking about me? Nice, I hope.' Arthur was good at mock gruffness. His trademark. Came in useful now and then. Having made his decision not to tell the women about Derek and Paul, there seemed little point in burdening them with his feelings. Man's job to shoulder that kind of thing; not woman's.

'Yes,' went on Janice, enjoying the moment. 'How are you at *billet doux* then?'

'Billy who?'

'A letter.' She dropped her voice to a husky, conspiratorial whisper. 'To a strange young man. Dah-dah!'

'You gone potty, Jan? What's she on about, mother?' He turned for guidance to his wife.

Elsie came to the rescue. 'The gent who brought Derek and Paul home last night. Flo thought it might be nice if we sent him a letter.'

'Thank-you letter,' expanded Flo. 'You're good at letters, Arthur.'

'Oh, I see. Yes, well. . . .' He nodded. 'Well, I s'pose I can handle a letter. What's his address?'

Both women stared at him blankly. Then at each other. Janice Scully leapt in quickly, her voice light and laced with mockery. 'Give it to Glad. She'll know. Take it herself, I shouldn't wonder.'

Elsie ignored her. 'Well, there's always a possibility. . . .'

'Sounds a decent sort of bloke,' said Arthur. 'Like to've met him meself.' Then as if he'd overstepped the mark, 'Did you say he was an American? A Yank? Somebody say that?'

'I did,' Flo said. 'When you came home. He's an American who goes on the wireless.'

'American,' mused Arthur. 'Don't sound right that.' Arthur Scully's opinion of Americans was roughly akin to the Spanish conquistadores' opinions of the Aztecs: rich, flamboyant and basically degenerate. In his personal league-table of world ratings they were pegged slightly above Italians and somewhere below Spaniards but the order was at any moment subject to change. 'Still, give it to him. Shows you can't always tell.'

'He was really nice,' protested Flo.

'I was on the roof,' said Arthur. This American nonsense was getting out of hand. 'Along with Mr Churchill.'

'Do you think Glad got his address?' Florence asked Elsie brightly.

'Well, she didn't say. . . .' began Elsie.

Arthur glowed. 'Mr Churchill said to me. . . .'

'Perhaps we could put an advert in the papers. You know, like they used to,' said Flo in a burst of inspiration.

'Mr Churchill,' boomed Arthur, 'was asking me my advice.'

The women fell silent and stared at him in open disbelief. He blinked at them sheepishly. His voice fell to a conversational level.

'Well, not exactly advice. He asked me a few things, sort of. . . .' His voice trailed away dismally.

It was no good; even his own kith and kin didn't seem to appreciate the honour of it. Priorities, that's what life was all about; priorities. It'd been the same the time he'd been on duty and the Foreign Secretary, Lord Halifax, Anthony Eden and Beaverbrook had come down to the Annexe to see the P.M. You'd have thought he was talking about some third-rate village cricket team for all the women cared. More interested in bloody film stars, they were. Priorities!

'That's very nice, love,' said Flo consolingly. She glanced across at Elsie. 'Arthur was talking to the Prime Minister.'

'Very nice,' said Elsie.

'Bit of an honour,' said Arthur offhandedly. 'Course, can't say too much about it.' He put his fingers to his lips. 'Be like dad, keep mum, eh?'

'Course, love. Still nice, ennit?' Florence knew when to be loyal.

They waited for him to go on, but he had lost heart. He walked moodily over to the window.

'Jack about?'

94

Jack was all right. He'd be interested. Now there was somebody who got his priorities right. He thought of Paul Warrender and the guilt hit him in the pit of the stomach. He hadn't told the women, but he could hardly keep it from Jack. It was his duty to let him know what was going on. Maybe together they could sort something out.

'Jack's in,' began Elsie hesitantly. 'He had a rough time last night though. I don't. . . .'

'His office got blown up,' helped Flo. 'He only just managed to get out in time. He did look ill.'

'He's not hisself,' admitted Elsie. 'You know how he felt about his office. And now . . . well, he's taking it hard.'

'Only to be expected,' said Flo.

Janice swung from the table and smoothed her skirt. 'Wish they'd hit my place,' she said. 'Do with a few days off.'

Janice worked for a garment manufacturer off Oxford Street which had been forced temporarily to shelve its *haute couture* line of goods to produce thermal underwear for the R.A.F. The loss of reflected glamour was total in Janice's eyes. She regarded it as a betrayal; a mean, underhand attempt to ruin her career and at the same time belittle her. There wasn't a moment of the day when she didn't feel a bitter resentment towards the faceless bureaucrats who had brought about her fall.

'Need a bit of cheering up, then,' said Arthur. 'All right if I nip round, Elsie?'

Elsie looked at him with a mixture of doubt and hope. 'It might. He seemed to want to be on his own, but. . . .'

'Worse thing,' said Arthur. 'Start brooding, that way. Once that happens, you might as well throw the towel in. Leave it to me.'

'It could be for the best,' said Flo comfortingly. 'Arthur's right. No use moping.'

Elsie nodded. 'Well, I suppose so.'

'Course I'm right.' Arthur turned at the door. 'Saw it in Egypt. Good lads. Soldier material. Cracked up in the heat, they did. Good sharp talking to and they was back on their feet in no time. That's all your Jack needs. Bit of chat.'

Sunday, 0800

The Warrenders' front door had been rocked off its hinges by blast during the night and it swung open at a touch. Arthur Scully gave it a good hard rap and peered across the parlour into the living-room and the kitchen beyond. The house was identical to his own. There was a pantry under the stairs and two bedrooms and a boxroom on the first floor, the boxroom being a bedroom for Paul Warrender, as the Scullys used theirs for Derek.

'Jack? You there?'

He edged inside making sure the door was wide open behind him, a time-honoured sign that you were a reluctant intruder. He trod warily. Only a couple of weeks back he had popped in to see Jack and, believing he was in the yard, had opened the kitchen door to surprise Gladys in the bath stark naked. He had retreated so fast he had banged his thumb in the living-room door. It was black and blistered still. To make matters worse, Gladys had insisted on making coquettish references to it afterwards, much to the mystification of the women.

There was a scuffling sound from the kitchen. Arthur opened the door. The little room was empty; the noise was coming from the yard. He leaned over the sink and peered out through the window. There, ludicrous against the mighty pall of smoke and flame sweeping the sky over the old Surrey, Jack Warrender was ripping the pages from the ledgers and files he'd rescued the night before and heaping them on a bonfire. The burning paper was floating up from the flames, still alight, and whisking away in the cross-current of wind across Nelson's Green towards Quebec Dock, the heart of the firestorm. Jack was jumping up at the stray pieces like a man possessed, slapping them down as if determined that none should escape, sparks showering him from head to foot.

Arthur watched in alarm. You didn't have to see the expression on his face to know he wasn't normal. His body was moving from fire to ledger with odd jerky movements as if he'd lost all co-ordination. Elsie had said he wasn't himself but this was bloody serious. Arthur had to think this out.

He pulled back from the window and padded through to the living-room. He was on his way back to the front door when he heard the sob. Again. Distinct. He glanced up the stairs and bent an ear. Wasn't Gladys or Paul, so where. . . ? He went back to the kitchen.

Jack Warrender, arms braced on the sink, head bowed over hunched shoulders, was sobbing uncontrollably. Arthur recoiled, faster even than when he had glimpsed Glad's soapy nakedness. Outside in the yard the bonfire blazed, snowing black flakes of charred paper. The sobs became a single keening groan.

Grasp the nettle, Arthur. Now or never. Come on, lad; can't be allowed to fester. Remember Egypt.

He manufactured a short, sharp cough. Jack Warrender whirled up from the sink, his eyes blood-red, tear trails etched in the ash covering his face.

'Leave me alone!'

'Can't do that, Jack.' Arthur stepped into the room, averting his eyes from the other man's shame. He drew up a small wooden stool. 'Here, stick yourself on there. You must be half dead, what I've been hearing about you last night.'

Jack turned his face away and stared angrily into the sink.

'Come on, Jack lad. Not easy, I know, but we've all got to make an effort. Sit down; tell me about it. Always better that way.' He allowed his voice to soften. 'Nobody's told me anything yet. Left me out in the cold, ain't they?'

Jack raised his head and stared blindly at the window in front of him. 'Walk out there! That's all you need do. Walk out there!'

It wasn't much but it was a start.

Arthur said quickly, 'Didn't have it all their own way, Jack. The R.A.F. gave Jerry a right old pasting.' No response. 'Always seems worse at night, I always say. You can't see what's happening. Like a pimple on your tongue. Feels ten times bigger than it looks, eh? Take my word, mate—the docks'll be back in business sooner than Jerry thought.'

Jack Warrender wiped his face on his shirt-sleeve without a

word. Arthur swallowed hard. Right, then. Shock tactics called for here. His voice when he spoke was harsh and uncompromising.

'I hear they smashed your place to pieces, then?'

Jack Warrender nodded.

'How bad?'

Jack shook his head.

'Well, was it flattened or just part of it or what?'

Jack turned from the sink and looked at him.

'You don't understand.'

'Course I don't understand, that's why I'm asking you. Bloody won't understand talking to myself, will I?'

'It ain't that sim . . . like that. Not just the bombing. Not only that.'

'Tell me.'

'Everything's gone. The docks, the offices . . . the . . . the . . . people.'

'What people?' Arthur asked, relentless.

'Charlie. My boy. The assistant. He left before me. He went home. . . . Saw him. . . . It *was* Charlie. I know . . . it was. . . .' The sentences were beginning to knit together. 'When I got out I walked . . . back. Bodies. Down by the edge of Lavender. A pile . . . of bodies on the tow-path. Burning, some of them. Burning. I looked.'

'Charlie?'

'I could just make . . . out. . . . It was. . . .'

'Would've been quick, Jack. Quick. Blast, see. Don't feel a thing.'

'There ain't nothing left now. That's what I mean. Nothing there for me. Nothing anywhere, don't you see?'

'Jack!' Arthur Scully pulled himself up to his full five feet eleven, slapped his hands on Jack's shoulders and gave him a damn good shake.

"S'all right.' Jack pulled back. 'You don't have to stay. Told you. Leave me alone.'

'It's for your own good, Jack. Snap out of it.'

Jack Warrender sank to the stool and gazed stupidly into

space. Arthur was at a loss. The lad was going off his rocker right enough. He needed a doctor. He tried one last tack.

'I come to talk about the boys. Derek and your Paul. Serious, Jack. Listen to me. We've got to talk.'

Jack Warrender was now well past talking. He looked vacantly at the floor at his feet.

'The lads could be in trouble, understand? That mean anything to you?'

Jack was no longer listening.

'Let me talk to him, then! Paul.'

Jack's bent back straightened and the face came alive. 'Fire's going out,' he said. He rose and stumped out into the yard without a backward glance.

Arthur watched him sift through the burning papers, obsessively raking the outlying pieces into the centre of the blaze with a stick. Treatment, that's what he needed. Fast. Nothing anybody else could do. Arthur went to the foot of the stairs and whispered, 'Paul.'

He received a grunt in response.

'You awake up there, Paul? It's Uncle Arthur.'

The boy peered down from the landing, still tousled with sleep. 'That you, dad?'

'It's Uncle Arthur. Your dad's. . . . He's just nipped out for a minute. Have a word, Paul?'

'I was just getting up,' lied the boy. 'Too hot to sleep.'

He came down the stairs in a pair of over-long pyjama bottoms and sat down half way. 'Something up, Uncle Arthur? Where's mum?'

'Next door with Auntie Flo. She'll be here soon. I asked your dad if I could have a word with you, Paul. Mind?'

'Mind? Nah?' The boy blinked the sleep away. 'What you want to talk about, Uncle Arthur?'

Arthur walked up the stairs and sat down just below him. 'Well, let's start at the beginning, eh? The football match. Let's start with the football match at West Ham. . . .'

Gladys stirred. Somebody was talking to her.

'Yes? Mmmmmm?'

Turned over. The voice went on droning in her ear. Not just one. Dozens of voices. Like when the lights went down at the start of the show.

The show! She snapped her eyes open. What time was it? God, they hadn't let her sleep through! She fumbled for the alarm clock. Eight-thirty! When? Night? Oh, no, they hadn't.... A thin chink of light glowed reassuringly under the sheet of blackout material pinned across the window. Morning! She sank back on the pillow.

Somebody was talking on the stairs, but she couldn't make out the words; didn't care. Her body felt totally relaxed; floating, weightless, sated with the first good sleep in months. Then the events that preceded sleep came tumbling home and she was floating no more. That terrible walk home to the Green. She shrugged herself into a sitting position and felt the first stirrings of alarm.

Something slid from the folds of the sheet on to the floor. She bent to pick it up. A visiting card. Melvyn J. Shaffer, Correspondent, American Broadcasting Network Inc. Melvyn J. Shaffer. She wondered idly what the J. stood for. She held the card between forefinger and thumb and blew to spin it like a child's windmill. It stopped with the blank side facing her. Only it wasn't blank.

In a clear, competent hand Melvyn J. Shaffer had written: 'Savoy Hotel foyer. Four o'clock. Tea.'

She shook her head. Americans! They were the end. Didn't they know there was a war on?

Sunday, 1000

The jangling of the telephone cut deep into his subconscious and Shaffer came awake with a start. Bright sunshine streamed through the windows, throwing the criss-crosses of anti-blast paper gummed across their panes into surrealist relief on the far wall. He gravitated upwards on one elbow but stopped abruptly; his body was stiffer than he'd ever known it, the muscles seized and sore, and as he touched his face and neck dry skin flaked into his fingers. His eyes, too, felt strange; the lids were tinder dry and as he rubbed them tears spurted remedially over singed lashes.

He swung his feet to the floor and reached for the old upright phone before the clanging of its English bell deafened him completely.

'Yes?'

'Mr Shaffer?' Cynthia Price, secretary to A.B.N.'s London correspondents since time began, was too well versed in American newsmen's behaviour patterns to be put off by ill humour. 'Are you properly awake, Mr Shaffer?'

'No, Mrs Price. I feel like hell and I need another ten hours—'

'I have Mr O'Keefe on the line from New York, Mr Shaffer,' she interrupted briskly.

'Tell him to go—'

'I'm putting him through. You have him ... now.'

There was a click, more clicks, then the asthmatic breathing that was a preliminary to every call from A.B.N.'s head of foreign news. Clarence O'Keefe was a caricature of the journalistic trade; a dumpy, hard-drinking, unhealthy, undisciplined, inspirational news-hawk who had served his time all the way up from two-desk newsrooms in mid-West hick towns to the city desk of the *Journal-American* before he switched to sound. It was a pilgrim's progress that had ruined his sex life, his marriage, his credit rating at the bank and his lungs.

'O'Keefe?'

'That you, Shaffer?'

'What time is it?'

'I'll tell you what goddamn time it is. It's come-up-with-some-action time. You drunk when you ran that piece of Aunt Martha's angel cake last night?'

Shaffer grunted as a nerve began to throb mercilessly between his shoulder blades. 'What are you talking about?'

'What am I *talking* about? That crap you filed last night is what I'm talking about. You wanna know what we're up against over here? I'll tell you. Fred Bate was on the air three times last night with the best damn coverage he's ever done for N.B.C., Murrow was on this morning for C.B.S. and Eric Severeid and

Larry LeSueur were backing up for him through the night. They just had Bill Shirer on from Berlin. You know what we had? We had noughts-and-crosses. Churchill is this, Hitler is that. Dowding is this, Goering is the other. Jesus, man, what kind of action do you need before you light up? You've got the end of the world over there.'

Shaffer closed his eyes and on the agitated scarlet screen behind the lids he re-ran the script he had originally written. 'We had a deal, remember? Play it the Board's way. What d'you want from me, Oke?'

'I want colour, son. I want graphic re-creation. I want what Murrow and Bate are giving the people — hell on earth in three-minute takes.'

'Go tell it to the Board. Go ask Vince Hirschfield. Then tell me for chrissakes what I'm supposed to be doing over here.'

'Don't make me take the Board's name in vain, son. I might say something I'll regret. Let me say this to you, Mel. Listen good, huh? O.K. Since Munich, we all went off the boil about the war in Europe — even C.B.S., and it's costing them thirty thousand bucks a month to keep that outfit of theirs working over there. But France and the Low Countries changed that some — and the Battle of Britain, Hitler bombing the airfields. We're getting kinda nervous over here. In the past couple of weeks Lindbergh's been getting the freeze. So's Joe Kennedy. And let me tell you this: you can have ten bucks of my hard-earned any time if Roosevelt doesn't pull Moanin' Joe out of London before winter. So — be what you're paid to be, son; grab yourself a little pride. Forget the fuckin' Board. I have. They make policy, but it's people like me carry it out — and policy can't change facts.'

'But Hirschfield—'

'Hirschfield's got himself an airblock in his ass. A little less time soothsaying and a little more chasing good hard news and he might still be sitting where you are. Take it from me, Mel — the politicking is over as far as this business is concerned. Last night changed all that. I'm calling off that deal we made. From here on in we give it to 'em straight — blood, sweat and tears, like the man said. You want in?'

Shaffer was on his feet. 'You sure you know what you're talking about?'

'No. I'm just another soft-hearted idealist burning to save the world. I said – are you in?'

'I can record inside an hour and play it over—'

'Oh, no. Not any more. We're in the instant news business now – just like the big boys. C.B.S. have been running a tight ship from Europe all year. No recordings. Matter of integrity, see? Everything comes over live, day and night. If we have to record you this end, different matter. You just carry your butt over to Langham Place and get it in front of a typewriter. Give me a nice round package. Last night, what you saw, how you felt, what the people did. And Mel. I want it on the eight a.m. bulletin, so remember you'll be going out to people sitting down to breakfast a billion miles from that war. They'll be going to church, carving a roast later on for friends come over to eat. They won't find it easy to see things your way, you get me?'

'It was a big night, Oke. I was in it up to my hairline. I still have the scars.'

'Keep 'em good and dry till air-time. We got the studio facility tied up with B.B.C. and the censor's scheduled to be there at eleven o'clock your time. A guy called Eric Warr and he's used to a bit of class. He's Murrow's censor, too. I'll call you eleven-fifteen. Get with it.'

The line went dead.

The studio was in the sub-basement of Broadcasting House, although by New York standards it would have fitted the description 'broom closet' better. To reach it, Shaffer had to pass an armed sentry at the sandbagged main door, cross a foyer laced with heavy iron screens and descend three levels, each sealed by a steel gas-tight door. On the lower ground floor the old B.B.C. concert hall had been converted to a cavernous air-raid shelter which doubled throughout the day and night as a dormitory for off-duty personnel, but as Shaffer picked his way through the basement corridors he had to step over dozens of blanket-wrapped sleeping figures, too late or too tired to find ground space in the hall. His accreditation pass was examined minutely several times, finally by a civilian sentry at the studio door. The man wore an arm-band and carried a shotgun and took his job seriously; the fact that he had seen Shaffer at least a half dozen times in the past week did not influence him in the conduct of his official function. This war, thought Shaffer privately, was going to create more self-serving bureaucrats than heroes or corpses; God help the post-war generation that had to live with them.

He opened his typewriter on the workroom side of the curtain which divided the small room in two; the other half was the studio. At this moment it was also a bedroom for three B.B.C. engineers who had bunked down under blankets on the floor. It was not exactly unusual. Ed Murrow claimed he'd made a broadcast a couple of weeks back with nine bodies on the studio floor; they all slept through his despatch.

'Last night the world came to an end,' he experimented. He cocked his head on one side, measured it for sound. The studio clock hit 1041 and he bent over the keyboard again.

'I know because I was there. I know because I'm alive and whole and I still have my faculties and they tell me I was there and it happened. You want to know something? I still don't believe it. I make the point, here and now, because, as you sit down to Virginia ham and real eggs, to freshly baked bread, to coffee that actually comes from the bean, to dairy cream and fresh fruit, in the Sunday morning peace and tranquillity of your American homes, you're going to find this pretty hard — even impossible — to believe; too. Maybe you have other things on your mind. Maybe you take the view that other people's wars are other people's business. Frankly, I couldn't find it in my heart to blame you because up to seven o'clock last night I lived on the sidelines myself.'

It ran out of him like blood from a punctured vein. The boys in the warehouse, Keeton's Road School, the frightened inhabitants of Nelson's Green — frightened, inexplicably, for each other, not themselves. He wrote of the night-club dancer who walked home alone through flaming streets rather than endanger his life.

'I couldn't tell you how those people fared,' he wound up, 'because I haven't been back into the East End yet this morning. Maybe some of them are still alive. I'll let you know. I'll go back today because I have to – *not* because I need to test my courage, *not* because I couldn't get the news some other way. I'm going back because I became part of the East End community last night, as sure as every individual in those mean, shattered streets was fused and bonded by heat and suffering to his neighbours. Today and tonight, those people will be waiting again for the discordant whine of the Dornier, the drone of the Heinkel and the nightmare scream of the bombs. They will watch their homes crumble, their friends die. But this time it won't be the end of the world. We know. We already survived it.'

Eric Warr arrived at eleven to check the script and O'Keefe came on the line at eleven-twenty. Ten minutes later it was all over. Warr kept his censor's finger on the cut-off switch in case Shaffer ad libbed on the agreed script but his interjection was unnecessary. For the first time in his professional career Shaffer felt total emotional involvement in what he had written; and intonation and emphasis gave his despatch more weight than he could have achieved with a sackful of adjectives. When he finished Warr winked at him complimentarily and, from New York, O'Keefe's stertorous breathing hacked into a chuckle of satisfaction.

'That's what I call *brio*, Shaffer. Encore. Get yourself back there at five this afternoon, your time, O.K? And keep it coming.'

He walked back to his car in Hallam Street, the backwater behind Broadcasting House where shrewder members of the American Press corps had rented apartments and/or offices. He rolled back the Morris Ten's primitive canvas canopy to admit the warm sun. There was no sound in the street, no hint of the carnage and destruction that lay just five miles east along the Thames. It slept in peace, sun flooding its western face, shadow dappling the east. From an open first-floor window the sad voice of an organ sang 'Bells across the Meadow' over the radio and, as Shaffer swung into the driver's seat, a couple in sober Sunday church clothes turned into the street with two little boys at their heels. The man wore black, the woman wore grey and the

children toy naval uniforms with wide square collars and miniature sailors' caps, trimmed with black satin bows. They marched
sedately and in silence as if taking part in a sacred procession.
Shaffer watched them in awe.

He drove along Regent Street to Piccadilly. It was with some
irritation that he had discovered before he left the apartment
that he had agreed to have lunch at midday with somebody
called Denzil Fletcher-Hale. At first, he couldn't fit the name to
a face, a meeting or even a moment of idle introduction; then
it came to him. Vincent Hirschfield's system of evening social
contact involved ploughing from one side of a crowded room
to another and back again at speed, a progress which allowed
him to tray-snatch at least four glasses of champagne, be seen
by the greatest number of habitués possible, indulge in a dozen
or so twenty-second conversations; attract the attention of his
hosts, say his goodbyes and push on to the next party. It was in
the course of one such assault on London's night-life that the
tryst had been struck with Fletcher-Hale. It had been on Shaffer's
second or third night in town at a party given by the Cunards.
Flogging his way in Hirschfield's wake through bejewelled *dé-
colletages* and a forest of powdered throats, Shaffer had found
himself staring at the boiled front of the tallest shirt in the
world. The guy inside it was around six feet five and lean as a
Redskin brave. Just short of the Cunards' tinkling chandelier, his
hair shone as though sheathed in gold and, at the other end of
him, impossibly small feet were encased in highly polished
Oxfords. Hirschfield had made his stereotype introduction and
prepared to plough on; but this character wasn't the casual
kind. An introduction was a preliminary to blood brotherhood
in his book; either that or he had a notion that American newsmen were useful additions to the old family armoury. He had
seized Shaffer's arm, produced a gold-ridged calling-card from
his pocket, wrote 'White's, Sunday, 12 noon' on the back of it
and posted it in Shaffer's cummerbund. Hirschfield had been
vague about him later on that evening. 'Denzil? Character.
Knows a lot of people. Use him.' Just that.

He parked in Albemarle Street and strolled across Piccadilly
into St James's. Hirschfield had membership at the Reform and

the Beefsteak and he had given Shaffer a basic training of sorts in conduct becoming a colonial in clubland. It didn't help much. He had grasped, but failed to understand, why no gentleman's club carried a nameplate at the door as a means of identification. He had learned where, as a guest, he could and could not sit; why the library and the reading-room were significantly different social venues where port was automatically — or never — served; why cash never crossed the bar; how the Anglo-Saxon aristocratic purity of one club was preserved as against the legal–financial professionalism of another or the political complexion of a third, and what it did to your standing in society to be blackballed by any of them. The New Brunswick farm-boy in him chafed at the watertight protectionism of the system but he couldn't suppress a sneaking suspicion that he might get to like life behind those anonymous façades if they ever let him over the threshold as a member.

White's had a more human scale than the Reform and the porter greeted him cordially; Shaffer put that down to the fact that anyone who dared cross the mat had to be top drawer. His *bona fides* was secured the second he uttered Fletcher-Hale's name. The porter behaved as he might if the king had strolled in with the House of Lords at his back; he disappeared in a cloud of promises and returned with the towering young man.

He looked taller, leaner; his hair shone brilliantly and Shaffer found himself wondering how anyone living with the English climate, especially in London, managed to hold on to a rich (yes, accent on the *rich*) Riviera tan. Fletcher-Hale came forward, a huge hand outstretched.

'Shaffer. Dear fellow. Delighted you could make it.' The eyes were cerulean blue, honest to the point of transparency; the face serious. As Shaffer was to discover over the next few days, Denzil had been blessed with all the equipment a fond providence can bestow on its favourites, except for two vital elements: quick-wittedness and laughter. He grimaced down on Shaffer with a tortured arrangement of mouth and eyes and brow which sought to convey his pleasure. The two men shook hands, loosely in Denzil's case as though he had been warned not to over-exert himself. He wore a dark suit with a faint stripe to it and a waistcoat (calling it a vest, Hirschfield said, was worse than pronouncing S'nt James's *Saint* James's). Across the waistcoat hung a gold chain supporting three gold medallions.

'Deuced early for lunch. Apologise. Green's waitin' in the dining-room. Appointment at two, d'you see.'

'Look, Denzil...,' Shaffer began. The young man's eyes widened slightly and Shaffer registered his first *faux pas*; first-name familiarity was virtually non-existent in upper-class English life outside the family circle. Oh, well; he was damned if he was going to grapple with 'Fletcher-Hale' all through lunch. 'Look, I'm sorry. I guess I missed something that night Hirschfield introduced us. You didn't say anything about....'

'Ah! Green? Hirschfield's idea. Called me on the telephone before we met at the Cunards. Introduce you around. A few types, d'you see. Somethin' to get your teeth into. Colour, what?'

Shaffer smiled tightly. 'Oh, sure. Fine. Colour. Well, that was real friendly of Vince. Thanks. Who exactly is Green?'

Denzil eyed him quizzically. 'Profiteer,' he said evenly. 'Black market, too, they tell me. Brisk line of business. Bounder, of course. Complete cad. Curious thing, doesn't seem to care. These chaps don't, y'know. Interest you?'

Shaffer squinted slyly down at his watch. He had to be at Broadcasting House at four-thirty latest; he had a date for tea at the Savoy at four with Gladys Warrender — if she deigned to keep it — and there was a note on the office diary at Hill Street that Duff Cooper, the Minister of Information, was personally handling a Press conference at the ministry's headquarters in the London University building at three.

'I don't have much time right now.'

Denzil patted his shoulder paternally. 'Nor Green. Has to be at Greenwich by two-thirty. Suit you both. Come.'

He led the way through to the dining-room. It was a light, airy room, not excessively over-furnished, but its graceful chandeliers, moulded ceiling, spotless white napery and glinting silver radiated an air not only of substance and well-being but of taste and tradition and calculated understatement. There were only three or four tables occupied so early in the day but

Shaffer identified Green instantly. The man had his back to them; only his shoulders and his head were visible but he might just as well have worn an electric sign above him declaring his unsuitability. He turned as they approached the table and Shaffer cringed as a Clark Gable moustache rose in greeting over large, china dentures.

'You'll be Shaffer, then.' The moustache sat uneasily over the upper dental plate; each word uttered caused it to dip and roll absurdly. Under it, the mouth was small and the lips pink and puckered with advancing age. Shaffer eyed the man's jet-black curly hair with open suspicion. He had to be fifty; fifty-five, maybe. The artist in vulgarity who had tried to slice twenty-five years off his age had the right to some kind of Academy Award.

'Hullo.' He edged around the table to the far side to avoid hand-to-hand contact.

Denzil flowed downwards into a chair, distributing his great height without effort. 'Freddie Green. Melvyn Shaffer, American Broadcasting Network.'

'*Captain* Freddie Green.' The moustache rose on the dental display, but aggressively. *Captain* Green was clearly not a man to miss out on essentials.

'Navy?' Shaffer pressed.

'Strewth, no. Army, o'course. Green Howards, actually.'

Denzil's head angled minutely in Shaffer's direction and for a second their eyes met. The opaque blue revealed nothing but, when they turned away, Shaffer felt as if he had received a two-hour lecture on the realities of English social handicapping.

'You people must be sweating it out, just now?' he said.

'Beg pardon?'

'Your regiment. The invasion. You're going to have a big job on your hands.'

'Oh? Aaaaaah – get what you're going on about. No – I'll miss the fun, damn bad luck. Invalided out, old son. Nineteen thirty-eight. Caught my packet' – he rubbed the small of his back with some fervour – 'out East.'

'India?'

Captain Green's yellow-beige eyes bounced from Shaffer's face to Denzil's and back. 'Not the kind of thing you go on

109

about it, is it? Bad form. That's the way we are, us English. Can't expect you to understand, though, you bein' an American and just unpacked your bags — eh, Denzil?'

Fletcher-Hale flinched without significantly moving a muscle of his face or body. Green missed it; Shaffer didn't.

A group of three men strolled into the room and made their way to a table in the window. One of them excused himself to his host and stooped at Denzil's shoulder. He nodded politely to Shaffer and Green.

'Might have something for you, care to drop in tomorrow,' he said.

'Thanks.' The young man indicated his guests. 'Do you know Gladwyn Jebb? Shaffer's with the American Broadcasting Network, and—'

'How d'you do, Mr Jebb. Freddie Green's my name. Captain Freddie Green. I think we have a friend in mutual : Mr Wilson.'

Jebb stared at him disbelievingly. 'I don't think . . . ,' he began coolly.

'Yes, you do,' urged Green, dentures awesome. 'I never forget names and I never forget titles. You' — he pointed a bony finger across the table — 'you are . . . no, gimme a minute, now . . . you are . . . gotcha, Private Secretary . . . right? . . . to the Permanent Under-Secretary at the Foreign Office. Now, am I right?'

'That's correct,' said Jebb politely. He flashed a sideways glare at Denzil who returned it squarely.

'See?' Green tugged at Shaffer's jacket sleeve. 'The old F.O. Never forget a title. Mr Wilson, our mutual, come to all my little dos up at Greenwich. Always there.' He lay back expansively in his chair, allowing his jacket to fall wide from a pink-and-white striped shirt and a green-and-white striped tie.

Shaffer broke the silence as Jebb moved away to join his party. 'You — er — thinking of working with the Foreign Office?' he asked Fletcher-Hale.

The shoulders of the dark suit rose and fell. 'Considering. One or two irons in the fire. Here and there. Fellow must do his bit. Office, desk, paperclips — not my line o' country. F.O. could be fun. Talked to Halifax about it. Said he'd do what he could.

Friend of the family.' He dried up, exhausted by the un-characteristically long speech.

'Told him — didn't I tell you, Denzil? — anytime he wants a cushy number, all he's got to do is come to Freddie Green.' Green waved his arms expressively and an ageing waitress floated to the table, interpreting it as a summons. 'I told him — I can use young men like him, all above board and official,' he went on, ignoring the waiting woman. 'I got my contacts to the highest level. One word from me and he could be classified in a reserved occupation.'

Denzil affected the scowl which passed for a smile. 'Kind of you. Other things to consider.' He gestured to the waitress and Shaffer and Green buried their heads in their menus. They ordered. When they finished, the wine waiter came forward and extended the wine list to Denzil. It never quite reached his hand; Green snatched it confidently.

'Right, now — let's see what they got on offer.' He hummed to himself. 'I think we'll settle for the white Bordukes with the fish and, after that, we'll go on to this Number Thirty-six, the Saint Emily-on.' The waiter cast a wide-eyed leer at Denzil, who nodded briefly. Green swung in his chair as the man walked away. 'And — er — we'll want the Bordukes cold and the other one room temperature, old son,' he called.

Heads turned at the window table. Shaffer slunk lower in his chair. Fletcher-Hale seemed not to have heard.

In the next quarter of an hour Green monopolised the con-versation. He was not easily interrupted or diverted and after the first few minutes Shaffer gave up trying. In the event, he was surprisingly well informed and it dawned on Shaffer that, for all his boasting and mindless posturing, his claims to having contacts in high places must, in some degree, be genuine. The invasion, he announced confidentially, was expected on the thirteenth and last night the order had gone out to prepare for it. Police, fire brigades, Voluntary Defence Force and ambulance units had all been notified to stand by. Operation Cromwell was the code phrase. Mark his words, the R.A.F. would be moving on the French and Dutch channel ports soon, 'doing up' the German landing barges.

What Churchill, the R.A.F. and, by inference, Captain Freddie Green would do to advance the war effort was lost to them at that moment; a siren wailed out the alert and Green slipped off his chair at once and fell on one knee beside it. He would have taken his precautions farther but a quick glance round the dining-room revealed that no one else had moved; at Jebb's table the lament had not even broken the train of conversation.

Green rubbed feverishly at his knee and pushed himself inelegantly back on his chair. 'Damn knee,' he grated. 'Just goes sometimes. Crack.' He looked at Denzil in silent appeal.

'Got that out East, too?' asked Shaffer solicitously.

'Bits and pieces stuck together with string and spit — that's me,' shrugged Green. He ducked his head in a forlorn attempt to observe the sky through the window overlooking St James's. 'Jerry starting early today again, eh?' He rolled dry lips one inside the other with a bony index finger.

Shaffer and Fletcher-Hale waited for him to resume his chatter and, when he showed no sign of doing so, made an unspoken pact to maintain silence. They heard the faraway whoomp-whoomp of anti-aircraft batteries in the Thames Estuary and, within minutes, the buzz-saw snarl of massed bombers. The first bombs hit ground miles away to the east and Green flattened his hands on plate and cutlery. He noted their stares and a stale imitation of a grin curdled around his mouth.

The dining-room steward came to Denzil's shoulder. 'I can serve the fish now, sir, if you care to begin. Or perhaps you'd prefer to wait a few moments?' His eyes crept involuntarily towards the ceiling.

'Now, I think,' Denzil said off-handedly. 'M'guest, here — got important work at hand. Appointment. Must leave before two. Right, Green?'

'Er — right.'

The sole was served and they began to eat. The activity seemed to generate a brave new spirit in Captain Green, and an appetite for confidences. One of his more important contacts, he revealed generously, told him last night that Churchill had thrown the whole of Whitehall into a tizz by ordering the House of Commons and the ministries to bring their lunch break forward by one hour so that Parliament would not have to sit late and present an even juicier target to German night bombers than they did to those attacking at random during the day. Green had personally decided to tailor his own day to this new format in the national interest.

A string of high explosives screamed to earth somewhere south of the river and burst with a violence that rattled the cutlery. Green fell to one knee again and this time, when he rose, made no attempt to cover his anxiety. 'Bloody close, that, Den,' he breathed, recruiting sympathy.

The bombardment in the east continued for nearly ten minutes and when it gave no evidence of advancing westwards the Captain returned to his confidences. The main course arrived and he enlarged on the extent of his business ventures and their relevance to the war effort. He had interests in aero-engine parts, glass-making, the manufacture of lathes and die-casting machinery, farming — 'big future in farming when this lot's over' — and what he termed 'ancillaries'.

'Green's bein' modest. Does sound work. What you might call Home Front stuff. Keeping the wheels turning. Eh, Green?'

'I wouldn't say that, Denzil.' Modesty sat uncomfortably on the pinched, improbable face. 'Yes, I s'pose you *could* say that, come to think of it. We do our best where we can, I always say. Now you take me,' he said, tugging again at Shaffer's sleeve. 'The war effort? I'm in it up to here. But that's only part. Only *part*. The people who're gonna win this war — the really *top* people — they have the worry and the cares and the responsibility, right? Your common soldier, he doesn't have any of that. Does what he's told — biff, bang, finish. Same with the women in the factories and the kids running wild all over the countryside, having a good time and giving people what for. *They're* all right. But your thinkers, your planners, your upper class and your upper middle class — left to it they'd get the same treatment as the rest. That's what these socialists they just let in the government want, see. Equal for everyone. But there isn't any equal about it, is there? I mean, who thanks the man who sits in his office till midnight figuring things out 'cause that's his duty? No one. Well, they've got some rights, the way I look at it. They deserve a few little extras now and then.'

'And you see to it they get them.'

'Only do my best,' said Green, lying back to show his pink-and-white shirt again.

'What kind of things?'

'The kind that make the difference, son. Your bottle of decent plonk or Scotch. Your full-fashioned stockings. Your sugar and butter and a little bit of meat that ain't mutton. Tyres for your car and p'raps petrol coupons. Things.'

'I thought that kind of thing was covered by government prohibition. Rationing.'

'Right you are.' The yellow-beige eyes contained no hint of suspicion and the Clark Gable moustache writhed in a generous display of indignation. 'And 'cept for me, that's the way it'd be for the duration. People in *need — real* need — getting nothing just so we can pretend we're all bloody equal.' The wine had raised red weals on his cheeks.

He expanded farther on the thesis of morality and patriotism over two large brandies. Finally, Fletcher-Hale checked him in mid-sentence and called his attention to the time. 'Ten to two, Green. Duty calls.' He looked at Shaffer. 'Has a pressing engagement. Top secret, shouldn't wonder — eh, Green?'

'Well.' Green got unsteadily to his feet. The knot of his tie had crept under the collar, as if ashamed to be seen. 'Can't say you're right and can't say you're wrong, see what I mean? Careless talk, right?' He raised a forefinger to his lips. 'Been a real pleasure as usual, Den. And I want to see you again, Melville, soon as you like. I'll get one of my secretaries' — he unleashed a vast, pantomime wink — 'to mark you down for my next little thrash up at Greenwich. Sometime this week, O.K.? No, don't get up.' Neither of them had shown a sign of doing so. 'Ta-ta.' He weaved uncertainly across the room and out of sight.

Shaffer shook his head. 'I don't believe it.'

Fletcher-Hale despatched his brandy. 'Rare bird, Freddie.'

Sunday, 1215

Dowding looked ill. At best an ascetic figure in the mould of his contemporary at Winchester, Stafford Cripps, he now seemed physically shrunken in the envelope of his uniform. At Bentley Priory the health of the commander of Britain's air defences had been the subject of concern for months. He was, as they all were, exhausted; that went without saying. But unlike Churchill, who seemed positively to thrive on the ravages of war, Dowding accumulated fatigue and stored it up. He drove himself without consideration; sometimes irrationally and, to the despair of his subordinates, obsessively.

He had established his private quarters just over a mile away so that he could arrive at the Priory promptly at nine o'clock each morning; by which time, his critics pointed out, many of the squadrons under his command had been in action at least twice. The Luftwaffe were no respecters of the British breakfast. It was an unfair jibe in many ways but it was seized upon by his detractors as an indication of his blindness to priorities. Dowding attracted criticism without effort.

At fifty-eight a man needed to conserve his energies, not dissipate them. At fifty-eight a man occupying the crucial role in one nation's fight-to-the-finish with another might have been expected to examine himself for personality flaws as he would his men. Dowding had no time for such introspections. Each night he insisted on being driven fifty miles to Redhill or Kenley to inspect progress in the research going on to improve the 'seeing eye' equipment for night fighters. The drive back, often in an air-raid, could take hours. And more likely than not, Churchill would be on the phone for him in his absence — demanding, inquiring, accusing. A phone call to Redhill would have achieved the same purpose but Dowding wouldn't hear of it. Now, he seldom visited operational fighter stations as he once had and his Cabinet critics claimed his overall grasp of the strategy of the air war was slipping from him. He was more distant, less flexible. His nickname — 'Stuffy' — was beginning to lose the bantering respect that had given birth to it.

The reaction throughout much of the service was the same: Stuffy wasn't up to it. As a consequence, Fighter Command, over which he had presided since 1936, was coming apart at the seams. Badly sited airfields; ineffective fighter armament; antiquated tactics; a lumbering, antediluvian organisational structure. The night of 7 September had seen those weaknesses coalesce into a single disheartening chaos as the Luftwaffe's Valhalla formations struck at London with impunity.

To cap it all, the much vaunted ack-ack defences had proved worse than useless. The sound locators for the fixed-azimuth system, already rendered unreliable by the Luftwaffe's method of desynchronising their engines, had a ceiling of only 15,000 feet. The Luftwaffe flew higher. The ninety-two heavy guns around London were unable to fire because they simply didn't know where the enemy was; an enemy that was filling the sky with aircraft! The order had gone out: shoot at random. Pea-shooters aiming at gnats in a darkened room.

The facts spoke for themselves: one cubic mile of space contained 5,500,000,000 cubic yards of air; the lethal impact zone of a shell was a mere few thousand cubic yards, and then for only a fraction of a second. With pot luck, it required a firing-rate of three thousand shells per second to achieve a one-fiftieth chance of hitting anything. The responsibility for solving that equation was General Pile's but its failure was yet another straw on Dowding's back.

Few of his officers could guess how many straws there already were. War smiles only on the victor and Stuffy had no scapegoat. Working virtually single-handed, he had been thrown into the front line with few weapons to sustain him. In 1936, when he was the most senior officer in the service and in line for an appointment as Chief of the Air Staff, he had been passed over for a rival, a junior, Sir Edward Ellington. The prewar code demanded that such a snub be answered by one's resignation. Stuffy's mistake had been not to proffer it.

Indignity was heaped on indignity. On more than one occasion he had been informed he was to be retired from the R.A.F.

Even as Goering mapped out his plans for the destruction of London, Dowding had been given the same blunt warning: he had six months, no more; then he would have to go.

But he was still there. The Chief of Britain's fighter force, on the second day of the greatest invasion threat England had ever known, was a man fighting not only for the lives of his depleted airmen and, implicitly, the lives of the millions they defended; he was fighting for his own, one hand tied behind his back and a vote of no confidence ringing in his ears.

At Bentley Priory, at midday on 8 September, the mood reflected the man.

Tom Russell was in the officers' mess. He had a half-hour break before resuming duty in the Filter Centre's operations room and he was beginning to wish he hadn't left it. At least, the activity there left no time for brooding self-examination of the kind his colleagues had been indulging in for the past ten minutes. Their anger — frustration, criticism, division of loyalties — was a microcosm of the whole of Fighter Command's present state of mind.

The Big Wing versus independent squadron interception. Mass assault versus free manoeuvre. Air Vice Marshal Trafford Leigh-Mallory versus Air Vice Marshal Keith Park. Twelve Group versus Eleven Group. My God, hadn't they got problems enough without turning on each other?

The voices rose, slanging and counter-slanging as the argument grew; as the argument always grew. Russell slunk deep in his chair, determined to stay out of it this time around. No victor ever emerged from this debate. The facts were indelible.

Keith Park's Eleven Group had the impossible task of defending south-east England and therefore were first in line to snatch the blood and glory of confronting Goering's taskforces day after day. Keith Park believed in independent fighter attack, in the freedom of individual squadrons to manoeuvre to find their quarries, hunt them down and, just as important, stay out of the Messerschmitts' gunsights.

Leigh-Mallory commanded Twelve Group and was responsible for the, so far, less-than-active defence of the industrial Midlands. For weeks he had watched his arch-rival, Park, dominate the skies and his pilots claim an impressive list of kills. It was a demeaning experience to be left on the sidelines, the more so for a man of Leigh-Mallory's ambitions. His sights were set on Stuffy Dowding's chair and he had no doubt he would get it. To that end he had refused time and again to send his squadron to Park's assistance in the early weeks of the battle, insisting that to do so haphazardly would merely add to the chaos and reduce the efficiency of the strike. Some weeks before, his most celebrated officer, Squadron Leader Douglas Bader, had outlined the strategic possibilities of what came to be called the Big Wing. Bader, a nerveless pilot of great skill, had lost both legs in a Tiger Moth crash in the early thirties, but when war was declared he had talked his way back into uniform and, finally, into a Spitfire cockpit. He was already an ace, a daring leader trusted by his men and a proved strategist. His idea was an equal-and-opposite reaction to the Luftwaffe's massive flight formations: fight might with might. Scramble squadrons simultaneously, form them up in a gigantic scimitar shape across the sky and hit the enemy on a wide front.

Leigh-Mallory had accepted the plan and ordered Bader to perfect it but the teething troubles were far from being resolved; it took precious time to get individual squadrons into the air and oriented to fit the attack shape, time that could not be spared. Luftwaffe bombers took less than twenty minutes to cross the Kent coast, hit London and turn back.

At the end of August Dowding had berated his group commanders and tacitly ordered Leigh-Mallory to comply with any request Park made for assistance, but the controversy still raged. Yesterday, Twelve Group had been scrambled at four forty-five and Bader had collected the Big Wing. His success over London was substantial, but then, so was Eleven Group's; and Bader had admitted himself that he still needed to cut his scramble time below three minutes. With thirty-six fighters to get off the ground, that would be some doing. According to the gossip, Leigh-Mallory had told Bader this morning: 'Your score justifies the experiment. Carry on.'

Tom Russell checked his watch and got to his feet. Dowding was holding court with Keith Park at this moment; no doubt the same argument was taking place there. Curiously enough, neither of them had seemed unduly ruffled when he saw them walking together earlier. The blow had fallen at long last and that must be a relief in itself. If the rumours he heard were true, Dowding had decided to conserve his already depleted groups. Six hundred German fighters had come over with the 300 bombers yesterday, a clear, naked challenge by Goering to an out-and-out duel; man to man, loss for loss. Perhaps Dowding, with Park at his shoulder, had divined Goering's intention and decided not to take the bait. A whole armada of invasion barges poised along the French and Dutch coasts might be waiting on just that premise.

He slipped out of the mess and closed the door on the endless argument. What they needed, all of them, was a couple of salutary hours in a cockpit with an Me 109 on their tail.

The thought pulled him up short. Damn right. What *he* needed was a ticket back to the real war.

Sunday, 1230

The portly figure poked at the rubble with his walking stick.

'This way, sir.' Harold Scott, Chief Administrative Officer of the London Civil Defence Region, waved a hand over the tangled mass of fire hoses. 'It's a little tricky, I'm afraid. Tallow. A candle factory nearby was hit during the night. A bit slippery, if you. . . .' He picked his way forward carefully and Winston Churchill followed, stumping heavily in his wake.

The crowds had gathered at every vantage point; on window ledges caked with brick-dust; on still-smouldering piles of debris; on the bonnets of ambulances and the backs of fire-engines. There had been no time for publicity but, in the East End, news travelled as fast as rumour. Buses had stopped running; trains were stranded on their tracks; dozens of roads were impassable, and the Underground was blocked. But the jungle telegraph that, in peacetime, could alert a whole neighbourhood to the arrival of the police within minutes was still intact. Momentarily the problems of survival were forgotten. The East Enders flocked into the streets for a glimpse of the man who was still preaching a message they could understand. Defiance.

A ragged cheer went up and swelled to a roar. Churchill surveyed them, his features pensive. Then, with a grin, he removed his black derby, placed it on the end of his walking stick and, holding it high above his head, twirled it expertly against the burning backdrop of the Surrey Docks.

'Are we downhearted?' he shouted.

Louder: 'Are we downhearted?'

'No!' roared the crowd. 'Noooooooo!'

Harold Scott smiled awkwardly, like a scene-shifter who has blundered onstage during an encore by the lead tenor. Churchill nodded his satisfaction and brushed away the solicitous hand of a senior police officer at his elbow. He retrieved his hat and jammed it on his head. From nearby came a sudden sharp explosion and the shredding sound of falling brick. The men at the Prime Minister's shoulder stiffened and crowded round him. General Ismay, head of the military wing of the War Cabinet Secretariat, said quietly, 'Your car's over there, sir.'

Churchill threw a cursory glance in the direction of the sound, shrugged vacantly and turned back to the crowd.

'Good old Winnie!' shouted a wag at the front. 'We can take it!' The catchphrase was Churchill's own, one of hundreds he had coined in the last few months.

He waved at the man and the crowd roared its approval. 'Who can take it? *We* can!' they roared. They added clapping to their shouts and Churchill raised his hand in the V-sign. That did it. The cheering was tumultuous.

Ismay held out a supporting hand and took the Prime Minister's arm.

'They're with me, Ismay.' Churchill pulled out a handkerchief. His eyes were running with tears. 'My God, they're with me.'

A woman shouted from close by: 'Look at him, he's crying! Winston's crying! Lord love him – you can see he cares, can't you?'

Churchill blew his nose hastily and waved his stick at Harold

Scott. 'Well, let's get on then, Scott. Lot to see.' And he strode off briskly.

They had to run to catch him up.

Sunday, 1515

The Press conference at London University was expected to be less than revealing but attendance was nevertheless high.

'Adolf Hitler's attack on the people and property of London', intoned Information Minister Duff Cooper, 'must be seen as the beginning of a sustained attempt to break the will and spirit of the British people. By concentrating his assault on London he has effectively given notice that the taking of innocent life — women, children, old people — is acceptable in the eyes of the German High Command. However, he and Reichsmarschall Hermann Goering are now in a position to count the cost of yesterday's blitzkrieg. During the daylight attacks, probably not more than six hundred planes flew over British territory. In the night raids the number of bombers and fighters used was not more than three hundred and fifty. You'll understand that it is too early yet to give complete figures, but German losses accountable so far indicate that one in six of their aircraft was destroyed. Much of this was due to the high endeavour and skill of the R.A.F.'s night fighter squadrons but our anti-aircraft defences shot with great accuracy last night and brought down twenty-one German aircraft.'

He added more in the same vein — reconstituted plum duff, someone growled — his features devoid of emotion, his eyes on the typescript in his hands. The bombing, he said, was described in a communiqué by the Ministry of Home Security as being widespread and indiscriminate in the later stages. Damage was severe but, judged against the background of the war, was not serious.

Tom Watson of International News Service who was sitting alongside Shaffer nudged the broadcaster and whispered fiercely: 'What d'you think he means by that? They only killed women and kids so it's not serious?'

When he finished his statement the minister sat down. Questions were fired at him at once from all round the room. Frank Pick, the Director-General of the Press Bureau, looked away as the minister's face creased uncomfortably. Pick, among other things, had been managing director of London's Underground and chairman of the Council of Art and Industry before Churchill propelled him into his first active war post. He was sixty-two years old, a distinguished businessman and a zealot; he was also the last man on earth to occupy the seat of power in what, after all, was a strategic part of the propaganda machine. To the Prime Minister's clear discomfort Pick had confided that he would not handle propaganda that did not conform with the truth and his own conscience. Hirschfield, who had lunched with him, said there was no love lost between Pick and his minister and, for that matter, between any two people in the curious polyglot group of writers, academics, businessmen, civil servants and well-connected nobodies who staffed the 'Minf' and its Press section. The British 'working Press', which might have been regarded as a natural source of manpower for such a critical role, had been ignored; unlike American newsmen they were neither socially nor politically acceptable. A few, largely editors, commentators and reviewers, found their way into government jobs but for the most part Fleet Street was represented either by its powerful newspaper proprietors — of whom Lord Beaverbrook was outstandingly the most dynamic — or by journalists who also happened to be Members of Parliament.

Cooper waved his piece of paper at his Parliamentary Secretary, Harold Nicolson, who shrugged non-committally. The unspoken message was clear to everyone in the room and the shouts for attention rose in volume. The minister had left no doubt in the minds of the Press corps that he viewed them and much of their work as counter-productive to British national interests. Before he arrived, Ray Daniels of the *New York Times* and Drew Middleton of Associated Press had cornered Harold Nicolson for an off-the-record assessment of the real damage of last night's bombing; they had received a polite hand-off.

Shaffer had been standing a few yards away and could understand why. O'Keefe had read him a snatch of Daniels's story in today's *Times*. Cooper must have seen it and loathed it.

'Danger was everywhere overhead yet there were those who adopted a fatalistic philosophy and went their accustomed way,' Daniels had written. 'Oddenino's and Quaglino's were filled with dancing couples, many in evening dress. Few taxi-cabs operated and they sold themselves to the highest bidder.'

Or, seen from the official British standpoint: while the Luft-waffe was blowing the blue blazes out of the working-class East End, the aristocrats of Mayfair were wining and dining, untouched by enemy bombs, and the only British workers in evidence were exercising their democratic right to indulge in a little extortion.

The wave of shouting rose higher, became more insistent. Pick folded his arms. Cooper bunched his hands on his knees, then rose, bent to whisper in Nicolson's ear and strode from the room. The newsmen subsided at once and returned to their chairs.

Pick climbed to his feet, a ghost of a smile on his normally pugnacious face. 'Gentlemen. Gentlemen. There will be no questions on the minister's statement. You can each collect a copy from the Press Room and you'll also find there copies of the communiqué issued by Home Security. Now I'm sure you'll want to know what R.A.F. Bomber Command was doing while Goering was pounding London. Between dusk and midnight we attacked the German invasion zone in France and Belgium and bombed selected German armaments targets – including the Krupp works at Essen.' He waved to a middle-aged man with a long, balding dome and glasses. 'If you'll give them the details, Waterman. . . ?'

Shaffer walked back to his car in Bedford Square with Edward Angley, the *Herald Tribune* correspondent. There was no smell of war in Bloomsbury.

'You believe them?' asked Angley.

'Why not?'

'Cop-out!'

Shaffer shrugged. 'Who honours the truth in war? You think Goebbels does?'

'It's our job to get at it. Too many Press conferences like that and we might as well pack up and go home.'

'Aw, come on, Ted,' Shaffer remonstrated. 'How many newsmen get to run around Berlin like we ran around here last night? It's so damn democratic it's insane. You may get the stand-off at this level' — he cocked a thumb over his shoulder back at the university building — 'but if you want hard-core fact you only have to go out in the streets and look. I got a read-through of your piece this morning. I wouldn't say you had too many censor problems, would you? And that man-in-the-street quote you used — what was it? "Berlin'll get it and twice as bad. Churchill will see to that. He's that sort of man." Now if I was checking you out, I'd give you hell for that. It's contentious, misleading and speculative. There's nothing to say Churchill would countenance this type of bombing of Berlin.'

'Let the people speak. That's my motto. Anyway, from what I hear, Churchill's gonna have his time cut out holding Parliament together if he doesn't hit Berlin after this.'

Four diminutive children stopped their game of spinning tops to ogle open-mouthed as the two Americans walked by. Angley gestured towards them. 'How many kids like that do you think these people will allow to die before they start hitting back, bomb for bomb?'

'Churchill's a politician and a strategist: not a bleeding-heart. He'll put tactics first. Anyway, I'm not convinced he's the type to retaliate for the hell of it.'

They reached Angley's car. The *Trib* man leaned on the open door. 'Murrow's kicking himself about yesterday. They tell me he and Vince Sheean and Ben Robertson spent the night in a ditch near Gravesend. Went down to the Thames Estuary in the afternoon looking for a story. Boy!'

'They didn't do too badly, the way I hear it.'

Angley studied his toes. 'That was a — hum — offbeat piece you did for A.B.N. last night. I had a call this morning from my office. What was it all about, they said. What was the significance and why last night of all nights?' He looked up, archly.

'Thanks, Ted. You're a real pal.' Shaffer slapped him on the arm and trudged away to his car.

She was there. Savoy Hotel waiters had a mortal fear of un-accompanied women and had buried her at a dark corner table with overhanging baby palm. She was stiff with nervous antici-pation. He grinned as he crossed the foyer; it was still only three forty-five. She was early. Very early.

'Hi,' he said. He held out his hand but she bobbed her head and kept her hands knotted in her lap. She wore dark-blue shoes which matched her dress, a white jacket with dark-blue piping and a crazy little white basin of a hat with a scrap of white veiling. Her eyes were dark as the blue of her dress and wide with suppressed excitement. He wondered if she'd ever been in the place before.

He sat down and dropped his raincoat on a vacant chair. 'Like your outfit,' he said courteously.

She looked around her and leaned forward anxiously. 'Is it all right?' she hissed.

'Fine,' he whispered. 'Why are we whispering?'

She blushed a bright pink; it touched the lobes of her ears. He said: 'You're early—otherwise I'd have gotten here. . . .'

The blush persisted and the tip of her tongue slipped briefly between her lips. It was an unconscious gesture but he found it strongly erotic.

She said in a rush: 'I thought—better come early because of the raids. I nearly didn't come when the siren went at dinner-time—er, lunch—but I thought, I can't have you wasting your time when you could be working. And you were very thought-ful coming to the club last night and that. So'—she twisted her head in a search for a wall clock, without success—'I'll just have tea, like I said I would, and then I *must* go. Mum'd worry if I'm not back by tea-time.'

'I'll take you home.'

'No!' Too quickly. 'No—I mean, it's all right. I'd rather you didn't.'

He opened a pack of cigarettes and offered it to her. She

shook her head. He said, lighting one, 'I'd like to meet your folks again.'

'You haven't been *writing* about us?' Her panic was communicable.

'I broadcast, remember? Anyway, what's so wrong with—?'

'Oh, you wouldn't! Promise me you wouldn't, unless you tell me first?'

He sucked on the cigarette to allay his discomfort. 'You make it sound not quite proper—like being in the Sunday papers. Isn't that what they say over here?'

'Nobody respectable gets in the papers, except politicians and film stars and people. My mum wouldn't know where to put her face if she thought you was—were saying things about her to millions of people.'

'There's nothing I could say about your family they could possibly feel ashamed of. I was proud to meet them. I hope you'll let me meet them again some time.'

She stretched her mouth beneath the ridiculous wedge of white veil. 'We'll have to see about that, won't we?'

An elderly waiter rooted himself behind Shaffer's chair.

'Tea and sandwiches? What'll you have?' Shaffer asked her.

Her face elongated and the lips formed a distended O. 'Could I have toasted scones? Do they have toasted scones? With . . . butter?' Mention of this luxury caused her obvious concern.

Shaffer cocked an eyebrow at the old man who twinkled over his busy stub of pencil.

'Buttered scones, madam? Certainly.' He ambled away.

She flicked invisible threads from the shoulders of her jacket and adjusted the hem of the blue dress over her knee. The action reminded Shaffer sharply of his wife. He said defensively: 'Are you engaged or something? Pretty girls are usually engaged.'

The question seemed to embarrass her. 'No.'

'They must be slow-witted, the boys in your part of the world.'

'The boys in my part of the world', she said primly, 'aren't the kind a girl gets engaged to if she has any pride. I'm not going to throw myself away on some East End labourer.'

He laughed before he could check himself and she glared at him angrily. 'I don't think that's anything to laugh at. You don't *know*,' she flared.

'Sorry.That was pretty rude. I didn't mean it that way. I just got through praising the spirit and courage of the East End to several million Americans and you tell me you wouldn't marry one of 'em.' He tapped the side of his head. 'I apologise. You're right. I don't know anything about your background.' The thought jarred awake the memory of his affair with the girl in the Hereford Street diner. 'Except. . . .'

'Except what?' She was alert with suspicion.

'Nothing. Just someone I knew once. Long time ago. She came from the East End, too.'

'People don't *come* from the East End,' she retorted tartly. 'That's where they end up when there's nowhere else to go. You don't think we live there 'cause we like it, do you? When people can afford to get out of the East End they go like a shot. You ask people in our street where they come from and they'll tell you where their mums and dads came from, that's where they *really* belong. Ask my mum and she'll tell you she's from Sydenham and dad is from Waltham Forest.'

'Like you said, I don't know about these things.'

She bit her lip. 'Oh dear, I'm ever so sorry, M— ... Mr Shaffer. I'm not quite myself today. You were saying about this ... person. ...'

'She worked in an office in Hereford Street. I came over here in thirty-two. Kind of holiday relief stand-in.'

Her eyes locked on his and the tongue came out again to play briefly between the lips.

'Was — were you engaged?'

He shook his head. 'Nothing like that.'

'But you were ... close?'

'Put it that way — yes.'

'Very? I mean, truly?'

'Some.' He regretted embarking on the subject and made a dismissive gesture with his hands. The waiter appeared with silver teapot and china cups and saucers and three sliced and toasted scones under a round silver dome. In a glass tray resting on ice in a silver dish were four curly rolls of butter.

'Oh, isn't it *lovely*!' Her delight sent a shiver through him. 'Shall I pour?' The waiter, who was about to do so, bowed and withdrew. She poured them half a cup of tea each, then refreshed the pot from a jug of hot water and poured again.

'You were saying about this girl,' she said without raising her eyes. She reached tentatively for the silver dish, raised the lid and gazed longingly at the toasted scones.

'It didn't work out.'

'Oh, that's a shame.' She scraped butter over the surface of one half of the scone as sparingly as if the supply was intended to feed a regiment. 'Why not?'

Why not? What are you supposed to say to a question like that? 'I guess it's better to let old flames die gracefully, huh?'

'You brought it up,' she flashed coolly. He was to learn that her reactions were always swift, always terrifyingly honest, always challenging, but at that moment the innocence of the remark stung him.

'I went back to Rome. We didn't plan on it lasting a lifetime.' He snapped it out coldly, like the punchline to a joke in poor taste. She froze, hands nursing the silver butter-knife and half-eaten scone; then she called up a tight little smile and set her chin.

'Oh, well. I s'pose she asked for it. That type of girl usually does.'

'She wasn't *that* type of girl.'

'I'm sorry. I didn't mean that. I shouldn't pry.'

'My fault. I spoke out of turn. It was a long time ago.'

She levelled a dispassionate stare at him over her teacup, held between forefinger and thumb with the little finger curled.

He set off on a new tack. 'Is it still burning down there?'

'Oh, yes,' she said airily. 'Fire's been going all night. I got soot all over me when I came out of the house just now. Mum came with me to the bus stop so I could wear a coat over my shoulders till we got past the smoke. This is the only good outfit I've got.' She set down her cup to flick more invisible specks from the white shoulders.

From a corner of the foyer a saturnine, long-case clock boomed a single stroke. She looked up at once. 'What time is that striking?' She slipped the last of the scone into her mouth with a flourish of fluttering fingers and dabbed at her mouth and chin with a damask napkin. 'That's not five o'clock, surely?'

He checked his watch. 'No problem. It's only four-fifteen.'

But the impetus to go was too great to resist. She folded the napkin into its original fan shape and slipped it back into the silver ring. 'That was really very lovely and I enjoyed it so much,' she said. She seemed to be reciting a lesson learned at her mother's knee. 'I must go, though. I've stayed too long already, really. You don't mind, do you? It's been so nice.'

She stepped around the table and made for the stairs up to the lobby. Her departure took him completely by surprise. He jumped up and followed her.

'Look, let me run you home as far as I did last night?'

'I mustn't put you to any trouble. The bus is quick enough and they're still running, you know.' She climbed the stairs and tip-tapped across the lobby to the revolving doors.

'If I get you a cab. . . . There're plenty right here. . . .'

'And pay what they're asking! No, thank you very much. I'd rather crawl home on hands and knees.'

He followed her into the courtyard. The grey and gold liveried doorman saluted and she ducked her head coyly.

Shaffer stood arms wide. 'I never knew anyone like you. Can't I do *anything*? There could be a raid any minute.'

She looked back at him over her shoulder. 'The bus stop's just across the Strand, not twenty yards. And there *is* something you can do. You can go back in there and finish off those scones. There's two left — *and* a little pot of strawberry jam. Shame to waste it at that price.'

'When am I going to see you a. . . ?' he began, but she closed her ears to him and hurried away.

He watched her turn the corner by the Savoy Taylor's Guild, shrugged helplessly and returned to the table in the foyer. The old waiter eyed him sympathetically as he dug into his wallet and checked the bill.

'Satisfactory, sir?' he ventured.

Shaffer measured him for double entendres. 'Yeah, sure. Quite satisfactory, thanks.' He dropped two half-crowns on the tray to show he meant it. He wished he had as much conviction as he had half-crowns.

Half way along the Strand in the car he realised he had forgotten to check the bus stop as he passed to see if she was still waiting; he cursed his selfishness but laid the blame for his preoccupation at her door.

He had a date at Broadcasting House and an open line to O'Keefe to fill. She'd already planted the seed: 'People don't *come* from the East End. That's where they end up when there's nowhere else to go.'

Sunday, 1955

Ian Russell skidded, feet wide, on the mosaic marble of the ground-floor corridor, grabbed the banister post and hurled himself up the stone stairs two at a time. He was still pulling on his brown hospital housecoat, his right arm half in, half out of its sleeve, three inches of cheese sandwich protruding from his mouth. He had barely hung up his jacket in the porter's lodge when the siren wailed and it had not died when he heard the wheeee-aaaah of the falling bomb. It must have hit somewhere very close; the lodge table rocked on its uneven legs and dust rose like smoke from burning toast on every shelf and surface.

For several seconds afterwards there was no sound; then his ears cleared with a sound like water rushing over boulders and it came to him; the crackle of burning timber, shouts, screams, an emergency bell. He ran.

On the first-floor landing Bertie Webber, the head porter, spotted him and bellowed: 'General surgical. Third. Well, don't stand bloody gawpin', lad!'

Ian swung on the banister post and leaped towards the second floor. Webber was crossing the landing in his wake but a long way behind. He had a stump of light steel below the knee of his right leg. Souvenir from the Kaiser.

On the second-floor landing Ian whirled on the next flight of stairs head-on into a quintet of wailing women. They were very old, very slow and their screams were little more than wavering ululations, almost in tune; almost in unison. Their eyes were on their quaking feet, measuring each step with one half of the mind, maintaining the chorus of breathless despair with the other. It was almost funny.

'Can I take you to the shelter?' he began, but his voice triggered five instantaneous screeches of such psychopathic terror that he flung himself against the wall to show he meant them no harm. They slip-slopped past him in their tatty slippers. He heard five more orchestrated screams as they encountered old Bertie on the landing below.

At the top of the stairs on the third floor a young probationer nurse was standing with her face buried in the cushion of one arm. She made no sound. Ian touched her lightly on the elbow and she looked at him. There were no tears.

'You all right?' he said anxiously.

'Down there.' She fluttered a hand along the corridor at her back. 'It's down there.'

He said gently, 'Do you want to come with me?'

She stared blankly into the serious young face and he brought one hand to his chin instinctively to hide the rash of adolescent acne. 'I think I want to be sick,' she said. He ran past her.

The corridor turned at right-angles ten yards from the staircase and, beyond swinging half-glassed double doors, opened out into General Surgical. Ian skidded to a halt.

The ward immediately beyond the doors was a mass of smoke and rubble – he couldn't even see bodies. The ceiling had collapsed and beyond the ward sister's desk on the right there was nothing at all, just a ragged hole in the brickwork where a giant had bitten through the corner of the building. He was breathing quickly, sharp little spurts of breath gulped and ejected as hysteria welled up and urged his stomach into vomitous contraction. He spat the remains of the cheese sandwich on to the floor, rubbed his mouth with his fist and hurled his shoulder at the double doors.

A muted, snuffling cry came to him weakly; somewhere under the choking mass of brick and plaster, he couldn't isolate the source exactly, there was someone left alive. Sweet Mary, Mother of God; the phrase ricocheted round and round in his head. Where to start? Where to look first? An electric cable fizzed and spat on what was left of the end wall of the ward, on the brink of the devastation; the sound sent his heart racing. Sweet Mary, Mother of—

The doors at his back exploded open and Bertie Webber hopped through. He pulled up short: 'Gawd!' he breathed. 'Gawd!' He snapped into action. 'Orright, son. 'Mergency phone, out there in the corridor. Straight ahead. Call operating theatre and tell 'em to get ready for a flood. Call the super and tell 'im—'

The door erupted again and the few square yards of unobstructed floor space were suddenly packed with people; three doctors, five nurses, the hospital superintendent, an A.R.P. warden and the almoner, who was instantly sick.

'Webber. Call the theatre. Tell them—' The super rapped.

'Lad's doing that, sir. Faster on 'is feet. Off you go then, son.'

When Ian came back there were three more doctors and two nurses and the first arrivals had strung a human chain across the rubble to a point where the ward floor dipped drunkenly downwards into space. A young doctor at the far end of the chain yelled to be pulled back. They hauled him in, wriggling like an eel on a line; his face was grazed and his white housecoat smudged and torn. He wore pyjamas under the coat.

He wiped dust from his lips. 'There are three beds missing on this side and about two from the far wall, I think. Someone had better check the quadrangle below if—'

'That's being taken care of, sir,' said the A.R.P. warden quickly. 'We got rescue men and ambulances standing by. Whole corner came down on top of 'em, poor old—'

'What can we do here?' snapped the superintendent. He was a small man, balding and shapeless in a tweed jacket and voluminous grey flannels. 'Can you hear if anyone's alive under that?'

'I don't think so.' The young doctor sucked a jagged cut in his forearm. 'Floor's very shaky, though. I could hear timbers groaning as I crawled out. It's not going to take much more of this.'

The superintendent swung on the A.R.P. warden. 'Can you get your rescue people to underpin the ceiling of the ward below? We need timbers, cross-members, right under this floor area.'

'Do me best, sir.' The warden dived through the doors.

There came a riot of clanging bells from the quadrangle below and the group ducked defensively. 'Fire brigade,' announced Bertie Webber calmly. The superintendent sent the almoner down to talk to them. She came back with a Red Rider, the leading fireman in charge of the appliance, the red flash on his helmet denoting his rank and the origin of the nickname.

The fireman reached into the helmet and scratched his thinning hair. 'Anyone alive?' he asked mechanically.

'We don't know. Perhaps,' said the super. 'We're trying to find something to support the ceiling in the ward below so we can get under this rubble. Can you help?'

'Do our best.' He gritted his teeth, his frustration apparent. 'Shouldn't stay officially, guv,' he said unhappily. 'Fire only, that's the order of the day. Rescue is down to Civil Defence. We got more fires'n we can cope with.'

'But dammit man, there may be someone alive under there!' The superintendent performed a little jig of anger. 'We can't do it without you.'

'Do what we can, long as they let me, guv. But I'm telling you now, if we get a fire call in the area the station'll have us out of here quick as you like.'

He looked up as a fireman's head appeared over the broken flooring at the end of the ward; his shoulders and trunk followed before the escalating ladder clanged to a halt. The fireman swung expertly around the ladder until he was hanging beneath it, then he released one foot from the safety of the rung and felt for a foothold on the edge of the sloping floor. It groaned mortally. He brought down his other foot and tested his weight, hands still clinging to the ladder.

'Watch that floor, Reg,' the leading fireman shouted. 'Don't put too much—'

His words were drowned by a satanic snapping: the floor roared and screeched and dipped out and down and several hundredweight of brickwork and plaster slid over the edge. From below came a metallic clatter as the avalanche rained down on the escape ladder and the rescue workers below. The fireman on the ladder was left dangling; he kicked himself back to the safety of the rungs with a violent pendulum swing of his body and disappeared downwards. The leading fireman was already out of the door.

'Oh my God, the stupid—' The superintendent bunched his small fists and turned to find an inanimate target on which to beat a tattoo; the A.R.P. warden came back into the ward and stopped inches from them. He looked about him quickly.

'We found some scaffolding round the back,' he said. 'It might do, if we can find someone to tell us how it works.'

'Leave it to me,' Bertie said crisply. He turned to the super. 'There's a warden at Lambeth Palace, sir. Sid Martin. He's a builder. Get that stuff up in a jiffy if they can spare him.'

'Send a car, an ambulance. Anything. Get him here quickly.' Bertie peg-legged away to a telephone.

'Doctor!' The super touched an elderly man on the shoulder. 'We can't spare all these people up here. Take the nurses back to their wards and get your doctors back where they're needed. Nothing we can do for the people under this until we can get to them. Nominate a team of six nurses and two doctors to stand by for when we get them out if anyone's alive and leave—er—' he spied the young doctor who had crawled out to the ledge—'leave Hawthorne here with me. You all right, Hawthorne?'

The young man grinned ruefully, the skin around his pale-grey eyes dark with lack of sleep.

The older man said, 'He's been on his feet for eighteen hours, John. He'd only just got to bed when this happened.'

But the superintendent was already preoccupied with other things. 'Thank you, Hawthorne,' he said vaguely.

He turned on Ian. 'How much do you weigh, young man?'

The racket from below indicated that Sid Martin's platoon of scaffolders were a long way from completing the job of supporting the ceiling; they had now been working at full stretch for well over three hours.

Ian Russell splayed his feet wide, found a purchase on two substantial lumps of masonry and took his weight on his insteps. The effort wrenched a sob of tension from him and a small dust storm gathered around his face. He was upside down, supported only by his feet, in the fifth tunnel he had dug in the rubble. He craned upwards, finding new holds for his feet, pushing at the crushed brick and plaster with his hands. This tunnel was nearly six feet deep, greater than his own height; it had taken nearly an hour to dig. He wriggled the last two feet to freedom and fell back on his knees, drinking in the air.

Hawthorne croaked, 'Alive?'

Ian shook his head. 'Don't know. Sometimes I think she is, sometimes. . . .' He left it unsaid.

The superintendent and the A.R.P. warden had left two hours ago after Ian's preliminary survey. He had crawled over every inch of the rubble, his ear tuned for the slightest sound, his thin body trembling, following as best he could the ward-plan drawing brought up from the matron's office. Five bodies had been found in the rubble in the quadrangle below, all dead. Up here in the ward there had been no sound for nearly three hours. Before Ian had begun his own reconnaissance four rescue wardens had worked for half an hour to clear the floor immediately around the doors. Three bodies had been recovered, but attempts to push out farther over the debris to find the last of the nine occupants of the ward had raised warning cracks and moans from the fractured floor supports.

'It's going,' the rescue team leader had told the super. 'Won't take our weight. We got to get that ceiling shored up.' They had gone below to lend a hand with the scaffolding.

Ian had worked on watched by the helpless Hawthorne whose

135

attempts to assist him had exacted terrifying squeaks of protest from the hard-pressed floor joists. Hawthorne weighed twelve and a half stones, three stones more than his spindly, narrow-chested helper.

Fifteen minutes ago Ian had located the woman.

Hawthorne stared up at the hole where the ceiling had been. The wardens had been up there — an old pre-med room — in the hope they might rig tackles and pulleys and raise the rubble from above, but the floor proved too weak to sustain their weight.

He said hoarsely, 'Let *me* try and get to her.'

Ian slithered across to him. 'Try if you like but it's too far out. I can hear it giving when I'm down there. I think you'd better tell someone the whole thing's going soon. They'd better be ready for it. Best we can do is rig up some kind of tackle from the corridor and get some straps round her body. I can't get her out alone.'

Hawthorne rolled up his sleeves. 'Give me a second. I'll see what I can do.' He inched out beside Ian on all fours and slithered towards the tunnel head. The floor groaned ominously. From the far end dust and small pieces of brick began to slide along the dip and out into the night. The doctor froze. 'No good,' he gasped over his shoulder. 'I can't make it.'

'Come on back! We'll get some tackle and I'll go down again.'

Hawthorne's report to the superintendent that one of the patients, a woman, might be alive brought him running. The rescue men rigged a rope and tackle to a steel grating in the corridor and Hawthorne threaded it through the tough canvas of a straitjacket to buckle around the patient's body. Ian squirmed back over the rubble and lowered himself headlong into the tunnel.

It was only slightly wider than his shoulders and punctuated with sharp angles of broken brick, ruptured steel bedframes, shards of glass and flakes of wood. His body and face were a mass of cuts and grazes and his shoulders and chest showed yellow bruising through the tears in his shirt, but he was too tired now to pay them attention.

He splayed his feet again to find support, plucked brickdust and plaster from the bottom of the hole and felt her face. Cold. He felt for the throat. A pulse? Last time he decided he couldn't feel it. Time before, he could. Try. Try again.

'Is that you, dear?'

Her voice shocked him so completely he lost his foot-grip and had to force his elbows painfully against the coarse tunnel-sides to prevent himself falling on her.

'Are you all right?' he whispered.

'You're late, dear,' she said weakly. 'I put your tea on an hour ago. It's all cold now.'

'Wait here,' he said without thinking. 'I won't be a minute.'

'Cold,' she sighed sleepily. 'All got cold.'

He wriggled back up the tunnel, felt for the straitjacket harness and bent his head to address the watchers clustered under a single light-bulb by the doors. 'She's O.K!' he whispered exultantly, his voice breaking. 'She's O.K!'

'What's her name?' called the superintendent.

'I don't know. She's old, I think.'

'They're all old,' sighed the superintendent. 'Ask her her name.'

Ian returned to her again, this time with the straitjacket held out below him. It took him half an hour to clear sufficient space to begin to wrap the canvas around her upper body and she remained silent throughout. He threaded the final buckle at last and tested the rope. It would have to do.

He bent his face within inches of hers. 'Are you awake?'

'Mmmmmm.'

'They want to know your name.'

'I had this funny dream. . . .'

'Yes, I know. My name's Ian. Ian Russell. What's yours?'

'Maudie. I'm Maudie. Who're you?'

'Ian. What's your other name, Maudie? Mrs what?'

'Mrs Dunn. You seen my Alfred?'

He pushed himself up into the air again. 'She says her name is Maudie. Mrs Dunn.'

The superintendent glanced at Hawthorne questioningly.

The young doctor made a face. 'I'd forgotten she was still in here. She should have been moved days ago.'

137

'What's her case?' snapped the super.

Hawthorne shook his head hopelessly, his voice low. 'Abdominal cancer. She hasn't got more than a week. Dear God!' He rubbed a hand across his eyes. 'Don't tell Ian.' He looked across at the boy who was peering down the tunnel anxiously.

The superintendent nodded. 'You're right.' Then louder: 'Very well, young man. We'll try to raise her. You'll have to go down there again, I'm afraid, and clear the way. It'll be a long job. Are you up to it?'

The boy grinned back at him. 'Last lap, sir. Easiest part now.'

At quarter to one in the morning Mrs Maud Dunn, aged sixty-three, a married woman of 40 Hadland Street, Rotherhithe, was freed from a tomb of rubble on the third floor of St Thomas's Hospital, Westminster, after a single-handed rescue operation by an eighteen-year-old assistant porter. All other occupants of the women's surgical ward were dead.

At 1 a.m., London *Daily Express* reporter Norman Smart made a routine call to the hospital as part of his air-raid round-up. They told him the story and he took it down, omitting the names of the hospital, the victim and the rescuer; had he put them in, the censor would undoubtedly have cut them from copy before it went down for setting. It was the lead to his story under a two-column headline on page one: HOSPITAL RESCUE. *Boy tunnels five hours to reach entombed woman.*

They put him in an ambulance ferrying blood samples to Hammersmith Hospital and he told the driver to drop him off near his home on Chelsea Embankment. Hawthorne and the superintendent watched it turn out of the gates.

'Chelsea Embankment, eh?' The super whistled appreciatively. 'That's hardly the address you'd expect for a hospital porter, is it?'

Hawthorne yawned widely. He was out on his feet. 'He's quite a hospital porter, I'd say.'

'Unusual, though, all the same. Who is he?'

Hawthorne turned on him and his tired eyes twinkled. 'Father's someone big in the Civil Service. Good family, by the sound of it. I'd say the boy's had a hard time.'

They strolled back to the main door. The sky to the east was flame-bright. 'What makes you say that?'

Hawthorne half turned to look back at the gates. 'He does. He's a queer one, all right.'

'Brave is a better word. That's what they'll call him in the papers tomorrow.'

Hawthorne chuckled grimly. 'I bet they will. But they don't know the meaning of the word and he does. He's fighting a war all his own.'

The super pulled open the door. 'He was fighting ours well enough tonight.'

Hawthorne stepped inside. 'I suppose so. But on his terms. The lad's a conscientious objector.'

Sunday, 2240

Grandfather Hodges was being awkward.

'He's wedged something against the door and he won't let anybody in.'

'Haven't you got *any* control over him?' Alfred Dunn asked the old man's daughter.

'He gets these moods,' said the woman. A gaggle of relatives around her nodded agreement.

'Well, it's a bloody fine time to get moody!' snapped Dunn. Nobody would dispute that. For the past fifteen minutes Alfred Dunn had been standing in the gloom outside Number 28 Baltic Street with the multifarious membership of the Hodges clan debating how best to winkle the old man from his locked bedroom.

'He does it for attention,' said a junior Hodges. 'Take no notice and he'll come out.'

''S'all very well,' wavered the elderly daughter, 'but he's got our ration-books in there. If he gets hit, what'll I do without ration-books?'

Alfred Dunn shushed them into silence. 'You're just as bad,' he said to the old lady. He turned to the others. 'All of you — out of here. Right away.'

'Not without me ration-books,' asserted the daughter.

'Look, I've got better things to do than bother about ration-books, missus,' snarled Dunn. 'I'll try once more and then that's it, right? No more messing. If your dad wants to play silly-buggers I'll get the heavy lifters down and go through the wall.'

'Don't you touch my home,' wailed the old woman.

Alfred Dunn turned his back on her and walked into Number 28. He climbed the stairs to the old man's bedroom and hammered on the door.

At 7.30 that evening, after a day's respite, any thoughts Nelson's Green may have had of sleep had evaporated with the siren's howl. And any glimmer of hope that the fires still raging in the docks could be contained were dashed when the invaders' bomb bays opened to dump hundreds of drums of petrol on to the blazes of last night. Ever since, without pause, waves of bombers had swept in over the beacon of burning London. Incredibly, after the blood-letting of yesterday, there were still people who refused to leave their homes. Whole communities had been cut off for twenty-four hours, isolated behind impenetrable walls of smoke and flame. Yet when the rescue services had reached them from the river householders had stubbornly resisted all attempts to get them out to safety.

The B.B.C. had been putting out bulletins all day: 400 people killed, 1,400 injured. Even the announcer himself, the cool and precise Bruce Belfrage, had broken down as he read it. Yet, clinging to the belief that lightning couldn't strike twice, the East Enders had not fled. True, some of them, their homes levelled, had made the trek to outlying reception centres but only because there was nothing left for them in dockland. The rest were prepared to sweat it out.

When the lightning struck again it was too late. Bemused with shock, they tried to make for shelters and Underground platforms in their hundreds, dragging children and ageing relatives through an unremitting rain of high explosives. Having scoured the maze of streets for hours to find a way out, whole families had disappeared without trace, blown to kingdom come within yards, sometimes, of where they started.

'Grandad!' Alfred Dunn stood back from the door, hands on

hips. 'You hear me? I want you out of there right now. Last time of telling, you hear? Your Mary's outside and she won't leave till you come out.'

'I ain't coming out and she can blooming well do what she wants,' bellowed Grandfather Hodges. 'Fat lot she cares, anyhow.'

'Look, there's a U.X.B. five doors away and if it goes up you go with it!'

'Don't care.'

Alfred Dunn put his ear to the door. 'What you doing in there?' Silence. 'I heard you. What you got in there?'

He heard a frantic scurrying and the clink of bottles.

'Bloody old cow's gorn and done it this time!' Grandfather Hodges' voice shook with outrage. More scurrying; drawers opened; furniture was moved. 'I had it. It was bloody here.' A howl of fury. 'It's gone! Pinched!'

'Will you open this door!' Dunn hammered on it again.

'Push off!' There was an odd, strained grunting from inside the room.

'You all right?'

'Uggghhhh! Uhhhnnnn!' The pitch of the sound changed. 'Aaaagh! Oh, bloody bleedin buggery! Oooohhh!' A bottle smashed to the floor.

Alfred Dunn raced downstairs and grabbed the first thing that came to hand: a coal scuttle. He went back, wound himself up and swung it against the bedroom door. The flimsy lock splintered. Grandfather Hodges was staggering around the little bedroom clutching his mouth. A bottle of brown ale lay seeping on the bedspread.

'Done for!' he mumbled. 'Me teef! Bloody done for!'

He pulled the hand from his mouth and held out his palm. In the middle of it sat a set of shattered dentures.

'You silly old. . . .'

'Only time I get, ain't it? Her bloody fault, always on me back. Ooooh, gawd . . . I bust me jaw.'

Dunn pushed him down on the bed and examined the damage. A trickle of blood ran from a cut lip. He would live.

The old man's daughter appeared nervously in the doorway.

'Serve him right. That'll teach him.' She pointed at the bed. 'Look at that coverlet! Well, you won't catch me washing *that*! Do it hisself, dirty old devil!'

Dunn threw his hands in the air in despair.

'Waits for a raid and when we've all gone he's into his drinking,' screeched the woman. 'Thinks I don't know! Cunning old bugger. Smell it on his breath. Drunk as a fiddler's bitch he was last night. Where'd you keep it then?' She rammed her face into the old man's. 'Found his water-bottle full of stout last time. Took it off him.'

The old man eyed her with simmering hatred. 'Who took me opener?'

She sniffed. 'Stopped you, didn't it?'

'Bust me teef I did, thanks to you. Starve to death if you had your bloody way, wouldn't I?'

'If you tried to open a bottle with your teeth you deserve to starve to death,' she stormed. She said to Dunn, 'He ought to be in an 'ome. Not that they'd have 'im.' Then furiously to her father, 'Oughta be in an 'ome!'

'Better off in one,' mumbled Grandfather Hodges, defeated at last.

Alfred Dunn pushed the old man out of the room and downstairs to the street. Once outside, he left them to it.

Part of the street had been taped off and the U.X.B. signs were in place. Twelve houses had been evacuated, including the Hodges'. Dunn had phoned the A.R.P.'s Central Control in South Kensington more than an hour ago but it might not be until after dawn before the small, hard-pressed group of Royal Engineers could even send a team to assess it. In the meantime the houses stood empty. They might stay that way for a week.

Their tenants would be left on their uppers, trapped like refugees at a border post where travel was denied them in any direction.

The Hodges family had dispersed, taking the incorrigible old man with them, and the street was virtually empty. Dunn debated with himself the safety of the Warrenders and Scullys at the far end of the street. Jack Warrender and his wife, Gladys, Flo Scully and the two boys were packed down in their Anderson shelter at the foot of the Warrenders' garden. Everyone else had gone off to the Tube or Rotherhithe Tunnel just after the U.X.B. buried itself under Bert Allan's grocery shop. They should be safe enough. The Andersons were uncomfortable, cramped, insanitary and claustrophobic, but the curved walls of corrugated iron bolted to rails and sunk into the ground behind a blast-wall of earth had proved their worth time and time again.

Dunn had heard that a couple of hundred people had formed up somewhere north of the river and begun the long march out to Epping Forest, carrying pots, pans and what bedding they could. Like medieval pilgrims they were picking up recruits as they went until the number had grown to uncountable proportions. Well, if that was their idea of shelter it wasn't his. One good stick of incendiaries, even by accident, and the whole bloody forest could go up. It was already tinder dry. He didn't have any time, either, for the bunch who had descended in droves on Chislehurst and settled themselves permanently in the sandstone caves there. Special trains had been laid on to ferry them back and forward to their jobs. Still, none of his business.

He stood still, feeling for the heartbeat of the street, a hollow pulsing in his ears. Didn't sound right.

His sense of unease crystallised into clairvoyant foreboding. He glanced back in the direction of the unexploded bomb. Stupid, but he began to listen for it. They'd been told what they sounded like: a click like the tumblers of a lock falling into place, a whirr, the hiss of escaping air from ruptured casing ... silence. He shook his head. Much more of that and he'd find himself alongside Jack Warrender in the loony bin.

The ground shuddered from the impact of some distant explosion in the docks. Bigger than usual that, he was thinking, and just. . . . The blast hit him from behind. He pitched forward, letting himself be rolled bodily along the street, holding his head. The thin blue A.R.P. overalls shredded around him and he gasped with sudden excruciating pain as his shins connected with a broken-off lamp-post. He grabbed at it wildly but missed and slithered to a halt in a pile of splintered timber. Something was pinching his ankles. He kicked savagely.

The sky was filled with flashing light, like pieces of floating silver in the Christmas baubles that you shook to simulate whirling snow. Caught in the white phosphorescence, broken glass sliced and swirled and clattered wickedly around him, driving deep into the timber, shattering on the stone.

Dunn clawed at his legs. A piece of rope, sent spinning like a bolas, had wrapped itself around his ankles. He sat up and reached down to free it. His hand touched a man's shirt-sleeve. With an effort he twisted his head to look down at it. There was no body attached. The washing line had been torn loose and blown down the street by the blast, its pegs refusing to release their charges. Knickers and vests were intimately jumbled with jumpers and socks and the whole day's laundry embraced Dunn as if clinging to him for protection. He ran across the road to the shelter of an out-house that had been blown across the pavement and half buried by the remains of the house to which it once belonged.

From there he surveyed the damage from top to bottom of the street. The explosion hadn't come from the docks. It was the U.X.B. under Bert Allan's grocery. The force of its blast had laid flat the four or five houses nearest to it and the tremor that followed had collapsed another six or seven. They leaned heavily against one another like fallen dominoes and, even as he tried to count them, began to slide to the ground, grinding their contents to matchwood.

Automatically he counted them off. The Hodges' place was first in line. Nothing remained of that. Next, Harry Evans'; next to that Mrs Bowen's. Then Ben Gardiner's, the Yates's place that was empty anyway after being half gutted by an incendiary weeks back, then. . . . Who? He tried to remember the street as it was just thirty seconds earlier. The picture wouldn't gell. Evans', Bowens', Gardiners'. . . . Yes; theYates's, old Ben Moffat's and then the Coopers' and the Bests'. Was that it? He edged cautiously from the shelter of the out-house, and began again, ticking them off finger by finger. No, there was another. The destruction ended abruptly at the Scullys'. Suddenly detached, it appeared to have received only minor damage. Yes, the Scullys' marked the extent of the damage. Which meant that another one had copped it, making a total of eight in all. The Warrenders' place, it must be.

The Warrenders' house had been peeled from its neighbour, leaving mirrors hanging and the trace pattern of stairways zig-zagging up the wallpaper. The bedroom fireplace clung like a black limpet to the Scullys' outside wall, no floor beneath it. Good God! He remembered the street's solitary Anderson shelter and started to run, but this time the pain in his ankle wouldn't be ignored. He limped at a tortuous pace around the worst of the wreckage until he found what must be the Warrenders' back yard. The Anderson was draped with plaster and tiles and slate but the main body of the house had fallen away from it into the street.

'Anybody there?' he yelled. He prised the steel blast barrier away from the doorway.

He heard Elsie Warrender's voice. 'Yes! We're all right!' She blinked as Dunn shone his torch into the gloom. 'We're all a bit deaf,' she said loudly. 'Bit deaf! That was a near one.'

'Did it hit anything?' asked Flo Scully, poking her head out.

Jack Warrender sat foetally in the corner of the shelter, eyes closed.

Dunn held out his hand to Elsie and hauled her up over the piled barricade of earth. Before she had a chance to see anything he said quietly, 'It wasn't a near one, Elsie.'

Her grip tightened on his arm. She swayed. She hadn't heard him, but the look on his face communicated more than enough.

'Oh my Gawd,' she said softly. Dunn put an arm around her shoulders, fearing she would fall.

Flo was scrambling up behind her, unaware of what Elsie had seen. 'Everything all right, Elsie? Elsie? What's the matter? I can't get up. Here, you boys, give me a leg up. Something's wrong. . . .'

She was bundled from the doorway and slid on her bottom down the mound of earth.

'Elsie, what is—' She stopped, transfixed.

'He got us,' Elsie murmured. She wasn't talking to Flo or to Alf or to herself; she was talking to the unheeding figure crouched back there in the shelter, for whom none of this had happened yet.

'He got us, Jack,' she said.

Her chin began to tremble.

Sunday, 2350

Shaffer pushed the script aside and checked his watch. O'Keefe was scheduled to open the line from A.B.N. at twelve-fifteen. Right now Fred Bate was on the air for N.B.C. Murrow was listening to him, elbows on the table, head in hands, cigarette dribbling smoke from the corner of his mouth — he had already been on for C.B.S. They had all seen a lot of each other tonight; hunting in the pack.

Murrow had pulled the string just after seven. They had met in the lobby of Broadcasting House as Shaffer was on his way out after putting over his late-afternoon file.

'Mel, you want to listen to Goering?'

'Don't tell me you're on *his* invitation list, too?' Shaffer gagged. Murrow had grinned good-naturedly. He had been top man for C.B.S. in Europe since 1937 and his circle of V.I.P. contacts was legendary. It was no secret that he had Churchill's ear, that he could come and go in ministerial corridors very nearly at will, that the homes of the great, the aristocratic and the influential were open to him. American newsmen, and particularly broadcasters, had never suffered the social hostility encountered by their British counterparts; they enjoyed remarkable freedom in their newsgathering activities and substantial advantages off the field of play, but Murrow was in all senses in a class by himself. His superiority was most evident in his relationships with professional colleagues. The way Hirschfield put it: 'He's so damn good, he can afford to help you out instead of cutting your throat.'

'No. They tell me he's broadcasting on Berlin Radio, seven-thirty. B.B.C. are laying on facilities. Interpreter included.'

They went back to the studio in the sub-basement and joined ten or so other correspondents who had drifted in to listen to the Reichsmarschall. They were prepared for propaganda; what they got was an invitation to go look up at the sky and prepare for a repeat performance of Saturday night.

'A terrific attack is going on against London,' boomed the Luftwaffe leader. 'Adolf Hitler has entrusted me with the task of attacking the heart of the British Empire. From where I stand I can see waves of planes headed for England.'

There was a stampede for the roof of Broadcasting House. Berlin Radio had announced several hours before that Goering was in personal charge of the raids and Intelligence sources had put him on the French Channel coast in the Pas de Calais, so any planes Goering could see would be over the English coast in minutes.

The first bombs – screamers, high explosives and incendiaries – fell at seven fifty-five. The bombardment was still in full swing. Shaffer had joined Murrow, Bate and Ben Robertson in Murrow's car and they drove to the East End. To the intense discomfort of his three passengers, Murrow insisted on removing the canvas top so that he could see in all directions – 'Heaven included,' Robertson observed drily – as he drove.

Shaffer's first instinct was to suggest they made for Nelson's Green, but Murrow was intent on seeing the effect Saturday's still burning fires were having on the German run-in along the Thames; he took them on a hair-raising guided tour of the Millwall, West India and Surrey Commercial Docks. At every crisis point they stopped to talk to firemen, police, wardens and bomb victims; to half-crazed groups of women staggering through avenues of flame with suitcases containing the few worldly goods they could muster. Several times they returned along a street on which they had driven minutes before only to find it sealed by a wall of fire where a house or factory had collapsed. Once, forced to backtrack along a narrow lane where flame towered hungrily over raging rooftops, Murrow slammed his foot on the brake and stopped the car inches from the brink of a bomb crater. They got by, but only just; the three passengers piling into the street while Murrow bounced the car on to the pavement beneath a sagging wall and tweaked it round the hole.

At ten-thirty they returned to Broadcasting House and tossed a coin for priority. Shaffer came last.

Eric Warr and the other duty censors, whose job involved the supply and selection of news as much as the suppression of it, kept up a continuous flow of facts and figures. Goering's 'terrific attack' on the heart of Britain's Empire had begun that morning. Between 1130 and 1330 there had been what Home Security and the Air Ministry described as 'promiscuous bombing' over Chester, Chelmsford, Colchester, London, Swansea, Cambridge and Newcastle. Tonight's raid on London was being repeated, on a smaller scale, right across the country; in the first thirty minutes after eight o'clock, Portsmouth, Newbury, Bristol, Peterborough, Bedford, Aylesbury and Brighton had been hammered. Between eight-thirty and ten-thirty, Bristol again, Hull, Grimsby, Newport, Brecon and Cardiff.

'What the hell's the guy trying to do — sink the whole damn British Isles?' fumed Bate.

He had received the thumbs up from his censor and vacated the seat in front of the mike. Shaffer gave O'Keefe a précis of his story, waited his cue and went on the air. It was a straight news report — it couldn't be anything else with the skies of London growling with enemy planes — and although it differed only slightly from the two earlier broadcasts, he was frankly overwhelmed by Murrow's presence and aware that his file was being weighed in the balance by two senior professionals who, in the main, had been competitive partners on dozens of assignments throughout the Battle of Britain. His eyes flickered over Murrow's face at several points in his broadcast, but Murrow's head stayed down, cupped in his hands, and the cigarette never left his mouth.

Shaffer signed off. Murrow's head came up and he peeled the cigarette from his mouth. It was dead. He lit another. 'This guy', he said to Bate out of the corner of his mouth, 'is looking to put both of us out of business, Fred. We have a choice. Beat him or join him. What do you think?'

Bate stuffed his script into a drawer in a side-table. 'I vote we join him. I'm too darned bushed to beat anyone.'

'Seconded.' Murrow got to his feet. 'We could go for a beer if they had a civilised licensing law in this country,' he said. 'But I know a bar across in Hallam Street where they keep an icebox full of Schlitz and Carlsberg, some decent Scotch and a mess of cheese and pickle. There's a phone, too, and the barkeep never sleeps.'

Shaffer eyed him with genuine interest. 'In *London*?'

Bate came up behind him and draped a raincoat over his arm. 'That's right,' he said, pushing Shaffer towards the door. 'The booze and the grub are free. Catch is — you have to play poker with the barkeep till breakfast. And believe me, he plays a mean hand.'

They went out into the corridor.

'Who is this public benefactor?' Shaffer asked, grinning.

Bate jerked his head at Murrow. 'Him,' he growled. 'You want to take my advice, Mel. Go home while you've still got a dime to your name.'

Sunday, 2355

Maud would understand. Nobody else would but that didn't matter; she would understand. She wouldn't have more promises to blind her. No longer be *lied to*. There'd been enough lies. What the hospital should've done was just let her go with dignity instead of giving her the daily dosage of hope and pain and despair and delirium.

Course, they'd stopped giving her morphine and that was as close as they'd come to saying it would soon be over. Morphine was held back for those who might recover, not for the likes of Maud. Night after night, day after day, little bits of her were being eaten away.

Please let her go, he'd pleaded with the doctors, but they had shown him no sympathy. Just excuses. He'd tried to argue with them: when someone's ill you don't let Nature take its course, you try to cure them. What difference is there here? Nature's running amok and it can only be cured by death. You tamper

149

with life — why are you frightened to tamper with death? Why make her suffer? If the only cure is death, cure her! *Cure her!*

Alfred Dunn rolled on the bed under the weight of racking thoughts. It would be his third consecutive night without sleep.

MONDAY
9 September

Monday, 0430

Shaffer leaped convulsively in his sleep as the phone clanged. The overdose of Schlitz with Johnnie Walker chasers and the side effects of nearly four hours of smoke-clad poker at Murrow's flat had rendered him semi-conscious before he even hit the sack; now it sealed him tight in vacuous stupor. Only his alarm system reacted mechanically to the phone.

'I've been ringing this for nearly five minutes and. . . .' There was some damn fool woman nagging at him from a thousand miles away. He fell on one elbow on the side-table, his lips touching the upright mouthpiece. He said numbly, 'This is a private number. Call in the morning.' He made to return the earpiece to its hook but the squawking rose from the other end.

'You still there?' he droned.

'I said . . . *it's me!*'

'Who's this?' He didn't really care. His eye strayed to the window where there seemed to be some kind of a thunderstorm clomping around the sky. Right. Lightning in big clumps — flash, flash, flash, flash. Thunder all the time. Must be right overhead. The woman was shouting like she was having a fit. 'I can't hear you,' he said. 'You'll have to talk clear and slow. There's a storm on right now.'

'MEL!'

He came awake. 'Rita?' No, she wouldn't make transatlantic phone calls at . . . what time was it?

'What time is it?' he yelled.

'I've been calling all day. Every half hour. I thought you were dead. I thought you'd got caught in one of those raids. Then I heard your broadcast tonight and I started in calling again but. . . .'

151

He tried to pull himself together. His first reaction was shock; the last time he had given brain-space to his wife and kids was forty-eight hours ago. Shock gave way to hideous guilt and, in his weakened state, guilt was instantly buried up to its neck in self-protective anger.

He shouted because the thunder outside was now deafening. 'What the hell are you doing – checking up on me? You think I'm over here having a good time?'

'You didn't call – not even the children. You didn't write. I saw in the *Times* Vince Hirschfield was home but you didn't even send a message through him. What do I have to. . . ?'

There was a lightning flash that turned night into day and a thunder roll that shook the bed, the side-table under his elbow, the floor, the pictures, the whole room. 'Hold it! Hold it!' he shouted down the line and dropped the earpiece. He stumbled to the window. It was a storm all right. A firestorm, courtesy of the Luftwaffe. He held up his watch to the hot, bright, orange sky and counted back to the first alert; seven fifty-five last night. Eight and a half hours. They'd been dropping bombs for eight and a half hours? He pulled the blackout curtains against the glare.

'There's a raid going on here, Rita,' he shouted. He changed his tone. She would just have to be reasonable. 'They've been dropping bombs here all damn weekend and I just fell into bed for a coupla hours' sleep.'

She didn't rise to that; it was a defensive position and they had both explored mutual defence roles till they knew them inside out. They'd stopped reacting instinctively towards each other years ago. Cool begets cool.

She said quietly, 'Is it your turn or mine?' An old domestic joke. He grinned in the darkness. Nice going, baby.

'You having a good war?' he drawled.

'Medium rare. The nights are the worst. You can't see the whites of their eyes. How about yours?'

'I make out.'

'I wasn't talking about your trophy wall. Are you suffering from anything mortal – aside from a cold bed, I hope.'

Nasty. 'I'm fine. How're the kids?'

'Gee. You *remember*!'

'Nuts. How are they?'

'Missing you between baseball and school and the movies — hey, did I tell you, they don't need sub-titles here? Come to think of it, they don't mention you more than twenty, thirty times a day.'

'I could get you for alienation, you know that?'

'I'll fight it to the Supreme Court.'

Long silence.

'Mel?'

'Yeah.'

'You missing me — you know, around the kitchen, that kinda thing?'

'You called me three and a half thousand miles to ask me that? This call is costing me a fortune. Or am I still paying the bills?'

Her gurgling laughter turned the flame high in his loins. 'You are till I can find time to look around for someone with more physical presence.'

It was a joke but it turned him cold. 'Don't count on it, baby.'

'Wow! I can feel your claws from here. What do you think you've got to worry about, husband? Or is that guilt reaction I hear?'

He glared at the window; it glowed pink and white.

'Sure. I just kicked this popsy on to the rug and she's got her eye-teeth in my throat. I'm all over love bites.'

He could hear the relief in her voice. 'Well, as long as I know you're being properly taken care of. Gee, you have no idea how tough it is for us frontliners, worrying about the boys back home and if they're getting their little comforts.'

'Love let me not linger.'

A real giggle that time. 'Ten out of ten. You must be O.K. I'll let the President know he's not to worry. He's been on the phone ten times a day asking how you are.'

'Rita.'

'Yes.'

'You want to let me get some sleep before the Luftwaffe come in through the window.'

'Pig.' Softer. 'O.K., hero. It's a big day tomorrow or whatever day it is over there. Just do me a personal favour, huh? If you want to get something hurt, make it the head. You can take it up there. Just stay covered from the neck down, especially *down*. Protect my investment.'

Salaciousness will get you everything. Keep the door locked till I get home.'

'Didn't I tell you? I threw away the key.'

'You better. Roger and out.'

'Remember the Alamo.' She put down the receiver quickly. That was the arrangement; she cut all the calls and that way there were no misunderstandings on either side. He fell back on the pillow.

Home sweet home.

Monday, 0900

Elsie Warrender turned the huge old mortice key in the lock of 25 Garfield Court, Chelsea, threw open the door and bent to scoop up the three pints of milk sunning themselves on the wide, white-scrubbed step. She paused, one arm full of bottles, one hand clutching her silver barrage-balloon-fabric shopping bag, the other grasping a brolly, a gas-mask in its brown cardboard box and the string bag of vegetables Mrs Russell had asked her to buy at the corner shop on her way in this morning. She paused and breathed the air and smiled gratefully at the stone-paved garden, sequestered behind its high railings, at the two beech trees and the shady seats that circled them, at the dahlias and chrysanthemums in their snug beds. Nothing had changed here, thank God. The birdsong was sharp and clean in the warm air; profligate, bursting with the joy of life. There were always birds in Garfield Court; a lot more in the back garden, of course, where there were more trees and long lawns and Miss Caroline's bird-bath and the long tails of nuts she strung together and hung from low branches in front of the french windows. It was all so . . . peaceful. No — she wouldn't tell madam about the bomb. Do no good and she'd get so upset. High-strung she was.

She went inside, nudged the door shut with one elbow and got to the kitchen in the nick of time; the gas-mask box and one of the milk bottles were sliding dangerously in her grip.

'Is that you, Elsie?' Elizabeth Russell called from the morning-room.

'Yes, madam dear,' she yelled. She looked at the kitchen clock and tsk-skked with irritation; five past nine already and they hadn't had their breakfasts, she'd be bound. Well, must get on.

'Had your breakfasts, madam dear?' she yelled again.

Elizabeth Russell swept into the kitchen in a full-length housecoat, mules, and a makeshift silk turban around her fading honey-blonde hair. Her smile was infectious; a torch that lit Elsie, the room, the whole house.

'How could you come, dear, today of all days?' she protested. She grabbed Elsie by the shoulders and studied her closely. 'It's been on the wireless all weekend and when I went to headquarters in Victoria yesterday they said the whole East End was on fire. It must have been terrible for you.'

'They wasn't wrong, madam dear. It was . . . well, if I started to tell you what it was really like I'd be talking all day and Mister wouldn't have his breakfast. Is he home?'

'Yes, he is.' Elizabeth made a face, mock-nasty; they had shared the same joke every morning for fourteen years, as they had shared the ritual of greeting, the pretence that Elizabeth *might* have cooked breakfast, the mutual relief of being in each other's company.

On the surface they had nothing in common. Elsie was fifty-eight years old, the daughter of a Sydenham grocer who could have done better for herself had she waited for the right man. She was quick, intelligent and blessed with the natural housewife's talent for making-do. She was a goddess of the knitting needles, she could sew beautifully, laundered clothes so that they came up like new, cooked like Escoffier and, unbelievably, seemed to enjoy every minute of her nine-hour working day.

155

Elizabeth was ten years younger, and a kinswoman of the Duke of Roxburgh. She was tall, slim, cool; beautiful by the standards of her day, which had called for large, soft eyes, a small, straight nose, a tiny mouth, good cheekbones and a complexion found only in pre-Raphaelite paintings. Her parents were still alive and lived in great style in a perfect Inigo Jones manor house in Lincolnshire. They had repeatedly offered to share their home, their good fortune, their geographical safety and their wealth with Elizabeth and her family, but their generosity had been rebutted by Charles Russell, whose own Yorkshire squirearchy had fallen on hard times during the Depression and willed him nothing but bank ovedrafts and petty debt. It was a pity; Elizabeth was to the manor born.

In the first few years the two women invested heavily in their five-day-a-week relationship; Elizabeth in a spirit of easy, classless friendship which hardened into childlike dependence, Elsie from sheer gratitude. Their bond, like their personalities, had matured. Elizabeth had made of Elsie Warrender a friend, confidante, surrogate mother-confessor, adviser and guide. Elsie's vision of Elizabeth was crystallised in her unchanging and unchangeable mode of address: madam dear. For her, affection, like all creation, was conditioned by a natural order. She would have resisted strenuously any suggestion of equality between them and, had Elizabeth insisted on it, their friendship would have suffered a mortal blow. In her own circle Elsie still referred to Elizabeth, in conversation, as madam.

Elsie boiled Mister's Monday egg the required three and three-quarter minutes, cut and buttered almost transparently thin Hovis slices for Elizabeth, filled a bowl with Farmer's Glory wheat flakes for Miss Caroline and made tea. She carried it all through to the morning-room and set plates and bowls and cups and saucers in front of them.

Charles Russell grunted from behind the *Daily Telegraph*, Caroline squeezed Elsie's hand so that her father shouldn't see and Elizabeth blew her a kiss. Elsie returned to the kitchen and began unpacking the vegetables. There was no formal lunch at Garfield Court most days — just a snack for young Mr Ian who got up late after working all night at the hospital and occasionally Mr Tom, who was an officer in the air force and came home when he could wangle a thirty-six-hour pass. Each day Elsie prepared dinner before she went home, setting the oven and scrawling instructions as to cooking times so that Elizabeth had only to serve. Occasionally, when the Russells gave dinner parties, she would stay on in the evening to serve at table and do the washing-up, but there had been little entertaining at Number 25 this year. Mister rarely got home much before eight o'clock nowadays. War work.

Elizabeth came back into the kitchen as Elsie unloaded vegetables from her string bag.

'Oh, Elsie — I didn't expect you to remember the *veg*.' She clicked her tongue. 'You're a wonder, that's all I can say.'

'You've got to eat. Everyone's got to eat.'

'I meant,' said Elizabeth, fascinated as always by her daily's dexterity when handling food, 'after what you must have been through this weekend. Are you all right?'

'You haven't finished your breakfast,' Elsie broke in sternly, eyeing the slice of brown bread in Elizabeth's fingers.

'I came in for the marmalade. No!' as Elsie turned at once to the larder, 'I'll get it. Tell me what it was like first. I couldn't help worrying about your boy Barry. All those terrible fires. Is there much damage?'

Elsie passed out a jar of Cooper's Oxford marmalade. 'I couldn't really say, madam dear. I was down the shelter most of the time. I saw more damage coming in on the bus this morning. Barry's all in one piece. Tired though. Worried about his Edie, I think. You know they got the old power station up the river? Fulham? I nearly died when I saw the smoke this morning. Could've hit you, easy.'

Elizabeth sighed. 'It happened about four o'clock. Charles got up. There were lots nearer than that. I don't know where, though.'

'Better you didn't ask, neither. Do no good to worry yourself about whys and wherefores. I said to my Jack this morning — he lost his office Saturday night — I said, "Do you no good worrying about bricks and mortar, my lad. Just be grateful you wasn't in it." Same with the house. But he's not hisself and that's a fact. He got this queer—'

Elizabeth broke in quickly. 'What do you mean, same with the house? What's wrong with it?'

Elsie clamped her lips in her teeth, annoyed with herself. She picked up a large, soil-encrusted potato and brushed it clean. 'It got hit, didn't it,' she said guardedly.

'Oh, my *dear*.' Elizabeth threw both arms around her shapeless friend and hugged her as the tears streamed down her face. 'Oh, my dear – why didn't you *say*? You come in here as though nothing's happened and let me babble on like a fool when you've. . . .' She hugged Elsie tighter.

The daily patted her turbanned hair. 'Now don't you go on like that. There's more'n enough tears been spilled for one day down our end.'

Elizabeth raised a tear-stained face and dabbed at it with a tiny lace hankie. 'But you could have *said*.'

"T'ain't no good saying when it's all over and done with, is it now? Anyway, the family's alive and kicking.'

'But the house. . . .'

'Flat as a pancake. Mr Dunn, he's the A.R.P. warden in the Green, he said he seen nothing like it. Unexploded bomb done it, he said. Blew down the whole row. Flattened it – wallop! – and left the house next door still standing. Like a hot knife through butter.'

Elizabeth felt for a chair, pulled one from the table and dropped into it. 'I've got goosepimples, look! I feel as if someone had just walked over my grave,' she said faintly. 'Oh, Elsie, what are you going to do?' Her face cleared and she looked up determinedly. 'You must come and stay here. *All* of you. We'll get things ready straight after breakfast.' She put a hand to her mouth thoughtfully. 'Now, you and your husband can have the big guest-room next to ours. Gladys can sleep in the—'

Elsie's face was round with incredulity. 'My lot? In *here*! Oh, no. That's lovely and thoughtful and bless you for saying it but I couldn't come imposing on you even if we hadn't got anywhere to go – which we have.'

Elizabeth fumed. 'How can you *say* that? Imposing! After all we—'

'There, there now.' Elsie drew up a chair beside her, her face soft, tone gentle. 'We already got places to go. We just moved in with the Scullys next door. Bit of a crush, but we aren't going to want for nothing.'

'But you could. . . ,' began Elizabeth tearfully.

'It wouldn't do. That's the start and finish of it,' said Elsie firmly. 'What do you think Mister would say, coming home tired to find my Jack in his chair? And Jack wouldn't feel right, neither. Be different if he was hisself.'

'What do you mean, himself?'

Elsie got up and returned to her vegetables at the sink. 'He's all right, don't you worry. Things just got too much for him, that's all. Having the office go up like that and then the house. That office was his life. That and his garden and his pigeons.'

'Oh, Elsie!'

'Some ways it'll do him good. Make a change. Get him out of hisself.'

'But you've lost *everything*!'

'Everything!' Elsie was genuinely amused. 'Bless you, we didn't have nothing to start with, did we?' She paused, potato in one hand. 'Makes you think, does that bomb. We never ever liked the place — the house, I mean, not the people. Nor the area. It was temporary, see; for the time being. Just till Jack got to know the job when he first started down at Baxter and Harvey's. Once he got on his feet, like, we were going to save up and put money down on one of them little villas out at Chingford. It's lovely out Chingford way. We even went out on the Green Line bus one Saturday afternoon and picked our spot.' She sighed and pulled herself back to the present. She scrubbed away at the potato savagely. 'Always the same with pipe-dreams, madam dear. You live with 'em too long. Kids grow up and you take a little bit out of your nest-egg here, a little bit there, and prices go up and up. One day you see the truth of it: just dreaming isn't never enough; you got to put your heart and soul in it, make it happen no matter what.' She turned her head and grinned. 'We got too comfortable down there in the Green, truth be known. What I reckon is, there's more fun looking forward to getting something than getting it. Now we got other things to look forward to.'

'I want to help you. Now don't say no. Don't say anything.' Elizabeth planted her hands resolutely on the table top. 'You can look on it as a loan. An interest-free loan. All you have to—'

'*Elizabeth!*' roared Charles Russell from the morning-room.

The two women exchanged looks. 'He'll be wanting his toast and marmalade,' said Elsie, and swung into action at once.

Elizabeth rose to her feet unsteadily. 'Damn and blast his toast and marmalade,' she hissed.

Elsie turned round in pure astonishment. 'Ssssh. You just sit where you are and leave him to me,' she said soothingly.

Charles Russell lowered the *Daily Telegraph* abruptly as Elsie came to the table with toast-rack and butter-dish. 'Is it too much to ask that I get breakfast at a civilised hour in the morning?'

'Sorry, Mister,' said Elsie without a trace of annoyance. 'I was helping madam in the kitchen.'

'What's she doing in there?' Russell growled moodily.

'Daddy, you're being unbearable again.' Caroline tapped him playfully on the wrist and he smiled ruefully. His daughter could do no wrong in Charles Russell's eyes; she was his one endurable and enduring link with a family which seemed to take positive delight in opposing his wishes, flouting his standards and rejecting his influence. Caroline was the only one he could honestly say bore evidence of being his child; Ian was Elizabeth reincarnated in a form and cast of mind least likely to find a respectable place in society, and Tom was quite beyond him — an impractical mix of engineer and poet, dreamer and worker, conformist and radical whose absurd ideas on the subject of social engineering verged on Bolshevism. He had learned to live at arm's length from the rest of them. In Caroline he had all he needed; daughter, fellow spirit, fellow scientist; the reflecting half of his intellect. When F. W. Winterbotham's Scientific Intelligence Unit and the Secret Intelligence Service decided to set up a preliminary monitoring station for Enigma — the ultra-top-secret decoding machine stolen from the Germans — Russell was invited to recommend men and women who might staff the venture sited at Bletchley Park, a scattering of huts five miles from Woburn Abbey. He was swayed by Winterbotham's opinion that 'when total security is vital, family ties prove more reliable than the most elaborate form of screening'. Russell had had no reservations about recommending Caroline for one of the most crucial roles on the project, that of translator. They now shared an additional bond of official secrecy.

'I have so little time at home,' he protested as Elsie swept out to the kitchen. 'That woman keeps your mother chattering all day. Why she has to start the moment she sets foot in the door. . . .'

Caroline's eyes sought cover in their own depths. 'She came, didn't she? She's a sweet woman and she works very hard and mummy likes her. Mummy doesn't have much, after all.'

Russell shook the *Telegraph* into shape and folded it to the front page. This was dangerous ground; they had tiptoed here before. A child had no right to question the intimate relationships of its parents; it was . . . unhealthy.

Elizabeth came back from the kitchen and sat down. She picked up the *Daily Express* and turned at once to the inside pages. She had no appetite for front-page news of war.

Russell said to Caroline, 'Did you hear the anti-aircraft guns last night?'

'No.' Caroline poured more tea for both of them. '*The Times* says London put up the biggest ack-ack barrage of the war, but I can't say I saw any of it out in the garden.'

'Hmmm.' His chin sank into his collar. There had been no anti-aircraft bombardment of the enemy in London last night, nor throughout Saturday night's holocaust. It was the reason he had been called urgently to Whitehall yesterday, to a hastily convened meeting of the Special Liaison Committee. His role was to co-ordinate the design and supply of highly complex technology for special projects. Officially he was attached to the Air Ministry under the protective wing of Air Intelligence, but the remarkable success of his squads of exotic boffins had earned a reputation, and appeals for help, from all the service arms.

Saturday night had been a disastrous baptism of fire for both the artillery defences and the R.A.F. Air Vice Marshal Keith Park's Number Eleven Group had been able to summon six squadrons of Blenheims and Defiants as night fighters but their performance against the enemy had been appalling. Not only had they failed to shoot down German invaders, they had often come dangerously close to shooting each other. Night fighting was in its infancy, an unpractised and seemingly impractical art whose relevance had been ignored for too long. In aerial dogfights at night fighter pilots found themselves totally disoriented by the competing light variables of ground-fires, searchlights, moonlight and the tracery of cannon-fire. Mission control and the orchestration of attacks, it seemed, were virtually impossible under present conditions. For the sake of simple preservation, the London artillery batteries under General Pile were ordered to remain silent and leave the skies free for the night fighters. In any event, Pile observed, his inner London defence would have achieved very little; he had only ninety-two guns in position, having farmed out the same number around the country to provincial cities which had come under German bomber attack in the preceding three weeks. At the end of the meeting Pile agreed to pull back his guns to strengthen London and Russell promised to throw the fighter problem into his brain tank.

'I said, why do you ask?' Caroline repeated for the third time.

He flexed his lips, their secret sign, and she turned back to *The Times*. He said to Elizabeth, 'I didn't hear Ian come in this morning. Where is he?'

Caroline said quickly, 'He came home early. About half-past two, I think.'

Russell bridled at once. 'If they hear he's been scuttling home early—'

Elizabeth looked up from her *Express*. 'He wouldn't *scuttle* anywhere, Charles. Don't be silly. They obviously let him off. He's an assistant porter, not a surgeon.'

'A commitment's a commitment,' Russell persisted doggedly. 'The boy has no sense of responsibility. No respect for me and my position. God knows, I tried my best with him.' He folded his paper and scraped back the chair. 'If he had an ounce of guts in him he'd be in uniform. I know the way his mind works. That hospital's a cosy little number; easy way out; makes no demands on his intelligence or his almighty *conscience*.' He spat the word derisively.

'I won't have you saying that,' Elizabeth snapped. 'He stands by what he believes.'

'He stands by the safety of his ignorant young neck.' Russell got to his feet, adjusted his black jacket and waistcoat and bent to brush crumbs from the immaculate creases of his spongebag trousers.

'Daddy, you'll be late,' said Caroline sharply. He glared down at her and met the mirror image of his own impatience. He softened at once.

'Can I give you a lift to Euston?' he asked her.

Caroline shook her head. 'I don't have to be in until tomorrow and then I shall be working overnight.'

Elsie Warrender beetled into the morning-room, clattered the dirty crockery on to a tray and returned to the kitchen. Russell watched her with mounting distaste. When she had gone, he snapped, 'Can't that woman leave us in peace for a second? A man has a right to some privacy in his own home.'

Elizabeth rose in her chair, her mouth set. For a moment she appeared ready to hurl the teaspoon in her fingers at his head. She exhaled slowly.

'That woman, Charles, lost her home last night. A bomb hit it. She could have been killed. This morning she hasn't a possession in the world. Her family's living in other people's houses. Her husband's ill and she's obviously worried sick about him. All that — and she still came in to work because she didn't want to let us down. Let *us* down.'

Russell slapped his thigh with the rolled paper in embarrassment. 'I'm sorry. I didn't know.'

'And I don't suppose you care much now that you do.'

'That's not true.'

It *was* true, he had to admit. He really didn't care. It would be hypocritical to try to convince himself otherwise. He had nothing in common with the woman and a great deal less to thank her for than his wife seemed to think. What she was doing to the fabric of his family was no less insidious and no less undermining than Attlee and his gang were doing to the social fabric of the country. Even Caroline had been subverted by her. And as for Ian and Tom. . . .

'Tell her. . . .' He paused. 'Tell her I'm most disturbed to hear of her . . . experience. Offer her my condolences.'

'She lost her home, dear,' Elizabeth said waspishly, 'not a pet budgerigar.'

'I am trying to be—'

'Have you considered telling her yourself?'

He drew himself up and fished out his fob-watch. 'If you'll excuse me, I'll get myself off. It's late. I'm obviously in everybody's way here.' He stumped out to the hall and they heard him collect his uniform of coat, bowler, umbrella and briefcase.

Caroline and Elizabeth exchanged guilty grins. The front door slammed. Caroline said, 'You *know* he doesn't understand.'

'He has to be made to. Honestly, he's so pompous at times I could throttle him. I think he really believes people like Elsie and her kind are ready to fight a war just to protect the privileges of Charles Russell and his tight little world.'

'You're a bit of old privilege yourself, dear,' Caroline said, eyes twinkling. 'Elsie and *her kind*, indeed.'

'Well, you know what I mean.'

'I think I do. I just hope *you* know what you mean, too.'

'Caroline!'

'Elizabeth!'

They both laughed. Even Charles Russell had to admit that Caroline had inherited that infectious laughter from her mother. Elsie popped her head around the door, made sure the coast was clear and came into the room, wiping her hands on a floral pinafore. She still wore her hat, a flat-topped narrow-brimmed black felt creation with three red plaster cherries on one side and a dazed green feather on the other.

'Mister gone then?'

'Yes, and good riddance,' said Elizabeth good naturedly.

'Poor man. Got a lot on his mind, I shouldn't wonder. You shouldn't go on at him the way you do, you two.'

Elsie stared at them, bewildered, as they roared with laughter. She sat down at the table and poured herself a cup of tea. Her eye fell on Elizabeth's copy of the *Daily Express*. In a shallow box that ran across the whole front page ran an extract from Churchill's famous speech of January.

'Come then, let us to the task, to the battle and the toil. Each to our part, each to our station. . . . Guard the streets, succour the wounded, uplift the downcast and honour the brave. Let us go forward together.'

She traced a finger reverently across the printed words. 'Oh, isn't he wonderful? I always said so. If anyone can get us through, it's him, I tell my Jack. He's got a lovely way with words, too. Makes you feel . . . oh, you can't do enough for him, can you?'

Mother and daughter fell silent. Caroline leant forward and ran her eye down the page. She suddenly stiffened and pulled the paper towards her. She read quickly through the opening paragraphs of a story at the bottom of the page under the headline : HOSPITAL RESCUE.

'I wish you could have shown this to daddy before he left,' she said quietly.

'Who's that?' Elizabeth propped her glasses on her nose and bent to look.

'It's about a hospital porter who rescued a woman during the raid last night. I think it's Ian.'

Monday, 1045

Cynthia Price was late, an historical event to rival Yorktown and the sinking of the *Titanic*. She rushed in, gasping apologies. A bomb had dropped on her home station at Wimbledon just before midnight, setting a District train on fire and paralysing lines in and out. Her mother had driven her to London in the family Austin Ruby.

'You should have stayed home,' Shaffer said apologetically, consumed for no good reason with the feeling that he had forced the woman to work against her better judgement.

'I haven't missed a day in fifteen years,' she retorted stoutly as if there was no achievement in life so noble. 'Besides, I change mother's library books at Harrods on Mondays.'

Shaffer pushed his typewriter aside. 'But your mother drove you in, you said.'

'Oh, but she couldn't manage Harrods. Not on her own.'

Shaffer felt a ridiculous compulsion to pursue this logic. 'Why not?'

Mrs Price directed a smile at him that wrapped him in a winding-sheet of pity. 'The raids, Mr Shaffer. She couldn't go inside knowing there might be a raid.'

'But she could've got hit just as easily driving you in to the office, couldn't she?'

'Yes — but that was an essential service.'

He gaped at her. She took off her coat and hat and busied herself at the percolator. One day, he told himself, he would peel back the layers around Cynthia Price and figure out the validity of that 'Mrs' label she wore so jealously. If there was a Mr Price, no one at A.B.N. had ever seen or heard of him. The indelicate opinion of all seven correspondents who had worked the London beat was that Cynthia had never met her man, never married him; he was the non-existent rod and staff that comforted her in her old maidenhood.

'Is there anything I ought to know?' she asked, spooning coffee.

'O'Keefe was on. I wrote it in the log.' Mrs Price logged every call, however irrelevant. She had a library of forty-six books, all bound in black leather and hand-tooled with A.B.N.'s imprimatur, running back over fifteen years of incoming phone calls. No one had ever ordered her to these lengths, nor applauded her for doing so independently, but she thought of her log as the linchpin of her career. She set the percolator and checked her precious black leather book.

Shaffer said defensively, 'I wrote in pencil so you could rub it out and do it properly.' Her copperplate writing was a byword.

'Hmm. Hmm. Hmm.' She read his scrawled note. 'It doesn't

say what Mr O'Keefe asked for, Mr Shaffer. I always put that in under "Subject of Call". What did he want?'

'Just the moon,' Shaffer said off-handedly. He lit a cigarette and regretted it at once. The stale taste of it awoke stale tastes all over; a combination of Murrow's hospitality and Rita's bile.

'What moon, Mr Shaffer?' Mrs Price pressed innocently.

'The one that's always just out of reach.' He chewed his lip. 'Did anyone ever call you Cynthia?'

She whirled round on her heel, colourless eyes wide with surprise behind her gold-framed spectacles. 'I should think not, Mr Shaffer. Not at the place of business.'

'No. I guess not. Just wondered. You've been here so long.'

'Mr O'Keefe's call,' she pressured him. 'About the moon.'

He said weakly, 'Joke, Mrs Price. Just a joke. He wants me to get a line on how the big boys run the war at the top. You know —a coupla quotes from Churchill, Dowding, Alexander, Eden. The usual bunch.'

She trapped her tongue in her teeth as she rubbed out his scrawl and wrote: 'Interview Mr Churchill, Marshal Dowding, General Alexander, Mr Eden.'

'Good,' she said, admiring her work from a distance. 'Won't that be rather difficult? I mean, they're very busy, I would think, just now.'

'No—not difficult at all,' Shaffer yawned. 'Impossible. O'Keefe's just running a temperature. Comes of working through the weekend without sleep. I'm getting to feel the same way myself.'

'You'll try, of course, though?' She was truly saddened by his irreligious attitude to the Great White O'Keefe across the water. 'I could check through the contacts book. . . .'

'So could I and it wouldn't do either of us any good. Take a tip from me, Mrs Price. From here on in, don't bother to write anything under "Subject of Call" till we've made it work. It's going to be a tough year for miracle-workers.'

He swung his feet up on the desk and pulled the phone into his lap. He dialled Denzil Fletcher-Hale's number. It rang a long time before the receiver lifted.

'Eight-oh-double one.'

'That you, Denzil?'

'Shaffer. Just goin' out. Top of the stairs. What can I do?'

'Look, Denzil, this is stupid, I know, but I have to ask. I want to talk to a couple of members of the government or someone like Dowding about the conduct of the war. I mean interview them. And I don't mean information ministers or second-layer civil servants, either. I just don't have that kind of contact and I don't want to have to go running round with my begging bowl to Murrow. Anything you can do?'

'Probably. Short notice, though. How much time?'

'The whole damn year if you can come up with a couple of top hands.'

'Not necessary, really. Few days should do. Call you later. Must fly. Seeing Jebb in ten minutes. That job, you know.' He rang off.

Shaffer left the office with Mrs Price's protestations that the coffee would be ready in two minutes ringing in his ears. He strolled along Hill Street and into Berkeley Square, bought a copy of the *Evening Standard* and checked the headlines. War was hell but in Fleet Street it still sold newspapers. The front page carried a four-column picture of King George against a background of a desolated row of houses. 'The King (in centre) inspecting air-raid damage in an eastern district of London, when he made a tour today,' read the caption. The king was in fact chatting with a serious bunch of East Enders. He wore a Field-Marshal's uniform and a wan smile.

The *Evening Standard* reporter had been tickled to death and felt duty bound to incite respect in his readers.

'The East Enders were quick to appreciate that the king had come among them while the firemen were still fighting the flames and the rescue parties still digging amid piles of debris. Pushing past a police sergeant, one woman tapped the king on the arm and shouted: "I'll bet old Hitler daren't go among his folk like this." '

A story on page two speculated on whether the United States–Canadian Joint Defence Board, about to meet in Washington, could channel American volunteer pilots into the war via the back door of the Canadian Air Force without breaching the Neutrality Act. Canada was already pumping men into England and there was a picture of the latest and largest group just arrived 'to fight in Germany', including two of the Dominion's Highland regiments. Among the grinning, bereted faces in the accompanying picture was a handsome man who towered head and shoulders above his comrades. Shaffer recognised him; the actor Gerald Kent, who had been Mae West's Broadway leading man in the thirties.

Meanwhile, life was brimming with timeless inanities. The secretary and proprietress of the South Ken Bridge Club had been fined for serving drinks after hours. Late-night tipplers using the one-roomed club had been required to ring the bell three times and whisper the password : Feeling Good. Butchers selling off-ration meat to housewives were threatened with Ministry of Food inspection. Two East Enders had been remanded in custody for looting during Saturday's raids; their haul was listed as a quantity of toffee, a piece of chocolate and a dummy chocolate carton, of a value of 9d. The magistrate had told them comfortingly : 'You two men are charged with looting and that is punishable now by death.' And on the main feature page a comedian by the name of J. H. Park gave thanks for the return of flat racing. 'For some the Blitz is at its peak,' he wrote. 'For us racing folk it has come to an end—from a business point of view. Saturday's meeting at Hurst Park breaks a spell that has lasted since 18 June.'

Shaffer walked back to Hill Street and climbed into the car. The Savoy American bar was the crossroads of the communications trade at lunchtime and, besides, he had to file something at five. O'Keefe thought it was a good idea to keep tabs on the people he had introduced into his Sunday morning story. Listeners were showing interest back home; ringing A.B.N., some of them, to ask if the boys in the warehouse and their embattled families were still alive. A few even called to ask if Shaffer could supply a name and phone number for the girl dancer who wouldn't let him take her home. 'Now that's what I call *real* interest,' O'Keefe had cackled. He would have to check out the scene at Nelson's Green. Later. He did not want to overdo that line.

As he approached the turnoff into the Savoy courtyard, he noticed a cloud of dust and trailing smoke rising a few hundred yards ahead where the Strand joined Fleet Street. He drove on around Aldwych until he was stopped by a line of police and wardens. The Royal Courts of Justice had been hit the night before and rubble littered the street. He left the car and walked on.

At the gates of Somerset House bands of firemen, wardens and rescue men were clearing away rubble from an obvious hit. A great gallery of lunchtime strollers stood in an arc around them. Many of them had brought packets of sandwiches to eat and flasks of tea or lemonade; surrounded by hooting cars and buses, by the unquenchable bustle of workaday London, by all the evidence of crude, destructive savagery and the promise of more to come — perhaps in the space of minutes — they stood contented, relaxed, even happy. Very few of them talked and that, thought Shaffer, might be a clue to some profound invisible sadness.

They stood as cattle might stand in the meadow adjoining a slaughterhouse, mildly curious but not alarmed.

Monday, 1300

Charles Russell squared his shoulders at the window overlooking the Embankment. Behind him, in the cool, sparsely furnished office, Mountford adopted the tone of the spurned fairy godfather.

'You can't expect decent commercial opportunity to lie comfortably with conscience in wartime, Russell. Can't be done. Had the same misgivings myself. But the plain fact of the matter is, like it or not, a fellow can't afford to let things slide on the grounds that maintaining his family in proper style is a form of profiteering. Dammit, it's not. Where'd we be, the country as a whole, if chaps like you and me decided to pull in our horns and sit on our capital?'

'You have a different attitude to these things,' Russell protested.

'Different attitude be damned. Precisely the same. Did my bit, just as you have; put hard cash into War Loans and be lucky to see my capital again, let alone a return on investment. D'you think the government's going to come along when we're destitute and say "Have a few thousand, old man, to keep you going"? Don't make me laugh.'

Russell turned into the room and pulled out his fob-watch. 'I have lunch at the Carlton at one-thirty,' he said uneasily.

'I can't promise this thing'll wait for you to make up your mind. Really can't. We're not dealing with gentlemen. You won't find gentlemen grubbing for profits at this moment.'

'But that's just my point, Mountford. Can't you see that? Men in our position—'

'Men in our position starve as fast as the next,' Mountford said with asperity. 'Besides, without the profiteers there'd be no private industry left. That's a fact. May strike some as hitting below the belt while the war's *on*, but just wait till it's all over and the country's bankrupt and private enterprise dead. What are they going to say then, ask yourself? Simple; they'll blame the middle class for failing to plan ahead, for sitting tight on their capital and not encouraging growth.'

'It's not the same thing,' Russell returned uncertainly.

'Exactly the same thing, old man. When the boys come home looking for jobs, it's not Clement Attlee they'll turn to for them. They'll be down at the labour exchanges, queuing at the factory gates, looking to the carmakers and the shipbuilders and the construction industry. The motto now may be "Keep them Rolling" but the question they'll be asking when they're out of work will be "Why didn't you keep them going?" You must see the logic of that.'

Russell came round his desk and perched stiffly on his chair. He harboured no great affection for Kingsley Mountford and reserved his judgement on the man's abilities as an administrator, but there was no denying his background; he was the third son of an earl, his aunt was a duchess, he had a private income of at least ten thousand a year and was impeccably acceptable. He had done the right thing, too, after Dunkirk; shelved his directorship with a merchant bank, offered himself to the Air Ministry, moved his family to the house in Yorkshire and volunteered the dozen or so shooting cottages on his estates in Norfolk and Somerset to the local authorities for evacuee settlement. He was a good sort, in that sense. Besides, they were fellow Wykehamists; they had fagged together in their first year and retained a slight friendship right through to Oxford.

'What would be required of me if' — he let the word hang for five seconds — 'if I decide to join you?'

'My dear old chap, if this fellow agrees. Let's not forget that tiny detail. I can only recommend you to him. Don't know him that well, as I said. Just met him at a party.'

'He might decline, you mean?'

Mountford shook his head, a sly grin lighting his weak blue eyes. 'Take leave to doubt it. Fellow's likely to be impressed by a man of your standing. Bit of a snob — not surprising in his case. You know the sort; sharp as nails. Crucify his grandmother rather than pass up the chance of making a bob or two, but greasy as hell and coarse as the devil's tickling stick. God knows where he was at school, if he ever went to school.'

'You make out a very good case for avoiding him like the plague.'

'Thought so myself. Had the same misgivings. But Hannan-Paynter introduced us; nothing wrong with Hannan-Paynter. And when I looked into it and found Lochandry and the Mountallans were already in and old Laughlan and a couple of his bank directors were on the main Melly-Greenmantle board — well, what else d'you have to know? Good men. Excellent families and you couldn't call them profiteers, now could you?'

Charles Russell breathed deeply, trapping the air in his chest to fuel a decision. He got up. 'Very well. When can we meet?'

'Up to him, but soon, I'd say. Maybe this evening. You'll have to give me an hour or so to talk to him. Busy now. Er — how much are you good for?'

Russell pressed his lips together in an expression of distaste. 'I'd have to think about that.' He knew exactly. Two thousand pounds at best; not more than that and only then if the bank agreed to advance the loan against his investment portfolio. He had to maintain a reserve at the bank; at least five hundred, for emergencies. With Elizabeth to account for there were always emergencies.

'Right.' Mountford got to his feet. 'Be pushing off then. I'm lunching, myself, at the Travellers'. Talk to you later.' He turned at the door. 'You're not ...' — he paused, searching for the right phrase — '... you're not averse to meeting him off the beaten track, I suppose?'

'How do you mean?'

'Pub, somewhere like that. Doesn't do to be seen on home ground with chaps like this. Not one of us. Business is one thing; parading him around one's club is another.'

'Of course. You're right.'

Mountford left and Russell washed his hands and face in the wash-basin, brushed his scrubby grey hair and telephoned the hall porter to have his driver bring the car to the entrance. He was closing the door on his way out when the phone rang.

'Russell? Beaverbrook.' The voice had a snarl to it that was daunting; a cutting edge that turned the broad transatlantic vowels into arrowheads.

'I was just going to lunch,' Russell said coldly. He had an intense distrust of the volcanic Minister for Aircraft Production, an illogical one in fact since it stemmed from a general distaste for all colonial entrepreneurs. Beaverbrook was a specific target, though; Russell regarded his newspapers — the *Daily* and *Sunday Express* and the *Evening Standard* — as the shock troops of the New Age of Vulgarity. His influence had grown like a rash during the newspaper circulation wars of the thirties, and with it his power. On the other hand, the man had recently been admitted to the War Cabinet; he had to be humoured.

'Wars don't stop for lunch, Russell,' Beaverbrook snarled.

'I don't have to be reminded of that ... sir. My lunch is a working one.'

'Don't believe in 'em,' returned the Beaver smartly. 'Work first, eat when you can. Listen — we've been talking about that night fighter problem. I've got a designer over here from McDonnell Douglas in the U.S. He threw out a few ideas and they sound good to me. I want you to get your boffins to kick 'em around. You understand me?'

Russell's lip curled. 'Verbal ideas, minister, aren't much good to my people. If he can commit his thoughts to paper. . . .'

'To hell with paper. It's an idea, not a goddamn foolproof work-study. That's your province.'

Russell eyed the clock. He was going to be late. 'What is his idea?'

'Simple. Good old American thinking-on-the-feet. We're equipping Eleven Group with Blenheims and Defiants for night interception. For why? Because we're thinking in compartments. Listen. The best fighters we've got are the Spitfire and the Hurricane, right? Best for climb rate, best for manoeuvrability, best for handling.'

'I don't see.'

'Nobody sees. The problem we've got is twofold. We don't have our best planes in the sky at night. That's one. Two is, solo pilots can't fly at night *and* stay out of trouble *and* blast the enemy. You with me?'

'I still don't see. . . .'

Beaverbrook's snarl took on a note of triumph. 'We take the Spitfire, O.K.? We work in a rear-facing seat with a gun turret for the second man. The pilot concentrates on finding the enemy and flying to order. The gunner takes care of the rest. What d'you think?'

Russell closed his eyes and conjured a picture of the baby-faced hobgoblin bent eagerly over his huge desk. 'Mitchell's design for the Spitfire was based on maximum airflow over the frame, sir. The mathematics are precise; they don't allow for fundamental changes in flow patterns.'

'You're saying I should mind my own business.'

'I'm saying, sir, that to introduce an enlarged cockpit and a bulb turret aft would radically alter the balance factor. You would be introducing, as it were, a basic flaw into an otherwise perfect design. In any event, the new Beaufighter design—'

'You mean you refuse to even think about it?'

'Not a matter of refusing—'

'Just lying down on the job. Leaving it to someone else?'

Russell flushed with anger. 'I'm prepared to ponder the impossible, if necessary, Lord Beaverbrook, but I consider it a waste of time and resources to send valuable scientific effort in pursuit of miracles.'

'Miracles! For you, maybe. This guy doesn't happen to agree with you. I guess the Americans are conditioned to taking miracles in their stride.'

'Then perhaps the problem is best left to *them*.'

There was a pause, the unearthly silence that precedes a volcanic eruption. 'Russell, I'm gonna remember this conversation. I'm gonna remember what you said and why. Meanwhile, I'll hand this problem over to my own people. That all right with you?'

Russell coughed nervously. 'I don't think I understand, minister,' he said. 'My permission is—'

'You don't, hey? Well, I just thought I'd ask, that's all—just in case you had some kinda conscientious objection.'

The phone clicked dead.

Russell stood with the instrument in his hand, unmoving. Just in case you had some kind of conscientious objection. It couldn't mean anything else. He knew about Ian. They *all* knew. The Cabinet, his own colleagues; probably every clerk in Whitehall. Sniggering behind his back. Pitying him.

Everyone knew.

Monday, 1500

Gladys Warrender stared at her reflection in the magnifying mirror of her compact. She scowled and stopped, focusing on a spot beneath her eye. She prodded it lightly with her finger. She repeated the repair on the other side. It hadn't shown itself completely, but it was there all right: a distinct puffiness, no mistaking it. She dabbed at an imaginary shadow with a ball of damp cotton wool. Look at her!

She clicked the compact shut and flung it on the bed behind her. And her hair! She had a constant battle with split ends but this was terrible. She'd washed it in stout but that didn't seem to have done much good. She tugged down a wisp across her face and sifted through it to prove her point until she was cross-eyed. She found nothing. She shook her head; well, it didn't have the bounce it once had. How could it, living like this? Enough to make anyone washed out, living in a coffin of a room with no air and dust everywhere. It was so hot at night that her one lipstick had begun to melt. On top of that, all the make-up she had left was what she carried in her handbag; the rest she'd have to buy again, which meant being fleeced on the black market if she was lucky. No underclothes, apart from what she stood up in; no dresses, shoes, hats. Nothing. Janice had let her borrow two dresses that must have taken hours to find in the bottom of some drawer; they were five years out of date. No self-respecting granny would be seen dead in them.

All right, the Scullys had been good to them, letting the whole family move in just like that, the boys top-to-toe in the boxroom, Arthur and Flo on a made-up bed in the front parlour and Elsie and Jack in their room next door. And there was no fun in sharing a room with Janice.

Course, most people would pray for neighbours like that, even in the Green, where acts of decent charity were part of what living was all about and not just insurance against the possibility of one's own bad luck. Even so, she couldn't help thinking that maybe they'd been *too* good. If the Scullys hadn't been there, or just never made the offer, it would have meant leaving the Green; packing up what they could and looking for somewhere else. It would have been an escape. A new start. Hundreds were getting out now. Things could never be the same here any more. Thank the Lord.

As a kid it had been different; it was good to be part of it all; everyone knowing everyone else. At Christmas and in the holidays whole streets used to have something going on — parties and games — and everyone was an uncle or an auntie. Even as children, though, they had known that East End life was unlike life anywhere else. Somehow they had been special, like gypsies and circus people were special.

Until the young chaps found themselves breaking their backs in the docks for a living and the girls realised with mounting horror that good old mum with her pinny and her mangle was the exact be-all and end-all of everything they could ever hope to be themselves.

Gladys fluffed her hair, her face determined. A new start. There was still time. And if the others wouldn't, she would. They'd soon follow. Right then, it was up to her! She got up and looked around the room critically. None of the big stars had had it easy; they'd had to fight their way to the top. Out of a room like this.

One day Carole Davis would look back on this and laugh.

She went downstairs imbued with a new sense of purpose or, as she preferred to think of it, Destiny.

There was a note on the kitchen table from her mother. Paul had gone out early and she was worried about a repetition of Saturday. The docks were still burning and the way things were Jerry could be back at any time. If the sirens went and Paul hadn't returned, Gladys was to tell Alfie Dunn and help find him. Gladys looked at her watch. It was getting on for four o'clock.

'Tea, dad?'

Jack Warrender was polishing the hob with a tin of Zebra, squatting in front of it with his back to her. He didn't seem to hear. He'd gone proper deaf since he was caught out on Saturday but mum said it wasn't that; he just didn't want to talk.

Gladys shrugged and put the kettle on.

'I'll make a cup, anyway. Always there if you want it. Uncle Arthur's gone to work, I suppose. Auntie Flo'll be round at Edie's. She's due any day now, must be.'

She turned to the bent back. Gently. 'Dad? I know you can hear me, dad. Please . . . just for me.' She bit her lip. She hadn't given a thought to him all the time she had been upstairs. 'Come on, dad.' She laid a hand tenderly on his shiny red scalp.

' 'S'all right, Elsie,' he said gruffly. 'Be all right.'

'Dad, it's me. Glad. Mum went to work. I've put the kettle on. Nice cup of tea, eh? You and me.' She bent to kiss the nape of his neck. 'Course it'll be all right. You see. It. . . .'

She straightened, aware of a coldness inside her; an icy

numbness. She tried to speak but the sound got lost somewhere at the back of her throat. Jack Warrender was busying himself with the Zebra, applying it to lumps of coal he had placed in an orderly row along the edge of the fender.

Gladys knelt beside her father and took him in her arms, rocking the pain away. He sat relaxed, quiet, unmoving – and then the alert went. As its first note swept out over the Green, Jack Warrender stiffened, pushed her away and climbed unsteadily to his feet. He was breathing heavily. He called for Elsie. Gladys took his hand and led him across to the couch and made him lie down. For ten minutes she watched him, but he did not move. He seemed to be sleeping. It was only then she remembered mum's note about Paul.

'Dad! Can you hear me? I've got to go out, dad. Just for a bit. Get Paul. Don't . . . don't. . . .' Her eyes filled with tears. 'Don't *do* anything, dad.'

In the street she tried to calm herself, control her trembling. She had to be strong like mum. They all had to be strong. Dad was drifting away from them. What could she do? How did you stop a man drifting clear out of his mind? She fought back her panic. Paul. Find Paul. Her strength seemed to be ebbing from her.

'You all right, love?' The voice came from one side, a bomb site. Barry! She blinked at her brother through her tears.

'Oh Barry. Barry. Thank the Lord you're—'

'Hey, hold on, Glad. What's the tears for, love?' Barry Warrender peered at her with difficulty. He wore the regulation oilskins of the A.F.S. and his face was half obscured beneath a helmet at least a size too big for him. Barry had joined the service two years ago and had been turned down for war service on account of his asthma. Essential non-active service for an asthmatic turned out to be the Auxiliary Fire Service with an eighteen-hour working day. Barry Warrender had seen his first real fire two days ago. To all intents and purposes that made him a veteran.

He struggled with something that looked like a wriggling sack under his arm. 'Hang on a tick Glad, I'm. . . .'

'What is it?' She stared at the shrieking, convulsing pink-grey thing as he tightened his grip. 'Barry, what is it?'

'Wrong way round, the little. . . . Come here! No you don't. Gotcha! Sorry, Glad. Only, if I put him down the little bugger's off like a shot.'

'It's a pig,' she squeaked.

'Piglet,' he corrected. 'The sow's back there somewhere. Won't find me trying to pick her up. What's all the crying about?'

Gladys shook her head. 'It's. . . .'

What was the point? There was nothing Barry could do. Anyway, he had enough on his mind with his Edie due any day now.

'It's our Paul,' she said. 'He's not indoors. You heard what happened Saturday night. Mum's worried sick he might do it again. You know what Paul is — in one ear and out the other.'

She stared with growing fascination at the wriggling piglet under her brother's arm.

'What are you doing with it?'

'Porky?' Barry slapped the piglet's rump affectionately. 'He's been bombed out. Back of Monmouth Street. Somebody's got a piggery on a patch of ground between the post office and the houses. Must be fifteen of 'em. Houses copped it and off the pigs went all over the bloody place, squealing blue murder. Here — want one?' He held it out.

Gladys retreated quickly.

'No, nor me,' grinned Barry. 'What am I supposed to do with him?' He patted the piglet on the head. 'Think they'd taken him down the reception centre?' His grin faded. ''Ere, Glad. You shouldn't be tramping around out here after Paul.'

'Never mind. I can look after myself. I promise if anything starts I'll go back.'

'Honest?'

'Promise,' said Gladys again. 'Just a little look. He's probably not far away.'

She didn't want to go back to the house alone, not with dad like that. She could have got used to a broken leg or arm — but something you couldn't see, in the head, that was terrifying. Mum would know what to do for the best. She'd be home soon.

High over her head the ominous droning sound began again. She looked up. There they were all right. Same as yesterday and Saturday. When were they ever going to stop? She held up her watch. She had been walking for an hour. Damn that kid!

'Pauuuuull!'

An hour? What *had* she been doing for an hour?

She couldn't remember.

'Pauuul?'

It was hopeless. Barry was right; there was no sense in walking in circles round and round the Green. She stopped and looked about her.

The Green? *Was* it the Green? She couldn't place. . . .

A crackle of blue and white flame lit the sky and she whirled. Where was she? She had walked from the house towards Lavender. No — after leaving Barry she had gone on past the docks office, or what was left of it and. . . . Wait a mo; couldn't have. She would have been near the Tunnel, that way. . . .

There was a muffled roar way over to her left; she started to run. Her stomach churned to the steady reverberation of the explosions but she couldn't stop. The streets here were empty, the houses gutted but incendiaries had started more fires. She knew she had to find somewhere; it was suicidal to go on.

She was calling stupidly for Barry when she stumbled across the sign. It lay twisted and half obscured under a pile of brick but she recognised the painting on it: The Half Moon. The last time she'd seen it, a year ago, was when Jack and Elsie had taken her there for a drink with Brian Carter. The front door was still in its frame but not much else was of a piece — except the two wooden cellar flaps lying flung back and she could see steps leading down into the darkness. She walked down. The cellar was damp and the smell of stale beer was everywhere, but it was protection. She splashed nervously to the farthest corner, sat on the concrete shelf that skirted the room, and adjusted her eyes to the gloom. In the putrid beery scum lapping the cellar floor rubber beer-pipes writhed like eels. Ugh! She settled herself against the wall. Could be worse. Could be worse.

From out of the darkness something floated gently against her shins. A sack? She shoved at it with her foot. Soft. It rolled on the tide of beer and the light caught a face. The flat open eyes of the dead woman followed her as she cringed against the wall. The echo of her own screams mocked her as she clawed her way back up into the street.

She ran without thought of direction or distance, without sensation and without hope. Her screams became breathless groans of horror and the tears refused to stop. Her shoes had gone and her feet were lacerated and bleeding as she ran. What sixth sense brought her home she never knew but suddenly there she was at the door of the Anderson shelter by the landslide of rubble that had once been the Warrenders' home.

The steel door banged outward. "A's Glad,' said a voice.

'Glad?' Paul Warrender balanced unsteadily in the sunken doorway, his eyes dazed. 'Glad?' He looked back over his shoulder. 'She's all white,' he said thickly.

'All right! Everybody's all right!' sang Derek Scully from inside. 'Tell her to. . . .'

Gladys dragged herself in and bent double. Oozing mud seeped upwards through the floorplanks, displaced by her weight.

'Glad . . . Glad. . . .' Paul stuttered. He made the mistake of touching her shoulder. The blow caught him under the ear and sent him reeling.

"Ere, hang about. . . ,' bawled Derek. He put the bottle of beer he was drinking down in front of him and twitched a finger at the corner where Paul lay in shock against the dirt wall. 'Whadja haveta do that for, your own bruvver?'

'You little bastard!' Gladys could have committed murder. 'Paul!' The boy scrabbled deeper into his corner, reaching backwards and upwards for the exit.

'Slor . . . slorr . . . slorry.' He fell backwards through the door and disappeared.

'Pole!'

Derek Scully sank down wearily on the wooden bench along the shelter wall, a solitary reminder of the bunks that had been removed. He looked at Gladys through one eye.

'Whassup?'

Gladys ignored him. Her legs were aching, burning. She pulled back the torn skirt, looking for bruises. At the top of her thigh was a yellow smudge that stretched all the way up to her hips. She examined it; touched it; gasped. It would show! At the club, it would show. It fell where her dancing tights would not cover it. An inch, perhaps, or more. . . .

'Nasty.'

Derek Scully swung himself upright. He kicked over the beer bottle as he did so. 'Nasty, that,' he repeated. His eyes took in the sweep of Gladys's thigh. 'Very . . . nasty. . . .' He bent forward over her. 'Give you a hand, eh, Glad?'

There was something in his fuddled tone that made her look up at him. Derek Scully unbuttoned his shorts and fumbled inside.

'Eh, Glad?'

The beer bottle had rolled to within inches of her hand. She picked it up and smashed it against the corrugated wall of the shelter.

'You come one step near me, Derek Scully,' she hissed, 'and I'll give you this right in your kisser.'

The boy braced back in the flickering light of the single bulb, his face bathed in its malarial yellow glow. Slowly he raised his hands until they were at shoulder height.

'Whas all that about then?'

'You know what it's all about, all right, you dirty little sod.' Gladys held the bottle under his chin as he edged past her, hands high.

He swung up through the exit. 'Just a pee, Glad. Just a pee.' She heard him laugh as he lurched down the garden.

The smell of beer filled the shelter, clinging to her clothes and her hair. Her dress hung in filthy tatters and the bruise on her thigh had stiffened the muscle of her leg. Oh, God. She was due on stage in less than three hours.

Monday, 1600

Arthur Scully retired to the small desk concealed behind a wooden partition in the main corridor and signed himself in for duty. The simple act of scratching his name in the log with that screeching, twisted nib had a miraculous effect on him; it was like building a blastproof wall between himself and the world outside. It was getting a mite overcrowded, that other world of his. There was Jack Warrender and Elsie to think of now, as well as Flo and that young bugger Derek. Gawd alone knew how they'd all muck in together, but one thing was certain; he could no more have told them to look somewhere else for a roof over their heads than fly.

He blotted his signature carefully and entered the time: 1601. He needn't have put the extra minute on, seeing as how he had walked through the door a good four minutes before he was due, but 1601 was the exact time of signing and nothing could alter that. Cheat the logbook and you never knew who or what you'd end up cheating next.

He returned to the head of the stairs and settled into his 'At ease' stance behind the machine gunner's rounded shoulders. The duty gunner was Bill Pitts, who had problems enough for six men. His wife and three kids had been evacuated to Peebles and his smallholding out by Westerham had been taken on by his father. The wife was playing around with some Scottish grocer up there by all accounts, and one of the kids, a boy of ten, had got on the wrong side of the police. Now word had come through that the smallholding was to be handed over to some big local farmer because Bill's dad wasn't running it efficiently enough to satisfy the new food production standards. Bill was a good man, though. Took his problems to Brigadier Hollis and then got on with the job. Nothing much the Marines could do about the wife and the kids but they'd had a paper sent to the farmer down in Kent and he was going to put a man on the smallholding to help the old boy out and keep things going till Bill could take up again when the war was over.

Could've got nasty. Bill said the rozzers had had to shoot a farmer down Hampshire way who wouldn't give up his land. There was always someone with bigger problems. But no man was ever alone in the Marines.

'Sar'nt Scully!' Brigadier Hollis's head appeared around the balustrade of the stairway from below.

'Sah!' Arthur raised the left foot and crashed it down, his thumbs rigid along the red stripes of his trousers.

Hollis came to the head of the stairs and held out a wedge of papers enclosed in a brown file-cover. 'Get these across to Mr Seal in the Cabinet Office at Number Ten, would you?'

'The tunnel, sah? Or. . . ?'

'Use the Foreign Office quadrangle. You'll get a signature and a rubber stamp on the warrant pinned to the file. Bring it back and give it to the adjutant, will you?'

'Sah!'

'Step lively' he would have told a messenger entrusted with the same task, so he did. The sun was glimmering through haze but there were no bombers in sight and no distant gunfire. Jerry was learning his lesson; bound to be. He wouldn't come throwing his weight around after the pasting the R.A.F. lads and the ack-ack gave him Saturday and Sunday. It was all in the papers, the way we'd seen him off.

He liked Number Ten; it gave him the feeling of walking a couple of centuries back into the past — a proud past. Houses had faces, much the same as people, and Number Ten always struck him as being a dead ringer for pictures he'd seen of old Mr Gladstone. Superior. He approved of that; Number Ten *was* superior, in spite of what Winston said about the man who put it up being a profiteering jerry-builder. It was common knowledge that the ceilings of the ground-floor rooms had had to be propped up with scaffolding; the effect of blast on the fabric was lethal and a bomb dropped within three or four hundred yards would probably bring the whole street down, some people said. Course, that was scare talk; any man in his right mind knew Jerry couldn't hit a barn door at ten yards' blank range. Still, the Cabinet were taking no chances. There was a lot of pressure on Winston to move into the Annexe and George

Rance said he wanted everything shipshape and Bristol fashion by the end of next week at the latest, so that Winston and his lady could move in permanently if they had to.

Arthur swung up a magnificent salute for the benefit of the young copper at the door of Number Ten and produced his pass, the prestigious grey government security card with his photograph stuck at the top. He clutched the brown file to his chest, implying that only death would part him from it, and the constable rang the bell. Frank Sawyers opened the door with his Sunday morning vicar's face buttoned on tight but at the sight of Arthur his left eyelid drooped fractionally in friendly salute. He beckoned him inside. The entrance hall looked like the foyer of a wartime club; about fifteen or twenty men were standing around waiting for audience, most of them in the uniforms of generals, admirals and air marshals; they didn't seem to run to much less than a brigadier-general in Downing Street. There was a constant stream of civilian clerks and Civil Service mandarins running and scuttling from office to office and up the stairs, and from behind closed doors came the clacking chatter of typewriters.

Sawyers shepherded Arthur into a corner and said quietly, 'Who's this for, Arthur?' He tapped the file.

'Mr Seal, Frank. He about, is he?'

'They're in the Cabinet Room right now,' Sawyers whispered. 'You want to wait or shall I give it to his secretary?'

'Orders is to hand it to Mr Seal, Frank. Nobody else.'

Sawyers winked. He said loudly, 'Perhaps you'd care to follow me, sergeant. I'll show you the way.' It was the first time Arthur had heard Frank's official Number Ten voice and it startled him; it bore no resemblance to his matter-of-fact off-duty voice at all. Frank had an official Number Ten walk too; he floated across the hall, led the way along a short passage and knocked at a brown-painted door. He opened it and ushered Arthur inside.

'Don't think much of the help round here, do they?' Sawyers contended with a wave of one hand. The Principal Private Secretary's staff-room was a gaunt, airless, cream-painted cell smelling of carbolic soap and Mansion polish. The single window was uncurtained, except for its folds of blackout material, and revealed nothing of the world outside through its frosted glass. There were four small tables around the cramped walls, each one laden with overflowing trays of files and a litter of paperwork. There were two half-full cups of congealing coffee on the corner of one of the tables; Frank removed them and sluiced them in the hand basin in one corner of the room.

'Can't stay,' Sawyers confided. 'Comings and goings all the time this afternoon, and His Nibs hasn't had his forty winks yet. He'll be right out of sorts if he don't get his head down soon. Hang on here and I'll tell Mr Seal soon as he comes out.'

He left the door ajar, threw Arthur a comforting grin and floated away noiselessly. It was a sobering experience, standing there right at the heart of the game, so to speak. The sound of muffled voices came down the passageway from the main hall, telephones jangled from every corner and the front-door bell pealed nineteen to the dozen. He had been waiting fifteen or twenty minutes when the voices in the hall suddenly died with the instantaneous cut-off that signifies the presence on parade of a senior officer; a new set of voices emerged, louder and more confidently at ease in their surroundings than the others. They became louder still and Arthur realised with quickening pulse that they were approaching the passageway. He tugged nervously at his jacket, smoothed the scarlet duty sash, adjusted his cap and balanced the file in his fingers to run at right angles to the stripe in his trousers.

The door was pushed inwards from the passage and Eric Seal held it wide for the Prime Minister and Mr Attlee.

They were inside before they saw Arthur and their conversation stopped at once. Winston Churchill shoved his chin forward pugnaciously, his mouth tight-lipped and angled. 'Who's this?' He looked very tired; ill. He glared short-sightedly at Arthur through eyes that were no more than trembling slits. 'Who's this?'

'Eight-nine-five Sergeant Scully, sah! Corps of Royal Marines attached to the Annexe, sah!'

The set of the bull mastiff face relaxed and the plump, fluff-fringed head nodded knowingly. 'Sergeant Scully, of course. One of Brigadier Hollis's Marines,' he confided to Attlee with a sweep of his hand along the perpendicular line of Arthur's uniform.

Clement Attlee's soulful, prayer-meeting features closed shyly around the pipe clamped in his teeth. 'Sar'nt Scully,' he said politely.

Eric Seal stepped forward briskly. 'You've got something for me, sergeant?'

'Sah! Compliments Brigadier Hollis.' He thrust forward the folder, flat to the ground, square to the body.

'What is it?' Winston demanded curiously. He took the file from Seal's hands and flicked through the papers deftly. 'Good.' He handed the file back to Seal. 'Hollis should have that funk-hole of mine ready by next week. Let the War Cabinet and C.I.G.S. have copies, Eric. And you'd better tell Mrs Churchill. She'll want to scout around her accommodation and the kitchens.'

Churchill turned on Arthur. 'Rotherhithe, isn't it, sergeant?'

'Sah! Nelson's Green, sah!'

The P.M. pointed a stubby finger at Arthur's polished belt-buckle and said to Attlee, 'We watched the bombing on Saturday night from the Annexe roof, the sergeant and I. He had a wife and son out there in the smoke and flames but do you think he'd agree to leave his post? Not even at my invitation. First man to flout an order of mine since I became Prime Minister.'

Attlee's eyes yielded no hint of his emotions behind the tiny black circles of his spectacles.

Winston propped his behind on the edge of a table. Seal flashed a look at him which conveyed the message that time was running against them and there was no provision for un-scheduled chats. The P.M. ignored him. 'Your wife and son, sar'nt. Are they well?'

'Fit and well, sah, thanking you, sah!'

'Your home is ... intact?'

Arthur felt the blush rise to his cheeks. 'All present and correct, sah!'

'And your neighbours?'

'House next door down, sah! U.X.B., sah! All alive though, sah!'

Winston nodded ponderously. 'Are they being taken care of by the proper authorities, sar'nt?'

'No, sah! Come to stay in my house, sah!'

Churchill looked meaningfully at Attlee. 'It must be very difficult for you and your good lady. Your home must be surrounded by devastation, sergeant.'

'Docks took a packet, sah. Houses down everywhere. Should've got out by rights, sah. Had to say no, sah. Got the job to think of, sah!' His cheeks now glowed a bright crimson that fell only a few shades short of the colour of his sash. His fingers quivered in his fists.

'Then you must do something for me, sar'nt, if you will.'

'Privilege, sah!'

Winston eased into a standing position with a grunt of pain. 'I went to the East End yesterday, to see the damage for myself. The destruction in some streets is total. But the people. . . .' He turned again to encompass Attlee in his audience. 'The people received me with cheers and laughter and the bravest of faces. They can be bombed and their homes destroyed and some of them will be killed – but the Narzees will never break their spirit. Not now. Not in this war. Sergeant – I want you to convey to your good lady my felicitations and my thanks to her for the part she's chosen to play. I commend her and you.'

He touched a vague hand to Arthur's arm but his mind had already moved on. His features drooped and his eyes grew blank and sightless; dead. A film of stubborn indifference settled like a shadow across his face as though the very life and soul of him had withdrawn to the innermost embrasure of his being; the last line of defence. He seemed suddenly to have forgotten all of them and, without another word, he limped from the room.

Arthur felt the air slipping out of him. Attlee nodded to him and followed the Prime Minister back along the passage.

Eric Seal rubber-stamped the warrant pinned to the file and scribbled his signature over it. He handed the paper to Arthur and bowed his head in response to the beautifully executed salute.

'I hope you'll tell your wife what the Prime Minister said, sergeant.'

'Yes, sah! Honour, sah!'

He marched back to the Annexe on a cushion of air.

Monday, 2000

He was growing accustomed to it, no mistake about that. Ten minutes after he wound up the second of his two pieces for A.B.N. in the studio at the B.B.C., Shaffer felt, rather than heard, the first bone-jarring tremors of bombs on the streets above. He didn't even go up to take a look around: only yesterday, he recalled as though it were weeks ago, Goering's broadcast had sent him racing to the roof to watch the action. He had caught the West End war bug: contemptuous familiarity. Like the rest of the lucky majority living north and west of the docks, he now took it as a matter of course that the bombs were not aimed to fall on *him*; the occasional one, maybe, dumped in panic by an off-course Dornier peeling away for home, but not in earnest. If you wanted to break a nation's spirit, break the spirit of the poor first – that was Hitler's philosophy and it had its comforts.

He had filed three minutes of news segments for the bulletin and a five-minute colour piece for the evening magazine wrap-up. O'Keefe was complimentary but probably only because he'd had a chance to catch up on his sleep; Shaffer knew he could have done better. He had built a set piece around the care and redirection of the victims of the weekend bombing. It was easy meat; the Ministry of Information had issued a statement on the subject and he had added a twist or two of emotional rhetoric. What the piece badly needed was ground-level observation and that he didn't have. He comforted himself that he had a right to take the easy way out for once. Half an hour in Nelson's Green could have brought the piece alive, but half an hour in Nelson's Green was something he couldn't face right now. Tomorrow maybe.

The raid had ended at six-thirty and he had chatted with a bunch of broadcasters and producers in the B.B.C. canteen. He drifted out into Regent Street a little after seven-twenty. The weather was holding but clouds had begun to gather around the westering sun. It was pleasant, cool; he decided to walk. When he drew level with the mock-Elizabethan façade of Liberty's department store, his mind jolted back to the girl in Hereford Street.

She had been more anxious than he to ensure that they were never seen together during their four-week affair, implying that his reputation was more vulnerable than hers. Soho was a rabbit warren, she used to say, and besides, it was on the way to Liberty's. She had never shopped at Liberty's in her life; they sold nothing she could possibly afford; but in her lunch-break each day she went there as others might have gone to one of the parks. She played the peculiarly masochistic game of watching other women buy; mentally noting the item, its price and quality, and comparing it with others on display. One day, one day, she had promised herself wistfully. . . .

He found Brewer Street and walked the narrow pavement looking for a pub they had adopted as their 'local' — The Chequer Board. The street was crowded with strollers and window shoppers and most of the bars and bistros were open. It was a holiday atmosphere, relaxed and good-humoured. He found the public house at last, dark-windowed and gloomy and uninviting on its corner site. The doors of the saloon bar stood wide and from inside came the locust babble of voices and the hangover stench of sawdust and smoke and stale wine and beer.

He slipped through the crowd into the snug and ordered a pint of bitter; he never cared much for the thin, warm English brew but it was an essential part of memory reconstruction. The alcove table they had used was empty. He squeezed in and sat back to watch the crowd at the small bar.

To hell with it. He shrugged off his coat and his hand touched the notebook in his inner pocket. He pulled it out, opened his fountain pen and doodled across the top of a page:

Dear Rita.

I guess you could say I have time just now to call you and the boys but I'm fresh out of nickels. This town wears me out. If things don't work out here I'll ask O'Keefe to pull me back to New York, and this time for a spell longer than seven months.

He read it through and grinned. Crap.

I'm not sure what I'm doing here anyway. That's no exaggeration. Half the people who live here don't know, either. I just left the B.B.C. and for ninety minutes there was a raid, a pretty heavy one (as they say over here). I had a couple of drinks in the canteen then came out for a walk. I guess there'll be more raids. There usually are. . . .

As if the reference had pulled a switch, sirens began to sound the alert. The talking in the bar ceased for the space of two or three seconds, then returned again to its original level.

. . . but nobody seems to care, except in the dockland area where air-raids mean getting blown to pieces. Here, up West as the Cockneys call it, they haven't learned yet what it means to get hurt.

A shadow fell across the pad and Shaffer looked up. A vast bruiser of a man, whose rolled-up sleeves revealed ham-size forearms mottled with red-and-blue tattoos, glared down at him suspiciously. He carried five or six empty pint jugs in one hand and a barman's cloth over his shoulder. A blue-and-white striped apron bulged over a belly swollen by years of devotion to his own brew.

'What're you up to, then?' he said brusquely.

Shaffer looked up, puzzled. 'I don't get you.'

'What you're writing in that book. Private, is it?'

Shaffer bridled. 'Yeah, it's private. What's it to you?'

'I don't know you, do I? You ain't been here before?'

'What's that got to do with—'

There was a giggle from behind the big man's back and a woman's hand appeared over the beefy shoulder, tapping it for attention. The barman turned.

'He's with me, Harry. Aren't you, dear?' The woman had red

hair, a red gash of a mouth and a red suit and high-heeled shoes, but those details became apparent only when the eyes had consumed, and recovered from, the blatant immensity of her breasts. Her whole being crystallised behind them; they strained up and out through a ruffle of white ruched cotton cut dramatically lower than good taste dictated. She set down a glass of some tawny concoction on the table and squeezed on to the bench beside Shaffer.

'Oh,' said the big man, apologetic at once. 'I didn't know he was a friend of yours, Doris.'

'You don't know all my friends, my boy,' she said, and winked grotesquely. The barman retreated to join his customers.

The woman pulled out a small green and orange box of cigarettes and offered him one. Shaffer came out of his spell and dug into his pocket for the Philip Morris.

'Aaaaeeeooowww!' she cooed, impressed. 'Don't mind if I do.' He lit it for her and she took the Zippo and inspected it with childlike fascination. He said, 'Thanks for the help. What was that guy talking about?'

'You're American!' she exclaimed. It was an accusation.

'Right. The barman. . . .'

'Oh, Harry. Got the jitters, ain't he, just like the rest. It was your writing, dear. Probably thought you was making notes of his top secret clientele.' She collapsed on the back cushion with a peal of laughter. 'In here! Top secret! Oh, lumme.' It took her some time to recover.

'I still don't get it,' he said. He was grinning, too.

'Spies!' she hissed melodramatically. 'Everywhere, aren't they? Eh? Eh?' She collapsed again. 'Sorry, dear.' She unearthed a red polka-dot handkerchief from the cavernous valley between her breasts with a little gesture designed to draw his eyes down admiringly. She watched him: beamed again when he looked up and caught her eye. 'We're a lot, we are, aren't we? War? It's a bloody pantomime. Oh, I bet you wonder what you let yourself in for, coming here.'

She dabbed the red handkerchief on her chin, then fluttered it professionally under his nose. Cheap perfume rose from its flapping folds. She tucked it back in her cleavage, taking her time to maximise his attention. She didn't have to work at it; he was totally absorbed.

'You on your own, dear?'

'I just came in for a drink.'

'Stranger in a foreign land, are we?' The giggle pealed out across the room. A couple of heads turned at the bar, drew their conclusions and returned to the conversation.

'I came back to look the place over again. I was here before.'

'Oh? Not first time then?'

'I was here in thirty-two.'

'Aaaaaeeeeoooowww. Int'resting.' Her vocabulary was so absurdly arch he found it difficult to keep a straight face. It would be impossible to caricature Doris.

'What do they call you then?'

'Name's Mel. Mel Shaffer.'

'Working or visiting?'

'I'm a correspondent here.'

Her jaw dropped. 'Not a newspaperman?'

'Radio. I'm a broadcaster.'

'Aaaaaeeeooowww. On the *wireless*. So that was what you was doing writing in your little book. *Wireless*.'

He sipped at his beer. It still tasted of sawdust. 'No. Just writing home.'

This was Doris's stamping ground. 'Married then, are we?'

'Some.'

The giggle rose and fell like a kite on a blustery day. 'Oh, you Americans kill me.' She lengthened her face and dropped her voice in imitation of his: 'Some.'

'That's what they all say, I guess, huh?'

She pulled a face at the implication that he had seen through her disguise and marked her down. 'Cheeky!'

'No slight intended.'

She slipped a big, soft arm through his and squeezed. 'Oh, I do love the way you Americans talk.' Again the imitation: 'No slight intended.' She raised the glass of tawny liquid to her lips and emptied half its contents into her throat with effortless expertise. 'What made you come here in the first place then? Not exactly Madame Tussaud's, is it?' She choked as the laughter rose and overwhelmed her again. 'Or p'raps it is, looking at some of them, eh?'

'I guess so.'

'Girl, was it, brought you? Thought so. I was looking at you from over there.' She gestured to a table where a well-dressed man had just sat down. 'And I said to meself: sentimental journey, that one, Doris. Raking the embers of his past is that one.' She pressed against him, her breasts yielding to his arm. It was impossible not to look down into them.

'Wasn't your wife, neither, was she?'

He gave fleeting consideration to the idea of bringing the charade to an end but rejected it: he hadn't felt so good in days. 'No, not my wife – er. . . .'

'Doris,' she reminded him, pressing back her shoulders to display the cleavage to brutal advantage. She dropped her voice to a seductive drawl. 'I think Mel is a fantastically . . . sexy name. Was that what it was all about, then, this girl?' She bounced him gently in the chest with the perfumed bust. 'A little bit of the other, eh? Yes. I can see that all right. It's in your eyes. Passion. All deep and cloudy. My dad was a passionate man – lumme, was he! Same colour eyes as you. Only had to look at a girl and she fell in a dead faint at his feet.' She giggled with such delicious enjoyment he had to join in. She winked at him. 'I know you,' she leered. 'You came in here with her on your mind and' – her hand fell almost unconsciously to his thigh – 'that naughty old thing down there' – she dropped her eyes to his lap – 'come over all funny, didn't he? I know. Just like my dad, you are. Lovely feller. Really missed him when he run off.'

The well-dressed occupant of Doris's table jumped with relief as a dapper man with faded blue eyes came into the snug. They shook hands awkwardly, sat down and began to talk in whispers.

Doris followed Shaffer's eye. 'Slumming,' she said knowingly. 'They're not regulars, them. Come in here behind someone's back, bet your life. Know the type.'

Shaffer nodded. His throat was dry and Doris's professional

pawing was having the required effect. 'Look, Doris...,' he began.

'I'm just around the corner, dear,' she whispered. 'When we finish our drinks, I'll get up and go out and you follow a couple of minutes later. I'll be waiting on the corner by the garage, all right? I'll keep in front and you just....'

He snatched a gulp of the beer. 'Doris.' He eyed her frankly. 'There's nothing I'd like better right now than to take you to bed and give you a night to remember.'

'But?' Professionals bruise easily. She'd been good to him, more so than convention demanded.

He put a hand on her upper arm and squeezed the soft flesh under the red jacket; the action brought his knuckles into intimate contact with the outer swell of her left breast. He kneaded it gently, persuasively. Her manner changed at once.

'Don't tell me you got to *work* tonight?'

'Right.' He grasped the straw; dropped his voice. 'There's a war on, remember?' The catch-phrase drew a reluctant titter from her. 'But that's tonight. There always tomorrow, O.K.?'

She was satisfied. She leaned into him, the bulbous gland pressing and overflowing his knuckles; she reached up her mouth to his ear and ran her tongue into its crevices and under the lobe. He almost changed his mind in that instant. The tongue, its work done, withdrew into the carmine slash of lipstick and she breathed: 'You'd better come back, old Mel, or I'll be frustrated for the rest of my life, wondering what I missed.'

'I'll be back all right,' he lied. 'Two can get frustrated.'

She ran her tongue around his ear again, then unthreaded her arm from his. 'Make sure you are, darlin',' she whispered. 'Come back really frustrated for Doris, promise?'

'Sure.' He squeezed her hand and she made a little pretence of shuddering with maidenly desire.

'First time in years I got all come over like this,' she breathed huskily. 'I don't think I'm going to be able to work tonight, now.' It was the greatest compliment she could pay a man. 'I'll go back and listen to the wireless and think of you.' She got to her feet and bent down over him, the huge appendages quivering in free fall. 'Give us a little kiss then.' Her tongue flickered out and found his, briefly. He knew the sensation of a dying man who has had the cup of life dashed from his lips. 'Like that, do you? Course you do. Just like my dad. You make sure you come tomorrow, eh? What I'm going to do for you, old Mel, I haven't done for a man in years.' She closed one eye. Unspeakable promise. 'And I'm counting on you to make a new woman out of me.'

She blew him a little kiss and tip-tapped, hips swinging, across the snug to the street doors. She turned, waved and blew another kiss. He grinned. She clacked away on her impossibly high heels.

He gave her a few minutes' head start, then got up from the alcove and walked towards the door. Before he reached it, a hand caught his wrist.

'Shaffer! Well, it's a small world and that's a fact.'

He looked down. The well-dressed man in Doris's seat looked uncomfortable. His companion with the pale-blue eyes managed a twitch of the mouth.

'Well, come and sit down, man,' Freddie Green said grandly, hanging on tightly to Shaffer's wrist. Then to his companions: 'I'd like you to meet an old friend of mine, gentlemen. Melville Shaffer of the American Broadcasting Network. Melville, let me introduce my old friend the Honourable Kingsley Mountford and his associate, Mr Charles Russell.'

Monday, 2000

On the black-painted glass walls of the porter's lodge Bertie Webber had gummed a clip of the story from the *Daily Express*: 'Hospital Rescue'. Below it was a second tearout from an early edition of the *Evening Standard* with a six-line reference to the rescue under a general heading, 'Heroes of the Blitz'. Below that was an embarrassing eulogy from the *Star* written by a woman: 'Saga of an Unknown Warrior'.

Ian grinned sheepishly. He had come in a whole hour early because, in truth, he could no longer bear the suspense of waiting to see what his reception would be at St Thomas's. His mother had cried; tears of pride after tears of sheer terror, she scolded him, and Caroline said jokingly he had no business putting Tom in the shade, particularly since big brother hadn't wangled a medal yet. He had waited as long as he comfortably could for his father to come home but at eight forty-five he had still not arrived. Ian couldn't have told the old man personally, but he would dearly have loved to watch his face when mother showed him the paper.

The superintendent had written a note of congratulation. In his own hand, not typed. So had the Senior Medical Officer *and* the Senior House Surgeon *and* Dr Hawthorne *and* Matron. Bertie watched him read them with a grin that was bursting to become laughter, as though he had organised the writing of each note himself.

'Think of that, then!' Webber said, smacking his lips.

'Jolly nice of them, Mr Webber. They shouldn't have.'

Webber, perched on his tall stool, looked down at the thin, nervous young face. 'Shouldn't? You're right, my lad. They know it, too. Not your job, unburying patients. They would've give up on her if it was left to them, wouldn't they? Not you, though. Only right everybody knows about it, too.' He tapped the cuttings with the backs of his fingers. 'One for your scrapbook, eh?'

'I don't have a scrapbook, Mr Webber.'

Webber bellowed happily at the *naïveté* of the boy. 'This rate, you'll have dozens, lad.' He fell serious. 'Super asked me this evening about your conchy thing.'

'Oh!' Ian's face fell. 'I hoped he might know. . . .'

'Everybody don't have to know; the 'orspital secretary and me, that's all. Anyway, he asked. Said he heard.'

'Was he . . . upset?'

Bertie Webber buried his face in an enormous mug of tea. He wiped his walrus moustache and flicked the waxed ends of the lip hair upwards. 'He was interested, that's all. Why shouldn't he be? Conchies got a bad name everywhere. Can't blame people. Take me. When the secretary told me you was coming — "'Allo," I thought; "lily-livered bugger." This, you see.' He rapped the metal extremity of his right leg with his mug. 'Twenty-two years old when I lorst that. Life over, manner of speaking. Good for nothing. Every man who did his time in the last lot got his scars. Some you can see, some you can't. Mention conchies and you think: I copped mine, why shouldn't he cop his?'

'That's not why I. . . ,' Ian began tentatively.

'Don't want to know the ins-and-outs, lad. All the same to me, whatever you think. You're young, see. Bright. Good education. You got all kinds of important things going on in your 'ead; ideals they called 'em in my day. Ideals. Well, I'll tell you, lad; down in the ranks where I was, we didn't have no ideals 'cause we wouldn't know what they was if they come up and bit us in the back of the neck. What *we* 'ad was – pardon the expression – the screaming bloody shits. Frightened? Terrified! Show us No-Man's-Land and we'd shit over nine hedges and splash the tenth. We'd've run a mile over broken glass to get out of it. Give our souls not to've been so bloody stupid signing on. Twenty-two, I was. November the third, nineteen fifteen. Second day in the trenches. All over. And now, what've we got for our trouble? The same bloody Boche running amok all over again. Don't ask me if I think my lot was worth it, lad.'

He frowned, concerned that he might have revealed too much of his private self. He slipped off the stool. 'Anyway, seein' as 'ow you're here, get on down to G Ward and report to sister. She's due for a break. Off you go.'

The G of G Ward stood for Geriatric but in the chaotic conditions of the past three days it had become a dumping ground for terminal women patients of all kinds. The superintendent, at his wits' end to find medical staff to cope with the hundreds of air-raid victims in Casualty and Surgical, had withdrawn the majority of the hospital's nurses from non-essential ward activities. G Ward was left to the ministrations of a sister called out of retirement and any casual help available, from clerks and off-duty laundry workers to telephonists and the old wardens. In drawing up his priorities, the superintendent grouped together advanced old age, terminal disease and terminal accident cases beyond the reach of further surgery. G

Ward just happened to be the most effective space he could find on the ground floor.

Ian came to the sister's desk and she took off her glasses. 'Thank heavens they sent someone. Look, my mother's all alone at home and I haven't been able to get away since breakfast. I must go. Matron said it was all right if I could get someone to stand watch. There are no special problems. If someone needs help, press this bell and someone'll come up from Casualty. Shan't be half an hour. All right, dear?'

She picked up her cloak and left before he could air his fears. He sat down and folded his hands on the blotter in front of him. He looked around. There were thirty-six beds crammed side-by-side with only eighteen inches between each. He shivered as he ran his eye along the faces propped on the bunched pillows; their complexions, for the most part, were yellow and age lapped in great folds of skin around their eyes and cheeks and throats. Several were crying – whimpering, really – but he knew this was not to be taken as a sign of crisis; old people, particularly women, whimpered all the time. Sometimes they were having dreams, Bertie said; sometimes they were talking to loved ones they imagined were standing by their beds, and sometimes they just made a noise as a sort of comfort to make sure they were still alive. When they couldn't hear their whimpering any more, they were dead. At some of the beds there were visitors, mostly men. It was long past the visiting hour but the hospital had waived the usual rule; bombing often forced visitors to travel for hours on end to get to the hospital and it would have been inhuman to turn them away.

He became aware that a man at the end of the ward to his right was trying to attract his attention. He got up and walked quickly to the bed; ten yards away from it he recognised the face on the pillow.

'Good evening, Mrs Dunn,' he said. He knew he was blushing. 'Are you feeling better?'

'This is him, Alfred. That's the young man.' The woman tried to raise herself from the imprisoning blankets but there was no strength in her.

The man got up from his perch on the side of the bed and

held out his hand. He was old and tired-looking and a little scruffy. He didn't seem to have washed for quite some time. Ian took the grimed hand.

'I'm Mr Dunn,' said the husband wheezily. 'I want to say—' He choked and began to cough; his chest heaved as the spasm took hold of him. He covered his mouth with both hands. 'Grateful. Both of us. Very grateful,' he gasped at the end of it.

'I'm just happy I could do something. Anyone would have. . . .'

The face on the pillow worked helplessly. 'He'll catch his death of cold, he will. Alfred's a warden. Don't know how to look after hisself with me not there.' Her face was skeletal; the eyes bruised with rings of dusty brown and yellow, the cheeks and temples hollow. Ian looked away.

'Now, you calm down and don't be so silly,' the husband said gently. He perched again on the side of the bed. 'You get yourself all worked up and they won't let you come home for another three weeks.' He turned to Ian. 'Tell her, Mr — er. . . .'

'His name is Ian. I like Ian for a name.'

'Tell her, Ian,' insisted the old man.

'You've got to do as your husband says,' the boy ventured timorously. He wondered if the husband knew his wife was dying.

'They're letting me out next week if I do as well as I'm doing,' the parched face said proudly.

Ian made the best of an encouraging grin. 'Good. Well, you mustn't exert yourself then, Mrs Dunn. Er. . . .' He looked around him. 'If you'll excuse me, I think I ought to get back to the desk. The telephone, you know.'

They nodded wisely and watched him make off down the centre aisle, his rubber-soled shoes squeaking loudly on the polished linoleum.

Alfred Dunn waited until the boy returned to his chair, then he bent over his wife and whispered, 'I got . . . them pills.'

'What pills?'

'Them pills I was telling you about last time. I heard about them from this — er — doctor I run into down the Green. *You* know.'

'They're very good here...,' his wife began diplomatically.

'Course they are.' His eyes searched hers for the slightest hint of suspicion. 'You don't get any better treatment than this nowhere. But like this doctor was saying, with the raids and all the casualties and that, they have to have their priorities, don't they? Poor devils who got knocked about, bleedin' and dyin', they're the ones who need the best attention and the proper medicines. Stands to reason. You're all right....' The gentleness in his eyes was almost liquid. 'You're going to be out and about soon.'

'I know,' she said weakly. 'That's what I mean. Don't seem right me having special care when some people—'

'No!' he interrupted quickly. 'Not taking anything from *them*. I got these' — he opened his hand and revealed a small red pill-box in his palm — 'on the black market.'

'Oh, you shouldn't, Alfred. Encouraging people like that.'

'It was for you,' he whispered softly. 'Only for you. Wouldn't do it otherwise, would I?'

'What do I have to do then, love?'

He had poured the glass of water when he first came in. 'Just let me lift you up here,' he groaned, taking the weight of her on his left arm. 'Now....' He looked down the ward towards the desk; Ian was flicking through a sheaf of brown cards. 'You got to take all three of 'em, O.K.? Here....'

She wriggled pitifully in his arm. 'It don't seem right,' she breathed. 'Don't seem right when other people need....'

He blinked his eyes several times, checking the tears of panic and pain. 'Trouble with you,' he said, clearing his throat, 'is you don't use your noddle, do you? Quicker you take these, the quicker you'll get better, the quicker you'll be out ... and, you silly old girl, the quicker they'll be able to give your bed to someone who needs it.'

'Oh-ah,' she said, satisfied, and let him place the tiny brown tablets on her tongue. She gulped at the water and he let her sink to the pillows.

'See?' he chided her. 'All done.'

Her hands twisted together on the sheet. He put his big, dirty paw over them protectively. 'Them pains starting again?'

She nodded through tight lips. 'Only a bit. Comes and goes. I'll be all right, don't you worry.'

'I know,' he said tightly, cupping her hands in his. 'I know you will.'

Exactly twenty-one hours and seven minutes after Ian Russell pulled her from her rubble tomb in Women's Surgical, Maud Dunn died in her sleep. The night sister called the porter's lodge to contact the superintendent; Ian answered the telephone and got the super from his bed. The night sister insisted, he said; she hadn't said why.

They walked together to G Ward and the sister took them inside the little box of canvas screens around Mrs Dunn's bed. Hawthorne was sitting on the locker, his thoughts a million miles away.

The super clicked his tongue. 'Was it really necessary, Hawthorne?'

'I'd like to have a post mortem done right away, sir,' he said.

'You haven't got me up to. . . .'

'I wanted you to check something, sir. I can't get anyone else. There's a riot down in Casualty. Open her mouth and sniff.'

The superintendent bent with a little sigh of annoyance, prised open the teeth and leaned close. He stiffened; straightened up slowly. 'Liver?'

'I don't know.'

'Sister?' The superintendent swung round on the woman.

'Absolutely nothing to do with me,' she snapped frostily. 'She had her usual injection when I came on at nine. Mr Packard did it himself. No one's been near her since.'

'Who was on duty before you?'

'Sister Gorman, sir. You know, the retired S.R.N. But there's nothing down on the treatment card to say. . . .'

'Damn it, sister, hold your tongue, will you? What d'you think, Hawthorne?'

'Hard to say. Educated guess? She was given a depressant in a range of three to five grains. Probably took a fair time to work through. I'd say she died of heart failure, probably induced by shock, about half an hour ago. Say ten o'clock. Dose must have been administered no later than eight-thirtyish.'

'Well?' The super glared at the night sister.

Ian blurted, 'I was here then. Sister Gorman went home to see her mother and. . . .'

'Yes, yes, yes. But what did you give Mrs Dunn, boy?'

'Nothing, sir. Nothing at all to anyone.'

The super stared at him keenly. 'Are you sure?'

'Honestly, sir. It was. . . .' He had a sudden flash of recall. 'Her husband — he introduced himself — he was here.'

'At eight-thirty?'

'He was here when I came in and he hadn't gone when Sister Gorman came back and relieved me.'

Hawthorne closed his eyes in despair. 'I suppose you didn't see him give her anything, did you?'

'Well, no. I mean, there were so many people. . . .'

The two men and the night sister watched his feeble protestations with calculating professional eyes. The superintendent turned away at last.

'All right, Hawthorne,' he scowled. 'Get them to take her down to Pathology and have Parrish open her up. Let me know right away.' He swung back to Ian. 'As for you, young man, I really don't know what to say.'

'I didn't think he'd. . . .'

'In a hospital in wartime,' the superintendent said slowly, 'no one can afford to stop thinking for a *second*. No one. Yesterday you saved a woman's life and you did so with courage and great devotion to duty. But it *was* your duty. Tonight you allowed that same woman to die helplessly because you—'

There was a roar and a cacophony of smashing glass. The super whirled and pushed out into the ward. 'My God! What's that?'

Hawthorne joined him and they stood stock still, listening. The crackling of burning wood and masonry rose from a whisper to a roar. 'West Wing,' shouted Hawthorne. He sprinted after the super. At the door he turned to look for Ian Russell.

The boy was still standing over the lifeless shell of Maud Dunn. He hadn't moved.

Monday, 2345

Charles Russell slammed the front door, unburdened himself of coat and hat, umbrella and briefcase, and opened the door into the drawing-room. Elizabeth was an inveterate wireless addict and spent most of her evenings there, knitting and listening indiscriminately. What he saw brought him to an abrupt stop. Ian was on his knees, head buried in Elizabeth's lap: his shoulders heaved with uncontrollable sobbing and his face, when he looked up, startled, was running with tears.

'What the devil. . . .' Russell began.

Ian jumped to his feet, ran blindly past his father and bounded up the stairs. Russell shouted after him, 'Ian! Come back here at once.' The order fell on deaf ears. 'Do you *hear* me?' he thundered again.

The only reply was the crash of Ian's bedroom door.

'Charles!' Elizabeth said crossly. 'Leave him alone.'

Russell sighed heavily. 'What was that all about?' He hooked out his watch. 'Isn't he supposed to be at the hospital?' Elizabeth got up and came to peck his cheek. He became suspicious at once. 'What is going on here?' he snapped. His temper had not improved on contact with Freddie Green in a disreputable public house in Soho.

Elizabeth gritted her teeth. 'He had to leave the hospital. Something happened and he was so upset. . . .'

'Upset! You mean he scuttled home early *again*?'

'No, I don't mean that, confound you! Oh, Charles—try to understand, will you? Listen to me.'

'I gave up trying to understand when he formally labelled himself a coward. I told him then—told *you*—that was the end of it as far as I was concerned. And let me tell you something else. Today I had his cowardice waved in my face by someone'—he gulped for breath—'. . . by someone at the highest level of government. A minister, if you please. *Conscientious objection!* I'm telling you, Elizabeth, my patience won't take much more of this. There can't be anyone in London who doesn't know my son is a publicly declared traitor to his country.'

Elizabeth caught his arm. 'You'll listen or I'll walk out of this house and never come back.'

He flinched as though she had struck him a blow in the face. Then his anger boiled over.

'Do what you have to do, Elizabeth,' he grated. 'And take your damned son with you!'

He swung out of the room, slammed the door behind him and burst into his study. Caroline was hunched over his desk; she jumped guiltily.

'What are *you* doing here?' he snarled.

'Oh, sorry. Thought you weren't coming in.' She was trying desperately to tear a sheet of paper from the scribble block he kept on his desk.

'What're you writing?' he demanded and moved nearer the desk.

'Nothing. Just notes.' She managed to tear the page free and folded it quickly. 'Sorry. I'll just. . . .' She walked to the door and waited for him to stand aside. He didn't budge.

'What's all this nonsense about Ian and the hospital?' he barked.

'Ian? I don't know. I thought he was there — isn't he?'

'Caroline,' he said warningly. 'Don't try to hide things from me. Please! Does that ... whatever you're writing have anything to do with Ian?'

Her laugh was forced. 'Good lord, no, daddy. Honestly, I didn't know he was home.' She performed a neat body swerve, ducked under his arm and out of the door.

He stared after her uncomprehendingly. Were they all mad? He went to the desk, sat down and pulled open one of the drawers. His eye caught the deep imprint of writing on the scribbling block from which Caroline had torn the top sheet and he picked it up, angled it against the lamp on his desk. He took the paper across the room to the drinks tray, poured whisky into a glass, dipped his finger in it and spread the liquid over the paper. Back at the desk he took a pencil and a pencil-sharpener from a drawer and ground the point until grains of carbon fell in a fine cloud on the whisky-sodden page. He found an old artist's brush and smoothed the grey scum. The imprint of the round, childish writing gleamed through whitely. He angled it to the lamplight again.

'Kiss of skin on holy scented skin ... embrace of heart and mind and limb ... no greater sweetness God denied His kind.'

What in the name of... ? He could read no more but anything else was unnecessary. It was a poem, if diseased carnal filth could be described as poetry. The child was out of her mind. No—she was clearly being manipulated by some swine, some ... Bletchley! Yes, that was obviously where she'd met him. She wouldn't know how to handle a direct advance. She was so young. Untouched.

Touched? If the swine had touched her... !

The door opened and Elizabeth looked in. She walked to the desk and placed a folded copy of a newspaper on the blotter. He dragged it towards him to cover the smudged page of the scribbling block. She didn't even notice it.

'I'm going to bed,' she announced levelly. 'You can come up when you want. But read this first. *Then* we'll talk about Ian.'

She walked out and closed the door behind her.

He looked down at the paper. It was the front page of the *Daily Express*. He turned it to look at the date: today's. She had folded it small to encapsulate one headline: HOSPITAL RESCUE.

He began to read. . . .

Monday, 2350

Eric Warr handed Shaffer the script with an apologetic twitch of his facial muscles.

'What are you doing to me, Eric?' Shaffer protested. He ran his eye down the blue-pencilled sheet.

'Sorry. We've been told to tighten up.'

Shaffer sighed with exasperation and settled down to assess the damage and the rewrite necessary to put it into shape.

'This is Mel Shaffer in London. It's midnight here and Goering's promise to devastate the heart of the British Empire is proving no empty threat. In the past three days his Luftwaffe has bombarded the capital with incendiaries, high-explosive bombs and landmines for the better part of twenty-four hours. In that time up to a thousand men, women and children have been killed and four thousand seriously injured — although this is a war of savage unpredictability and no one can guess, yet, at the bodies that lie waiting to be uncovered beneath the rubble of the East End.

'The bombing is described by the British as indiscriminate, which is typical understatement in a country where war has a vocabulary colder than British reserve. A few minutes ago I received the text of an Air Ministry statement analysing the reasons for this. Germany, it seems, is sending over successive relays of aircraft operating independently. At no time has an intensive attack been delivered by a large force. Since the Germans are also operating at very high altitude, any degree of accuracy in selecting their bomb targets is virtually impossible. [Now, plain truth is a rare commodity in war and confession, in the mouths of government agencies, is usually aimed at camouflaging other facts too dangerous to admit — CENSORED.] The Ministry of Information also advise me that, and I quote, "Some concern has apparently been felt by the public about the activity of anti-aircraft guns and our fighters during night attacks on Saturday and Sunday. It's emphasised that in fact the ack-ack guns were engaged throughout both nights, working in conjunction with searchlights."

'But — and this is the big but — those German planes flying so high that they couldn't hit their targets also flew too high to be caught in the beams of British searchlights.

'Similarly, the night fighters were up on both nights [according to this statement — CENSORED]. It is emphasised here, too, that, and I quote again: "Neither Britain nor Germany has solved the difficult problem of being able to engage the enemy during night operations unless favoured by such conditions that they can be brought out clearly in the beams of searchlights. It is almost impossible for fighter machines to pick out enemy bombers or fighters in the darkness where both are travelling at between two and three hundred miles an hour."

'[Now, again as the East Enders would say, there's no smoke without fire. It's been common gossip for the past three days among Londoners crouching in their shelters under the Luftwaffe's barrage that the city's inner anti-aircraft defence has been strangely quiet at night. In fact, unless I miss my guess, it's been totally silent. Add to that this unsolicited technical explanation of the difficulties of night fighting and we arrive at a poignant tactical truth. The concern felt by the population of this capital is justified. At this stage of a brutal, innovative war there *is* no defence against night attacks by small groups of bombers and fighters operating independently of one another. By day the R.A.F. are proving themselves masters of the air. At night, they are powerless. So are the anti-aircraft guns. CENSORED.]

'Whether the ordinary citizen is aware of this state of affairs or not seems irrelevant. Morale, here, is not generated by facts and figures [true or false—CENSORED]. Morale is an accident, produced out of the national hat by a process of osmosis no one seems to understand. It is part of the pink glow of unreality that requires life to go on under the constant threat of instant death. It permits a court of law, for instance, to charge a man for giving vent in public to his anxieties about the conduct of the war, but holds as not particularly unpatriotic a demand by professional footballers for more pay for their services on Saturday afternoons to compensate for the wages they lose by missing a half day at the factory.

'Tomorrow, no matter what hell Goering's planes unleash between now and dawn, the workers will stream back to their offices and workshops, their wharves and warehouses, sometimes without the benefit of a night's sleep. For instance, tonight I went strolling in Leicester Square, the entertainment hub of the West End. The bombs had been falling for a couple of hours but as I passed the Warner Theatre, a famous local movie house, I heard the booming of an organ and several hundred voices raised in song. I went inside. The audience were resigned to staying the night and were doing what makes people everywhere feel good in any crisis : opening their hearts and their throats and raising the roof in song. After the recital Warner's

American managing director in London, Max Milder, led them downstairs and served them coffee. When I left everyone was settling down perfectly happily to sleep on the stairs. Tomorrow they – and hundreds of others caught out in restaurants, cinemas, clubs and the few live theatres still open – will find somewhere to wash and brush up, snatch a breakfast sandwich at a café or snack-bar, thumb a lift to their place of work in a private car or take a bus and get on with the job of seeing it through.

'[Others, less lucky, will tramp the streets looking for homes for themselves and their families. When a house is destroyed by bombs there is no benevolent official hand outstretched to whisk the homeless to sanctuary. Local authorities provide rest centres and food and blankets and medical attention, but their ministrations are strictly short-term and their bounty limited. A place in the country, far from the carnage, is the dream of every victim, but unless he can produce a willing relative or friend ready to accommodate him and his brood, or pay inflated rents for cottages or hotel rooms, he is very much on his own. That's another side of the British character that tends to mystify strangers: if there's fighting work to be done, they'll stand shoulder to shoulder to the death. But in a plain case of personal survival, an Englishman is expected to stand on his own two feet and make the best of it. Where the homeless go, how they survive, is beyond this reporter's range of experience – and there are no government guidelines to help our understanding. CENSORED.]

'Real or unreal, life goes on, maximising the potential of every bare second of living, minimising the dangers. Tonight, at this very moment, dockland is once again a raging furnace, new bombs heaping coals on the embers of those fires that have blazed for three days. [Waterloo Bridge is on fire. Hungerford Bridge. Charing Cross Station, that emotive geographical centre-point which marks the heart of the heart of London, is burning. And from all over I hear first-hand reports of destruction from those who escaped to tell the tale: Islington, Camberwell, Battersea, Bromley, Fulham, Kensington, Westminster, Paddington, Woolwich, Wimbledon, West Ham, Esher. The Führer has left his mark tonight. CENSORED. MANY OF THESE ARE KEY POINTS AND CANNOT BE QUOTED.]

'Yet, crazy as it may seem, the question these people are asking themselves tonight is not, how long can we take it? but, how long can Hitler keep it up? There's a world of courage between those two question marks.

'This is Mel Shaffer reporting from London. Good night and . . . sleep well.'

TUESDAY
10 September

Tuesday, 1100

Paul Warrender kicked the half-brick in a fast, rattling volley
along the gutter and hobbled after it, one foot on the kerb, the
other below it. Ahead of him, Tooley Street rose to its junction
with London Bridge and across the river lay the City and another
world.

Paul was much concerned with the world outside this morning. Not because of the raids—only old women and girls cared
about getting bombed—but because he couldn't stand another
day in the Scully household. That silly old bugger who thought
he was still a sergeant in the Marines, and his loony old woman
shouting 'Ooooh!' like an owl with a pin up its arse every time
a lorry backfired in the street; them and bloody Derek, sodding
off on his own and getting into trouble.

It was the old man who'd done it; really cheesed him off, this
morning. 'Don't mope around the 'ouse all day, lad,' he barked
like he was on a barrack square. 'Do something useful. Go out
and look and learn. Had my way, you'd be in uniform, lad of
your age.' And he leered that silly bloody old-fashioned look of
his like he knew something no one else did. It was that what did
it.

Paul had run all the way from Nelson's Green, breathless and
sweating profusely in the warm morning sun, to the Army
Recruiting Centre in the old meeting-hall on Jamaica Road.
There were a lot of men there and the young ones looked him
over and told him to scram but he stuck out his chin defiantly
and told them to go home and play with their dolls, which was
what Derek always said. They laughed at that and one of them
slung him a Woodbine and a W.V.S. granny, nice old geezer,
brought him a cup of tea in an old tin mug. He enjoyed that bit;

waiting and drinking tea and listening to the chat of the men and the dirty jokes about girls in the blackout and randy wardens. But that didn't last long and the queue wound through the doors and into the hall and there, waiting behind this green curtain with a sodding great stick under his arm and a face like a peeled beetroot with a ginger moustache, was this Guards sergeant-major who didn't talk like normal people but half shouted and half screamed like he'd got his balls caught in the mangle.

'What's *this*, what's *this*, what's *this*!' the silly bugger screeched.

Paul ignored him because he wasn't sure it was him the old sod was going on about or the bloke in line behind him, but then the big stick came out from under his arm — more like a pole than a stick — and poke, poke, poke it went in Paul's ribs.

''Ere, mind out with that!' he had shouted.

'You watch your lip, little boy, or I'll run you through with it, smart like.' The C.S.M. demonstrated by numbers: 'In, two three. Out, two three.' The stick passed harmlessly between Paul's body and arm. 'Come on, then. Out you go and stop wasting the army's time.'

The men who had so cheerfully drawn him into their company only minutes before now turned to laugh; they were still only civvies but they could appreciate the dangers of flouting a sergeant-major's humour.

'I come to join up,' said Paul stoutly.

'We don't run no *nursery* regiment yet, little boy. Not that I *knows* about, little boy.'

'Don't call me little boy.'

'I'll call you something *else* you don't hook it out of 'ere, snappy. *Get orf!* I want to see your raggedy little arse leave this place like lightning, *greased* lightning, and I want to see it disappear round that corner out there like it got shot out of a three-point-seven. *Gitcha!*' He whacked the stick across Paul's backside, grabbed his shoulder in one great, ginger, hairy hand and propelled him out to the pavement.

Paul backed away angrily, his face flushed with shame, his eye on the bristling beetroot face.

'T'ain't your bloody war, mister!' he bawled lamely. 'An' if it was, we'd bloody well've lorst the bugger by now!' He ducked as the sergeant-major took two threatening steps forward, turned on his heel and legged it around the corner towards Tooley Street.

Rotten old sod. When he was out of danger he stopped beside a shop window and inspected himself in its reflection. He could've passed easy for seventeen. Well, easy enough; they wouldn't know no different. Too bloody glad to get anyone to volunteer, they were. His eye fell on a box of uninspiring-looking sweets; V for Victory Gums, read the label. He turned away hurriedly; there had been a box of those hidden under his bed, untouched and burning a hole in his conscience, when the bomb had mercifully wiped out the house and the evidence. That was the last time he'd go nicking with Derek Scully, thank you very much. Derek just loved nicking, that was his trouble. Bloody barmy.

He stopped to watch a bunch of firemen, dirty faced and dazed with exhaustion, directing hoses at a towering column of oily black smoke on the far side of a mountain of rubble. The area had been fenced off with tubular steel posts and rope. He didn't ordinarily stop and stare at fires; he wasn't interested. He didn't fancy himself as a fireman or a rescue worker or a warden : Barry, his brother, said fire-fighting was a lousy job and it was a diabolical liberty he couldn't go in the army like he wanted to but They wouldn't let him.

Paul's eye glazed and his mind fled from the boring bleak world of Tooley Street to the wild, blue, romantic skies – or, at least, to the skies described with such vivid power every week in 'Rockfist Rogan, R.A.F.' – his favourite serial in one of his weekly comics, *The Champion*. Rockfist was a fighter ace, the most brave and deadly pilot in the R.A.F. – he shot down at least one Nazi plane every week and usually two or three in fantastic life-or-death dogfights 'over the patchwork quilt of dear old England'. But in between, he was also the heavyweight boxing champion of the air force and he never lost a fight, although every week the war almost got in the way to make him too late to get in the ring or he had to get back from occupied France after being shot down by a dozen Messerschmitts who didn't fight fair. He was great, was Rockfist. A lot like Paul, too; never did what he was told by snotty-nosed know-alls like group captains who didn't understand what fighting was all about. He always proved them wrong, regular as clockwork, but every week the group captain seemed to forget how right Rockfist had been the week before and made a silly bloody fool of himself all over again.

Paul held his arms wide like Spitfire wings and engaged an imaginary Heinkel. 'Da-da-da-da-da-da-dut!' he stuttered, firing invisible cannon into the shattered hulk of the helpless aircraft. "Ey, you, you silly little bugger. Piss orf! Wanta get yourself singed, do you? Bugger orf!' A rescue man in a white tin hat came across the rubble mountain at him, waving his arms. Paul stuck out his tongue and dodged away.

The trouble was, real life wasn't cheerful like comics. Even in that story in *The Adventure*, 'His Father was a Nazi,' about this English schoolboy who was forced to be a Nazi spy but got round it every week and did Jerry down instead, even in that it was never really *gloomy*, like it would be in real life. Paul liked the war stories best, not the sort they had in *The Wizard*, like 'Vengeance of the Three Lost Men,' because that was just about blokes running around in England trapping Fifth Columnists — that was boring — but the ones where it happened a long way away, like France in 'Leader of the Lost Commando.' *The Hotspur* was best, all things considered, although he could never admit it to Derek Scully because Derek thought it was a snob comic for stuck-up ponces. The reason was it had mostly public-school stories in it and they were fantastic; all the boys liked each other, except for the odd bully or what they called 'cads' or 'rotters', who generally got what was coming to them. Everyone was always *doing* something; nobody ever mooched about kicking bricks along gutters and the weather was always brilliant hot or brilliant cold with tons of snow. 'The Baffler in the Black Hood' was about a school on the north-west frontier of India where the boys were fighting Nazi agents trying to stir up the tribes; 'Cadger Collins' was about this tramp who was pretty funny and ran this posh public school; and 'When the Luckstone

Gleams Red' was about a school fighting for survival against a former pupil who was trying to ruin it. But the best of all was 'So Smugg Won't Talk, Eh?' which was the latest series about Red Circle, this terrific public school which was the best at sports in the country and where everyone had brothers who were fighter pilots or commandos or Royal Navy frogmen — all officers, of course — and incredible things were always happening. Captain of the School was Cripple Dick Archer, so called because he pretended to be crippled and used a crutch when he first arrived at school, but now everybody knew he was the greatest athlete in the world and had done work for the Secret Service. Smugg was the Fifth Form's master and a thick old twit — just like the group captain in 'Rockfist Rogan' — and the lads were always doing him over and making him look stupid. Cripple Dick Archer never did anything Smugg told him but he always let Smugg take the praise when things came out right anyway because he was so brilliant and decent he didn't have to prove it to anyone.

Paul had never met anyone like Cripple Dick or Rockfist but it was his mission in life to find where they were and go there as soon as possible. It was nowhere near the East End, that much he could say with certainty. All the stories happened in the country. On the other hand, the only country he knew well was the patch around Southend, where dad used to take them to the seaside before the war, and Chelmsford, where he and Derek had been evacuated. Cripple Dick would've run a mile from Southend but Paul had high hopes of the countryside around Chelmsford when he first saw it. On closer inspection he realised it was just boring old greenery like everywhere else and no sign of Red Circle or anyone decent; just nagging old women and their tight-lipped husbands saying, 'Get your feet off that chair,' and 'Have you washed properly?' and 'What time do you call this?' They ran away from Chelmsford after two weeks and three days. Derek stuck his boots in the night-soil tank before they left and tramped stinking muck all over the old woman's front parlour armchairs and couch and up the stair-carpet and all over the sheets and pillowcases on the bed. Serve her right.

A bus braked into the kerb right beside him and he looked

up, tempted. The conductress was upstairs and there were four or five passengers standing down below, so he nipped aboard smartly and pushed past two of the standing passengers and kept his eyes open. Beside him, two old grannies sat in deep conversation; the one immediately below had her arm through the handle of a basket and a handbag on her lap. Protruding from the basket was her ticket. It took him a good three minutes to angle himself into position to slide it free but he managed it without drawing attention to himself.

The conductress clattered downstairs, dyed blonde hair in a black net, eyes like a cat on the prowl. 'Orright you.' She spotted him and weaved through the crush. 'Where's your fare, then?' She could smell his kind a mile off, her eyes said.

Paul held up the ticket and she deflated angrily. 'Well, I don't remember giving you one,' she snapped, and returned to her platform.

The bus ran through Cannon Street, past St Paul's into Fleet Street and the Strand. When it stopped in Lower Regent Street the conductress spied him again but this time with a look of supreme triumph. 'That's the end of your stage, mate!' she yelled. 'Off you go.' He didn't mind.

There was nothing much about London in comics but he couldn't help feeling that he was nearer Cripple Dick Archer in Piccadilly than he was anywhere else. Everyone was busy in Piccadilly and well-off and good-looking. There were sandbags all over the place and strips on the windows just like the East End but otherwise you couldn't believe you were in the same country. He drifted along the shop windows, marvelling at the displays of goods. One shop displayed silver cakestands piled with muffins, 'Freshly baked English muffins,' the notice said, and he felt good; Cripple Dick was always eating muffins, toasted on a fork in front of his study fire by the boy who was lucky enough to fag for him and his friend, A. P. E. Carew.

He walked as far as Green Park and then stopped. He didn't know what to do next. There was no fun being in the West End alone, not if you had no money in your pocket. Then he thought of Gladys and remembered she was due at the club before twelve for a rehearsal. So she'd said. He asked the way of a commissionaire outside the Ritz and got a fast clip round the ear for his trouble. The newspaper seller on the corner was more helpful.

A woman in a faded pinafore was on her knees scrubbing the entrance when he reached the club and she ignored him pointedly when he asked if he could go inside to find his sister. He decided she was deaf, stepped round her and pushed through the glass doors. He took both flights of steps down and emerged under an archway in a sour-smelling room lined with glass panels. There was a balcony and lots of twisty bits of metal painted gold and silver, and electric lights with showers of glass hanging from them. The whole room was one big mirror and in the middle there was a round sort of slippery floor with steps down to it and a bandstand with no band on it. A thin man was prancing about like a ponce in front of a half dozen girls, humming some song and breaking in occasionally with 'There and so and so and *so!*' Paul's eye fell on the girls' figures and ran quickly downwards; he blushed to the roots of his hair. They were wearing no skirts! Just kind of little knickers, all tight and showing off everything they'd got. He turned away, but the thin prancing man stopped and snapped, 'Now who's *that*, may I ask?'

They all looked at him and he felt their eyes in the back of his shoulders. He swung round, still blushing. 'I'm looking for my sister. Gladys Warrender.'

The giggling and cackling that followed this simple statement was cut short by the thin man who waved his hands limply, said in a funny voice, 'Oh my *God* – now it's a *crèche!*' and minced away in disgust. The cackles grew and the girls crowded round him. He wondered what Rockfist Rogan would have done in a situation like this.

'What're you doing, big boy?' one of the girls said, prodding him in the chest with her elbow. This was obviously very funny because they brayed with laughter fit to bust.

'Is Gladys here yet?' he asked uncomfortably. 'I know she had to work this morning and I thought. . . .' He lost courage.

'Well . . . if you're Gladys's brother you're a natural born dancer, aren't you, ducky?' said the girl with the elbows.

They just grinned at him this time and he felt good. 'Oh – I'm not so bad, I suppose,' he retorted, his lips only just holding back the funny side of it.

'Oooooooh! Full of it, ain't he?' exclaimed the girl. She straightened the wide band of shiny black silk around her waist and raised one knee experimentally, admiring her shapely legs. 'Going to stand in for Glad, are we then?'

He stuck both thumbs in the band of his shorts and puffed out his chest. 'If you can keep up with me,' he said daringly. Two could play at that game.

'Right then,' the girl flashed challengingly. 'All right then. Into line, you lot. Ron!' A bald head appeared over the top of an upright piano, mouth open. ' "Tea for Two",' ordered the girl crisply. 'From the top. Two-bar introduction and put a bit of snap in it, will you?'

Paul found himself surrounded. A hand threaded through his arm and clamped on his wrist first from one side, then the other. With their arms and hands laced behind their backs, the girls came to attention and waited as Ron tinkled his introduction. As he reached the last few notes of it, the girl with the elbows shouted, 'And one and two and *Tea* for *Two*...,' and up came six left knees, thighs perfectly parallel to the floor; waggle, waggle, waggle and ... *kick*. Paul nearly fell over backwards but there was no stopping Ron and no stopping the girls who high-kicked all the higher when he struggled to keep up with their rhythm and failed. '*Boy* for *you*...,' shouted the girl and the music swallowed him up and he flung up his leg almost as high as theirs and gasped and grinned and gritted his teeth all at once.

Don't come yet, Glad, he chanted over and over in the back of his dancing head. Don't come yet. Don't come yet.

He wouldn't have swopped this for the Captaincy of Red Circle and a Spitfire thrown in.

Tuesday, 1130

There was a note addressed 'Mel Shaffer A.B.N.' on the rack in the sub-basement studio at Broadcasting House when he checked in to run through his midday file. It said: 'Some of the guys are getting together tomorrow in the bar at the Savoy. Objective: a little straightening out on this censorship crackdown. Time: around 1 p.m. Try and make it.' It was signed 'Ted Angley.'

Shaffer slipped the paper into his pocket; he'd make it all right. Eric Warr's blue-pencilling of his script had made him ten minutes late on the line to New York last night.

It had been a bad night all round. Back at the flat he had lain for two hours on the bed, fully clothed, trying to convince himself he was not playing mental footsie with Soho Doris and not trying to make up his mind to go find her. Some things they didn't issue coupons for in this country; what Doris sold was a genuine pre-war article. In the end he fell asleep and dreamed he was digging a grave for Rita in Hyde Park, with bombs whistling all around them and Petey yelling for ice-cream soda.

There was no word yet from Denzil Fletcher-Hale; Mrs Price had been on the phone from Hill Street at nine-thirty to remind him that Mr O'Keefe's message in her black book still had nothing under the 'Action Taken' column.

He drove over to the Ministry of Information at London University and picked up the mid-morning fact sheet. Forty-seven German bombers and fighters shot down; thirteen British fighters were missing but three of their pilots were safe. The Air Ministry were going to make a statement on secret counter-moves being made to combat enemy night bombing but, no, they wouldn't be revealing what they were. The first U.S. destroyers transferred to Britain were physically handed over in a port on the Canadian eastern seaboard yesterday, and there were details available, three days late, of the R.A.F. bombardment of Hitler's invasion fleets along the French and Belgian coasts. That last item gave Shaffer pause. Freddie Green had 'predicted' that raid at lunch on Sunday, just a few hours, presumably, before the bombers took off.

The plain facts of war, he thought uneasily, were becoming bland; too predictable. O'Keefe had already volunteered the same opinion. 'Keep the hard facts for news slots,' he said. 'Statistics three times a day is like eating hamburger every meal for a month.'

The culinary simile set him thinking.

He sketched out a light reflective piece on food rationing. 'Even the king and queen have ration books,' Mrs Price had told him with great pride. It wrote itself; every American could grasp the inadequacy of one pound of meat per person per week, eight ounces of sugar, four ounces of butter or fat, one egg, one ounce of cheese, two ounces of tea, and a system of 'points' which permitted the housewife a choice of luxury foods like rice, jam, biscuits, dried fruit and tinned stuffs at the rate of twenty points a month. A diet like that would have caused a riot in Sing-Sing.

'I haven't seen an orange, a lemon or a banana in the shops since I arrived here,' he wrote. 'And they tell me onions are next to unobtainable. Fresh fish isn't rationed, except by its scarcity, and Mrs Britain is learning to sweeten her tooth with saccharine rather than sugar and coat her children's sandwiches with margarine, not butter. Like everything else, food is the responsibility of a ministry here and the Ministry of Food takes space in national newspapers, on hoardings and wallposters to put across its own recipes for getting the best out of the less-than-perfect. They try hard but, like even the best chefs, they can get it wrong. Some of their formulae for using powdered egg and milk to make scrambled eggs and similar dishes have earned the ministry a national reputation for indigestion. The ministry, in fact, is as much the Ministry of Taste as anything else. For instance, it prohibited the sale of white bread here on the grounds it didn't have enough vitamins. The new bread is officially called national wholewheat; the unofficial name is less than wholesome.'

It even raised a slow grin on Eric Warr's face as he ran over it. He made no amendments, but offered the observation that his wife had tried the powdered scrambled eggs recipe and the result was a cross between sorbo rubber and reinforced lavatory paper.

O'Keefe liked it too but wasn't about to let him relax on his laurels. 'Those two kids you talked about Sunday. That dancer. You seen them again?'

'Not yet.'

'Go find 'em, Mel. The people want to know, remember?'

After the drive through dockland with Murrow on Sunday night he should have been prepared for it but his growing indifference to statistics had blunted both his memory and his sense of perspective. He crossed London Bridge and ran into the East End through Tooley Street and Jamaica Road. The area was still burning in places and driving was a mad game of chance; to skirt a whole city block of crushed houses or circumnavigate a crater it was necessary to circle, turn, double turn, backtrack and circle all over again. When he cornered into Redriff Road on the last leg of the trip to Nelson's Green, his mouth went dry; here and there a house or part of a house stood in solitary splendour against mountains of masonry and fallen timbers but, where the bulk of the Surrey Commercial Docks had been, there was little or nothing to be seen but pillars of smoke and floating ash. Dock gates were closed to traffic, water ran in wide eddies across the road where water mains had burst and the smell of escaping gas was strong. Twenty yards short of the fire station at Pageant's Wharf in Rotherhithe Street, a policeman stopped him and told him he could take the car no farther.

'Can I make it on foot?'

'No point, son,' said the bobby firmly. 'No one in these houses no more. Everyone's been turned out. Unexploded bombs mostly, and them fires still burning in the old Surrey. Couldn't leave people to burn, could we?'

'I'm pretty sure these people I'm looking for are still there,' Shaffer persisted. 'Baltic Street, Nelson's Green.'

'If they are, they're asking for trouble,' said the policeman flatly. 'All right. Go if you must but don't say I didn't warn you.'

He came towards the street over the smouldering remains of the old timber warehouse that abutted from Albion Dock. He couldn't quite fix the geography in his mind at first; Saturday night had not exactly been the perfect time for sight-seeing. Then he saw the wreckage. Where the terrace of little houses had been there was only rubble. Where Number 14 had stood the wind blew unopposed from the river over an avalanche of devastated brick and tile. A knife had descended and sliced it dead, cutting it flesh, bone and sinew from the house on its right. Number 12.

He broke into a run along the cobbled street and stopped where the devastation began. He had not noticed it on Saturday night but the wallpaper in the Warrenders' living-room was mottled brown and yellow; strips of it still clung to the right-hand wall. A bedside lamp hung from its cord in the front bedroom wall socket, stirring forlornly in the breeze. The kitchen sink leaned drunkenly over a ruptured gas cooker and here and there he could make out the remains of chewed picture frames, fractured plates and cups and saucers, charred clothes, upholstered furniture. The flapping of paper drew his eye down to the far corner; a book lay open and the wind was turning its pages. Shaffer climbed over the debris, bent and picked it up; it was H. G. Wells's *War of the Worlds*. It lay open at the first page of Book One, Chapter 16: 'So you understand the roaring wave of fear that swept through the greatest city in the world just as Monday was dawning. . . .'

Shaffer realised with a start that his primary emotion was one of professional annoyance; it shocked him. He'd liked these people; in Gladys's case, more than *liked* — but their deaths stirred no more regret in him than any other story that had strayed just out of reach. He slammed the book hard on the palm of his hand in frustration and swung round to climb down to the street.

The girl was watching him, weight on her right foot so that the left leg bent slightly at the knee, mannequin-style. He knew at once that she had fallen into the pose quite deliberately; had held it carefully and with some patience for the moment when he would turn. Her hair was black, rolled high at the front and full on her shoulders. She was taller than average height and she loved her body; her hands lay featherlight on her thighs, stretching occasionally to caress the silky material of the yellow dress she wore. She swayed slightly on spiky-heeled shoes; the movement despatched a rippling through her body that rose through her hips to her flat belly and on up to her bust. When it reached her shoulders she tossed her head and the curtain of black hair billowed and swung and fell back into place.

The full scarlet mouth parted and strong white teeth flashed more than a greeting. 'You looking for someone then?' she asked innocently.

He waved a hand self-consciously at the ruin of Number 14. 'The people here. I met them Saturday night. Are they...?'

'Oh, you'll be the American.' She shifted her weight expertly from one foot to the other, throwing one rounded hip forward; she rested a long, smooth, red-nailed hand on its curve, palm outward, forcing her elbow upward and her breast into taut outline against the yellow dress. He stumbled inelegantly over the rubble and jumped down beside her. She didn't move but when he turned to face her a tiny tremor of muscle-control ran along her arm and rippled the straining cotton at her breast. Her eyes floated slowly up from his feet and came to rest at last in his eyes. She made Soho Doris's jocular technique look like the advances of a novitiate nun.

He said quickly, 'The Warrenders. Did they...?'

'You're Glad's friend, aren't you? The broadcaster. You got them all of a tizzy, know that?'

He watched her face hypnotically. The full lips had a trick of over-forming words as though preparing to suck them; when she stopped talking they fell into an exotic pout that flexed perceptibly as though cushioning the psyche against a snatched kiss. She ran the tip of her tongue under the curve of the upper lip.

He snapped out of it, but not without her being aware of the effort it took. 'Are they all right? Were they ... hurt?'

'Care, do you?' She lowered one perfect eyelid by less than a millimetre.

'Yes or no?' he snapped, irritated by the mounting awareness in his loins.

She studied him with mild amusement and brought the pouting cushions together in a dismissive blow-kiss. 'Say please, like a gentleman, then.'

'Please!' He exploded.

She threw back her head and laughed; the sound was all in

her throat; low, bubbling. 'Poor love. You're really worried, aren't you? Well, there's no need. They're all right.'

'Where are they?' he snapped.

'With us.' She angled her head in the direction of Number 12, the small house next door to the heaped rubble.

'Can I . . . ?'

'Course you can. Liberty Hall, here.'

He started for the front door. She watched him until he was forced to turn and wait for her, then laughed again, shook her black hair and strutted past him. She opened the door and walked in without turning her head. He followed her.

In the ten-by-eight-feet front parlour a double bed claimed much of the space. A gramophone with a horned trumpet loud-speaker had been playing a disc and the turntable revolved the record with a sibilant hiss of approaching exhaustion. Shaffer switched it off on his way through. The living-room was instantly recognisable. From the dusty green plant on the tall stand to the Radio Rentals wireless receiver, the scrubbed table and hardwood chairs, the single-bar electric fire – even down to the scattering of brass and copper knick-knacks on the mantel-shelf – it was almost a replica of the Warrenders' home. But the wall abutting the crushed Warrender house had split like an over-ripe plum from the ceiling to a point two feet above the wainscoting; rags and rolled newspapers had been stuffed hurriedly into the crack and a bucket was lodged by the wall to catch dripping water from a fractured pipe. It was a miracle, he thought, that the place still stood.

The girl waved her arm grandly. 'You can sit down if you can find room.' She lit the fuse of that long, slow smile. 'Lovely, isn't it?'

He looked about him, puzzled. 'You said Gladys. . . .'

'Staying here,' she pouted. 'She's gone down the club, though. Rehearsals, she said.' Her look implied that she didn't believe it for a moment.

'Oh.' He balanced himself on a corner of the table. 'You expect her back soon?'

'Depends, doesn't it?'

She fell automatically into the mannequin pose again. For a

moment they simply looked at one another in silence. She moved a step nearer, hands falling to her thighs.

'You want a cup of tea?'

He shook his head. 'What's your name?'

She gurgled deep in her throat; amusement laced with satisfaction. 'Janice. Janice Scully.' She raised her left hand and stretched the fingers wide so that the glint of the gold ring on her marriage finger caught the sunlight streaming through the window.

'Married,' he said coolly.

'If you could call it that.' Her eyes came up from examining the ring and stabbed his. 'Geoff is in the army. Egypt.' She judged the pause beautifully. 'Big brave soldier, see. Like his dad. Haven't seen him for over a year, have I?'

'He live here too?'

'His old man's house. I just married into it, see what I mean?'

She ran her hands up her body and under the fall of her hair, caught the black sweep of it and twisted it up and round experimentally on top of her head. He watched the act with blatant hunger as he was expected to. She never let her eyes leave his. When he stirred in sheer physical reflex on the table edge, she performed a slow pirouette in front of him, leaning back from the hips so that the yellow dress developed horizontal folds of tension across the flat belly. The whole act was so gauche it was hysterical. Pathetic. But, then, so were his reactions.

He moistened his lips. 'You – er – work around here?'

She came round to face him again and shook her head.

'I was going to be a singer, wasn't I? Geoff was keen on that. That's why he married me.' Again the burning pause. 'Among other things.' The lips rounded to the cushioned pout, leaving no more than a peep-hole at its centre. The pout flexed subtly, exposing the soft pink underbelly of the lips.

And, outside, the siren growled, then moaned, then raised its voice to a faltering whine, then howled its full-throated warning.

Shaffer reared off the table edge and their bodies closed. His arms slipped under hers and his right hand clamped powerfully on the long, cool neck. But she was quicker. The cushioned lips widened over bared teeth and lunged at his mouth, engulfed it and sucked it into hers. Her tongue darted through his lips and forced a writhing passage deep into his mouth; her hands fell to his waist, pulled open his jacket and dug down fiercely behind the belt. He felt for the fastenings at the back of the dress and, as his fingers began to pluck at them, she arched her body in a spasm of need and thrust her pelvis hard into his loins. He heard, felt, tasted the sob that burst from her mouth into his and answered it with a low moan of carnal gluttony.

Her head wrenched back suddenly; she stared at him, eyes opaque, teeth parted, searching his face. Then she relaxed and the slow smile harried him. 'You've had a lot of practice, haven't you?' she whispered tauntingly.

He lunged at her with his mouth but she pulled back farther, toying with him.

'Impatient, too. Just a minute.' She slipped from his arms and swung the nest of chairs away from the table. She dropped on one knee and pulled him down beside her. 'Safer under here,' she whispered, slipping the jacket from his shoulders. 'Cosier too.'

She wriggled expertly and the dress slipped down over her shoulders.

'Can you manage the rest?' Her mouth was on his ear.

Janice Scully was an artist; a demanding, inexhaustible, ravenous, voluptuous, insatiable artist. When he had nothing left, no spark to light another fire, Shaffer fell into a stupor of total collapse that became a soft-coloured oblivion and finally sleep. He woke with a start, alone. The siren was howling the 'All Clear.'

She was in the kitchen, making tea. They drank it in silence; Shaffer in the inevitable mood of self-condemnation that always followed a sexual encounter outside his marriage bed, Janice in a dreamy state of perfect relaxation. When he finished his tea he got up.

She said coyly, 'You aren't going to leave it like that, are you?'

He grinned in spite of himself. 'You mean you can do that more than once?'

She blossomed with genuine delight. 'Was it nice, then? I mean . . . better than you had before?'

He shook his outstretched hand in front of his face. 'Wow!'

'Better than little Gladys, was it?'

He stiffened. 'It's not like that,' he said sharply.

She winked. 'Coming back for more then?'

He looked at his watch. It was one-forty. 'You want to give me a raincheck?'

'What's a raincheck then?'

'It means yes but I can't give you a date and time.'

She got to her feet, came to him and caught his lips hungrily in hers. 'Not too long then, all right? You've give me a taste for it now.'

'Not too long,' he agreed.

The sun was still shining. He trudged wearily across the rubble of the old warehouse and out towards Rotherhithe Street. buttress in time; twenty yards to his right Gladys side-stepped He only just managed to hurl himself back around a corner a stream of black water and hurried towards Baltic Street, her brother Paul at her side. He let them pass, then sprinted back to the car. God! If she'd recognised the car. . . .

When he arrived in Hill Street Mrs Price was in a high state of excitement herself.

'Mr Fletcher-Hale called while you were out,' she told him. 'He says to tell you that Mr Green is holding a reception at his home tonight in Greenwich. He's given me the details. You're invited and Mr Green says to bring a guest if you like. There'll be a lot of influential people there, Mr Fletcher-Hale says, and you might meet someone who can help you with what you discussed with him.' She lowered her voice. 'He means the matter Mr O'Keefe wanted.'

Shaffer threw his jacket over the back of his chair and leaned into the leather gratefully. He ached all over. 'Call him when you've got a minute, Mrs Price, and tell him I'll be there.'

It was only two-thirty. In two and a half hours he had driven to Nelson's Green, met Janice Scully, run amok and taken leave of his senses, his frustrations and his guilt complexes. He felt absurdly free; refreshed, restored. The Warrenders were alive and maybe even well and Gladys was. . . .

He chewed thoughtfully on his lip. Gladys was where she should be; occupying a place in his mind, not his conscience.

Mrs Price wrinkled her nose. 'Can you smell scent, Mr Shaffer? Funny, I could swear I smell scent.'

Tuesday, 1450

Flying Officer Tom Russell cupped his hands round the flaring match and lit Caroline's cigarette. She leaned back in the rustic wood chair and closed her eyes, savouring the sharp bite of the tobacco.

'My God, you wouldn't think there was a war on, would you?' she sighed, stretching deliciously in the warm sun.

'You speak for yourself,' he retorted. He lit his own cigarette and swallowed the last of the beer from the pewter tankard.

He had been surprised to get his sister's call; they had been working within thirty miles of one another since July, Tom at Dowding's headquarters at Bentley Priory, Caroline at Bletchley Park, but neither had considered it politic to chat or write letters, and certainly not to meet. Both were aware of the strategic delicacy of their work and had chosen the easy path of refusing to discuss it with anyone; recognition of the existence of a wall of secrecy around life defined new attitudes to family relationships. When she called he had agreed to meet her for lunch at a village pub conveniently midway between them, but not without certain misgivings. He knew very little about Caroline's job and nothing about her personal life; he suspected her call had been precipitated by professional or private crisis and he had prepared himself all through lunch to tell her to work things out for herself. The crunch hadn't come. They had eaten in the garden behind the pub, surrounded by people and loud conversation. Caroline had devoted herself to an enormous plate of sausage and mash and a dessert of apple crumble and their talk had been limited to Elizabeth and Ian.

He snatched a glance at his watch. 'Can't be too long now,' he said gently. 'Must be back about three-thirty.'

'Mmmmm,' she said vaguely.

'Oh, come on, Caroline. What's it all about? You can't go on spinning this out for ever.'

'Pig,' she said good-naturedly.

'Well. . . .' He sucked smoke deeply. 'If it's the job. . . .'

'I know. Don't tell me.' She held up one hand like a police-man on point duty. 'You don't want to know. Not your business. Hush-hush. Top Secret.'

'I only meant to say—' he began.

'I know what you meant to say,' she said moodily, 'and I can't really blame you. It's just that. . . .' She clenched her fists. flattening the cigarette in her knuckles. 'Oh—it's like living with a lock on my tongue. Daren't talk, daren't even *think* of talking. About anything—in case something slips out about'—she gestured with her head in the direction of Bletchley Park—'that place. We don't even talk to each *other* most of the time. The motto at Bletchley Park is "Have faith in no one". . . .'

'Really?' Tom said seriously.

She clicked her tongue. 'No, of course it isn't, you idiot. I mean it's in the air, unspoken, something you feel the moment you walk through the door. And as for anyone working on the really secret projects. . . .'

He made a face. 'Look who's talking. . . ,' he said pointedly.

'Sorry.' She dropped her head. 'Stupid, isn't it? We're on the same side, we both *know*, we're both working on secrets in one form or another, yet we—'

There was a nervous cough behind them and Tom whirled in his chair. The landlord stood watching them. He had a tray in his hand and the bill trapped against it.

'Sorry, squire,' he said. 'I give you as much time as I could. Way past closing time, see.'

Tom grinned with relief. He took the bill, slipped a ten shilling note on the tray and told the man to keep the change. They got up and strolled together to the front where Tom's snazzy little white M.G. with its belted bonnet stood next to the anonymous black Austin 'Tilly' Caroline had borrowed from the motor pool.

He took her hand. 'I've been a real help, haven't I?' he said apologetically.

She squeezed his fingers. 'I should've known better. Big girl like me. Daddy would have a fit.'

Tom grimaced at the mention of his father. 'Look, if it's anything *really* serious. . . .'

She laughed without humour, perhaps with a note of self-derision. 'What's *really* serious, Tom? I don't know — perhaps this is just ordinary everyday simple serious.'

He glanced at his watch again. 'There's not much. . . .'

'No, there isn't, is there? Not much time for anything any more. Here today. . . .' She shrugged. 'Do you love anyone, Tom?'

He was taken aback. 'How d'you mean — *love*?'

She chirruped impatiently. 'I mean *love* love, bonehead. Is there anyone for whom you feel deep love? Is there anyone you would die for, rather than they should die?'

'My God — what kind of a question's that?' He felt uncomfortable and looked it. She smiled at him and made him feel worse. 'Sorry,' he said sheepishly. 'That public-school education coming out again. That's *your* problem, is it? Someone you' — he found it difficult to apply the word in its correct sense — '. . . love?'

She sighed. 'Does it show?'

'I dunno,' he retorted. 'I suppose it might for anyone who can recognise it. I don't. Is it fatal?' He tried to make a joke of it. It fell flat.

'I think it is. I think it's terrible.' She placed her hands on either side of her face. 'Like not being able to talk. I can't talk about . . . this. Not to anyone.'

'Well, surely. . . .' He coloured all the way to his ears. 'Surely you can talk to *him*?'

She looked at him, puzzled, then the penny dropped and her eyes misted and her throat bobbed threateningly and she leaned her face into his shoulder. 'Oh, God, Tom, I wish I could tell you. I wish I could believe you'd understand.'

'Hey, hey.' He put his arm round her shoulders, self-consciously looking around him to see if anyone was watching. 'Look, old kid, I'm not that much of an idiot. Tell me about him if you like.'

Her shoulders shook. He held her until she stopped crying. She found a handkerchief and buried her face in it; blew her nose sharply. He watched as she dug in her bag for a compact, studied her face in its mirror and dabbed at her cheeks with the powder puff.

He said unhappily, 'It can't be that bad. If. . . .' He bit his lip; he had to say it. 'If he's married or something. . . .'

She looked up at him. She had control of herself now. 'Or something?'

'Well . . . I mean. . . .'

She stood on tiptoe and pecked his cheek. 'You'll be late and they'll carry on the war without you. You'd hate that, wouldn't you?' She got into the Tilly and wound down the window. 'You won't say anything to daddy or mummy about. . . ?'

He snorted indignantly. 'What d'you think I am?'

The landlord, leaning heavily on the bar of The Baker's Arms, watched the two cars reverse and drive away. He nudged his wife who was busy pulling a pint for one of the favoured group of drinkers who joined them each day for a quiet after-hours chat.

'What d'you think of *that* then?' he prompted.

'Little affair going on there,' she snapped primly. 'Somebody's wife and somebody else's husband, I shouldn't wonder.'

'Ah — bit of nookey on the quiet, eh?' chuckled the postman over in the corner. 'Nothing like a bit of nookey in wartime, I always say. Comfort for the troops.' He placed three dominoes in succession on the table before him and his opponent, the grocer from across the street, sniffed irritably.

'Bloody good luck to 'em, is what I say,' growled the grocer, searching his pieces for a comeback. 'Pilot, that boy is. I bet he's seen a thing or two, poor young devil. They say these

231

fighter boys don't last more'n a month to six weeks before Jerry gets 'em. Bloody good luck to him. Live while he can.'

'Bletchley Park, she's from,' said the landlord knowingly.

The wiry grey head of the village constable rose with interest at the end of the bar. He gave his attention to his pint of mild and bitter, then asked, 'You say Bletchley, Fred?'

' 'At's right, George.'

'Now, how would you know that? I never see either of 'em in here afore. Have you?'

'No-o-o,' said the landlord doubtfully.

'Then how d'you know?'

'They was talking about it, that's why,' returned the landlord cuttingly, piqued at this unreasonable doubt. 'Out in the back. Two sausage and mash and apple crumble and tea,' he added, enumerating the menu on his pudgy fingers as though such fine details lent substance to his claim.

'What was they saying about Bletchley then?'

The landlord looked uncomfortable. 'I don't go round earwigging my customers, George,' he insisted stoutly. 'How'd you like it if I came round earwigging what *you* was talking about?'

The policeman stared him down. 'I got nothing worth your listening to, my old mate, have I?' he said. The official tone was unmistakable. 'Now, let's have it, George. What was they saying out there about Bletchley Park?'

The landlord cleared his throat. 'I don't know, do I? Something about working together. Hush-hush, *she* said. Secrets. Something about being on the same side. Something like that.'

Tuesday, 1600

The fever had been on him through the night and it grew worse with daybreak. The hoarse voices in his head had been joined by others; a wild, unintelligible argument raging in a language he had never heard before. He wished they would hurry up and tell him what to do; he was tired of waiting. The voices had the solution, of course; they were just being awkward, stringing him along so that when they sorted it out they'd look even cleverer. Any minute they'd tell him; he sensed that. Mustn't stop listening, though, or he'd miss the whole point.

Jack Warrender had left the house early; that way he knew he wouldn't be bothered by anyone. He walked for a long, long time but nowhere in particular. After a while, the voices got louder, deafening; shouting at each other. How was he supposed to make out anything? He held his hands to his ears to dull the racket. They were torturing him. Preparing him. He slumped down on a low brick wall. The shouting rose to a crescendo. They were all around him, screaming at him from every direction. . . .

They stopped. His head rang like an empty steel ball. But with silence. He waited. Where was it then? The answer? Silence. They'd gone, left him alone! Nothing was any different. No, it couldn't be! He must have missed something they said.

He hardly noticed Alfred Dunn. The warden sat down beside him wearily, staring ahead.

'I've bloody had enough,' he said. 'More'n enough. . . .' He glanced at Jack. 'I spend my life asking people if they're all right. *You* all right?'

Jack Warrender was far from sure. All he knew was that he was alone at last. No voices. And no solutions. He could see why, clear enough. There had been no one there all along. Just him, trying to win time, pushing away what he didn't want to see. Little old Charlie was still dead. There was no job. They were all going to be killed. His mind was quite suddenly startlingly clear. He didn't want any part of it. He didn't *have* to accept anything and nobody could make him. Nobody.

'Maudie's dead,' Dunn said with terrible sadness.

Jack's body jerked as if he'd been electrocuted.

'Elsie!'

He had said Elsie, hadn't he? He gripped Dunn's shoulder, twisting the cloth of his jacket, pulling him off balance. 'Elsie? Dead?' He shook the stupid man.

'No! No! No!' Dunn broke free, pushed him away, face

flushed. 'Christ almighty, you gone bleedin' mad? Who said anything about Elsie — bloody lunatic.' He stood up angrily. 'Maud!' he shouted. Then softly : 'My old Maudie.'

'What?' Jack was still puzzled. 'I thought you said. . . . Maud?' He bowed his head. 'Thank God!' Then, with the shock of realisation, 'Sorry, Alf. Strewth, I'm sorry. I didn't mean. . . . You know what I . . .' He half stood up, sat down again. 'I'm sorry.'

Dunn shrugged hopelessly. 'No need to go off like that. What's the matter with you, anyway?'

Jack shook his head. 'I dunno, Alf. I think I'm going off me rocker. What you said, just then. I was thinking of Elsie and. . . .' The shock had drained his face of colour. 'Elsie dead, I thought you said.' His shoulders sagged.

Dunn rejoined him on the wall. 'Go around acting like that and they'll stick you away. Fat lot of good that'll do Elsie and the rest,' he said accusingly. 'Anyway, I wanted to ask you something. Not going to go off again, are you? 'Cause if you are, I won't bother.'

'Bit shaky, that's all.' He caught Dunn's enquiring glance. 'No, course not. I ain't been myself, Alf, that's the long and short of it. If you hadn't've come along, I dunno what I might have done. Something really daft.'

Alfred Dunn cut him short. 'Try and forget about it, that's my advice. Now then, do you want to hear what I was going to say?'

'Yes, course. 'Ere, I really am sorry about your Maud, Alf. I thought she was getting better.'

'Walk down to my place,' said Dunn. 'We'll talk on the way. I'm a bit pushed for time. You up to it?'

'I'll manage.'

They began to walk back through the Green.

'I was just coming back from Deptford,' said Dunn. 'Wanted a word with the Chief Warden but he wasn't there. You're a bit off the beaten track, aren't you?'

'I just walked. Didn't think about where.'

'Lucky I saw you. I'd never thought about it, otherwise.'

'Thought about what?'

234

'You takin' over.'

'Eh?' Jack Warrender stopped but the other man jerked his head.

'C'mon. I haven't got much time. Things to be done.'

'What you mean, taking over? Taking over what?'

'Wardening.'

'Me? Warden?' Jack shook his head. 'Nah, not me.'

'Couldn't you do it then?' Dunn said provocatively. 'Minute ago you was going on about havin' no job. Well you can have mine. Warden for Nelson's Green. Three pound five shilling for a seventy-two-hour week, twelve days' leave a year, three weeks' sick pay. Free overalls, helmet and the rest. Tea up the hut's free. Talk is they'll be issuing free boots and waterproofs end of the month. Not exactly office manager standard but it's a job. Someone's got to do it. Still, if you don't want to....'

'Well, it's a thought, grant you that.'

'You know the Green, everybody knows you. Lots of experience handling people from around here. Couldn't be better,' said Dunn. 'You'll be in Group Control before the year's out.'

'I don't know much about it,' Jack said uncertainly. 'Read about it, but how it works....'

'Easy. Ten wardens' posts to the square mile, which means you'd have just the Green. Start duty by assembling at the main posts; that's Deptford for round here. Post Warden checks you out. He's responsible to the District Warden and him to the Chief Warden and the whole lot is sorted out by Group Central Control in some museum or other over at South Ken. Only time you need phone 'em is for a U.X.B. What you can and can't do is all spelled out in the book they give you. Bit like being a rozzer, I suppose.'

'But what about you? You can't leave, Alf.' They reached Dunn's house and went inside. On the living-room table a case lay open, half packed with clothes. Others were scattered around the room, as if awaiting a final selection. Jack shook his head. 'You're upset, Alf. Move away, yes. I can understand that. But you can't just up and go.'

'Why not? Nothing here for me now — you know that. If it

235

hadn't been for Maudie I'd have left the bloody dump years ago. Funny; you can live in a place all your life and never feel you belong. Don't feel right. Out of place here, Jack. Out of place.'

He picked up a pile of clothing and dumped it in the open case.

'You're just going through a bad patch,' Jack persisted. 'Like I was. Don't mess your whole life up because of one rough patch.'

Dunn shook his head bitterly. 'I'm not upset. I'm glad. Glad Maudie's out of her misery. Glad I don't have to worry about her no more.' He stared hard at Jack. 'You understand what I mean?'

'I think so. Nobody's place to tell you you're wrong.'

'They will though,' said Dunn quietly. 'They will.' He turned away quickly. 'Anyway, up to you now. Here!' He tossed over his tin hat and Jack caught it awkwardly. 'That's yours. Try it on.'

Jack Warrender balanced it on his head. 'Fits.' He grinned. 'Must be an omen.'

Dunn piled the rest of his A.R.P. kit on a chair. 'All you have to do is go down to Deptford and see a bloke there called Braithwaite. Sign you on straight away.'

'Look – are you all right? There's nothing. . . .'

Both men smiled at once.

'Bloody hell, you've only had the hat on for two seconds and you've got the patter off perfect. Keep a penny for me everytime you say that and I'll be a rich man.'

Alfie Dunn had changed in the instant. He was almost light-hearted. Well, more light-headed than light-hearted. That was it. Offhand. Maud's death would have come mighty hard to him, although he had been living with it for over a year now. Elsie and Flo said she'd been with the doctor so long now she must be on the mend, but he'd never believed it. Maud Dunn had wasted away to nothing.

Anaemia, they said, but that was for the benefit of the neighbours. It was cancer all right. The hospital tried to send her home once, but Dunn said No. Couldn't look after her in his job, he said. It was something a lot deeper than that though. A lot simpler. He couldn't bear watching her go. Jack felt an overwhelming compassion for Alf Dunn. Nobody liked him but, God knows, he'd had a lot to shoulder and he'd taken it well. Imagine if it had been his Elsie. Jack shuddered at the thought.

'Got a few more bits to sort out,' said Dunn. 'You going to Deptford then?'

'Reckon I might,' said Jack. 'But think first, Alfie. You've been in the Green fifty year and more. Second thoughts, Alf, eh?'

Dunn slung a pair of underpants into the case. 'Had them. Second, third, fourth and fifth.' He clumped upstairs.

Jack Warrender looked down at the case. Funny how easy it was. Make up your mind and off you toddle. Turn your back. Gone. He folded a pair of trousers Dunn had screwed into a bundle. Everything was in a mess; the shirts were unwashed and crumpled and stuffed one on top of the other; it didn't look like the act of a man who had thought it all out. More like a man who had no future at all. He noticed a bundle of pictures wrapped in a towel and bent to look. They were bent and torn. He smoothed them out, stacking them in a neat pile. The top one was of a young boy, blurred but recognisable. Jack picked it up. Derek Scully! He'd been a good-looking kid then, before his face got thin and those ferret eyes sank too deep to make out what he was thinking. Must have been — what? — five or six years old when it was taken. Derek Scully. What was Alf doing with a picture of. . . ?

Jack ferreted through the rest of the pile. There were four more of the boy. Two of them were wrapped in tissue paper, one also had Flo Scully in the frame, another had been torn straight down the middle, cutting off half the boy's arm, but showing a background of sand and sea. Alfie had never had kids of his own; never seemed to care for them much. Didn't make sense.

Unless. . . . No, it was *unthinkable*. He dropped the bundle in alarm. Just in time. He whirled away from the case as Alfred

237

Dunn came down into the living-room. He picked up the first thing that came to hand: a pair of boots. 'Want these?'

'Chuck 'em in,' said Dunn. He dropped a toothbrush, razor and soap into the case. 'Reckon that'll see me all right.' He snapped the old case shut and swung it from the table. 'Right then. Braithwaite. Remember his name. Big bloke, not half bad. You'll get on all right.'

The two men stood awkwardly, facing each other.

'Alf, I don't know what to. . . .'

'Hear that siren a few minutes ago?' Dunn said brusquely. 'Here.' He picked up the tin hat and plunked it on Jack Warrender's head. 'You won't get paid for it yet but you have to start somewhere. Out you go, lad.'

They stood in the doorway. The first flashes were lighting the sky downriver.

'I'm going this way.' Dunn nodded up the street. 'That way's your beat. Down Pond Street, along the alley and on to the wharf, back from there to the gasworks. Christ, I don't know if that's still standing. Then into Drabble Road, back behind the post office into. . . .' He smiled bleakly. 'When the raids get going you won't see your hand in front of your face. But you'll get the idea.'

Jack Warrender held out his hand. Dunn looked at it for a moment as if unsure, then shook it.

'Best of luck, Alf.'

Alfred Dunn nodded. 'We all need that, Jack. Some more'n others.'

Tuesday, 1900

Elizabeth Russell fell into a chair, kicked off her shoes and propelled her green uniform hat across the room. The W.V.S. headquarters in Victoria had despatched her to a rest centre in Southwark the moment she reported in this morning and she had been on her feet all day. She lay back and closed her eyes. Duty!

Duty, in her judgement, was a physical property, like good

looks or good manners or wealth; to have the good fortune to be born with it implied an obligation to exercise it for the common good no matter what the cost. Had it been socially proper for a woman to don a flying suit and helmet and squeeze into the cockpit of a Spitfire, she would have volunteered to do so with only a passing shudder, if that was her duty. She had no feeling of nobility about it, no sensation of being in a state of grace; it was simply a responsibility, bequeathed by her class. Since it called for no emotional commitment, it was also unnecessary to pretend she liked what she was called upon to do.

She felt genuine sympathy for the homeless women and children she had to deal with but by no stretch of the imagination could she sustain that sympathy for long in their company. Unlike her, they had no sense of duty at all, no manners and very little gratitude. They were noisy, dirty—though they couldn't help that—and at times excessively rude. One woman, mother of a brood of five begrimed little children, had sipped a mug of tea from the urn, pulled a face and hurled the contents at Elizabeth's feet. 'Call that bloody tea, missus?' she'd shouted so everyone in the centre could hear. 'No better'n gnat's pee, that. Too bleeding much to expect lah-di-dahs like you to make a decent cup of rosie. Can't make tea, what *can* you do?'

Mary Kettringham, the local organiser, explained that the woman's husband had been killed when their house was bombed last night and they had nowhere to go; no family or friends with whom they could lodge. That made it understandable, but not admirable. Later that afternoon Mary had come to her again, leading two of the smallest infants by the hand. She'd been very hesitant—and so she should have been! Could Elizabeth *possibly* put the family up for just a few days?

Elizabeth had very little experience of lying, except for the little white lies a mother tells her children when all else fails, but she drew on reserves of deceit she never knew she had. She said her daily had also been bombed and she'd promised all the space in the house to Elsie, her husband and two children. The lie had troubled her through the rest of the day and all the way home; it was only when she reached the security of the paved garden in Garfield Court that she divined an excuse that satisfied her; it was her duty to think of Charles and Ian first and to hold open the option she had offered Elsie. Duty was always a thoroughly satisfying reason for doing anything, even something that seemed consciously irregular.

She heard footsteps on the stair and called out, 'Is that you, Charles?'

Ian's head came round the door. 'No. It's me.'

'Darling!' She held out her arms to him without getting up and he came to sit beside her and dropped his head on her shoulder. She crooned, 'Are you feeling better now? I hated to have to go out this morning but you know I had to.' She didn't add: it was my duty. Ian knew that. He was her son, in every sense.

'I'm O.K.,' he said dully.

'What are you going to do tonight?'

'I dunno. Go back, I suppose.'

She cradled his head in her arm. 'Darling, you mustn't let it get you down. It was the shock, that's all. I'm sure the superintendent and Dr Hawthorne will be the first to admit they spoke without thinking. They know what you did for that woman. They're proud of you. They wouldn't have put it in the paper otherwise, would they?'

Ian choked, near to tears. 'How could I know. . . ?' He couldn't go on.

Elizabeth kissed the top of his head. 'Sssh, darling. I'm proud of you, anyway. So is daddy.'

Ian shook his head violently on her shoulder. '*He* doesn't care! He thinks I'm a . . . coward.' The word came out explosive with tears. 'He just won't understand. Even the Board of Examiners understood. They listened and they knew I meant what I said. They don't let you off fighting if they think you're just a . . . coward.'

'Daddy's just. . . .' She groped for a word, any word, that might rationalise Charles's pig-headed obduracy. '. . . upset.' It was the best she could do. She added hastily, 'He has a great deal on his mind, darling. More than you know. And he has all of us to worry about.'

'He's only worried about himself,' Ian blurted, sitting up. 'He thinks he's the only one who can be right. It's *his* ideals that matter, *his* standards, the way *he* feels.'

'That's not true—' she began.

'Oh, mother, it *is* true and you know it. He's more concerned about what the neighbours think or that bunch of pen-pushing militants in Whitehall. He'd change overnight if I joined up. He wouldn't think: Good, the boy's thought it through and changed his mind. He'd only be happy because I was doing what *he* wanted. Because I was doing what everyone else is doing. He's just like all the other sheep. Follow my leader. Never get out of step.' He twined his fingers together, his bottom lip jutting.

'That's not what he thought last night,' she said quietly.

'That's *always* what he thinks,' Ian rejoined sullenly.

'I made him read that story in the *Daily Express*. He wanted to come to your room and talk to you but I wouldn't let him. He felt terrible about the way he spoke to you last night. Very proud, too.'

'I bet.'

'Darling, don't use those dreadful American expressions,' Elizabeth snapped testily. 'And don't make the mistake of being what you accuse your father of.'

'I'm not anything like him,' he countered defensively.

'He thinks *he's* the only one who can be right?' she emphasised reprovingly. '*His* standards, *his* feelings are the only ones that count? You're exactly the same. You've decided you know best, better than him or me or the government or anyone else and you're sticking to your guns no matter what. That's true, isn't it?'

'It's a different thing,' he grunted, slouching on the arm of the chair.

'It's always different from one's own side of the fence,' she said briskly. 'Take it from me, darling, he's not proud of the way he treated you and he's waking up to the fact that he hasn't behaved as he should over a lot of things. But then, neither have you, so you're both equal. For the first time, last night, he understood what you're doing down there at the hospital, what you risked for that woman . . . because you felt it was your. . . .' That word leaped to her lips again; she gave voice to it with only the slightest hesitation, '. . . duty.'

'I don't believe it.'

'Then you're a little fool. Because he said to me, "That boy's got a lot of courage. I don't think I could have done it. It's as bad as being in the front line." And I told him, "He *is* in the front line. The war is in the streets now and he can't run away from it. More to the point, it's in the hospitals." He really does understand, darling. I promise you.'

The front-door bell rang once, twice, three times in urgent succession. Elizabeth looked up with impatience. 'That can't be your father. He said he'd be late this evening. Be a dear and go see who it is, will you?'

She heard the voice, official, gruff and measured. 'Ian Henry Russell?'

She heard his, 'Er. . . .'

'Who is it, darling?' she called protectively, jumping to her feet. Ian ushered a burly purple-faced man of about fifty into the drawing-room. He wore his Anthony Eden square on his head and slid it off by way of his chin when he came in. His raincoat was an aged buff-coloured Burberry, blotched with stains along the sleeves as though he had been up to his elbows in darkest crime.

'Detective Sergeant Pearce, m'm,' he said uncomfortably.

'I'm Elizabeth Russell. Why did you use my son's full name just now?'

The detective allowed a cough to rumble deep in his chest. 'Inquiries, m'm,' he explained.

'But what could you possibly want with Ian?'

'Talk to the lad, can I?'

'Yes. I take it I can stay?'

He made what might have been intended as a courteous little bow; it came out as if he were reacting to a twinge of lumbago. He looked at Ian. 'You work up at the hospital, sir?'

'Yes, I do.' Ian looked petrified.

'Not your regular job. I mean to say, not the job you'd be doing if you wasn't. . . .' He looked anxiously at Elizabeth.

'If I hadn't been a conscientious objector,' Ian finished for him. 'No. I'd be at university. I'm at the hospital because I refused to go into uniform.'

Detective Sergeant Pearce produced a large notebook, opened it, folded one side over the other, took out a pencil, licked the end of it and wrote something in a round, painstaking hand. 'What I thought,' he said to himself.

'What is this all about?' Elizabeth snapped imperiously.

The purple face twitched unhappily. 'Ask the boy, can I, m'm?'

'If you'll explain what you've come for, yes.'

Detective Sergeant Pearce licked his lips, then the stub of pencil. 'Up at the hospital last night. . .,' he began slowly.

Ian jumped in instantly. 'It was nothing to do with me. I only just said hello to the woman, and the husband said—'

The detective held up the stub of pencil. 'Whoa, there, boy. Got to get this down.'

Elizabeth flared, 'My son has a right to have a solicitor present when you take a statement, sergeant. I won't have him treated like a common criminal, I won't. . . .'

The purple face creased in a twitch of indignation and the tongue came out to lick the faded grey moustache. 'I haven't said nothing about *criminal*, have I?' he demanded. 'I just said inquiries. This 'ere boy of yours is a witness, that's all. That poor woman he saved, God rest her soul, was' – he snatched a quick look of confirmation at an earlier leaf of his notebook – 'was administered poison by a person or persons as yet unknown. This lad 'ere might've seen who done it. Right, lad?'

Tuesday, 1930

When Shaffer wound up his news file O'Keefe nagged him again about picking up the threads of the Saturday night story – the boys in the warehouse, the little old ladies in the little old grey street, the chorus girl who wouldn't let him take her home. The listeners were still calling in about these characters, he said. Shaffer had struck a rich seam of paydirt in Nelson's Green and he had a responsibility to get off his butt and go mine it some more.

'Besides,' O'Keefe drawled laconically, 'the Board sent me down a tablet of stone today. They like that stuff you're sending.'

'They did what?'

O'Keefe sucked his teeth, loudly. 'No kidding, Mel. I guess they're thinking about joining up with the good guys.'

'And I'll be drafted from the floor for President!'

'No. On the line. I told you Sunday to play it straight. What do you think I was doing – shoving my ass in the fire? I know these guys. They move the way the next dollar moves, right? You helped but they listen to Murrow and Bate, too, and they even read the papers now and then. Most of all they read the schmuk sheet.' The schmuk sheet was a daily digest of listeners' phone calls and letters. 'The people are breaking their hearts about the English war. That's what they're calling it – the English war. That's a big step nearer home than the European war. And you're getting a big audience, friend. The Board like that.'

Shaffer went back to Brook Street, showered and put on a dark-blue suit and soft white silk shirt. He got out the car and drove east. Like Murrow, he gave little thought to the dangers of driving and, had he been asked, would have offered the opinion that he was safter in a driving seat than he was on foot or crouched under a table in the apartment. In fact, of the four alerts reported today, he had been consciously aware of only one. He had been on his way back to Hill Street from Grosvenor Square in mid-afternoon when a lone Heinkel roared low over the city. It dropped no bombs but peeled away to the north-east and disappeared unmolested. According to the Air Ministry, many of these solo missions were straightforward reconnaissance flights to check on damage done the night before. Certainly, Goering seemed to be learning his lesson about the massive daylight bombardment of London; it paid psychological dividends but came expensive in planes and aircrews. There was more profit in sneak attacks on scattered provincial cities where British fighter cover was less organised and stretched thin. Anyway, London was a sitting duck at night; the scuttering fires of earlier raids created a perfect flarepath for Luftwaffe flight commanders leading their packs westward along the Thames and simply added to the problems of interception by R.A.F. Blenheims and Defiants.

Ben Robertson of C.B.S. was openly prophesying a blitzkrieg of London lasting at least three months and, although the majority of the Press corps felt that was over-estimating the staying-power of the Germans, no one was eager to cover his bet. The R.A.F. had bombed Berlin again last night and raised fires in the suburbs. One bomb made a hit less than a mile from the Tiergarten, according to O'Keefe, who had read over a wire-service snap from Pierre Huss, the I.N.S. correspondent in Berlin. He quoted Goebbels's radio: 'Churchill's Cabinet of criminals carries the responsibility for further intensification of this aerial warfare.' Robertson could be right. Hitler's fury at this unexpected assault on the Fatherland, and Goering's burning humiliation, might well force the Luftwaffe to continue bombing London long after the High Command deemed it either sensible or productive.

He allowed Rita into his mind one last time as he crossed London Bridge, then tuned her out to make way for Gladys. Freddie Green's invitation for his party at Greenwich had been for two. Midway through his talk with O'Keefe, Shaffer decided he would take Gladys Warrender with him. A gesture to a good story.

He left the car again near the ruin of Pageant's Wharf fire station and walked through the gathering dusk to Baltic Street. The fires were still burning fiercely in the Surrey Commercial Docks, branding the lowering sky with sunset pinks and bronze. The stench of smoke and escaping gas lingered in the narrow streets. He had been debating what sign-language he could use if Janice Scully opened the door to him — assuming she was prepared to keep her mobile mouth shut — but the question didn't arise. Florence Scully answered his knock, twittered nervously and drew him inside. Mrs Warrender was in the kitchen, peeling potatoes; the two women fussed him to a seat at the table and insisted on making him a cup of tea. Gladys was upstairs, said Elsie Warrender; she clattered away to fetch her.

Shaffer sat uncomfortably in his chair at the table, his right foot tentatively exploring the scene of his matinée performance with Janice. Florence Scully retreated to the kitchen to watch the kettle boil and from upstairs he heard an exchange of urgent whispers.

Shaffer got to his feet as Gladys appeared in the frame of the little staircase. Her face was flushed with irritation and he thought, in a moment of panic, that Janice Scully had talked after all. He said defensively, 'I'm sorry if I called at a bad time.'

Elsie went into the kitchen. Gladys eyed the closed door as though she knew her mother's ear was at the keyhole and said very quietly, 'My dad'll be home in a minute for his supper.'

'I promise I won't get in the way. I only came to—'

'He's still not right, my dad,' she whispered, her eyes pleading. 'He'll get all upset, finding a stranger in the house.'

Elsie Warrender tapped at the kitchen door, poked her head through and carried in a tray with teapot and cups and saucers. 'There you are,' she said. 'Nice cup of tea. You too, Glad.'

'Oh, mum!' fumed her daughter.

'Sorry, I'm sure,' Elsie retorted, mock offended. She explained to Shaffer, 'She don't like me calling her Glad in front of strangers.'

'Mum!' burst out the agonised Gladys again.

'Sorry we haven't got anything to offer you except tea. And not even in our own house. I said to Glad, you're the last man on earth to worry about things like that. I can tell.'

'That's got nothing to do with it,' Gladys snapped.

'Oh, yes it is,' her mother said sharply. 'That and my Jack. She's worried you'll think he's—'

'Mum, stop it! I'll go right upstairs this minute if you don't.'

Shaffer raised his hands. 'Look, this is my fault. I just stopped by to ask your daughter to come to a party. I—'

'I've got to go to work,' the girl interrupted.

'It's only for an hour or so. I could run you up-town to the club right after.'

'No, I wouldn't have the time.'

'Oh, yes you would,' Elsie Warrender said firmly. 'You can dress now—you got nothing else to do—and you don't have to be there till ten o'clock. She'd love to go, Mr Shaffer. Do her the world of good to get out of here for a bit.'

They were still arguing when the kitchen door opened and Jack Warrender came into the room. Gladys was on her feet at once and came round the table to him. The old man submitted to an embrace and patted her hair.

'Watch it, old love,' he said hoarsely, 'I'm not made of wood, you know. Fair out on me feet.'

The level tone of his voice made Gladys step back and search his face. It was grimed with smoke and sweat and deeply lined but his eyes were clear and steady and twinkling with the old gruff good humour.

She said anxiously, 'Are you all right, dad?'

He slipped off his warden's helmet and dusted his blue uniform overalls. 'Course I'm all right. Be a sight better when I get a cuppa rosie inside me. What about it, mother?'

Elsie's face softened. 'Never could get in the door without asking for his cuppa, could you?' She bustled away to fetch more crockery.

Jack Warrender held out his hand to Shaffer. ''Bout time I said thanks for what you done for my boy Paul,' he said, his eyes not quite meeting the American's. 'I wasn't meself the other night. I told that Paul, "You should've been dead by rights." Would've been if *you* hadn't happened along. Young terrors, them two.'

Shaffer shrugged awkwardly. 'It was just luck.'

'Yes. Lucky it was you and not someone who'd turn tail and run a mile. Lucky you had guts. Me and my missus—'

'Please,' Shaffer protested. 'Let's forget it.'

'Never forget that night's work, son,' said Jack Warrender. He eased himself into a chair as if every bone in his body was broken. 'You just come to say hullo then, did you?'

'He come to take Glad out to a party,' explained Elsie, bustling back into the living-room. She poured a cup of tea and set it in front of her husband.

'Oh? That's — er — very nice,' he said. He set himself at the milky beige liquid, sucking noisily.

Gladys pouted. 'I'm not going, though,' she said.

Jack Warrender put down his cup and wiped his lips with the back of an oil-stained hand. 'You go on up and get dressed and enjoy yourself, my girl,' he said gruffly. 'Nothing for you here, is there, mother?'

'Just what I told her.'

Warrender tapped Shaffer on the arm. 'There'll be raids again tonight, son,' he said. 'Better watch out for yourself, the two of you.'

'We'll be careful.'

'Not up to you, son. Up to Jerry.' His eyes darkened. 'Three shelters around here got direct hits last night. Three of 'em. Women and kids, mostly. They're still digging 'em out. The buggers even bombed a maternity hospital they was telling me down the hut. Babies! Crying in the wreckage, waiting to be dug out. By Gawd, if I could get my hands on that bloody Hitler—'

'Father!' Elsie warned.

He relaxed. 'Mother's right. Don't do no good to let Jerry get under your skin, eh?' He waved a firm paternal arm at Gladys. 'Go on, girl. Get up them stairs. I want to see you dressed and down here in ten minutes, all right?'

She obeyed him meekly.

Warrender winked at Shaffer with quiet satisfaction. 'She'll be all right now I'm on the mend. You made a big hit with her, son. When Glad won't talk about something, you know she ain't got nothing else on her mind — and she ain't uttered a single solitary word about you. Not a solitary word.'

The alert sounded as Shaffer pointed the car up the hill to Blackheath. They looked at each other but said nothing. Freddie Green's house was an impressive white-painted mansion nestling behind high walls on the brow of the heath; they drove through a set of magnificent gates, along a curving driveway and parked on a wide shingle frontage. Fifty or sixty cars were already in place, their chauffeurs standing in little groups among them. Huge black Rolls-Royces and Bentleys mingled with camouflaged Humber staff cars and sporty open-tops; the world beating a path to the Green door did so in style. Beyond the cars the ground sloped away to smooth lawns, a water-garden and an orchard, and beyond that to the river and a fearsome backdrop of burning dockland. To the left the Thames ran black between scarlet licks of fire along the loop of Bugsby's Reach; behind it the Isle of Dogs blinked with a thousand pockets of unconquered flame where the West India and Millwall Docks were wreathed in their fourth night of agony.

They crunched across the shingle to the cavernous portico and the east wind brought them the first faint coughs of anti-aircraft gunfire.

They were received at the door by a butler in white tie and tails and Gladys instinctively put a hand to the simple pale-blue day dress she wore. To Shaffer's discomfort, she had confessed in the car that it was one of Janice's; all her own clothes had perished in the destruction of Number 14. The butler bowed stiffly, closed the door, pushed back the voluminous folds of blackout curtaining and wrote something in an open book on a table by the door. He led them across the white marble hall-way.

Gladys whispered urgently, 'I hope it's not *dress*.'

The butler drew open two studded oaken doors and stood aside. There were at least three hundred people in the huge room, two-thirds of them in uniform. A makeshift bar of trestle tables covered with sparkling white linen ran the length of one wall and servants moved among the guests balancing trays encrusted with glasses.

Gladys's face registered wonder, apprehension, betrayal. 'I *said* I shouldn't come,' she hissed at him. 'It *is* dress.'

Shaffer smiled down at her. 'Uniforms. Let's go introduce ourselves,' he urged encouragingly.

He singled out Denzil Fletcher-Hale without difficulty. The smooth gold mane glowed a foot and more above the heads of the mass. The young man's startling blue eyes were constantly on the move, checking faces, voices, actions; some sixth sense made him look in Shaffer's direction and he waved, patted his companion on the shoulder and weaved through the crowd to join them.

'This is Gladys Warrender,' Shaffer said.

Denzil studied her face solemnly, took her hand, brought his lips to within a quarter inch of her fingers. 'Charmed. Can I get you something? Champagne's the thing, I think. Here.' He leaned out across a trio of bald heads and neatly lifted two glasses of champagne from a passing tray. Gladys beamed nervously and sipped, still unsure of herself.

'Anyone I should talk to?' Shaffer asked.

'Fellow here works at Air Ministry. Top man. Could get you to Dowding. Have to see. Good turnout, don't you think? Hand it to Green. Doesn't miss a trick.' He waved generously. 'Air marshals, generals, admirals, civil servants, M.P.s. Take your choice.'

'How the heck does he do it? I mean ... *Green*!'

Fletcher-Hale scratched his chin with a slim brown finger. 'Chap's a patriot, what? Three or four nights a week. Open house. Every fighter station in the south-east. Chaps off duty drop in, take a drink, bite to eat. Has a swimming bath down below. In the cellar. Heated water, old boy. Paradise for pilots.'

'But the guy's a two-faced sonofabitch. You told me yourself, he's a profiteer. They must know that.'

'War on,' Denzil said gently. 'Nobody cares. Drink his booze. Eat his food. Use his pool. Hale fellow. Sound businessman. War effort stuff. You know the form.'

'You telling me generals and admirals just come here for the booze?'

'Not at all. No place like Green's. Everyone comes here in time. Meeting point. Generals and M.P.s. Admirals and Whitehall men. Industrialists and the Press. Exchange ideas. But off the record. Talk business. Off the record. Useful. Green's useful, too. Get anything you want. Don't have to like him.'

Shaffer shook his head. 'Profiteering's O.K. if you spread the profits around some, is that it?'

Denzil patted him on the shoulder. 'Can't expect you to understand. One thing at a time, that's the way it is. That's war. Today, let him play. Doing his bit. Tomorrow?' He shrugged. 'Scandal, perhaps. Revelations. Crookery. Up in the courts. Name in the papers. Bang goes his business. Clang! — door of the cell. Exit Freddie Green. Takes time.'

Gladys's eyes were riveted on a figure to her right. 'Oh,' she squeaked. 'There's—' She caught herself in time. Denzil followed her gaze, allowed his eyes to flicker over the man from head to foot and back again, then turned to her, his face serious. 'Friend of yours?'

'Oh, no,' she said, flustered, cheeks glowing redly. 'I just see him where I work from time to time.'

'Gladys is a dancer,' Shaffer volunteered.

'Aaaah,' breathed Fletcher-Hale, seeing light. 'Queer chap. Introduced me to his wife, two, three times. Confusing. Always a different lady.' The agonised smile played around his long face. 'Promising career. Make the Cabinet before long, I hear. Odd johnnies, politicos, what?'

Shaffer jumped as he was grasped from behind by two bony hands and he swung to find Freddie Green's moustache dipping and rolling on the crest of the display of dentistry.

'Melville!' Green grabbed at Shaffer's hand and pumped it energetically, his eyes fixed on Gladys. 'Who's the little friend, then, eh? What's your name, girlie?'

'This is Gladys Warrender,' Shaffer said coldly.

'Got something to drink, have you? Course you have. Just a minute.' He took the glass from her hand, sniffed it, sipped it, wrinkled his nose. 'They give you the plonk. Should've known. Always serve the plonk when the lads're here. Don't know what they're drinking half the time, do they? Shame to waste a good year. You come with old Freddie, Gladys. We'll find you something worth the time and trouble.' He put an arm around her shoulder. 'And there's a couple of people you ought to meet, pretty girl like you. You mind, Melville?' he said, with a stab of the yellow–beige eyes.

'Not if the lady doesn't.'

'Oh, well,' said Gladys, drunk with attention. 'I don't want to. . . .'

'Your host, Freddie Green,' Denzil said politely.

'Oh. You've got a lovely home, Mr Gr—'

'Captain, actually,' cut in Freddie. He threaded his arm through hers and led her away. Shaffer heard: 'Army, not navy.

Sherwood Foresters. Caught my packet in India. Damn bad luck. . . .'

Shaffer said, 'Will she be all right?'

'Here? Naturally. Too many people.' It would have been unthinkable for Fletcher-Hale to lower his standards to the extent of winking but he managed to convey the impression all the same.

'You take that job with the Foreign Office?' asked Shaffer conversationally.

'Not really.'

'That's great English directness. What does not really mean?'

Denzil balanced his chin on the rim of his glass. 'Not my line of country, I fancy. Very decent of Halifax. Jebb's a good sort. But . . . no. Think not, all in all. Brainy chaps they're looking for. Grey matter. Planners. Big stuff.'

'They didn't like the way you shaped up?'

'Lord, yes. At school with half the fellows there. Decent outfit. Not for me, though.'

Shaffer weighed him clinically. He had a welling suspicion, born in the first hour of their lunch at White's on Sunday, that Denzil Fletcher-Hale was the biggest, most calculating phony he had ever met; that, sometime, somewhere, the young giant would be able to keep up the idiot pretence no longer and would collapse with a bellow of amusement at the gullibility of the human species.

He decided to play along. 'How many shots are you allowed before they drag you into uniform and send you up front?' he drawled sarcastically.

'Don't actually know,' Denzil said, scowling profoundly. 'Good point that. Must ask Halifax.'

'You decided against the air force too?'

'Awfully cramped, airplanes, old boy.' Denzil stretched his arms above his head, achieving a height of about nine feet from toes to finger ends. 'Don't make a plane to fit, d'you see.'

Shaffer fought off the temptation to giggle. 'What about the army?'

'Yes. Have to be the Guards. The Blues. The old man, you know. His regiment or nothing. Difficult. Can't stand horseflesh.

252

Never could. Got a seat like a badly filled sack. Appalling.' There was no twinkle in the blue eyes; no quiver around the lips to suggest the containment of an improbable joke.

Shaffer sipped his champagne. 'You know, the war could be over before you make up your mind, Denzil.'

'D'you think so? Really?' He was utterly serious and not a little alarmed.

Shaffer swallowed his disbelief for a few more minutes. 'Look, tell me something. Isn't it against the law for a healthy, well-educated. . . ?'

'Hah!' Denzil's long, lean countenance trembled on the very brink of real humour. 'Eton, old boy! Education? Hah!'

'But isn't it against the law not to do something? If you're not in uniform don't they send you down the mines here, or make you a firefighter or a warden or something?'

'Never actually asked,' Fletcher-Hale said slowly, lower lip clamped contemplatively in his teeth. 'Sound move, though.' He drank deeply from his glass. 'Miss the war?' he ruminated. 'Must get organised, what? Sorted out. Intelligence chaps asked me over again. Said I'd look 'em up. Must ring them. Tomorrow. Definitely. Decent types.'

Shaffer gave up. 'Look, I want to grab some air, Denzil. This is worse than the army–navy game. Will you keep an eye on Gladys and that creep Green?'

'Creep! Hah. Good one. Creep! Yes, of course. Leave it to me.' Denzil scythed off, lifting over the crowd like a Spanish galleon on an Atlantic swell. Shaffer walked back across the hallway and into the night air. It was dark now and dozens of searchlights fingered the low cloud, interlaced like a moving picket fence as far as the eye could see, east to west. Upriver the mounting east wind bent the uncountable patches of flame to its will; downriver, the pitch black sky was pierced at intervals by spitballs of light. He lit a cigarette in cupped hands and kept the glowing tip concealed; it was unlikely the Luftwaffe invaders would see a cigarette end from ten thousand feet or even bother to look when there were a thousand raging fires to guide them to their targets, but showing lights was one of England's seven deadly sins, indelibly registered in the national

253

consciousness, and he was as brainwashed by the psychology of observing it as anyone.

He walked to the lawns and watched the searchlights bob and weave hungrily. From time to time a flash of silver would catch in one of the beams but invariably disappeared just as quickly. There was no gunfire that he could perceive; the spitballs over the estuary seemed to be the limit of the anti-aircraft defence ring and it was quite impossible to judge from the drone and occasional diving whine whether the aircraft up there among the fingers of light were 'ours' or 'theirs'. To his left the night belched a hundred blips of bright white flame, pretty as a bursting firework, and seconds later the snappety crackle of explosions followed. Incendiaries. Somewhere down there men and women were rushing about the streets, into gardens, climbing on roofs, forcing a way into locked schools and shops and factories, to deal with those raindrops from hell. Some of them would have only blankets; most would grab a bucket of sand to suffocate the fizzing life from the torchbombs. If only a third of the bombs ignited, and that was the official count, there would be thirty new fires for the luckless A.F.S. to deal with, or ten new fires and a resurgence of twenty old ones.

A gust of laughter penetrated the solid walls of the house and rose over the guttural snarling of the planes. The leap-frog game. The young men in air-force blue with their animated children's faces flushed with effort and single-minded commitment. Target for tonight — another of the pat catch-phrases. Target for tonight: hell raising. Mind-blowing games, as much food as they could bolt, and liquor-laced oblivion. For tomorrow we die. Or maybe somebody else died as these kids sat tight in Spitfires while bombers rained T.N.T. on the uncomprehending suburbs of Berlin or Hamburg. Heaven protect Captain Freddie Green: criminal accomplice, universal uncle, public benefactor. In the final analysis there was no such thing as *The* War; just a host of well-regulated private ones, sectioned off and classified according to geography and social status. Freddie Green made bits and pieces to make planes fly young men into battle to kill other young men. Jack Warrender donned a tin hat and wandered the streets waiting for the skies to fall. Gladys flashed a pair of shapely gams on a night-club dance-floor. Mel Shaffer and his kind picked the bones clean of edible meat. Denzil would locate his little area of the fight, too; a safe and prestigious corner far from flying shrapnel where well-bred men could find the essential peace and quiet to get on with the 'real work' of apportioning the expenditure of lives. Denzil's kind would all, in time, earn a sash of the Royal Victorian Order or the Order of St Michael and St George, kneel before their sovereign and accept – with due modesty – the thanks of a decimated nation.

Shaffer found the shelter of a box-hedge under the house wall before he bent, shoved the butt of the cigarette under his heel and ground it out. He was straightening up when the front door opened. Three men rustled out through the layers of blackout curtaining and came down the steps.

'All right, then. Off you go.' Green's voice. 'Just do what you're told and you got nothing to worry about.'

'Except the coppers and the wardens and firemen. And bloody *people*, Fred. Every bugger's a nark, these days. Everyone.'

'Keep your heads down and use the kids. Nobody gives a tuppenny toss about kids. Worst thing can happen to them if they get caught is they spend a night in a rest centre.'

A third man said, 'If they keeps their mouths shut, Fred. Allus that. Some get scared and run. An' if they got stuff on 'em, down their shirts or in a sack or somethin', silly young sods get nicked red-handed and chat their bloody heads off, don't they, eh?'

'So what?' Green again. 'What do they know about you? Nothing. No names, no pack drill, my old son. Remember that and you're safe as houses. Just do like I say: never meet the kids before or after a job until they're all in one place and you can see they haven't brought company. Only work an area when the raids're on and not where there's fire. Check up on the kids you use, and if they look like causing trouble, drop some black on 'em and tip off Old Bill – no copper ever believed a kid. Use the navy ambulance for getting the stuff out and nothing else; always the ambulance. Never let yourselves be seen with the kids and never let 'em come to the ambulance, remember that. Make 'em dump the stuff where you can drive round and pick

255

it up clean. And never forget one thing, lads: you don't come hooking your crook round me. Never! You got anything to say to me, you talk to Billy Sutcliffe down at the wharf. Got it?'

'Yeah, we got you, Fred. But we'd sure as buggery like to know one thing, mate. You know — just between us three.'

Shaffer could imagine the Clark Gable moustache wriggling over the china dentures. 'All right. What?'

'Well. . . .' The man was clearly at a loss for words. 'There's this house and them bleedin' toffs in there and the way you go on, Fred — big bloody cars and racehorses and swanky places you go and flash clothes and ... well, everyfing you want. I mean, you're the guvnor, right? What we was finking was, why you have to bother wiv nicking tea and sugar and butter and stuff like that from warehouses? I mean, where's the sense in it, seeing as how you—?'

The man's speech was forcibly stopped; he sucked in air in a hiss of pain. Green's voice came out of the blackness, low and grating. 'Don't tell me what's sense and not sense, Jigger, or I'll begin to think you're after my job, lad. And you give me cause to worry about what you're thinking and whether you're doing what I tell you and I might get very bleedin' narked. And then I'd be forced to nobble you, lad, wouldn't I, and that'd make me very vexed.'

'Ow, leave orf, Fred!' gasped Jigger. 'Aaaah!' He exhaled his relief. 'I only asked, guvnor. That's all.'

'Well, in future don't bleedin' ask. Do what I tell you. And one more thing. Concentrate on the foodstuffs; that's the line I'm interested in. Perishables. You wanta nick clothes and shoes and stuff, nick it on your own time, not mine.'

'All right, Fred. We'd best be getting on.'

'Right you are, Jigger,' said Green. There was a pause. The searchlights careened the sky and a muffled boom of artillery fire sounded from the estuary. 'They'll be over again, any minute now, I'll tell you that for nothing. Be at it all night too. You lads get moving now you'll do yourselves a bit of good tonight. Buzz off then.'

Footsteps crunched away along the gravel drive. The door opened and closed. Shaffer let the breath run out of his chest. He experienced no sense of shock; no moral indignation, no revulsion. If anything, he was faintly amused. Freddie Green was not only a loud-mouthed, vainglorious, self-seeking crook, he was a greedy one too; the supply of 'unobtainable' rationed goods that kept his reputation for hospitality intact was going to hang him, one day. By the neck. There was no greater sin in time of war and, as he recalled from a newspaper story yesterday, the penalty for looting was death. A country that learned he was using kids to do his stealing for him would have little compunction in screaming for the hangman's noose. Green must know that. What in blue blazes persuaded him it was worth the risk?

He waited thirty seconds longer, then slipped through the door and the blackout material. He walked back to the big room and found Denzil in the far corner, watching the leap-frogging pilots. Gladys was among them, apparently adjudicating some kind of long-distance leap, because she had a notebook in one hand and was scribbling in it with a pencil. The last young fellow on the line made a spectacular running dive, zoomed over the end man and collapsed in a heap on the floor. There was a wave of cheering. Shaffer pushed his way towards them. He arrived at Denzil's shoulder as Gladys presented a bottle of champagne to the victor, tied a sash of white ribbon with a champagne cork on one end around his neck and kissed him on both cheeks. The cheers were deafening.

Denzil looked down and angled his head. Shaffer looked to his right. A tough-looking, spare, grey-haired man in a black suit was talking animatedly to a naval captain and two brigadiers. He recognised him at once. It was the man who had occupied Doris's table at the pub in Soho. 'Charles Russell. Chap I mentioned. Air Ministry. Could be useful. Want to meet him?'

'Why not.' Shaffer looked at Gladys; she had no need of him for the time being. She'd just been made Queen of the R.A.F.

Denzil led the way to Russell's group. The grey-haired man was saying, '. . . new generation fighter plane. Gladiators are still in service on aircraft carriers because we just haven't been able to reproduce *exactly* their take-off/landing characteristics in a mono. . . .' He stopped instantly when he saw Shaffer and his cheeks flushed. Denzil inclined his head to the captain and the senior army officers and something in his face worked the necessary magic. They nodded with what appeared to be understanding and turned away. Denzil performed the introduction.

Charles Russell's mouth tautened at the mention of A.B.N. 'You're a journalist,' he accused. 'I'm afraid I'm not permitted to talk to journalists.'

Denzil said easily, 'Favour to me, Russell.' Shaffer waited for Russell to reject the invitation out of hand but the hard mouth relaxed perceptibly. 'Oh, well.... Dammit, Fletcher-Hale, you make it confoundedly difficult.'

Denzil patted his shoulder encouragingly. 'Tit for tat, Russell.' He bent his head to the older man's face level. 'Green's let you in, yes? Investment project, I hear. Kingsley Mountford and his chums.' He touched his nose significantly.

Charles Russell blushed to the roots of his grey hair. His jaw jarred his teeth together and two muscles twitched high on his cheek. 'Yes, all right,' he said less forcibly. 'Do what I can, I suppose.' He swung on Shaffer. 'What d'you want?'

'I'd like to talk to Dowding—' Shaffer began but Russell broke in at once.

'Out of the question. Now that really is out of the question. I have no influence with a man like—'

'Bags of influence,' Denzil protested. 'Churchill listens. John Dill listens — told me so himself. Everyone listens to you, Russell. Even Beaverbrook.' There was nothing in his face to suggest that mention of Beaverbrook's name carried any ulterior significance whatsoever, but even Shaffer looked up at him quizzically.

Russell coloured again. 'You've approached him officially?' he asked Shaffer.

'No point. Ministry of Information says no. No to everything. Even no to talking to Battle of Britain crews. Don't ask me why.'

'I *know* why,' Russell retorted tartly. He sighed. 'I'll do what I can but I promise nothing. In the end, it'll be up to him.'

Shaffer slipped him a pasteboard card with his office and home telephone numbers inscribed. 'I'd appreciate it,' he said.

'Yes. Well, if you'll excuse me....' Russell nodded to Denzil and pushed into the crowd. They watched him go.

Shaffer said, 'Will you tell me a secret, Denzil?'

'Have no secrets, old boy. Open book.'

'Then how come people jump through hoops for you? What've you got that makes a guy like Russell bend?'

Denzil's face was a picture of tortured self-examination. He thought until deep lines crossed and criss-crossed his brow. He shook his head. 'Facer, that one. Can't say I know. Chap can only ask. One has chums, of course. School. Varsity. Family links. One's clubs.'

'Russell a member of your club?'

'Russell, no. Friend of a friend.'

'Were you blackmailing him back there?'

'Blackmail?' The word was clearly not in his vocabulary.

Shaffer pressed the point. 'You pulled Beaverbrook on him. I know. I heard the inflection. You were telling him you knew something.'

Denzil examined his face as though he thought the American mad. 'Inflection? No inflection. Why inflection? Nothing to know. All above my head, old boy. Science, that's Russell's game. Brainy chap.'

He was saved from further cross-examination by the explosive arrival of Gladys and an escort of five panting, red-faced young airmen. One of them took Gladys's hand lightly on his, bowed low before Shaffer and placed the tiny hand in his palm.

'Your princess, your Lady of the Tower, your Guinevere, your gentle maid — returned safe and sound, good sir.'

Shaffer ducked his head in suitably regal manner. Gladys turned impulsively and kissed all five of them on the cheek. They affected to swoon at the touch of her lips; one fell pole-axed into the arms of the others and they dragged him away, heels scuffing the marble floor.

'Well. No need to ask if you enjoyed yourself,' Shaffer grinned. 'Glad you came?'

'Oh, yes!' Her face was flushed with happiness, her eyes shining. 'I'm sorry I was such an old killjoy. I wanted to come, really, all the time. I was just....' She eyed Denzil uncertainly. He averted his face politely and she finished in a whisper. 'I was just terrified my dad would be ... funny ... like he was before.'

He showed her his watch. 'It's after nine-fifteen. I guess I ought to drive you into town now.'

Her face fell. 'Oh! Yes. I suppose you ought to. I was ... the time just flew, didn't it?'

Denzil's face turned down to her, giraffe-like. 'You'll come again? Always something going on.'

'Mr — Captain Green said I was to come up any time I wanted. And do you know what he said?' Her eyes were round. Shaffer shook his head. 'He said if I was to call him up first he'd send a motor car to pick me up. What would they say in the Green, a motor car picking me up?'

Shaffer forbore to mention that a motor car would not get as far as the Green — if the Green itself was still standing after tonight. The first ominous grunts of high-explosive bombs had shaken the house on the hill a few minutes earlier. Gladys seemed not to have noticed.

'Going to town?' Denzil cocked an eyebrow.

'Yeah. We'd better leave now. Gladys has to be at work at ten.'

'Good. Take me, too. Had enough. Café de Paris, isn't it? Fine. Take supper there. Watch your show.'

As the car pulled out on to the dark heath road a brilliant orange flameburst stained the sky over the City of London.

'Poor devils,' breathed Denzil softly. 'Landmine.'

Tuesday, 2350

The platform was bathed in a cold, white, soulless glow, the muted light of an aquarium, and a silver disc of moon filled the jagged hole in the roof of Victoria Station.

Trains lay hunched and silent along the tracks, survivors of the day's obstacle race, windows blank under a coat of dark-blue paint. The crowds had gone, leaving the inevitable sea of litter, the dank smell of dead cigarettes and sweat. It was the sadness of a deserted circus ring.

The flashlight flickered briefly in the doorway of a urinal and snapped off.

'Come on, let's be having you,' said the elderly policeman to a lurking figure in the shadows. A grizzled old man scuttled out, stood still. Flicker.

'Ain't doing no harm. Can't you leave a body in peace?' He clutched a greasy bag at his waist and, still mumbling, made for the exit. Another uniformed man ushered him through the half-closed gates.

The concourses of London's mainline stations were a natural and traditional rallying point for the city's down-and-outs, drifters and runaways. They were warm, they had benches and their rubbish bins yielded up a dazzling array of discarded food and newspapers suitable for bedding. Most important of all, they were quiet. The regulars arrived around midnight and dossed down in their chosen spots until they were moved on by the porters at dawn. Regulations didn't permit dossing, of course, and vagrants were required to be moved on, but rather than play an endless, heartless game of tag with the pathetic huddlers, the police had traditionally turned a blind eye and most of the station authorities had followed suit. But that was before the emergency was declared. The phrase, "Aven't you got no 'ome to go to?' now had a new chilling quality to it. The gentlemen of the road had joined the growing army of dispossessed. Most of them took to the Tube station platforms now but others, more restless, had learned that war could bring rich pickings if one knew where to look. In the confusion of the reception centres, stealing a bewildered family's ration books while posing as a 'helper' was like taking candy from a baby. There was always a good price for ration books on the black market. Looting was a dangerous game, but who was to say picking up a few trinkets in the street was looting? Most profitable and easiest of all was nicking from the bodies of bomb victims as they lay dead or nearly dead.

War had changed all the rules. The police no longer allowed loopholes in the regulations. Each night now the stations were patrolled and the 'residents' summarily ejected 'for their own safety'.

The lamp flickered again. Without a word, half a dozen men swung from their benches and gathered their rags around them.

261

'C'mon. C'mon, you know the rules.' The policeman addressed no one in particular. An old woman, eyes darting, hand clutching a half-eaten apple, peered at him from behind a newspaper kiosk, scampered towards him, stopped, half turned, turned again and bolted for the exit as if late for an appointment.

'All right, blue eyes. Up you come.'

The sleeping figure did not stir. The policeman prodded a shoulder. Still no movement. One of the policemen watching from the exit shouted, 'A stiff?'

The constable shook his head. Louder now to the recumbent figure: 'Room service!' The man blinked open his eyes and sat up abruptly. He was unshaven and his hair was matted but his clothes, apart from being badly creased, were of better quality than those of his colleagues. The policeman bent over him and sniffed. 'Sleeping it off, eh?' But there was no trace of alcohol. 'Sorry. You can't stay here, old son. Where d'you live then?'

The man shook his head vaguely.

'Well, wherever it is, you won't get a train from here till seven at the earliest. Got anybody who'll put you up?'

Again the man shook his head.

'Bit of a mess you're in, aren't you, cock? Got any money?'

'A ... little....' The man rubbed his eyes. 'Can't I just sleep here? I won't do—'

'There's a few places might still be open. My advice is: see if you can get a cheap hotel. Paddington. Know Paddington?'

'Yes.'

'Best place. But you can't stay here.' The policeman helped him to his feet. 'Out in the fresh air you'll feel better.' A thought struck him. 'Want to telephone anybody? Telephone over by the left luggage.'

The man didn't want to telephone.

At the gate the other policeman swung back the metal grille. 'Have a bit of trouble, did you, mate?'

'No ... I just ... well, I suppose....' The still-dazed figure swayed.

'Thought as much. Look, Sandy's going off in a couple of minutes, Fred. Car'll be picking him up. Hold on.' He leaned out through the gate. 'Which way you going, Sandy?'

The police driver came up and glared at the man. 'Harringay,' he said.

'Live anywhere near there?' asked the gate man.

'No. I'm afraid. . . . I'll be all right. Thanks, anyway.'

Almost imperceptibly, Sandy's hand eased the door forward until it closed the gap to a few inches. 'Excuse me, sir,' he said. 'Would you mind telling us your name?'

'Name?' The man looked helplessly at the half-closed gate. 'Name?'

'Your name, sir.'

'Harris.'

'Harris,' said the policeman. He nodded, his hand still on the gate.

'Have you any identification? Driving licence, identity card. Something like that, sir?'

The man fumbled in his jacket. 'I don't seem to. . . .'

'Something up, Sandy?' asked the policeman with the flash-light.

'No, just wondered. Hang on a tick. Won't keep you a minute, sir.' He disappeared into a tiny box-like office and there was a rustling of paper. He reappeared, looking at pages pinned beneath a bulldog clip.

'Harris . . . Harris. . . .' He shook his head and looked up apolo-getically. 'Sorry about that, Mr Harris. Missing persons, that kind of thing.' He was still staring coldly above the grin. 'You're all clear.'

'Clear? Oh, yes. Thanks.' The gate scraped back and the policeman waved a hand. 'Hope you find somewhere to stay.'

The man stared out into the night as if reluctant to move. Then, with a nod, he began to walk away.

'Looks as if he needs—' began the officer with the flashlight but his colleague held up a warning hand.

'Mr Dunn!' he called out. The man turned, realised his mis-take too late and tried to resume his walk.

'Mr Alfred Dunn?' said the policeman insistently. The trudg-ing figure stopped. The police driver went over to him and took his arm, almost sympathetically. 'It is Mr Dunn, isn't it?'

Alfred Dunn nodded distantly. 'Knew it couldn't last,' he said brokenly. 'Don't know why I bothered. Feel better now.'

'This way, Mr Dunn.' The policeman gave a sideways glance at his colleague. 'We only had your description arrive this morning. I wasn't sure.'

Dunn nodded. 'Feel better now.'

'Don't say anything, sir. Best not to, yet. You haven't been formally charged.'

Alfred Dunn's eyes took in the iron barred gates.

'Better now,' he repeated.

WEDNESDAY
11 September

Wednesday, 0930

Ian Russell munched contentedly on a piece of fried bread. No one could cook like Mrs Warrender but her fried bread was poetry even by *her* elevated standards; soft and fluffy inside, crisp and golden-brown outside. She had made him a plate of potato fritters and Spam cutlets, piping hot tea, and produced a ramekin of blackcurrants picked fresh from the garden. He hadn't been so hungry in days; not since he dug Mrs Dunn out of the ruins of Women's Surgical, anyway.

Everything was all right again.

Last night Dr Hawthorne had come to him and apologised, and when he passed the superintendent in the corridor an hour later the little man stopped and chatted with him in the friendliest fashion. He hadn't actually said he was sorry, but you couldn't expect a man in his position to admit he had spoken out of turn. The police were looking for Alfred Dunn, said the super, but so far without success. Ian was allowed to go home at two-thirty and he was in bed by three. By eight o'clock he was up, bathed and famished.

His father was finishing breakfast when Ian came down and there had been a brief, uncomfortable but very genuine offer of *pax*. It was no good expecting the old man to be something he wasn't, or could ever be, but he'd gone an awful long way towards setting the record straight. With much clearing of his throat, occasional blushes and his eyes fixed unwaveringly on his breakfast bloater, he'd opened his heart an eighth of an inch and confessed his pride in his son's achievement. He was also deeply aware of his failure to understand Ian's position; his . . . er hum . . . conscientious objections to taking human life. They must talk more about it, he said. Silence between grown men

265

never solved anything. Meanwhile — er hum, er hum — he had to call in at the bank on his way to Whitehall and he couldn't afford to be late because he had a very important technical conference at. . . . It didn't matter; Ian was too happy.

He munched on the last bite and lay back in his chair. Life could not more perfect be. Well, almost. . . .

Elsie Warrender's ear was attuned to the clink of knives and forks on china plates and she came in from the kitchen to fetch his 'empties' when he laid the cutlery to rest.

'Couldn't've had much sleep, Mr Ian,' she said busily.

'Don't really need it, Mrs W. I feel really quite good this morning.'

'Thank Gawd somebody do,' she retorted. 'Your dad's down in the mouth again and your mum ain't been this late to the table since she was ill last January twelvemonth.'

Elizabeth called from the stairs. 'Elsie? Is that you, dear?'

'Yes, madam dear,' shrieked Elsie, hurriedly tidying the cloth around the mistress's place-setting.

Elizabeth looked tired, strained. Elsie knew at once there was something wrong; she had put on make-up, dressed, and combed and brushed her hair. She was ready to go out.

'I wish somebody'd tell me what was going on in this house,' Elsie grumbled. 'Mister getting his own breakfast and you should see the mess he made. Mr Ian up early, too.'

Elizabeth turned on her son. 'Has Caroline phoned, Ian?'

He looked bemused. 'No, she hasn't. Why?'

'Nothing,' Elizabeth said absently. 'Finish your breakfast.'

'I have finished.'

'Mmmmm.'

Elsie and Ian looked at each other and the daily jerked her head meaningfully. Ian scraped back his chair. 'I think I might just go down to the hospital for an hour,' he said. 'Just to get some air.'

'Mmmmm,' said Elizabeth again.

When Ian had gone Elsie sat herself at the table. She rapped it hard with her knuckles. Elizabeth jumped.

'What're you worrying yourself sick about now then?' demanded Elsie.

Elizabeth stretched her lips resignedly. 'I didn't want people to get upset over nothing,' she said.

'Not doing much for you, is it? Come on, let's have it.'

Elizabeth studied her hands. 'Caroline said she was working last night. It's the first time she's had to work overnight so, when Charles got home at ten-thirty, I made him call her office — well, it's a sort of country house place — to see if she was all right.' She picked up a fork and twisted it in her fingers. 'She wasn't there. The duty officer said she left as usual at six o'clock. He said she wasn't on the duty roster for last night at all. Then he phoned her digs — but she wasn't there either.' She dropped the fork weakly. 'Honestly, Elsie, I don't know what to think. Where could she have gone?'

Elsie pursed her lips judicially. 'I can see what's in your mind, madam dear. Suspicions. Some young man you think it is, don't you?'

Elizabeth nodded numbly.

'Well,' Elsie squared her shoulders. 'It was bound to come, you can't say it wasn't. Twenty-three years old Miss Caroline is. I was married and nursing me first at her age.'

'She doesn't . . . *know* anything. She's so . . . naïve.'

'You were naïve yourself. So was I. Two days before I married my Jack I still thought babies come from under goosegog bushes; that's how much my mum told *me*. Miss Caroline's got a head on her shoulders. She wouldn't do nothing silly, not her.'

'You can't be *sure*. She's so impulsive.'

'Then there's nothing we can do except wait, is there? Now, what I'm going to do is make you a nice fresh cup of tea and a bit of toast and marmalade. All right?'

Elizabeth nodded helplessly.

'Course we will. She'll turn up. Mark my words.'

Ian propped his bicycle on the outer wall of the porter's lodge at St Thomas's and went in. Reg Poynter, the head day porter, was eating a jam tart and poring over the racing column of the *Daily Herald*. He looked up when Ian appeared in the door.

'What you doin' here this time of the day, lad?' he said, licking a wedge of strawberry jam from the corner of his mouth.

'Oh, just came out for some air,' Ian replied cheerfully. 'It's a lovely day.'

'In your place I'd be in my kip. Be on again at eight tonight, won't you?'

'Yes, Mr Poynter.'

'What I thought.' He made a mark on the open newspaper, then looked up again. 'Do me a favour, would you, lad?'

'Certainly. Anything you like.'

'They got some burn patients from last night up on F.5. Mr Sinclair ordered some dressings up from Hammersmith. They're in them three boxes. See? There in the corner. Take 'em up for us, would you?'

Ian grabbed the packages and made off along the corridor and up the stairs. He backed through the swing doors of F.5 and dropped the dressings on the day sister's desk.

'For Mr Sinclair,' he said. 'He ordered them. Dressings.'

'He's along the ward,' said the sister without looking up. 'Take them to him, there's a good chap. He could probably use some of them now. One box will do.'

He walked the length of the ward to a bed near the end where a canvas screen had been rolled into position. He stood outside it, waiting. Through a break in the canvas he could see Sinclair leaning across the bed and a nurse's hands clamped on a terribly burn-blistered arm. He looked away.

Suddenly, from behind the screen, came a piercing scream, a sound so terrifying it chilled the blood in his veins. He bent to peer through the crack in the canvas but from behind him a voice called hysterically, 'It's her arm! Oh, God—mind her arm!'

He swung on his heel so fast the box of dressings leaped from his hands and went skidding across the floor. Before his eyes found the face, he knew it was Caroline.

'But we thought you were working,' he said again. He was repeating himself for the third time in five minutes. She had refused to listen to him at first; not until he had gone to Mr Sinclair to ask if the woman was all right.

When she was convinced all was well, Caroline fell back on

268

her pillows, exhausted. Her face was heavily bruised and her shoulder and back bandaged. She wouldn't say why.

'We thought—'

'I know what you thought,' she said woodenly.

'But if you got bombed at Bletchley, why did they bring you here?'

'Oh, go away, Ian. Please!'

'But it's only luck I came in this morning. If I hadn't. . . .'

She stared at him blankly. 'I don't want you to get hurt. Just go away and leave me alone.'

He said impatiently, 'You're in shock. It's all right. I've seen it happen in burn cases before. Just relax and—'

'Go away!' She almost screamed. He looked up guiltily. The day sister was watching him sternly from her desk but she didn't get up.

'Look, Caroline. I've got to phone mother. She'll be out of her mind with worry if she doesn't know.'

Caroline conceded defeat. Tears welled into her eyes. 'Silly baby,' she choked. 'Silly baby.'

'I only want to help.'

'You can't help. Nobody can help. It's all gone wrong. They won't let me see her any more now.'

He looked perplexed. 'See who any more?'

'Yvonne.' She closed her eyes tightly against the flowing tears. 'Yvonne.'

He looked back across the ward towards the bed hidden behind the screens. 'The woman who screamed, you mean? That one over there?'

'Yvonne,' she sobbed.

'But I told you she'll be all right. Mr Sinclair's looking after her himself. He's a surgeon. Jolly good one, too.'

She stopped crying. Her mouth worked to choke back the tears. She sniffed. He gave her his handkerchief and she blew her nose.

'Phone mummy then. You have to, I can see that.'

'I won't if you don't want me to.'

'No. It doesn't matter. Tell her. She'll be worried.'

'Father will too.'

She brought the handkerchief to her face and staunched a renewed wave of sobbing. He waited for it to stop. She lowered the handkerchief at last.

'Would you let me . . . say something to you?'

'Anything. Anything at all,' he said eagerly.

'I don't think I'm going to be able to tell mummy, or . . . daddy. I don't know what to do but I have to tell someone.'

He felt deeply touched. 'Anything. Really. Anything.'

'When the bomb fell last night I was in a little flat off Black Prince Road. That's not far from here.'

'I know,' he said quickly, 'but. . . .'

'I wasn't working. That was . . . a lie. Stupid lie. When we left work yesterday I came home with Yvonne. I . . . stayed with her last night.'

His face registered blank incomprehension. 'But why? You could've practically walked home from Black Prince Road.'

She reached for his hand, found it, squeezed the fingers tightly. 'We were together when the bomb fell on the house.'

'It was rotten luck your both getting burned like that. I mean, fantastic you weren't killed but. . . .' He trailed off. 'I don't understand. Why didn't you come home? You could have called me here at the hospital. I'd have come to fetch you.'

She said softly, 'I wanted to be with Yvonne.'

'Yes, I know,' he said gently, 'but you shouldn't have put her to the trouble of making up a bed and. . . .'

Caroline's eyes were fixed on the ceiling. Her brow was smooth, her voice soft but firm. 'She didn't make up a bed, Ian.'

'Oh, you were still up, you mean?'

'No,' she said with great precision. 'We were both in her bed. Do you understand what I'm saying?'

Wednesday, 0945

Paul Warrender was wearing a tie. Worse, a jacket, a stiff-collared shirt, boots that shone and trousers with a crease in them he wished he could cut his throat with. As Derek Scully would have put it, a right Charlie. He still didn't know what it was all in aid of. The last time he'd been forced to get togged up like this was when Auntie Betty had been buried over at Basildon, but, as far as he knew, nobody in the family had snuffed it lately, so why all the dressing-up? The old man had spent half of last night ironing his warden's overalls and polishing his stupid helmet till it shone.

'Just you wait and see,' was all he would say when Paul asked him where they were going.

'Ready, lad?' Jack Warrender gave a final tug to the sleeves of his overalls and spat into his palm to flatten an imaginary stray wisp of hair at his temples.

Paul nodded glumly.

'He does look a right little toff,' said Flo Scully admiringly. The boy squirmed in the centre of the living-room. Auntie Flo had scrounged the clothes from the W.V.S. They didn't fit proper.

'Dad...,' pleaded Paul. Derek had gone out straight after breakfast. If he was to come back and see him like this. . . .

'Right,' said Jack. 'We're off. Sure you don't want to come?' He looked at Flo.

'Arthur's on at four,' she said. 'Has to start travelling at two. Travels so bad. Love to, though, if I had the time.'

'Pity Arthur's got to get his head down,' said Jack. 'Right up his street.'

'Dad!'

'Off we go then.'

Paul kept between his father and the wall as they walked to the top of the road, matching his pace exactly to obscure as much of himself as possible. They turned into Garnett Street. To his relief it was almost deserted. They crossed it and approached the church.

The girls were sitting on the wall outside Terry Rainbow's bicycle shop. The sweat oozed from Paul's collar.

'Er—dad? It'd be quicker if we took a short cut down one of the side roads,' he said desperately.

'Short cut? You don't know where we're off to,' said Jack. 'How can it be a short cut when you don't know where we're going?' He half stopped. 'Your mum didn't let it slip, did she? You haven't guessed?'

They were less than thirty feet from the girls but they hadn't seen him yet. They were giggling about something, jostling each other. There was still time. Rosie Taylor and that funny piece, Sylvia Somebody-or-other. Derek said she flashed herself on the swings over in Redriff Park. Right pair they were. Couldn't be worse. Paul's face was a mottled crimson.

'You all right, son?' Jack stuck a finger inside the lad's shirt collar. 'Not choking you, is it?' He wiggled it experimentally. 'S'all right. Excited, eh? Bit of a mystery? Won't keep you guessing for long.' He took out his Woolworth watch. 'Better step on it. Might miss 'em at this rate.'

It didn't matter any more. They'd seen him. The girls stopped giggling and watched in silence as they drew near.

The heavy serge jacket had become a suit of armour and his legs had forgotten how to walk properly. His tie was flashing like a circus clown's and his boots had begun to squeak. They had!

Squeak, squeak. He twisted them awkwardly, putting his weight on the instep.

Squeak, squeak.

Rosie nudged her friend, who choked and clapped a hand to her mouth. They stared at him poker-faced, bottling their mirth under bulging cheeks.

Squeak, squeak. His collar was crackling, his trousers scraped loudly against his legs. He could hear it! Squeak, crackle, rasp. They drew level with the girls. Rosie's lips formed a perfect tight circle of cheap cherry-red lipstick. She placed her hands on her hips and, arching her body, swooned into the shoulder of her friend, panting ferociously.

The other girl shook her head dreamily from side to side, eyes half closed. Then they both collapsed with laughter.

'Couple of young admirers you got there all right, son,' said Jack as a shrill wolf whistle followed them. 'See what dolling yourself up can do?' He chuckled. The back of Paul's neck was as bright as Rosie Taylor's lips, but the ordeal by fire wasn't over yet. The seat of his trousers hung baggily behind him and there was no way he could hitch them up without drawing attention to himself. He died slowly until they turned the corner. He was considering the relative possibilities of the Foreign Legion and the Merchant Navy when his father took him by the shoulder.

'Over there! Bet your boots! Spot on, we are. Knew they'd come this way.' He nodded towards an avenue of people formed up at the far end of the road. The crowd began to stir and jostle for position. 'Spot on!' repeated Jack Warrender with satisfaction.

If he fell ill, really ill, thought Paul, he would have to go to hospital and if it was bad enough by the time he came out they would have forgotten. Not even Rosie would take the micky out of somebody who had been ill, if it was bad enough. He tried a feeble cough.

'C'mon, Paul. Through there you go.' Jack Warrender grabbed Paul by the elbow and drew himself to his full height, flashing the helmet like a badge of office. Reluctantly, the crowd parted for him.

'There's the car. See? No number plates. Get it now?'

Paul felt the stirrings of ear-ache; definitely. His throat was sore as well.

'Blimey,' said his father excitedly. 'If only Arthur could see this. There, look! Not the car at the front, the other one. They're getting out now.'

Paul looked bleakly at the huge car. All around it were policemen and blokes in suits, only they didn't look as stupid as him because theirs fitted better than his did. There was a lot of rushing about opening car doors and waving of arms like there'd been an accident. Then another bloke with a fancy uniform got out with a plump woman dressed in bright blue. The crowd began to shout and clap and both of them smiled, looking round, embarrassed, as if they didn't know why they were there.

'There you are,' cried his father triumphantly. 'Got a good view, son?'

'What's happened?' Paul thought it was stupid but his dad had taken his helmet off and was holding it tight under his arm. What was occupying him now was the prospect of the walk back. They'd be waiting. Wouldn't turn down a chance like that. If him and dad was to cut across the back of Trotter Street and do a dogleg behind the church, they'd miss them. Unless, of course. . . .

'Happened?' Jack put his arm round the boy's shoulders in a clumsy gesture of solidarity. 'Tell you what's *happened*.' He broke off with a look of alarm. His face clouded. From the back of the crowd a group had begun to boo. 'Bloody Bolsheviks!' muttered Jack grimly. 'Bloody hell!' He craned his head to the rear for a better view and put on his helmet officiously.

'Any more of that,' he communicated to the person next to him, 'and I'll. . . .' He left the threat hanging in the air. But the booing died under the weight of rousing cheers as the couple walked forward from the car.

'They film stars or something?' said Paul with quickening interest. If they were he could tell the girls about it and that might take the edge off. Maybe he could get an autograph. He clutched at the straw.

'Film—!' His father laughed hugely. 'Bigger than your film stars, Paul. Ain't a film star born could hold a candle. . . .' He shook his head. Relented. 'That *there*,' he said proudly, 'is the King and Queen of England.' He looked down at his son as if he had presented him with a new three-speed racing bike.

'King and queen,' said Paul. 'What they doing here then?'

'They've come to have a look around. See how we're doing. The king and queen! Didn't expect that, did you? That's why I kept it secret.'

'What they here for?' asked the boy again.

'Told you, look around.' Jack pushed the boy forward. 'Here, get a good look, so's you can tell your mum. Take it all in.'

'Must be barmy,' said Paul. 'Coming here.'

His father didn't hear. He had taken off his helmet and was waving it with an accompanying 'Hooray.'

'Did they used to come here before then?' persisted Paul. He'd never seen his dad like this.

'First time to my knowledge,' said Jack. 'Here. Wave me helmet.'

The boy swung it limply. 'If they didn't come here before, what they come here now for?'

'Smart. He looks real smart!' said Jack. 'Now that's what I call smartness. That's a field-marshal's uniform, that is.' The couple had stopped at the barrier of people and the police were clearing a path for them.

'He's shaking hands. Half a mo. . . .'

Jack Warrender edged forward. The alert whined threateningly. The men in suits began to run around and, as the crowd fell silent, somebody in a blue uniform waved at the car and it swung in a semi-circle but became instantly hemmed in by the crush.

Jack Warrender sucked on the whistle he had placed between his teeth. This was tricky. In theory, he was still in charge when the sirens went but there was a lot of scrambled egg down there, not to mention the king and queen. The crowd began to break, flushed away by the police.

Someone spotted Jack's gleaming tin hat. 'You! Warden!' A finger beckoned.

'Warrender,' he said, breaking out of the crowd.

'Get these people out of here, Warrender,' said the man. His authority was beyond discussion. 'Move them out. No'—he looked around him—'shelter, is there? Shelter here, man?'

'End of the road. The police station.'

He was waved to silence. The man spun on his heel and spoke to someone at the king's shoulder. There was a heated debate, then the man looked back at Jack. 'Straight away, understand?'

Jack Warrender understood. With Paul trailing at his heels, he led the group along the street and into the police station. He stood back to let them pass. The desk sergeant jumped to his feet.

'Shelter!' snapped Jack. 'For Their Majesties.'

The sergeant grabbed his helmet, stuck it on his head and saluted. 'This way—er—sir.' He broke into a trot and led the way to a door. It opened on to a flight of steps leading to a basement. The group filed down. Jack and Paul brought up the rear.

The man who had given him his orders turned on the stair-way. 'What is this, Warrender?'

'Canteen, sir. I think,' hissed Jack.

'Good. Now then, Warrender. No more people down here. You stand guard here. Don't move an inch, understand? If you know where they can get that car under cover, tell them. The police will take care of everything else. All you have to do is guard this door. You won't have a more important job if you live to be a hundred. Clear?' The man looked up at him commandingly.

'You just leave it to me, sir.' Jack Warrender's jaw set firm.

'Oh, and by the way, can you get someone to make some tea?'

'Tea, sir?'

'Her Majesty has expressed a desire for tea,' said the man.

'Do what I can, sir.'

'Good man.'

'Paul?'

'What?'

'Tea.'

'You what?'

'Tea. The queen wants a cuppa tea. Nip down them stairs and tell one of the canteen women to make some tea. Tell 'em it's for the queen. Any funny business, they can come and see me. Go on then! Move!'

'Me?' Paul was open-mouthed. 'Down there?'

Jack Warrender glared at his son. 'Tea!' he snapped. 'You know what tea is, don't you?'

Wednesday, 1200

Palfrey, the Oxford don who had co-ordinated development of the 'leaf' incendiary, was droning his report on its success rate. Russell had already read the report, discussed it at length with Bomber Command liaison and agreed with them that the 'leaf' had only limited potential as a short-term irritant. Palfrey's baby was a celluloid card three inches square, in the centre of which was a hole containing an incendiary film enclosed in cotton wool. The cards — Berlin radio had chosen to call them 'leaves'

276

—were self-igniting and gave off an initial pulse flame about three feet high. The effects were mildly satisfactory but no more than that. They had been dropped on harvest fields; forests and dry pastureland in Westphalia, Hanover, the Harz mountains and southern and central Germany causing quite useful conflagrations. Unfortunately, their flames would ignite only light wood constructions, tinder-dry ground growth or trees. They had been designed for saturation use on military store dumps, arsenals and open trucks in railway marshalling yards.

Russell closed his ears to the monotone. He was feeling better, a little more sure of himself now. He had dropped into the bank in Piccadilly at ten o'clock and outlined his request to George Peterson. He had expected the indrawn breath, the shaking head, the tut-tut-tut of professional scepticism and he got it in full measure; but the introduction of Kingsley Mountford's name worked wonders and the revelation that the project already had Lochandry, Mountallan and Laughlan on the board clinched the bank manager's acquiescence. A project with war effort importance and such eminent City men on hand had obvious investment attractions. Yes, he thought two thousand *was* rather a lot in Russell's present situation but in view of the security offered by the house in Garfield Court and his impeccable borrowing record, the bank would be prepared to advance him the loan. Freddie Green's name never once entered the conversation.

'Of course,' droned Palfrey, without the slightest change of inflection, 'there were bound to be hazards. Maintaining the lightweight quality of the device, and therefore the effectiveness of its dispersal over wide areas, placed upon us the burden of. . . .'

The American, Shaffer, had called his secretary while he was at the bank and Russell had talked over his request with Leigh Ashton, the Director of Foreign Publicity at the Ministry of Information. Ashton confirmed Shaffer's credentials and urged 'careful co-operation'. It was important, he said, to bear in mind the Prime Minister's injunction that face-to-face interviews with pilots and aircrew were of doubtful propaganda value and if Shaffer's approach to Dowding involved a request of that nature the answer would be No. On the other hand, his was an influential voice just now and Winston was equally anxious to recruit American public opinion to the British view. Dowding himself had undoubted publicity potential if he was prepared to allow it to be harnessed.

'... higher, more strategic target yields hoped for, are not, as of this moment, visible. Nevertheless, the chief scientist assures me that, given more time. . . .'

That chat with Ian this morning had gone rather better than he could have hoped. Damn the boy for a thoughtless young ass, but that newspaper story. . . . He had mentioned it off-handedly to his secretary, knowing the speed of the office grapevine, and, within the hour, the news was all over White-hall. Brotherton, his counterpart at the Ministry of War, actu-ally called to ask if the 'hero of the hour' was indeed his son, and Mountford drifted in later to compliment him on a darned good show.

Now if only this confounded nonsense with Caroline could be cleared up, he would really begin to feel his old self. She was a good girl; *his* girl; there was too much good in her to be wasted on some ridiculous escapade. She had too much sense. Those calls, last night, to Bletchley, though . . . sinister. She was lying to them; that was clear enough, but Elizabeth, as usual, was over-reacting. Everything would work out for the best.

'Turning to the question of the combustible quality of the material used and the possibility of advancing the point of ignition. . . .'

His secretary appeared in the door and stood patiently, wait-ing to be noticed. Russell held up a hand and Palfrey dropped his papers to the table.

'Someone to see you, sir. They say it's very urgent.'

'Cabinet Office?' He had sent the P.M. a layman's outline on the 'seeing eye' equipment designed for installation in the new night interception aircraft, the Beaufighter, which De Havilland were now promising for operational use in October. The new secret weapon sounded impressive on paper but its prototype in use with the anti-aircraft defences was falling short of expectations.

'I don't think so. They just said it was very. . . .'

He sighed and got to his feet. 'Carry on, Palfrey. I apologise, gentlemen. I won't keep you long.'

There were two men waiting in his office; the elder was obviously an ex-officer. He wore a bowler, a dark coat, a regimental tie and his shoes were buffed to a perfect shine. The second man was twenty years younger; his anonymous raincoat was creased and old and belted too tightly at the waist. He held a battered brown trilby in one hand and a blue folder in the other. It was the younger man who spoke first.

'Charles Russell?'

'Yes.' He resented the omission of 'Mr'. Damned modern generation.

'We have a few questions for you.' No 'sir', either. Who the devil did the man think he was?

'I don't have the time. You'll have to make an appointment. Ask my secretary—'

'Please forgive the interruption, sir.' The older man inclined his head courteously. 'A matter of some importance. My name is Maconachie. This is Inspector Lubbock. We're both with the Security Police.'

Something cold crawled through Russell's bowels. Green? His involvement with Green? He should have given more thought to it; much more thought. Perhaps it was illegal; at the very least incompatible with his position at the Air Ministry. He clutched nervously at his tie and waved them both into chairs facing him across the desk. 'Ah—sit down, gentlemen. I'm afraid I can't offer you anything in the way of—'

Lubbock's intense, disagreeable face tightened. 'You hold a position of high trust here,' he rapped.

'I'm a permanent under-secretary to the—'

'Secrets pass across your desk regularly. All kinds of things.'

'They do, but I don't see what it has to do with—'

'With what?' The response was whiplash fast.

'With. . . .' He swallowed hard. 'With your work as— ah. . . .'

'You're in constant communication with the Prime Minister. With the Cabinet. With senior officers. With the Chief of the Imperial General Staff.' His questions were all unequivocal statements.

'Yes. Yes, I am.'

'You co-ordinate top secret work on weapons of war — torpedoes, bombs, detection devices, guns ... that kind of thing.'

'I do. But, look here — ah — Lubbock—'

'Do you ever take work home with you?'

'Sometimes. Not highly classified material, of course, but one can't do a job like this on a nine-to-five basis. But what's all this about?'

'You have a son Ian. He's registered as a conscientious objector.'

'I don't see what that. . . .'

'Where is your daughter Caroline?'

The question shocked him so completely he couldn't speak for several seconds. He said lamely, 'What do you mean?'

'You called Bletchley Park last night and asked to talk to her. She wasn't there and' — he consulted a paper in the blue folder — 'you gave the impression you expected her to be there. You asked the duty officer if he was sure your daughter wasn't working last night.'

Russell's hands were shaking and he could do nothing to stop them. 'A childish prank. The girl is—'

Lubbock consulted his file. 'Caroline Russell. Twenty-three years old, double first at Oxford.' He looked up. 'Childish prank?'

'I resent this. This is private family business and I have no intention of—'

'Where is she?'

Russell clamped his hands together in his lap. 'I don't know. I don't . . . know.' He felt weak. 'I think she might be having an affair. Dammit, I don't know.'

Lubbock shot a glare at Maconachie. He said icily, 'Your daughter, or a girl fitting your daughter's description, was seen between the hours of twelve forty-five and two-fifty at a public

280

house called The Baker's Arms in Milton Bassett.' He looked up again from the file. 'That's about sixteen miles from Bletchley Park. I take it' — his voice took on a pandering tone — 'you know what happens at Bletchley Park?'

'Yes.'

'Because you recommended your daughter to one of the scientists there?'

'Yes.'

Lubbock exchanged another look with Maconachie. The older man was stretched out easily in the chair, arms folded.

'Yesterday afternoon, following information received, the licensee of The Baker's Arms was taken for questioning to Buckingham police headquarters. He overheard a conversation over lunch in the garden of the public house between your daughter and a man in air force uniform. He was foolish enough to discuss what he heard in public.'

'Oh.' Russell had a mental picture of the scribbling block and the indented writing he had exposed with whisky and carbon. So he was a flyer, was he? Just the sort of romantic nonsense she'd fall for! Damn her stupidity; her blind *naïveté*. The swine was probably married into the bargain.

'Do you know who that man might be?'

'No. I don't.'

'No idea at all?' Disbelief underscored every vowel.

'None! I said, no!'

'I see. In the course of her conversation over lunch, the woman answering your daughter's description talked about her work at Bletchley Park.'

'Nonsense! That's absolute rubbish. Caroline's totally aware of the obligations imposed—'

'She mentioned . . . secrets. She talked about being unhappy. I imagine you know that she's engaged on top secret work. You might also know it's so secret even my colleague and I can't be told what it is.' Lubbock's stare was piercing; his eyes seemed to cut through to the back of Russell's brain.

'She just wouldn't do anything stupid, if that's what you're implying. I know her.'

'But you don't know she has a *friend* who meets her for lunch

281

at a country pub and you don't know where she was last night and you don't know where she is now. How well *do* you know your daughter?'

'Damn you! That's inexcusable!'

Lubbock sniffed, unaffected. 'Your daughter has discussed in public matters covered by the Official Secrets Act nineteen—'

'You don't *know*. Not for sure.'

Lubbock flicked up another page in his file. 'Austin Utility van, number 45 HB 66, signed out at Bletchley Park motor pool by Leading Aircraftsman J. Turner to Miss Caroline Russell, Technical Wing.' He looked into Russell's eyes. 'Signed out 1200 hours, signed in 1528 hours yesterday. Mileage recorded would cover a drive to Milton Bassett.'

'But you can't take the word of a common publican.'

Lubbock's face drained white. He controlled himself with some difficulty.

'We don't take people's words for anything.' He lowered his eyes deliberately, then flashed them head-on again. 'Not even yours.'

Russell flinched. 'I meant—' he began.

Maconachie said quietly, 'The publican knew nothing, Mr Russell. He just heard something he didn't understand and tried to make himself important by bragging about it. He bragged to the wrong man.' He wrinkled his nose. 'The village constable.'

'Well, there you are then. She—'

'It was your daughter all right. And she used the word secrets. She was clearly discussing Bletchley. Now, that's a potentially indictable offence, you see. I don't have to tell you why. Important thing now is to find that chap she had lunch with. I saw your face when Lubbock brought it up; you've suspected something . . . an affair, you said.'

Russell nodded heavily.

'No idea who he is?'

'No.' He couldn't bring himself to tell them about that poem. God – what on earth had possessed her?

'Ah.' Maconachie looked regretfully at his companion. 'I'm afraid we'll have to ask you to accompany us to Bow Street, sir,' he said. 'We'll need a statement and it'll have to be given in the presence of two witnesses other than Lubbock and myself.'

Russell reached for the phone but Lubbock craned across the desk and clamped his hand across the receiver. 'No phone calls. You'll have the right, later on, to call a solicitor and you'll be able to consult him before you make any statement involving your daughter. Meanwhile—'

'I was going to call my wife to see if she'd heard from Caroline. She might be. . . .'

The two Special Branch men eyed each other warily.

Maconachie said apologetically, 'Sorry to have to put you through that, sir. Your daughter's in hospital. No – she's all right. Slight burns, nothing serious.'

Russell recoiled in his chair, his mouth wide with shock. 'But why didn't you say so at the beginning? My God, man, I want to see her. Where is she? What hospital?'

Lubbock said sharply, 'You can't see her yet. Not yet. Later today, maybe. We need a statement from her first.'

'But how did she. . . ?'

'She was found in a burning house in Black Prince Road, just off the Albert Embankment. Several flats there, mostly bed-sitters. Firemen pulled her out and took her to—' He stopped.

Russell glared at him uncomprehendingly. 'Black Prince Road? What was she doing there? What. . . ?' He stopped himself. The flyer! They'd been. . . . He said, 'How? I mean . . . where was she found?'

Lubbock's lips parted then clamped tight again. 'She was in bed at the time. Bedclothes caught fire. She was lucky. If there'd—'

'Was she . . . alone? In the bed?' Russell blundered on.

'No, sir,' said Maconachie gently. 'She wasn't. The other . . . occupant of the bed is also in hospital.'

'Who is he? In the name of God, who is he? I want to know his name. I'll have him cashiered. I'll have him—'

The Security men said nothing for the space of ten seconds, then Lubbock sought refuge in the blue file.

'Wasn't a man, Mr Russell.' He sounded almost sympathetic.

283

'Woman name of Yvonne Coutance. French. She works at Bletchley Park too. Cryptographer.'

'But I don't understand.' For a moment he scented a reprieve, relief from the nightmare, then the hideous implication of it flooded him. He smashed his hands to his cheeks.

Maconachie banged home the final nail. 'I'm sorry, sir. Really terribly sorry. But we have our duty to do. Your work is crucial to the war effort, too important to take chances with. For the time being, until we can get this thing sorted out, I'm required to tell you that you must consider yourself under suspension. You'll be permitted to go home if you'll give us your parole but I can't allow you to return to this office. You will seek no contact with any member of any ministry or government or service agency and you'll tell your family nothing. In the meantime, your work here will be carried on by your deputy.'

He collapsed downwards into the chair; sat there, waiting for salvation. None came. The two men looked down at him and Lubbock made a gesturing motion with the fingers of one hand.

Russell raised his eyes. 'I still have a meeting going on in there,' he said helplessly.

Wednesday, 1300

The weather, a defensive shield since before dawn, had begun to fragment with each penetrating ray of sunshine. At Bentley Priory much of the morning had been given over to tracking Luftwaffe reconnaissance aircraft. After the bombardment of last night it was, as one wag put it, like shooing seagulls off the deck of the *Titanic*. For over an hour three Spitfire squadrons had searched for an interloper who had been tracked across half a dozen counties, only to find it was an R.A.F. Blenheim. The R.T. waves had crackled with a number of highly spiced suggestions on the subject of what Operations Control could tell the Observer Corps to do with their binoculars.

It had, if nothing else, reduced the tension. In the next few hours, if the pattern of the last few days held true, there would be little opportunity for banter in the face of Goering's afternoon visitors. The first counters in the roulette game were already neatly stacked to one side of the grid-ironed tracking table in the Filter Room and the girls stood ready to be called into play.

Tom Russell had taken advantage of the lull to borrow a typewriter for half an hour. Laboriously, he drafted the letter he had been mulling over for days. If he had had any doubts about the decision, they were dispelled by the reports of last night's losses. Pilots were at a premium and he was a natural pilot, not a damned croupier.

... and therefore, though aware of the critical role played by the officers and staff at Bentley Priory, and not wishing in any way to imply that my request reflects other than gratitude at having shared in the overall effort. ...

He rested his fingers. One mistake now and he wouldn't have time to start again until tomorrow.

They were scraping up pilots from anywhere; flying schools, aero clubs, cadet training units — and they weren't far from the bottom of the barrel. In the two weeks from 24 August to 6 September — last Friday — Fighter Command had lost 295 kites. Another 117 were little more than colanders. One hundred and three fighter pilots killed, 128 wounded; and Dowding had less then 1,000 pilots left to juggle with. The Command was losing one tenth of its effectiveness *each week*. At that rate it would all be over in a couple of months. No matter how fast Beaverbrook whipped them off the production lines, planes were so much furniture without pilots to sit in them.

In August a new crop of trainees had been wheeled out of the operational training units; kids again. But there were no skirmishes awaiting them as they had been promised, no Red Baron 'blooding' in one-to-one combat. Those kids had gone down still wet behind the ears, bounced out of the sky by storms of Me109's flown by experienced Luftwaffe pilots whose fuel gauges told them they had half an hour to fight before turning for home and no time for personal heroics. The kids hadn't even learned to stay alive. No wonder Dowding had avoided a slug ging match with the Luftwaffe; all he would have had left were coloured counters to play with.

'. . . I feel I must stress my desire to be part, not of the larger, but the smaller sphere. . . .'

The Brylcreem Boys. After Dunkirk, that was what the army called them. Brylcreem Boys. It must have looked that way to troops on the beaches, stupefied with lack of sleep and unprotected as the Stukas whistled around them virtually unmolested.

Dowding again; refusing to be drawn, knowing how little he had. First France and then Dunkirk. Dowding's battle with the Air Staff over the question of defending France had done more for him in Fighter Command than anything else — at least among those who were prepared to view the picture as he saw it. Three hundred R.A.F. pilots had been either killed, wounded or captured in that débâcle, and still the French had asked for more. He'd stuck his chin out then, no matter what they said about him; stuck it out at a time when even Churchill was dithering under the weight of contradictory advice from every side. The battle is to come, he had written to the Air Staff. The fighters were needed at home. Dowding had won and Churchill concurred. The French High Command saw it as a monstrous sell out — and used it to justify their final capitulation to the Germans.

With some regret, then, I feel my contribution may be more properly exercised in the role for which I was originally trained. I shall willingly accept any active station you consider me best suited for. I await your advice and trust that the inspiration for this request is seen not as dissatisfaction with my present post, but rather. . . .

Rather what? Boredom? No, more than that. An appetite for excitement? Glory? Precious little of that, either. Sleeping in stinking flying boots and moth-eaten parkas in some dingy cardboard hut or draughty tent was a long way from glory.

So *what* then?

Tom Russell's two fingers poised over the keys. He looked at his notes. Maybe he had gone too far. The whole damn letter was already pompous enough. Oh, well.

'. . . but rather as a need, in the Prime Minister's words, to "take one of them with us!" '

It wasn't right. He'd never been good at letters. That was Ian's field. But it would have to do. He addressed it to his commanding officer and sealed it quickly.

Wednesday, 1315

Shaffer walked through to the American correspondents' special bar behind the Embankment entrance of the Savoy Hotel. It was packed. Edward Angley was talking heatedly with Larry LeSueur and Ben Robertson but he came across at once when he spotted Shaffer.

'I better warn you we'll be playing dirty,' he said pugnaciously. 'Couple of the guys invited Harold Nicolson to lunch and they're bringing him down here for a drink first. He won't like it.'

Shaffer shrugged. 'What can he say? He's on our side, isn't he?'

'Unofficially. Duff Cooper makes the rules.'

'You should've kidnapped *him* then.'

'Fat chance.'

Angley went to the bar and bought a couple of beers. He brought them back and they found a table. 'We're getting the bum's rush all over. Syd Williams was down in the East End for U.P. this morning. The king and queen were on a tour and he was a bit late. He saw the crowds in the street but no royals. When he asked around someone said they just disappeared.' He took a swallow of beer. 'The alert had just gone. Syd kept looking and a couple of plainclothes cops showed him off the premises.'

'So they took shelter somewhere.'

'So O.K. – why keep it under wraps? Anyway, Knickerbocker got the same thing down at St Paul's. He was just cruising around and there was this Royal Navy bomb crew and all the rest at the bottom of the cathedral steps. They wouldn't let him within a hundred yards. It's crazy. The ministry guys won't say a thing, either.'

'The key point syndrome,' Shaffer said. 'There isn't a square foot of this town they can drop a bomb in that doesn't have a key point within spitting distance. The way they see it, publicising what got hit just tells the Luftwaffe how close they got to the target.'

'So they say,' growled Angley. 'But we're not here to feed people with guessing games. Anyway, the British lose out in the end. Talk about miles of rubble and burning real estate and people back home get a picture of the whole damn town lying in ruins. Censorship works two ways, Mel.'

He got to his feet as Ray Daniel and William Humphreys of Associated Press entered the room with Harold Nicolson between them. The crowd at the bar parted and Daniel urged his guest forward. Nicolson was what Murrow had described as 'artistically impeccable'. His dark-blue suit was set off by a blue polka-dot handkerchief, a white shirt and a floral tie almost American in its intensity. The thinning hair qualified him for the role of hard-pressed parliamentary secretary but soft eyes, a generous mouth and flailing Gallic hands marked down the writer and dreamer. He clearly felt at home among them.

They shared a couple of jokes, a raucous toast was drunk to Hitler's downfall and another round was ordered. Ray Daniel called for white wine; German, as it happened, since, like most hotels in London, the Savoy had been forced to stock what they could get when the French wine industry began to run down in 1939.

Edward Angley reached forward and clinked Nicolson's glass with his own. 'Toast, Harold. How about one to . . . the Ministry of Misinformation?'

Nicolson's smile faded, hung troubled between incomprehension and distrust, then bloomed again. 'I don't think I get the point of that, Ted,' he said pleasantly.

Angley looked down at his feet. 'You get it all right.'

Ray Daniel chipped in. 'O.K., Harold, you're covered. Nobody leave the room.'

The bar echoed with laughter, including Nicolson's. When it subsided the Englishman raised his glass. 'To better times.' They sipped uneasily. Nicolson faced Bill Humphreys. 'I have the feeling I'm being — what's your expression? — set up?'

Humphreys glared across the bar at Angley. 'You're on the team, Harold. We just needed to talk, that's all.'

'We're always talking. Aren't we?'

James Reston, the *New York Times* correspondent, settled himself on the edge of a table. 'It's not the talk, Harold. It's where it gets us. Since Sunday night your people have been making our jobs as near as dammit impossible. Now we know word has gone down the line to the censors to cut back on strategic facts. That much we go along with. But the way they're *interpreting* the rules is crazy. We'd like to talk about that.'

'I can't deal in emotive speculation,' Nicolson said uneasily. 'Why don't you try to be specific.'

A dozen voices opened up in unison and Angley held his hands in the air. 'Hold it. One at a time. Syd?'

Sydney Williams hooked a thumb over his back. 'Why'd the police throw me out of the royal tour of the East End just now?'

Nicolson registered concern. 'I can't imagine. What happened?' Williams told him. Nicolson produced a small looseleaf notebook from his inner pocket and wrote swiftly. 'I'll look into that.'

Reston drawled, 'Add the St Paul's Cathedral time-bomb to your list, Harold. Same kind of situation. What're you hiding down there?'

Nicolson's pen hesitated over the paper fractionally then flowed on. A half-dozen other cases of aborted coverage went into the notebook. He looked up. 'I can't explain any of these at the moment but I'll do what I can. I warn you, though — there might be valid explanations and I may have to tell you there's nothing to say. Don't expect me to breach the rules.'

Shaffer snapped the Zippo to a cigarette. 'We're getting nowhere over here, Harold. We're in the middle of the biggest bombardment in history — and one that reflects well on the British — and we're tied hand and foot. I don't see the point. We can't run emotive speculation in place of news.' There was a titter at his manipulation of the government man's phrase.

'The point', said Nicolson gently, 'is that you want more than it's safe for us to give.'

'Safe nothing!' snapped Angley. 'The Luftwaffe were over London four times yesterday, photographing the damage of the night before. I bet they know more than you do, right now, about what's busted and what isn't.'

Nicolson straightened visibly. 'You know as well as I do, Ted, that what you file to America doesn't just rest there. It's picked up by British — and German — correspondents in New York and sent straight back to base. As far as the Germans are concerned, Goering's getting enough of it his way without our helping him further.'

'And the British papers?' drawled Daniel.

'Don't be deliberately myopic, Ray,' Nicolson snapped. 'The British papers work under tighter reporting restrictions than yours — but we can hardly prevent them publishing extracts from *American* papers, can we? We have morale to protect; national morale. You don't protect your people by pouring down their throats every detail of every outrage with names, dates and addresses.' He turned away angrily, then swung back again. 'The way things are in Fleet Street at this moment, the British Press is a bigger nuisance than Hitler.'

'Can I quote you on that, Harold?' someone asked lightly.

Daniel slammed his hand palm flat on the bar. 'You go ahead and quote anything you hear in this room and I'll personally beat the shit out of you.'

He put a hand on Nicolson's sleeve. 'O.K., Harold. This is Bumsville, U.S.A. It was a lousy trick we pulled and I'm personally sorry it had to be you. You're one of the few guys in that jam factory down there who understands our problems. We don't just want to *talk* about them; we want them solved. We want the right to publish information, as and when it happens.'

'But that's what you get,' protested Nicolson mildly.

'We get the bombing of the invasion ports on Sunday, three days late,' said Shaffer. 'Who were you protecting there? The population of Berlin?'

'Just a minute, Mel,' said Daniel. 'Harold, you've been around the Civil Service beat long enough to know what happens when some guy at the top sends a set of rules down to some guys at the bottom. Every level they pass through, the rules get multiplied by two. Time you get to the bottom, you can't see the intention for the letter. We're asking you. Please — go back there and take a look at the way the censors are playing the rule-book.'

Nicolson stared around him at their faces. 'All right,' he said at last. 'I'll take a look. If we are guilty of over-interpretation, I'll get something done, I promise you.' He raised his glass again and studied the half-inch of lemon-bright wine. 'I repeat. To better times.'

They all drank. The Americans were busily restoring a social atmosphere when the barman tugged at Daniel's sleeve. 'Call for you, sir,' he said, pointing to the booth in the corner.

Two minutes later Daniel came back to join the group. His face was set hard. He reached for his glass and raised it in Nicolson's face. 'To better days, Harold, just like you said. But don't hold your breath.'

Nicolson raised an elegantly quizzical brow.

Daniel gestured to the telephone. 'Leigh Ashton's called a Press conference for two-thirty. Priority. Wouldn't say what the hell it is but he didn't have to. My office took a call from New York two minutes ago. Message just reached them over the tickertape from London. It says the Germans bombed Buckingham Palace Monday night. There's an embargo on the information for two hours. You want to comment, Harold?'

Wednesday, 1415

With a croak of tortured metal the mechanical digger bent and scooped, bent and scooped, a parody of a skeletal water-bird dipping for food. Swinging unsteadily, it choked, shook, swallowed and regurgitated brick and stone and wood and glass into the backs of waiting lorries. A bulldozer jerked forward as its back was turned and retreated, leaving another pile of debris.

Bend, scoop, swing, shudder, jerk, swing, scooooop. . . .

'Doing a good job, them demolition lads,' said Arthur Scully over the noise. 'Good job,' he repeated awkwardly, as if unsure that he had chosen the right words. 'All the same, bloody heart-breaking.'

'They take it out to Sheppey; somewhere like that,' said Jack Warrender.

The two men were standing on the pavement outside the Scully house watching the removal of the remains of Baltic Street. The lorries, diggers and bulldozers had moved in at dawn and were now nibbling at the sandwich of rubbish of what had once been the Warrenders' home. Beyond it stretched an anti-septic swab of levelled ground where the rest of the row had been. It seemed to hold more promise than regret.

'Sheppey,' said Jack Warrender. 'All this goes out there, dumped in the marshes. New towns built on it one day. Funny to think of a bit of my house under somebody else's.' He shook his head. 'Wonder what's under all that lot? Never found half the stuff. Few pots of Elsie's, couple of pairs of trousers. Found me razor.' He pointed at the digger. 'Just where he's having a go now, lying there, it was. Good razor, too. Blade sharp as a whistle. Got something else they don't know about.' He grinned at Arthur. 'Our Glad's bag. Full of bits and pieces. Gawd, you ought to see it — jars of this, tubes of that. Stuck under a bit of bedstead. You see her face when I give her that. House going she can take, but without her "face" she's like a lost soul. I've hung on to it. Shouldn't have, really, but it'll be like giving her a Christmas present. Better'n anything I could've bought. Daft, ain't it?'

A shattered wireless slipped from the jaws of the digger and disappeared into the quicksand.

Arthur felt uncomfortable. He still wasn't sure about Jack. No doubt of it — he'd been going barmy when he talked to him in the kitchen of Number 14 a couple of days back, but suddenly he'd changed. Arthur couldn't be sure if he was just barmier or flat exhausted. Watching his home being carted away like a dustbin full of rubbish didn't seem to worry him at all. He hadn't mentioned his job or what had happened to him in the docks; all that stuff about Charlie and the files he'd burned. Nothing.

'Takes some; leaves others, Jack,' he said. 'Look at that. Stopped right against our wall. Could've been in that lot, you, Elsie, Paul.' He nodded sagely. 'Lucky, Jack. Bloody lucky. Makes you think.'

Jack shook his head. 'Don't worry me. Should, but it don't.'

'Bloody war,' said Arthur Scully. It wasn't a clean bloody war any more. Somehow it was different up on the Annexe roof, with *Churchill* there; everything seemed to make sense; war was *war*. But this wasn't what Winston had to deal with – fractured gas mains, burst water pipes, half-cold meals. No meals at all. The Warrenders losing their house, girls sobbing over lost hand-bags, kids searching for toys in rubbish heaps. It wasn't armies any more; men fighting men. It wasn't war.

In the living-room Arthur poured them brown ale in cups. It was warm and flat. Jack rolled his shirt-sleeves up to the elbow. Sipped. Nodded. Wiped an imaginary moustache of foam from his mouth and winked at Arthur. They gave themselves to the job in hand, making it last.

'Dunn,' said Arthur. He used the word savagely. 'You talk to Alf Dunn about Derek? And your Paul? Right bloody mate *he* turned out to be.'

'Alf ain't that bad,' said Jack mildly. 'All right, bit queer – pushing off like that, but, well. . . . He did some good work. As a warden. Give him that. There's no saying he wasn't right about them kids, Arthur. Just trying to tip us the wink.'

Arthur Scully simmered over his beer. 'Maybe you're right. Wouldn't like to say. Couldn't stand the bloke meself – never could; never will. So what do we do? I had a word with Derek. He denied it, o'course. Point blank.' He shook his head and his voice dropped. 'He was lying. You talked to Paul?'

'He wouldn't say anything, either. Just clammed up like he did with you. Shouldn't be saying it, you being the boy's father, but Derek's the one who always starts things off. We both know that. Paul just tags on. Course he's as much to blame. . . .'

Arthur drummed a fist gently on the table. 'No, you don't have to make allowances. I've been thinking about Derek a lot the last few days. I've had me eyes shut to him too long. Haven't watched the way he's going. Can't blame Flo, she's had enough on her hands. Can't blame the boy, either, s'pose. If the blame lies anywhere it's with me, fair and square.'

'Can't blame yourself. Young lads go their own way, whether you like it or not.'

'Got no respect, that's the root of it. I can see it when I talk to him. One thing I always had was respect for me elders and betters. Rank, I mean. Authority. We all have to face up to it in the end. Best to do it with good grace. That way you have a right to it yourself. With Derek. . . .'

'Paul's the same,' said Jack, desperately anxious to shoulder some of the blame. 'When I took him to see the king and queen.' He paused. Maybe this wasn't the right time to regale Arthur with the more impressive circumstances of the occasion. 'Just up the manor. Think it meant anything to him? Just stood there, he did. Not a flicker.' He sipped his beer. 'Times change, Arthur. Changing so fast now you can't keep up. After this lot, respect'll be a thing of the past.'

'Wouldn't argue with that. But Derek's getting to be a bloody handful. Needed a heavy hand from the start, he did. Same old story, ennit? Came home on leave after a year away, spent two weeks with Flo and got called back. Next thing I know, Flo's carrying. Didn't see the lad till he was seven months old. After that it was a week here, week there. Bloody good life, the Marines, don't get me wrong. But not for Flo and the boy. Sometimes feel I never was his father, not proper.'

Jack Warrender downed the rest of his beer in a gulp. Alfred Dunn's collection of pictures of Derek Scully; the physical resemblance — it all added up. But what point was there now in blurting it out?

'Lack of kip,' said Jack. 'What've you had since you got home? Three, four hours? Them blasted ack-ack guns are enough to drive you daft. That's what it is, take it from me. You're a bit low. We all are.' He clung to the straw. 'Ever see the buggers hit anything?' He swung the contents of his cup with a circular motion, swilling the beer around.

Arthur nodded glumly. 'When the bombing started, this last

lot I mean, I thought: right then, here we go. Here comes your knockout punch. If we're left standing afterwards, Jerry may as well pack up. Well, we didn't go down for ten, Jack, never thought we would, but up town there's a lot of talk. You get to hear things. What I'm trying to say — and don't get me wrong — is, if this lot goes on much longer the spirit's going to be knocked out of us before we get a chance to hit back. You heard about them barges across the Channel? Word is they could invade any time. Word is' — he leaned closer, unable to resist the temptation to repeat a heresy — 'we wouldn't stand a chance. Jerry would be in London in seventy-two hours once they got ashore. And what's between here and the coast to stop 'em? Some of the brass, the top brass, are beginning to argue with the Old Man. See it in their faces when they leave him. Black as thunder.' He shook himself. 'Bet your boots he's got something up his sleeve, though, old bugger. Softly softly catchee monkee. Next couple of days, eh, Jack?' He hoisted himself to his feet. 'The old one-two!' he said, punching air.

'The old one-two,' repeated Jack Warrender loyally.

The picture of Derek Scully wouldn't go away.

Wednesday, 1415

Shaffer reached the Ministry of Information in Bloomsbury a quarter hour early. He had left the Savoy immediately Ray Daniel broke the news and had driven to the office in Hill Street. O'Keefe came on the phone briefly, demanded to know what the hell the Limeys thought they were playing at but signed off when Shaffer told him a Press conference had been called for two-thirty.

It was a bizarre situation. The news of the explosion of a time-bomb at Buckingham Palace in the early hours of Tuesday morning had hit the tapes in New York at 9.41 eastern daylight time. It was followed by a special note to editors: 'The above story must be held in strict confidence until 11.30 a.m. eastern daylight time.' O'Keefe and a dozen city editors in New York were gnawing their finger ends to the bone; the delay meant the story would be too late for the main news bulletins or the early editions of the afternoon papers. The British Embassy in Washington couldn't say what the delay implied.

Shaffer spotted Jim Brebner, the director of the News Division, as he crossed the lofty marbled main hall of the university building. He went over to shake hands. Brebner introduced a slim, elegant, good-looking young man with whom he'd been in earnest conversation.

'You know Tom Driberg, I suppose?'

Shaffer did, but only by reputation. Driberg was the real name and the deft, acidulous hand behind William Hickey, the social columnist of the London *Daily Express*. He was also one of Lord Beaverbrook's golden boys and a hardworking acolyte in his master's causes. It was no coincidence that Beaverbrook regarded the Ministry of Information as a rest home for incompetent milksops, and that the abrasive Hickey column was constantly firing barbs into the ministry's thick, but sensitive, hide. Driberg's fine-boned narrow face broke into a smile; it made him look ridiculously young.

'Come to do battle with the troglodytes?'

'Thanks a lot,' said Brebner with mock severity. 'It's nice to know we're loved and respected down here.'

Driberg laid a hand on his shoulder. 'Of course you are. Fêted on all sides. Lauded. Applauded.' He made a show of admiring his own dialogue. 'I must remember that for later. They like to be told they're wonderful, you know, and one runs out of ways of saying it.'

'What's the hold-up?' Shaffer asked Brebner shortly.

Brebner looked uncomfortable. 'Perhaps you'd better come down to Room Eight till Duff arrives.'

'Aha!' drawled Driberg accusingly. 'Sticking you out of sight, out of mind. What d'you know, Shaffer, that's so dangerous?'

Brebner drew them both towards the stairs leading down to the bomb-proof, gas-proof, air-conditioned War Room of the ministry. 'Later, Tom,' he cautioned. 'Let's go where it's less public, shall we?'

The War Room had the reputation of being the safest hole in the ground in all London, a fact which the British Press had found worth recording more than once. Its staff maintained contact with the inside world of government, civil defence, the services, and acted as go-betweens and sieves for the outside world of newspapers and radio. In a line across the centre of the room were the 'pig pens', private phone boxes with direct lines to the Foreign Office, the War Office, Admiralty, Air Ministry and other strategic departments of government. Nearby, other pens held six reserve switchboards in case the central exchange was put out of action. A tall, thin, elderly man was lying back in his chair in the Foreign Office pen and Brebner bid him good afternoon and introduced the two journalists.

Driberg commented sympathetically on his narrow little world, hedged in like a latterday Prisoner of Zenda. 'Yes, indeed,' said the Foreign Office man languidly. 'Any night you can see an admiral, a general, a senior civil servant and one of our own mandarins sitting in a row in these little boxes. I always feel as if we were the opening scene in a revue — about to step out simultaneously and sing a number.'

Brebner urged them through to Room Eight, the Press Room, and its serried ranks of chattering teleprinters. He led them to an office behind a glass screen plastered with newspaper cuttings and fading brown and yellow official communiqués. He dropped into a chair.

'All right, Tom. You can listen but not talk. You're here as a guest.'

Shaffer raised an eyebrow quizzically. 'Guest?'

'His master wants him to write about the way we work, so Tom came down for this Press conference Duff Cooper's giving for American correspondents and Fleet Street editors.'

'You'll note the billing there,' Driberg interposed mischievously. 'American correspondents are infinitely more important.'

'You mean you haven't put it out to Fleet Street yet?'

'Only to editors,' Brebner said cautiously.

'Let me into the circle,' protested Driberg. 'What is *it*?'

Brebner shrugged. Shaffer said, 'A time-bomb exploded on Buckingham Palace early Tuesday.'

Driberg came upright in his chair. 'I don't believe it.'

'Well?' Shaffer aimed at Brebner.

297

'It's true enough.'

'Then why the block on releasing the story in New York?'

'What block?' Driberg snapped.

'Came out on the tapes at 9.41 New York time with a qualifier to hold publication till 11.30. No explanation.'

'Aaaah. I think I see.' Driberg's eyes glittered. 'America's more important but some jug-eared buffoon over here — and maybe not a million miles from where we're sitting right now — this buffoon realises he has to tell the British Press too. So he gives America a racing start and keeps Fleet Street waiting so both stories come out at roughly the same time. Am I warm, Jim?'

Brebner groaned. 'Don't ask me. I only work here.'

'What happens now?' Shaffer pressed.

'There's a facility for one American, one British reporter to look at the damage at three-fifteen, then they share their information through me for general news bulletins and stories and, later on, the rest can go to the palace for feature material. That's the plan.'

'I volunteer,' said Driberg quickly.

'No, you don't,' Brebner retorted. 'You're a guest.'

'How about me?' Shaffer rapped.

'O.K., I suppose. First come. We'd only have pulled names out of a hat. The easiest way will be to send the Press Association man with you for Fleet Street. He's upstairs now. I've just seen him.'

'Can you get a hold of him? Now, I mean? I'd like to skip the Press conference and check with my office before we go to the palace.'

'I bet you would,' sighed Driberg regretfully.

In an attempt at a short-cut to High Holborn through the narrow artery of Lamb's Conduit Street, Shaffer was caught in a mile-long traffic jam. A horse had collapsed and died in the shafts of the milk-float it was pulling and had, as its last gesture to deserving humanity, overturned itself, the float and several hundred pint bottles of milk. By the time the mess was cleared, he was too late for a diversion to Hill Street and drove directly to the palace. He stopped the car by a phone box in Birdcage Walk and called Mrs Price.

She was, she said, out of her mind with worry. Mr O'Keefe had just called again with a message. A flash had just been received over the tapes from Berlin claiming that Buckingham Palace had been bombed by the Luftwaffe. A.B.N. and everyone else in New York intended to use the German version of the story right away. The British embargo still had thirty-five minutes to run before it could be lifted. No one was prepared to wait.

Were they all right? pleaded Mrs Price. Were the king and queen safe?

'They were walking in the East End this morning,' Shaffer said, flashing a look at his watch. 'Don't worry. They're fine.'

He drove to the gates of the palace, showed his accreditation and Brebner's rubber-stamped ministry pass, and was allowed to drive into the courtyard and park under the south-west wall. He saw the Press Association man waiting by the arch under the stern eye of a police inspector and joined him. They were taken through the Quadrangle to the main entrance. All Shaffer could see at this stage was a couple of shattered windows and a few pools of glass.

An equerry in naval uniform welcomed them with not too much enthusiasm and led them along dark, carpeted corridors to what he described, with a flourish, as the Belgian Suite. Everything in the room – mantels, chairs, couches, tables, pictures and ornaments – lay under a choking layer of white dust and flaked plaster. Two men stood talking in the centre of the room and one of them came forward and shook the newsmen by the hand. He was tall and pink and sandy-haired and wore a silver pencil on a loop around his neck.

'Brebner sent you, did he? Good. I've been told to show you round. Been piecing things together.' He ushered them to the window. 'Bomb fell out there, near as we can guess at about 0140 in the early hours of Tuesday morning. Think it was a two hundred and fifty pounder. Obviously a deliberate attempt on the lives of Their Majesties.' He looked very solemn. 'It went down about ten feet out on the terrace, there; you can see where it forced up the stone slabs.'

They went outside into the sunshine. The lovely little green world hidden from the public behind the high walls was a revelation. Wide stone steps ran down from the terrace to lawns of the finest, smoothest Cumberland turf and then to a setting of trees and stream and bridge and winding paths and lavishly cultivated flowerbeds. The ministry guide, following Shaffer's eye, grabbed his arm and turned him to the business at hand.

'What do you think of that?' he said, pointing proudly.

Jagged chunks of masonry, some of them weighing several tons, lay where they had been tossed by the falling bomb. Some of the building's massive stone columns were broken and cracked.

'Bits of that brickwork and stone', the guide said chattily, silver pencil swinging, 'flew right over the roof here and came down in the Quadrangle.' Shaffer nodded. The P.A. reporter was writing down everything. They strolled across to a lurching wall and the guide slid carefully through a half-open door. In the deep end of the dust-rimmed swimming pool, the twisted steel remains of a diving-board shivered up from the cracked bottom tiles. Overhead, the roof had caved in, leaving ruptured steel supports black against the sky.

'There's a deep shelter under the pool,' said the guide. 'Wasn't touched. Absolute miracle. The whole staff was down there. The end of the building by the squash court was blown right out. See there? Smithereens.'

A set of steps and a balustrade leading to the terrace fronting the Belgian Suite had been literally pulverised.

Shaffer looked up to the first floor. 'Aren't they the private apartments?' He could see furniture, largely undamaged but covered like everything else in dust and debris, through smashed window panes.

The guide nodded eagerly and the P.A. man flashed perfect shorthand over the page of his huge, lined notebook. 'Could well have killed them.' He had second thoughts. 'God forbid.'

'Anybody killed?' asked Shaffer.

The ministry man pursed his lips in frustration. 'No. Lots of staff here, of course, but they were down in the shelter.' He thought for a minute. 'The sentry at the north-west corner was blown off his feet, though.'

'And the king and queen and the family?'

'Ah. They went down to Windsor at the weekend. I thought they'd tell you that at the ministry. Weren't you down in the East End today when the king and queen were there?'

Shaffer shook his head. He remembered Syd Williams's experience. 'Did they know about this bomb then?'

The guide beamed. 'Their Majesties? Of *course* they did. Not going to let *that* stop them, are they? I mean — one bomb!'

The Press Association man said, without looking up from his flying pencil, 'Anything happen down East today? I s'pose we covered but I'd better make sure.'

'My dear chaps, you should have *been* there,' preened the guide.

'Were *you*?' interrupted Shaffer.

'Naturally.'

'Go on.'

'Well, they were meeting people and talking when the alert sounded. Raid! *They* didn't care, of course. Quite happy to carry on strolling but the police got them off the street quickly and into a shelter under a police station. There were about thirty people there already, I'd say, and, my goodness me, weren't they *astounded*! They stood up and clapped and the king — he was wearing a field-marshal's uniform, by the by — sat down in a bare wooden chair, cool as you please, and the queen beside him. The king leaned back and folded his legs as though he were sitting by his own fire, and lit a cigarette. There were some ladies in white coats there, too. They were from the police canteen, I imagine, and one of 'em got busy to make Their Majesties a cup of tea, but the "All Clear" sounded before it was ready. But, do you know what the king said? He said, "That's the 'All Clear', but I'm going to wait for some of this tea." I swear to you as sure as I stand here. That's what he said. Cool as a cucumber. And everyone clapped again, of course. Marvellous! Really splendid!'

The P.A. man's pen was eating paper at breakneck speed; it

occurred to Shaffer he might even be recording the indrawn breaths and the swoops of the silver pencil on the black silk cord.

'Where are the king and queen now?'

'Ah! Not at liberty, old boy, I'm afraid. Can't tell you. Sure you understand. But they won't be far away, take my word for it.'

Shaffer sniffed. 'No. I guess not.' He was being unreasonable, he thought. Somewhere there had to be people who felt the same way about Roosevelt and Eleanor. The P.A. man slapped his notebook shut pointedly and looked around for an exit. The guide said, 'I suppose you've got enough, you chaps?'

'I've got to file my story first to Mr Brebner,' mourned the agency man impatiently. A suspicious thought struck him and he glared at Shaffer. 'So've you. Can't file till you've given what you've got to everyone else, you know. That's what being on rota means.'

Wednesday, 1615

The house in St James's Place would have been an ideal address for a serious publisher or a firm of discreet solicitors. Its soot-blackened red brick and high, vaulting gables offered incontestable evidence of integrity, solidity and responsible purpose. Denzil Fletcher-Hale rang the bell, showed his slip of paper to the belted, spatted, pistolled sailor who opened the door and was taken in tow to the second floor.

A handwritten piece of card on the old oak door advertised: DONITE. And in a much smaller hand below: Captain W. H. S. N. Dysart, D.S.O., R.N.

The sailor knocked, a rhythmic tattoo that could have been a signal, and there was a delay of several seconds before a grunt pierced the oak. The sailor swung back the door and Denzil drifted into the room.

Captain W. H. S. N. Dysart, D.S.O., R.N., was, physically, a credit to Naval Intelligence and all it stood for but he had not been designed to fill a naval officer's uniform. He was small and painfully thin with the face of Sherlock Holmes (complete with black widow's peak) and knobbly wrists and hands. The face hinted, in fact, at a history of some wasting disease, so hollow was it, but the eyes were diamond-hard and flickered like Aldis lamps as if burning off an excess of energy from the soul. He jumped to his feet with alarming bounciness and held out his hand. Denzil took it and awarded it a limp response.

'So!' the little man exploded. He plopped back into his leather chair as abruptly as he had risen from it. Denzil waited courteously for an invitation to sit. It didn't come at once; Captain Dysart allowed his signal-lamp eyes to flicker to the summit of the golden hair and travel down again. He took his nose between finger and thumb and rubbed it energetically. 'Well, sit you down, man.' Denzil subsided elegantly into the single chair facing the desk.

'Friend of Broadribb's, are you?' It was a single shot across the bows; accusative, implying that any friend of Broadribb was automatically open to suspicion.

'Aaah, Broadribb.' Denzil nodded to himself, confirming a flash of intuition. 'One of your chaps?'

Dysart seemed momentarily nonplussed by the switch of interrogative roles. 'My A.D.'

'A.D.?' Denzil's face settled into a scowl of incomprehension.

'Assistant Director. O.N.I.T.E.' Dysart trapped his nose again between finger and thumb.

'Ah—O.N.I.T.E.?'

Dysart flashed impatience. 'Office of Naval Intelligence Technical Espionage. You sure you know Broadribb?'

'School chum. Not close. Decent sort?'

'All right.' DONITE flailed his fingers impatiently at being trapped into domestic gossip. The fellow appeared to have no sense of place or position, especially his own. Another amateur, obviously. The world was full of amateurs.

'Broadribb says you're looking for a place.' It was another accusation but Dysart was put out that it seemed not to have found its mark.

'Decent of him. Few irons in the fire, though. Know some of your chaps. Chums, you know.'

'Who?'

'Bobby Curzon. Dean-Highsmith. Randall. Chevening.'

Amateurs. All amateurs! 'You have any idea what we do here?'

'Not a flicker,' Denzil drawled disarmingly. 'Mustn't pry, what? Careless talk, that sort of thing. Decent mess though, they tell me.'

'Wardroom,' spat Dysart.

'Is it really?' Denzil's friendly stare was uncontaminated by either curiosity or understanding. The Director found it impossible to meet it for more than a few seconds at a time. He opened a folder and glared down at it, his skeletal head, crowned with a top-dressing of thin, brilliantined hair, bent low over the typed pages.

He looked up. 'What's your line?'

Denzil blinked. 'Line?'

'Job. Profession. Source of income.'

'Hah!' The tall young man winced. 'Job, profession . . . see what you mean. Yes. Father's heir, d'you see. Income . . . modest allowance. Tough nut, the old man.'

Dysart sighed. It was all down in the file but he had asked the question to hurt. The fellow was inviolable. 'No job. No profession. Private income. Ye'd be better off in the army, man.'

'Could be. Yes, certainly could be.'

'Don't you have any ambition? There are thousands – *thousands* – of young chaps standing in line to join this office. Know that, do you?'

'Can't say I do. Not informed. Good men, are they?'

Dysart gave his nose a tremendous yank with the finger and thumb. 'Ye silver spoon's no good to us here, Fletcher-Hale.'

'Really?' He might have been passing the time of day or propping up one end of an inadequate cocktail party exchange.

'The requirement here', Dysart gritted, damping down the fires, 'is a keen brain in a professional naval officer's uniform. I have more inspired amateurs than I know what to do with. Sure you understand.' He folded his arms conclusively.

'Get your drift,' Denzil droned easily. 'Priorities, what? War

304

on your hands. Don't fit your frame. Deuced good of you to give me your time.' He began to rise.

Dysart took a mouthful of lip and chewed on it thoughtfully. 'Wait a minute.' He chewed some more. 'Registered for service, are ye?'

'Registered?' Denzil seated himself again.

The little man's cruelly defined Adam's apple bobbed with irritation. 'Registered! Know what registered means, don't ye?'

"Fraid I don't. Not up with the argot, what?'

'Registered! Ye've got your papers, man. Required to report for duty in the armed services. Got them, right?'

'Ah — registered!' The dawning removed the pained expression from Denzil's olympian brow. 'No; can't say I have. Thing to do, is it?'

Dysart's exasperation became a clinical suspicion. 'Everyone's registered, man. Every able-bodied man. You able-bodied, are ye?'

'Never given the matter much thought, actually. Some sort of test?'

'Medical! Ye look A. One to me. Nothing wrong with ye? No' — the idea had occurred to him seconds earlier — 'no history of, what you might say, *illness* in the family?' The man was clearly a fool but it might, of course, be hereditary. Couldn't blame him out of hand for that.

Denzil frowned. 'Gout, I dare say. The old man's prone to it. Runs in the family. Grandpère suffered the dickens.'

The Director lowered himself into the security of the back of his gaunt leather chair. There was no hope for this one; none whatsoever. He took refuge in the file, running his eye down the clumsily typed documentation prepared by the oaf Broadribb. There was something ... something.... Not in the file. Something the fellow had said. What the devil...? He looked up sharply. Got it!

'Say ye know Dean-Highsmith, do ye?'

'Dean-Highsmith?'

The Director took a grip on his overflowing temper. 'One of ye chums, ye said.'

'Ah, yes. Dean-Highsmith. Good sort. Polo player. Met at Hurlingham.'

Captain Dysart creaked forward in the chair. 'Close chum is he? Good friend?' His teeth were showing, top and bottom.

'Could say that. Close enough.'

Dysart sucked air deeply through his nose, unsettling the build-up of matter in his sinuses. He spun the chair, opened a drawer in a steel cabinet at his back, withdrew a red folder and turned back to face the desk. He opened the folder lovingly, caressing its stiff cover. Dean-Highsmith, Patrick Winford, Roderick.

'Hurlingham, ye say ye met him?'

'Best of my recollection, yes.'

'By accident, so to speak? Never seen him before?'

'Dean-Highsmith? Lord, yes. Same staircase at Oxford. Oriel. Joined a couple of clubs together. Usual thing.'

Dysart was bent low over the file as though guarding against the possibility that a magic wind might appear from nowhere and snatch it from him. He grabbed his nose again for comfort. 'Clubs, eh? What sort of clubs?'

Denzil shrugged. 'Never any good at names. Just clubs. Chaps getting together, you know. Drinking, mostly. Bawdy songs. Talking shop. That sort of thing. All the same.'

The chair creaked again as Dysart loomed even farther out over his desk. 'Belonged to The Link did ye?'

'The which?'

'The Link. Dean-Highsmith was a member.' He stabbed a finger down on the paper in front of him. 'In his file. Member of The Link.'

'Ah – The Link. Yes – seem to remember something or other. Let me think.' He propped his chin in his hands and gazed blankly at the far wall. 'No! No good. Can't remember. But I dare say you're right. What was the idea, this Link thing?'

Dysart's teeth displayed greedily. 'Oh, student stuff, of course. Continental affairs. Travel club, perhaps.'

'Ah – The Link!' The painful smile. 'With you now. Certainly. The Link. Chaps' fathers joined, what? Dean-Highsmith's family were in. High-powered, they tell me. Yes, bunch of us joined.

Some sort of exchange thing; England, France, Germany. Went to Heidelberg one summer, thirty-seven I fancy. Could've been thirty-six. Bags of fun. Larking around. Decent types. Well connected. Whale of a time. Yes. The Link.'

Dysart lay back, gorged with satisfaction. He allowed the thumb and forefinger another tug at his nose, then brought the curtain down on the display of teeth. 'Like to keep these things in mind, ye know. Detail. Important.'

Denzil rose to his feet and the Director followed suit automatically in an attempt to win back some of the stature he had lost in the young man's unrolling height.

'Wasted your time. See that. Deuced decent of you.'

Dysart came around the desk and opened the door for him. 'My dear feller, nothing of the sort. Delighted ye came. Bound to see ye again.' They shook hands.

When he closed the door again, Dysart scuttled around his desk to his chair, his uniform flapping voluminously around his bony limbs. He grabbed at an internal telephone.

'Jamieson? Got something for you. Heard of a feller name of Fletcher-Hale? Denzil Fletcher-Hale?' He waited and a slow grin creased his face into tramlines of triumph. 'Thought not. Just had the bounder in here. One of Dean-Highsmith's fellow travellers. Yes! Of course it's The Link.' He listened again, the smile widening. 'Just doing one's bit, you understand. Always ready to help. His file's here on my desk. Give it ye if ye'll send somebody round to collect it.' He stirred the brown manila folder with one hand. 'No use to me now, is it?'

Wednesday, 1700

Ian Russell had spent the late morning and all afternoon in Hyde Park. By any standards of peace or war it was the sort of place to take troubles to; big enough to be alone in, sufficiently populated to remind a man of his membership of the human race. Not that he wished to be reminded of that, just now, to any marked degree; humanity, as far as he could see, was just another word for other people's problems.

It was easy to concentrate on nothing in Hyde Park on a mild weekday afternoon, but rather more had been happening in the park today than was normal. Just after dawn, according to one spectator he asked, about a dozen anti-aircraft guns had been driven in on low-loaders and swung into position on their old circular concrete emplacement pads. By the time Ian arrived, hot foot and guilt-laden from Caroline's bed on Ward F.5, Royal Engineers had roped off whole areas under the trees and begun the work of camouflaging each gun nest. The new arrivals had clearly affected the disposition of the barrage balloons moored in the park and, throughout the afternoon, their crews constantly raised and lowered the shiny silver Dumbos to achieve a perfect pattern of obstruction at varying altitudes over the canopy of summer-green trees. Between gun post and balloon winding-gear, control centre and listening post, plotting centre and radio dug-out, an army of trucks and Land Rovers fussed and fumed, their interiors jammed tight with officers and occasional civilians. Twice Ian spotted a large Humber staff car cruising meditatively around under the trees. Inside sat an elderly officer with the scarlet flashes of War Office rank on his cap and collars. Wherever he drove, an attendant Land Rover shadowed; as the great man's car passed each gun emplacement, the Land Rover would stop, an officer would leap to the ground and fling orders, threats and taunts at the sweating, bare-backed gun teams.

The unusual activity had drawn swarms of spectators to the park; in addition to the regulars – the homeless, the old, the lonely and the idle – shopping housewives had been lured by the bustle and swing of the military from their haunts in Marble Arch and Knightsbridge and Park Lane. Lunchtime strollers had come to join the crowds; nurses with prams who would not normally have strayed from the eminently respectable walk-ways of Kensington Gardens; whole bands of aimlessly nomadic children, and rougher hunting packs of teenage boys looking for excitement or trouble or both; and off-duty servicemen, de-lighting in the sweated labour of the artillerymen. It had about it something of a carnival atmosphere, a disconcerting light-heartedness that was almost, but not quite, a throwback to hot summer Sunday afternoons before the war.

Ian watched the ebb and flow of it but only as a man might fix on the vague movement of fish in an aquarium to aid his concentration. Caroline had not left his mind for a moment; she refused to go away. The top and bottom of it was he should have telephoned mother. There was no excuse for that; no escape from the irresponsibility of cowardice. At the hospital he had picked up the phone in the porter's lodge; actually inserted his finger in the first number on the dialling ring – then dropped the instrument as though it were burning a hole in his hand.

What stopped him was the realisation that he didn't know what to say. What could he tell her? What had he actually grasped from those five minutes of conversation with Caroline?

Eighteen years of life under his father's roof, at prep school and in the authoritarian orthodoxy of Winchester – the *family* school where Charles had excelled and Tom had been a pan-jandrum of sporting achievement – had done nothing to prepare him for emotional maturity. He had always thought of himself as reasonably sophisticated, although under closer examination that claim just didn't stand up. If sophistication was the passing of dubious novels around the dormitory from hand to sticky hand; if it was the manipulation of Latin tags to describe carnal improprieties; if it was the sniggering of ignorance in sheltered places . . . he was sophisticated. That was the seamy side of sex, he supposed; probably simple lust. He had never quite grasped how or why it was generated and he was still totally ignorant of the applied mechanics of physical contact. He was not alto-gether blind, though. Like everyone else, he knew that some boys developed strange passions at school, often in extension of hero-worship, and that they took curious physical forms that everyone pretended to understand but never did. There was a lot of talk, but it was talk that exploited ignorance; it resolved nothing. On the other hand, Winchester had always made much of love as an instrument of social and cosmic respectability : love of parents, love of country, love of God. Preached in chapel, it emerged as a message of self-glorification, like doubling one's prep voluntarily to get good exam marks.

He could hardly take 'love' as a text for a sermon to his parents on the subject of Caroline's torment. There had to be

a very much simpler answer in her case. After all, she was ...
well, a girl. So this ... feeling she had for the woman with the
burned arms — Yvonne? — must be perfectly honourable and
perfectly decent.

Yes. Then why had she asked him if he *understood*? Even in
her agony she had managed to envelope the words with hor-
rendous implication. Friendship required no understanding.
Being in bed with another woman? Yes. That did. A little.

He rolled into the grass and buried his face on interlaced
fingers. He was a long way from the anti-aircraft guns. A world
away from the idlers and gawkers. Caroline was ill. He should
have seen that from the beginning. Mentally ill. Probably the
pressures of the job only she and father were allowed to talk
about. Even mother was kept in ignorance of what Caroline did
at Bletchley Park and it was tacitly agreed that she would never
ask. A job that important could. ... The siren howled and the
distant crowds scattered.

He bounced restlessly to his feet, dragged his bicycle from
the long grass and began to push it towards the Serpentine.
There was no point in holding the truth from them, if there was
a truth worth disclosing. They had to be told and he had to do
it. What he couldn't explain he would have to leave to their
imaginations.

There was one bright thought; at least he would have to tell
only his mother. With luck, he could be out of the house and
on his way to the hospital before father got home.

The 'All Clear' sounded as he wheeled the bike into the potting-
shed at the bottom of the garden. He lingered there, comforted
by the sight and touch and time-dried smell of the detritus of
his childhood; the rocking-horse Elizabeth could not bring herself to give away; the push-chair in which Nanny Bell had once
aired him daily in Battersea Park; a dislocated pinball board, a
present from father one Christmas; old cricket bats and stumps
and pads; his first football boots, diminutive and now cast-
iron hard. He automatically connected all of this with happier
days but, in truth, times past had been no better than time
present. He had throughout his growing up seemed always at a

loss, always stranded in the outfield, watching the play closely but seeing only chaos; he had never learned the social ground-rules so obvious to everyone else. Caroline had *always* known the ground-rules.

His watch told him it was five-thirty. He left the shed, ducked under the sweeping branches of the sycamore that shielded it from the upper garden and stopped with a tremor of surprise; Elizabeth and Charles were seated at a table on the terrace. Elsie Warrender was pouring tea. He quailed at the thought of reciting his story to both of them, but squared his shoulders and walked on.

Charles Russell offered no greeting. Elizabeth angled up her face to be kissed but it was a gesture born more of habit than reflex affection. The atmosphere was abrasive with expended temper and it was not difficult to see that his mother had been crying.

'Sit yourself down, Mr Ian,' Elsie ordered sharply, telegraphing messages. She grimaced at him and the sight of her made him smile; her black felt hat with its attendant fruit and feather decor had slipped forward over her brow, its constant hatpin stabbing the air like an antenna. It made her look a little tipsy.

She produced a cup and saucer and poured him tea while Charles and Elizabeth fixed their eyes sightlessly on the dark side of eternity. His father wore the stone basilisk of his leave-me-alone-or-else mask, a certain sign of thunder in the air. His mother was toying with a leaf-thin cress sandwich that never quite reached her mouth. She had fallen prey to the hypnotic influence of the teapot.

'Been out then?' Elsie asked, twitching wickedly.

'Only the park.'

'Good for you. Cooped up in that hospital all night.'

'Yes, I suppose so.' He glanced left and right at his parents but they held rigidly to their private grief. He summoned up all his courage. 'Is Caroline. . . ?'

Charles Russell's chair scraped back on the laid stone. 'I'll be in the study,' he said abruptly, and stamped indoors.

Elsie raised her eyes to heaven. 'He's gone,' she informed Elizabeth. No response. 'What about you then?' she asked Ian.

'I'll have to be at the hospital earlier tonight,' he said in a rush.

She recognised it as a lie before he completed the sentence but she wouldn't give him away. 'You'll want a proper tea then, won't you? Cress sandwiches aren't going to keep your spine from your belly all night.'

He shrugged uncomfortably. 'It's all right, Mrs W. I can get something from the mobile canteen.'

'Like fish you can! I'm not having you walk out of this house without something inside you. Not at my time of life.'

He wondered idly what her time of life had to do with his appetite. 'Well, just something simple.'

'You'll get what you're given,' she retorted and swept away to the kitchen, her work shoes squeaking on the polished parquet. He waited until he heard her timpani of pots and pans and cutlery from the kitchen before he turned on his mother.

'Have you heard anything from Caroline?' He had intended it to be innocent, offhand, but the words came out in a strangulated burst, like sandpaper wrenched from the walls of his throat.

Elizabeth blinked nervously but kept her face turned away. 'No. I'm sure we will. Later.'

'Look, mother. I don't think she'll be—'

Elizabeth's porcelain gentility shattered. 'Ian *please*! Don't be tedious. I really don't think you have the right to interfere in your sister's affairs—' She gulped on the word and her pretty face bunched with frustration and anger. 'Oh, *do* let me have a moment to myself, will you? It really isn't any concern of yours.'

Ian sat back in his chair, uncomprehending. 'But all I wanted to say was—'

She shot to her feet angrily. 'I really can't argue with you tonight, darling. I just can't. I'm going to—'

'But I haven't *done* anything!' He was angry himself now.

Elizabeth pulled herself together with an effort. 'I'm going to lie down, darling. Tell Elsie she must go as soon as she's finished getting you something to eat. It's too bad of us keeping her here so late. I'll be in my room if. . . .' She left the 'if' in exhausted suspension.

He watched her go and let resentment burn in her wake. It was father's fault; it was always his fault. Everything would be perfect in the house if it weren't for him.

Elsie Warrender came back on to the terrace and planted a tray in front of him. She raised the lid of a silver warming dish and revealed a mound of golden scrambled eggs. He was momentarily astonished; no one had been given so heaped a serving of precious eggs since war began.

'Gosh — that's a bit much, isn't it?' he breathed.

Mrs Warrender had her coat over her arm. She slipped it on. 'Only two eggs there,' she said soothingly. 'Don't you worry yourself. Mister brought three dozen home last night. In a box, straight from the farm. You can tell. Fresh as daisies they are. He won't miss two and you need your strength.'

'*Father?*' Ian gaped incredulously.

"S'right. Must've been given 'em by someone.'

'But he's never brought anything like that home before.'

'Then, this is the first time, ennit?' she retorted, tapping the end of her nose reprovingly. She picked up her barrage-balloon shopping bag and her brolly and her gas-mask. 'My hubby's on watch tonight,' she said proudly. 'Better get back and give him his supper.'

He let her go inside, then called out, 'Mrs W.!'

She poked her head around the french windows.

'Why did my father come home so early today?'

She waggled the brolly at him. 'Now would I be the one to ask him *that*? All I know is, he come home about half-past two or just after and he was spitting blood, he was. Right do, him and your mum had out here. Raised his voice to her. Never heard the likes of it in this house all the years I worked here.'

Charles Russell heard the boy trudge upstairs to his room, then down again. From his study window he watched him cross the lawn and duck under the sycamore's hanging veil to the shed to fetch his bicycle. Thank God, he didn't know. Of all the hospitals they could have taken her to in London, it had to be St Thomas's! She and Ian could have met — easily. Talked.

Caroline might well have been so close to a state of collapse that she confided everything. Thank God.

He refilled the glass from his last bottle of Black and White.

At Bow Street he had been treated with pained civility as though they had already found him guilty of the worst kind of treachery and only the formality of a judge's black cap was left outstanding. They had permitted him a telephone call to George Choker, who had responded at once. Seconds after George arrived things began to look brighter. There was no question of his client giving a statement, he pontificated, when the subject under investigation was his daughter and he was being asked to furnish what could only be second-hand information or, at best, speculation. Neither was acceptable in law. Secondly, his client was covered by the Official Secrets Acts and so was his daughter, as the Security Police officers were at such pains to explain. Secrecy worked both ways; in the Russells' case it imposed on them specific responsibilities not to discuss their work, in either a professional or personal sense, except before a properly constituted court of inquiry or in the presence of their superiors. That instruction did not include policemen.

'Close shave, that, Charles,' George said with a mock swipe of the hand across his brow when they stepped back into the benevolent sunshine of Bow Street. 'Good thing about the Secrets Acts; they're so damned wide open to interpretation nobody's really sure how to apply them in this sort of case.'

Russell had answered with tired protest. 'But that's the point, George. This *isn't* a case.'

'Oh, yes, old boy, it jolly well is. Careless talk . . . remember? At worst, they could get Caroline on that one. Are you sure you don't know who this fellow is she met at the pub?'

'No.'

'Pity.'

Russell had wished at the time that Choker would display less obvious enjoyment of his work; lawyers seemed to take such evident relish in the misfortunes of their clients. The more agonising the quandaries, the better.

A little after two o'clock George had established officially that Caroline was at St Thomas's. They drove there at once, only to discover that Caroline and 'another patient, a woman' had been collected by R.A.F. ambulance just before noon and taken to an undisclosed destination for 'specialist treatment'.

George had been amused; professionally, he could see the funny side of it. 'Blighters! Yield an inch, take a mile. Tell us where to find her, but only after they've spirited her off. Playing with us, Charles.'

George had raised the tempo and the morale but, in essence, he had changed nothing. Russell had deliberately withheld from him the connection with Freddie Green, and that was an oafish, blundering sin of omission because, as he realised later, if the Security Police suspected him of any impropriety at all they would plod the inexorable investigative path into his personal life and wind up at his bank manager's door. Two thousand pounds! What couldn't the disagreeable Inspector Lubbock do with that knowledge?

His suspension was also unchanged. George had discussed the point with a chum at the Law Society whose view was that in wartime, under the prevailing conditions of the Blitz and the fear of imminent invasion, it would be little short of impossible to defend the temporary suspension of a vulnerable civil servant 'pending further investigations'. An hour after George Choker dropped him at Garfield Court, Russell called Bow Street and spoke to the gentlemanly Maconachie, who admitted he and Lubbock had invited Caroline 'to discuss certain areas of confusion'. No, there was nothing to report. The situation could not be said to have materially progressed. Caroline was resolute; she refused to discuss anything relating to her job or her family. She would not reveal her relationship with the Frenchwoman, Coutance. She was, thought Maconachie, 'a little overwrought'. Russell did not waste his breath on an appeal to be allowed to see her. Maconachie was only doing his job.

He poured neat Scotch down his throat with reckless indifference to its probable effects. He had already drunk two glasses and his eyes no longer focused properly. Another glass and they would more than likely close; a fifth would bring a welcome oblivion. Well, he deserved oblivion for as long as he could hold on to it. The working classes were right after all;

some things in life just could not be borne with sobriety. And why in damnation should they be? Where had stiff-necked burden-bearing brought Charles Russell, gentleman; gentleman's son? Answer: to his knees. Perhaps even to his stomach; that was the level at which the Freddie Greens of this world conducted their personal and commercial affairs and he was now their toady. He gulped the tawny fire. He had already been bought. Last night, when he got home from Green's house at Blackheath, he had found a box of eggs in the back seat of his car. Three dozen eggs! Would that, in a time of national emergency, be accounted more or less than thirty pieces of silver?

He gulped the last of glass three and poured glass four. He was getting better at it; perhaps he had more resistance to liquor than he credited himself with. Bubbling fire in the head and the arteries; something like that. Poetic, almost. One could appreciate what the common man saw in drinking to excess. The secret was . . . yes, the secret was that remaining sober was the excess. Spirits didn't drown the sorrows — stupid phrase; he would never use it again — spirits demagnified them. Exactly. Demagnified.

He took a fresh glass and upended the bottle over it, splashing a few drops of Scotland's blood on the carpet in the process. He carried both glasses to his desk and slopped them down on his blotter. Nothing to deserve any of this. Honest life filled with hard work and loyalty to his class and his country. Same thing, really. Wholly unfair.

Stupid girl. Just a stupid, thoughtless girl.

He paused with glass four at eye level. Tomorrow, tell Elizabeth about Caroline. Not today. Not tonight. Too much hurt today. Poor Elizabeth. Not strong. Couldn't understand his suspension. Had to tell her that, of course. Internal investigation, he'd said. Very hush-hush. All turn out in the end.

Silly girl. Silly, stupid, blind girl.

Elizabeth? Yes. Elizabeth couldn't understand the suspension. On and on with her questions. Why this? Why that? Made him angry in the end. Lost his temper. Made her cry. Poor Elizabeth.

The glass dropped from his fingers, rolled sideways on the blotter and ran a complete circle, neatly discharging liquor in a perfect arc. He felt his eyes closing and laid his head experimentally on the backs of his hands, waiting for oblivion.

Silly child. Blind, thoughtless child. . . .

Wednesday, 2130

Shaffer ripped the last page from his typewriter and re-angled the desk reading light to fall on the three sheets.

Lousy. It was too emotional. It was also — what was O'Keefe's obscenity? — fucking the flag. He read the first page with his mouth twisted into a self-conscious leer. Page two was no better. He was supposed to be a reporter.

And there, at the end, the worst of it.

'I repeat, because repetition is now the only effective weapon against constitutional deafness, that inventive isolation is no guarantee of exclusion from this war. The Lindberghs and the Kennedys protest too much and in their protests I hear conditioned minds bending before the inevitable. Adolf Hitler will not stop short at Britain if he ever gets both feet firmly planted on these shores. He will look West, beyond even the Atlantic Ocean which Senate Foreign Relations Committee chairman Key Pittman tells us we might allow Hitler to control if needs be. America is the real challenge and the German Chancellor would be the last man to pass it up. International power is his goal and the vested wealth of the United States is a sprawling goldfield just waiting to be harvested. Each bomb that falls on this United Kingdom is a whistling promise in Washington's ear. Only a fool or a deaf-mute could fail to comprehend the warning.

'Last Christmas, with his country newly at war, King George the Sixth quoted these lines from a little-known piece during his radio message to the nation :

And I said to the man who stood at the gate of the year:
'Give me a light that I may tread safely into the unknown.'
And he replied : 'Go out into the darkness and put your hand

317

into the hand of God. That shall be to you better than light and safer than a known way.'

'The darkness is now all about us and there is no safe diplomatic way to perfect peace and happiness; no light to lead any country safely to the gate of another year.

'America could do worse than put its hand into the hand of God.'

He shook the sheets into an orderly stack, bounced them speculatively on the desk top and glanced at the office clock. O'Keefe would be opening the line to the studio at Broadcasting House at 2330. He folded the sheets carefully, smoothed a razor edge across the middle, then slowly tore them to shreds. He dropped an hour of his life into the trash-can in a flutter of scraps.

He rolled another piece of paper into the typewriter and, without thinking, wrote:

'This is a letter to my wife, the first I've had a chance to write since I got here.

'I've been thinking about her and our two boys a lot lately. You can put that down to many personal reasons I can't go into on the public airwaves but also because I live from day to day in a world that belongs to women and children. Sure, the firefighters of London are men; the wardens, the police, the creators and manipulators of war. All men. But here in the heart of London, at the end of the fifth day of its bombardment, it's the women and children who arrest the eye, tune the ear, occupy the heart of any observer.

'I guess my wife and I think of our kids as most American parents do: protectively. We worry when they're out of sight, despair when they're sick, die a little when they're threatened by real or imagined disaster. I don't suppose the English are any different but they've learned lessons, this week, we shall, I hope, never have to learn.

'Firstly, they've had to accept that kids adapt to war much quicker than adults. There's little or no schooling around this town for boys and girls left behind by the national evacuation schemes, so adaptability is pretty important. It can take some macabre forms. Bomb sites — the mess of flattened rubble and brick left behind when a German bomb has crushed a house or an office block — have become playgrounds for dozens of neighbourhood kids. Sometimes their games grow perilously close to the real thing: one or two of them have found unexploded bombs, U.X.B.s in the argot of the times, and reported them to the authorities. A couple of youngsters accidentally detonated bombs . . . but the bombsite games go on. Parents, as one matter-of-fact East End mother told me, can't be everywhere.

'Toys are not scarce yet, but they're no longer the toys that brightened our childhood. The kids of nineteen forty have a wider choice. Imitation Sten guns are available in the shops here; rifles, helmets, rubber commando knives and bayonets. But that's . . . well, kid's stuff in this town. A boy with pretensions to being ahead of the field will have a collection of bric-à-brac from shot-down enemy planes or he'll be able to boast a chunk of the fin of a German bomb. When a Messerschmitt is blown to earth, the authorities are pretty quick on their feet in sealing off the area around it. They need to be. Marauding kids can strip a plane in five minutes flat. This particular collective art form has naturally roused tremendous interest in aircraft spotting. There's even a magazine, *Aircraft Spotter*, to keep the kids on their toes.

'For those who do get to school, classes are large — sometimes as many as sixty or seventy children to a classroom. Discipline is rigid and schoolteachers often elderly, in the absence of younger men away in the armed services. Schooldays too are subject to constant interruption; from actual peril — another alert, the drone of Heinkels and Dorniers, the crunch of falling bombs — as well as continuous, unannounced air-raid practices and gas-mask drills. It's a little difficult to take drill seriously when your days and nights are under constant threat from the real thing.

'My wife and I would worry about how little the boys were getting to eat if they lived here in London and I suppose it must be said that, compared with average American boys and girls, these youngsters are pale, thin and obviously underfed. Rationing apart, diets here were pretty spartan anyway; the war just made it official. Yet, walk down any street where life still goes on and you'll find tubs on street corners set aside for uneaten scraps. Pigswill bins they're called; designed to keep the nation's bacon growing out on the farms.

'I've met mothers here who couldn't tell me at any time of the day or night where their older children were. During the day many mothers are working — munitions factories, aircraft and tank-building plants, for instance, are often totally dependent on female labour now — and London, through a teenager's eyes, can be a magical place to roam in. Gun-sites and barrage balloons dominate parks and green spaces; convoys of army, navy and air force trucks flood main highways; vast fires run across whole city blocks with fire-engines every thirty yards and firefighters poised like flies aloft dizzily tall ladders; and they only have to lift their heads for the ever-present skyscape of incoming bombers, artillery fire and dogfighting Spitfires and Messerschmitts. At night the sensations multiply a hundredfold.

'But for me, the abiding presences of this time are the weary little groups trudging the streets, night or day, their belongings in hastily packed holdalls and paper bags, their household pets on leads or quivering in a child's arms, a baby-carriage weighed down by burdens too heavy to carry. Women and children. Behind them, their homes may have been demolished or rendered unsafe by local damage or an unexploded bomb or burst gas and water mains. Ahead of them lies a search for a night's sleep — a barn, a protective hedgerow, a cottage if they're lucky. The eldest child will usually act as scout, ranging ahead a couple of miles to locate a convenient stop-over and perhaps use his or her tender age as an instrument of persuasion.

'The women are often in tears, robbed of the essentials of life they have always taken for granted: husband, home, security, protection. The kids are more resilient. As I said, they adapt to war conditions quickly. Perhaps with an ease that is also frightening.

'For children, war is an adventure when it's necessary to stare it hard in the face. At other times it's just a backdrop, brightly coloured, excitingly lit, against which they have to cope with the tedious monotonies of being young in a grown-up world.

'It would be comforting to think they were learning lessons that will insure tomorrow's generation against the insanity of war. But I take leave to doubt it.

'It will be a mansize job for these kids to adapt as quickly to the peace.'

Wednesday, 2355

The final 'All Clear' had gone at half past eleven, but before that, as the bombing slackened off, the Warrenders and Scullys left the shelter and went back to the house. Arthur was on shift and Jack still out on his rounds of the Green. Flo and Elsie, Derek and Paul had settled down for what promised to be the first full night's sleep for almost a week.

Elsie found she just couldn't nod off without Jack beside her, no matter how hard she tried. Flo had lent her a hop pillow but all that seemed to do was make her sneeze. She tried counting sheep and found instead she was counting the 'crump, crump' of anti-aircraft fire. Each battery seemed to have its own peculiar note. One, coming from somewhere over near Redriff Park, sounded like sacks of coal being dumped from a lorry; another, near the river, crackled like burning fat; and a third she couldn't place, though it was very near, seemed to have a hollow metallic echo like a dustbin lid being banged. In the end she found herself actually holding her breath if one gun missed its place in the sequence.

Derek Scully could hear them too, and arrived at his own interpretation. They were firing lazily, which meant the planes were going. That was good. The rescue blokes would work on, of course, and so would the firemen, but the rest would grab the chance of a few hours' sleep in case the buggers came back. He stared at the ceiling impatiently. Paul Warrender's feet jogged his elbow every time he turned over.

He peered over the sheet at him. He was flat out, useless bugger. If he'd had his head screwed on and showed a bit of guts he could've been in on it, but his performance on Saturday had put paid to that. Like a bloody chicken with its head cut off, he'd been. Running around in circles, twittering about his sodding hand! Big soft nellie. If that bloke who found them had been a rozzer they'd have been right in the cart. Derek strained his eyes down the bed; Paul Warrender *looked* asleep.

'Pole?' he whispered.

No response. Great! He wasn't in the mood for explanations. He slipped from the bed and pulled on his trousers and shirt. The boxroom was pitch dark, but that didn't worry him; he knew it back to front, inside out, like a tomcat knows its own backyard. He crossed to the door, carrying his plimsolls, and eased it open. No problem. Down the stairs without a squeak; he was particularly proud of that and quietly bet himself there wasn't a cat burglar in the Green who could do better.

The door at the bottom of the stairs was open. He craned around it, eyes narrowing to pick out the lie of the land. The blackout curtain on the yard window had never quite fitted and the rosy glow from outside shone across the room into the front parlour and on to the old bed his mum used. He started to move forward, but something checked him. Christ, she was awake! He could see her eyes open. Staring at the living-room window they were. No mistake, she was awake.

He half toyed with the idea of bluffing it through on the pretext of going for a pee or looking to see if Jack Warrender was O.K., but the trouble with that was all bloody hell would break loose when he didn't come back.

If he could make it across the living-room he could wriggle into the kitchen and out into the yard. It wasn't as he'd planned it; the back door was stiff and needed a hell of a jerk to get it open sometimes. Couldn't be helped. He wasn't going to miss tonight.

He slid around the door and dropped to his knees. At full length, he was lower than the bed; even if she turned round the chances were she wouldn't see him. Using his elbows like they did in the commandos, he dragged himself slowly across the lino, holding his breath. His plimsolls hung from his mouth by their laces, hovering dangerously an inch above the floor. But he was there. He slithered into the kitchen and stood up. Now, the door; one hard jerk. Pull! It didn't make a sound. He grinned at the darkness.

Out in the street he drew in half a dozen gasps of breath and began to run.

Paul Warrender waited. If Derek had gone for a pee he was making damn little fuss about it. Most times he woke half the house clattering down the stairs. After five minutes he knew something was wrong; Derek was up to something. Paul got up and banged his ankle against the bed as he groped for the door. Halfway down the stairs there was a creak from the tell-tale stair.

'Glad?' Elsie Warrender hissed from the front bedroom.

'It's me, mum.' Paul couldn't see anything.

'Paul? You all right? Need the lav?'

'No, I.... You alone, mum?'

'Dad's not back yet. Sounds as if Jerry's going. Can you see? Here, I'll light a candle.' The match flickered and Elsie, illuminated by the trembling flame, swung her feet to the ground and sat on the edge of the bed in her winceyette nightie. She looked old, thought Paul. The low flame threw deep shadows around her eyes and made her hair look thin and strangely dead.

'Everything O.K., mum?'

'Me? Right as rain.' She shook her head; bit of a fib. 'Just can't drop off till your dad comes home. He'll probably want his cocoa, anyway. You like one, lovey? Won't take a minute.'

'No. No thanks, mum. Just nipping out the back.'

'Go on, then. Don't catch cold.' Elsie lighted the stairs for him with the candle and climbed back into bed.

Paul sat on the cold seat in the privy watching a flickering pattern of light dance through the broken slats. A spider's web was stretched from the door's rusty hinges to the cistern yet somehow he hadn't broken it when he came in. He blew on it and the small black spider scuttled across to investigate, pausing resentfully halfway as if aware it had been fooled. Paul watched it move slowly back into its lair and thought of Derek Scully. How in hell had he managed to get out without mum and Auntie Flo waking? Where was he off to? He hadn't said anything. If he'd gone back to the docks on his own he must be potty after what happened on Saturday. Risking your life for a handful of mouldy old tea you wouldn't get tuppence for! Unless he was out with a bit of stuff. Hmmm — he'd always been a bit that way; always talking about tarts and tits like he was having it away left, right and centre. Big talk.

One time, over near Greenwich Pier, they'd met three girls and Derek had suggested they go into a shelter and see if there was anything down there. The lights weren't working but they'd lit a fire out of some old papers and stuff and one of the girls had grabbed Paul around the waist and imprisoned him on the bench until he put his arms around her. She'd smelled of something that reminded him of Brasso and kept biting his ear until it filled with spittle and he'd gone deaf in it.

After ten minutes of that, he got pins and needles in his legs and gradually eased her aside; she wouldn't stop moaning. Derek had got one girl sitting on his lap while the other one stroked her hair. The girl sitting down didn't have a stitch on, not even her knickers, and apart from his socks neither had Derek. He was bouncing the girl up and down and she kept giving out little groans as if he was hurting her. Then she threw her head forward and choked on a scream and fell back on his chest. It was the single most exciting thing Paul Warrender had ever seen.

Not that it did him much good. His girl had reached for her handbag and stuffed some chewing gum in her mouth and smoothed her dress without even a glance at the others. He had made a poor attempt at re-establishing contact but she'd just stared at him.

The memory of it sent an uncomfortable tingle down the inside of his legs.

He went back into the house convinced there was something wrong with him and grunted in reply to Elsie Warrender's whispered goodnight. He slipped beneath the sheets filled with a wretched unease.

A foot brushed his cheek. He came awake.

'Sorry, me old tater,' hissed Derek Scully. The foot was cold and clammy. 'Disturb the beauty sleep?'

'Where you bin?'

'Bin? What you mean, bin? Bin here.' He tugged at the sheet.

'Like bloody hell. I saw you go out.'

'Nosey sod.'

'Well, where then? Never said nothin'.'

'Don't have to tell every bugger where I'm goin'.' Derek bounced his head on the pillow.

'Might have told me. Would have told you.'

'Nothin' to bother about, old cock. Nothin' at all.'

'Know what time it is?' Paul tried to keep his voice at whisper pitch.

'Three thirty-seven,' said Derek. 'Next question.'

Paul came up on one elbow at the end of the bed.

'You bin with some tart?'

'Do me a favour. Tarts? Ain't got the strength to raise me hand, never mind anything else.'

'Where then?'

Derek blew an exasperated breath of air. 'If you must know, I've been walkies. Down the docks.'

'You haven't! Not—'

'With Jigger Kemp and Charlie Rowthorne,' said Derek. 'Mates of mine.' He snuggled into the pillow wickedly, knowing the strength of the seed he had sown.

'Jigger...? Charlie...? Bloody hell! They're villains! You been with them?'

'Like I said: mates. We had some business. Don't worry yourself about it.'

'Nicking?'

'Keep your bloody voice down, twerp! Want the whole house to hear?' Derek tugged violently at the sheet and it slipped down to Paul's waist.

'They'll stick you inside!' Paul whispered defiantly. 'Clink!'

'Sod off! It's war, ennit? What do you think they're doing where Geoff is then? Pinching and looting and raping, that's what war's all about. If you want to be a choirboy, you got yourself born in the wrong bloody place. Too sodding soft by half, you are. Get you nowhere, unless you fancy the dole queue. Look at your old man; mine. What've they got to show for anything? Bugger all! Catch me going that way.' He sniffed. 'Sweet dreams.'

Paul Warrender sank back on his pillow of rolled overcoats. What was wrong with him? Soft? Yes, soft. He felt his eyes tingle. He *was* soft. Scully was a shit but he was right.

Derek raised himself up on his elbow.

"Ere,' he hissed. 'Wouldn't mind a bit of the raping, would you?'

THURSDAY
12 September

Thursday, 0700

'Never right, Elsie, never right,' said Flo Scully with feeling. 'Two ounces a week! Blimey, my Arthur could drink that on his own, never mind the rest of us.'

She poured three mugs of tea, upending the pot over the strainer until the very last golden drop trembled through it. Flo had made a point of never grumbling about rationing. Fair's fair and everyone gets their share, was her way of looking at it. But two months ago the Ministry of Food had brought in tea rationing and the allowance just didn't *make* allowance for the fact that the precious liquid was now not just a time-hallowed way of punctuating the day, but also a sedative, a balm and a restorative against the rigours of war. Tea reassured the homeless, soothed the bereaved, calmed the frightened, refreshed the weary. It was the all-purpose, unfailing analgesic.

'One spoon for each person and *none* for the pot' the Ministry of Food had cheerily punned. As far as most East Enders were concerned, at the rate tea was consumed in their homes the advice would have been good for three days.

'I've got one packet left,' said Elsie, spreading a generous supply of dripping over the hot toast and passing the plates round the table. 'Should do us till Sunday if we take it easy.'

The two women and Jack Warrender had risen early, leaving the rest in bed.

Flo sniffed as she sat down. 'Still seems daft to me. How much tea you had come into the docks, Jack, before all this lot? Must have been millions of tons.'

Jack nodded over his dripping.

'So!' went on Flo, showing a rare indignation. 'Who's keeping it all then? That's what I want to know. Couldn't have drunk all that lot, could we?'

'Does seem a bit funny,' admitted Elsie. She ladled a teaspoon of Tate & Lyle syrup into each cup in lieu of sugar. The tea thickened to a rich liquor.

Elsie liked her cup of tea. Always had. The July rationing had been a blow. Four ounces of bacon or ham a week; twelve ounces of sugar; 1s 10d worth of meat a week for each person over six; two ounces of cooking fat; four ounces of marge and two of butter. She had learned to live with it and, apart from the fact that eggs had disappeared from the shops entirely, she had made do, using substitutes with the ingenuity of a castaway on a desert island. But there was no substitute for tea. The Kitchen Front was beginning to feel the strain.

Jack Warrender dabbed his mouth with the back of his hand. There was a twinkle in his eye. 'Shouldn't moan, Flo. There's other things. Got fish, f'r instance.'

The allusion wasn't lost on them. Both women raised their eyes to the roof and Elsie clutched her nose. It had been a couple of weeks back when Flo, after queuing at a fishmonger's in Bermondsey, had seen the last three portions of hake she'd had her eye on for the past hour scooped up by the woman in front. Determined not to go away empty-handed, she had bought what was on offer, whale meat, and had served it up as a treat for both families at tea. The thick rubbery steaks, despite valiant attack, had remained virtually untouched until Paul, in desperation, had spoken for all of them. The government's latest addition to austerity living had become a standing joke.

'Whale meat again,' crooned Jack Warrender.

Janice Scully pushed through from the front parlour, a copy of that morning's *Daily Mirror* in her hand. Janice was always up early, always out first to buy the paper as if she expected to see a picture of herself all over the front page. She only bought it to read the comic strips – Jane and Garth, and Captain Reilly-Foull in Just Jake. She never bothered with the words.

'Well, then.' She was particularly bright-eyed and bushy-tailed this morning, thought Jack. 'Heard the news, have you?' she challenged.

Jack tapped his lips thoughtfully with a spoon. 'Don't tell me, let me guess. Tommy Handley's a German spy? No. You're on "In Town Tonight"? Er — Vic Oliver's lost his fiddle? No? I give in then.'

'Tea, love?' prompted Flo.

'Well, if you don't want to know,' Janice flounced.

'Go on, Jan. Tell us,' said Elsie. She didn't really want to listen; she had too much on her mind. Flo had gone round to see young Edie again yesterday and she said she thought the baby would come any time now. She was already getting the pains and that mother of hers was making the poor girl feel worse. Then there was Barry; he wouldn't be able to come home at a minute's notice to be with the girl when her time came. That boy was looking really ill now; tired and drawn, and his hands shook all the time. Madam dear would allow her to rush off the moment Flo phoned through, of course, but madam dear was another worry. Fair sick about young Miss Caroline, she was. *And* that husband of hers. Something really funny going on there.

Janice leaned over the table. 'The rozzers picked up Alfie Dunn. He's in the nick.'

Jack spilled tea in his saucer. 'You what?'

'Picked up dossing on Victoria Station. They were talking about it round at Willoughby's when I went for the paper.'

'Get off!'

'That's what they said.' Janice sipped a mouthful of tea and made a face.

Flo's face was white as a sheet. 'Whatever did they do that for?'

'Killed old Maudie,' said Janice flatly. 'Gave her some pills while she was in the hospital. Willoughby's said Dick Harris told them.' Dick Harris was a station sergeant at Rotherhithe. 'Alf didn't deny it. Owned up clean, Dick said. They locked him up in Wormwood Scrubs.'

'Bloody hell.' Jack subsided into his chair. 'The silly bloody ... onion. I knew something must've been up but. . . .'

'If he done it, he done it for the best,' Elsie said loyally.

'Best or not he's up for murder,' said Janice.

'Yes, but. . . .' Jack realised Flo was no longer with them. He looked round. She was standing over the kitchen sink, scrubbing mechanically at a saucepan. Damn and bugger it! Them pictures of Derek old Alf had taken with him. It was true then. Alf and Flo. While Arthur was away, Alf and Flo had. . . . He caught himself.

"Bout time you was off to work, ennit Jan?' he said sharply.

Janice sniffed. 'I can take a hint.' She took her coat from the hanger behind the stairs door and knotted a headscarf under her chin. 'No peace for the wicked.' She clip-clopped down the backyard, her shoulderbag swinging jauntily in one hand.

'Mother!' Jack prompted. Elsie looked up from the barrage-balloon bag into which she had stuffed her woolly gloves, hand-bag, identity card and gas-mask box. 'I'll walk you to the bus stop.'

'Well, give me a minute, love. I haven't got. . . .'

Jack glanced over his shoulder to the kitchen. He got to his feet. 'I could do with a walk,' he said, jerking his head at his wife. 'Nice morning for a walk.'

'Walk?' She looked at him stupidly and he gathered up her coat from a chair.

'Walk,' he confirmed heavily. He shoved her protesting into the front parlour where Arthur snored under a twist of blankets on the makeshift bed.

Florence Scully wiped the saucepan until it shone. Wiped it again. When the front door closed she got out her hankie to wipe away the tears.

Thursday, 0830

Shaffer had been up since five-thirty. The 'All Clear' had nudged him off the edge of unbuttoned sleep to wide-open wakefulness and he got up to yawn and scratch by the window and watch the sunrise vie for attention with the flameglow. There were no fires to be seen from the windows of the apartment, there rarely were, but the clouds danced with wriggling shades of orange and scarlet and plumes of black smoke hung like violated serpents in the still air. And over all was the soundlessness, the hollow silence. Shaffer had begun to fear the silences more than the thunder of bombardment. Silence was a threat, a tactile substance, a winding-sheet of ice around the bowels. Silence took on a droning sound at dawn.

There had been no pleasing O'Keefe last night. The piece on the kids received a grudging, 'Yeah, not bad,' but he returned to his demand for a straight interview with a 'top name' on the conduct of the war.

'Like Churchill?' Shaffer had interposed sardonically.

'Who was the last correspondent to ask him?' O'Keefe shot back. 'I'll tell you. Nobody. And for why? Because they all figure the way you do he's gonna say no.'

'Because he *would* say no. Period.'

'O.K., so somebody else.'

'Attlee. Go ahead, tell me Attlee.'

O'Keefe didn't rise to the bait. 'Not Attlee. He couldn't make Armageddon sound worth buying tickets for. We want class. That first. Status. But a guy who runs his own show his own way. Get my meaning?'

Shaffer jumped into it feet together. 'How about Dowding?'

'Now you're thinking, Mel,' O'Keefe had snapped briskly. 'Dowding – fine. When?'

He got the Morris out of the lock-up and drove over to Hill Street at 8.45. The morning papers gave him his noon news file; London's inner defence ring of anti-aircraft guns had opened up last night with the fiercest barrage heard since the Blitz began. According to a communiqué issued by the Air Ministry and the Ministry of Home Security, ninety German planes had been shot down in what Goering had intended should be a super-blitz of the capital. That news shared the headlines with the text of a broadcast speech by Churchill; Hitler's plans for an invasion, he announced, were nearing completion; barges and ships were massing in ports all the way south from Hamburg to the Bay of Biscay and a secondary force was in readiness to attack from Norway. The invasion could be launched at any time and next week should be regarded as 'very important'.

Shaffer reached for the trash-can under his desk at once but the pieces of last night's rejected emotional essay had been removed by the cleaning woman. He sighed. Just as well. Keep it straight. He completed the piece before Mrs Price arrived, flustered and embarrassed once again at the failure of the public transport system to get her to work on time. Shaffer called New York and left a message with the overnight man to open a line to the B.B.C. at ten-fifteen.

Thursday, 0915

The crash of the front door woke Charles Russell with a start. His head jerked upwards and the movement filled his neck, shoulders and back with a delta of channelled pain. He gasped, opened his eyes, then closed them again with hydraulic suddenness as the morning sunlight streamed off the polished table by the window and stabbed straight to his brain. He was sprawled over the desktop, his arms swinging anthropoidally free, his face flat to the tooled leather.

He slid backwards until his hands could get a purchase on his head without stitching more pain across his back. He slumped in the chair. All night? Had he been here all night?

From the kitchen he could hear the thunderous morning concatenations of Elsie Warrender and an accompanying ululation that occasionally took verbal form in endless repetition of the same line: 'Who's taking you home tonight/After the dance is through?'

What could Elizabeth have been thinking of to allow him to sprawl in here all night like some alcoholic down-and-out? Surely she had the sense to. . . .

The patterns and sequences fell back into place. Caroline, her R.A.F. lover, Maconachie and Lubbock, Black Prince Road, the Frenchwoman, suspension.

Yes, he remembered last night now. He rejected Elizabeth's sympathy, her offer to try and grasp the reasons for his suspension. Confound it — what else could he have done? Told her the truth? She'd fretted; he'd turned to the last bottle of Black and

White and. . . . Elizabeth was still in ignorance. Dear God—
they must let Caroline come home. If Elizabeth didn't have her
back under her wing again soon, she'd go out of her mind.

'Who's taking you home tonight/After the dance is through?'

He clambered shakily to his feet, clutching at the chairback
for support. The light was unbearable. He stopped in front of a
mirror and shuddered; he looked disgusting. His hair was matted
and standing out from his head, his jaw was a black–grey
smudge, his eyes bloodshot and gross with suffering, his lips
cracked and dry. He bent to the drawer of his desk and found
a couple of Aspro tablets. He swallowed them and gagged on
the bitter taste.

Practicalities. Firstly, he had to know what Caroline's friendship with that woman meant. Secondly, it was essential he find
the officer she lunched with at the pub at Milton Bassett on
Tuesday. Thirdly . . . no, he had to face it; Elizabeth must be
told. That was inescapable. He clasped both hands to his face.

'Who's taking you home tonight/After the dance is through?'

Could he? He dropped his hands and turned back to the
mirror, challenging the thought face to face. The Warrender
woman was—for all her irritating imperfections—clearly
worldly; wise in an earthy, fundamental sense. She had known
Caroline for most of her life. She was Elizabeth's confidante.
Could he possibly. . . ?

No, the idea was outrageous. To confide in an unsophisticated,
possibly illiterate charwoman would be an act of gross folly.
She would quite probably boast openly about it to her family
and friends; and, of course, the master–servant relationship
would be destroyed for ever. He would never be able to face her
again. Unless . . . unless he could cross-examine her cleverly;
lead her to believe the conversation was a perfectly innocuous
one; draw her out. Yes, that might work. Wise? Yes, she was
that; but intelligent, no. He was on his way to the kitchen
before his natural caution could change his mind again.

Elsie Warrender dropped a saucepan in her surprise when he
came round the kitchen door. She grabbed it in time to arrest
its fall from the table to the floor and slapped a restraining hand
over her heart.

'Lumme, Mister, you scared me out of ten years' growth.'

He looked confused, then the allusion dawned on him and he reached a hand to his stubbled face. 'I . . . I'm sorry, Mrs—er. I worked rather late in the study last night and I—er—I seem to have slept there.'

Elsie Warrender swung into action at once. She lifted a large breakfast cup and saucer down from the Welsh dresser and rattled the kettle which was already singing on the hob of the kitchen fire as though to hurry its natural processes.

She turned back to him and her eyes narrowed. 'You sure you're all right, Mister?'

His head seemed about to burst. He leaned on a handy chair and Elsie pulled it out and lowered him into it.

'I think perhaps I've overdone things in the past few weeks.' He groaned, head in hands. 'My work, you know.'

'Just exactly what I told madam the other day. "He's looking really peaky," I said. I said, "If ever I saw a man who needed a tonic," I said, "it's him. He'll come down with a chill or 'flu or something, one day," I said, "and he won't know what hit him. No resistance, he'll have." '

She swung on the black iron kettle as steam rose in a steady column from its spout. The tea-caddy snapped open and she slid the teapot to within range of the kettle. Russell closed his eyes and nursed his face in his hands.

Elsie slipped a plump tea-cosy over the pot and took knife, fork and spoon from a drawer. 'You'll want your bloaters now, I suppose, will you?'

'No!' The idea revolted him. 'No. Some toast, I think. Just . . . toast.'

He didn't see her stare at him; it was just as well, for he would have been horrified at the pity and shrewd understanding in her eyes. She set a cup of tea at his hand and busied herself slicing two rounds of bread and slipping them under the grill. He sat, face in hands, until she pushed the buttered toast and the jam dish under his nose. He looked up quickly, blinking.

'You belong in bed, Mister,' she said reprovingly.

His irritation reared at once but he clamped it down. 'Yes . . . perhaps you're right, Mrs—er. . . .'

'I know I'm right. The way you're going on, you're heading for a breakdown.' She dropped into a chair, facing him across the table. 'You men won't be told. Think you know better, don't you?' She was waggling her finger at him like a kindergarten teacher admonishing a recalcitrant toddler. 'It's the blinking war, I know. Important, your work is, madam told me. But it's no good your thinking you're any different to anyone else. And what good will it do if you get yourself ill and can't go to work for' — she waved her hands in the air vaguely — 'oh, for months p'raps?'

'Mrs ... er ... You're a gool friend of my wife's. *No!*' He stopped her interruption. 'No, I know you are. She speaks very ... highly of you as a person as well as an employee.'

'Well, I don't know about that. I just....'

'Yes, yes,' he said impatiently. 'Natural modesty. I think perhaps I've failed to recognise that in the past. Too wrapped up in my work. I want you to know I was ... shocked to hear your home was bombed.'

'Madam said we could come and stay here,' Elsie interjected with real pride. 'I couldn't have that, o' course, but she offered and I know she wouldn't have unless you said it would be all right first.'

He was astounded at the revelation but fought to keep his features in a sympathetic mould. 'Yes, yes, of course. If there's anything we can do in the way of....' He couldn't bring himself to mouth the hypocrisy. Elizabeth must have been out of her mind.

'We'll manage, thanking you anyway, Mister,' she said soothingly. 'We're not the only ones.'

'Your husband ... your children.... They're...?'

'Father was hit hard at first. Got over it though. You wouldn't know he was the same man.' She trapped her tongue in her teeth and made a practised clicking noise. 'But, course, you don't know my Jack, anyway, do you?'

He cleared his throat to cover his embarrassment. 'No, I don't think I've had the pleasure.'

'Well, he's O.K. And Paul, that's my youngest, and my girl

Glad – Gladys . . . they're like rubber; bounce right back again, don't they, youngsters?'

'Ah – yes, they do. Your daughter is. . . ?'

'Almost the same age as Miss Caroline. Glad was born in May, Gemini, and Miss Caroline in January, Aquarius. Course, your girl's a lot brighter than my Glad – that's the Aquarian side coming out, I always say – but Glad's got a lovely nature; very sweet, she is; do anything for you. I tell her a lot about Miss Caroline – you know, the way she won all them prizes at the university and writing all them clever things in her – what she wrote to pass her exams.'

'Her thesis,' he said mechanically.

'That's it. Thesis. Madam did say at the time. Glad was ever so interested but not envious, you understand. She hasn't got an envious bone in her body. We're proud of Glad, me and Jack . . . like you're proud of Miss Caroline.'

Had his mind been more alert and his preconceptions about Elsie Warrender less biased, Russell might have discerned in those last six words more than an innocent compliment; instead, he rose to it eagerly.

'Yes, we are proud of her, naturally. But then, you know her as well as my wife and I, I suppose. You've watched her grow up. Become . . . a woman.' The fractional hesitation told Elsie more than Charles Russell would have believed possible.

She leaned forward on her plump forearms. 'I was meaning to ask but I didn't want to push myself where I wasn't wanted. Miss Caroline. She's . . . well, all right, is she?'

He tried to ignore the pounding in his temples. 'That's an odd question, Mrs – er. . . .'

'Well, I mean, you not hearing from her for two nights. I only wondered.'

'I'm sure she's told her mother where she is,' Russell said stolidly. 'Women do tend to . . . club together, after all, don't they?'

She nodded quickly. 'Oh, yes.'

'Something a man . . . a father, can never hope to grasp. The – er – close friendships women develop for one another.'

'That's true, yes.'

336

He crunched on a piece of toast. 'I expect you do?'

'Eh?' She was at a loss.

'Understand. I say I expect you understand the — er — *basis*, yes basis, for relationships between women.'

'Depends what sort. Me and Glad is one thing. Me and madam is different again as chalk and cheese. You mean like madam and Miss Caroline, do you?' Again he failed to catch the subtle emphasis.

'Not altogether. I was thinking more — generally.' He waved the piece of toast. 'I mean, women — young women, shall we say? — they develop what one might describe as — er — indelible affinities for other — er — women. Friendship, no doubt, in the first instance but later on something more ... tangible?' He attacked the toast noisily.

'I don't rightly know what you mean, Mister. But if you're saying do girls get all mixed up where their feelings are concerned, the answer is yes. My Gladys. ...'

'No, not quite that.' The woman was either ignorant or obtuse. He should have allowed instinctive first impressions to prevail and kept his problems to himself. 'I was thinking that perhaps — er — the emotions of young women at the — um — formative stages of their adult lives incline — in an experimental sense or out of a feeling of insecurity — towards other — er — women. Er — rather, that is, than men.'

She swept the cosy from the teapot and poured him another cup. His eye naturally followed the progress of the teapot and she used the diversion to study his unwashed, unshaven face.

'I don't rightly know, Mister, and that's a fact. You aren't worrying yourself that Miss Caroline—'

He dropped his toast on to the plate. 'Good God, Mrs — er ... how could you possibly think a thing like that? I thought we were having a purely — er — academic and — um — impersonal discussion. If I'd thought for a second that you imagined we were actually discussing my *daughter*. ... Really, I can't believe you honestly entertained such an idea.'

She sat bolt upright in her chair. 'Beg pardon, I'm sure.'

'The idea's ridiculous. Absurd. You know Miss Caroline well enough to. ...'

'I must be getting old, Mister,' Elsie said consolingly. 'Can't see my hand in front of my face first thing in the morning sometimes. The idea!' She poured herself a cup of tea and contemplated it seriously. 'You're right, though, about young women, come to think of it. Crushes, they have. Don't know what they're doing one minute to the next. It's being in-between, I think. Feeling in ways they never felt before and not knowing why. They want to feel needed, see? Important to someone. Sometimes, another woman can make it. . . .'

'You don't think there's something fundamentally . . . well, *incomplete* about . . . such women?'

'Naaooww.' Her scorn was manufactured with difficulty. Elsie Warrender was a whirlpool of conflicting emotions and doubts herself at that moment. 'Kids learning to be grown up, that's all.'

'But — er — when the other party to the — er, huh! — contract is a woman of some maturity, surely it implies. . . .' His haggard face fell in folds around sunken cheeks.

She became horribly afraid that he was going to press her for a conclusive answer. She stood up. 'Lumme, look at the time. It's after half past nine. Madam'll skin me if I don't bring her her cuppa. And you'll want to get yourself spruced up, Mister. I'll run you a bath when I take madam's tea up and—'

'I'll take my wife's tea,' he said curtly. 'Then I'll run a bath myself.'

Elizabeth had to be told. Now. Right now.

She peeled back her sleeping mask when she felt his weight descend on the side of the bed. He had not brought her tea in the morning since the first year of their marriage. Her eyes registered surprise, then resentment, then coldness.

'Where's Elsie?' she asked bleakly.

'In the kitchen. I thought I'd bring your tea myself.'

She ignored the proffered cup and he set it down on the bedside table.

'What on earth have you been doing?' His appearance suddenly hit her and she felt a twinge of remorse at her initial callousness. 'Are you ill? Oh, you look terrible, Charles.'

338

'I fell asleep at my desk in the study. It's not the most comfortable way to spend the night.'

'You must come to bed. You don't have to go to the....' She
stopped herself, but not in time. The look on his face showed
how deeply the imputation had struck home. She said quickly,
'Has Caroline...?'

'No. She hasn't. Look, Elizabeth; about Caroline—'

'What's wrong? Oh, my God, Charles, what's—'

He couldn't do it. He just hadn't the strength, the self-
confidence, the anger to tell her. He snapped defensively, 'Why
do you *always* anticipate the worst? She's a grown woman, for
heaven's sake. She can take care of herself.'

'You know that's not true! We've always looked after her.
She relies on us, especially you. What else do you expect me
to think when my daughter cannot be found for two nights
running? After lying to us about what she was doing and
where she'd be. Don't dare accuse me of anticipating the worst.
I *know* something's happened to her. I can *feel* it. If she can't
bring herself to keep in touch with us it's because she's afraid
of you.'

'Rubbish! I won't have that. Caroline and I—'

'Precisely. She wouldn't hurt you for the world. There *is*
something wrong and she's worried it'll affect her relationship
with you.' Elizabeth caught her knuckle in her teeth and rocked
in silent agony in the bed. He raised one hand to touch her but
dropped it again at once.

'I'd better run a bath,' he said heavily. 'I have some calls to
make this morning.'

He closed and locked the bathroom door behind him and
turned on the taps. He watched his image fade in the mirror
as steam stole sinuously over its surface. There was one more
slim, slim hope. Tom. The pub at Milton Bassett was as close to
Bentley Priory as it was Bletchley Park. Perhaps, just perhaps,
the air force officer Caroline had met there was somebody
known to Tom; somebody he could trace, if necessary, by a
process of elimination and the help of a duty roster. Tom
would have to be handled carefully. They had never got on,
never achieved any kind of understanding on which a normal

relationship, father and son, could be based. Tom was independent to the point of pig-headedness; he would certainly do nothing to compromise Caroline although it was equally true to say that he had little in common with his sister and had shared nothing of any importance with her since childhood. From the day he went away to prep school, Tom had closed the door on close relationships within the family to the extent of leaving Ian to fall on his own feet when they came together briefly at Winchester.

He punched fist into palm. Dammit, he couldn't call Tom. Lubbock and Maconachie had made it clear that he was expected to avoid contact with any government, civil or service agency. Tom would be suspect immediately if he were to call him now. The only alternative....

No!

Then what else? To sit and wait for the forces of circumstance to overwhelm him? Throw away his job, his reputation, a whole life's work? For what? To spare Tom the discomfort of perhaps half an hour's inquisition by Lubbock and Maconachie? Was the sacrifice of his career worth that?

He began to strip off his crumpled shirt and trousers. If he couldn't contact Tom personally, then there was no good reason why he shouldn't ask Maconachie to do so. Come to think of it, the policeman might already have investigated the possibility himself by now. Of course. And Tom had nothing to fear one way or the other.

He stood naked in the hot room, the taps' roar alluring and reassuring. He looked into the mirror. The steam had eaten away his reflection from head to foot. He did not exist.

Thursday, 0950

Larry LeSueur was on his way out to breakfast after a night spent feeding C.B.S. from the studio. They met in the lobby of Broadcasting House and swapped gossip. LeSueur had had feedback on Shaffer's 'Letter to my Wife.' 'That was a lousy thing to do to your friends,' he growled. 'Every wife in the Press corps will expect the same treatment between now and Thanksgiving.'

Eric Warr was already in the studio and Shaffer handed over his typed script. In the fifteen minutes before air time, Warr produced a stream of more up-to-date information and together they spliced it into the original. There was still no word on the St Paul's Cathedral time-bomb and a call to Ray Daniel at the *Trib* office came up empty-handed; if the confrontation with Harold Nicolson yesterday had produced any effects, they weren't as yet visible. The story of the palace bomb was prominent but rather less so than his instincts had led him to believe; in fact, it was played so coolly in text that he felt slightly chastened. He had expected the ministry to pull out all the stops on this one; use it to build a bridge between the terrible suffering of the East Enders and the conspicuous freedom from harm of the rest of the population.

He mentioned his theory to Eric Warr who shook his head decisively. 'I wouldn't let you say that, Mel, if you were to put it in a script — and not just because it's potentially harmful to morale. I don't happen to think it's true. Oh, I know what some people are saying in the East End and I can't blame them. But I swear to you there's no official pressure to play up the Buck House bomb. I'd know if there was. I'd probably be encouraging you to paint it with rainbow colours. But we don't have to *sell* the royals to our people. What do you expect them to do — stagger out of the rubble with blood on their faces? The East Enders don't want that — not for a minute.'

Shaffer accepted the point but felt his opinion was partially reinforced by the editorial in Lord Beaverbrook's *Daily Express*.

The Nazis will crow [it read], claiming that not even the King of England is immune from the attacks of the glorious Luftwaffe. But Englishmen will say, instead, that they are as sorry for their king as they are for the neighbour who has had a night visitation. The bomb that struck the palace is most certainly the unluckiest throw the Germans have made so far in this war. For it binds more tightly still the king to the people.

341

Now this becomes a Neighbours' War. The working man, the king, the working-class mother, the queen, the private soldier and his colonel are all in it together.

When the line opened from New York he was grateful for once to be told that O'Keefe had gone home and was sleeping the sleep of the totally exhausted. He had been on his feet – or his generous backside – for nearly four days with only an occasional nap on the couch in his office. He had been ordered home and told to stay there for thirty-six hours. The producer handling Shaffer's file played back a half-hearted sigh when he finished his read-out. 'Don't bother to make the five o'clock file, Mel, unless Hitler stops by for tea at the Ritz. We've got a special running on the Russian situation.' He didn't have to add: Because I wouldn't want to waste my time on more garbage like this.

Eric Warr's lower lip disappeared into his teeth and a flush of amusement burned his cheeks. He said, when the line clicked off, 'I think they're looking for a more interesting war, Mel. He sounds as if he's had a bellyful of ours.'

The calling light on the telephone blipped and Warr picked it up. He handed it across the table and got to his feet politely. 'For you,' he said and disappeared around the curtain.

Gladys was defensive. 'It's me,' she said meekly. 'I didn't want to interrupt but the lady at your office said I should call you at the B.B.C. and she gave me the number. I knew I shouldn't really.'

'You should. Really. I'm through here. Where are you?'

'I'm at the club. They told us to be here sharp at nine when we finished last night but they wouldn't say why. They're closing down for a few days – well, they *say* a few days but you don't know, do you? I thought I ought to tell you because, well. . . .'

'In case I came along expecting to find you there,' he finished.

'Yes,' she said weakly.

'So – you're on the breadline, huh?'

'Oh, no,' she protested at once. 'They gave us two weeks' pay in advance. They're very good like that.'

'I was joshing you. What're you doing today?'

He had touched a nerve; he heard her catch her breath. This was the real reason for her call. 'Well, I suppose I ought to get back to Nelson's Green. . . ,' she ventured slowly. It was a speech designed for interruption. He obliged.

'Why go back? You have something to do there?'

'Well . . . not exactly.'

He made it up as he went along. 'Fine. You've got a day off; I've got a day off. What do you say we take the car out of town? Get some good clean country air. We could take a picnic basket and—'

'Oh, a picnic!' It was the breathless squeak of the child whose daydreams materialise the very second she inspires them. It was followed by instant caution. 'Er—I don't know that I should.'

'You should. For my sake. I've been slaving away here non-stop for days without a break. I'm falling apart for air and relaxation . . . and good company. You wouldn't let me down, would you?'

'Oh, no!'

'Good. I'll pick you up in half an hour, at eleven o'clock. Corner of Carlos Place, opposite the Connaught. Do you know it?'

She said she'd find it.

Thursday, 1055

Mrs Price had told him about picnic hampers from Fortnum's, although she wasn't sure the war hadn't put an end to such sybaritic indulgences. It hadn't. An awesome personage in black jacket and waistcoat and striped pants produced a basket for two at only twenty minutes' notice. He apologised for the indifferent sparkling wine which nowadays deputised for the champagne of pre-war days, but he was sure Mr Shaffer appreciated the problems involved in trying to maintain standards in such hazardous times. Mr Shaffer did. Readily. The chicken sandwiches were, of course, fresh, said the personage gravely, and the tomatoes, celery, radishes and lettuce were all English.

The cutlery and napery could be returned with the basket at the customer's convenience. The miniature pork pies were the best available *hors d'oeuvres* and the dessert gâteau should ideally be kept wrapped in its grease-proof shroud and protective box until required for consumption. The double thermos flask of tea was, perhaps, a liberty – by no means the convention at Fortnum's – but conditions of war were such they recognised that the niceties of tea-making in the open air were probably temporarily inconvenient. He left it to an elderly woman to put a price on this inadequate package and accept the 15s 6d in sordid currency of the realm, but he accompanied Shaffer out into Piccadilly and saw him to his car.

He was five minutes early at Carlos Place but she was already there; chocolate-coloured beret, flimsy green cotton coat, chunky wedge-heeled shoes. She noticed his appraising stare as the Morris pulled into the kerb and looked down at herself. 'Is this all right? I had to borrow from Janice again.'

'You look great. Let's go.'

Mrs Price had also been the Baedeker for plotting his course and destination. Avoid Epping Forest, she advised. Too many homeless evacuees. Avoid Essex. Not terribly scenic. Don't go north. Berkshire would be nice. Or Kent – no, Kent was full of Battle of Britain airfields and therefore German bombers. Lovely, of course, but dangerous.

He left it to Gladys and she chose Kent, Hitler or no Hitler. There was a tiny village off the main London–Maidstone road near West Malling where her mother and father and a whole posse of relatives had gone each summer to pick hops, she said. Hops? The things they put in English beer to make it taste like beer, she explained. Hop-picking had been the East Ender's traditional summer holiday since time immemorial. She hadn't been since 1938 but she would dearly love to see the village again.

He wouldn't have found the main A20 to Maidstone without her. There were no signposts along the way, not even at major road junctions; they had all been uprooted months since and taken away for storage. Even the ancient stone mile-posts, dating back to the Canterbury pilgrims, had been defaced to confound

344

and delay any potential German invasion force. For the first time in his life Shaffer gave serious consideration to the true value of an ordinary, everyday, well-marked road system, to the free, uninterrupted passage of traffic, to the unremarkable right of a citizen to go where he wanted. The more he considered it, the more depressing the alternative became. This country had tossed aside the privileges of traditional organisation; that and more. Not only could a man get lost in his own country, but his freedom to move around in it was questionable. All his freedoms were questionable, for the moment anyway, except the freedom to fight and the freedom to die. That probably lightened the psychological load in the long run — unless you happened to be a Churchill, an Attlee, a Bevin, or a Dowding, and you were juggling those freedoms for maximum effect — snatching them away here, granting them there; withdrawing them, re-issuing; godlike as long as you didn't brood too deeply on human fallibility. What in damnation did politicians do, any of them, when they lost the way? When they woke up one morning and stared into the shaving-mirror and thought: Why did I do what I did yesterday and what am I expected to do today? How did they console themselves when their decisions cost a few thousand lives, lost a country, yielded more ground to the enemy, brought the hissing vituperation of the people down on their heads? What could a Chamberlain do, apart from resign, to compensate for wrong-guessing the opposition and drumming up a war? Maybe they were all so goddamned egotistical they never questioned their right to decide the fate of their fellow men. Oh well, chaps, tomorrow's another day.

'I think Farningham's down there,' Gladys shrilled over the wind's roar but she looked and sounded so uncertain he braked the Morris and pulled on to the gravelled frontage of a substantial-looking roadside pub. His request for directions to West Malling evoked an instant airfrost of hostility from the twenty or so farmworkers and local tradesmen drinking beer outside. His accent didn't help but even Gladys's intervention did nothing to allay suspicion; if anything it made matters worse. The German spy and his English fifth columnist slut; the conclusion was written all over their round, disingenuous faces. What use was a war if you couldn't confront the enemy occasionally? A young woman relented and reeled off a complicated route of left and right turns but the crowd began to rumble menacingly and Shaffer pulled back on to the road. This was not the day to end up in some inarticulate village constable's lock-up.

The incident loosened their humour and as the car put distance between them and the pub the sheer lunacy of it gave them both a fit of the giggles. Once started they couldn't stop; and when Gladys guessed at a turn that might lead to West Malling and they wound up, instead, at the gate of a hop field, they fell back in their seats and spilled tears of laughter. Back they went along the lane until Shaffer found another, equally narrow lane, hedged to a height of nearly twenty feet on either side. They followed it for miles as it snaked up and down, looping crazily back and forth over the hidden landscape, while both of them roared helplessly. At one point Gladys was almost overwhelmed. They had passed two farm entrances on which the wily owners had painted out the name but left the word 'Farm', and when they came upon a third her shriek was so piercing it took her breath away and she clapped a hand to her breast.

He brought the Morris to a sliding halt and leant over her, concerned. He took her hand and searched her face anxiously; and in that instant their laughter died as abruptly as it had begun; they grew still, their eyes locked and questioning. She waited but he made no move; then she touched her hand lightly to his face and drew it downwards. He crushed his mouth on hers, wound the slim young body in his arms and. . . . He pulled away, swung back to his seat and engaged gear again. 'Sorry. I guess I shouldn't have. . . .'

'No!' She was shivering slightly. 'It was my fault. I . . . made you. I thought you . . . wanted to. Now I feel terrible. Let's go back.'

At the end of the lane, on the elbow of yet another bend, was an open gate and through it he could see stubble and stooked corn. He roared down to it, swung in and brought the Morris to a halt under the sheltering hedge ten yards inside the cornfield.

'Now you listen to me good.' He grabbed both her hands and forced her to face him. 'Don't ever make the mistake of doing

346

my thinking for me again. O.K.? And don't tell me how I feel or what my emotions are. You couldn't know back there what I was feeling. Who the hell do you think you are? If I didn't feel—' He stopped abruptly. She was smiling. 'What's so damn funny?' he snarled.

'You are. You're like a little boy.'

He flung himself back into his seat. 'Why do women think the way to a man's heart is through his babyhood? I'm no little boy, sweetheart, and what I felt for you back there was—'

'I know,' she said simply.

'Then for chrissakes, why the big production?'

She smiled down at her hands and then fully into his face. 'I just wanted to be sure, that's all.'

'Sure of what?'

Her grin was infectious. He felt the dormant stirring of idiot hysteria.

'What kind of a man you are.'

'And what does that mean?'

Her eyes were wide and clear and joyously honest. 'You know well enough what it means.' She fluttered her fingers with wicked satisfaction.

'I'll be damned if I. . . .' His voice broke and the first giveaway giggle squeezed out of him and deflated his temper. Her clear young voice peeled with laughter and she fell forward on his shoulder and he held her to him, one-armed. When they stopped rocking she reached up her face and pecked his cheek with gentle intimacy.

'Come on,' she said, swinging her legs out over the stubble. 'I've been starving for miles. I'm dying to see what a Fortnum's hamper looks like.'

Thursday, 1330

Denzil Fletcher-Hale draped his impeccable length in the arch linking the bar with the Savoy Grill and adopted a mask of tactful indifference while his host upbraided the *maître d*. They were well matched for social combat but it was inevitable that

347

Colonel Tristram de Wolffe should win; it was no more than one expected of the Savoy's unparalleled service. A guest was always right and a member of the staff clearly in error in any situation where their points of view were at odds, as on this occasion when de Wolffe claimed imperiously that his secretary had booked a table for one forty-five and the *maître d* was unable to find written evidence of the fact in his reservations log. As it happened, de Wolffe had confided to Fletcher-Hale, he'd quite forgotten to book a table but Denzil was not to worry; 'leave it to me'. After a seemly period of token resistance, the *maître d* bowed low and apologised for the shortcomings of his staff and waved them into the Grill. While they argued, a table had been set up in a corner, and chairs, cutlery and napery magically produced. Fletcher-Hale watched this discreet performance with mild amusement and, when the *maître d* handed them into the care of a trusty old waiter, he slipped the good fellow a oncer behind de Wolffe's ramrod back.

Their first few minutes at the table were not private. Harold Nicolson was lunching at the next table with Erika Mann and they both greeted Fletcher-Hale with some warmth. De Wolffe was a co-ordinator at S.O.E. and a difficult man to introduce to anyone of normal social sensibility and impossible to coax into the briefest verbal contact. He knew Nicolson by name through his connection with the Ministry of Information but a recital of Miss Mann's antecedents — her father Thomas Mann, the celebrated German novelist; her husband, the poet W. H. Auden — added only a twitch of suspicion to his glare of blank disdain. Noël Coward presided with deft command over a table for eight, three stunningly beautiful girls among them attracting every male eye in the room, and he stood and threw a click-heeled bow which clearly embodied a message only he and Fletcher-Hale could comprehend. De Wolffe's sole concession to involvement of any kind came when a man in undistinguished herring-bone grey crossed the room to shake the young man's hand. De Wolffe snapped to his feet but his reaction stemmed from the first word of Denzil's introduction : '*General* Spears,' and not the explanation that he was head of the British Mission at General de Gaulle's headquarters.

They settled at last and Colonel de Wolffe instructed his guest in the vagaries of the menu. The old waiter, poised for their order, displayed no emotion but his jaw squared fractionally; he and Denzil were old acquaintances and it was his personal view that only the *chef de cuisine* knew the Savoy menu more intimately.

The food and wine ordered, de Wolffe ran a prurient eye over the faces in the room. His voice was pitched low.

'Had a *billet doux* from CIGS,' he said, pronouncing the initials of the Chief of the Imperial General Staff as a word. 'Seems he has a pretty high opinion of you, Fletcher-Hale. Friends at court?'

'John Dill? We mix socially. Sound man. Like him.'

De Wolffe's pale-grey eyes searched the brown face for further clues. 'Do I take it you approached him with a view to joining . . . our little band?'

Fletcher-Hale displayed surprise. 'Met him last at Sibyl Colefax's. Dinner. Lord North Street. Talked a lot. War. That sort of thing. Two, three weeks ago. Might have mentioned something. Can't say.'

De Wolffe bunched his lips and ran his tongue round his teeth. He had no personal social contacts of rank himself and ordinarily mistrusted those who had but he was genuinely intrigued by this indolent young hound's Malthusian sphere of influence.

'Sir John's letter reached me yesterday,' he said. 'Coincidence, I suppose, but I also received a call this morning from the' — he dropped his voice to whisper level — 'the Prime Minister's office.'

'Really?' Even Denzil's curiosity was aroused momentarily, then his face sagged into the agony of a smile. 'Ah! Desmond Morton, yes?'

'The P.M.'s private assistant. Yes — as a matter of fact it was.'

'Thought so. Met him at the Camroses last night. Cocktails. Keeping an eye on me, he said. Mentioned we were lunching today. Knew you by reputation. Pitched it rather strong, did he?'

'Said something about your considering' — de Wolffe edged

his chair nearer and his voice sank again to a whisper – 'an offer from Dysart's people at Naval Intelligence. Correct?'

'Manner of speaking. Dropped in yesterday. Had a chat. Decent types. Get along. Nothing settled.'

De Wolffe clamped his hands together and the muscles in them jumped convulsively. 'Amateurs, Fletcher-Hale! No-hopers. Take my word. Sea cooks the lot of 'em. Place is a funk-hole for third raters. Now then. . . .' He froze as the sommelier opened the wine and poured for his acceptance. He waved the fellow on without tasting and waited for him to retire. 'We could use a chap with your . . . *ahum!* . . . style at Special Operations Executive. Professionals, you understand. The best. The cream. You have any languages, do you?'

Fletcher-Hale grimaced. 'French, of course. Never too bright at Latin. Missed the boat at Greek.'

'Excellent! French. Very good. Know the country?'

'France? Paris, of course. Deauville, Monaco, Nice. Fond of Biarritz.'

De Wolffe's clenched hands leaped excitedly. 'Couldn't be better. French speaker. Knows the country.' He seemed to be addressing an imaginary appointments board. 'Tell me about yourself. Eton, right?'

'Yes.'

'Colours?'

Denzil sighed modestly. 'Cricket.'

De Wolffe's eyes widened slightly. 'Made the Lord's match, did you?'

'Yes.'

'Hmmmm. Fletcher-Hale. Fletcher-Hale.' De Wolffe's eyes closed and he summoned a clouded recollection. 'Wait a minute. D. W. K. Fletcher-Hale. Thirty-one? No. Thirty-two. Third wicket down?'

'Second,' Denzil admitted reluctantly.

'You scored your ton, am I right?'

'A hundred and twenty-three. Caught and bowled.'

'Exactly! Harrow, myself. Watched the match that year. Surrey were after you, weren't they? But you went on to

Oxford. Got your blue of course. Seem to remember you toured with the M.C.C. Colts a couple of seasons. Good reports.'

'Lot of luck,' Denzil said dismissively. 'Better team that year, Harrow. Off form on the day.'

'D. W. K. Fletcher-Hale,' De Wolffe mused to himself. 'D. W. K. Hundred and twenty-three in the Eton–Harrow match. Caught and bowled. Well, I'll be damned.' He brought his face uncomfortably close to Denzil's. 'Look, old fellow, this makes a whale of a difference. Brothers under the skin, after all. Can't allow you to throw your talents away on Dysart's bunch. Wouldn't be right. With your form you can take your pick, make no mistake about it. Take your pick of the best.'

'Matter of doing one's bit.' Denzil shifted awkwardly on his chair.

'For the rest, yes. Absolutely. But don't fool yourself this is just another conventional war, Fletcher-Hale. We'll learn a lot this time round. This'll be an Intelligence war, my boy. Scientific. We're not going to win this one with cavalry charges and siege infantry. Penetration from within, that's the scheme. Guerilla tactics. Misinformation. Striking at the enemy's morale. The knife across the throat.' He made a sickening squelching noise. 'That's what our chaps are designed for. Tough little group. You couldn't do better.'

The waiter approached and lifted their sole from the bone on a wheeled trolley. Fletcher-Hale made a few experimental probes with a reluctant fork. De Wolffe lunged at his with the aggressive confidence of the fencer. He gulped contentedly and chewed.

'What do you say?' His mouth was full.

'Honoured, naturally. Attractive idea. Like to think about it; meet some of your chaps. Arrange that?'

'Like a shot. First class people. You'll like them. Now, let's see . . . we have a Q. tactics manoeuvre on next week.' He raised a finger to his lips. 'Not too far out of town. Have you picked up and driven out, what do you say? I think we can lay on a decent lunch as well.' He lifted the bottle of Rhine wine from its cooler and shook his head. 'Offer you something a little more drinkable than this, too. Tell you what I'll do. On Monday I'll call—'

'Hey, Harold.' The cry came from the centre of the grillroom; it was loud enough to turn every head and even brought de Wolffe's monologue to an abrupt halt. He looked up in irritation.

The man was American, clearly upset, and bee-lining for Harold Nicolson's table under a head of steam. Nicolson got to his feet uncertainly.

The American pulled himself up short at the table and made an attempt at a stiff bow to Erika Mann. 'I apologise for interrupting your meal, ma'am.'

'Not at all.'

Nicolson introduced his guest. 'This is H. R. Knickerbocker of the New York *Journal-American*.'

'I have to talk to you, Harold.' Knickerbocker was trembling with rage. 'I just got through beating my head against a wall with your people and—'

Nicolson signalled for a chair. Knickerbocker sat down. He lowered his voice but not sufficiently to exclude Fletcher-Hale and de Wolffe.

'I've gotten the best story in the world and your censors won't let me run it. I hear some of the guys talked with you yesterday and you said you'd work out some kind of deal for—'

'I said I'd look into it, that's all. I made no promises.'

The American hunched forward on his chair. 'O.K., O.K. You'll look into it, but that isn't going to do me any good right now.'

'What's your story? If I can—' Nicolson turned suddenly to his guest. 'I'm sorry to drag you into a trade tussle, Erika. Forgive me.'

'Don't worry about me,' she smiled. 'I'm enjoying it.'

Knickerbocker looked uncomfortable. 'Yes. I should've left this till later,' he said apologetically. 'I guess I lost my temper.'

'Your story. . . ?' prompted Nicolson politely.

'The time-bomb outside St Paul's Cathedral. I know it's there —we all do. And I know it can go off any time. That bomb could lay the place flat, destroy one of the greatest pieces of church architecture in the world. Why can't the American people be brought in to share my anxiety?'

'I honestly don't know. I'll try to find out.'

'*Trying* to find out takes time, Harold,' Knickerbocker appealed. 'But that isn't all. I wrote a story today about the destruction in Bond Street and the Burlington Arcade. Every American who knows London can identify with those two places. So why won't the censor let it through? You know, this is basic stuff, Harold. You're asking us to work with a gag in our mouths.'

'Who is that dammed American?' de Wolffe whispered acidly.

'Newspaperman. Knickerbocker, New York *Journal-American.*'

'Damn silly name.'

Nicolson looked at his watch and waved an arm at the hovering waiter. 'My bill, please.' He said to his guest, 'I really think I should settle this right away, Erika. Do you mind?'

'No, of course not. I didn't expect to commandeer you for long. Anyway, I have some shopping to do.'

Knickerbocker's eye flashed over the neighbouring table and his eyebrows arched when he saw Denzil. 'Hi,' he said guardedly. Denzil dipped his head in greeting.

'Know the fellow?' hissed de Wolffe.

'Friend of a friend,' Denzil sighed. 'Excitable chaps, Americans.'

Thursday, 1445

Food had never tasted so good, or wine so delicious. The white wine was warm, of course; the damp cloth in which Fortnum's had swathed the bottle had dried in the sun, but no connoisseur ever drank a prime vintage with more satisfaction. They ate in the shade of a half-built cornstook and she talked until the sun came round to bathe them free of shadow.

She told him the truth about her father's breakdown and how the past two nights had brought him new strength and peace of mind.

She talked with compelling *naïveté* about herself. Her life seemingly was a tapestry of dreams; reality a vulgar, intrusive sham. She knew every major American film actor, believed all the publicity material, could name every big movie of the last ten years and quote word for word the more memorable lines. The club was fairyland; the West End paradise. The fact that she and her family were homeless, destitute in every practical sense, seemed not to worry her. The shock of seeing rubble where once there had been a home had been numbing, horrifying in its deeper implications, but now the shock was over and forgotten. The Warrenders were in free fall. Her mother, she said proudly, hadn't missed one day's work with the family she 'did for' in Chelsea and no one had as yet given thought to looking around for somewhere else to live. They would manage. Things would work out.

The family had its ups and downs but everyone else was in the same boat and there was comfort in that. The war made everything normal seem so unimportant. The best thing was to live for the moment, that's what her dad had told her. Be like the kettle and sing, she laughed, like in the Vera Lynn song. Now there was a case in point, Vera Lynn. There was always Vera on the wireless when they needed cheering up. And Jack Warner and Tommy Handley. Shaffer had to search his memory; Warner was a Cockney comedian, lately popular for his droll working-class monologues. Tommy Handley was the linchpin of a B.B.C. comedy show called 'ITMA' – the initials originally intended as a cheeky sideswipe at Hitler. 'It's That Man Again' – which had half the nation glued to its sets throughout the winter months.

No, said Gladys dreamily, the *real* things didn't change. Had he seen that *lovely* picture *Night Train to Berlin*, with Rex Harrison and Paul Henreid and Margaret Lockwood and had he. . . ?

He let her talk without interruption. They had lain apart at first, divided by the spread of white tablecloth and the litter of crockery and cutlery, but as the food disappeared and the talk and the wine relaxed her he inched closer and finally took her hand in his. She didn't seem to notice. The satin coolness of her skin excited him and he drew nearer, staring at her as she talked, watching her lips move, her eyes change colour with the passing moods; then in the middle of one of her rambling reminiscences he curled an arm over her shoulder and pulled her down to him. He caught her mouth in his, forced the lips wide; felt and heard her hiss of expectancy, then the weight of her leaning into him. The simple cotton dress she'd worn under the coat yielded under his hand as he moved from breasts to thighs; she didn't flinch as his fingers curled into her but her arms tightened around his neck.

Afterwards they lay in breathless silence, her body quaking under his, her face buried in the hollow of his throat, shutting out the possibility of contact, eye to eye. Then he rolled away and she pillowed her head on his chest. Her hair spilled in an ebony pool across his shirt; the perfume of bitter-sweet oranges. Along the wall of the half-made stack a fieldmouse poked a twitching nose, sentry-like, from a barricade of stalks and two bees hummed in furtive anticipation over the remains of a chicken sandwich. If he was ever called to account for this war, he thought, this is what he would remember first.

'What are you thinking?'

She sighed sadly. 'Oh, things.'

'You want to be a little more specific?'

She chuckled softly, but without amusement. 'You'd be embarrassed. You'd play the little boy again.'

'Try me.'

She sat up and he saw the tears gathering in her eyes, but she was still smiling. 'It's like a film, that's all. You know, you can see it happening and it's lovely and nothing else exists. But you know it'll end. The lights go up and you go outside and there's the real world. It's always there — waiting for you to come out.'

He pushed up on one elbow, puzzled. 'What does that mean?'

'It means I know you're married.'

The simple directness of it, cool and unemotional, momentarily snatched the breath from him.

He couldn't match her coolness. 'Why didn't you say something before? Why let it go as far as' — he looked down at the crumpled Fortnum's tablecloth where they had lain — 'as far as this?'

Two tears crumbled over the brink of her lashes and strayed

down her cheeks. 'Because I love you,' she said simply. She saw the panic in his face. 'No — that's not a threat. I'm not going to make you . . . do anything about it.'

'What do you mean — do anything?'

'You know. I wanted you. I wanted to be part of you. Just a little part. Just once. You don't have to worry I'll make a nuisance of myself.'

He grabbed her savagely and pulled her down to him, her tears flooding his cheek. Why in God's name had he. . . ?

Three black specks high in the heat-stained sky broke formation, their vapour trails diverging like streamers loosed from a retaining pin. One dived earthwards, pulled out at zero height and headed towards the cornfield in a low hedge-hopping run. The others banked crazily and headed eastwards.

She spoke into the soft flesh of his throat.

'I just want to pretend for a little while. That's all. Just pretend till the lights go up. Then I'll go away.'

'I don't want you to go away,' he said harshly. Yes I do. I want you to go away right now. Never come back. Never be anywhere I can find you again; think about you. Goddamn the whole stinking mess.

Two of the vapour trails turned in a great loop and flew inland again, diving to find the level of their hedge-hopping comrade. Another speck, much smaller, sat unswervingly on their tails. The hedge-hopping plane was now audible; about four or five miles away. He jumped to his feet and hauled her after him, tucking his clothes in place hurriedly.

'I think we'd better get out of here,' he snapped. He pulled her towards the car in a stumbling run but she turned, waved a hand towards the remains of the picnic.

'The basket and—'

'Forget it!' he yelled. The plane's nasal snarl was loud now; urgent. 'Come on!' They reached the car as the plane broke over the hedge on the far side of the field. He hurled her down and dived on top of her, shielding her body with his. The bomber screamed overhead, its shadow blipping over them. He pulled her up again and pushed her into the car. He reversed wildly, swung the Morris out into the lane and accelerated away.

'What are you doing?' she shouted at him.

'Moving target!' he roared over the rush of air. 'Keep down in the seat!'

From behind them came a shattering staccato burst of cannon fire and he ducked involuntarily. A second plane zoomed overhead, followed by another. He saw the Hurricane bank suicidally, heard the patter-patter of gunfire again.

Ahead of them the road divided three ways around a triangle of long grass. He pulled right into an even deeper tunnel of hedgerow-bounded lane. A hundred yards on it widened and then opened dramatically into a village high street. Two bombers and the pursuing Hurricane seemed to be revolving on a mad carousel above them. Shaffer skidded the Morris to a halt, dragged the girl from her crouched position in front of the seat, ran her across the road and pushed her into a ditch. Her body bounced savagely as he lost his grip of her and he heard her gasp. He flung his arms about her and pulled her close.

Along the street, maybe twenty yards away, was a tiny stone bridge over a stream which ran into a pond where white ducks paddled unconcernedly. Behind it a pub squatted, red brick at ground level, whitepainted wood at the first floor, a thatched roof. Opposite was a row of cottages, pocket-handkerchief gardens ablaze with late-summer flowers. Over a belt of trees he could see the bell-tower of a little church and, to one side, the railings and yard of what was probably the village school. Ten yards along the ditch was the wall of a shop decked with brightly painted tin signs advertising Reckitt's Blue, Robin Starch, Bovril and Andrew's Liver Salts. The picture stayed on the retina of his memory for years afterwards in perfect resolution and detail.

The planes above dived yet again and he saw one German bomber under pressure suddenly swing and lift. He heard no explosions — later he thought he might have been temporarily deafened — but there was a slight puff of energy and the pub subsided to the ground like a burst balloon. Only in the last split second before it settled did it seem to lose its shape. I'll huff and I'll puff and I'll blow your house down. In the dream-like slow motion of the moment, the wolf's line from the old fable came bounding into his head.

He jarred his face on the back of her head as he ducked. The planes whined into a climb and he ventured another look. It *was* a school. Had been a school. There were no trees to hide it now. But there was nothing to hide. A stretch of railing stood untouched and an arch and a wall fluttering with paper and a line of hat-pegs stranded in the ruin of a cloakroom, but that was all. He could see the church now. It was whole but one window gaped black where stained glass had been sucked out in the blast.

He felt her struggling, pushing against him and realised he had her in a bear-hug. He let her go. She stood up and he followed suit. From a long way away came the ringing of a bell; an ambulance or a fire-engine. The front doors of four of the cottages opened simultaneously and without a glance to right or left the householders ran into the street. The road from the church was suddenly alive. An R.A.F. fire-tender whoofed to a halt beside the school; another clanged past it and raised a cloud of dust as it braked alongside the pancake debris of the old pub. An ambulance followed it and behind that a delivery van with a temporary canvas sign stuck to its side: Civil Defence.

Eight years later, when Princeton invested him with an honorary Doctorate of Letters, the Dean singled out his despatch from that summer's day, 'Somewhere in England,' as the most powerful, most evocative, and perhaps the most influential piece of radio reporting the country had ever heard. But in the moments, the hours that followed, his professionalism deserted him; he functioned only as a digging tool, reasoned with the single-mindedness of the face-working miner. First at the pub, where they located three bodies before they found the landlord. A doctor had to amputate both his legs above the knee before they could free him. The school was out for the summer holiday, luckily, but a caretaker was believed to have gone there to sweep and dust. They found him alive, bent double under a blackboard which had fallen on him just seconds before a wall collapsed around him. The blackboard saved his life but not his right arm. Across a high wall from the school, just thirty yards from the church, the vicarage had sustained a direct hit. They found the vicar, a pale little man in his late thirties, scrabbling on his knees in the rubble, the shirt slashed from his back but his dog-collar intact. He was inarticulate. They dug where he knelt and found the remains of the bathroom. His wife had been giving their three young children an all-in-one austerity bath. All four of them were dead.

It was three-thirty when he looked around him for Gladys. He found her in one of the cottages surrounded by a platoon of pathetic old people and dozens of empty teapots and mugs. When she was sure there was no more to be done she allowed him to lead her to the car. She remained silent all the way to Nelson's Green. At the end she didn't even say goodbye.

It was a little after five-thirty and Florence Scully had only just arrived home. She seemed a little subdued herself but clucked around like a mother hen when she saw Gladys's frozen stare and, when Jack Warrender came in for his supper, told him to entertain Shaffer while she put the girl to bed. It was an anticlimax both of them were grateful for.

Warrender listened gravely to the story of their picnic and at the end of it shook Shaffer by the hand. It was acutely embarrassing; he couldn't help wondering what the old man would have said and done if he'd been privy to the scene that preceded the action. If anything he was as vaguely innocent as his daughter; probably more so.

They both heard the clatter of heels in the paved backyard but Shaffer had his back to the window and decided it would be bad mannered to turn around and stare. He expected to see the worn, practical figure of Elsie Warrender; Janice Scully's arrival was all the more a shock because for several hours he had successfully blotted her out of existence.

'Well, now — who's this then?' Janice drawled, falling automatically into the mannequin pose. She was wearing a green blouse open to the third button and a tight-fitting black skirt. A bag swung from her shoulder. Her head was covered with a square of silky material but when she saw him she swept it off and shook the black curtain of hair free.

Jack Warrender eyed her warily. 'Yes, well, this is Mr Shaffer and, Mr Shaffer, this is the Scullys' girl, Janice. Married to their boy, Geoff.'

Shaffer went through the pantomime of rising to his feet and extending his hand. She watched him, amused; delayed her acceptance of the handshake until he was suitably humiliated. Only Florence Scully's clattering descent on the stairs saved him from total disintegration.

Florence made tea and they sat around the tiny table. Shaffer was pressed to tell his story again; Florence marvelled, one hand clasped nervously across her stomach, and Janice filled every hesitant gap in the monologue with a series of mocking exclamations: Oh, no! You didn't, did you? Oh, that was *brave*! No — I can't *bear* it! Both Jack Warrender and Florence seemed to treat the interjections as perfectly genuine.

In the end Shaffer could stand it no longer. He got to his feet abruptly and flicked up his watch. 'I'll have to go, I'm afraid. I've got a broadcast to do tonight.'

Flo went to the kitchen and returned with something basin-shaped wrapped in a scrap of white cloth. 'Man like you with no one to look after him don't feed hisself properly, I'll be bound. You take this with you. Do you the world of good.' His protests were fluttered away and he took the wrapped basin self-consciously. She made no attempt to enlighten him as to its contents and he didn't feel he could challenge the mysteries of English working-class hospitality by asking.

He offered his hand to Jack Warrender and then, as she rose, reluctantly to Janice. She looked down at the hand then up into his face. She said, 'You couldn't give me a lift could you, Mr Shaffer?'

Jack Warrender's eyes narrowed suspiciously. 'Where you bound for then, girl?'

Florence Scully pushed at him diplomatically. 'Don't be nosey, Jack. None of our business, is it?'

Janice turned on her with an ingratiating smile. 'S'all right, mum. I don't mind. I'm staying with Maureen Thompson down near Blackfriars for a couple of nights. She's just about due.

Like Edie. Only her Brian's away in the navy. Destroyers. Couldn't let the girl cope on her own, could I?'

'Course you can't love,' agreed Flo. 'You'd best pack a few things then. Quiet though. Glad'll be asleep up there by now.'

Janice moved to the staircase. 'I won't make a sound,' she whispered. Her eye caught Shaffer's. 'Course, if Mr Shaffer can't wait, though. . . .'

'Oh, I'm sure he don't mind, long as you hurry up. Do you, Mr Shaffer?'

At the car he dropped her case in the back seat and held open the rear door for her. Janice opened the front passenger door, winked in his face and squeezed into the seat with the maximum display of stockinged thigh. As he turned into Jamaica Road her hand reached across the gear lever and stretched lightly on his knee.

'Phew!' The low gurgling sound rolled in her throat. 'I better phone Maureen at the Corner House and tell her where I'm supposed to be for the next few days.' She tightened her fingers on the swell of his thigh.

'And nights.'

He exhausted his arguments and his anger too quickly not to be aware that he was secretly glad she was there and prepared to cling for as long as it suited her. Even as he gave vent to his guilt and frustration he knew he could say nothing that would make the slightest difference. He might lie to himself but he was an open book to Janice Scully. She let him shout and threaten, but her long, capable fingers maintained their shameless kneading of his thigh. And when he invoked the name of her husband, in one final relentless bid to salve his conscience, she laughed openly.

'Geoff? I don't owe Geoff nothing. Tell you that himself if you asked him.' She touched a finger to her lips. 'Well, maybe not to *you*, he wouldn't. He knows all about your kind, our Geoff.'

He halted the Morris to allow a convoy of tightly battened army trucks to cross the junction from Tower Bridge. Three of them carried peremptory notices on their tailboards: 'Danger.

Keep Your Distance.' Half a dozen others were towing field guns; his knowledge of armaments was too limited to define their type and role. A clutch of Military Police motorcycle outriders weaved in and out around the trucks, swanky in white crash helmets and belts and gauntlets.

'What kind is my kind?' he rasped.

'Wouldn't you just like to know.' She nudged his arm with her shoulder; playfully, but as always with a sexual insistence that required no translation.

'Oh, to hell with him — and *you*, dammit!'

Again he was aware of his unquenchable appetite for her; of a chemistry that transcended simple physical lust. Her preposterous posings were as transparent as her venality, her insincerity and her self-absorption, but she overflowed him, penetrated and pervaded him, scoured him of all the finer pretensions.

'Go on then,' she goaded. 'Ask me nicely then.'

'You can go get yourself—'

'Say pretty please like a good boy.'

Boy again! He yielded. 'O.K., tell me.'

'Please?'

'*Please!*'

She stretched across the seat as he let in the clutch to cross the intersection and nibbled his ear. Her breath was hot mist on the angle of his jaw.

'Our old Geoff was all show, know that? Like at school, he was the one who got all the girls and scored all the goals and was the best swimmer and the best at running and jumping and that. He could fight, too; got that from his dad. Wallop you soon as look at you, from the time he was ten years old. Cosher, they called him at school. Nothing up here, mind you.' She tapped the side of her head with a long index finger. 'But brains aren't no use when the only thing what counts is show. See what I mean? You can't *see* brains. You can't stand in front of a mirror or a bunch of girls and make your brains bulge like muscles. That was our Geoff. Look at me, ain't I fantastic? Everyone knew he'd go in the army and it stood to reason he'd kick and bully and bitch his way into a few stripes. They give him his crown in April last year. Youngest C.S.M. in the army, he was.'

'Great,' Shaffer gritted. He braked the car and pulled up behind a jam of traffic on the approach to London Bridge.

'Yeah,' she drawled. 'But not where it counted.'

He flashed a look at her. The smile no longer prowled the corners of her lips and her cheeks stretched taut over the big bones. He looked front again and the penny dropped. He let the grin flower triumphantly and choked with grim satisfaction.

'Well, well, well. The playgirl of the western world . . . struck out, did you, honey? What was he — too small for you? Couldn't hold the fort?'

She swung on him, her teeth bared. For a moment he thought she was going for his throat with those strong white incisors but she plunged her talons into the sensitive skin of his groin instead and pouted mockingly when he leaped with pain.

'All show he was, like I said. Old Geoff couldn't hold nothing, not even with both hands. He must've been standing behind a tree when they were handing out the lead for the pencils. Not a trickle. Know why he married me?'

'Surprise me.'

The talons stabbed again and he winced. 'For a thick idiot he wasn't stupid, old Geoff. He knew the way things were and he knew he couldn't advertise it or even let people *think* it. Comes of having your brains in your feet, see. Anyway, he looks over the field and he sees old Janice and he says to hisself, "She's the ticket for me. She'll only go to someone who can give her her oats regular. Everyone knows that. So any man she marries must have it where it counts, right?" That's what he thought.'

'Powerful brain, your husband.'

'Powerful be buggered. But I had to hand it to him; he was more bloody cunning than a den of foxes. Before we were married, he never touched me once. Well . . . I mean not *that* way. He led me a dance, that man. I was dying for it, the way he had me going. Couldn't get to church quick enough.' She leaned back in the seat and twisted her hair in a pony-tail on top of her head. 'He even tried a whirl on our wedding night — just in case there'd been some overnight miracle and he'd found his manhood under the pillow.' She turned a bright, hard smile on him. 'No such thing as miracles. Didn't know what to do with hisself, poor little sod. And the way I worked on him that night, I knew there wasn't anything *any*one could do for him.'

The line of traffic edged forward. Shaffer said, 'I still don't see why he married you. If you'd talked to anyone he knew. . . .'

She drew his eyes to hers, challengingly. '*That's* why. Old Geoff could size up people shrewd enough. He knew I wouldn't talk. I was too much like him. All show, see what I mean?' The smile reappeared for a second, jauntier than ever, and when it failed, came to a pout that sucked with vacuous symbolism at the air between them. With any other woman he might have felt a degree of pity; with Janice there was only one emotion and its roots lay in passion, not civilised feeling.

'You could have left him.'

'Why? He was leaving me, wasn't he? The army. Once he'd done his turn, showed off, he was free to go. Any other girl might've gone to pieces but he knew old Janice'd find her level. Proud as punch, old Janice. Couldn't stand being made to look stupid, she couldn't. He knew what I'd be up to the minute he cleared off. Told me so hisself. Never said a word about it that first night, never once, but when he was packing up his kit the morning he left for Aldershot he gave me the old tip-and-a-wink. He knew I wouldn't be lonely for long.'

'My kind?' he growled.

She let her hair fall to her shoulders and held her left hand high in front of her face, fluttering the finger on which the slim gold wedding band glinted feebly.

The old confident amusement bubbled deep in her throat.

'What other kind is there?'

He began touching her in the elevator, pulling the rich, distended curves of her backside into his crotch, toying with shaking fingers at the third button of the green blouse. She pressed hard into him, urging him on, moving lasciviously left and right across the rigid cord of flesh. At the door of the apartment, as he fumbled for the key-chain, she freed the buttons of his shirt.

They made love on the floor within arm's reach of the phone. It rang twice.

Afterwards, she led him to the bathroom and bathed him with distracting attention to detail. Then she climbed in, facing him, and they lay touching but without intent, eyes closed.

She was a good cook. She made him something called Shepherd's Pie from the meagre provisions she found in the kitchen and reminded him of his declared intention to write a late-night file for A.B.N. He already had the line: 'Somewhere in England.' He went to the typewriter and she made him tie on a bathrobe. She lit the coal fire, tidied his desk, kissed him on the mouth with intoxicating promise and took herself off to the kitchen.

He wrote quickly, easily and with an olympian confidence that comes rarely to the sausage-grinders of information. He reduced Gladys's function to that of a stoic, selfless stranger who happened along the way; otherwise the story told itself as it happened. He had difficulty containing it within the three-minute slot format. When he finished he became aware that the air was ripe with the bouquet of baking.

In the kitchen Janice, swathed only in a towel, was handing a large round tin from the oven. A chocolate cake glowered inside, its shining surface split with a heat-slashed grin of invitation.

He came up behind her and pulled her into him. Her throaty chuckle of satisfaction was instantaneous.

'Dunno which end you're hungrier most, do you, love?' she breathed over her shoulder. 'Let me put this down. Then' — she twisted her face and took the end of his nose in her lips — 'you can make a meal of both of us if you want.'

Thursday, 1830

There was no accounting for it but Charles Russell seemed dead set against letting her see madam at all today. Elsie seethed with frustration, convinced on the one hand that Elizabeth was really ill, aware on the other that Russell felt he'd made a fool of himself in the kitchen this morning and was determined to keep it from his wife. He insisted on taking up her elevenses, her lunch and the mid-afternoon tea and biscuits Elsie prepared and he went back to fetch the tray each time.

The telephone rang continuously through the day and Russell snatched it up each time, on one occasion beating her to the instrument by inches. At other times he prowled around the house like a cat with its ear to the wainscoting, anxious for the least tell-tale patter of scuttering mice. He was waiting for something; easy enough to see that. Waiting with his heart in his mouth and his hands wringing and his eyes closing for lack of sleep. He was like Jack the day after the bombing got to him; a pin dropped behind him on a velvet cushion would have had him jumping six feet in the air.

He made no attempt to resume their conversation although she heard him refer twice in consecutive telephone calls to 'my daughter Caroline'. Several times Elsie scraped together the courage to go to him and tell him outright that she knew what was worrying him and he ought to talk about it but each time something came up to stop her; a ring at the front-door bell, a telephone call, a boiling kettle, the baker rattling the kitchen door; always something.

Young Mr Ian got up very late, too late to want his early afternoon snack; he came into the kitchen for a glass of milk and a biscuit and hung around, spaniel-eyed, but when she asked him what was troubling him he gulped and stammered and made an escape to the garden. He sat on the old swing under the sycamore for the best part of two hours, alternately studying his trailing feet and the window of the master's study. The shame was those two never talked to each other, in spite of what madam was saying the other day about Mister being proud of that story in the paper. Being proud wasn't enough. Jack was proud of their Paul, not that he had anything to be proud of, but he didn't love the boy or play with him or listen or talk to him just out of pride. A father didn't need pride as an excuse to show what he felt. There was no getting to the bottom of that man Russell. Ian could be a real son to him if he gave him half a chance. Master Tom, too, once upon a time, but he was too old to care. He didn't need no father now. Never would again.

At six-fifteen the telephone squawked and Russell pounced on it while prowling through the hall. He seemed more than usually agitated this time and tried to shout at whoever was at the other end without actually raising his voice above a croak for fear she should hear. In the middle of it Mr Ian opened the side door from the garden straight into Mister's bowed back and Elsie – peeping across the hall from the kitchen – thought Russell was going to have a heart attack. He clapped a hand over the mouthpiece and roared at his son, 'Get out of it, damn you! Get out of here when I'm taking a confidential telephone call!'

Ian leaped as if he had been struck in the face. He raced upstairs and within a minute was racing down again, his night-duty woolly jumper over his arm. He swept out of the side door and broke into a run across the lawn to the potting-shed. Elsie watched and her heart went out to him. If people would only stop and think before they spoke in haste. Russell had gone straight to his study from the telephone and she could hear him going through drawers, rustling papers. He came back into the hall a couple of minutes later and pulled on his coat. He put his head around the kitchen door and said to her severely, 'Now, my wife's not to be disturbed under any circumstances, Mrs – er. . . . Is that understood?'

'Yes, sir. Course not.'

'Well, be sure . . . *nobody* wakes her. You'll be leaving soon, won't you? It's late. We both think you should leave earlier now, with the bombing and so on.'

'Very kind I'm sure,' she said. 'I'm just finishing off.'

'And you won't wake. . . ?'

'I'll be quiet as a mouse, sir.'

He was torn between sinister doubt and the urgency of his errand. 'Yes, well . . . I'll be going. I'll see you tomorrow perhaps, Mrs – er. . . .' He stood uncertainly in the doorway. 'The – um – little talk we had this morning. Debate. Not the kind of thing I'd want Eliz . . . my wife to – er. . . .'

'Wouldn't dream,' Elsie reassured him warmly.

'Good. Very good. Till tomorrow then.' He withdrew at last.

She gave him five clear minutes' start, then beetled upstairs to Elizabeth's room. She tried the door, opened it silently, tongue in teeth, and jolted to a halt.

'Elsie, dear! Charles said you'd gone.' Elizabeth lay back against a sea of pillows, her spectacles perched on the end of her nose, a book open in front of her. She removed the glasses at once. 'Why did he say you'd gone?'

'You probably didn't hear him right, madam dear,' said Elsie diplomatically. 'You're not well, I can see that.'

Elizabeth scuffed the air with impatient hands. 'Oh, for goodness sake, Elsie, don't *you* start. I feel bad enough letting him talk me into staying in bed as it is. There's absolutely nothing wrong with me. I'm just a little' — she gritted her teeth — 'just a little low, that's all.'

Elsie came to the bed and plumped the pillows. 'It's that Miss Caroline again, ennit?'

'There *is* something wrong, dear, I know it. Charles is so ... so ... mule-headed. He refuses to believe *his* daughter could be ... well....'

'That's why I came up.' Elsie perched on the bed and reached across the coverlet to pat Elizabeth's hand. 'He's just gone out and he might come back soon. He told me I was to go home so I mustn't stay long. What I wanted to say was ... he's been acting very funny all day and I know it's something to do with Miss Caroline.'

'What is it?' Elizabeth jerked up from the pillows.

Elsie pushed her back firmly. 'Now don't you get all worked up. I didn't hear what he was saying on the phone but I know *he's* worried too. He came and talked to me in the kitchen this morning. Thought he was being very clever, he did, but they're like babies, men. Can't come right out and ask when they've got something worrying their insides out.'

'What did he say? Oh, Elsie, please!'

Elsie raised a warning finger. 'Now I won't tell you anything if you don't behave yourself. No use getting all hysterical. Won't do no one any good.'

Elizabeth sighed. 'You're a dear good friend and I'm a stupid idiot. I'm sorry, Elsie. You're right. Tell me.'

'You was saying to me yesterday — about Miss Caroline — about her ... well, having a young man she hadn't told you about.'

'Yes. But I don't know that. I ... just feel. ...'

'I know. Well, I don't think it's that.'

'Charles told you something! He knows!'

'He didn't tell me nothing. But he's got some bee in his bonnet and from what he said I think I know what he's worrying about.'

'Oh, Elsie!'

The warning finger was raised again and Elizabeth steeled herself, her mouth tight.

'Did Miss Caroline ever talk to you about her friends?'

'Only people she knew around here. Not really friends. Never about ... men friends.'

'*Women* friends.' Elsie let the word sink home.

Elizabeth looked confused. 'She's not the type to make friends with other women. She never was. At school she had a couple of special chums, but never anyone her own age. She isn't. ...'

'I don't mean girls her own age. I mean *women*.' Elsie paused, praying that silence would speak for her.

'I don't follow. When you say women. ...'

'The girl's never had no boy-friends. That's a bit funny at her age, I'd say, wouldn't you?'

Elizabeth opened her mouth to protest but closed it sharply again. Her face drained. 'What are you saying?'

'I'm not saying anything, madam dear. I'm just going on what Mister said in the kitchen this morning. Take hold of yourself for a minute and just listen. Girls is funny and the brighter they are the funnier they are. They get ideas, see? Their minds run on faster than their bodies can follow and they get sort of ... led astray. Lots of girls do. It's' — she groped in the air with beckoning hands for the word that eluded her — 'it's ... experimenting, if you like. Trying out their feelings.' She paused. 'You was away to school, wasn't you, when you was little?'

'Yes.' Uncertainly.

'You know what I'm talking about then. Didn't you ever come over all ... you know, trembly, about some girl you thought was really smashing?'

Elizabeth's face cleared with relief. 'Oh ... you mean *crushes*. Of course. Every girl did. It's a phase. But....'

'But you grew out of it.'

'I remember exactly when. This girl ... the one I ... she was captain of lacrosse. Beautiful girl. Married a boy Charles knew in the Foreign Office. I had to take a message to her one afternoon and' — she clicked her teeth — 'Elsie, it sounds so ridiculous. I'd never even *spoken* to her. Admiration from afar! Anyway, I went to her study and handed her this note from the house-mistress and ... my dear, I was absolutely shaken to my *roots*. She had dirty fingernails. Really *black*! I went right off her. Instantly!'

Elsie said quickly, 'Some girls didn't ... grow out of it, did they?'

Elizabeth frowned. 'Of course they did. Everyone did.'

Elsie Warrender clamped her hand protectively over Elizabeth's. 'Some girls take longer to grow out of it, that's all.'

'But ... you don't think Caroline... ?'

'Mister thinks so. That's what's in his mind and my guess is someone put it there. He's been told something.'

Elizabeth slumped on the pillows. 'Oh, dear God.'

Elsie tightened her grip on the slim white hand. 'Now don't you give me that I-don't-want-to-talk-about-it stuff. There might not be anything to it. You know what men are. But if there is, you've got to square your shoulders, my girl, and get a grip on the situation. If you don't, nobody will. Mister can't.'

'What in God's name can I *do*?'

'Well.' Elsie swivelled the bedside clock to keep an eye on the time. 'Your Caroline will be coming home soon. Won't be easy for her. She'll need mothering, that girl. She won't know if she's on her arse or her elbow, will she? Mr Ian not knowing anything. Mister all out of sorts and moping around the house. That and the bombing. You can't just lay back and pretend it'll go away. Deep down she'll want someone to talk to or she'll go pop. You're the one she'll turn to, natural like.'

'I couldn't.'

'You'll have to. That's your clear duty, the way I see it.'

The word sank its teeth into her and Elizabeth pushed up against the pillows. 'I don't deserve your friendship, dear. I really don't. Bless you.'

Elsie got to her feet. 'Friendship go fiddle!' she said with mock severity. 'Prize catch I am, I'm sure.'

'I wouldn't be able to get through this if I didn't know I could turn to you. I mean that, dear. You're the best friend I've ever had.'

Elsie pointed to the clock, her embarrassment intense. 'Look at that time then! Ten to seven. My Jack'll be home and gone again before I get back. And there's *me* talking about duty.'

Thursday, 1945

Charles Russell's long stride devoured the pavement of the Embankment with a mechanical intensity that could well have been interpreted by the few homeward-bound workers he passed as a healthy sign of respect for Hitler. As the craters and bomb-sites of Chelsea and Westminster and Kensington graphically illustrated, no one was safe any longer. A man had a right to run, if necessary.

But Russell's preoccupation was not with the German Chancellor, or with his blitz of London. He had far more insidious enemies to contend with; in order of potency — Caroline, Elizabeth and himself. Enemies within; dear enemies whose worst follies were committed in the name of love. Caroline: ruining him professionally for reasons she couldn't hope to grasp. Elizabeth: threatening him with her suffering, accusing him with her *naïveté*. Bad enough, perhaps, but bearable. He could have muddled through; prevaricated, lied, protested; kept his sanity intact and Elizabeth's. Somehow.

But there was no hiding-place now. He had sped headlong to his doom, snapped up that wretched instrument, dialled, asked as a matter of urgency to speak with the Prime Minister personally, received audience, been ordered to Downing Street at eight o'clock. He could not withdraw; all escape routes had closed behind him. He had elected to expose the family frailties and by so doing would mark down the Russells as social pariahs for all time, outsiders tarred with the indelible canker of uncleanliness. He had appealed to Churchill as the cornered rat appeals to the cat; the best he could hope for was a swift and uncompromising end.

Parliament Square was almost deserted; the House no longer sat late into the evening and government offices not immediately connected with the active waging of war closed promptly at five. As he turned the corner into Whitehall the first signs of life stirred to prove that Hitler was not entirely forgotten in this place. Messengers flitted like rumours across empty pavements; a lone despatch rider turned his motorcycle in a wide circle round the Cenotaph and roared away towards Trafalgar Square; figures in Homburgs or bowlers, black briefcases clutched to their black coats, slipped from the stately doors of government. Some would have the seniority to command a chauffeured journey home in comfort, but there were remarkably few who enjoyed that privilege. The rest would aim their steps for Charing Cross Station or Waterloo or London Bridge in the hope that the train that brought them from the suburbs that morning would be available to take them home tonight — unless a wandering Heinkel had placed its bomb-load across the railway line, of course, in which case the service would be suspended and the travellers would be trailing back to their offices for a painful night's sleep. In four days, surprisingly accurate bombing had cut scores of major rail links between London and the south.

He turned into Downing Street at three minutes to eight and presented his Air Ministry pass to one of the policemen. The two sentries on either side of the sandbagged entrance neither came to attention nor spared him even a half curious glance; he didn't have the look about him that generated suspicion. A woman, Miss Watson, he thought, one of the four private secretaries, answered the ringing bell and rooted him to a spot a few yards short of the door of the Cabinet Room. He heard voices as she opened the door; Churchill's, pontifically, someone else's with rather less vigour. The woman backed out and beckoned Russell into the room and closed the door behind him.

A typist sat at a small desk to one side of the huge Cabinet table, a reading light burning over her upright machine and a sheaf of three half-foolscap lengths of paper in the typewriter between carbon copying sheets. There was no other light in the room. On either side of the Cabinet table, sprawling in their chairs, sat Jock Colville, another private secretary, and Brendan Bracken, disagreeably referred to in Civil Service circles as 'Winston's chief Myrmidon'. Bracken did the work of the P.M.'s parliamentary private secretary but had chosen not to assume the title, preferring instead the freedom of being regarded as a close political colleague. Winston had made him a member of the Privy Council in June and even the king had admitted to being disturbed by the appointment. It added to the ridiculous legend, of course, that he was the child of an illicit but stormy Churchillian love affair. At school at Sedbergh the young Bracken had never quashed rumours of this tempestuous link, and the story had followed him through his career in the City and politics. In fact, he had been born in Ireland and received much of his education in Australia but such facts merely added to, rather than subtracted from, the fantasy. But in no way could it be said to have done him particular harm.

Two other of the Myrmidons were present; Professor Frederick Lindemann, former Professor of Experimental Philosophy at Oxford who ran S. Branch at the Admiralty but was now a special assistant to Winston, and Major Desmond Morton, another aide but one less known to Russell. He had been an Intelligence mandarin of sorts so he wore his profile naturally low but his influence was considerable. These two stood on either side of the silent woman typist.

Churchill was wearing evening clothes and carpet slippers. The inevitable cigar sprouted from the fingers of one hand and as Russell came into the room he gestured violently with the weed and displaced a wedge of white ash on to his already well fouled waistcoat.

He was in full flow: '... but the act is the act of a madman and the reasoning, if reason he employs, is that of the coward.'

The typist's fingers flashed at great speed over the keyboard but no sound emerged from the impact of keys on paper. The machine was quite silent.

'No' — Churchill stomped the length of the Cabinet table and returned again — '. . . if reason he employs, is that of the blackguard. Blackguard.' He tasted it and jammed the cigar full in his mouth. 'Good. Blackguard.' He squinted short-sightedly into the gloom beyond the table. 'That you, Russell?'

'Yes, sir. I apologise for the interruption. Perhaps you'd prefer it if I came back later.'

'No. Stay. I address the House next week and . . . never mind. Gentlemen, this is Charles Russell. You know each other, of course, Lindemann. All of you? Yes, yes, of course you do.' He gestured to the typist. 'Where it all begins, Russell. These gentlemen are good enough to submit themselves to my rhetoric and pepper it with facts. I was never adept at affixing words to paper myself. Dictation has been the saviour of my career both as a writer and a politician. Couldn't function without it. Millions of words.' He seemed transported by the concept and turned on his heel, waving his cigar in a sweep of movement as though swinging a mental butterfly-net to imprison a lifetime of verbosity. 'Millions.'

He turned again, feet planted unevenly to settle his great weight. 'Have to talk to Russell. My compliments to Sawyers, if he's still here, Jock. Ask him to crack a bottle of champagne. You fellows deserve it. If he's gone to the Annexe, you'll find it in the room behind his pantry. Give me ten minutes, would you?'

He dumped himself into a chair at the midway point of the table when the speech team left. He sat with shoulders hunched, an overflow of chins propped glumly in one plump palm. The single reading light under its green bowl encapsulated his disgruntled baby's face in soft highlights and pale shadow and threw a bubble of saffron light on to the table through the half-full brandy balloon at his elbow. The rest of the room was lost but for the knife points of silver and gold where the lid of an ink-well or the frame of a picture momentarily trapped a flicker of lamplight.

Russell waited nervously. A minute passed. Two. From some-where in the gloom a clock ticked holes in the silence. He peered around him and his eye fell on the typewriter and the speech he had interrupted. He couldn't read the words but the layout of the sentences was intriguing. The typing did not run from one side of the paper to the other; it was couched in the form almost of blank verse; some sentences contained only one word, others two or three or as many as eight.

'What do you think of my speeches, Russell?'

The growl took him completely off balance. He jumped ner-vously, tense as a schoolboy caught at midnight in the head-master's study ogling the next day's exam papers.

'Ah – I'm hardly alone in thinking ... they're superb, sir. Masterly. They've rallied—'

'Words are important, you think?'

'I think so, sir, yes. At this moment, critically important.'

'They've been the making of me. They also contain the seed of my destruction.' The old man nodded sadly into his brandy balloon. 'They've exalted me and they've brought me to my knees. Many times. Society has a conspicuous facility for forget-fulness, Russell – in all areas of human endeavour but one. Politics. People have never forgotten my speeches, the good or the bad. They've never forgiven me my errors. I lack frivolity, you see. I lack the skill of some of my confreres' – his eyes twinkled mischievously and he stared up at Russell, head tipped back to employ the half-moon shape of his spectacles – 'to bathe the air with meaningless verbiage as one might cover that wall with wallpaper.' He jammed the cigar back in his face. 'Hm. Hm. Hm.' He nodded enthusiastically to himself, as if he were lodging the phrase in a mental niche for possible future use.

He took his chins in pudgy fingers and pressed and moulded them reflectively. 'My words will win or lose this war, I think. And if I lose....' He sighed. 'They'll see to it I'm the laughing-stock of the twentieth century.' He took off his glasses. 'Sit down, man. Sit down. Forgive me, I'm tired. I miss my after-noon nap.'

Russell perched himself on the edge of the nearest chair.

'Well, out with it, then. What is this nonsense about your daughter?'

He listened without interruption as Charles Russell stumbled through his story, occasionally prodding the black-framed spectacles around the sheet of paper with the chewed end of his cigar. Russell came to the end and sank into the heaven of silence. Churchill glared down at his spectacles for several minutes then leaned back in his chair.

'I suppose you've told me everything? Left nothing out?'

Russell shook his head vehemently. 'Nothing.'

The chubby hands came together with a little plop of exasperation and kneaded a ball of invisible dough.

'Do you really believe your daughter would put the work at Bletchley in jeopardy?'

'No, sir. She's quite incapable of that kind of foolishness.'

'Hmmmm. You imply a knowledge of your children I wouldn't dare claim of mine. However....' His mouth clamped in a diagonal of pugnacious contemplation. 'The Security Police have their duty. That's clear. I can't – I won't – obstruct them in it. But you say this fellow Lubbock point blank refused to investigate the possibilities at Bentley Priory?'

'I can only tell you, sir, what he told me: that he was not prepared to "waste his time chasing my intuitions". Those were his words.'

The Prime Minister exhaled sharply through his nose. 'He may be right, of course. Dammit, Russell, this is an infernal bloody nuisance. Have you talked to your son?'

'No, sir. It was a condition of what the officers termed my parole.'

'Parole!' Churchill squinted across the table. 'Do you have any reason to believe your son is in a position to furnish any facts relevant to the case?'

Russell squirmed on his chair. 'If he were given the freedom to investigate the whereabouts of his fellow officers at lunchtime on the day in question...?'

'Spy on them, you mean?' There was an unmistakable edge in the voice.

'Spying is not the word I'd choose to—'

Churchill waved him to silence. 'Spying is an enterprise best left to those trained for it,' he growled. 'Look here, Russell. I want you back behind your desk where you belong. At the moment that's my prime consideration; my only consideration. For that reason I shall instruct the Security Police to address their investigations to your son. But I feel bound to warn you : if nothing comes of it. . . .' He gazed down at his hands. 'This other aspect of your daughter's . . . trouble. What do you make of it?'

'I'm at a loss, sir. I . . . I have no reason to suspect.'

'Yes, yes. I'm not prying, you understand. Just . . . preparing you for the worst – if it comes. Children are damned unpredictable at the best of times. Do your best with her. Spend some time with her. We should, you know. Men in public life. . . .' He waved one pudgy hand in a gesture of mutual sympathy. 'The Frenchwoman Coutance we can deal with. She's clearly a troublemaker. Her value to us isn't worth *that*.' He snapped his fingers savagely. 'Damn de Gaulle and all his acolytes.'

He brooded, his shadow stretching dimly across the table. 'Very well, Russell. Go home. I shall speak with the Security people myself tonight. Hold yourself in readiness for tomorrow. And if it goes against us. . . .'

Us. The implication didn't escape Charles Russell. He rose to his feet and settled the chair in its place at the table. 'I can't tell you, sir, how—'

Churchill sliced his hand through the air imperiously. 'Don't thank me, Russell. Just pray God we've taken the right step. Now – tell Miss Watson to show Lindemann and the others back in here, would you? Good night to you.'

Thursday, 2245

Shaffer hung around impatiently outside the studio door until the red light clicked off. Ed Murrow had just finished his last file of the day and he and Fred Bate were planning supper in Charlotte Street. It was a favourite haunt; the Greek and Italian restaurants clustered in the narrow artery off Tottenham Court

Road conjured miracles from the bleak rations they were permitted and were seemingly quite happy to stay open late into the night as long as the customers came. Charlotte Street was therefore a magnet for late-night people and for the journalists and producers of Fleet Street and the B.B.C. in particular.

Ray Daniel had strolled along to the studio to join the group which included Ted Angley, Syd Williams and Ben Robertson. Murrow threw open an invitation to Shaffer but he made an excuse about having problems with O'Keefe at A.B.N.

'You hear about Knickerbocker's thing with Harold Nicolson?' asked Murrow, lighting a fresh cigarette from the butt of the old one.

'No. What happened?'

'What didn't!' Ray Daniel spluttered.

Murrow killed the old butt. 'He squared up to Harold in the Savoy Grill today. Went off like a roman candle about his story on the St Paul's bomb being spiked by the censor. You have to hand it to Nicolson. Got straight up from the meal, went back to Minf. with Knickerbocker and pounded a few desks.'

'Did it work?'

'It worked all right,' put in Robertson. 'Half hour later the story went through.'

'With a few tickles here and there.'

Shaffer said, 'Why the change of heart?'

'Call it common sense,' Murrow drawled with a slow smile. 'They went to see Cyril Radcliffe. He'd held it up, or one of his people did, because the rules say no time-bombs can be mentioned.'

'See what I meant about every rule multiplying by two the lower down the heap it goes?' interjected Daniel. 'Crazy!'

'Anyway, they O.K.-ed his bomb story. Then they got around to the rest. The censor wouldn't let him run a section on the bombing of Bond Street and Burlington Arcade. Why, says Nicolson? Because of the way he wrote it, says Radcliffe. What way was that? Interpretively, says Radcliffe. Seems Knickerbocker wrote that Bond Street was "that street, comparable to Fifth Avenue and the Rue de la Paix" and the censor held that might indicate to the Germans other desirable objectives. Can you beat that?'

'I wouldn't try. So where does that leave the rest of us?'

Angley grinned. 'It leaves us flat on our butts looking stupid,' he drawled. 'While we were all down there at the Savoy yesterday, shoving Nicolson through hoops, my own side-kick Frank Kelley was filing for the *Trib*. Look at this.' He produced an early edition of Friday's *Daily Telegraph*, opened it and folded it into a square. The story was headlined 'London hitting back with all its Strength.' It was datelined 'New York, Thursday.'

The *Telegraph*'s New York correspondent quoted at length from Kelley's story in today's *Herald Tribune*, a review of the thunderous anti-aircraft gun barrage thrown up at the German invaders on Wednesday night. Halfway down it drew attention to the ingenuity with which Kelley had dodged the British censor's ban on revealing place names.

He described the explosion of a bomb 'near Nash's nobly planned street' and his New York editor easily identified it as Regent Street. Once into the style Kelley found no difficulty in getting his meanings across to the censor's blind-eyed satisfaction. 'London's most Parisian café will reopen its doors within a few days,' he had written, and, 'A high-explosive hit a block of luxury flats in John L. Balderston's favourite square.' The editor had reminded readers that Balderston was the playwright who wrote *Berkeley Square*.

'Cheeky bastard,' Shaffer grinned.

'How d'you think I feel?' Angley growled good-naturedly.

'Anyway, it was fun while it lasted. I guess things'll be a mite easier from here in,' Murrow said. He swung on his coat, patted the pockets and looked around him. 'O.K. What do you say we go fuel the fires of artistic merit?'

'I'll drink to that,' said Fred Bate with feeling.

'You'd drink to anything,' retorted Robertson.

They trooped out.

Eric Warr stayed behind to read through 'Somewhere in England.' At the end of it he let the pages fall to the desk. 'They're going to hate you for this in the morning.' He hooked his head after the departed correspondents.

'Like it?'

Warr slid the pages across the table to him. 'I've handled a lot of words in the past year, Mel. A lot of good words. You develop pretty high standards when you're dealing with chaps like Ed. But I'll say this — and I really mean it: if anyone who hears this in America tonight doesn't think at the end that they should be in this war, there's no hope they ever will. It's. . . .' He grinned. 'It's a fine piece of reporting, Mel. Pieces like this change history.'

Shaffer shrugged. 'I've been too long in the business to believe that. Words are cheap. Always have been. It's like the B.B.C. motto: Nation shall speak peace unto nation. Great concept; fine ideology. Looks good over the front door. Except I don't happen to believe it. Words — communication — on paper or over the air . . . they start more wars than they end. Trouble with this business is it reminds people who ordinarily wouldn't know, people who could be living happily in their ignorance, that the world's one hell of a mean place and gets meaner by the day. Think about it.'

Warr threw a tired, angular smile. 'I'd still sacrifice a month's pay to make sure this goes out tonight.'

The internal phone buzzed and Shaffer took it up. The line was opening from New York. He winked at Warr.

'Your money's safe, Eric. Tonight we save the world.'

O'Keefe was back on the job and his reception of the file was effusive. He was feeling good. Even better, the Board was feeling good. He ran over the latest wire messages from Berlin and listened with evident glee to Shaffer's story of the Knicker-bocker–Nicolson confrontation and its outcome.

On the way up to the lobby Shaffer dallied with the idea of following Murrow and the rest to Charlotte Street but on the steps of Broadcasting House his mood reverted quickly. The ack-ack barrage was in full swing again and the city streets echoed and re-echoed to the clapping thunder of the guns. Searchlights slid across the low smoky cloud layer with a new voracity. For the first time in a week, he suspected, it might be more danger-ous up there under a Heinkel's flight-deck blister than in Nelson's Green.

Nelson's Green. The word association should have leapt from there to Gladys, then back to the field near West Malling, then on to the piece he had just filed and with it should have rolled waves of remorse. No remorse, though. Nothing. Nelson's Green rang only one bell right now: Janice Scully. The sound was clear and uncontaminated by echoes of guilt.

He walked back to the Morris in Hallam Street and drove home.

She must have come to the door every time the elevator whirred because he hadn't fetched his key-chain from his pocket when the door swung open. She let it stand wide and with practised ease fell into her own parody of that ridiculous mannequin pose. He laughed and she caught his finger-ends with hers and drew him over the threshold. She was wearing one of his shirts. Just that.

She pulled the unbuttoned neck of it wide then dropped her arms to her sides and wiggled from hip to shoulder. The shirt slid miraculously over the undulating curves and fell to the ground. She raised her naked arms in the air with a triumphant smile.

'I've been practising,' she breathed throatily. 'What would *you* like to practise?'

He showed her.

Thursday, 2315

The sound came to her in her sleep, a chinking noise looking for a dream to belong to and finding none. Chink-chink. She yawned and raised her hands high above her in the bed and watched the play of light over them from the window. Chink-chink. She raised her head off the pillow. The living-room? No, the kitchen. Chink-chink.

Who?

It was not a question that came with fear panting on its heels. There had never been burglars in Nelson's Green; nothing for burglars here. Less now. Gladys Warrender had been brought up to sleep securely behind unlocked doors, to place keys casually under the mat or over the lintel of the back door, to leave money for the baker or the milkman openly on the backyard window-ledge. Nobody thought of it in terms of universal honesty or put it down to a profound trust in the constancy of neighbours; it was simply the way things were. There had always been thieving in the East End but thieving was crime and crime was work and work of that kind was conducted up West or in the country where the big houses were and the jewellery.

Who?

She sighed and swung her feet to the linoleum, taking care not to disturb the blankets on Janice's side of the bed. Then she remembered; Janice was away for the night. Some girl at Black-friars was having a baby and Janice had gone to be with her, she had said when she came up to pack a bag. Well, it was un-christian to think it but that didn't sound like Janice for a minute; wasting her time, hovering round some poor lumbering dumpling of a pregnant woman. Janice hated pregnancy. She'd cross the street to avoid a pregnant woman. The idea of it, of carrying the fluttering life and weight of an organism inside her, made her feel physically sick.

Chink-chink.

The stairs creaked halfway down and she bit her tongue; it would be criminal to wake her mother and Auntie Flo. They both worked all hours God sent them and neither slept easily. Since Number 14 was bombed the arguments had raged about whether they should sleep down the shelter all night, every night, or just during the alerts. Flo and Elsie had cast their votes to stay at home and in their beds and to hell with Hitler. Elsie reasoned that, having claimed Number 14, lightning was not going to strike twice within an area of inches; it stood to reason.

Chink-chink.

'Who's that?' she whispered from the gloom of the living-room.

There came an answering whoof of expelled air and the clang of a spoon dropping in the sink. The black mass of the kitchen door swung open towards her and she sensed a figure in its frame.

'That you, Glad?'

'Dad?'

'Phew! Turned my hair white you did.' The breathy whisper of relief. 'What're you doing up, girl? It's a quarter past eleven. Thought you was asleep.'

'I heard you dinging about down here.' She pulled Janice's quilted cotton robe more tightly around her. 'What's up?'

He laid a restraining hand on her arm and drew her into the kitchen to avoid rousing Flo Scully in the front parlour. He shut the door, drew the blackout curtain over the window and set a match to a night-light the size and shape of a bun. He floated the wax on a saucer filled with water. 'There. That's more like. Here. Have a cuppa.' He poured from Flo's small brown and white china teapot, the one reserved for intimate drinking groups of two or three; the pot held only six cups.

'Everything all right, dad?'

'Right as anything, I suppose.'

Outside the sky flared scarlet and gold, then brightened to an intense white that survived for nearly a minute. There was no bang. The light penetrated the blackout curtain and threw shuddering reflections on the kitchen walls. Jack Warrender stopped with the cup poised at his lips.

'Nasty bugger that one. Landmine.' He swallowed a mouthful of tea. 'Not our manor, though. Isle o' Dogs I'd say.'

'Is it bad tonight?'

His laugh was forced. 'What we come to, girl? Is it *bad*. You know—a week ago we was half out of our skins if we heard a bomb drop ten mile off. Ten *mile* off! Now they're coming down thick and fast and you want to know if it's bad.'

'I meant. . . .'

'Know what you meant, girl. Same for me. If they're hitting Nelson's Green, that's bad. If they're hitting Jamaica Road or Bermondsey or Shadwell or Limehouse or Stepney, that's not so bad. I got relations up Shadwell way—you know, your Auntie Dinah and the kids. Your mum took a real shine to old Dinah; we both did. But you can't let considerations like that rule you with this going on, can you?'

'Is it then? Bad, I mean?'

Jack Warrender upturned the mug on his lips, drained it of

383

tea and poured himself another. 'Wouldn't be here if it was, would I? Our electricity up the hut copped it. We already lost the water when that main went bang in Redriff Road, so the lads are nipping home for their cuppas when they can.' He hooked a thumb over his shoulder in the direction of the Surrey Docks. 'There's fires out the back here again. St Katherine's got one, probably two, and there's a big 'un along Silvertown way. Beckton Gasworks got hit, someone said up the hut, and they called up a couple of ambulances to the Minories about half past eight so they must've got plastered down there too. Old ackack going a fair treat, though. Marvel to me your mum can sleep through it.'

Gladys sat back on the circular wooden lid of the boiler. 'I think *you're* a marvel, I really do. You walk about out there with all that going on and—'

Jack Warrender brushed aside the compliment impatiently. 'Easier for me. I'm out there doing something. Your mum and Flo — you kids — tied to the house, not knowing—' He bit off the thought. 'Had to do something, didn't I? Job gone. Office gone. The old Surrey in smithereens. When we get this bugger Hitler beat, we can think of getting back to rights again, but for the time being we do what we have to. Anyway....' His eyes were dark-ringed in the scuttering flame of the night-light. 'You was nearly took yourself today. When that young chap of yours was telling me—'

'He's not "my young chap"!'

'Hold hard, girl. No need to be bashful. I got eyes in my head, y'know. I see the way you look when you talk about him. There's no reason to—'

'He's just an acquaintance, that's all. I wouldn't even have met him if mum hadn't pestered him to come and fetch me at the club Saturday night. I was just being . . . friendly.'

'Strikes me there's more to it than friendly. On his side, anyhow.'

'You're seeing what you want to see.'

The tired old eyes glinted. 'P'raps I am. I'd like to see you and Paul out of this.' He waved his hand around him at the tiny kitchen. 'Man like that could give a girl a *real* life. Travelling the world, seeing the sights. Nice house. Kids going to decent schools. You'd live the way I always dreamed you would. P'raps in America. You'd like that, wouldn't you?'

'Dad!' It was a warning and he heeded it. There was a break in her voice that threatened anger or tears; he couldn't be sure which.

'Sorry, girl. Didn't mean to pry.'

'It's not that.'

He quaffed deeply from his mug. 'You're not holding back on your old dad, are you?'

'Don't know what you mean, holding back.'

'Wouldn't say that if you'd seen yourself when young Shaffer brought you back tonight. Face like death. Cold? Corpse, you were. Hands like ice.'

'That was different. It was ... shock.'

He dug into a pocket for his pipe and lit the black ashes of hard-packed shag. 'Changed your mind about him, have you?'

She folded her arms protectively across her body.

He sucked on his pipe. 'Didn't tell your mum what happened this afternoon. Thought it best. Got worries enough, she has. The bombing wasn't all that happened though, was it? Tell your dad.'

'There's nothing to tell.'

'That's what I said to myself last Sunday. Nothing to say. Hold your tongue, Warrender, I says. Keep it all locked up in your head. Don't bother no one else. Zombie, I was.'

She gulped the last of her tea and put down the mug. 'I better be getting back to bed,' she whispered.

He pulled her face towards his and planted an affectionate smack of a kiss on her forehead. 'Had enough, have you, girl? Can't blame you. Same way myself when I was your age. Old people carping on about whys and wherefores – gave me the pip. Go on then, up you go to bed.'

She turned away then quickly back again and flung her arms round his neck. 'I wish I'd meet someone like you.' She buried her face in his shoulder, the tears spurting.

'Me? You must be out of your tiny mind, girl. Ten a penny, the likes o' me. Now – that young Shaffer—'

'No!' It was a muffled squeak, a cry of pain. He hugged her tightly. 'Please, dad. No more. Don't talk about him any more.'

Thursday, 2355

Barry Warrender reared back at an angle of forty-five degrees and tried desperately to tip the oversize helmet back from his face with jerky, hiccupy flicks of his head.

It was bloody impossible. The last time he'd snatched one hand away from the crackling nozzle of the hose to shove the stupid helmet back on his head he'd nearly copped one. The hose had taken over and picked him up like a rag doll. Nearly had him on his back.

'Den-i-i-i-s!'

He bawled with all the power of his lungs, which wasn't much. He'd been choking a lot tonight; more than usual. The doctor said there was something in your mind that willed an attack to come when you didn't feel too good in some other way; like if your feet ached or you were dog-tired or your muscles got stiffened up or you had a splitting headache. Barry had all those miseries and several more that hadn't been medically catalogued yet. For at least a quarter of an hour now he had been embroiled in a tug-of-war with the lashing hose; unaided, isolated from the rest of the team by snarling, bone-cracking flame-walls and smoke thicker than black candy-floss. His wrists ached so much now as they twisted for grip on the branch that he sometimes let himself wail with pain; no one could hear him. No one.

'Den-i-i-i-s!'

Denis Hastings, his Red Rider, had stationed Barry alone nearest the river; all he had to do was damp down one wall of the warehouse with the wind at his back while the other four tackled the rough part. But the wind had backed right round fifteen minutes ago and it was now in Barry's face. So were the tongues of flame. Nobody had come round to check he was all right; they couldn't be sure he was alive or dead unless they could see his jet of water – which was a damn sight more than

386

he could; he had no idea if he was spraying the warehouse or ground-creeping flame. Lost his sense of direction long ago.

'Den-i-i-i-s!'

There should be two men to a branch by rights but the team was three blokes short; one in hospital with first-degree burns, one half paralysed from being crushed by a cord of timber over at Quebec Docks, and one had just hopped it. Just took off and disappeared.

'Denis! Turn the sodding pressure down, for Gawd's sake!'

He couldn't keep this up much longer. Hands and wrists and arms and shoulders numb with agony. Wouldn't do what he wanted 'em to do. And that bloody helmet! He'd swopped his with Terry Hagan because Terry's was two sizes too small but it was still like a bloody coal-scuttle on Barry's head. He bent forward over the branch, twisted his thumb upwards without loosening his grip and shoved the helmet backwards, backwards, wriggling his chin over the strap.

Thank Christ. The smoke came at him like an express train, under pressure. It reached down into his lungs and wrenched great hacking gasps from him.

'Denis! I can't bloody hold it! I can't. . . .'

He could feel it tearing loose from his hands like a boa constrictor fighting for its life, but he knew it was suicidal to let go. Left to itself, the hose and its lethal brass-tipped branch and the spiked holding handles would whip everything in its path.

The coughing shook him again and this time, as he bent double with the agony of it, the hose performed a sideways thrash; his feet slid in the mud and he crashed flat on his back. He clung to the branch for dear life, still hacking and gulping, welding himself to the murderous thing.

Behind him he heard a snapping explosion like the cave-in of an overheated roof and a storm of showering brick and gravel plunging into water. Where the hell was that? The river was supposed to be behind him. For Gawd's sake!

He knew he had only seconds left to get away from that hose. A picture of Edie flashed into his mind, looking down at him in her swollen-bellied nightie, and he made his bid. He wrestled up on one knee, made it to his feet, then hurled the branch from him and ran blindly in the opposite direction, towards the river. He ran towards the air, sucked down the first cool God-given draught of it, tripped over a boulder of debris and threw out his hands to cushion his fall.

But they didn't touch. He fell, fell, clawing at air, shouting — then he hit a boiling torrent of foul, clinging effluent and went under; toppling, rolling, swallowing the muck. He reached the surface once but there was no air above him now; his helmet banged hard at the curved roof of the sewer and he went under again. Before he lost consciousness he tasted the stench of rotten eggs.

FRIDAY
13 September

Friday, 0115

Emptying the 'slops' in the working areas of Floor B. was a powerful disincentive to troublemaking among the military at the Annexe. Slops was officially a job for janker-wallahs, soldiers who had earned punishment duty for a range of sins which fell under a wide-open section of the Army Act covering 'conduct prejudicial to good order and military discipline'. Slops was George Rance's homely aphorism for the collection and dispersal of urine and faeces — or 'night soil' as it was termed in Standing Orders. It was a thankless task of the lowest menial order and the luckless groups of men trapped into it each night experienced genuine shame at being seen reaching under beds and into 'sanitary lockers' for the pot-bellied chamberpots issued to the War Rooms complex.

The exercise was unavoidable, for there were no formal sanitary arrangements at the Annexe and not even the most primitive system for pumping water into the drainage system. At first the loathsome job had been performed each morning when the night staff retired to bed and the day shift took their place, but George Rance's antennae had picked up early warnings of muttering rebellion among the men on the grounds that at such a time of day their labours were visible to virtually every man and woman, soldier and civilian in the place. The effect on their morale and common dignity was irreparable. So slops had been switched to the dog-hour of one-fifteen in the morning with the men's wholehearted approval. It made the job no less hideous and destroyed a decent night's sleep into the bargain but at least they retained some shred of self-respect.

The threat of being rewarded for misconduct with a spell on

slops deterred the Marines' natural excesses magically and good behaviour was the rule rather than the exception; so much so that crimes that might otherwise have been overlooked were seized upon readily to ensure a continuous supply of labour. This morning, for instance, the four unfortunates in harness had been guilty of such magnified follies as laziness (failing to 'square' the folded sheets and blankets of their bed-blocks to utter geometric perfection), slovenliness (a smudge of metal polish left in one corner of a brass belt buckle), inadequate preparation for guard duty (parading with 'weights' slung in the hang of the trousers above the gaiters to ensure a neat 'fall') and unsoldierly conduct. This last was the closest thing to a crime the Annexe could find to pin on a man. The Marine concerned had had the bad luck to be caught selling one of Winston's discarded Corona Corona cigar butts on the corner of Great George Street. This was a popular business venture among some members of the Annexe staff. When conducting meetings in the Cabinet Room, Winston had the habit of flicking his ash, and finally the smouldering butt, on to the floor behind his chair, rarely using the ashtray provided for anything more than concentrating his gaze when thinking. The memento value of 'an actual Churchill cigar' was so high — at least ten shillings on the free market — that it was not unknown for some imaginative entrepreneur to pass off any old cigar butt as the real thing. The practice was, of course, frowned upon and an order had gone out forbidding any unauthorised person from collecting litter of any description left behind in the Cabinet Room after a meeting; but cigar butts continued to sell briskly in Great George Street.

Arthur Scully commanded the slops party each morning without a thought for its impact on his morale and social standing. If anything, he was harder on the men in the knowledge that they could regard any military requirement as less than their duty. Arthur didn't hold with free thinking.

He gathered them together by the sentry post at Windy Corner and was about to march them down to the Hospitality Room when there was a decisive clacking sound from the door on his immediate right.

'Watchit!' he hissed softly. 'Smarten up there.'

The circular slot on the door turned from 'Engaged' to 'Vacant' and edged open. The sentry came to attention and presented arms.

Arthur snarled, 'Party!' The four jankers men stretched to the 'At ease' position. 'Party ... *'shun*!' Four heels crashed to the brown linoleum as George Rance slipped sideways into the corridor, one hand propping open the door.

Winston Churchill emerged from the tiny room and stopped when he saw the men. 'At ease, Sar'nt Scully, please,' he said, an amused twinkle in his eyes.

'Party—stand at ... *ease*!'

Glory be—he remembered his name!

Arthur threw up a shiveringly rigid salute and the Prime Minister fluttered his hand. He was leaning heavily on a stick and the cigar in his mouth streamed a wraith of blue-grey smoke.

'What is your duty?' he asked.

'Slops, sah!' spat Arthur. Then, explanatorily, 'Sanitation, sah!'

The P.M. viewed the collection bucket with wrinkling distaste. 'Unpleasant job, sar'nt. There's much to be done here before we can call it home.' The smile was genuinely sympathetic.

George Rance had gone back into the room and emerged with the Prime Minister's portable toilet. He lugged it across the corridor to a large wooden cupboard, unlocked the door and swung it inside. He turned the key in the lock again while the four members of the slops party did their best to suppress twitches of astonishment. It was no secret that Winston had a private loo; no secret that he had it carried into his private toilet across the corridor from the Map Room; but what truly mystified and fascinated the military staff was that he always took George Rance with him and rarely spent less than an hour in there behind the 'Engaged' sign he had had specially fixed to the door. The interpretations these nightly visits bred at first were, in some cases, little short of scandalous. The kindest imputation was that the old man was now so enfeebled and ill he could no longer relieve himself unaided. The unkindest were also unrepeatable. There were other confusing factors involved which bedevilled rational explanation; like the smell of cooking sausages that occasionally emanated from the room.

It was to be four years before the Annexe staff penetrated the secret of Winston's loo; four long years of war before they learned that the room in fact housed the Prime Minister's 'hot line' to President Franklin D. Roosevelt in the White House in Washington. Inside the 'toilet' was a large double cupboard in which Winston installed a comfortable armchair. With the doors of the cupboard wide, he could sit and watch George Rance at a small desk, the telephone to his ear. When George signalled to him that Roosevelt was on the line, Winston would take the instrument — but not a moment before. Delays on the transatlantic line were often interminable and the President more often than not engaged in matters of state when the London calls came through. Since Winston regarded it as loss of face to sit endlessly on an empty line awaiting the favour of a reply, he employed George to function as his third ear, and when the delays became excessive had a small hotplate wired to one wall where his talented aide could grill a snack of his favourite sausages.

The portable loo was Winston's private joke against the prying curiosity of the staff. He had always been an acute student of camouflage.

Winston gazed with the experienced officer's self-confident amusement at the rigid 'Eyes front' paralysis of the slops party. 'I should say, Sar'nt Scully, wouldn't you, that if these gentlemen were ordered to this duty for the duration' — he paused to watch the ripple of horror cross one Marine's face; his grin widened — 'they would see to it the war ended by Sunday night at the latest.' The men's taut faces relaxed perceptibly.

'Sah !' agreed Arthur.

George Rance's grey old face twitched solemnly. 'There's General Pile in your quarters, sir,' he prompted.

'Pile? Yes. Yes, of course.' The Prime Minister seemed reluctant to leave. He bounced his stick rapidly three times on the floor, summoning up the energy to move. 'Very well.' He turned away and limped heavily along the corridor to the archway leading to his room. He turned and looked them over again. 'We all have responsibilities we would like to shirk, sar'nt,' he growled, his lisp smudging the string of sibilants.

They heard him shuffle to his room, heard the general's 'Good morning, sir!' and Winston's answering growl, 'A moment, Pile, if you would. Let me get into bed first, and I'll be at your disposal.'

Then the door shut.

Friday, 0730

Shaffer woke in a dream, a muted skein of sound rippling the surface of his sleep, a hand at his throat. He wrenched free and for a moment lay trembling on the indefinite borderline of consciousness. He keyed in to reality slowly; the room, the low cloud beyond the criss-crossed window panes, the interruptus of the alert siren; Janice Scully's outflung arm and hand.

He checked the time on the travelling clock by his bed and pushed his fingers back through his hair. The lady had reason to be tired, he mused drily. So had he. Three times she'd woken him in the course of the night, the last time around dawn. Hell's flames, she was. . . . So who was complaining? Allowing for the English mind-block about sex, Janice had probably grown up believing that babies came gift-wrapped from a central baby bank at the friendly neighbourhood nursing home and, if she were telling the truth, her soldier husband had contributed very little to her adult education; but, against all odds, she had picked up techniques that outdated 3000 years of Oriental pleasuring. By any measure she rated genius-status in her chosen craft — and there was no doubt in his mind it *was* her craft. She had chosen it with enthusiasm and graduated with honours.

He hauled himself into a sitting position and reached for his robe; it had slipped to the floor along with most of the bedclothes. It was uncanny and maybe unnatural, too, but he felt fine. Fit, fresh; fighting fit and bitter-lemon fresh. No guilt gnawing away in back of his skull; no burned-out taste in his mouth; no sickening remorse. No reason. The sensational thing about Janice was that she didn't need a diet of pretence to satisfy some phony self-respect before she went for a roll in the hay and, afterwards, she sought no promises, no binding investment. Janice was like a sheet or a blanket or a pillow; an integral part of the natural machinery of sleep at night, an item of furniture during the day.

He rolled over the side of the bed so as not to disturb her and padded across the carpet to the sitting-room. He inched open the outer door and picked up the morning half pint of milk and the newspapers. He made coffee and sat down in the kitchen to drink it, the papers strewn across the tabletop.

Knickerbocker of the *Journal-American* had grabbed himself a sizeable slab of the London front pages this morning, one way and another. His persistence on the St Paul's time-bomb story had won a victory in which the British Press was now sharing and his clamour for the right to specify damage areas also appeared to have yielded universal fruit. The time-bomb that landed in Regent Street on Wednesday earned a lot of coverage and the same story revealed the existence of the 500-pounder half buried in Dean's Court near St Paul's churchyard. The *Express* threw in a lot of incidental detail about specific buildings destroyed and the *Daily Telegraph* ran a list of nine City churches damaged by bombing and itemised hits in Berkeley Square, Rotten Row and the Strand. The door was ajar.

But it was Knickerbocker's late despatch to the *Journal-American* last night that riveted Shaffer's attention and rated the more prominent headline. 'Invasion today is U.S. Tip,' ran the *Express*. 'But it's rough in the Channel.'

Shaffer ground his teeth furiously. What the hell were they doing? Why had they allowed Knickerbocker to run the ultimate scare story when they'd turned down everyone else? The piece was almost word for word the one he and every other American correspondent in London would have written at the end of last week, given the freedom to file. They had all tried it for size a second time when Churchill broadcast his invasion warning on Wednesday and once again every file had been slashed to shreds.

The hottest tip [wrote Knickerbocker] is that the German

invasion of England is coming tomorrow, Friday. This is the opinion of the most knowledgeable people. It is considered that the Nazi Caesar is going straight for the nearest point on the south-east coast, which is Dover and its vicinity. The accumulation of shallow-draught small craft in German-held ports opposite the south-east coast now seems to have reached saturation point for harbour facilities.

The *Express* had wisely strangled the story at birth by preceding it with a paragraph pointing out that high winds in the Channel invalidated the likelihood of an invasion by towed barges, but that would not pacify O'Keefe. There were precious few newsbreaks to be had in this stage-managed war and exclusive material was the only weapon A.B.N. could use to hammer away at the market superiority of the big networks. If Knickerbocker had done a deal with Murrow or Fred Bate. . . . No — he didn't want to think about that.

The rest of the news on the front pages was either several days old or enlargements of Anti-Aircraft Command's continuing 'box barrage' of incoming enemy raiders. Fewer German planes were getting through to London, the papers claimed, and the barrage was probably responsible in the main for reducing the number of casualties from 400 killed and 1400 injured on Monday night to 40 killed and 170 injured on Wednesday, the début of the great gunfire show.

The spectre of an early call from O'Keefe was taking powerful shape but he banished it instantly on reading a three-paragraph story tucked away at the bottom of a page. J. Edgar Hoover had assumed personal charge of an F.B.I. investigation into a suspected sabotage of the Hercules gunpowder plant at Kenvil, New Jersey. The plant, which handled British and U.S. war contracts, had been rocked by four giant explosions yesterday; fifty people had died and at least 200 were injured. O'Keefe would have his hands full where it mattered most. Still, it would pay dividends to check out the invasion story; if only to spot the leak.

The table jumped under his forearms and the coffee cup performed a nervous little dance in its saucer. He twisted round towards the kitchen window; it offered him only a view of the inner well of the apartment block but across the enclosed space lay a sinking cloud of white dust. He tiptoed quickly across the living-room and slipped out of the door into the corridor. Beyond the far end of Brook Street, rising to a frothy bubble several hundred feet above the ground, was a column of black smoke. The air shivered with heat around it. Could be Hyde Park. Chelsea, even.

'Hullo, old son. Close to home, is it?'

Archie Fisk, the amiable party-giver who had kidnapped him the previous Saturday, bent round the angle of the banister from the landing above. He was wearing pyjamas embodying an all-over design of chubby red hearts on an apple-green background, a pair of leather slippers and a muffler of great length marked with longitudinal stripes of white, black and purple.

'Hi.' Shaffer pointed along Brook Street. 'Couple of miles off, I'd guess. Big one, though.'

'Really?'

The pyjamas flowed down the half flight to Shaffer's level, the huge scarf streaming behind.

'Damn nasty for someone, that.' Archie pursed his lips ominously. 'No chance with one of those things, you know. Bang — all over. Might as well write them off, poor devils.' He turned with an expression of professional diffidence. 'They've made me chief firewatcher here, you know. The building, that is. Bit of a bind at first. Ate like hell into the evening wassailing and so forth.'

'Yeah,' said Shaffer, in neutral.

'Got the hang of it, though. Hit on the idea on Wednesday night — you know, when our chaps started putting up the old bang-bang. Tremendous stuff. Whoom, whoom! Had some of the boys and girls in for a tot or two — well, you know them, of course, from last weekend: Roly, Sarah, Phil, Tommy, Vera, Dot.... Yes, I bet you remember Dot all right.' He nudged Shaffer with a playful elbow. 'Took a shine to you. Sporting girl, Dot.'

'So the barrage began and...?'

'Yes. Well, the boys and girls weren't going to sit it out in some damn shelter, old son, were they? Wouldn't get Dot and Vera and Sarah down *there* in a hurry. So—nothing for it, herded the lot of 'em up on the roof. Against regulations, of course; they should have had tin hats, gas-masks too, but what could I do? Anyway, as luck would have it, incredible night's entertainment. Fireworks? Weren't it, old son. Loved every minute. Couldn't get enough. Came down to the flat when the "All Clear" went around half past five. On the phone Thursday afternoon, soon as they woke up. More, more, they said. Encore. Well, I ask you; what better? Made 'em firewatchers, all seven of 'em. Wouldn't miss a night, not one of 'em. Love it, old son! Love it!'

'You're running all-night parties up there? On the roof?'

'Parties? Well, yes dammit, of course they're parties. We keep the old wary eye askance for wandering wardens or a nosey bobby, have to, naturally. But it's war work, old son. National interest. Nothing in the rules to say you can't make the best of it.'

He tightened the muffler at his neck. The low cloud had brought a sharp wind with it and the first hint of winter's chill. The column of black smoke was beginning to bend at right angles, half way up. The firewatcher eyed Shaffer in the manner of a stockman assessing the sale-ring value of a specimen of prize beef. 'Don't suppose you'd care to join the duty roster yourself?'

Shaffer shook his head violently. 'Sorry. I'm up to here. In my line of work, you never know where you'll be next—or when.'

'Yes, of course. Pity. New blood, that sort of thing. Still, you'll pop in from time to time, I dare say. Just for a noggin.' His eyebrows climbed into his hairline. Shaffer accepted the invitation and made his excuses.

Janice was still asleep, her innocence in repose a standing joke to untrammelled virtue. He let her lie, performed what he now understood was called 'a stripwash'—a standing bath applied with a flannel from a washbasin filled to a depth of five inches—and shaved and dressed.

The phone was ringing as he unlocked the office door. He threw his coat across the desk and flopped into the chair.

'A.B.N. Shaffer.'

The voice was so timorous he couldn't make any sense of it at first.

'Can you speak up, please? I didn't get that.'

'Um — Mr Shaffer? Is that you, Mr Shaffer?'

'That's Mrs Warrender, right? Gladys's mother?'

The voice swelled with confidence at once. 'Oh, Mr Shaffer, thank goodness. I thought I'd got the wrong number. Then, when you came on, I thought—'

'Anything I can do for you, Mrs Warrender?'

Long pause. 'Well, I shouldn't be ringing really because I haven't told madam or anyone and if Mister found out I'd. . . .'

'Look, why don't you start at the beginning. You're speaking for a friend? A neighbour?'

'No, not exactly. Oh, I feel such a fool, now. It's just that . . . well, you see, these people I do for, this family . . . three days ago their Caroline, that's their daughter, went off to work and she hasn't been heard from since. Her mother, that's madam who I do for, can't eat or sleep or do nothing. Dunno where to put herself. I just couldn't watch her go through it another day. There's something funny about it, see.'

'How d'you mean, funny?'

'I think Mister, madam's husband, I think he knows but he won't say anything to her.'

Shaffer leaned back into his chair. What was he supposed to do about it? 'What do you want me to do, Mrs Warrender?'

'Well, that's the trouble. I don't rightly know what you can do. I just thought, he's a journalist, Mr Shaffer, he might know some way of finding out where she is. I didn't really think what I'd say to you, if you want to know God's honest truth. I'm just trying to help, that's all.'

Shaffer sighed wearily. 'Why should the husband hide it from his wife if he knows something?'

'He's funny, that's all I can say. I dunno for sure but I think he's been laid off.'

'Laid off?'

'You know, lost his job. Got the sack. Anyway, he's been home since Wednesday dinnertime and touchy as anything. I mustn't say too much, I know, but there's something rum about it because he's very important.'

Shaffer's instinct developed an itch. 'Important? In what way?'

'Well, if you think it's all right. . . .' Her voice withered to a barely perceptible murmur. 'In the government, sort of like. You know, Civil Service. Very high.'

He kept his tone level. 'O.K. Let me get this straight. He's a top civil servant. He's been kicked out of his job—'

'I think! I only *think*, Mr Shaffer. He hasn't said nothing.'

'Fine. He's maybe lost his job and his daughter's disappeared. You know where he works, Mrs Warrender?'

Another long pause and the sound of something, perhaps her fingers, drumming on the receiver. 'Aeroplanes. Yes, I think madam said once about his being in aeroplane work or something.'

'The Air Ministry?'

'Yes. That's the name of it, I'm sure. Something like that.'

He pulled a scribbling block towards him across the desk. 'Now you say the girl's name is Caroline, right? What's the address?'

She recited it.

'Now, the name of the father.'

'Russell, he's called. Mr Charles Russell.'

The pencil skidded across the pad and its point snapped. Shaffer tightened his grip on the phone. 'Would you repeat that, Mrs Warrender?'

'Charles Russell. C-H-A. . . .'

Friday, 0855

Elsie scuttled off the Embankment into Garfield Court, her heart banging away under Flo Scully's brown wool coat. Shouldn't-a-done-it, shouldn't-a-done-it, shouldn't-a-done-it; the chant rolled over the screen of her mind to the rhythm of her heartbeat. They'd find her out; throw her out. There'd be a row and Mister would turn on madam and blame her as well. It wouldn't help

399

anyone in the end; just hurt them more. Why did she do it!

There was a large black Wolseley saloon by the kerb outside Number 25; no one who lived in the East End could mistake the look and smell of a police car and although it carried no sign Elsie identified it at once. She ran across the paved garden and let herself in. She heard their voices in the drawing-room; the door was half open and someone was standing by it with a hand on its closing edge as if keeping a bolt-hole free for escape. She tiptoed into the kitchen and put down her barrage-balloon bag and brolly and slipped her coat on the hanger behind the door. She spread some vegetables on the table to make it look as if she were suitably engaged in the work of the day, then edged to the door, a Brussels sprout in one hand, a topping knife in the other. For the last twenty seconds of these preparations she had held her breath in an effort at perfect silence and when she came to the door she thought she would burst. She had to hold her nose to let the breath flow noiselessly from her mouth. Shouldn't-a-done-it, shouldn't-a-done-it, shouldn't-a-done-it.

The second she saw the police car she had prayed they were bringing Miss Caroline home but the first few snatches of conversation from the drawing-room ruled out the possibility of that miracle at once.

'. . . might have made your daughter's position less vulnerable, sir.' A stranger. Probably one of the policemen.

'Where *is* Caroline? Oh, for God's sake, Charles, make them tell me where she is.' Madam. Poor dear creature.

'With respect, madam.' Another stranger. 'Your husband already knows where your daughter is. We made no attempt to conceal that from him.'

'Charles?' Elizabeth Russell clearly couldn't believe her ears.

'What's my son doing here?' Charles Russell, savagely changing the subject. 'Tom?'

'I'm not going to talk to anyone about anything until I can talk to you in private first.' Mr Tom. Good lad; you show 'em.

'I'm afraid that's not possible, sir.' The first stranger. He sounded sad and put-upon and beginning to wish he'd never heard of Charles Russell.

'Do I have to enlist the Prime Minister's aid a second time?'

Charles Russell. The Prime Minister! Elsie developed a sour taste in her mouth and realised with a start that she was chewing the raw sprout.

'That's up to you.' The second stranger. Hard, flat voice, soft as the front wheel of a steamroller. 'The Prime Minister, as we understand it, called for speedy action. He didn't recommend curtailing the investigation. We're expected to produce a full report. A copy will go to the Prime Minister. His request ... sir.' That 'sir' came a little too late to be well meant. The speaker didn't want Mister to be comforted. He wanted to hurt.

'I don't understand, Charles. Tom, for God's sake—if you've got anything to say that'll change their minds, bring Caroline home.... Anything at all....'

'Mother, please! You don't know what you're asking.'

'I think I should tell you, sir'—the put-upon copper again—'that we're obliged to remind you that anything you say in this room may subsequently be taken down in the form of a statement.'

'Will you let me talk to my son alone if I give you my word to repeat to you everything he tells me?' Mister.

'No.' That steamroller voice. Sneering, this time. 'I reminded you once before, Mr Russell. We don't take people's words. Not even yours.'

'Don't talk to my father like that.' Mr Ian. There was a scuffling sound and the youngster's heavy breathing. He wasn't having a go at one of 'em, surely?

'Leave him alone!' Madam. He *must* be having a go.

'Stop it! At once!' Mister. All strong and don't-you-dare-disobey-me. The scuffling stopped. 'Ian, go upstairs ... old chap ... and put some clothes on.'

Mister, all gentle; saying more than the words gave away. Mr Ian must have trailed off upstairs to his room because there was a lull for a full minute; Elsie could feel the prickly atmosphere all the way from her spy-hole behind the kitchen door.

'Very well.' Mister in command now. 'Tom—tell these gentlemen what they want to know.'

'I'm not going to tell—'

'You're going to do as I say, Tom.' Ooooh — that was a turn-up. Not raising his voice like he always used to; very quiet and reasonable. Like a proper dad should be. 'Inspector Lubbock, if you wish to make a note of what my son tells you, please do so. Tom, what is it you've refused to tell the police?'

'I didn't refuse! Well ... only to the extent of saying you had a right to know first. Dammit, that's only fair.'

'Go on.'

'Mother?'

'Tell them, Tom. Tell them quickly.' Poor madam dear.

'O.K. It was Tuesday. About eleven o'clock, I suppose. I was at Bentley Priory, on duty, when I got this call.'

'Call? Telephone call?' Lubbock.

'This telephone call. Caroline asked if I could meet her and—'

'Was that an unusual request, sir?' the nice copper interrupted.

'I don't know what you mean by unusual.'

'Did your sister often call you at Bentley Priory? Did she often meet you?'

'No. It'd never happened before.'

'Thank you, sir. Carry on.'

'She was pretty low, I could hear that. Down in the dumps. She said she wanted to meet and could I make lunch? I said it would be difficult — and it was. I had to get someone to cover for me. Anyway, I said—'

Charles Russell broke through in a rush. 'Are you about to tell me *you* had lunch with Caroline on Tuesday? At a pub called —er....' Snap, snap of his fingers.

The nice copper volunteered. 'The Baker's Arms. Milton Bassett. *Did* you, sir?'

'Well, yes.' Mr Tom sounded puzzled. Elsie understood how he felt. It was beyond her, all of it. 'But—'

'You can prove that, of course ... sir?' That nasty bugger, Lubbock. Oh, he hated this family for some reason, you could hear that.

'I keep a sort of travel log for my car. I put the journey down to keep a check on the petrol I use. That's all. No — I arrived first and I talked to a — er *huh!*' — just like father — 'a girl who was waiting for a bus in front of the pub. And I suppose the landlord ought to recognise me. He came with the bill after we'd had lunch in the garden behind the pub. The damage was seven shillings and tuppence, I think, and I gave him a ten bob note. Told him to keep the change.'

'Oh, my God, oh my *God*.' Mister. He was laughing. Laughing.

'And that's all?' The thin-gutted swine!

'Isn't that *enough*?' Madam.

'Yes.' The put-upon man sounded very genuine and sad. 'Yes, I think that *is* enough, Lubbock.'

'We'll have to check the—'

'Yes. We'll check. But I'm sure we'll find everything's in order. I'm sorry we had to bring this on you, Mr Russell. It's . . . just very unfortunate.'

'I still don't understand. . . .' Madam sounded completely lost.

'We'll still have to interview the officer you say covered for you at Bentley Priory and—' Lubbock!

'That's enough . . . I think, Lubbock.' The first copper, throwing his rank around, but cannily. He knew human nature well enough, that one. Knew when to call a halt. 'Your daughter was removed to an R.A.F. hospital near Cambridge, Mrs Russell. She's perfectly well and there's no reason why she shouldn't be home in a couple of days if—'

'Days!' Elizabeth Russell was appalled. 'Why not now?'

'That's up to her doctors, Mrs Russell, but—'

'Then I'll go up there myself. Right away.'

'Elizabeth! Wait a moment!' Mister again. There was a change in him, anyone could hear that. Found his feet, that man had. Come a long way since last night. 'I don't think these gentlemen are in a position to do anything about the hospital. Leave it to me. I'll talk with the—'

'But they said you *knew*. They said you were told where she was.'

'Mr Russell's right, madam. I think that's best left in his hands.' The nice one. 'We'll submit a report but I think it'll be a little thin. Circumstantial evidence leading to conclusions not borne out by subsequent investigation. Happens often, I'm bound to say. One of the hazards of wartime police work. Biggest enemy we have is coincidence and there was rather too much of it for comfort in this case.'

'But what about Caroline? She must be. . . . Oh, Charles, she must be so alone. So frightened. . . .'

'Leave it to me, darling. Leave it to me.' Darling! He'd never said that to her, not in all of Elsie's fourteen years at Garfield Court. *Darling!* Charles Russell. 'Gentlemen, let me show you out. I think we've wasted enough of your time as it is.'

Elsie dodged to the other side of the kitchen table as feet tramped across the marbled floor of the hall. The nice copper and Mister were talking together in a relaxed, friendly sort of way but too quietly for her to hear. The conversation trailed away out into the front garden and presumably across the pavement to the car because it was some minutes before a door slammed and the engine revved and Mister's feet stamped back into the house. The front door shut and madam called from the drawing-room.

'Charles! Charles!'

She heard them come together in the hall, the subtle whisper of clothes brushing clothes, arms slipping around shoulders and waists. Lovely! That's what they needed, both of 'em.

'Charles. . . ?'

'Now listen to me, my darling. We've had enough drama to be going on with. And on empty stomachs, too. Good God, child, I'm starving. Before we do anything else, I've got to get something inside me. D'you think Elsie's here?'

'Elsie!' He called her by her name!

'Elsie, d—' Elizabeth began.

'Yes, madam dear! Coming!' she shouted. Far too loudly.

Charles Russell said he had never tasted bloaters so beautifully cooked in his life and when Elsie brought in the toast and marmalade and the tea he made her sit down at the table with them. Mr Ian was grave and very nervous but Elizabeth was beginning to look her old self again. She smiled behind her hand when Mister invited Elsie to pour herself a cup of tea and sit down.

'Mrs. . . . Elsie. We've been through a very bad time in this house in the past three days and I think you've probably taken the brunt of it,' Russell said. He couldn't look her in the face, just yet, but he was doing his best.

'Oh, I didn't do nothing, sir—' she started.

'My wife told me about the—er—little talk you had with her last night before you left.' He stopped and a blush raised two bright spots of crimson on his cheeks. 'I want to thank you for that. Oh—yes,' he waved his hand at her discomfiture. 'It was very, very thoughtful and. . . .' He snatched a guilty look at his wife. 'I should have told her myself, of course.' He reached forward and touched Elizabeth's hand lightly. 'I feel I owe you an apology, as well as my thanks—*our* thanks.'

Elizabeth nodded encouragingly and he smiled.

'I've been something of a . . . tartar, I'm afraid, this past year or so. Easy enough to blame it on my work, I suppose, but that's just not good enough. My daughter. . . . Caroline will need all of us when she comes home. She's been through a . . . nightmare. The fact of the matter is. . . .' He looked at Elizabeth again for help and she urged him on with a little twitch of her nose. 'I'm not altogether sure I can deal with Caroline's—um—problems alone. She's always liked—been close to you. I'd very much appreciate it if you would consider helping her where you can and—'

'There's nothing I wouldn't do for that child,' Elsie broke in breathlessly. 'Anything at all. You don't have to ask, Mister.'

'No, of course not. You're . . . one of the family . . . Elsie.'

He was floundering now, his cheeks burning; they were all grateful when Tom thundered down the stairs from his room and breezed in, fresh in civilian sweater and his old cricket ducks. He gauged the atmosphere shrewdly and came behind Elsie's chair and dropped a kiss on the crown of her black felt hat.

'How's your husband, old Elsie?' he asked softly. 'Mother told me.'

'Better thanks, Mr Tom. Got over it now, Lord love us.'

Russell said wretchedly, 'If there's anything I can do. Anything at all. . . .'

Tom walked around the table and sat down beside Ian.

'If Elsie thought there was anything we could do, she'd tell us, wouldn't you, old Elsie?' He winked at her. 'Is this a meeting of the Inner Cabinet or can anyone join in? Pass the toast and marmalade, brother. Is that butter or marge?'

Elsie made to rise at once but Elizabeth pushed her back into the chair with firm hands. 'No you don't, dear, you sit where you are. He can manage perfectly well by himself.'

Elsie's discomfort was obvious. Russell said to her kindly, 'We've all taken far too much advantage of your willingness, Elsie. I more than anyone. Well, that's going to change. You told me you're living with neighbours. We've plenty of room here....'

Her guilt burst its banks and overflowed into her face. She clenched her hands on the table in front of her, the knuckles white.

'Oh madam dear!'

She was on the brink of tears. She couldn't bring herself to address Russell direct. Shouldn't-a-done-it, shouldn't-a-done-it, shouldn't-a-done-it pounded her heart in her ears.

'Elsie!' Elizabeth took the clenched hands in hers. 'What is it?'

'I was so worried! I didn't think. I was so worried.' She gulped back the flood. 'This morning. I came early, see, and looked in to see if Miss Caroline was back and she wasn't and. . . .' She pulled her hankie from her sleeve and blew her nose resoundingly. 'I did a very silly thing.'

A flicker of disenchantment crossed Russell's face but he kept his voice gentle. 'We've all done a great many silly things, Elsie. You don't have to be afraid.'

'Oh. . . . I wish I'd never a-done it,' she wailed helplessly.

'What did you do, old Elsie?' Tom leaned forward.

'I went down the Embankment to the phone box and I ... I called this man who helped find Paul and young Derek Scully when the bombing started Saturday. He's an American. He goes on the wireless and—'

Russell broke in harshly. 'What's his name?'

'Mr Shaffer. He's a—'

'Melvyn Shaffer?' Russell gripped her arm, his fingers tight on the soft flesh. 'The American correspondent?'

'Yes, him. He was so kind to us, I thought—'

Charles Russell released his grip and lay back in his chair, his face hovering between anger and resignation.

Elizabeth said quickly, 'Do you know him, Charles?'

'Yes, I know him. We met at . . . he asked for my help.'

'What did you tell him, Elsie?' Tom repeated more firmly.

'I asked him if he could find out where Miss Caroline was.'

The silence that descended on them was tactile. It seemed to Elsie Warrender that all the air had been sucked from the room and replaced with icicles. She mumbled, 'I'm ever so sorry. I just wanted to help.'

Tom was the first to recover. 'Can't be helped, can it? You mustn't blame yourself, old Elsie. You did it for the best. Problem now is: how do we undo the complications?'

'I think you'd best leave that to me,' Charles Russell said gruffly. 'I know how to handle these people.'

'He's not like that, honest,' Elsie said defensively, watching Russell's face for storm signals from the corner of her eye. 'He wouldn't—'

'He's a journalist,' Russell said with judicial severity. 'His job is to pry. It depends, of course, what you told him.'

'Charles!' Elizabeth protested.

Russell pursed his lips unhappily. 'Yes, well . . . I suppose it doesn't make much difference at that. We know each other. He and I met socially, as it were. I have no doubt he knows as much about me as I do about him. More, possibly. These people have sources of information. Contacts. If he. . . .' His face changed suddenly; hope grew, erasing the deep lines around his mouth and jaw. 'We were introduced by a . . . mutual friend. Young fellow. Good family. Well connected. Perhaps he might. . . .'

He slipped his watch from his waistcoat pocket. 'Nine thirty-three. I think I have his home number in my book. Excuse me.' He pushed back his chair, stood irresolutely for a moment, napkin swinging in one hand, then left the room. They heard him go into his study and shut the door.

'Well, that was quick.' Tom took another round of toast and smoothed margarine on it sparingly. 'Am I particularly dim or is everyone baffled?'

'Don't be flippant, Tom,' Elizabeth said reprovingly. 'You don't know how serious it is.'

'Do *you*?' he retorted accusingly.

'Well, not exactly. But I'm sure your father knows what he's doing.'

'Oh, Gawd, I wish I'd never a-done it,' moaned Elsie.

'Now, you're not to go on about it, dear,' Elizabeth ordered. 'The very least of our problems is that some journalist is running around London half-knowing something that doesn't concern him. If Charles knows someone. . . .'

Ian rose. He should have told them. . . .

'Are you all right, dear?' Elizabeth came to him and kissed his cheek with passionate protectiveness. 'That Lubbock man didn't hurt you, did he?'

'No, of course he didn't. There's nothing wrong. I just thought I'd get some air.'

'You don't want to wait till your father comes back?'

'It'll be all right now. Long as Caroline comes home soon. Father'll fix it, he always does.' It was too late now.

Elizabeth inspected him with a nursing mother's eye; if only it were still possible to look through his serious grey eyes and see into that over-active mind as she had when he was a child. But the eyes were mirrors now; clouded mirrors.

Tom made a loose fist and punched his brother in the fleshy part of the upper arm. 'Give me a sec, brother, and I'll come along for a breather. I could do with it.' He pushed the last of the toast into his mouth and licked a spot of marmalade from the corner of his lips. He bounced to his feet. 'What I need is the company of a bright spark like you; full of beans and whizz-bang.'

Ian grinned in spite of himself and Elizabeth gave them a joint hug. 'Don't be late for lunch,' she admonished. 'Elsie isn't going to stay on tonight so dinner will be late.' She tapped her breast. 'I'll be cooking it.'

'Oh, no!' Tom blurted in mock horror. 'Anything but that!'

'Now I'm not going out of this house without getting your—'

'You'll do what you're told, Elsie,' Elizabeth said comfortably. 'You'll be away at five on the dot to be back in Nelson's Green for your husband's supper. It'll be a change for him to have you to talk to for once.'

The study door banged and they all exchanged glances. Charles Russell came in and studied them cautiously. He waited for effect, then allowed a smile to blossom thinly. 'It may be all right. Fingers crossed, hmmm? This fellow thinks he might be able to get a word with Shaffer right away.'

'Oh, thank Gawd for that,' breathed Elsie. 'Honest, I don't know where to put meself.'

'I think the best thing you can do is—'

Elizabeth never finished her homily. The room shook and a trio of ground-level thunderclaps ricocheted around in the street outside.

'Christ! That was close.'

'Tom! Language!' Elizabeth was grateful for the diversion. 'I didn't hear the alert. Is there a raid on?'

Tom came back from the window. 'Can't see anything. Yes, mother, there *is* a raid on. You're the dizzy end, you really are. It sounded about two minutes ago but you were far too concerned with your clutch of cheeping chicks. Wasn't the local siren, though. Sounds like one of them might have slipped in under the fighter screen.'

The respectable conventional hush of Garfield Court closed round them again and they gave up straining their ears for clues of further combat.

Charles Russell consulted his watch again and dusted the arms of his black jacket. 'I shall be going in to the office this morning,' he said with the suspicion of a smile on his lips. 'The officers will have informed the minister by now. I mustn't keep him waiting.'

'Oh, Charles, dear.' Elizabeth threw her arms around him. He submitted with ill-disguised embarrassment. The others averted their faces and Elsie dodged round the pair of them to dash to her kitchen. She heard Ian and Tom going upstairs and a moment later the unmistakable tweak of lips on lips in the hallway. The front door was opened and there was a furious whispering, then. . . .

'Goodbye, Elsie!'

She recovered just in time.

'Goodbye, Mister!' she shouted.

Friday, 0945

'Hey, Denzil. Coincidence. I tried to call you a coupla minutes ago. Your line was busy.'

'Yes. Something came up.'

'Dowding?'

'No. No, not exactly.'

'Here we go again. What does "not exactly" mean?'

'Difficult. Deuced difficult. Need your help, Shaffer. Personal matter. Delicate.'

'Fire away.'

'Understand a lady called you, what? Early this morning.'

'Lady? We got a crossed line here?'

'A Mrs Warrender, Shaffer. Elderly person.'

'Mrs Warrender? O.K., sure—she called. How d'you know that?'

'Just talked with Charles Russell. Remember? Chap at Freddie Green's the other night?'

'I know who he is, all right. What was he calling you for? Turning the screw?'

'Screw? Don't get the drift.'

'Forget it. What did he want?'

'Family's compromised, Shaffer.'

'You bet he is.'

'Don't think you grasp the nub. Not Russell, old boy. His daughter.'

'Caroline?'

'Precisely. Girl's in a bit of a fix.'

'That's not the way Mrs Warrender tells it. The way she sees it, Russell got kicked out of the Air Ministry and—'

'All changed. Just now. Russell will be at the ministry in an hour. Call him there if you like. He'll explain.'

'I'm not calling anyone, Denzil.'

'Please yourself. Matter of honour, my way of thinking. Lady's name at stake. Fellow does what he can.'

'Look, how do I know any of this is true?'

'My word, Shaffer. Good enough?'

'That's one hell of a way to put it.'

'No other, what? Russell's a white man. Straight as a die. My father knows his family. Yorkshire stock. Couldn't lie to me. Gave me his word.'

'Goddammit! This is the only country in the world where they believe a guy because he gives his word.'

'Of course.'

'Of course *nothing*. Look, Denzil, exactly what are you asking?'

'Nothing at all, really. Just drop in for lunch, one pip emma, twenty-five Garfield Court.'

'Russell's place?'

'Yes. Spoken for, are you?'

'No. I can make it. Why?'

'They'll explain.'

'Isn't this all a little too involved? I mean, if the guy wants to get his daughter off the hook—'

'Asked my help, Shaffer. Said yes, naturally.'

'You going along, too?'

'Wouldn't leave you stranded, old boy.'

'We-l-l-l ... O.K. I'll be there. But don't think the old school tie crap is going to work with me. If he's—'

'A lady. Just a lady, Shaffer. Simple case of honour.'

'If you say so.'

'I do. You have my word on it.'

'Oh well, that makes everything peachy, right?'

'Come again?'

'Nothing, Denzil. One o'clock.'

'Pip emma. Twenty-five Garfield Court.'

'I'll see you.'

'Cheers, old boy.'

Friday, 1130

Shaffer devoted twenty minutes to hammering out a letter to Rita after the call from Fletcher-Hale. Maybe there had been a trigger for the decision somewhere in Denzil's exposition on honour and personal integrity.

He composed himself as he would before writing a persuasive despatch for O'Keefe, his concentration neatly divided between content and impact. Rita, after all, was just another consumer in the great marketplace of mass communication; she wanted to be swayed or intrigued or lulled with comforting background noise like the rest of them.

Mrs Price plied him with coffee and silence in the belief that he was engaged on the solemn business of A.B.N. and he sent her out to buy the midday editions so that he could address an envelope without exciting her curiosity.

The alert sounded as he was sealing the letter. When Mrs Price returned he excused himself by saying he had a couple of house-calls to make. He slipped the letter into a pillar-box in Berkeley Square and experienced a sense of relief that was almost physical. Now that hadn't been so painful, had it?

He had parked the Morris in Bruton Street, a lot farther from the office than usual, but for some reason the streets were alive with automobiles this morning and every inch of space around Hill Street had been taken. The regular Friday shoppers and trippers, Mrs Price explained; even now, with every paper in the land carrying horror stories of destruction and instant death and the wireless pouring out the saga of London's torment across the nation, the Friday shoppers were teeming in from the suburbs and the country for their weekly jollies. According to Mrs Price, 'jollies' were an integral part of middle-class suburban life and would be conceded only as a last resort. A morning's shopping at Harrods or in the cluster of department stores along Oxford and Regent Streets, coffee and scones and gossip in one of a hundred bijou watering holes, lunch, a round of speculative 'trying-on' in the dress shops in Bond

Street and off home in time for hubby's tea. Jollies. The perfect curtain-raiser to an English weekend.

Shaffer was on the point of turning the corner into Bruton Street when his eye was arrested by the figure of a man indolently poised on a folded umbrella in front of a car sales-room display window. It was the set of the shoulders, the almost Oriental imperturbability, that drew his eye; then other characteristics — the angle of the head, the pronounced jut of the jawline — checked him in his stride. He crossed the street and stood behind and slightly to one side of the man who was obviously entranced by the automobile on show, a superb late-twenties Rolls-Royce limousine with polished brass coach-lamps, lush rosewood and leatherwork and an open driving section for the coachman turned chauffeur. The window-shopper continued to gaze at it lovingly, apparently unaware of Shaffer's presence; then he said, as if to his own reflection, 'They're making tanks and scout cars now, they tell me.'

Shaffer came closer. 'I know which I'd rather have.'

Leigh Ashton, Director of Foreign Publicity at the Ministry of Information, nodded glumly. 'Ever have a car like that?'

'You must be joking.'

'Oh, I don't know. You Yanks are rolling in money. Anyway, there isn't an American car built that's much smaller than that.'

'You've been watching too many gangster movies.'

'Hmm. P'raps I have.'

Shaffer looked at his watch. 'I was about to drive down to Bloomsbury — in my Morris Ten, if you're interested. You want a lift?'

'Hmmmm?' Ashton was still hypnotised by the Rolls in the window. 'Nice little buggy, the Morris.'

'You want a lift?'

'Might as well.' Leigh Ashton tore himself from the window with some effort. 'You know something, Shaffer? I have an uncomfortable notion we've seen the last of that kind of excellence.'

'What else do you expect in wartime?'

'No, I don't mean for the duration. I mean for ever. When this lot's over no one's going to build that kind of car. Say it costs a thousand guineas today. Next year, twelve hundred. The year after, fifteen hundred. Peace carries a pretty high premium.'

'They'll find ways. You don't run down a whole industry just because of a war. Look at Germany. Flat on its butt in nineteen eighteen. Today. . . ?'

'We're not German.'

'It wasn't meant as an accusation.'

'Sorry. Touchy. I meant the English don't worship the concept of work as the Germans do. Different priorities. Nothing noble about sweated labour, no matter what the trade unions say.'

'Somebody's got to make something. You're a trading nation, aren't you?'

'Hmmmm. Maybe we are. We're in a state of . . . what do they call it? — metamorphosis? Shedding our skin. You can't put back what you've thrown aside.'

'You sure as hell can't live naked — not in this climate.'

Ashton frowned severely. 'You can afford to joke about it. Americans are different. You haven't been a nation long enough to find a shape. You're adaptable, flexible. You yield to pressures and circumstances; re-form around them. No traditions to peg you down; no rules you're not prepared to change.'

Shaffer said, 'If I'd known it was a wake I'd have walked on by. What's the big gloomy secret?'

They reached the car and Shaffer held open the passenger door to his companion. Ashton stared down at the car as though seeking courage and inspiration, failed to find it and slouched into the seat, propping his umbrella between his knees, hands folded on its handle.

Shaffer got in, started the engine and pulled into the traffic. He turned into Berkeley Square and headed up Berkeley Street towards Piccadilly.

'I said what's the big secret? Or is it classified?'

'Everything's classified, you know that,' Ashton called out over the rush of air.

'I'll put it down to professional *ennui*, then. The propagandist's dilemma. How long does it take before you start doubting what you say before you say it?'

'Rubbish!'

'That's the word. You read the Knickerbocker story on the invasion in the *Express* today?'

'Now that really *is* rubbish.' He was serious.

'So it's rubbish one of your people let through. Don't tell me there wasn't a damn good reason for it. The way I see it, either Churchill wants the Nazis to know he knows, or he wants Roosevelt to use it to beat Congress over the back of the neck, or he wants the world to know he doesn't care because the R.A.F. have blown the German invasion fleet out of the sea. Don't tell me....'

They had reached the junction with Piccadilly and a policeman on point-duty raised a white-gloved hand. Shaffer braked to a halt as the stationary traffic line held up in front of the Ritz roared away towards Piccadilly Circus. He turned to Ashton to enlarge his argument when the throaty scream of an aircraft engine at maximum pitch pierced the hurly-burly of the street. They both looked up at once but saw nothing. The traffic surged on, although the bobby directing it was now temporarily off-duty, hands shading his eyes to look up into the grey scum of light cloud. The scream became a whine and then a guttural snarl and there followed in quick succession the thunderclaps of the explosions; three, maybe five.

'God almighty!' Ashton threw out an arm, narrowly missing Shaffer's face, and pointed out over Green Park. 'They've got the palace!'

The policeman appeared suddenly to become aware of the situation and with an almost Parisian flash of arms brought the traffic to a halt.

'Go on. Go on!' yelled Ashton and dug into his inside pocket for his wallet. The constable raised a hand to them angrily but hesitated when Ashton raised his identification card and waved it wildly in the air. One look at it and the bobby signalled them on. Shaffer turned right and accelerated down to Hyde Park Corner. The tell-tale smoke plumes were already writhing in the wind; bowing at the waist as they loomed over the high brick walls of Buckingham Palace, flowing down to the tree-shaded walks of Constitution Hill.

'It *is* the palace!' Ashton was in a frenzy. 'Hurry, man. For God's sake!'

Shaffer brought the Morris to a skidding halt on the park side of the street across from the palace gates and bounced it over the kerb and under the trees. Ashton was out and running before the car rolled to a stop. Shaffer followed him. Between the boarded-up statue of Queen Victoria and the palace gates the road was torn by two smouldering craters and a rash of smaller holes where shrapnel had ducked-and-draked crazily on impact. Half a dozen people on the far side of the road by St James's Park crouched in the paralysis of shock. An old woman lay face down on the grass behind a tree, holding her hat with both hands. By the palace gates a man lay prostrate, one arm curled over the back of his head. Ashton reached him and dropped to one knee. Shaffer came up to hear him saying, '. . . sure you're all right?'

'Yes. I was just leaving. I'd been inside. I'd just got through the—' He gagged and Ashton leaped to one side smartly.

'Come on!' He led the way through the gates. There were no policemen. In the arch ahead of them across the courtyard they heard the bellow of voices and Shaffer noted another column of smoke climbing from what seemed the very centre of the building, but both sentry-boxes were empty. 'Wait here!' shouted Ashton as they reached the archway. He strode into the smoke.

Shaffer gazed around him. The hard-standing of the courtyard was a carpet of shattered glass and chunks of masonry and tarmacadam lay like volcanic dust in every direction. Detail flooded in on him. Five small birds, sparrows maybe, lying like discarded rags around a rainwater pipe. The branch of a tree, snapped from its mother bole, perilously balanced on the slope of a roof, leaves blackened. A bicycle, snatched from some discreet hiding place, lay in the very centre of the courtyard, one wheel still spinning, one wheel gone. A bowler hat, black and whole, was wedged in the empty frame of a second-floor window. Beyond the yard and across Buckingham Palace Road a third-floor bow window yawned wide as a smile without teeth and from it a curtain, miraculously spared, waved tragically for help. A delivery van had mounted the pavement below it and buried its nose in a shop-front. From Admiralty Arch, way down The Mall, Shaffer heard the ringing of bells, then a reprise from the Victoria end of Petit Curie. A green army fire-tender tyre-screamed through the gates of Wellington Barracks.

Ashton came stumbling back, his face and clothes smudged and soaked, his eyes rimmed red. 'They think there were four or five hits,' he gasped, gulping air gratefully. 'Nobody knows if—'

'Are the king and queen here?'

'Yes. I think so. Yes. They are. Look, p'raps we can lend a hand till the firemen get here. But I'm binding you to absolute secrecy about anything you see or hear. Good enough?'

'Agreed.'

Ashton framed the word mechanically. 'Agreed. You'll get wet. There are two craters in the inner quadrangle and one of 'em's got a burst main in it. Water's shooting up about ten feet in the air. The guard's doing what it can. Come with me.'

The place was a shambles. Blast had sucked and blown every object that was loose or free-standing from its place. They crunched every foot of the way over a carpet of glass shards, smoke swirled in dizzying eddies, the stench of gas was everywhere and, before Ashton could warn him, Shaffer stumbled into a wall of water. He couldn't see it; it was just there. There were a dozen voices, all shouting, the grunt of men bending muscle to the limit of endurance, the hiss of breath, the splash of fountaining water on sodden clothing.

Shaffer turned to find Ashton but he had disappeared. He groped in the smoke and again walked into the fizzing curtain of water. Ashton loomed up and grabbed his shoulder.

'Over here! Over here, Shaffer!'

The smoke thinned and the water became only a swish of energy and he knew he was inside. They crossed a room, a carpet crackling with broken china and glass and brickdust, and came into a corridor. An officer appeared from the other end and made at once for Ashton.

He eyed Shaffer warily and said quickly, 'They're all right.'

'You sure?'

'I've just spoken with the equerry. Thank God, they're all right.'

Ashton prompted, 'Hurt? Were they...?'

'No. Near miss, though. The king was in his study about thirty yards from the Quadrangle. He was talking to his secretary. He's badly shaken, but he's O.K.'

'Anyone else hurt?'

The officer stared deliberately at Shaffer. 'I don't think I can say any more. I appreciate your prompt action, but....'

Ashton's jaw jutted angrily for a moment, then he relaxed and his arms fell to his sides. 'Yes, right. Quite understand. Nothing we can do anyway. There are your firemen.' The jangle of bells from the courtyard pealed deafeningly. Ashton raised his voice. 'We'll be going then. Sure we can't...?'

The officer swung on his heel and strode away. At a point where the corridor branched he stopped and pointed. 'That way,' he snapped. 'You'll get out to the courtyard if you walk straight through. All right?' He waited for them to join him and watched them trudge away, water slopping down their trousers and overflowing their shoes.

Outside they lingered by the three fire-tenders; watched the exhausted young men of the A.F.S. run out their hoses and tag on to the branches before advancing through the arch.

'I'm sorry you—' began Ashton.

Shaffer was wringing out his trouser ends. He straightened up. 'Don't apologise to me for being on the doorstep the day they bombed the king and queen of England.'

'I meant what I said, you know, Shaffer. Until I have clearance, you saw and heard nothing. You weren't here.'

'And if you get clearance?'

'That's another matter.'

'That's good enough for me, friend. Forty-eight hours ago — goddammit, almost to the minute — I was standing right here, waiting to look over the Tuesday bomb damage. By invitation. A little late coming but you asked me in. Nobody's gonna tell you to hush up a dive-bomber attack on the palace, you know that, Leigh. You have any idea what this story's worth when it hits America? Two attacks on the king and queen in one week? Man, you couldn't begin to guess! I'll tell you what that bomber just did. It just tuned out Ambassador Joseph Kennedy and Colonel Lindbergh and every other American mother's son who thinks Hitler might just be Saint Francis of Assisi in jackboots. You're not going to miss out on that kind of publicity. Churchill won't let you.'

'But we'll wait and see, O.K.?'

'Sure. As long as one of your sidekicks doesn't hand it on a plate to Knickerbocker first.'

'That's unfair.'

'So's love and war, Leigh. Let's have a sign of faith, huh? Or — er. . . .' He grinned good-naturedly. 'Or maybe you'd care to walk back to Bloomsbury like that.'

Ashton's grimed face parted in a nigger-minstrel smile. 'O ye of little faith! What is it?'

'What else happened in there?'

Ashton's grin faded. He pondered, turned and slouched away. Shaffer followed.

'All right,' said Ashton wearily as they neared the gates. 'There were five bombs in all, they think. Two in the Quadrangle, one hit the chapel. I think that one was probably a direct hit. Couldn't see much in the time I had. These two' — he pointed out into the road where army and A.F.S. men were sealing off the approaches to Buckingham Gate — 'make five. There were a few incendiaries, according to the officer of the guard, but they fell in the park. You heard the rest.'

Shaffer grinned happily. 'My lips are sealed . . . till around midnight, I'd say. But it wouldn't surprise me if you were feeding this out to Fleet Street within the hour.'

He was right. Winston Churchill made the decision himself.

Friday, 1235

Flo Scully woke Jack Warrender from his sleep with a light touch on the shoulder but it was sufficient to set his nerves leaping. He blinked up from his swaddling of grey blankets and reassured himself he was no longer in the nightmare that had been tormenting him. 'You, Flo? What time is it?'

'Edie's coming due, Jack. I just sent young Paul for the doctor. I'll go round to be with her meself but I thought you'd better know first.'

He pulled himself up on one elbow and pawed the sleep from the corners of his eyes with a shaking hand. 'Where's young Barry then? Does he know?'

Flo unlaced her pinafore and rolled it into a neat bundle. 'I told Paul to leg it down to Pageant's Wharf when he's been to tell the doctor.'

Jack grunted to a sitting position. 'There ain't no bloody Pageant's Wharf no more, woman. I told all of you that nights ago. Copped it, didn't it. Barry'll be down Jamaica Road more likely, or out on some fire or salvage. Don't be silly, Flo. He can't do nothing, now can he?'

'Well, I only did it for the best.'

He nodded, exhaustion settling back on him like a mantle. 'Sorry, old love. Tired, you see. Didn't get in till after seven. How's young Edie then?'

'She's home. Her mother came round to say she was near her time. Said she wanted to stay but I said it was better she went home. Look, I better get over there now; there's no telling with babies. I remember Elsie when she was carrying young Paul. Another four or five days easy, old Doctor Flack said, but I knew different. You remember, don't you? Elsie caught short in the middle of Borough Market that Tuesday afternoon? I said to meself—'

'Are you going or not?'

'I'll tell her you'll be round then, will I?'

Jack Warrender grunted assent. 'O.K. You can tell her, though I'm buggered if I know what I'm supposed to do.'

Flo clip-clopped away down the narrow staircase and he pulled on his vest and shirt and trousers and went down to the scullery to wash and shave. The water was cold; the gas main which had taken all yesterday afternoon to repair must have

420

been hit again or developed a crack that reduced pressure to nothing.

Flo had lit the fire in the living-room so he set a kettle on it to boil and went down the yard to the privy. It was in a sad state of repair; constant blast had parted its wooden planks at the seams, and the lavatory bowl, already an antique, had cracked from top to bottom. When he flushed it, water ran out at his feet and soaked his carpet slippers.

He used the hot water from the hob kettle to wash and shave and make his usual giant breakfast mug of tea. It was new, the mug; Elsie had bought it on her way up West on Tuesday morning to replace the old Edward the Seventh coronation mug, treasured all of their married life, which had been lost in the bombing. He sat at the table and swallowed the orange-coloured fluid. That's better. Nothing set a man up like a cup of tea first thing.

He should have gone to see young Edie before, though like as not her mother would have taken the hump. Snotty number, that Mrs Wilcox; got ideas outside her reach and Gawd help Barry if he couldn't do something about them. Still, Edie herself had got expectations enough for Barry. She was going to push him and shove him till he made something of hisself, she said, and the way her face lit up and her fists went tight and her chin stuck in the air when she said it, you could tell she wouldn't take no for an answer. Still, many ways, that might be the making of Barry. He wasn't no great brain, saying it as shouldn't about his own flesh and blood, but he was quick and he'd got a touch of the old manner about him; you couldn't help liking him. Edie was all for Barry learning a trade and she'd go out to work to support him till he got his articles; that was the plan; she was always talking about it. Never a word about babies like it was only natural for young couples to talk. Then out of nowhere she was suddenly carrying. Precious quiet she'd kept about it too; till she was six months gone. He hadn't noticed himself and neither had Barry, the way Elsie heard tell. Proper Gawd-help-us Barry was sometimes. And where was he now?

Last time he'd seen the boy was when Thompsett's garage

went up over by Lavender Lane. Wednesday night? No, Tuesday night or early hours Wednesday morning. Strewth, there wasn't no way to keep check of time no more. Night and day was all the same. Barry had been hanging on to a branch with a kid who didn't look much older than young Paul and the hose was kicking behind them like some live thing. Fit to drop, Barry looked. Saw his father, cocked his head in greeting and then got on with his fire. First time in a week they'd met. He probably hadn't seen Edie much, either. Bloody war.

Edie. He remembered his promise to Flo and got up and pulled on his navy-blue overalls because he could button them to the throat which meant he didn't have to put on a tie. He knocked back the rest of the tea and went into the kitchen to wash the mug; he was drying it when he heard Arthur open the door from the parlour where he and Flo slept.

'Cuppa char, lad?' he called out.

'Jack? Yeah, ta. Won't say no.'

Arthur wore his uniform trousers and braces, slippers and a vest. He always slept with the trousers between two boards under the mattress to ensure a perfect lasting crease but he avoided donning his jacket and boots for fear of messing them up. Arthur always washed first too; never came to the table without he was shaved clean, scrubbed till his neck glowed red and his hair slicked down flat with water. Flo kept a washstand bowl filled night and day, special like.

Arthur stationed himself in front of the mirror, pulled back his shoulders ruthlessly and displayed his teeth for inspection.

'Flo's gone off round Barry's,' Jack said, shoving the kettle back on the hob. 'Our Edie's due.'

'All right, is she?' Arthur drew a comb forward along the line of his parting to achieve a more precise flash of white scalp between the grey hair.

'Just going along meself. Must be O.K., I'd've thought. Healthy girl. Plenty of fat on her. Choose her time right though, didn't she? What a bloody week to pick to have a baby. I ask you.'

'Nothing wrong with babies, Jack,' Arthur retorted in his best sing-song barrack square manner. 'Don't hold with babies being blamed for getting born.'

'Well, now then . . . I wouldn't bring no baby into the world voluntary with *this* lot going on, I can tell you. Having the choice, o'course.'

Arthur turned his back on the mirror and pushed his hands together behind his back in the braced 'At ease' position. 'Jack, lad, we got problems enough without not having babies. Ain't never heard of no problem ever being solved by an *un*born baby. Have you?'

'Well. . . .'

'Well nothing. That Edie could be having herself a Prime Minister or a B.B.C. announcer like Alvar Liddell or a general or an artist right this minute, for all you know. Years from now he could come into his own, that baby.'

Jack Warrender paused on his way to the kitchen. 'Be a bugger if it's a girl.'

'Vera Lynn is a girl, Jack,' Arthur said gravely.

'S'pose you're right.'

The kettle began to sing and Jack took it into the kitchen and added hot water to the pot. He came back with Arthur's mug full.

'Ta.'

'Best be getting on round there then. Elsie'll give me what for if Edie gets took short and me not there.'

Arthur slurped his tea. 'Doctor know about it?'

'Paul's gone to get him. He'll be lucky to find him. Poor bugger's been worked off his feet the past few days. Flo should've told him to call the midwife.'

'Don't need no midwife with my Flo around. Bringing 'em into the world or laying 'em out for the next – you can't beat Flo.'

His shiny red face lengthened. Can't beat Flo for bringing 'em into the world, nor even having 'em herself. Derek. Got to face up to it. Boy was his flesh and blood, carried his name; had Flo's mark on him. He'd thought long and hard, off duty and on, waking and sleeping, and in the end he'd come to his decision because there was no other. The boy may not seem like his but he *was* his.

Sort of accident of nature, like picking out the wrong baby

from the nursing home and taking it home and bringing it up not knowing it was somebody else's. Boy needed help and by Gawd he'd have it, all there was to give. First things first, though. . . .

'You talk to Ronnie Hayes, Jack?' He snapped it out, covering his shame. Ronnie had been a mate of theirs in days gone by until he'd joined the Force and set himself apart from ordinary men.

'Saw him last night.'

'What'd he say?'

'All he said was they was looking for looters and they was thinking some of 'em might be young kids, that's all.'

'And a rozzer stopped you to tell you that for fun, did he? And waited around for me this morning 'cause he felt like a chat, eh?' Arthur expanded his chest mightily.

'Well, there's nothing to say. . . .'

'It's young Derek for sure, I'll take my oath. I wouldn't like to say about your Paul.'

'Not my Paul. He wouldn't.'

'Can't tell with kids, Jack. Young buggers get into everything. You just watch 'im, that's all.'

'What're you going to do about it?'

Arthur squared his shoulders resolutely. 'I had a yarn over the Royal Sovereign yesterday with Bob Turton. He—'

'You didn't know yesterday . . . did you?'

'You forgot what Alfie Dunn said last Sunday? Poor old bugger. I asked Bob what he'd charge to take young Derek down to Eastbourne on one of his runs.'

'He's got that carter's business, right?'

'That's it. Three lorry runs a week now. I'm sending the boy down to Flo's cousin. She's got a little boarding-house down there. Always said she'd be pleased to have us down for a stay. Hardworking woman. Keeps a good clean house. And she won't hold with no nonsense from Derek, either.'

'Well, I dunno . . . ,' Jack began slowly.

They heard feet on the stairs and Gladys looked down at them from the archway. She was wearing pyjamas and a dressing-gown.

'Dad—can I go too?' She looked guiltily at the two men. 'I'm sorry, Uncle Arthur, I couldn't help hearing. Do you think Mr Turton would take me?'

Arthur Scully darted a glance at his friend. 'All right with you, Jack?'

'Well, I dunno what your mum'll say, girl....'

Gladys came down into the room and kissed him on the cheek. 'Please, dad. I don't want to . . . stay now. I've got a little money from the club and when I pay mum I'll still have enough for a fare and something for Aunt Flo's cousin. Just for a week or two?'

Jack Warrender nursed his chin. 'Well, I suppose it's best for all concerned. You'll have to ask Bob Turton, though. He might not....'

'Leave him to me,' said Arthur. 'Be glad to make a bit on the side, won't he? Leave it to your Uncle Arthur, my ducks.'

Gladys beamed at him gratefully. 'I'll get dressed and go round to Edie's,' she said brightly. 'When were you thinking of sending Derek, Uncle Arthur?'

Arthur eyed Jack again quizzically. 'Tell you the truth, love, I told Bob this Sunday. He's leaving about half past five.'

'Pheeeew!' Jack wrung his hands. 'Your mum won't like that, Glad. I mean, walking out with only two days' notice.'

'Please, dad! Please!'

There were days when life sneaked up behind you and whispered in your ear that times were getting bad, thought Jack Warrender as he trudged over the broken pavement of Rotherhithe Street. There was Elsie, bless her, working herself to death, and here was Edie having a baby and Glad sliding off to Eastbourne with not so much as a by-your-leave. He should have been firmer. Told Glad to wait. After all, Bob Turton made three runs a week and she could go on his next trip easy enough, once she'd had a chance to talk it over with Elsie. Families should stick together. Course, the trouble with Glad was she'd got herself in a pickle over this young Shaffer. It was a pound to a penny she was on the run from some tiff they'd had.

His mental ear jolted him into an awareness of the world

around him. The low-pitched 'whooomp' brought his head round in a flash and he felt the ground heave. Over by Southwark Park somewhere, that sort of northern corner between St Olave's Hospital and the bandstand. He increased his pace.

Bloody hell! He broke into a run for a few yards but his wheezing chest soon dragged him back to a jog-trot. Bloody hell! Barry's house in Fenner Road wasn't a stone's throw from the park, just behind Keeton's Road School. When Jerry got the school Saturday night, Elsie said, the shock had taken the tiles off the terraces for half a mile round. If the baby was coming and.... He urged his leaden legs on, his heart pumping in his mouth. Hope to God young Paul found the doctor and got him round there quick. Not far for the doctor to go to Fenner Road from the surgery in Skipper's Place.

He hobbled the length of West Lane across Union Road into Cherry Garden Street, the blood roaring in his ears, sweat trickling under the heavy-duty cotton of his overalls, his tin hat bouncing insanely on his smooth skull. Thank God! Thank God! It wasn't Fenner Road; it was way over to the left, in the park probably. He turned right into the narrow street and hammered at the door of Barry's tiny cottage. Flo came down to let him in.

'Is she all right?' he gasped.

'Course she is,' Flo snapped. 'Bloody Hitler!'

'Doctor come?' He slid the tin hat from his head and wiped his glistening scalp with a handkerchief.

'No, not yet. And I don't suppose he will with *that*.' She pointed along the street to the flame-speckled cloud of grey smoke rising from behind the houses in Southwark Park Road.

Jack narrowed his eyes to judge geography and distance. 'Bloody closer'n I thought. Not Cornick Street, is it?'

The thought struck them both at once. 'Skipper's Place!'

'Look, you get back up there,' he said, suddenly official, the warden with a job to do. 'Stay with her and I'll go see what I can do.'

'There's dozens of families down Skipper's Place, Jack. Dozens of little kids.'

'And there's a doctor. Don't forget he's there. Go on. Up you go and make sure Edie's all right. I'll be back.'

He marched quickly down the street and diagonally across Southwark Park Road to the curving entrance of Skipper's Place. He knew it was going to be bad – that voice in his ear back there had told him already – and when he reached the inner bend he heard the hungry crackling of flames and the slip and slide of collapsing brickwork and caught the dry mustard stench of burning masonry. The whole length of the little hidden-away backwater came into view and he nearly pulled up short; the bomb had brought down three, maybe four houses in the terrace and fired a fusillade of flying debris and metal all around it. Bits of wall lay in the street, pitting its surface where they had struck; spearheads of glass and plate-size discs of ceiling plaster and scraps of wood and china and clothes and ... a six-inch square of bloodied flesh, splattered across a gatepost. Hairy flesh. Dog or cat. Gawd almighty! Jack Warrender spat to clear his throat and ran towards the dust and smoke.

A screech of tyres came from behind him and he turned in time to see the doctor's old Singer saloon bang its front bumper into the remains of an amputated water tank. The doctor had obviously struck his head on the windscreen on impact because a trickle of blood ran down his forehead as he came over to join Jack Warrender.

'What happened, Mr Warrender? Do you know if. . . ?'

'I just got here. We'd better watch out. You stay here and I'll go have a look.' He made for the edge of the crater which had once been a narrow pavement and a house.

'Be careful!' the doctor called after him.

Jack worked his way around the crater's steep sides, then down into its maw. Nothing. A tangle of fallen brick and wooden spars and the top of somebody's garden shed. From above he heard the jangle of bells and then the boom of a fire-engine's motor, then scampering steps. A row of faces loomed over the rim of the hole and one of them yelled, 'Anything?'

'Nothing yet. Can't see proper. Can you get someone down here with breathing equipment?'

'Bert!'

There was a delay of no more than seconds, then a pair of black waterproofed legs slithered down and a fireman dropped beside him, ghoulish in breathing-mask. The fireman waved him upwards towards the street and he went gratefully.

A Red Rider took his wrist and hauled him up the last few feet. 'You were 'ere quick, mate,' he said. He brushed away some of the brickdust and dirt from Jack's overalls. 'Passing, was you?'

'The houses!' Jack gasped. 'The rest of the street.'

The leading firemen patted his arm comfortingly. 'Easy, dad. Don't lose your lid. There's nobody here. All been gone since Monday. Had the whole lot evacuated after the Keeton's Road bomb. Don't you worry then, dad.' He laid a kindly arm around Jack's shoulder as the old man's eyes spurted tears.

'Thank Gawd.'

The doctor came to join them.

'I saw the flash from down the road. I moved my surgery over to the old chapel on Drummond Road a couple of days ago. You all right, Mr Warrender?'

Jack reached into the swirling torrent of activity behind his eyes; held his hands to his face to pin it down. Something. What was it? Why was he here? Why had he come to Skipper's Place when. . . ?

'Paul! My boy Paul. He came down here to call you round to our Edie. He came here. He . . . oh, bloody strewth!'

A shout had come from the pit and two firemen raced to the tender and carried something back to the edge. More shouts.

'Doctor! Come here, quick!'

All three of them ran, the doctor so quickly he had to be restrained on the brink of the crater or he would have fallen in. The masked fireman was lying face down on the far wall of the hole, his hands scrabbling away at earth, sand, gravel, stones and twisted piping. His arm waved, beckoning for help, and three more firemen slithered down to join him. Two shovels were hurled deftly through the air; the others used their hands as tools.

'Got 'im!' One of them yelled suddenly and waved to the Red Rider, his right hand grasping a slim wrist.

The firemen hand-shovelled and scraped away the debris until an arm was visible; then a chest, a leg, the back of the head. Jack could see little from where he stood, but the voice told him over and over it was bad.

The doctor slipped his belt through the handle of his bag and looped it round his neck. He lowered himself gingerly into the pit and scrabbled over the rubble to join the firemen. He opened the bag, produced a stethoscope, applied it.

'He's alive!'

He ran his hands over the body, limbs and head with great gentleness. 'We'll need an ambulance,' he shouted. 'One of you. Quick as you can.'

The Red Rider waved to one of his men who clumped off at a run along the rubble-strewn street.

'Who is he?' Jack croaked. His tongue seemed to have swollen and filled his mouth. 'Can you see who. . . ?'

The Red Rider took him by the arm and drew him over the edge of the crater, holding him steady in powerful hands. They reached the firemen, who parted to let them bend over the slim young body. Jack Warrender closed his eyes tightly then opened them wide, praying for mercy but he knew what he was going to see. That little voice, whispering in his ear; times were getting bad. He forced himself to stare at the bruised white face.

The doctor said, 'He's got a broken arm and leg. Probably concussion. But I think he's going to be all right. Do you. . . ?'

Jack's tears rolled like giant translucent beads down his cheeks and into the collar of his overalls.

'Oh, Paul,' he said softly.

They led him up out of the pit and sat him down on the running-board of the fire-tender. The Red Rider stayed where he was, unspeaking, until Jack Warrender was out of earshot. Then he turned to the wall of the crater and kicked out with his boots and swore with a fury that raised the tendons of his neck and surged blood into his face.

The doctor looked up, startled. 'He'll be all right, man. I said he'll be all right.'

'You say the name was Warrender? The old man? The kid?'

'Yes. They're patients of mine. Why?'

'Is there another son?'

'Yes. You probably know him. Barry's attached to—'

'Pageant's Wharf?'

'That's right.'

The Red Rider dug into his pocket and produced a packet of Woodbines. He lit one and puffed it into life. His hands shook.

'They found his body in Limehouse Reach less'n fifteen minutes ago. Got caught up in the piles on West India Dock pierhead. He's been drowned.'

Friday, 1255

Tom Russell lay at full stretch on the lush, clipped grass of St James's Park, his chin wedged comfortably on folded forearms, a long-stemmed grass jutting springily from his mouth. Ian lay beside him, face to the sky, eyes closed.

'I just remembered something,' Tom said drowsily. The sun was slightly obscured by cloud, but he felt hot, satiated.

'Mmmmmm?'

'I'm going back to flying duty. I got the C.O.'s O.K. last night.'

Ian rolled over on one side and searched his brother's profile. 'But it was a promotion, wasn't it? Bentley Priory?'

'So they said.'

'Have you told mother and father?'

'I forgot.'

Ian snapped off a stem of grass and sucked at it nervously. 'Do you have to go back?'

Tom's head rose and fell decisively.

'Why?'

'You wouldn't understand.'

'Don't treat me like a kid!'

Tom angled his head round fractionally, then restored it to the comfortable perch on his forearms. 'Nothing to do with your age.'

'Oh, I see. Conchies wouldn't understand, you mean?'

Tom sighed with exasperation. 'Let's forget it, shall we?'

Ian rolled on to his stomach, weight propped on his elbows

and forearms. 'Sorry. It's getting me down, having to excuse myself all the time. I'm shut out. Even the family.'

Tom slipped a tattered Player's packet from his pocket and lit a cigarette. The familiar blue and gold cardboard box with the bearded sailor's head encircled at its centre was now nearly six months old. Packaging for what were now described as non-essentials was scarce and every tobacconist's shop carried a plaintive notice to smokers inviting them, in the national interest, to take out their cigarettes on purchasing them and leave the packets with the tobacconist. The austerity measure had started a vogue among young R.A.F. officers for 'vintage' cigarette packets; the older they were, the more keenly they were prized. The Ministry of Supply would have been positively proud of them — for the wrong reasons. Among fighter pilots the ageing packets were regarded as talismans, fateful vessels in which their very lives were wrapped and held forfeit. A man with a six-month-old cigarette packet had been favoured by the gods; if *it* could survive, *he* could survive. Tom slipped the packet carefully into his shirt pocket and drew deeply on the cigarette.

Ian watched him with undisguised envy. Tom had been blessed with all the virtues, the natural ones of form and shape and strength and courage and co-ordination, as well as the acquired ones : social ease, sartorial elegance, adaptability. He had won medals and applause but it meant nothing to him; at school Ian had watched him closely in that final glorious year before university and he had never once sensed cockiness or elation or self-satisfaction in his brother's demeanour. Tom also had the greatest, most benevolent of all virtues : he was blind to his own.

'You're having a rough time, aren't you?' Tom was not good at close-quarter relationships and was uncomfortably aware of Ian's superior intelligence.

'I made my bed. I'll have to lie in it.'

'You make it sound as though it's some kind of . . . well, punishment. It wouldn't have anything to do with the old man, I suppose?'

'Oh, you know father. Traitor to the purity of English fighting tradition — that's the way he sees me. Not *me*, he doesn't recog-

431

nise individual views and opinions. He sees people as blobs in a sort of ocean of massed humanity. Blobs don't count; they only have an identity in relation to the mass. A halfway decent blob gets into uniform with the rest and tackles the Hun, the other mass of blobs. Father doesn't even believe Germans are human. He thinks they're either caricature tyrants like Hitler and Goering and Goebbels, or they're semi-anthropoid monsters weighing twenty-five stones apiece in jackboots and steel helmets. If you said to him, "Well, look — most of them are like us and they feel as weak and scared as we do," he'd laugh you out of the house. I mean — I can understand people like him in one way but at the same time I . . . oh, you know what I mean.'

'I think so, but it wouldn't do you any harm to remember the old man went through *his* blood-letting too. He learned his patriotism the hard way. Bayonets in the guts between the trenches. Hand-to-hand fighting. Saturation shelling. Nothing very poetic about his war.'

Ian flicked the grass in his mouth with his forefinger. 'You haven't heard him from my side of the fence.'

'That's true but . . . hell, Ian, I'm hardly likely to hear it from your side, am I? I can only *respect* what you feel. I can't *understand* it.'

'Don't worry, you're not alone. Neither can he. Caroline tries a bit. I think she has a glimmer of — I don't know, fellow-feeling maybe — but she wouldn't show it. Father's girl, isn't she?'

'Mother thinks—'

Ian laughed hollowly. 'Bless her, she'd put her head in the fire if someone told her the king and queen thought it was a good idea.'

'She's on your side, dammit!'

'She's on *everyone's* side; mine, yours, father's, Caroline's. But she doesn't grasp why I did what I did. How can she think *you're* doing the right thing if she believes *I* am? That's what I mean. She thinks in blobs too. If you're eighteen and able-bodied you should be out there killing along with the rest. It's only natural.'

'All right!' Tom flicked ash savagely over his shoulder. 'I'll tell you why she can do it. It's called loyalty. Stupid, damned,

432

old-fashioned, blind loyalty. It's something that comes with giving birth to another human being. No strings attached — and no long-winded philosophical bullshit for or against. She comes down on your side, right or wrong. And mine. And Caroline's. She doesn't have to think or read books or listen to speeches. She *knows*. If you were in danger she'd lay down her life for you. Not because it was morally right or a question of duty. She'd have to do it because ... because. ...' He hurled the half-smoked cigarette into the distance. 'Father's the same behind all that bull.'

Ian's face drained. He said softly, 'You think I'm pretty low, I suppose. I deserve that.'

Tom grabbed his wrist and shook it angrily. 'You deserve a good kick up the backside, brother. You're supposed to be the bright one in the family. Bright? My God! You don't *see*, do you? The time for thinking, for raising moral doubts and hammering out judgements, is *before* you go to war. That's our right; yours, mine, mother's, Caroline's, father's. But once we're in that's it, finished. When I'm in a position to offer my life for yours or mother's or the poor devil on my wing who's just about to get a hundredweight of German lead up his tail — *that's* the time to stop thinking because the only thing left is to *act*. The way mother would act if you or I were in danger.'

He let go of Ian's wrist and rolled back on his stomach.

'I'm going back to my squadron because I can't stay away. I don't have a rational explanation for it. All I can tell you is I can't spend another month watching symbols being scooped around a map table. My C.O., the chaps I serve with, everyone tells me I'm doing an important job and I'm a self-indulgent twerp to walk out on it — and I know they're right. But I have to go back.'

'I know.'

Tom looked up sharply. 'What d'you mean — you *know*?'

Ian probed the grass with a finger, disturbing an ant in its jungle of green stems. 'Just that. I understand. I feel it too, the way you do. I want to join up.'

Tom pushed himself up on one arm. 'I don't think that's very funny.'

'It's not meant to be.' Ian couldn't look at him. He trapped the ant in a laager of crushed grass stalks and watched it struggle. 'It was O.K. while it was a long way away. You know, the war. Then they began bombing the airfields and mother started worrying about you and. . . .' He broke one side of the laager and allowed the ant to escape. 'I knew I was right. That didn't change. I still believe it's wrong to take human life on somebody's political whim. I can't wipe that out. But things change. I got a letter this week from Tim Bayfield, chap in my house at school. He's joined the navy. Said he'd heard that Bryce —you know, the hurdler who nearly pipped you to the *victor ludorum* in your last year?—Bryce lost a leg at Dunkirk. Infantry.'

Tom nodded. 'I know. But why now? Why didn't you do something about it before?'

Ian shrugged, his head still bent over the grass. 'Pride, I suppose. I thought: Here you go, Russell, ready to follow the rest of the sheep. Convictions aren't worth a damn, are they? I thought if I held out for a few weeks I'd change my mind again, you know, come to my senses. It didn't work out like that.'

Tom looked at his watch. 'Hey—it's ten past one. You know what mother said about lunch today. You feel up to it?'

Ian shook his head. 'You go,' he said slowly. 'I'll see you.'

Tom dropped back on to the grass. 'I'll treat you to a snack later.' He slipped the old cigarette packet from his shirt and lit up again. 'Why did you let me rave on at you like that, you stupid little tick?'

'You know what it's like when you're not sure of yourself. You provoke an attack to gauge the wind. I dunno.'

Tom let smoke curl from his mouth into his nose. 'And I suppose it makes you feel better, does it? Having someone tear you to pieces? Lord, you're a deep 'un, I'll say that for you. So— what now?'

Ian shook his head.

'At the hospital the other night . . . we had a bomb. Took the side off one of the wards, brought down the ceiling, killed . . . oh, just poor old people. We managed to get one of them out, half dead. An old woman. Then we discovered she was going to die anyway. Terminal cancer. That shook me. It seemed so hope-less. Then, next day, someone gave her poison. Her husband, they think. Couldn't let her suffer any more, I suppose. He gave her some pills. That really did it for me. Really finished me. I didn't know at the time; I just went to pieces and howled like a kid. They blamed me for letting it happen. *Me!* I'd have gone crazy if it hadn't been for mother. She was an absolute brick.' He looked into his brother's eyes. 'But it sort of woke me up. I should have told mother then. Father too, but I didn't. This thing over Caroline — you don't know what it's been like at home for the past three days.'

'Believe me, I can guess.' Tom pointed the cigarette at Ian's head. 'You still haven't told me what you're going to do.'

Ian rubbed a hand over his face helplessly. 'I rather hoped you'd. . . .'

Tom got to his feet and hauled his brother after him. 'When in doubt, do it.' He pulled him towards the bench where they had leaned their bicycles. 'No more second thoughts, brother. Do you have any preferences? R.A.F.? Navy?'

'I thought the army. The Sussex, if they'll have me.'

Tom stared at him in genuine astonishment. 'The old man's outfit?'

'Well, I thought I might as well.'

Tom slapped an arm round his brother's narrow shoulders. 'There's a recruiting office in Victoria,' he grinned. 'Let's see if they've got any vacancies for apprentice heroes.'

Friday, 1315

Lieutenant-Commander Donald Jamieson closed the file for the fourth time in less than half an hour and gazed sombrely from the window along Northumberland Avenue to Trafalgar Square. There was much he had cause to regret : the denial of a com-mand at sea, especially at a time when German U-boat wolf patrols were decimating British merchant convoys; an emer-gency Admiralty posting so soon after he had settled Amy and the children in Portland; a desk instead of a bridge-deck; paperwork in place of action. Worst of all, secondment to Naval Intelligence in a role for which he was not suited or prepared to admit an aptitude. It was no way to fight a war, playing policeman-cum-spy.

He flipped open the file Dysart had called him about two days ago. He would have to make a decision today. Tomorrow — early — active Security Police inquiries would need to be set in train. The whole shabby caravan of deceit and accusation and unremitting pressure would rumble into motion and he would have to live with the consequences.

He lit his pipe.

The general public didn't care a damn about aliens' rights and with the Blitz at its height would have roamed the streets in packs howling for their blood if someone had put them up to it. The *Daily Mail* headline his deputy had pinned to the noticeboard in the main office outside said everything about the current attitude towards Britain's thousands of German, Austrian and Italian nationals: 'Intern the lot!'

The cry had been taken up around the country and the government had opened its attack on the Home Front on 22 May with the extension of Defence Regulation 18B which effectively gave the Home Secretary *carte blanche* to imprison anyone likely to endanger the realm. The Treachery Act had been rushed through Parliament to facilitate instant trials and mass detention and, inevitably, the whole wretched pantomime had suffered from unseemly haste and bad organisation. Sir Oswald Mosley had been arrested on 23 May, and by 30 May his British Union of Fascists had been summarily dissolved and its publications banned. A Member of Parliament, Captain Ramsay, had been arrested too for his membership of the allegedly anti-semitic Right Club, but by some ludicrous parliamentary *droit de seigneur* he was still permitted to table questions to the House.

By August 1600 of His Majesty's subjects were under detention without trial awaiting tribunals yet to be set up to adjudicate their individual cases. Hundreds of them were living in the most appalling conditions; a tented compound near Sutton Coldfield in the Midlands and a derelict, rat-infested cotton mill in Lancashire were only two of the bolt-holes hastily provided.

If that had been the worst of it, Donald Jamieson might have found a salve for his unruly conscience but his own position was particularly distasteful.

He had been appointed to a newly created office of investigation after the arrest of Admiral Sir Barry Domville, former chief of Naval Intelligence and an officer held in the highest respect in the service. Domville's sin was that he had been chairman of an Anglo-French-German organisation called The Link. Its ideals were militantly right wing, nationalistic and isolationist but there was no doubt that many of its aristocratic—upper middle class—professional recruits had joined the ranks as eagerly as they would have sought admission to an exclusive club. The Link was now well represented in the seedy emigré camps and a Conservative M.P. had already raised his voice in the Commons against the imprisonment of Englishmen without trial. He was wasting his breath, of course. No one was prepared to listen. It was the open season. Anyone was fair game. The Arabian explorer H. St John Philby had recently been arrested.

Jamieson brushed a stray flake of tobacco from the file cover and flipped it open again. Fletcher-Hale, Denzil Whitlock Kentersham. Even his name, with all its historical family echoes, was against him in a situation like this. It marked him down as aristocratic, élitist, privileged, protected; it wouldn't matter a damn whether he harboured pro-German views or not, the nomenclature alone condemned him in Jamieson's eyes.

His case, if he could advance one, would be examined with suspicion and great brevity; there would be no time for the long-drawn-out processes of law. The Security Police would deal with it summarily and make their recommendation or arrest based on the subject's ability to prove his innocence. Fletcher-Hale was, however, in an invidious position; one could say almost that he was damned from the beginning. He had confessed membership of The Link. By the standards of summer 1940 that in itself was enough to support an arrest.

Jamieson removed his pipe and knocked it out on the ashtray. No more time. It had to be done. He reached for the telephone and called for an outside line. He dialled a number.

'Inspector Maconachie, please.' He waited. 'Maconachie?

Good afternoon. Jamieson. I'm afraid I have another one for you from our end.'

Maconachie's faultless propriety cracked a little. 'Emigré or. . . ?'

'Sorry. English. Very.'

'Oh Lord, not another.'

"Fraid so. I've been stewing over his file for two days. Have to move on him. Nothing else I can do.'

'Then I'll be straight with you, Jamieson. I hope you have a case, that's all I can say. If he's the victim of another whispering campaign or. . . . Dammit, I've just cleared up the worst kind of circumstantial case you could imagine only this morning. Top government man. Seemed absolutely open-and-shut but . . . my God, we came near to making absolute damn fools of ourselves.'

'I don't think you'll have too much trouble with this one. He admits to membership of a proscribed organisation.'

'Admits! Under pressure?'

'No. Voluntarily.'

Maconachie grated out his disbelief. 'To whom?'

'Dysart. DONITE.'

'How'd *he* come into this?'

'He was interviewing the man as a possible Intelligence officer.'

The policeman's tone changed at once. 'Was he, by God! All right. Can I have the file? There's not much I can do with it today, I'm afraid, but Lubbock and I might be able to get around to him some time tomorrow.'

'Fair enough. I think he'll wait.'

'Why should he run?' Maconachie retorted drily. 'If he was idiot enough to admit it without considering the consequences, he's not worrying unduly now. Right. Let me have the file by messenger this afternoon, will you? Do what we can.'

Friday, 1330

Shaffer liked Elizabeth Russell on sight. She was wearing a silver-grey silk dress, so perfectly cut that it seemed to anticipate her every movement, and a light pastel-pink scarf of some diaphanous material lay loosely around her neck, untied. She had about her that quality of aristocratic Englishness he had previously encountered only in the novels of Henry James; hauteur tempered with warmth, distance bridged by wry good humour. She called Elsie Warrender from the kitchen to be introduced and the daily wiped her hand on her apron before shaking his and bobbed what might have been a curtsey to Denzil Fletcher-Hale.

Charles Russell arrived late and Shaffer was momentarily grateful that Denzil was on hand to relieve the barometric pressure. Russell was a deal more relaxed than when they had met at Freddie Green's house in Greenwich but he had obviously been apprehensive of the meeting all morning and his sails were set for battle. He shook hands with the kind of rigid formality royalty reserve for the heads of unfriendly states and his attempt at a smile of welcome was grotesque. Denzil appeared to be quite unaware of this cold undercurrent and launched at once into a discussion of Russell's collection of nineteenth-century East Anglian watercolours. It was enough to break the ice and they went to the table as two distinct conversational groups, Russell and Denzil, Shaffer and Elizabeth.

The food was excellent and reduced the pressure even further. Talk turned first to the Blitz, then, at Elizabeth's instigation, to America's role in the war. The two groups became one. Elsie Warrender cleared away the remains of the main course — 'mutton dressed as lamb', as Elizabeth described it proudly — and served apple pie and 'mock' cream. Denzil finally introduced the subject they had all skirted with such diffidence.

'Mrs Russell. . . ,' he began.

'Elizabeth. You must call me Elizabeth.'

Fletcher-Hale bowed his head gracefully. 'Elizabeth. Have to talk over this ... difficulty, what? Shaffer here, good chap, delighted to help. Eh, Shaffer?'

Shaffer swallowed a cream-topped slice of apple pie and nodded uncertainly. 'Sure.'

'Well, that's really awfully kind of you, Mr Shaffer. I'll confess to you, we were a little worried when Elsie told us she'd called you on the telephone, weren't we, Charles?'

'Er — *huh*! Yes. A . . . little concerned.'

'Best intentions,' Denzil smoothed easily. 'Fine woman. Shaffer knows the score. Seems to me, nub of the matter so to speak, get your daughter Caroline home, *tout de suite*.'

'Oh, absolutely,' breathed Elizabeth.

'Um — yes, indeed.' Russell fidgeted with his spoon, clearly unhappy at the form the conversation was taking.

'Know where she is, do we?' Denzil probed delicately.

'She's—' began Elizabeth, but Russell cut in imperiously.

'They've been treating her at an R.A.F. hospital near Cambridge. I've spoken to the group captain in charge this morning. He's prepared to release her at once. There's . . . er. . . .'

Elizabeth leaned forward anxiously. 'There's what, dear?'

Russell looked awkwardly at Shaffer, who took the cue. He made to rise. 'If you'd like me to leave. . . ?' he began.

'Don't be silly, Mr Shaffer. Of course not. Tell him we're more than grateful to him, Charles,' she ordered.

'Er . . . exactly,' Russell floundered. 'More than grateful. Um . . . it's a little difficult. Caroline's . . . experience left her rather nervous, the group captain tells me. She doesn't want. . . . She'd prefer to make her *own* way home. . . .'

'Charles!'

'Yes, yes, I know,' he said testily. 'We can't allow that, but the group captain feels it might ease the transition for her if . . . er *huh*! — a friend were to fetch her and bring her home. Rather than . . . my wife or me.'

'But I don't understand.' Elizabeth was stiff with apprehension. 'What's wrong with her? Why can't I. . . ?'

Russell glared at her balefully. 'The child feels . . . compromised, of course,' he said, his cheeks reddening. 'I really don't think it's necessary to go into it here. The problem is to find someone prepared to go to Cambridge; someone sympathetic who can put her at ease and persuade her that the best thing is to come home where she belongs. The group captain thinks that part of it might be — well, hazardous.'

'But. . . .' Elizabeth bit her lip.

'Simple enough.' Denzil came to the rescue with immaculate understatement. 'Trust me to take it on, Russell, would you?'

'Well, I hadn't thought. . . .'

'Obvious choice, what? Friend of the family.' He inclined his head respectfully in Elizabeth's direction. 'No previous form. Know nothing of her troubles. Besides — absolute fluke — have to be in Cambridge tomorrow, myself. Pick her up. Buy her lunch. Ease the burden. Bound to talk. Loosen up. Feel better for it.'

'Oh, would you really?' Elizabeth clutched at his arm.

'Certainly. Glad to. Must go, anyway. Visiting a chum.'

'May he, Charles?'

'I think we should consider it a little. . . .'

Shaffer leaned back in his chair. 'I don't want to butt into your personal affairs, Russell, but since you asked me here. . . ?'

Russell eyed him suspiciously.

'I have a car and my petrol ration as a correspondent is a shade better than most. If Denzil can drive—'

'Drive? Certainly,' interjected Fletcher-Hale.

It was settled.

Russell had been snatching worried glances at his half-hunter throughout the meal and, having conceded the battle, made his excuses. He must get back to his office, he said; so much time had been — he looked unhappily down the table at Elizabeth — *wasted* over the past few days and he might have to be away from London overnight. He got up from the table and went out into the hall. He reappeared seconds later with an opened letter in his hand.

'Elizabeth. When did this arrive?' There was tension in his voice; everyone in the room detected it.

Elizabeth's finely tuned sense of disaster was triggered immediately. 'It must have come with the post this morning. The man was late again. Why. . . ? Is it. . . ?'

Russell raised a comforting hand. 'Nothing, my dear. Perfectly all right.' He stood in the frame of the door and ran his eye down the short, typewritten letter again to make sure he hadn't imagined it.

It was from the bank in Piccadilly.

Dear Russell,
   I regret to say that head office has countermanded my

441

decision to advance you £2000 as discussed in this office on Wednesday morning. I really must apologise profusely but I am sure you recognise that, in these times, matters of lending policy are subject to executive sanction guided by Bank of England dictat.

Your disappointment, I assure you, is matched by my embarrassment on this occasion. I must inform you, therefore, that I have not despatched a banker's draft in favour of Melly-Greenmantle. You have my apologies for the delay in confirming this.

George Peterson's flourish of a signature had not been influenced in any way by his professional embarrassment.

Elizabeth said again, 'What is it, dear?'

'Nothing. Really, it's nothing. A business matter. But I would' —his eyes signalled to Fletcher-Hale— 'I would like to talk to our friends here for a moment. If you'll excuse us.'

Denzil and Shaffer followed him across the hallway to his study. Russell closed the door and turned the key in the lock. He straightened up and slipped the letter into his inside pocket.

'This has been rather ... unpleasant for you, gentlemen. I'm sorry.'

Denzil lounged on the end of the desk. 'Nothing to it, Russell. All's well, what?'

'I want to ask a favour of you,' Russell went on doggedly. 'We met, Shaffer, under circumstances that. ... This man, Green, Freddie Green. I thought you should know I have no connection with the fellow.'

Denzil's face registered bewilderment. 'Curious thing. Told you at Greenwich. Heard Freddie'd taken you under his wing. Business project.'

'Oh, good heavens, no. Nothing came of it, Fletcher-Hale. Couldn't permit my name to be associated with someone of Green's stamp. Not in my position.'

'No business of ours anyway,' Shaffer drawled mildly.

'The favour. You mentioned a favour,' pressed Denzil.

'Well, yes. There is a favour. Shaffer, really. I'd deem it a very generous service to me ... and my family' —he threw in the

442

family as an afterthought – 'if you could – um – forget that incident in Soho, at the – er – public house.'

Shaffer's amusement was temporarily too great for him to conceal. He straightened his face with difficulty. 'I don't drink in Soho,' he said slowly. 'I don't know anyone who does.'

Russell breathed his relief and his tense grey face brightened. 'Then I'll leave you both to discuss the details of Caroline's – er – repatriation?' – it was his little joke and they pretended homage to it – 'with my wi . . . with Elizabeth.'

They watched him leave, then returned to the dining-room. It was a monument to English cool, thought Shaffer, that Elizabeth refrained from asking what Russell had discussed with them. It would have been beyond Rita to resist the temptation to listen at the keyhole. The only way to mark Elizabeth Russell's uniqueness was to put her on a pedestal. What in the name of human unpredictability had made a woman like that marry a man like Charles Russell?

Mrs Warrender served coffee – or one of those substitutes for coffee that in wartime England came out three-quarters chicory. It said a lot for any woman that she could neutralise the taste of bad coffee but Elizabeth managed it somehow.

Russell had been gone no more than twenty minutes when the phone rang in the hall. Shaffer immediately checked his watch; three-fifteen. He was letting things slide. He had told Mrs Price where he could be contacted during lunch; promised he would leave at three.

Elsie Warrender yelled from the hall, 'I'll get it, madam dear,' and Elizabeth suppressed a smile.

'Yeees? Yeees?' The daily's telephone manner was, to say the least, loud. They heard her snatch her breath then, voice dropping, 'Jack? Is that you, Jack? What are you doing calling me at . . . ?'

Shaffer and Fletcher-Hale did their best not to listen but Elizabeth made that *politesse* virtually irrelevant by straining her ears to catch every word. The pause was a long one, maybe two or three minutes, then: 'Yes, I heard you, love. I heard. You go be with him and tell Flo to stay with Edie. I'll be round to see Paul soon as. . . . Now don't, Jack. *Don't*, there's a good old

443

feller. You just wait and I'll come quick as I can. You hear me? That's my lovey. Now you go off, then. All right? Bye bye, love.'

They were all three of them watching the door before she put down the phone. She pushed it open and leaned one-handed in its frame. Her cheeks glinted with twin rivulets of tears and her felt hat lay drunkenly across her forehead, but her mouth was braced and her shapeless, work-aged body stood straight as a young aspen.

'Could I go, madam dear?' There was a fracture running through every word.

'Of course, Elsie. Why? What is it?'

The daily opened her mouth to speak, closed it quickly, swayed wildly. Shaffer caught her before she hit the floor.

Friday, 1600

The bones of the right leg and arm had been set, the shoulders strapped, a good two dozen lacerations and contusions and bruises cleaned, breached, iodined and patched. Paul Warrender was a flour-faced stick-insect strung between wheels and pulleys and frames but he was alive and, with the drugs beginning to wear off at last, almost *compos mentis*.

In the corridor outside the tiny side-ward where they had parked him for peace and quiet and convenience, Elsie fell into Jack's arms with a withering blubber of despair. The sight of her husband crouched on that bench, his overalls daubed with mud and his bald head streaked with muck and sweat, was more than she could bear. But her collapse didn't last long; she had done most of her weeping at the Russells' and most of her soul-searching in Shaffer's car on the way from Chelsea to St Olave's Hospital, and at the very moment her own racking sobs subsided Jack's began. His tears streamed on to the now muddy-brown shoulder of Elsie's borrowed coat and plopped on the green-painted wall behind. They both felt much better after that.

They looked at Paul first through the circular window in the door but when the doctor had finished fiddling with the dressings he allowed them in. Jack had wept himself dry but he was racked from time to time by sudden shuddering afterthoughts of sobbing and it was one of these, alarmingly magnified in the small room, that brought Paul round. He opened his eyes and Elsie clasped a hand to her abdomen. They waited, breathless, their hands meeting as though contact would generate life's electricity to rouse the child. There was scarcely a square inch of his face that wasn't black, mauve or yellow and the once bright blue eyes were bloodshot and drained of colour. The eyes narrowed, focused, moved through 180 degrees and fixed on Elsie and Jack. A puzzled expression clouded the fragile brow, then evaporated to make way for a shy, pained smile.

'Where's Derek?' Paul whispered.

They were both so overjoyed they took no notice of the words but clung instead to the glorious sound; they both spoke at once: 'Don't you ... mustn't waste your streng ... try to do too much ... hold still, old son ... want the doctor? ... drink of water. ...'

Paul didn't hear any of it because his mind too was riveted on a fixed point; the only thing that mattered.

'Bet Derek never got hisself bombed.'

His eyes travelled the length of his body and broken limbs and the tired smile grew in brilliance and satisfaction. 'Broke anyfing, did I?' he asked eagerly.

Elsie and Jack exchanged glances.

'Well, not so's you'd know, darlin',' Elsie began comfortingly. Paul's smile withered at once and became a pout of protest.

'He said ... someone said, I got an arm 'n' a leg busted and me shoulder pulled out and. ...'

Jack saw at once what was needed and grabbed Elsie's hand and stopped her from issuing the stout denial she was blowing herself up for.

'Right you are, you young tearaway,' he said, and he bent over the bed and winked outrageously so Paul would know they were sharing a secret understanding. 'Have to keep you in splints and plaster for weeks, like as not. Proper do that's going to cause down the Green, I'd say, wouldn't you? I mean, you won't know where you are, what with perfect strangers coming up to you every minute of the day asking how you got an arm 'n' a leg in plaster and then you telling 'em and them saying, "Oh, the boy what copped that high explosive all on his own down Skipper's Place, eh?" I bet you'll get sick and tired having to tell the tale over and over. Young Derek'll be proper narked he wasn't in on it, bet your life.'

Paul's smile widened with each word until it stretched beyond the point of bearable pain and he winced with tormented delight.

'I s'pose he'll say he was with me,' the boy whispered hoarsely. 'But he won't have the proof, will he, dad?'

'That he won't, son.' Jack turned away and smudged the tears with a stroke of his overall cuff.

Elsie leaned forward over her son in an agony of maternal solicitude; every instinct in her made her want to clutch him to her, smother the bruised face with her kisses, but caution restrained her inches from contact.

'Don't you worry about young Derek,' she urged. 'He ain't within a mile of you, lovey. The doctor said you was a proper little soldier. Brave as anything. He said you didn't utter a sound, not once, the whole time they was patching you up. Never seen nothing like it in all his born days, he said. Proper proud of you in here they are.'

Paul sighed with pleasure and allowed the engulfing waves of it to form around him and mount inside. His eyes closed and a snort of tranquil exhaustion escaped his open mouth. 'Derek. . . .' was the word that followed him into his dream.

Jack leaned forward to raise the light blanket more protectively over the boy's chest but Elsie touched his arm at once and shook her head. They tiptoed to the door and looked back at him longingly.

'He'll be all right then, mother.'

'Course he will.'

Jack slipped his arm through hers and held it imprisoned reassuringly tight against him. 'Young tearaway,' he breathed.

She leaned her face to his and kissed the side of his nose. 'You and me got to take real proper care of him from now on,' she whispered brokenly. 'Now Barry's . . . passed over, we've got to be real careful with young Paul.'

446

She heard the sob building up in his chest and pulled his old face close to hers. 'It's no good going on, old love. Won't bring the boy back, will it? We got to be strong and we got to think of the living. We got responsibilities to our own, haven't we? There's Edie to think of now — and Barry's baby.'

'I . . . know. I know . . . you're . . . doing it for . . . the best . . . ,' he gulped helplessly. 'I just can't . . . get it straight in me mind . . . we won't have . . . Barry no more. All the time . . . I wasted . . . not being with him . . . not going over to . . . have a chat now and again . . . all the time. . . .'

She took him in her arms and he buried his head in her shoulder.

'Barry wasn't the kind for regrets, now was he?' She was having difficulty keeping her voice level and the tears from drowning her every word. 'What he'd want is to know his baby and Edie was going to be properly looked after. And that's what we're going to do, don't make no mistake about that. You got yourself another family to take care of, Jack, my lad. No use your thinking you can let things slide for the rest of the war. You've got to get back on your feet again. Get back to a real job when this lot's over. You're going to be important when they get the old Surrey back to work again. Man like you, your experience, can't be done without. Stands to reason. We'll all be relying on you.'

The sobs were cut off as if by a switch and he raised his head from her shoulder, his bloated red eyes on hers.

'Right hero I am,' he mumbled, cuffing away the tears. 'Cry baby, more like.' He pulled himself upright and cupped her face in his hands and kissed her. 'I got out of the habit of saying things to you, Elsie. You know, how I feel and that. Bloody silly, letting old age make you embarrassed to tell your wife she's . . . well, you know. Times like this, though. . . .' He came close to yielding again to his tears but sniffed them back. 'I got a lot of love inside here for you. You know that. Even though I don't say. There all the same. You're right about what you said too. I've got a lot on my hands now, one way and another. Responsibilities.' He tried a grin. 'Keeps you young. That's what they say, ennit? Responsibility keeps you young.'

447

She caught the loose skin of his cheeks in her hands and pinched it comfortingly. 'Nothing old about you, you rascal,' she whispered fondly. 'Haven't changed a bit since we was courting.' She looked up at his glistening bald skull and ran a finger through the fringe of grey-white hair at his ears. 'Well, you had a bit more on top in them days, that's all.'

They giggled through their tears until Elsie recalled where they were and with a worried glance at Paul raised a finger to her lips and pushed him gently through the door.

Elizabeth Russell got up from the bench at once and folded Elsie in an embrace. Instinctively the older woman returned it.

'Is he. . . ?' Elizabeth began, bending to peer into Elsie's face.

'He's got the broken arm and leg, like they said, and his shoulder is all bandaged up and his face' – the memory of it brushed a shadow across her eyes – 'you wouldn't believe it. But he came round and he talked and now he's gone to sleep, bless him.'

Elizabeth put a hand to her heart and breathed hard. 'Oh, I can't tell you what I've been *thinking* while you were in there.'

Shaffer and Denzil, who had insisted on cramming his towering bulk into the back seat of the Morris to allow Elsie the comparative comfort of the front passenger seat, had borne witness to Elizabeth's watching brief. She had sat with her hands in her lap and her eyes fixed on eternity, not daring to talk to either of them in case a chance sound from inside the ward gave some hint of what was happening. Throughout the journey from Chelsea she had heaped herself with reproach, blaming her thoughtlessness and selfishness for Paul's injury; the Russells, she said, had robbed Elsie Warrender of fourteen years of her life and for a pittance. Luckily, Denzil had proved himself once again to be equal to the task and had calmed her down before her self-castigation drove them all crazy.

Shaffer had played the part of chauffeur and he had played it willingly, much to his own surprise. They had been at the hospital for the better part of half an hour before he actually looked at his watch and realised he had no hope of making the five o'clock file. He called Mrs Price and ordered her to assure

O'Keefe that he would be in the studio at Broadcasting House with the midnight file at eleven o'clock tonight.

Shaffer allowed Elizabeth to unburden her soul, then asked Jack Warrender if he would like to be driven home.

Elsie broke in at once. 'No, Mr Shaffer, we ought to go round to Edie's right away. If you could run us over there. . . .' She checked herself. 'Well . . . our Glad is there, you see, and I think she's. . . .' She flashed an S.O.S. at her husband. Jack Warrender took Shaffer's elbow and drew him along the corridor away from the others.

'Don't like to say this, Mr Shaffer, seeing as how you've been so good to us. . . .'

Shaffer protested but the old man patted his arm paternally. 'No, you done us proud. Never a thought for yourself, always ready to help out, and you a busy man with a lot of worries on your plate. No, fact is our Glad come down this morning and asked straight out if she could go away for a couple of weeks. Nothing permanent,' he added quickly. 'Just need a rest, she does. Got all tied up in herself. Worried, that sort of thing.'

'Is she ill?' Shaffer felt a stab of mortal fear. If he were responsible for making her run headlong for the hills he had a duty to tell the old man. The Warrenders had gone through enough.

'No. She's fine, don't you worry yourself. Me and Elsie—my wife—we talked about what just happened to Paul and about Glad wanting to go away and we decided we won't tell Glad just yet. The way things've worked out, she'll be better off down Eastbourne—but a pound to a penny she won't move an inch if we told her about Paul. Be different if the boy was hurt bad but he'll be on the mend in a few days and then we'll tell Glad —in a letter, like. P'raps get Paul to write and tell her hisself. That's the thing.'

'But your son Barry. . . .'

Jack Warrender's tongue appeared between his lips and he controlled himself with difficulty.

'Can't tell Glad about Barry, Mr Shaffer. Go to pieces right away. Close they was, her and him. And she'd want to stay to look after Edie. Doctor was saying to me he can't afford to have

449

Edie told about Barry till the baby's born and there's no way he'd be responsible otherwise. No — it's best Glad gets off down Eastbourne. She'll hear soon enough.'

'If I can help in any way....'

'You could help best by steering clear of young Glad, that's all, son. Terrible thing to say, I know, but that's the truth.'

'Well, I'll drop you off along the way then.'

'No need, son. We just got to walk out of the hospital here, across Southwark Park and up Fenner Road. 'Sonly a step. Besides....' He dropped his voice and half turned away. 'You oughter get the madam back home. She's in a real old tizz, anyone can see that. And the gent, Mr Leatherdale.'

Shaffer didn't correct him; Denzil would have been the last to complain.

Jack Warrender walked back to the group. He allowed Elsie the floor. He didn't want to talk any more; there'd be time enough for that later on, keeping up appearances for Glad and Edie and making sure no one left in the Green got to hear and dropped the wrong word before it was due. He had been an open man all his life, open as a book. Never held back the truth because in the end it did nothing but harm. And look at him now; he couldn't tell Glad or Edie about two things that mattered more to them than life itself. He was going to have to carry that load himself, along with that other load he'd taken on a couple of days ago; the burden of knowing that Derek Scully wasn't Arthur's flesh and blood at all. How open was that then, Jack Warrender? Best friend you ever had, old Arthur, and you can't share the plain truth with him.

If God struck him down now where he stood, he'd know why.

It was four forty-five when Shaffer, Denzil and Elizabeth returned to the car for the drive back to Chelsea.

Shaffer was mapping out his story before they passed through the hospital gates.

Friday, 1645

Derek Scully pulled on his best grey flannel trousers, his best white shirt and the Fair Isle pullover Auntie Elsie had knitted for his birthday. Sunday-best clothes and boots, the old man had said, 'cause he wasn't having no son of his going visiting up the hospital looking like the devil's mucking brush.

Well, sod him. Who wanted to go to the bloody hospital anyway? He could just imagine what that little bugger Paul was going to get out of a busted arm and leg and all them cuts and bruises; everyone was already rushing about telling him he was a little hero. He'd be bloody unbearable by the time he came out.

He stared at himself in the kitchen mirror; bloody ponce, he looked, and he'd look the same way on Sunday night when they shipped him off to Eastbourne with Bob Turton. And Gladys. He grinned at his reflection. Yeah. Glad was coming too. That was a bit of a bonus. Wouldn't mind a bit of old Glad, give him the chance. His grin faded. Bloody Eastbourne. Alfie Dunn was to blame for that; him and Ronnie sodding Hayes, turning him in to the old man.

He looked in through the living-room door and checked the clock. Quarter to five. Another fifteen minutes. What he needed was to *do* something. Something that'd make him feel better. Something he could think about when he stood over Paul's bed being told how big a hero he was. Something. . . .

The idea came to him in a flash and it was so stupendously brilliant he had to laugh out loud. Brilliant. Bloody brilliant. He poked his head out of the kitchen door and made a fast recce of the yard. The old man'd gone to work and the others were either down at Edie's or safely out of sight and sound.

He ducked back into the kitchen, swung the lid of the copper aside and reached down. His fingers touched the small cloth-wrapped square and he brought it into the light. Twenty-five quid. He counted it again to be sure. Twenty-five quid. He stared at it, then stuffed it back. Safe there for the time being. He'd worked hard for that and they'd got him cheap. Twenty-five quid! How many jobs had he done for that? A dozen maybe. Four a night; five last night, if you counted going back to the tea warehouse twice. And whose neck was it? His. Jigger Kemp and Charlie Rowthorne never came within a mile of the lads till the nicking was over and done and even then they always hung about, waiting, till the swag had been dumped at the appointed places, and then they drove up in the old navy ambulance. Derek knew their game, all right; spotted it straight away Wednesday night. Didn't trust the lads, didn't Jigger and Charlie.

He knew the colour of their necks. That's why he'd followed them. Bloody hard going it was too and if it wasn't for the fact they'd worked Stave Dock that first night he wouldn't have been able to keep up, but the ambulance had to stop and start a dozen times with all the fire and flame going on and finally it turned into a yard just a mile away by St Mary's Church, just downriver of Elephant Stairs. He could have been an Indian in the cowboy pictures the way he wriggled and crept up on them and he knew right away what the measure of it was because who should pop up out of this office there but Billy bleeding Sutcliffe. That explained a lot, that did. Derek had a grudging respect for Billy Sutcliffe. He'd been a real villain all his life and some people said he carried a knife and wasn't afraid to use it if the money was right. Being Billy Sutcliffe, Derek knew there was big money involved in this nicking from warehouses. Billy only came in on big money jobs.

Twenty-five quid!

On impulse, he dug a hand into his trouser pocket and brought out the coins he kept wrapped in his handkerchief. Just pennies, but. . . .

He slipped outside, made sure the coast was clear, and ran swiftly round into Rotherhithe Street, dodged smartly into the cover of what had once been the warehouse in Lavender Yard and scuttled in a wide arc. He came out through the break in the wall into Acorn Walk and ran to the phone box by Silver Street church. He waited for a whole minute when he got inside to catch his breath. Wanted to have it right, didn't he?

The idea was so beautiful. Jigger and Charlie had told them all it was on again tonight, except this time they'd have to cross the river because the target was West India Docks. They were to meet at half past ten in the south-east corner of the South Dock on the short side of Junction Dock. The way in was through Chipka Street, where the wall was down.

He slipped the pennies into the slot and raised the receiver.

His finger trembled on the dialling ring; excitement, not fear. He'd always wanted to ring Scotland Yard; always wanted to hear the rozzers say it from the other end. He dialled: WHItehall 1212. It buzzed.

'New Scotland Yard.' Just like the pictures!

'I want to talk to the Information Room.' He knew that was the drill because he'd seen that on the pictures too.

The voice at the other end lost some of its mellifluous formality. 'Whatcha want then, son? Come on, be slippy.'

'I want the Information Room, like I said.' He was going to have no truck with nobodies.

'Look, son, I'm warning you. Wasting police time is a prison offence. Get me? You tell me—'

'Bugger it! I want to report a robbery.'

'Where? When did it happen?'

'Hasn't happened yet – but it bloody will if you don't pass me on to the Information Room quick.'

'Hold on.' The formality returned. Another voice came on.

'You want the Information Room, son?'

'Yes.'

'Go ahead.'

'I want to report a robbery. Tonight. West India Dock. They're going to have a go at the sheds around Blackwall Basin.'

'Who is?'

'Kids mostly. But the geezers you want are called Jigger Kemp and Charlie Rowthorne, but they ain't the governors neither. Anyway, you go up there half past ten tonight, mob-handed, and you'll pick 'em up. And if I was you—'

'What's your name, son?'

'If you don't know, copper, I'm buggered if I'm going to tell you. You writing this down?'

'Course I am.'

'Righto. Jigger and Charlie pick the stuff up in a navy ambulance after the gang's nicked it. They'll be coming down Manchester Road into East Ferry Road and then into Chipka Street, 'cause that's where they get through into the dock. The kids, I mean. The wall's down there.'

'You know a sight too much for my liking, son. Why don't you tell me who you are and where you live and—'

'Bugger off, copper! Do me a favour, will you? I told you what they're going to do but I haven't told you the best yet. They take the stuff, Jigger and Charlie, down to a place called Melly-Greenmantle's yard down from Elephant Stairs near the church. The bloke waiting to unload the stuff is called Billy Sutcliffe. You ask the local rozzers about Billy Sutcliffe and they'll tell you.'

'If you're having us on, son. . . .'

'Why should I have you on? There's more bloody fun in topping that mob, I can tell you.'

'You said half past ten tonight?'

' 'Sright. And I'll give you this for free. Billy Sutcliffe is a right bloody villain around our way but he never worked a job on his tod. Always got a governor, Billy. So you look for the sod in charge of Billy.'

'All right. Now, you listen to me for a second—'

Derek cut him off and leaned back into the steel frames of the kiosk. Hadn't taken more than two minutes. Two minutes!

Strewth, there'd be bloody ructions up Chipka Street tonight.

Friday, 2155

The bombing had started at nine o'clock but so had the ack-ack barrage, splattering the milky, moon-bright sky with angry orange flowers and rolling its thunder along the warren of East End streets.

Jack Warrender saw the searchlights pick out a formation of German bombers well over to the east and fondle them lasciviously all the way in to a spot over the City. The gun-crews redoubled their efforts and suddenly down the beams slid a shower of silver rain. He waited for the cannonade — pa-bam-bam-bam-boom — like a roll of drums, but he saw no flashes.

It was good to be out in it. He'd tried to sit with Elsie for half an hour but he hadn't got her turn of mind and looking at her was like looking at Barry. Once he started that the nightmares

454

came out of the cupboards. Barry floating in the water with his arms up and his hands praying for help and no one coming. Barry being sucked down and fighting for life. Barry giving in and letting the river take him down. The pictures had him jerking up from his chair till he didn't know what to do with himself but Elsie just sat there with one eye on her Bible and the other on Edie across the little room in her bed with her great big tummy heaving up and down with the life waiting to come out of it. Elsie knew what was making him jig up and down but she wouldn't comment for fear of making him look small in front of Flo; and, course, she couldn't be sure Edie wasn't awake and listening. They were doing just like the doctor said : telling her nothing till after the baby was born.

Elsie had popped into St Olave's about eight o'clock to see Paul for ten minutes but he'd been asleep and snoring fit to bust, which the nurse said was a sure sign of recovery from shock. Jack had looked in himself an hour later but the boy was out to the wide again after having his bed made and taking some soup through a straw. He'd asked for some Ovaltine for the first time since he was an Ovalteeny seven years ago and more, and they'd given him a big mug and popped his pills in it for good measure. Young Paul wouldn't be losing his sleep tonight, that was for sure.

He searched the face of his old Woolworth's watch at a distance of three inches and slipped it back in his pocket. Up and down, Elsie and Flo were, all the time, trying to get that baby born. Edie wasn't going to have it easy, Elsie said, because of the baby being the wrong way round or something and they'd have to be careful because ten-to-one the little skip would pop out with the cord round his neck. The doctor had said Elsie was to call him the moment the baby looked like he was due, but Flo said if she and Elsie couldn't deliver a baby on their own after all the kids they'd brought into the world, they might as well give up.

He stamped along Fenner Road for twenty yards, then back again. There was a prayer he'd remembered from when he used to go to the Congregational church as a boy, but it came to him too late to speak it over Barry's memory and, anyway, he could only remember a couple of lines:

> O Lord, from whom all blessings flow,
> Bless these Thy children, here below. . . .

He repeated it, moving his lips but allowing the words to emerge only as a purr of sound. There was a lot more to it than that but seeing as how the Almighty had been hearing it every Sunday regular for thirty or forty years from millions of people who reeled it off word-perfect every time, He'd likely take it as read from someone who'd forgot. It could serve for Paul too, though he wasn't a hundred per cent sure if Paul qualified, being in hospital and getting the best of treatment, like. Elsie had had her little pray, up in the bedroom on her knees by the chest of drawers where she'd hung her Cross, and she'd come down looking a lot better; but then, she knew more about praying than he did and there was a fair chance the Almighty would listen to her because she was a regular and already had His ear. Jack wasn't too well versed in the business himself; he always felt out of it at christenings and weddings and funerals, not knowing whether he was supposed to be on his feet or his knees or his bum and being treacherously deaf to music. But his dad had been exactly the same and he'd said all through his life that religion was more than a little bit like bringing up babies: a woman had a natural-born gift for it but men, with the best intentions in the world, could only stand around and look like they knew what it was all about.

Another bomber was caught in the searchlights' web and the gun batteries roared at it, pocking the moonlit sky with their bad breath. Again a stream of silver rain curled down from the plane's belly but this time there were no bangs, just a brittle crackling. Incendiaries. He waited for the glare. It came.

The window went up in Edie's bedroom. Flo's head poked out and searched the horizon before focusing on Jack's black tin hat.

'You. Jack?' she hissed mightily.

'Yes.'

'She's coming on. Elsie says to put a kettle on downstairs.'

He started for the door but stopped suddenly. 'You'll want more'n a kettle for a baby, Flo,' he said seriously.

Flo stifled a chuckle. 'Teach your grannie to suck eggs, would you, Jack? We got the water for the baby on the boil up here, you old dillwall. The kettle's for a cuppa for me and Elsie.' The window slid down with a muted sigh.

Barry had put new sash-cords in that window only a month since. Only a month.

Jack boiled the kettle, turned it down to a low gas to simmer, kept it there for twenty minutes, then hissed up the stairs to ask for further instructions. The only reply was Edie's groaning but there was nothing new in that. Eventually he made the tea, stacked pot and sugar-bowl and milk-jug and cups and saucers on a tray and bore it all up the stairs to the tiny landing. He tapped the closed door of Edie's room with his boot but no one came. He tapped harder and once again the only response was one of Edie's quivering moans. He wedged the tray against wall and door and managed, finally, to turn the door-handle. He nearly knocked over the milk-jug in the effort but he steadied himself in time and padded noiselessly into the room.

The sight of it stopped him dead, tray poised and forgotten in front of him.

Elsie was on the far side of the bed and just behind Edie's head, holding on to her clenched fists with one hand and bearing down on her tummy with the other. Flo was on one knee by the bed and she was pulling something out of ... well, something was in her hands. There was only the light of a candle to guide them; it flickered a frail orange glow around Elsie's anxious face and Edie's dilated tummy and Flo's face and glistened on the little wet black head and the body sheen of the baby.

Then Flo was on her feet, quick as a flash and businesslike, and she turned the little skip upside down, her capable fingers imprisoning its feet, and whacked its little bum cheek – whap, whap, like fish on a marble slab. The baby choked and gurgled and wailed and Flo laid it on its back in a nest of clean white towels set up on the ironing-board beside the bed.

Flo spared him a brief glance and said without a trace of con-

cern, 'Well, you certainly took your time with that tea, Jack.
Put it down then and go on downstairs where you belong. No
place for a man up here.'

He came to himself quickly, lowered the tray on to the chest
of drawers and went back to the door. At that moment the sky
beyond the houses across the street blushed white through the
blackout curtaining.

He turned away and closed the door, but on the stairs he
stopped and tried to remember how Elsie made the sign of the
Cross.

> O Lord, from whom all blessings flow,
> Bless these Thy children, here below. . . .

No dad, poor little skip. Born with no dad and christened
with incendiaries.

Friday, 2345

Shaffer was yawning when he came into the studio and the
affliction rubbed off on the duty censor whose rumpled hair and
fly-away collar and tie prophesied imminent total collapse. Only
the nature of their exhaustion separated them and, in that,
Shaffer was way out in front. Janice had cossetted him, fed him,
pleasured him – he could no longer think of it as love-making
and was now mildly amused to realise she was treating him as
little more than a vessel for her own satisfaction. He was feeling
completely light headed, even a little drunk; he had been grateful for the excuse to leave her.

The censor read through the piece, nodding appreciatively
between his yawns, one hand permanently ruffling his hair as if
to massage his brain into wakefulness.

Janice had sat at Shaffer's shoulder as he typed it, fascinated
by his flow of consciousness and, he thought, a little intimidated
by the process of converting to dramatic journalese the mun-
dane experiences of people she knew and understood. It was
funny, she said, seeing young Paul Warrender being made out

to be a hero, clever the way it was done, but a bit put on, really. Back in the Green every mum and dad would breathe a sigh of relief that it hadn't been their son, but that's as far as they'd go. The things Shaffer wrote about Paul, the ideas he expressed and the way he tied them together to illustrate the torment of a whole nation struck her as no better than story-book fiction. She said so.

'You're making that up,' she accused at one point. 'He only got caught in an air-raid. He didn't *do* anything. He wasn't even killed.'

O'Keefe listened to the run-through without interruption and followed it with his highest accolade. 'Not bad.' He chuckled when Shaffer told him he would be recording the piece at the London end 'for personal reasons'.

'I don't wanna know your personal reasons, Mel,' he growled. 'But it's O.K. with me. The kid deserves a memento.'

Shaffer looked across at the censor and grinned weakly. It was bad enough that O'Keefe had guessed he intended giving the recording to young Paul as a keepsake, but at least he would hold his tongue; it would be terrible if the story went the rounds at Broadcasting House and ended up being retold in the American correspondents' bar at the Savoy. Gestures like his could end up as permanent jokes about the anxiety of some people to immortalise their contribution to the war effort.

He went on the air. The story rang true.

He ended: 'Anyone who found himself in London this week might be forgiven for thinking that England doesn't need help to throw back the tide of German ambition. They have their bow of burning gold: it's called the will to win. They have their arrows of desire: an unshakeable conviction that they are defending the right. And their spirit of cheerful acceptance is a chariot of fire.

'Young Paul, who should have died today but survived against all odds, is a reflection of the spirit, the conviction and the will. And perhaps something else; that unquantifiable ingredient handed down to warring nations by God or Fate or Providence: bounteous good luck.

'The boy was dug from the ruin of a drab, unlovely street in a quarter of London no legislator could be proud of. Tonight he lies in hospital, pieced together and made whole as, in the years ahead, the street itself must be made whole.

'The real challenge for young Paul and for his parents, for London and its defenders, for England and her leaders, does not lie in resisting the enemy and defeating him. That will come; in time, with help, against all odds. The challenge lies in making the broken body whole again. And the mind.'

He went back upstairs, through the layers of blast-proof doors, between the lines of sleeping bodies in the corridors, to the foyer with its armed sentries and protective screens. Brilliant moonlight bathed Regent Street, softening its jagged outlines and the pockmarks of devastation. Above him the searchlights ran their finger-ends across the face of heaven and the shellbursts of the anti-aircraft guns outshone the moon.

SATURDAY
14 September

Saturday, 0900

Denzil Fletcher-Hale rang the bell and retreated two formal steps backwards. There was a pronounced delay before his signal was answered but then the door swung wide. He averted his gaze at once and pivoted on one foot to turn to face along the corridor.

'Oh, I say – frightfully sorry. Expected Shaffer.'

The girl was wearing a towel, if 'wearing' were the appropriate word in the circumstances. It was a simple hand-towel and formed little more than token cover for the midsection of her ample contours. The top of it barely met requirements. She made a sound in her throat that was uncannily like water running out of a bath, but pleasant, fired with incomparable good humour.

'Oh, there you are then. Denzil, aren't you?'

'Ah. . . .' He blushed. Ridiculous of him, of course, but he was just not prepared. He pivoted a little farther round to avoid any possibility of head-on visual contact. 'Shaffer. Is he. . . ?'

She chuckled again. What a jolly girl.

'He had to run, love. Gone to his office, he said, then he's off on his rounds, then he's going down Stepney. Busy little bee, isn't he?'

She beckoned him with a twitch of her head and he stepped over the threshold, taking care to give her as wide a berth as possible. She watched him with unconcealed amusement and, as he came alongside her, edging crabwise to take up the minimum amount of space between them, she thrust out one hip with dramatic suddenness and doubled up with laughter when he flinched. The laughter temporarily loosened her hold on the ends of the towel and the upper half slipped an inch or so. Denzil's head whipped away again, concentrating his attention fixedly on the far left-hand corner of the room. Having passed

461

her he strode quickly to a comforting window and set himself in front of it, staring out.

'Awfully sorry,' he repeated unhappily.

'Oh, you are a one,' she teased.

He heard her cross the room and enter the bedroom and released the breath that had built up in his chest. Awfully jolly girl. Never thought of Shaffer having a. . . . Well. . . .

She emerged from the bedroom and he sneaked a guilty half-glance over one shoulder. Relief. She was wearing a robe.

'He said you can take the keys.' She jangled them in her fingers enticingly. 'And the motor's parked in the garage behind the block. He said you'd know where to find it.'

'Well, thanks frightfully. . . ,' he began. He covered the distance between them in two vast strides and held out his hand for the keys but she snatched them into the palm of her hand and made a protective fist around them.

Her lips formed a scarlet cushion and her big brown eyes widened with bold interest.

'You're ever so *brown*,' she breathed. Before he could pull back, she had taken his hand in hers. Her fingers ran lightly over his golden skin. 'I bet you didn't get brown as that down Southend, did you?'

The lips were pulsing somehow; curious effect. And her fingers. He felt very odd; couldn't put his finger on it exactly but . . . very odd. He slipped his hand free with what he hoped was not too obvious a display of bad manners.

'Wintered at Antibes, hot summer here,' he explained gently.

'You what?' She settled her body in one sinuous undulation, supporting an elbow in one hand, her chin in the other. Deuced odd feeling.

'Ah — I don't quite get you, er. . . ?'

'Name is Janice. You can call me that, seeing as how we've got a mutual friend.' Her smile was a constant challenge. Really, an *awfully* jolly girl. 'You said you wintered in Onteen. What's Onteen?'

'An-tibes.' He pronounced it with greater clarity. 'Little place, south of France. Chaps go there for the sun.'

Her eyes widened. 'But there's a war on in France. It was on the news. Dunkirk and that.'

'Little before Dunkirk. Miss it this winter, of course. Fearful bind, war.'

She stared at him silently for a moment, then began to shake with suppressed laughter that finally became too much for her and found an outlet in deep, merry, tinkling peals. *Frightfully jolly girl. Was she Shaffer's ah. . . ?*

'Know it, do you?' he asked politely.

'Know what?'

'Antibes.' The laughter threatened to bring tears to her eyes.

'Gawd! Do I know Antibes!' She held her hands to her face, relieving the aching cheek muscles. 'You're a card, you are. Do I know Antibes! I haven't been farther than Southend and I only been *there* twice. In all my life I haven't—' She stopped and the mouth pulsed elaborately. 'How old would you say I was, then?'

Denzil was absolutely stumped. 'Age you mean?'

'Age I mean, yes. What d'you think?'

He blustered. It was absolutely out of character in him; never found occasion to resort to it before but ... yes, blustered. What on earth did a fellow say?

'Eighteen? Would that be about it?'

'Oh!'

She was off again, bending at the waist this time, hands clasping her stomach, shuddering with laughter. This time the tears really did come.

'You old smoothie! I know what *you* are. My mum used to talk about men like you. Mashers they called 'em in her day. That's what you are, all right.' Words were engulfed with sobs of delight. '*Masher!*'

The robe, bound round her with a loosely tied belt, began to part under the strain and he backed away respectfully. She didn't seem to notice and was now so consumed by merriment that she had lost temporary contact with the world of social prudence. He cleared his throat loudly. Couldn't allow her to compromise herself. She heard nothing.

'I say — ah — Janice. . . ?'

The mention of her name had a miraculously arresting effect. She looked at him, smoothing tears from her eyes, suddenly serious.

'*Janice*, is it? Well. . . .' She slipped both hands under the fall of her long black hair and lifted it in a tail to the top of her head. 'Janice, is it?' She raised one bare foot, took a springy step to the side and performed a nymphlike arabesque. He retreated another two steps backwards, astonished. She came to a halt facing him, allowed the hair to fall back on her shoulders and crossed her arms in front of her, hands resting gently on the swelling curves of. . . .

'Well. Must be going. Long drive. Hold-ups along the way, I dare say. Better—'

She caught his elbow with both hands and danced around him as he tried to pass, forcing him to turn with her if he was to retain his balance.

'Must go . . . long drive . . . must be going . . . long be driving. . . .'

She sang it, the street chant of a skipping child, her bold face bright, long legs kicking high. At length he began to feel dizzy and held up a protesting hand. She made one more turn to propel her in another arabesque and fell spread-eagled, but expertly, into a deep chair. The fall exposed a length of limb and Denzil found to his concern that he was staring at it openly. He pulled himself together at once.

'Awfully nice meeting you.. . .' He made hastily for the door.

'Denzil !' She was out of the chair and running for the bedroom. He swung round, alarmed. She turned in the doorway and dropped a ridiculous curtsey. 'Old Mel said you was to take me with you. Chaperone, he said.' She winked wickedly. 'Gimme two secs and I'll be dressed.'

'But—' he started anxiously.

'No buts,' she pouted. 'It's Shaffer's car and I'm his. . . .' She grinned slyly. 'I'm his representative, right? Besides, you never know what you'll be getting up to with a girl like that on your hands, do you? I mean. . . .' She pulled the robe tight around her with unmistakable emphasis. 'She could throw herself all over you. That'd give you a right turn, wouldn't it, eh?'

The laughter pealed out again and was cut short by the slam of the bedroom door.

Denzil returned to the window. What on earth was all that about? The girl might throw herself all over him? Give him a right turn? Totally baffling. Quite mad.

But ... the corners of his mouth twitched upwards involuntarily ... she was a deuced jolly little thing.

Saturday, 1000

Tom Russell stared at his kit piled neatly on the stripped mattress of his bed. Suddenly it was all over; months of comradeship, almost brotherly closeness, and it was over in the time it took to strip a bed and pack a bag. A couple of the chaps had dropped in to say 'Cheers!' but only for a second. No time. No reason, either. Easy come, easy go. They'd pretended he would be dropping in again from time to time to say hello but they didn't really believe that and neither did he. In a couple of months perhaps none of the old faces would be here.

When it happened it happened quickly, thank God. The C.O. had been damned good, not only in rubber-stamping Tom's request for transfer to active duty but in fiddling a return to his old outfit, 672 Squadron at Coltishall under the command of Squadron Leader Douglas Bader. The lads had ribbed him about that in the mess last night. Smack bang into the heart of the controversy; right into Bader's lap. And since Bader was Leigh-Mallory's blue-eyed boy, Russell was roundly condemned from that moment on as a Big Wing man.

Idiots.

They'd struck up the old song before he escaped to bed.

> The Hurricane pilot is something
> That most other pilots are not.
> When most other pilots are pissing about
> The poor bugger's put on the spot.
> The Spit may be handsome and luvverly,
> Like a better-class cabriolet,

> But when it comes down to shifting the shit
> Which bugger carries the day?

Officially he was not due to report for duty to 672 until 0800 hours on Monday morning and he had a thirty-six hour pass in his pocket to prove it, but he couldn't face London again. He wanted to get to Coltishall as soon as possible, locate the machine allocated to him, have a chat with his plumbers – the aircrew responsible for keeping him aloft – and talk to Bader. If he checked in by mid-afternoon he might even be airborne by Sunday.

Saturday, 1200

The Oxo tin was on the back shelf of the pantry, under the stairs. By stretching on tip-toe Florence Scully could reach it with the tips of her fingers. She inched it towards her, squeezing a passage for it through an array of bottles and jars behind which it had been strategically hidden. She took it to the table and opened it.

Hooks, eyes, sequins, buttons; buttons of blue bottled glass, big as marbles; big green mushroom-shaped leather buttons; mother-of-pearl buttons, coal-black buttons; hundreds.

She had played with this tin when she was a child, knew its contents as old friends, had added to the collection over the years. She never used them, even when she was desperate; she had a proper sewing basket for common running repairs. Somehow, she couldn't bring herself to rob the Oxo tin.

She shook the tin gently, poked into it with a finger and touched the paper. Ten ten-shilling notes. She took them out and put the tin back in its place. Five pounds. It was a lot of money. Taken her a long time to save; sixpence here, shilling there. Saving for a rainy day. She folded the notes neatly and put them in her handbag.

Elsie had taken a bus up to Borough Market and she'd said not to worry about making her something to eat because she'd not be back till after she'd been to the hospital to see young Paul.

That was what had put the idea in Flo's mind; visiting Paul. Arthur's dinner was in the oven and she left a note for him explaining why she wouldn't be there. She'd never done anything like that before but she knew he'd understand. For the fifth time she moved the scribbled note to the middle of the table to be sure he couldn't miss seeing it.

Dear Arthur,
  Have nipped out to visit Paul at the hospital, see how he's doing. Won't be long. Dinner in oven. Stew. If you get up early, carrots may be bit hard, so turn gas up for few minutes. Love, Flo.

It was the first letter she'd written him since their courting days and she felt funny about it. Maybe she should have made it a bit more ... well, affectionate. She had compromised with the 'Love, Flo.' Just writing it had made her think in a way she hadn't thought for donkeys' years. Funny word, love. For the youngsters, really. Arthur would be the first to say so. He'd never been one for that kind of thing. 'Love, Flo' she'd written determinedly. Why not? Nothing wrong with that. Two wars and two kids and still together. *Two* kids? Oh, Arthur love....

She took the Tube to East Acton. She bought a *Daily Express* but it was full of war and she read it only out of a sense of guilt at the money it had cost and to fill her mind; stop herself thinking.
  When she came down from the Tube she was in strange country and she had to ask the way. It turned out to be a five-minute walk along Du Cane Road. She was hot and worried. What had possessed her to make the journey in the first place? All she had to go on was something Janice had said. Janice could have been wrong, easy enough. And she still had to think up lies for Arthur when she got back. How she couldn't get in to see Paul. What was it she'd worked out? She'd forgotten. Visiting hours. What if Arthur mentioned it to Elsie and it was all wrong? He'd want to know.

She stood before the huge double gates of the Scrubs and rang the bell at one side. A window opened.

'Yes, luv?'

'Don't matter,' she mumbled in sudden panic.

'Eh? Come a bit nearer, luv. Can't hear.'

'No, 's'all right. Just. . . .'

It was a mistake; a stupid silly mistake. What difference would it make? Arthur's carrots would be hard. She ought to get back.

A small door opened within the frame of the larger one.

'That's better,' said a cheerful, portly man as he squeezed out. 'Now then, my old china — what can I do you for?' Jokey.

'It don't. . . . Well, yes . . . I. . . .'

'Sorry, luv. No one here. Just me. All the er . . . blokes are gorn away. Who you after then?'

'Gone?' Flo stared at him, alarmed.

'What's 'is name? Not that it'll help much, but . . . your hubby, luv?'

'No,' she said sharply. She took hold of herself. 'No — a friend. Friend of a friend.'

'See. Name?'

'Dunn. Alfred Dunn.' She couldn't retreat now.

'Dunn,' hummed the porter. 'Hang on.' He forced himself back through the narrow door and reappeared with a thick ledger. 'Place has been taken over, luv.' He ran his finger down ville.' He snapped the ledger shut. 'Might not be there now, Hush-hush. Dunn . . . Dunn. . . . Gotcher! Pentonville. Lucky, you are. One of the last we had, he was. Last on me list. Pentonville.' He snapped the ledger shut. 'Might not be there now, o'course. Know it?'

Flo shook her head. She wanted to go home.

'Past King's Cross. Up by Islington, luv. Ask around.' He smiled sympathetically and closed the door. His eyes appeared through the window. 'Worth a try,' he said. 'Couldn't have got far. Lucky.'

There was no jolly porter at Pentonville. He was small, thin aloof, frightening. 'Dunn? Never heard of him. Place full of people; moving 'em out as fast as they come in. Try the Home Office.' His weasel face worked irritably.

She got angry then, angry because she was scared.

'Dunn!' she snapped stubbornly. 'Is he here or ain't he?'

'Look here, missus—' the thin man began imperiously.

'Don't you missus me!'

The man sighed. 'Visiting hours are suspended, all right? Don't matter what you say—'

'Bugger it!' she shouted. 'Bugger visiting hours! I'll sit right where I am then!' And she did; on the ground, back to the doors.

'Don't be daft!' The man tried to peer down at her. 'Won't do no good.'

'Sit here then!'

She settled herself for a long wait. The *Daily Express* made an inadequate cushion but she didn't care. Discomfort or no, she wasn't going to be choked off by the likes of him. After fifteen minutes the door opened. A man came out with the Weasel and looked down at her.

'Madam.' The new chap was young, no more than thirty. 'Making a scene won't get you anywhere.'

Flo folded her arms. 'Took me three hours to get here. Not going now. All I want is to see someone.' She lifted her head and held the man's stare. 'He's a criminal but he's still a human being, no matter what you say. Stuck in there, nobody come to see him. Wouldn't treat a dog like that.' She struggled to her feet and the young man helped her. 'No use your thinking I'm going, 'cause I'm not.'

The Weasel whispered something in the other's ear. He was waved aside. The young man said diplomatically, 'Mr Dunn is here, madam, but you must appreciate we can't let visitors come and go at all hours of the day and night. There are fixed times, but we've had to suspend them for the moment. In a week, maybe—'

Flo butted in. 'Look, son, times don't make no difference. It's people we're talking about, not times. Clocks was made for people, not people for clocks. Please, I don't want to be awkward. I don't want to upset anyone. I've come a long way and. . . .' She swayed on her feet and both men grabbed at her before she fell.

'Are you all right?' The young man turned to the Weasel. 'She can sit down inside. Get her a glass of water.'

He led Flo through into the gatehouse and eased her into a seat. The Weasel came back with a glass of water and she drank from it.

'Feel better,' she gasped. 'Come over all of a flush. Sorry. Don't know what happened.' She leaned her head against the rough wall behind the bench. 'Got to see him. Really have. Just once. Wouldn't forgive myself.'

'Madam, I've tried to explain. . . .'

'I know, I know. Regulations. Always regulations.' She looked pleadingly at the young man. 'Please. Never asked for nothing in me life I felt so bad about. You don't know what it'd mean if you was to let me see him.'

'You're not a relative, are you?'

'She ain't. I hascertained that,' said the Weasel officiously.

'A friend. Just a friend. He's got no relatives I know of. Nobody,' said Flo.

The young man capitulated so suddenly she wasn't quite sure she'd heard him correctly. He turned to the Weasel. 'Wheel Dunn along to visiting.' The thin man swung on his heel and disappeared, shoulders rigid with disapproval.

'The visiting room is just down the corridor, madam,' the young man said kindly. 'Wait a few minutes and Mr Dunn will be brought along. I'd be obliged if you'll keep it short.' He made a tight smile. 'I'm breaking the rules for you.'

'Thank you.' Flo touched his arm. 'I'm ever so grateful. I won't tell anyone, honest.'

She counted to a hundred then walked down a corridor to the door marked 'Waiting Room' and tentatively pushed it open. Alfred Dunn was sitting at a table in the small, bare room. Behind him stood a man in uniform who nodded her to the chair facing Dunn, then shifted his gaze to the far wall.

She could only see Alfie's head and shoulders; there was a little wooden screen erected halfway along the table to prevent them touching. He didn't look well. His hair was cropped monkey-short and his eyes seemed black with lack of sleep.

'Hallo, Flo,' he said almost in a whisper. 'I knew it was you. You shouldn't have come.'

'I had to, Alfie. When I heard about ... about Maud. I didn't know what to do. They haven't got it right, have they? I mean, you didn't do for your Maud like they say?'

Dunn seemed to have no existence beyond his own head.

'I knew what I was doing, Flo. Only reason I left was I couldn't stand the thought of being picked up in the Green. Everybody knowing.'

'But if you tell them you done it they'll put you away, love. You mustn't say you done it. We'll speak up for you. Lots of people in the Green will. We could get a solicitor for you. Anyone can have one. It's the law.'

'Flo!' Dunn put a finger to his lips. 'Don't go on, old love. I know what you're trying to say but it don't make no difference. I'll do things my way.' He glanced round at the warder, but the man was oblivious to all earthbound life.

'But I can't go home leaving you here.' She crumpled the brim of her hat on her knees. She felt sick. The table smelt of carbolic and Alfred Dunn's face and hands were so white they looked as if they'd been scrubbed transparent.

'We made a promise, Flo. Remember? Both of us. Kept it for a long time. Don't bugger things up now; not now. What's happened is my problem. I don't need any help.' He bit hard into his lip. 'I don't want you coming here again, Flo. For everybody's sake. If you do come, I'll tell 'em I won't see you.'

She remembered and fumbled in her bag and brought out the ten ten-shilling notes.

'Ay, ay!' The warder stepped forward swiftly and plucked the notes from her hand. 'Can't do that, ma'am.'

'He'll give 'em back,' said Dunn. 'Don't worry. But you might just as well throw them away as give 'em to me.' He stood up unsteadily. 'Don't need money here, Flo. Don't need anything. Good of you, though. The thought, like. Thanks for worrying about me. Now forget, eh?' He stared down at his hands. 'Don't think of me. Don't think of this place. Don't think of Maud or anything. Think of Derek, Arthur. Yourself. I loved my Maud,

Flo. Her and me was. . . .' He grimaced at the warder. 'Got to go now. Remember what I said. I meant it, Flò. And if you want to use the money, buy some flowers for Maud's grave. Do that for me, eh? But don't ever try coming back here again.'

He turned away and the warder jerked open the door, tossed the folded ten-shilling notes on the table in front of her and shoved Alfred Dunn out into the corridor. Their footsteps clattered away and died behind a final clang of steel.

She smoothed out the ten-shilling notes. Five pounds would buy a lot of flowers; enough for a whole funeral. She couldn't stop herself shuddering at the thought.

Saturday, 1400

Northumberland Avenue drowsed in a spill of sunshine that ran sharp as an arrowhead from the Embankment all the way to Trafalgar Square. Lieutenant-Commander Jamieson allowed the last of the cold tea to settle in his stomach, then took the chipped enamel mug to the wash-basin and flushed it under the tap. He upended it and dried his hands.

Amy had called just before lunch to say that Allan had chickenpox and the doctor had quarantined all three of them. The married quarters were cramped enough without being turned into a prison for three out-of-sorts young children and she wanted to know if he could possibly find the time to. . . .

There was no time. He was due for a forty-eight-hour pass in two weeks' time but that was all. They had no conception of the meaning of the phrase 'compassionate leave' in Naval Intelligence. She was far from impressed. He couldn't blame her. The call had disturbed him sufficiently to make lunch irrelevant; declining appetite was the cross every absentee father had to bear. It was different at sea. A naval officer was doing what he had been trained for when he was on the bridge of a destroyer. A father could mollify his conscience when there were several hundred nautical miles between him and his responsibilities. It was—

The phone rang and he slid into his chair.

'Maconachie here. Is that you, Jamieson?'

'Oh, hallo.' Relief. He had thought for a moment it might be Amy again.

'We got around to your D.R. 18B this morning.'

'Oh. Fletcher-Hale?'

'Yes. We've been down there for nearly three hours. I think he's flown the coop. No sign of him. Looks like he packed a toothbrush, few clothes and ran.'

'Oh Lord. Have you put out an All Points bulletin on him?'

'Yes. Just now. Anyway, nothing we can do for the time being. Must have got the wind-up. Dysart probably tipped his hand.'

'Doesn't seem very likely. He said the chap was a complete fool. Didn't seem to think his membership of The Link amounted to anything important.'

Maconachie's chuckle was harsh. 'On my side of the game, Jamieson, you expect them to play the innocent. The complete fools are usually the cleverest. Anyway, we've informed the local C.I.D. and asked Edinburgh to keep an eye on the family home. Softly, softly. We'll keep a watch on his clubs, the flat, his known haunts. Don't worry yourself. We'll get him.'

Saturday, 1430

The train began to slow. Wedged in the corner of the compartment, Shaffer dropped the early evening newspaper into his lap, arms aching. The single naked bulb made it impossible to read anything more than six inches from the eyes.

He squinted through the small square cut in the latticework of netting glued over the blue-painted glass of the window. If his homework was correct, this was the Bank.

This morning he had mastered the Bakerloo line to Watford, an experience that did little for his peace of mind and even less for his personal hygiene. He had got back to the apartment just after midday; crushed, perspiring and smelling like a damp sheepdog. A shower, a quick snack and ten minutes poring over a map of the Underground and he had set off once more from

Bond Street, vowing never again to deprive himself of the Morris, no matter how humanitarian the reasons.

The headlines shrieked up from his lap. No trouble reading those: 'LONDON'S SEVENTH NIGHT OF RELAY RAIDS.' The bombing of the palace and the strength of the ack-ack barrage the previous night were the two big topics of the day. The king had replied to the Prime Minister's message of congratulations on his escape with the words: 'Like so many other people we have had a personal experience of German barbarity which only strengthens the resolve of us all to fight through to victory.' Shaffer had squeezed that into his morning bulletin.

He flicked open the paper. Downing Street hit by incendiaries; a fire-bomb on the roof of the House of Lords; the Piccadilly Hotel, Somerset House, the Strand; not to mention an impertinent explosion 'close to the London home of a well-known legal peer'. Shaffer grinned. Perfidy!

By comparison, the East End had fared no worse. *That* was where the real significance lay. Either by design, or under the influence of General Pile's fanatical anti-aircraft barrage, or both, the Luftwaffe was widening its favours to include the whole city, totally nullifying the psychological wedge it had driven between East End and West in the past week. It didn't say much for the perception of Hitler's so-called fifth column, nor Lord Haw-Haw's much vaunted information network.

'We can take it,' Churchill had said, but a lot of people down-river had, up to now, been asking just who 'we' actually were.

Another stop. Two more to go. Shaffer tugged a pencil from his pocket and made a note on the margin of the newspaper reminding himself of the piece he had intended to write for the last four days. The fifth column. He'd mapped it out after reading H. G. Wells's open letter condemning the government's treatment of aliens in Britain. The behaviour of the authorities was, to say the least, extraordinary. Fifteen to twenty thousand German refugees — many Jewish — had fled to England between 1933 and the summer of 1939. Many of them had been rounded up and interned in May and June. Dozens had committed suicide at this final crushing blow. The restrictions were now even tougher. Anti-alien feeling had even led to a First World War v.c. being refused permission to join the Local Defence Volunteers because he had in his distant family past a trace of foreign ancestry. The national mood was verging on hysteria; his own confrontation with the crowd at Keeton's Road School had underscored that. Aliens. In the wrong place at the wrong time. The wrong street; the wrong country. Well, it was the best line he had. Both today's assignments were non-starters.

Workers' Playtime. He stared into the gloom. He could see O'Keefe now, handing the tape to his secretary as he always did when confronted with a file that made too great a demand on his sense of proportion.

'A Funny,' she would say, handing it back with an interpreter's disinterest. Irony and satire were the two areas in which she back-fielded for O'Keefe.

And then, of course, he'd spike it.

A pity. Watford *had* been funny. Workers' Playtime. There *should* be room for it among the blood and thunder.

Lovebody & Son, Ltd., formerly makers of novelty ashtrays, wall-plaques and artistic chinaware and latterly producers of electrical condensers, deserved fleeting recognition in anybody's war. The B.B.C. had invited Shaffer to watch an amateur talent show from the factory floor. In fact, it had turned out to be a dry run to select acts due to appear in a programme later in the day. It said a lot for the producer's clairvoyance that he had decided the performers weren't quite braced for a straight live transmission.

On a wooden platform raised above a sea of headscarves and caps, the hopefuls had trooped before the producer's jaundiced eye, their voices tremulous in the face of imminent stardom. Dilly Flynn, the buxom 'canteen sweetheart', trilled an incomprehensible lyric to an awestruck audience, unaware that backlighting had rendered her dress totally transparent. She sang four encores before the producer became aware of the real nature of her audience appeal.

Then Harry the Mimic who, after laborious explanation, still couldn't appreciate why his mime of Charlie Chaplin was unsuitable for the wireless. He retired hurt and angry, mumbling of 'favouritism'. Next on was a comedian complete with a flashing bow-tie and a line in patter that would have horrified Max Miller. He was dragged offstage by a production assistant at the climax of what promised to be a fascinating account of a chorus girl and a camel's hump.

Reluctantly, Shaffer had left before the final selection. His departing image was of the works' manager trying to placate an irate member of the audience who came close to decapitation by an energetic tap dancer's flying shoe.

He'd had another pressing engagement in the East End. It had turned out to be a ticket to hell.

Tilbury Shelter was more than ten miles from Tilbury Docks and no one was quite sure how it came by its name in the first place. Commercial Shelter or Stepney Shelter would have been more geographically accurate, situated as it was between Stepney's Commercial Road and Cable Street, a few hundred yards from the point where Whitechapel Road merged with Aldgate. But it had been Tilbury to the shelterers of the First World War and Tilbury it still was.

Shaffer had heard veiled references to it from the day he arrived back in London, but they had taken their place along with other, more immediate, horrors. Hirschfield had been obscure when he had raised it with him. He had merely wrinkled his nose as if dismissing some unnatural aberration that good taste forbade as a subject of conversation. Denzil hadn't been much more forthcoming and it was left to the lugubrious Archie Fisk to reawaken Shaffer's professional interest. Archie's friends knew the Tilbury shelter well.

'Shelter-slumming, old boy. Never been?'

Archie's regard for good taste and social morality was by no means as inhibiting as Hirschfield's. Shelter-slumming or shelter-crawling, as the *demi-monde* termed it, was a fast-growing recreation for those comfortably off and bored with the West End. It involved organised trips to the biggest public shelters in the East End. The biggest and, by definition, the most sordid.

Tilbury had reared its ugly head in veiled newspaper reports and questions in the House of Commons. Shaffer had decided he had to see it, but he had felt like an eighteenth-century fop visiting Bedlam.

It was ten storeys high. Flanked by half-crippled roads and smoke-drenched railway arches, it towered like some evil cathedral over the most decadent slum of London's poorest neighbourhood. He had looked for a door in the wall that encircled the building and found, instead, a hole knocked through the brickwork. A steady trail of humanity wound in and out laden like native porters. Nobody paid him the slightest attention as he jostled through the crowd.

The soldier was in full battledress and carried a rifle. 'Business here, sir?' His eyes narrowed warily as he took in Shaffer's clothes. 'You official, sir?'

'Official? Well, sort of, I guess.' He handed over his identity card and Press accreditation.

The soldier studied them, handed them back. 'Normally need a ticket, here. Reckon it'll be all right. American paper?'

'Radio.'

'Plenty of places better seeing than this hole. Don't judge a cup of tea by its dregs, know what I mean, sir?'

There was a faint humming, as if from a wasps' nest. It came from the small doorway Shaffer judged to be the entrance to the shelter proper.

'Don't get me wrong,' he said placatingly. 'I'm not here to criticise. Nothing like that.'

The soldier shifted the rifle-strap on his shoulder and ran his eye down the line moving steadily backward and forward from the shelter. 'It's bad all right.'

Shaffer angled his head at the doorway. 'I'm not asking for a guided tour, but. . . .'

'Sorry, sir. 'Gainst orders. Like to help. Door's back of us. Two levels. Official. Unofficial. Unofficial's in the basement.' He shook his head as if to excommunicate even the thought of it.

'Unofficial?'

The soldier broke off to intercept a small boy who was about to dodge inside with a bundle of newspapers.

'No you don't. Off you go, sonny Jim.' He clipped the boy expertly around the ear. The child wheeled smartly into the line leaving the shelter before the guard could grab his newspapers. 'He'll be back, little bugger. Go on tryin' till my back's turned.'

'What's so wrong with newspapers?'

'Newspapers? Nothing. Bloody Commie papers they are. Not allowed. They try and sneak 'em in all the time.'

Shaffer made a last effort. 'The entrance, then, maybe. Give me two minutes and I promise I won't ask anything you can't answer.'

The guard relented. 'All right then. Two minutes. Over here.'

It *was* a cathedral. Steel girders soared at intervals of fifteen feet in giant arches over raised platforms flanked by aisles of pounded earth. The main hall was oblong in shape and every square foot of it was packed with bodies, dense as the hold of a slave ship. The air was heavy with a damp, fetid musk.

'Fifteen thousand people,' said the soldier, measuring the lake of humanity. 'Not all here, o'course. This is the visitor's parlour.'

'Visitors?'

'The basement is what you'll want to see. Down the steps at the end. Careful how you go. And if you get into any trouble, best thing is sing out, loud as hell. But only two minutes.'

'Fine. One thing, though. This official, unofficial stuff. I don't get it.'

'Nothing much to it. Two floors, right? Top floor was took over by the borough. That's official. Wasn't good enough, though. Commies wanted the bottom floor 'n' all. That's private. Owned by someone. Legal. Storerooms full of food. Commies marched in and everybody else followed. No facilities, nothing. Two bogs . . . latrines, that is, for five thousand women. Nothing for the rest. Keep horses down there, the owners do. Half a dozen of 'em. Even they'd complain if they could talk. See for yourself. Russian ambassador came down here to see for himself. God knows what he thought. He was bottle-green when he came up.'

'The ambassador came here?'

'On his own two feet. Triumph for the working classes, see?'

'It's O.K. if I go down there?'

'Wouldn't advise it without a gas-mask, but there you are. Got this far, might as well go the whole hog. Now, I'd better be getting back. That little bugger with the papers is about due for another shot. On a piece of elastic, that one.'

The soldier turned on his heel and left Shaffer to it.

The train was virtually empty now. One station to go. He decided he'd walk from Holborn. He needed air; even the stale air of a hot city Saturday.

In the end he had stayed twenty minutes on the basement floor of Tilbury Shelter. Twenty minutes. When he left he had slipped the soldier a pack of cigarettes in lieu of a medal.

There were no words. That was the trouble; he could see the pictures, but there were no words. There was no shortage of smells either; they still clung to his shoes. But words ... words were inadequate.

Saturday, 1455

The music room had been a late Victorian addition to the Georgian house and the architect had done his best to display contempt for the classic simplicity of the earlier period. Deep flying buttresses supported curved red brick on the outside and huge neo-Norman-style windows, crowned with stained-glass roses of violent hue, lent it the atmosphere of a back-street chapel inside. Captain Freddie Green had never considered it an appropriate place for music; he played no instrument himself, nor did he encourage his guests to do so. When he felt the need to add the scraping of fiddles and cellos to the social cocktail of booze and chatter he hired professional musicians. He was a conventional knees-up man himself and appreciated a good pub piano, but in the age of wireless and gramophone records he couldn't see the sense in manufacturing your own. Besides, the music room was the most suitable area in the house for a study. Not an office; he had one of those over at the front of the house looking down on the river. No, a study was something else; a place for putting things you liked.

He had bought the bust of Napoleon first, not because he admired him — to tell the truth he'd only associated the bloke with brandy until an antique dealer he'd got in with told him about the Napoleonic Wars and Josephine and so on – but because it was going cheap and he liked the shape. The same dealer told him he could fix him up with a line in Roman emperors and Greek gods, too, all in the same shape, and they came on tall stands in black marble which made a very handsome effect. He had thirty-seven of them now, in a semi-circle on the curved wall, staring into the room with their blind eyes; thirty-six assorted gods, warriors, emperors, politicians, poets and philosophers, and in the very centre, slightly bigger than the others to strike a balance, one of himself.

The walls on either side of the door leading in from the main hall were covered with bookshelves from floor to ceiling and there were little wheeled ladders on rails to help you reach the higher shelves. The books were all bound in faded leather and on the odd occasion he'd climbed up to have a casual sniff around the titles seemed to be mostly in a foreign language. Not his doing, the books; the last incumbent had acquired those and thrown them in as a job lot when he sold the house. They added atmosphere, which was what it was all about, after all. They went well with the Romans and Greeks, with the two tiger-skin rugs, with the stuffed heads of gazelle and lion and zebra and reindeer and the fat dark-brown furniture with black leather seats he'd picked up in a country house sale. The polar-bear skin draped over the settee was new but it added the perfect finishing touch. Well, it wasn't finished, not properly. He'd given his agent instructions to look around for half a dozen tasteful stuffed birds in glass boxes, like they had in the British Museum, and ten or twelve settings under glass of mounted tropical butterflies, nicely framed so he could hang them on the walls like pictures. He already had too many pictures.

He stood at the centre of it all, his back to a blazing log fire, distinguished in his silk smoking-jacket. A good quality fag in the old tortoiseshell holder – touch of the Noël Cowards – set the seal on a first class lunch. He could not be more at ease, he thought, and dammit, why not? He deserved it.

There was a gentle knock at the door and Wally Parrott stuck his head round and intoned, 'Two persons to see you, sir.'

Nothing new. Never a minute to hisself these days — but he wasn't knocking it. He had all the time in the world for people now.

'Who are they?'

'Persons, sir,' repeated Wally, wrinkling his nose.

Stuck-up old shitbag! He was that way with anyone who hadn't got a pearl handle to his moniker.

'Wheel 'em in, Wal.'

Parrott flinched. He always flinched when his master used the familiar diminutive. He rued the day Freddie Green discovered his first name was Wallace and not Charles, as he had claimed.

They were rozzers, Freddie knew that straight away. They had a habit they just couldn't resist of looking around a room before they came into it as if they expected to find blokes with guns behind every chair. They wore plain clothes, which made them look even more hangdog and underpaid and nasty. He came at them over one of the tiger-skin rugs, his hand out. They wouldn't shake, which told him they were here on real business.

'What can I do you gentlemen for then?' he said cheerily. You had to keep it cheerful or they'd screw you to the floor in the first ten seconds, the bastards.

'Albert Edward Green?'

Arresting talk! He ran his tongue over the upper set of dentures and fingered his moustache. Stay calm. Make the sods work for it.

'I'm known about here as Freddie Green, matter of fact,' he replied chattily, 'but you could say Albert Edward was right. That's what's on the birth certificate.'

The one who'd done the formal bit stuck his hand out, palm up. 'May I see your identity card, sir, and your passport, if any?'

'Course you can.' He turned away to ring the bell over the fireplace and bit deep into his lip with the upper chinaware. Identity card. Passport. Bloody hellfire! He pressed the bell and turned to them again.

'Would you gents care to let me in on the secret? Like who you are?'

'I think you know who we are, Mr Green,' the older one said, like he was chewing gravel. He dug into his pocket and produced a wallet. He flicked out a card with his picture stuck in one corner but Freddie didn't bother to look at it.

'What d'you want my identity card for?'

'It's the formal proof of identity, sir.'

'And my passport?'

'The same, sir.'

Freddie stuck the knuckle of one forefinger between his teeth and bit on it. He strolled to the centre of the room, planted his feet squarely on the tiger and sized up Napoleon. They *knew*. No bullshit; no looking for loose ends to tie up. They knew. Plain as a pikestaff. He could waffle on for a couple of hours but that wouldn't get him far. He could call Dougie Estonis on the grounds he had a right to have a lawyer present but they'd scrub around that, sure as eggs. Cut the cackle and get to the nitty-gritty, that was the best thing. Do like he'd always planned he would if the time ever came.

He stuck the cigarette holder in his breast pocket and stubbed out the fag. He looked over his shoulder at them as he did so and let 'em have the old teeth, full throttle.

'All right, gents. We know where we stand, I can see that. What's the charge?'

The two men glanced at each other quickly, then the older one said, 'Are you prepared to make a statement, Mr Green?'

'Could be, old son, yes. Depends on the circs. First, though, you tell me why you came. I won't play stupid, honest.'

The officer cleared his throat. 'My name is Ronald Trotter, detective inspector, Savile Row police station. Before you say anything, I have to warn you that anything you say may be taken down and used—'

'Yeah, yeah, yeah; I know all about that. Just tell me who?'

Trotter cleared his throat. 'Do you know two men called Bernard Kemp and Charles Rowthorne?'

Freddie's eyes fluttered shut then open again. He sighed and gave the chinawork an even better show. 'O.K., so it was Jigger and Charlie. What else?'

'Do you know a man employed as a wharf superintendent at the Melly-Greenmantle yard in—'

'Billy Sutcliffe? Yeah, I know him.'

Trotter stared at him in bewilderment. 'You admit knowledge?'

'Why not?'

'We have statements from all three men substantiating the existence, between them and you, of a—'

'They work for me.'

Trotter's face became a marshalling yard of tight parallel lines. He pressed on. 'A number of youths were apprehended in the course of looting at a warehouse in—'

'West India Dock,' Freddie said helpfully.

'I think I must caution you, Mr Green, that the penalties involved in cases of looting fall under the—'

Parrott's knock at the door cut him off. The old man's head appeared. 'You rang, sir?'

'My identity card and passport, Parrott. They're in the study. Top drawer of the desk. Get 'em and be slippy about it.'

The butler withdrew.

The inspector said, 'As I was saying, Mr Green, under the—'

Freddie waved at the drinks cabinet. 'What's your poison?'

'No thank you.'

'Mind if I do?' He helped himself to a generous gin. He swallowed a third of it quickly. Better. 'Right you are, gents.' He sank into one of the overstuffed armchairs and folded one leg over the other. He eyed them critically. 'Detective inspector, are you? What are *you*?' He indicated the other with his glass.

The younger man looked at his superior. 'Detective sergeant.'

'Well, you could both be superintendents by tonight.' He upended his glass again. 'Sit down, eh?' They remained standing. 'Please yourselves. All right. Got me all ends up. Witnesses, clues, everything—right? Well. I'm going to tell you something and then if you've got any sense you'll scoot back to Savile Row and you'll tell your chief. And if *he's* got any sense he'll have a chat with Number Ten Downing Street. See what I mean? Now then....' He drained the glass and set it on the table at his elbow. He lit another cigarette and fixed it in the long holder. 'We got a right little facer here, you and me. You come along here thinking, "'Allo, all nice and simple. Cut and dried." Right? Course you did. Well, it ain't, see. You want to know where all the stuff that got nicked went to, don't you? Well, I'm going to tell you. Straight out. I'm—'

Parrott returned with the identity card and the passport. The inspector snatched the documents from his hand as he passed and studied them minutely. He seemed satisfied. Parrott whirled, outraged at the grotesque manners of the visitor.

Freddie waved at him airily. 'Go get me the visitors' book,' he ordered. 'The red leather one.' The old man went out again, this time leaving the door ajar.

Freddie resumed his oration. 'So, then, where were we? Oh, yes—where the stuff went. Well, I'll tell you. I give it away.'

The faces of the two men registered total disbelief. Green grinned at them good-naturedly.

'Don't believe me, eh? Why should you? Well, I'll help you prove it, lads. Help you prove it. I give it away all right and I'll admit I had my reasons, but they weren't none you could put a finger on, tell you that for nothing. You ask around here about me—the local rozzers, the wardens, the council—they'll all tell you the same: Freddie Green's is open house, day and night. Parties all the time. Boys from the fighter stations come up for a swim in my swimming-bath downstairs. All the time. Officers only, o'course. Then, three nights a week, I have my little soirees, don't I? One tonight, matter of fact, if you're interested. They all come to Freddie's: generals, admirals, air marshals, politicians, the captains of industry, dozens of your civil servants. Champagne, good grub. Love it, don't they? Get a little comical by the end of the night, most of 'em. You know, a bit pissed. And when they leave, there's a little something for the missus or the girl-friend or the kids. On the back seat of the car, see. Surprise, like. But I'll tell you something else; they never bring it back. None of 'em.'

Parrott re-entered the room but this time he gave the visitors a wide berth and clutched the big red book to his chest until he reached Green's chair. He handed it over with a smile of achievement.

'Off you go then, Wal,' Green growled. 'And shut the door behind you this time, eh?'

He bounced the leather-bound book in his hands, then ex-

484

tended it to the inspector who took it gingerly. The policeman opened it and his colleague craned over his shoulder. Their eyes widened and they gazed blankly at each other.

'What precisely does this. . . ?' began Trotter.

'Every geezer who ever stepped through my front door is down in there, old mate,' Freddie gushed expansively. 'His name, his rank, where he come from, what time he arrived and the time he left, the number of his staff car, his driver's name and. . . .' The dentures burst through, pressing back the lips. 'And down that column on the right you've got the little present he took home. Booze, sugar, butter, eggs, coffee, tea, fruit — fresh or tinned. All of it. Well, then, what d'you say?'

Inspector Trotter closed the book with a snap. 'I don't believe any of this. I'll. . . .' His mouth formed an epithet but he bit it back. 'I'll have this lot checked out before the night's out. Don't think you're—'

'Don't think nothing, me old mate. It's all in there. Give the boys a ring, eh? Ask 'em what they been up to at Freddie's.'

The detective sergeant tugged urgently at the inspector's sleeve and they turned away for a whispered consultation. The inspector swivelled round. His face was red.

'I'll keep this book for the time being, Mr . . . er . . . Green, and I'll give you a receipt for it. The identity card and the passport too. I'm going back to Savile Row right away but' — he glanced at his colleague — 'my sergeant will stay with you. If you don't mind.' The last words were an attempt at sarcasm but they rolled off Freddie's brilliantined black head like water off a duck's back.

'He can take his coat off, then, can't he?' said Freddie. Nothing they could do, either of 'em. Nothing anyone could do. Got 'em all by the short-and-curlies, hadn't he? See 'em suck the juice out of *that*.

'I must ask you to agree not to leave this house, not to attempt to contact any members of your staff, or make any telephone calls. When the time comes, your solicitor. . . .'

Freddie waved both hands. 'Easy on, old mate. Won't do a thing, straight up. Don't need a solicitor, now do I? I mean, don't need anyone. Not now.'

Saturday, 1500

Jack Warrender had spent all morning making his rounds of the
Green and he'd been looking forward to his dinner. He was late
getting in and Arthur had already started. Flo had left a note, it
seemed, saying she was off round to St Olave's to visit young
Paul and she'd left a hotpot in the oven. Seemed funny, her going
to all that trouble with the hospital just around the corner, but
that was women for you. He and Arthur got stuck in.

In a way it was a slice of luck, Flo taking it into her head to
go off like that, because it gave him and Arthur a chance to talk.
Privacy had become a pretty rare commodity in the crowded
little house these past few days. As often happened, they seemed
to have been thinking on the same lines. Derek and Gladys
getting ready to leave the Green had started it off; it was as if
the fact of their going had broken a spell neither man had ever
thought to challenge. They'd be getting out. Shaking the dust.
So – why shouldn't the others? Elsie and Flo. And young Paul,
when they let him out. And Edie and the baby. They'd mulled
it over and Jack remembered his cousin Sid Bartram who had a
little rope and dye works over at Taunton. Sid had done well for
himself and he had a lot of friends around the West Country.
Maybe he could find a place for the women to stay. Jack said
he'd phone him, first chance he got, but Arthur had said what
was wrong with right then, so they'd finished up and gone down
to the phone-box by the church. Sid was a real joy, he was. Got
a cottage, he said, right out in the country with a meadow and a
river on one side and old farm buildings and wheatfields on the
other three. Bit cramped, though, he said, for six people. The
cottage only had six rooms. Cor blimey – six rooms *cramped*!

Their elation lasted as far as the living-room table and the
remains of their Lancashire hotpot. All fine and dandy – except
now they had to tell the women. That clobbered them for a
minute or two because, as Jack said, he and Arthur would have
to stay on in the Green whatever happened, wouldn't they?

Arthur said he wouldn't let down His Nibs — he meant Mr Churchill — for all the tea in China.

They sat there, stumped, for a good twenty minutes; then Arthur pounded the table with his rolled-up fist and said he'd got it. He'd got it, all right. Brainstorm.

They talked it over and examined it every way up and it was still flawless in its guile, harmless in its execution and, best of all, took the whole issue completely out of their hands. They decided to face the women with it tomorrow, giving themselves a full night to sleep on it and rehearse their lines.

That's how they'd left it. Jack felt happier than he'd done for months. Arthur buttoned himself into his uniform and slipped his old black mac over it and set off for the night's work at Storey's Gate. He was looking tired, damn tired, thought Jack, and it was going to catch up with him if they made him work seven nights a week for the rest of the war the way they were doing now. Not that he didn't feel a bit groggy himself, come to think of it.

He was slipping down to Deptford to make his report to Post Warden Braithwaite and he'd got as far as the corner of Roper Street when he came over faint. Not just faint, either. Seeing things. Strewth. He drew a hand across his eyes. Not them bloody voices again! His face was running with sweat. It was all over his hands.

'Hey, dad! Dad, you O.K.?'

His legs buckled and he grabbed at a rainwater pipe on the wall beside him. It was the voices again, all right. Seeing *and* hearing.

'Hey, come on, me old mate. You're out on your feet.' An arm, a strong young arm, encircled his waist and took the weight of him.

He felt the strength and the warmth and he choked out, 'Barry? Is that you, son?' He couldn't help himself; he started to cry. Barry wrapped his other arm round his father and stood there in the open street hugging him.

'Sorry, dad. Sorry, old dad. Tried to get you at the house. Didn't want to give you a turn. I just. . . .'

Jack pulled back and peered through the tears at his son. He grabbed both his hands and held on to them in case they disappeared.

'You young ... pup. Lost me ten years' bloody growth, you have. Young pup.' The relief came up from the pit of his stomach again and overwhelmed him. He buried his face in his hands.

'Hey, dad. Dad! Come on. Sit down.'

The strong hands pulled him a couple of steps forward, then forced him downwards. Barry lowered him on to the kerb and dropped down beside him. 'Gawd, dad. It's been a right bleeding shambollick cock-up, start to finish. I was—'

'Don't matter. Don't matter what it. . . .'

'This sewer went, see. Right behind me. Couldn't see the bugger. I went in arse over tit, right in it. Stink? Strewth, you never in your bloody life smelled anything like it. Anyway, I thought I'd copped it. Just carried me along, see. But they say me oilskins saved me; blew up like a barrage balloon. Would've had it. Couldn't breathe and I was swallowing muck and shit a ton at a time. . . .' He stopped and threw an arm around his father's shoulders. 'Here—you listening, are you, dad?'

Jack nodded dumbly but he didn't raise his head. 'Keep talking, son. I'm listening. Every word.'

Barry gave him a hug. 'Nothing much to tell. River police pulled me out. Drifted about a mile downstream. Next thing I know I'm in hospital. Well, sort of field hospital; place they run up outside of West India Dock to take care of emergency cases. Gave me an injection, didn't they? Out like a light. Come round this morning and they got me in a proper bed in a proper hospital down Plaistow way. Quack comes up to me and calls me Hagan. Hagan this, Hagan that. Know what happened, dad?'

'I'm listening, son.'

'Me bleeding helmet, that's why. Wasn't mine. Hagan was on my team and he had this helmet coupla sizes too small so I swapped it for mine which was three sizes too big for me. Anyway, his helmet was still too big but I never did get round to changing the bugger. That night, out on the fire, my bloody helmet had Terry Hagan's name inside it and his had mine, see? Terry was the body they found with *my* helmet on. They picked him up out of the river and thought it was me. Didn't check up. He'd got stuck on the—'

Jack clutched at his hand. 'I know. We was told.'

Barry said, shame-faced, 'Bloody pantomime, beginning to end, but nothing I could do about it, dad. How'd mum take it?'

Jack pushed himself to his feet, using the boy's shoulder for purchase. 'Your mum', he said mock sternly, 'took it like I did.' He wiped at his tear-stained face with the grimy sleeve of his A.R.P. overalls. 'Bloody liberty, we thought. Both of us. You ever get killed again, you hear me, and I'll take a bloody dim view of it.' The smile sliced his face and he buried his head in Barry's shoulder.

'You know what they say about bad pennies. . . ,' Barry began, but Jack stopped him, pulled away.

He wagged a finger solemnly in his son's face. 'Walking out on your responsibilities, that's what you were doing, all right, young bugger,' he reprimanded. 'Saw that straight off.'

'Eh?'

'Responsibilities. You know what they are, don't you? *Dad.*'

'What d'you mean?'

'You heard, cloth-ears. *Dad*, I said. Responsibilities, a *dad* has.'

'You what?' Barry's slow-spreading grin matched his father's. 'You mean. . . ?'

'Boy,' Jack burst out. 'Lovely little feller. Blue eyes. Lots of hair. Bloody sight better looking than you. Takes after me.'

Jack grabbed at his tin hat but he was too late. Barry snatched it from his head and sent it spinning down the street. It clattered to the ground and rolled clanging into the gutter. Barry scampered into the street after it, plonked it on his head and danced a jig along the pavement.

Jack took the hat off the boy's head and dusted it with the sleeve of his overalls. 'Government property, that,' he grinned.

'A *boy*! How much did he weigh?'

Jack slapped him fondly on the cheek. 'Right bloody father you are. Fat lot of good being dead when your son's born. Had to deliver the little bugger all on me own, didn't I?'

Saturday, 1615

Gladys Warrender reached the public telephone-box by the church, let herself in and paused with her hand on the instrument. For goodness' sake, think again. She thought again; for several minutes. It would do no good; it could make things infinitely worse. After all, he had nothing to lose and she had nothing to gain. He was married and ... perhaps he even had children. What did she expect him to do? The sick longing that had brought her this far was no more than childish curiosity; yes, a need to know, to watch his face while he said what he had to say. Stupid!

She let the pennies fall and dialled the number.

'Yeah.' Terse, unwelcoming. He was probably working.

'It's me. Gladys.'

'Oh!' Unprepared for that. Thought he'd seen the last of her. 'Gladys, I'm sorry about—'

'I don't want you to be sorry. Nothing to be sorry about. I just wondered.... Well, I'm going away tomorrow. To Eastbourne. That's down on the south coast. I don't know when I'll be coming back.'

'I see.'

'I wasn't going to do anything ... call you. Then I thought: that's wrong. I don't like running away from things.'

'I know.' Still no help from him. Didn't he want to finish it properly? Like a man?

She said in a rush, 'I'd like to see you before I go. Today. I just want to....'

'Where are you?'

'Near home. In the phone-box. If you can't get away....'

'No. I'll get away. Can you come up to town?'

'Yes. The buses are....'

There was a smile in his tone. 'Yeah. I know. The buses are still running. Can you meet me at the Savoy, say at six-thirty? Same place?'

'I'd have to borrow one of Janice's dresses.'

'I don't suppose she'd mind. Six-thirty then.' He wanted her to ring off.

'All right. Half past six.' She put the instrument down, clutched her handbag and pushed out into the street. If she cut across the park she could pick up a bus in Jamaica Road. It was too early yet but she could do some window-shopping in the Strand or Piccadilly. Anything to get away from Nelson's Green for a few hours. There was nothing to keep her here.

Derek Scully pinned himself back-to-the-wall like Pat O'Brien did when he tailed James Cagney to the mobster's hideout. What was she up to then? He had seen her leave the house as he mooched back from the hospital for the second time in two days and the temptation to follow her had been far too enticing to resist. Besides, he had a right to know, didn't he? They were going away together, weren't they? They'd see a lot of each other in Eastbourne. He had a right.

She set off towards the park and Derek peeled himself off the wall and tiptoed in her wake, a hundred yards to the rear. She wouldn't even smell him. He would be on her heels every step of the way and she wouldn't even guess.

Crikey! This was turning out to be a real old caper.

Saturday, 1630

Denzil Fletcher-Hale lounged in the small window-seat overlooking the neat lawns and paths of the quadrangle of King's College, a slender glass of amontillado dwarfed in one brown hand. He had a real affection for this place – treacherous as it might be for an Oxford man to admit it, even to himself. He enjoyed coming here. Of course, the setting itself was by no means the prime reason for his feeling of well-being whenever he walked through the gates. He was free here, released. It was. . . .

Henry Chatterton burst through from the staircase and pushed the uneven door shut with a light shoulder charge.

'Damn thing. I really must get the porter to look at that door. Sorry to make you wait, old chap. The cattle were being particularly *faible* this afternoon.'

Chatterton's cattle were the members of his special operations group; men and women handpicked for their muscular and linguistic virtues rather than their academic excellence. They were all young enough to wear the mask of ordinary students but they would graduate in less than a year and pursue their Ph.D course at a large house near Maidenhead. It would involve such fine Italian touches as unarmed combat, knife throwing, garrotting and the use of explosives.

'Oh good. You got yourself a drink.' Chatterton poured a glass of the tawny liquid and dropped his shapelessness into a deep leather chair. He was in his mid-fifties but looked older as all academics look after the first quarter century of drilling learning into reluctant young minds. His long hair was still youthfully golden but he squinted tightly behind pinched round spectacles and his cheeks sagged as if too tired to support the weight of age. He wore a holed grey cardigan over a plaid shirt and a Harris tweed jacket over that. Nothing about him seemed to be co-ordinated; his long legs stretched crookedly in creaseless green trousers and his shoes were an offence to the cobbler's art.

'Sorry about the short notice. Things went rather too well. That fool Dysart got off the mark like a shot and if it hadn't been for the Naval Intelligence chappie — what's his name, Jamieson? — sitting on your file for a couple of days you might have found yourself in the pokey already. Special Branch have been round to your flat this morning. Turned the place upside down, I'm afraid.'

Denzil shrugged. 'Well, it's working, that's the thing.' Me Shaffer would have been stunned at the metamorphosis in Fletcher-Hale's manner and intonation; not to mention Freddie Green, Charles Russell and half of London's clubland-and-cocktail set. 'You know I like coming down here.'

'So you say. Your business, old chap.'

Denzil grinned; it was a simple display of pleasure, not the tortured fixity of expression so familiar to his London acquaintances. 'Our business, Henry. I get home at night sometimes and wonder if I'll ever be able to unfreeze my face again. Or keep it straight when some damn fool asks me a stupid question expecting a stupid answer.'

Chatterton studied his sherry. 'You're not letting it get you down, I hope. Difficult — yes, I'll give you that. But you understood that from the beginning and you've had practice enough since Oxford. Your second year, wasn't it, when Rufus recruited you? That's six years. God — how the time flies.' He snapped out a watch from his breast pocket and flinched at the evidence. 'I've got a group in ten minutes. Can't be long. Keep it short. I suppose you're covered till you get back to London?'

'Too well for comfort, allowing for my role as the amiable dolt. I'm picking up Charles Russell's daughter tomorrow and taking her back to London.'

'They reinstated Russell, I'm told. Bloody mess. So what's so uncomfortable about that? Pretty girl, is she?'

'Never met her. But I'm towing a friend of Shaffer's at the moment. We're putting up for the night at the University Arms.'

'Worried?'

'Only for my virtue. She's a girl. Damned attractive one at that. Try playing the insensitive cold-blooded oaf with a long-legged panting brunette under your nose some day, Henry. You'll split your sides if you don't blow a blood vessel first.'

Chatterton smiled wanly. He had no experience in the field of heterosexual relationships.

'Well, make sure you keep your hands clean. I can't afford upsets just now. All coming together and God help me if it got out that we'd used our own brothers-in-intrigue to get you shipped out. Special Branch'd blow its top right in my face.'

Denzil slid into a lower lounging position and swung one great leg over the other. 'What's the drill?'

'Well.' Chatterton got up to refill his glass. 'We'll shove you on the New York plane on Tuesday morning. Be a little ticklish getting Special Branch to think it was their own idea but leave that to the Home Secretary. I'm afraid we'll have to drag your dear *mère et père* into it; look decidedly odd if the family didn't rally round the son and heir. You won't have to face them, though. We'll spare you that.'

'Thank God,' breathed Denzil. 'Father's bad enough but my mother would swallow the whole of Special Branch at a gulp.'

'The New York side is perfectly straightforward. You won't have a thing to do for the first three days, so play the tourist. Shouldn't be difficult. Look up a few old cronies—I'm sure you have plenty—lunch at the Algonquin; stay on the circuit where you can be seen. On Saturday morning a couple of bruisers will come bashing on your door. Friends of ours—F.D.R.'s personal blessing—but they'll say they're F.B.I. and they'll slip you off to Washington.'

'Awfully cloak-and-dagger, isn't it?'

'You're supposed to be an unsuitable alien at this point, old chap. Just play the fool as usual. They needn't know too much. In Washington you'll be handed over to the Immigration Service, just in case someone's cheeky enough to follow you. They'll take you to Intrepid.'

'Sounds ominous. How intrepid is he?'

'Very. His name is William Stephenson and more than that you needn't know. Suffice to say, he's our key man and he controls everything we've got running over there—interception, decoding, surveillance, strategy, political and public affairs, string-pulling, Press relations, lobbying—the whole shoot.'

'And which of his pockets do I fit into?'

'Maybe all of them—depends the way the wind blows. But Intrepid'll channel you into the Bund. Not straight away, of course. He'll probably float you into the America First movement initially. Your line of country. Big business, the Republican aristocracy. Blue Book people. It'll be up to you to find your way from there to the German Embassy. Shouldn't stretch your resources. They feed out of the same trough these days. Your being booted out of the country should set you up with them very nicely thank you. And play up The Link angle for all you're worth—without dropping that club-headed act of yours, of course. An English blueblood drop-kicked off the home turf for belonging to an anti-semitic organisation isn't a bad qualification; but an anti-semitic blueblood who hasn't brain enough to tell the difference between night and day is even better. The Hun will like that. Your job is to encourage them. The quicker you can get them to use you the better. The moment they start manipulating you against us, you start earning your bread and butter.'

Denzil sipped his amontillado. 'How jolly.'

'It's what you're used to.'

'That's what makes my face ache at the prospect. I was hoping the chinless wonder act was on its way out. Oh well.'

'Won't last for ever.'

'Just the duration.' The young man's smile was wide. 'At least I'll be out of the Dysart–Jamieson–de Wolffe circle. Honestly, Henry, I thought they'd never bite. I don't know what was worse, dangling carrots in front of the Intelligence community or doing the rounds of the services. And as for Freddie Green. . . .'

Chatterton had drifted into a state of mental suspension but he snapped out of it at once. 'Dammit – I knew I'd forgotten something. Green's a dead 'un.'

Denzil closed his eyes in an expression of pained disbelief. 'I don't think I want to know. If you're about to tell me that all those ghastly parties at Greenwich, all that eavesdropping and snooping, all that tittle-tattling behind the backs of the high and the mighty. . . .'

'You're being short-sighted, old chap. You did sterling work there. Essential work. Know thine enemy is a fine sentiment but know thine own is a useful prerequisite. I can appreciate your feelings. I was ready to slip in someone there to replace you but. . . .' He waved his glass dismissively. 'C'est finis.'

'Don't tell me some clod-hopping local bluebottle went tramping in on his size tens and got him for showing lights after dark. Because if they did I think I'll go out and. . . .'

'No. Nothing like that. The idiot was running a gang of kids. Stealing from warehouses. All those goodies he was slipping into our high-falutin' friends' knapsacks. I got a call from London an hour ago. They're mulling it over now.'

'I'm glad I'm going. That could've been messy.'

'It'll be messy anyway. Still – nothing for you to worry about. What time d'you expect to be back in London?'

'Oh, I don't know—four o'clock perhaps. I'm picking up the Russell girl at eleven tomorrow morning. Why?'

Chatterton manufactured a wolfish smile. 'I'll tip off the constabulary. I'd rather they picked you up right away than wait another day. Must have you on that plane on Tuesday.' He stood up, hand out. 'Got to be going. Duty calls.' They shook hands.

'Till the clouds roll by,' Denzil grinned.

'*A bientôt.*'

Chatterton gathered up an armful of books, wrenched open the door and turned thoughtfully.

'You might persuade the American—Shaffer—to let you have a few names. Contacts in New York. Wherever. Might be useful. You never know.'

Denzil nodded. 'I will. I don't see why not. I've already used him, his car and his petrol coupons and now I'm traipsing round the countryside with his girl.'

Chatterton arched a shocked eyebrow, the don incarnate.

'Really, Fletcher-Hale. That's quite indecent. I trust you don't intend using *her*?'

Saturday, 1700

His secretary had gone home and he indulged himself with the mild panacea of irritation at her lack of consideration. It was unreasonable of him, he knew; he had telephoned from Bletchley to say he would be late, if he actually came back to the office at all, but a secretary had a moral responsibility to support her superior at all times. It was well known throughout the ministry that he made no allowances for himself; Charles Russell was a synonym for blind commitment to duty. She should have waited.

He offloaded his coat and hat and carried his briefcase to the desk. The visit to Bletchley had, of course, been precipitated by personal motives, but Winterbotham, Caroline's chief, had gone out of his way to make things extraordinarily easy for him and their conversation had led on to more critical matters. The Scientific Intelligence Unit, under Winterbotham's direction, was playing with a set of variables which could—the scientist emphasised the tenuous nature of the game — *could* lead to their using Enigma for what Winterbotham termed 'diversionary measures'. He wanted more scientists, four at least, men who had been engaged in university research projects involving the orientation of high-frequency radio beams. Russell had promised his help as a recruiting officer.

He shuffled the contents of his case into a neat bundle and locked them in the wall-safe beside the desk. He looked at his watch; Fletcher-Hale would be in Cambridge; he had told Elizabeth he would be putting up for the night at the University Arms and would collect Caroline for an early start on Sunday morning. Russell pondered. He ought to call Elizabeth. His hand hovered over the telephone. No! It was early enough to make plans for the evening. Take her out. Dinner. Yes. Dinner. That little French place she liked off Piccadilly. What was it? La Petite Estelle. As his hand closed on the telephone it rang shrilly. He snatched it up.

'Russell.'

'Thought you'd still be there, Russell. Beaverbrook.'

Russell's sensation of well-being and simmering goodwill evaporated instantly.

'Can I help you, minister?' he asked stiffly.

'Hey — this is a friendly call, Charles. Don't give me the freeze before you hear me out.' Was that irony? Sarcasm?

'I really don't know what you mean, minister.' He would give no ground to this man.

'Look, Charles — you mind if I call you Charles? — I had a chance to talk with my boys about that Spitfire modification idea. They tell me it's pure fruit sauce. Well, I'm not a man who can sit on his pride when he's in the wrong. So make the most of it — I'm trying to say I should've listened to you the other day instead of bawling you out. You were right, I was wrong.'

Russell's surprise was genuine. He was at a loss for something to say. 'That's really very ... kind of you, minister. But I'm sure I was at fault myself. I'd had a rather difficult few days and—'

'Sure. Sure. I guess we've talked that side of it out, right? I saw the test-flight rundown on the Beaufighter today and that kind of puts the whole thing in a different perspective. That plane's about to change the course of night fighting, Charles. You can quote me. Goering's on ice till he can come up with something better. He won't know what's hit him.'

'That's excellent, sir. I'm delighted.'

Beaverbrook hesitated and it came to Russell in a flash that the conversation so far had been only an excuse for what was to come. He steeled himself.

'Look – er – Charles. . . . About your boy.'

'Ian?' The word was out before he could control it.

'Right. I read the story but it didn't mean anything to me till yesterday. Came up in conversation with Christiansen – you know my editor at the *Express*? He was talking about doing some kind of follow-up but I told him to lay off. Thought you'd prefer it that way.'

Charles Russell's breath escaped through his teeth. 'That was very thoughtful indeed. I don't think it would do the boy any good, in the circumstances, to—'

'You don't have to say it. I'm a father myself. But you've got reason to be proud of that boy. It took a hell of a lot of guts to do what he did.'

'Yes. We're . . . his mother and I are very proud. It hasn't been easy for him.'

'Nothing about war's easy, Charles. You've had your share of problems. Winston told me yesterday about your . . . set-to with the Security people. I told him he should have come to me right away. I'd've told the sonsofbitches where to put their goddamn investigation. I want you to know, me to you, that there's nobody I trust more in this war than you. You hear that?'

'You're very . . . very generous, minister. I—'

'Keep in touch, Charles. We've got a lot to do this winter, you and me. And let me know how that "seeing eye" gadget works out in the Beaufighter. We're going to need it.'

He rang off abruptly.

Russell called Elizabeth at once.

'Oh, darling—' she began, but he cut in.

'Lord Beaverbrook has just been on the telephone. He'd heard about Ian. Elizabeth, he was *extremely* complimentary. I must say, after the way he— He apologised, too. You see — it's all coming out right, just as I said it would. At Bletchley, last night, Winterbotham was kindness itself. Said he understood completely and we weren't to worry. He said he had complete faith in Caroline and when she's ready to go back to work—'

'Charles!' There was a break in her voice; tears.

'What is it? What is it?' Oh God, not more.

'Oh, Charles — Ian's—'

'What's wrong with him?' He had a nightmare vision; a bomb, the boy's mutilated body, blood.

'He's all right, dear. He . . . he's joined the army.'

Russell gaped at the receiver as if it had come alive in his hand. 'He's what?'

'He's joined the army. Well, he's been to a recruiting office in Victoria. Tom took him yesterday. He signed some papers and he — Charles, he said he'd wanted to do it for weeks. Darling, I don't know what to think, I really don't. Tom says it's what he wants but he's such a baby and. . . .'

'If it's his decision then we have to accept it.' He was afloat with elation. It was unworthy of him but he couldn't help conjuring with the prospect of telling Beaverbrook. He had that opportunity now, of course. Keep in touch, Beaverbrook had said. It had been a social invitation as much as a pact between professionals.

'Oh, darling, I know. It's just that, coming on top of everything else. . . .'

'What else?' That unspeakable fear again; a spectre rising from the back of his skull.

'It was just after you left the house yesterday. Elsie had a phone call from her husband. Their son Paul . . . such a little boy . . . he was caught in an air-raid.'

'Is he alive?' He would never be able to face Elsie Warrender again if the child was dead.

'Yes. Mr Shaffer drove us all down to the hospital in Southwark Park. He's very badly injured but the doctors say he'll mend. Mr Fletcher-Hale came with us too. You really must thank both of them, Charles. I don't know what I'd have done if they hadn't been here. Elsie was a *ghost*.'

He dropped with relief into the chair. 'I should have come home last night, but you know how important I thought it was to talk with Winterbotham about Caroline. My secretary *did* call you, didn't she?'

Elizabeth, her burdens shed, was becoming more herself. 'Yes, of course she did, dear. I'm sorry, but I've been waiting all day for you to call. I suppose I've just got things out of perspective. I wanted you to talk to Ian, you see. I just couldn't grasp what he'd done. I thought, "He's done it for us. He's done it because he thinks we're ashamed of him." It kept going round and round in my head.'

'He wouldn't,' Russell said emphatically. 'He wouldn't do that. Not even for us.'

'He doesn't seem to want to talk about it. He went to his room when they got back and I think he was writing letters. Then Tom went back to Bentley Priory and Ian went to the station with him. He must have come back before he went to the hospital last night because his bike was here, but I didn't see him. And I haven't seen him at all today. He must have left the house before nine. Oh, Charles, I've been so worried.'

'Now you listen to me,' he said firmly. 'It's nearly ten to six. I want you to get yourself ready. I'll be home in twenty minutes if I can get a car. Run me a bath and get out my dinner jacket. We're eating out tonight.'

'But Ian—'

'Ian's just proved to both of us that he's a man, my darling. Don't give him cause to regret it. He'll be perfectly happy on his own. He's got a lot to think about. Anyway — when was the last time I took you out?'

'I don't know. Months, I suppose. Oh, Charles, do you think you should?'

'Not a matter of thinking about it. I've already booked a table,' he lied.

'Where?' At the greatest moment of crisis in her life, Elizabeth would always have time to consider social detail.

'La Petite Estelle.'

'Charles, that's lovely!'

All wounds were breached, the battle won. He would have

wagered a fortune her mind had emptied of all unrelated matter to make way for the supreme task of deciding what to wear.

'Darling, you could have given me more notice,' she scolded, but she was talking now only to fill the gaps between her own thoughts. 'You'd better come along home, then. I'll begin running the bath at about six-fifteen.'

'Why don't you wear that dark-blue thing you bought in Paris last year?' he said with a grin. 'It cost me a fortune.'

Saturday, 1845

The foyer of the Savoy Hotel was already crowded with dinner-jacketed and uniformed men and their evening-gowned women, and the halfway house of the tea lounge echoed with their light-hearted chatter. Gladys was marooned in the same overhung corner. She was more than just uncomfortable; she was alarmed. She hadn't expected this high tide of celebrants. Shaffer took half a dozen strides towards her before he noticed the dress. He winced. It was the clinging yellow creation Janice had worn on the afternoon of their matinée performance under the table.

She got to her feet as he approached.

'Sorry I'm late,' he said quickly. 'I was at the B.B.C. You want to go somewhere else? I forgot they started early here.'

'No. It's all right. I thought you might have got held up. All these people....' She looked around her. 'I feel so—'

He put a hand on her arm and she withdrew it instantly. 'Let's sit down. Would you like a drink?'

'No. I can't be too long. I ought to be back to help mum and Aunt Flo.' There she went again; rushing him. Making it difficult. Why did she have to say that? Mum and Aunt Flo wouldn't need her.

He said gently, 'I'm sorry you have to leave.'

'It's best.' She sighed. 'I wanted to tell you it doesn't matter ... what happened. I wanted to....'

He leaned forward urgently, his voice low. 'Don't go. Stay where you belong. If you're worried about my butting in where

I'm not wanted, I'll keep to my own neck of the woods. You don't have to go.'

She smiled nervously. 'No. I have to go. It's all fixed up.'

'Unfix it.'

'Why?' That unflinching honesty of hers was harrowing.

'Because ... look, Gladys. I don't have the right to ask anything. I—'

'Do you have children as well?' Bull's eye.

'Yeah,' he sighed, and fished for a cigarette to give his hands something to do. 'Two boys. Ten and four.'

She nodded; swallowed hard. Of course he had children. 'I didn't want to phone at first. I wasn't going to but when I thought about going away tomorrow....' She blinked hard, crushing back the tears.

'You could stay ... with me.' He hadn't meant to say it, and regretted doing so the moment the words came out, but she saved him further self-deception by shaking her head vigorously.

'You don't mean that, Mel. Don't say what you don't mean. Please!'

He hunched back in the chair and started a mental hate campaign for the happy, relaxed evening-outers thronging the tables around them. They'd be going into dinner soon, their priorities neatly arranged; wine, song and, later, the other side of the triangle.

'I meant it,' he growled stubbornly. 'I'm not trying to say I could do anything about—'

'Your wife and children?' God — why did she have to lay it on the line in all its naked inevitability?

'Yeah.'

She looked around her to make sure she was not being over-heard. 'If things were different....' She slid a small white-gloved hand across the table and caught his. 'I'd say yes.' She made a face, tried a smile. 'There. Now you really know what sort of a girl I am.'

'Then why... ?'

The gloved hand reached up and touched his lips, silencing him. 'I didn't say that for the reason you're thinking. I wanted you to know....' The hand dropped and so did her eyes. 'I wanted you to know I really meant it when I said I . . . loved you.' The eyes came up again to find his. 'I do love you, Mel. I wouldn't care if . . . knowing you had to go back to your family. I'd just stay with you till you had to go.' Her eyes drifted out over the waiting diners. 'But I've got mum and dad to think of.'

'You could—'

'I couldn't do anything. And I'm not going to.' She looked around for her handbag and bent to take it from the floor by her chair. 'I just wanted you to know, that's all.' She began to rise.

'Wait!' He grabbed her hand and pulled her back into the chair. 'Just . . . just have one drink. Stay another five minutes. I promise. Just one drink.'

She smiled. 'All right. Just one drink.'

He signalled for the waiter.

When Gladys turned into the courtyard approach to the Savoy Derek stopped. Bugger it—what was she going in there for? He looked down at his pressed grey flannels and his Fair Isle pullover and judged shrewdly that he had as much chance getting through those revolving doors as he had of paying his way inside. He should've brought that twenty-five nicker he had hidden in the copper, he thought. A crisp oncer in the hand could do miracles with lah-di-dah doormen, even in a place like this. Still. . . . He looked around him enviously at the huge gleaming limousines and the elegant twerps they were disgorging at the hotel entrance. One day, mate, he told himself; one bloody day he'd be up here stepping out of a Rolls himself. One day. . . .

His wandering eye crystallised on a face just across the courtyard on the corner of the Strand. The man was dressed in his Sunday best, easy enough to see that, but his Sunday best was East End. So was his face. With a little jolt of surprise Derek recognised him. Tubby Rosen! What the hell was he doing here?

Now there was a turn-up. George 'Tubby' Rosen was chairman of the Stepney Tenants' Defence League, a known Communist and one of the loudest voices raised against the government in the face of Hitler's bombing of the East End. Agitator, Derek's dad called him. Bloody Bolshevik. Derek had heard Tubby Rosen working up the crowds down Stepney way and Wapping and Canning Town and Silvertown — all the places where the bombing was worst and the people suffered most. He'd had willing ears to preach to, as well, and not just because of the bombing alone. Down West Ham, the borough council was socialist through and through and what Arthur Scully termed 'bloody pacifists, the lot of 'em'. The borough council had refused to build shelters in advance in the holy name of turning the other cheek so the people who lived there had caught it proper when the bombs began to fall. Tubby and his mate Phil Piratin, another Communist who was a member of Stepney Council, had found out that the government had been stockpiling papier mâché coffins around the East End in town halls and warehouses, just waiting for the worst; and outside London they'd had pits dug and tons of quicklime stored for mass graves. Phil and Tubby had gone bonkers when they heard that and they hadn't worried about keeping it quiet, either.

Derek had heard one of Tubby's speeches down on the Commercial Road only the other day. It was about 'the bosses' war', as Tubby called it. 'Our people are dying like rats down here,' Tubby had yelled to the gathering, 'because the Tory bosses refused to spend money to build us proper deep shelters, while the government and their girl-friends sleep cosy in double beds, two to a compartment, in deep shelters! Comrades, it's about time we took 'em over.' Tubby knew all the griff about what was going on up West. Come to think of it, he even mentioned the Savoy; that and the other hotels. He said they laid on special shelters underground for their clients, all fancy and done up like bedrooms.

Tubby directed a final searching look at the crowds, then turned and scooted along the Strand. Derek, on impulse, followed him, saw him duck down the steep gradient of Savoy Hill.

Derek followed him right around the block and came out in the sweeping curve that ran in front of the Embankment entrance to the hotel. Derek pulled up in surprise. Blimey! There were about a hundred people just waiting on the pavement there, just down from the door. East Enders, the lot; a few kids among them and some women who looked as if they were heavily pregnant and a couple even carrying babies in their arms. He crept up and slipped into the crowd. And at that moment the siren sounded.

There was no time to ask questions; it seemed like they'd been waiting for the siren because there was a great cheer and Tubby Rosen shouted from the front, 'O.K., comrades. In we bloody go!'

The crowd surged around the entrance and a grey and gold uniformed doorman held out his arms wide. 'That's enough,' he yelled. 'You can't come in here.'

'That's where you're bloody wrong, mate,' shouted a voice. Phil Piratin, Derek judged. He got his elbows working and burrowed to the front rank of the mêlée. Phil was standing with his hands on his hips, eye to eye with the doorman. 'If you want to know,' Phil roared in his speechifying voice so everyone could hear, 'there's a law what says you have to give people shelter when the siren goes. That's government law.'

The doorman looked as if he'd swallowed a hot potato whole. 'This is a hotel, friend,' he said reluctantly. 'You can't come in here. There's a public shelter along the way. You go—'

'We're bloody coming in here,' bellowed Tubby Rosen and he waved his arm and shoved one of the pregnant women in front of him. The doorman caved in at once. Derek was on Tubby's heels and burst through into the foyer. Straight away a couple of the women whipped out ropes and a man shackled them to two pillars. The rest of them milled around in the hallway and Phil started up chanting, 'We want shelter! We want shelter!' They all joined in and so did Derek. He was enjoying himself better than he had for years. What a bloody lark this turned out to be!

There was a scuffling of feet on the carpeted stairs and half a dozen nobs in black jackets and striped trousers came down all at once in a bunch. One of them, obviously the boss because he looked like the Lord Mayor of London or a duke or something, tried to talk to Tubby but Tubby wouldn't stop chanting; then some of the scruffs nearest the door went quiet and they all turned round to see a police sergeant and three bluebottles come in from the Embankment.

At this Phil started chanting even louder and that gave the rest of them courage. The toff went over to the police sergeant and Derek wriggled through the crush to hear what they said.

The toff said, 'I'm Hugh Wontner, the managing director here. Can't you do something about this, sergeant?' Derek was disappointed. The toff didn't seem a bit scared; just sort of cheesed off.

Phil Piratin suddenly waved his arms for quiet and everyone stopped chanting. The sergeant's voice came over loud and clear.

'You're a hotel, you see, sir,' he said firmly. 'You come under the Innkeeper's Act. If a *bona fide* traveller comes in and asks for a meal — and these people look like *bona fide* travellers to me — then you're obliged to serve 'em. Now, if they're making a row or breaking things or causing a disturbance, we'll escort them out. Otherwise they're clients of the hotel and should be treated as such.'

Some of the women up front started shouting, 'We're hungry. We want something to eat,' and Tubby shouted, 'This way. Let's go and surprise the Archbishop of Canterbury and his girl-friend in *flagrante* bloody *delicto*.'

They charged off and Derek swerved through the stragglers to join them. Behind him he heard the toff say, 'Very well. Perhaps the rest of you would come with me.'

Tubby headed into a bar and as they came in a bunch of blokes standing around having drinks stopped and stared at them. They looked funny; their suits were different to the toffs' and the East Enders', and Derek remembered the American who'd copped him and Paul down the docks on Saturday. Yeah, they were Americans all right.

There wasn't much happening in the bar so Tubby shooed them all out again and they followed the stream being led downstairs by the toff. Phil was up front when the toff opened a door and led them into a huge room decked out like a shelter but fantastically comfortable with bits portioned off and little bunks inside. Derek read the little cards fixed to the partitions. The Duke and Duchess of Kent, said one. Lady Diana Cooper, said another. Blimey!

'If you would be good enough to wait here,' said the toff, 'I'll see to it you all have a cup of tea.' But that wasn't good enough for Phil. He obviously knew the lie of the land because he grabbed a couple of the women and shouted, 'This way!'

The toff tried to reason with them but Phil and half a dozen others shot across the underground shelter and made for a door on the far side. Derek nipped after them smartly, determined not to miss the fun. He slipped through the door and pulled it shut behind him.

Strewth! It was a huge room and there were tables all around and hundreds of people in fancy clothes were sitting there and about fifty were dancing in the middle. An orchestra was playing and Derek twigged it with great awe – cor, that's Carroll Gibbons, that is. He knew about Carroll Gibbons and the Savoy Orpheans. Everyone did. They played on the wireless all the time, 'direct from the ballroom of the Savoy Hotel'. He was an American band-leader, Carroll Gibbons, and really famous. They had two pianos; one played by Carroll himself and the other by Ian Stewart. That was on the wireless too. Derek held his breath; they might even see the singers; George Melachrino and Ann Lenner. Tell *that* to Paul bloody Warrender and let him stuff it up his pipe! Better than any stupid bomb.

Phil was raising his voice but only a few people near the door seemed to have heard him and when one of the pregnant women grabbed a waiter and shrieked about wanting a table and something to eat, her voice was drowned by a crackle of applause and the band played a big chord and a bloke in a black suit and bow-tie came on and started talking. Everyone sat down and the band took up a tune and the announcer said, 'Ladies and gentlemen, Vic Oliver!'

Vic Oliver! Derek hugged himself in a delicious agony of excitement. Vic Oliver. There wasn't anyone didn't know *him* – he was on the wireless even more than Carroll Gibbons. Nearly as funny as Tommy Handley, Vic Oliver was. Yeah – and there was that fiddle he always played in his act.

The comedian bowed, studied his audience and drew the bow speculatively across the strings of his violin. The instrument whined like a kicked dog and everyone laughed. Phil Piratin didn't laugh. He shouted at the top of his voice, 'Why don't you go back to Germany, you bleeding Kraut!'

The comedian lifted the bow from the fiddle and peered out over the footlights into the darkness. He put out his tongue.

'Thank you, Sir Adrian Boult,' he gagged. The whole room dissolved in laughter and Derek saw Phil's face go taut.

'Capitalist vermin!' shouted Phil. 'Safe in your bloody hole while they're burning the East End. You wait and bloody see. Our time'll come. And you won't—'

'I've heard of first-night nerves,' drawled Oliver, smoothly, 'but this is ridiculous. If you want to sing, Sir Adrian, give me a tune I can play.' The cheers that followed were thunderous and Phil swore and jerked open the door back into the shelter. Derek followed them out reluctantly with Vic Oliver's voice at his heels, 'Forgive him, ladies and gentlemen. He's so shy about asking me for advice. Now I've come here tonight to introduce a little number I rattled off in my bath this morning. I call it Beethoven's Ninth Symphony after my beagle-hound, Fritz Beethoven, who....'

It was all caving in; Derek could see that right away. The women stood around looking like they wished they'd never come and Tubby Rosen was making speeches at the hotel toffs in black jackets and trousers. Phil went up to Tubby and grabbed his arm and pulled him aside and Derek heard Tubby say, 'We should've waited till later on when they was all down the shelter. No bloody good if the place is empty, is it? I vote we go.'

And there was no argument. Phil said, 'We did what we come here to do. You're right. Let's go. We can call the newspapers later.'

They had finished the martinis Shaffer ordered and he had persuaded her to have another. They heard the shouting but paid no attention to it at first; it seemed a long way away and they had other things on their minds. The waiter who brought the refill bent to Shaffer's ear discreetly.

'I apologise, sir, for the — ah — disturbance.'

Shaffer looked up. 'What is it?'

'A number of persons came into the river entrance a while ago, sir. But there's no cause for concern.'

Gladys leant forward. 'Who?'.

The waiter looked pained. 'East End persons, I'm told, madam. I gather it's in the way of being a demonstration.'

Shaffer flipped a note on to the table. Gladys was already on her feet. 'Thanks,' he said. 'We won't need the drinks.'

In the lobby Shaffer saw Larry LeSueur and went over to him. He was surrounded by half a dozen men Shaffer recognised as Fleet Street news-hawks.

'What's the commotion?' he asked.

One of the newsmen broke in. 'Tubby Rosen and Phil Piratin —couple of our pet Bolsheviks. They tipped us off they were going to invade the place. Silly beggars went in the back way and the hotel won't let us down there.'

'Then let's tell 'em we want in,' Shaffer snapped.

'Easy, Mel.' LeSueur laid a hand on his arm. 'The fun's over. One of the assistant managers just told me they're on their way out. Don't waste your breath. This is one story even Knickerbocker won't get past the censor.'

Shaffer grinned. 'Right. Er. . . .' He turned to find Gladys. There was no sign of her. He slammed the flat of his hand on his thigh. She was the last girl in the world to turn down in face of a story. A goddamn stupid story he couldn't even file!

She got through the lines of defence by claiming her mother was among the invaders downstairs and she wanted to persuade her to leave. They thought that was a good idea. When she reached the rear-entrance foyer the crowd had left. Some of them still stood on the pavement outside, talking excitedly about what they'd done and seen, but it was getting quite dark and the bulk of them were trailing away to a deep shelter down the road.

She had to run to them with an excess of East Ender's fellow feeling; an urge to help, pacify, sympathise, but now it seemed a waste of time. She thought about going back to Shaffer. No — there was nothing more to be said. Last goodbyes were awful and she might cry again. She couldn't do that to him.

She went out on to the pavement and thought seriously for a

moment of going to the shelter with the invaders but decided against it. She turned towards Savoy Hill but a face caught her eye in the half light across the street and she turned to stare.

Derek!

He was never part of *this*, surely? She opened her mouth to call his name but thought better of it. He was in trouble again, a pound to a penny. And there was Aunt Flo back at Edie's, not knowing. Well, there was nothing else to do. She couldn't leave him alone but she couldn't make herself known, either. She would just have to keep an eye on him from a distance. It was the least she could do.

Saturday, 2025

They'd switched off poor old Piccadilly Circus and taken Eros away from his perch in the middle of it to keep him safe till the war was over, but Derek felt an undeniable thrill as he and Harry Killingbank came into the circle from Lower Regent Street. He was a right gent, old Harry. They'd met up at the shelter and were thinking of going down with the rest of the retreating invasion party when Harry said only rats belonged down holes and why didn't they take a gander up the West End while they had the chance.

Right you are, Derek had said, quick as a flash, and Harry had told him not to worry about spending-money because he just got paid yesterday and he had a pocket full of ackers. They were companions-in-arms, after all, said Harry, and if a bloke couldn't buy a comrade a drink after what they'd been through there wasn't much point, was there?

There was a lot of traffic about, buses and taxis and big cars full of people like they'd seen up the Savoy, but the 'All Clear' hadn't gone yet and they both heard the guns banging away downriver and saw the flashes in the sky where the bombs were dropping. They didn't care. They'd been through it, hadn't they? Thick and thin. Take more than a couple of bombs to frighten *them*.

They crossed the circus and Harry dug Derek in the ribs and

said how would he fancy a bit of arse. Plenty down Brewer Street, he said. Prostitutes lining the walls from end to end and they didn't care about the bombing, either. With a bit of luck they could find one to give 'em both a jig; one price for two short times. Derek said that would be a real giggle and they walked on more urgently, their appetites rising.

Gladys stopped to gentle the heel in her shoe; it was rubbing painfully and she could feel a blister developing. She sensed the man before she even saw him or heard his voice and straightened so fast the bones of her back clicked.

'Where you going then?' said the voice. He was a sailor; young and ridiculous in his new cross-creased bell bottoms and his saucily angled hat. H.M.S. *Swiftsure* said the legend in gold around the hat-brim.

'I'm waiting for my husband,' she said at once. 'Don't you dare....'

'Strewth! Sorry, miss.' The sailor took a step back as if warding off a blow. 'I thought you....'

'I know what you *thought*,' she snapped sarcastically.

She peered round him and watched Derek and the other man push through a pub doorway.

'You shouldn't be left waiting out here,' said the young matelot protectively. 'Don't know who might come along.'

'I'm all right. You just go about your business,' she said. He was easy to deal with. Probably seeing Soho for the first time. Whoever picked him up tonight would fleece him of every penny he had, silly young fool. They all had to learn the hard way.

He swung his hand to his hat-brim in a little salute. 'As long as you'll be all right,' he muttered, backing away.

Can't stand around here, she thought when the darkness swallowed him up. Must keep moving; look as if I'm going somewhere. She set off briskly along Brewer Street, head down, coat pulled around her. This was the wrong dress to wear in a place like Soho, she meditated, touching Janice's clinging yellow silk. Open invitation to some people. She reached the end of the street and turned again. Not quite so fast on the way back. If they came out as she reached the pub there'd be hell to pay. Derek would cause a scene. He'd love that.

On her fifth consecutive passage along the street she began to panic. This was terrible. What if a policeman stopped her and asked her what she was up to? What if one of those evil painted faces in the doorways followed her and accused her of trespassing on other people's territory? It would be so embarrassing. And what if...?

The doors of the pub were suddenly flung wide and voices erupted into the night. She heard Derek before she saw him, backing away, fists flying. The other man came out backwards all of a rush, trod awkwardly on the edge of the kerb and sat down with an oath in the gutter.

'Bleeding capitalist shit!' he roared at the closing doors of the pub.

'Come out and fight like bloody men, you scum!' bawled Derek.

But nobody answered the invitation and Derek helped his friend to his feet and brushed him down. After a while they started to giggle and then they laughed as though the joke were on the drinkers inside. They slapped arms around each other's shoulders and lumbered away in the opposite direction to Gladys's patrol, singing 'Show me the way to go home,' in loud, vulgar voices, pretending to be drunk.

Oh, that *Derek*. Just wait till she got him home and told Uncle Arthur. She set off after them, taking care to reduce the clicking of her heels on the pavement to a minimum. They staggered the length of the street, elbowing passers-by off the pavement, interrupting the song from time to time to roar with inane glee at people who crossed the street ahead of them to avoid a confrontation. They turned left into Wardour Street and she gave them time to get away before she turned the corner. They were a long way ahead, about a hundred yards; she couldn't see them but she could hear them. They stopped to argue heatedly with one of the prostitutes in a doorway but apparently drew no satisfaction from the exchange because they began shouting obscenities and the woman clacked away hurriedly down a side-street.

From a long way behind Gladys there came a thundering of anti-aircraft guns and the whoo-whoo-whoo whine of Dorniers and the kindling-snap of incendiaries. She clung to the wall but hurried on, trying to keep Derek in view. She saw them suddenly dive to the left as if they had made a last-minute decision not to go on and when she reached the corner they had disappeared. She ran thirty yards to yet another corner and heard their voices again; they had turned into the narrow canyon of Berwick Street and were upbraiding another lady of the night when the plane roared over, almost at roof height. It left a clatter of incendiaries behind it but their spitting explosions were drowned by another plane roaring low on the tail of the first. Then two more, then. . . .

Derek and his drinking partner were dancing in the middle of the street, their arms raised, fists clenched, screaming at the planes, their insane cavortings illuminated by a blinding greenish-white glare where an incendiary had ignited in the gutter of a low roof. Then Derek and the man and the road beneath them and the rambling old buildings on either side disappeared in one booming, ear-splitting gulp of sound. They just disappeared as if they had been shadows on a screen erased by light.

Then the blast reached her and hurled her across the street into the gutter and the sky rained brick and glass and wood.

She tried to shout his name but nothing would come out and she scrambled to her feet and stumbled into the dust-cloud and the crackling furnace-heat of smoke. For a moment it cleared, swirled away on an eddy of self-generated wind, and she stopped. The buildings had been blown away. Just blown away.

And in the street where Derek and his friend had been there was only a vast smoke-belching hole licked by flame-tongues.

They'd just evaporated as if they'd never been there at all.

Saturday, 2100

The party, as usual, was going with a swing and the young detective sergeant showed signs of wishing he could join in; at least go out to the big room and have a look. But that would have been against orders. Freddie Green had a pretty good idea what Detective Inspector Trotter had whispered to him before he left for Savile Row. Freddie had had to go to the lavatory a couple of times and the sergeant had insisted on standing right outside the door so it made sense he wasn't going to leave him alone for a sec. Well; didn't matter. He still wasn't planning on running anywhere. No need.

About an hour ago the double doors of the music room had burst open with a wham of exploding energy and a line of young R.A.F. lads had come charging through dancing their own version of the Carmen Miranda conga. The young sergeant must have come close to having a heart attack because he came out of his chair like a stuck pig, shaking all over with shock. The lads danced on round the room, shouting to Freddie to tag on the end of the line, but the detective moved across to make sure he didn't and when they conga-d back out again into the hall he closed and locked the doors.

Freddie lit his tenth cigar. He wasn't smoking every one all the way down but it gave him something to do, clipping the ends off and balancing the length of them in his fingers. When the cigars got small it somehow made him feel small, so he chucked them in the fireplace and started another.

The doors bulged, without sound this time, then settled back again. There was a discreet knock and the sergeant went to the door. A voice came from the other side and he unlocked them at once.

Trotter was not alone. There was an officer in uniform with him; one of the big boys, Freddie decided, from the silver braid on his peaked cap and the lumps of silver on his epaulettes. Behind him were two men in lounge suits; both were middle-aged and grey with faces harder than Freddie's marble busts.

Trotter came in and stood on one of the tiger-skins. He waved to the two men behind him. 'These gentlemen would like to talk to you, Mr Green.' He stepped back respectfully. Freddie noted that the red leather visitors' book was trapped under the uniformed officer's arm.

'Albert Edward Green?' one of the terrible twins opened.

'You a rozzer?' Freddie shot back.

'We're not policemen, no,' said the other. They seemed to have a gentleman's agreement about who should talk and when.

'You've told this officer the history of your – er – hospitality in this house,' said Tweedledee, the one who'd spoken first. 'You offer that book' – he pointed at the red leather tome – 'to corroborate your claim. Is that true?'

'I'm saying, son,' Freddie grinned, 'that there's been a lot of high-ups been taking stolen goods when they've come here. They're all in the book. Matter of fact, if you was to go out in the big room – that's what we call the ballroom here – you'll like as not see one or two of 'em in there, knocking back the booze and having a good time. Why don't you go have a look? Ask them, if you like.'

'We've been into the ballroom,' said Tweedledum severely, as if the remark were an imputation of inefficiency.

'Then you've seen, haven't you?'

'Why did you keep this record?' Tweedledee.

'Insurance, son,' winked Freddie. 'Fire, accident, flood, tempest and the old Act of God.'

'You were contemplating blackmail?' Tweedledum.

'Leave orf!' Freddie was amused. 'Blackmail? Why'd I want to blackmail my mates? You tell me, son. Like that, we are, me and them gents in that book. Come here more'n once, all of 'em. You take a gander down them pages and you'll see. Come back all the time, don't they? Mates, see.'

Dum and Dee looked at each other sadly.

'You sought pecuniary gain?' Tweedledee.

'Come again?'

Tweedledum translated. 'Were you hoping to persuade the – er – gentlemen to whom you made gifts to afford you certain considerations? Create business opportunities for you?'

Freddie shook with amusement. 'How's a general supposed to give me a leg-up in business, eh? You think fighter pilots got money to throw around? Strewth, you don't know much, do you?'

'You realise the seriousness of your proposition, I trust, Mr

Green.' Tweedledee showed signs of heading towards an arrange‐
ment.

Freddie did his best to help. 'Well, son. I'll tell you. You an
me are men of the world. We can see situations clear, right
Now if I was in your shoes, being a man of the world like, I'
ask myself : What's going to happen when old Freddie here goe
up before the beak — saying, as it might be, at the Bailey — an
they asks him about his giving all this stuff what got nicked t
blokes who're the cream-of-the-cream, leaders of the countr
and running the army and the navy and the air force. Well, fas
as you like, the old beak's going to say : Who are these bloke:
then? What are their names? Stands to reason, dunnit? Gott
come out. Bound to. Wouldn't be right otherwise.' He touche
his nose with a magisterial finger. 'Wouldn't be serving justic
would it? *That's* what you've got to consider, being a man of th
world. Big case it'd be, I'd say. Newspapers there in hundred
every day, picking out new names; wondering who's next. Ca
see it, can't you? Stands to reason.'

Tweedledum and Tweedledee studied each other, their e:
pressions of alarm perfectly matched. They turned to the un
formed officer and he looked like he'd swallowed a razor blad
Inspector Trotter was trying not to appear as if he wanted t
say 'I told you so.'

'Mr Green,' Tweedledee said at last. 'You are making som
very serious imputations here on the characters of gentleme
held in the highest regard in public life. Your accusations ma
be true. They may not. What is important, however — *critical* –
is that this country is at war. The normal processes of law an
order cannot be expected to function at their normal ... er –
pace. It would be invidious, mortally — er. . . .'

'Wounding,' offered Tweedledum.

'Wounding — er — to the war effort if your — um — reckless sug
gestions were made public. My colleague and I—'

'Have considered your case thoroughly in the past few hours'
interposed Tweedledum quickly. 'It's clear to us and our princ
pals that the matter must be considered under the requirement
of the Official Secrets Acts—'

'Contravention of which,' Tweedledee added nastily, 'in time of war, carries the ultimate penalty.'

'Death,' intoned his twin.

Freddie's face flushed with good humour. 'Right you are, gents. Just what I thought. Question now is — where?'

They looked at each other doubtfully.

'Where?'

'S'right. Where? Australia? South Africa? South America? Where you gonna stick me away then? Seems to me you wouldn't want me hanging around dear old Blighty, now would you? Might talk, eh? Might get pissed one night and blab it all over the place. Can't be sure, can you? Gotta keep me tucked somewhere safe, I'd say.'

The two men shared another agonised glance. 'Ireland,' said Tweedledum.

'North or South?' queried Freddie.

'North, of course,' snapped Tweedledee.

Freddie lay back in his chair and sucked on the cigar expansively. 'Not bad, I s'pose. Bloody raining half the time but not bad. Got interests in the Province ... but I s'pose you know that. Useful. Got to have a base, haven't I? Can't run me business over here without having a base. Right?' He eyed them coolly.

Tweedledum nodded resignedly.

'Thought you'd see it my way, son. All for the best, I always say. After all, I'm in the war effort, I am. Don't want to bugger up the war effort, do we?'

Saturday, 2240

Shaffer slopped another four fingers of Johnnie Walker into the glass and fumbled for his handkerchief as the overspill spread on to the copy-paper beside him on the table. The paper was empty; his head was full but the whirling images up there defied captivity and translation. He held up the bottle to the light of the table lamp and inspected the damage. It had been three-quarters full when he sat down to stare at the typewriter keyboard a little after nine o'clock and there were now less than three fingers left. He'd drunk it neat; water was a heresy and the English had yet to catch up with the invention of ice. Maybe eight inches of raw Scotch. Could he take that much?

The insistent moistening of his eyes and a consequent refusal to focus suggested he couldn't. He bent over the machine again and frowned threateningly at the keys. They swam in horizontal confusion. He straightened up, rubbed at his face with both hands, tried to focus again, failed, and got up. He made for the bedroom, stopped, wheeled, snatched up the bottle of Johnnie Walker and draped himself across the bed.

Pillowspin. He opened his eyes wide, took another slug of the spirit, belched loudly and felt better. His eye fell on a flimsy nightgown slung across the back of a chair. Janice. Where the hell was Janice? No — don't think about her; she might come back. Didn't matter where the hell she was; he was in no shape for her tonight. Maybe he'd never be in shape for her again. Janice was a survivor. Janice would never crawl like a stricken rat into a hell-hole like the Tilbury Shelter. Janice would never feel the need; life had to be bearable to be worth preserving, in her book. Janice was human; the cringing, scrabbling, stinking, bestial troglodytes of the Tilbury Shelter had been stripped of all human criteria; they were mutants, animals of a half-lit subworld who had taken over the domain of the sewer-rat and subverted themselves to the rodents' instincts. A billion years of natural selection had gone into leading them to the age of enlightenment and they'd slunk back into the primeval slime in four days. God bless humanity.

Who the hell cared anyway? Not Janice, wherever the crazy broad was. Not the government. Not him. Not Gladys. . . .

Yeah. Gladys cared. She was the type.

Why did she have to take off that way, just because he turned his back on her for one stinking minute? One stinking story. Trouble was, there were no stinking stories tonight. Just jumbles of meaningless images, shapes without words to comfort them. Nothing for O'Keefe. Goddamn O'Keefe.

The telephone jangled on the table at his elbow and he pretended he hadn't heard it. It kept on jangling and he remembered Denzil and told himself he ought to pick it up. He picked it up.

'Mel?'

'Oh. Hi, Rita.' Oh. Hi, Rita. She'd love that!

Her voice was strained, anxious. 'You O.K.?'

'Sure I'm O.K.'

'You sound like you've been hanging one on. Is it that bad?'

'What else do you expect? They kill people here.'

'Sorry. I didn't want to call at first. . . .' Women never wanted to call at first; they just waited for the second wave of intuition. *Then* they called. 'But since you were playing the don't-call-us-we'll-call-you routine in reverse I decided I ought to try. You're still paying the bills.'

'Great.' He didn't want her to know for sure he was canned.

'Well, beggars can't be choosers, I guess,' she said uncertainly. 'Great is not bad for a hero up to here in blood and thunder.'

'I didn't mean it that way.'

'I know you didn't, honey. I'm just a little overstretched, that's all. The radio's running over with all the gory details. I thought I'd run a check on whether I've still got a meal ticket.'

'You have. I'm glad you called.'

'So help you God?'

'So help me God. Look, I'm tired, sweetheart, and I'm trying to make a piece work for O'Keefe. It's been a long day and I'm running out of road. Kids O.K.?'

'As ever. Missing poppa, like their mom.'

'Missing you.' Self-pity rolled over him like a shroud. 'I'm missing you one helluva lot, Rita. Christ, I am!'

She didn't reply at once and he wondered if she'd gauged anything too profound from his uncharacteristic wave of love-you-till-I-die. 'Keep missing me. I'm not the roses-and-cream type they have over there but I sure as hell can cook. Can *they* cook?'

'I haven't had the time to find out.'

'Great. Keep your eye on the flag and remember Westchester. And get some sleep before you fall down. Promise?'

'Promise.'

'I love you.' She didn't give him time to reply.

He got up and went into the living-room; sat down and glared at the typewriter. The sheet of paper on the roller was still blank.

SUNDAY
15 September

Sunday, 0845

Death and overwhelming grief were no match for the implac-
able ordinariness of the English Sunday. The ticking of the clock
cranked night into day with perceptible mournfulness and the
hidden sinews of the house — water pipes, cistern, gas pipes,
chimney — seemed to sigh with mutual unease. Sunday was a
day made forfeit to the deepest depressive element of the English
character; a day of rest laden not with relaxation and renewal
but with *ennui* and black reflection. It was a hiccup in the week
that formed no part of what had gone before or of what was to
come.

Jack Warrender consoled himself with the thought that this
was by far the worst Sunday he had ever known. He had been
backwards and forwards to the A.R.P. post several times during
the night but Chief Warden Braithwaite had finally told him to
take the day off. 'You're no use to me in that condition,' he
snapped morosely, trying to conceal his sympathy.

He was right there, thought Jack wearily. He had been on his
rounds when Gladys came home, her clothes ripped and bloodied
and her hair like a thatcher's sheave, but Elsie told him she'd
never known a scene like it in her life. Poor old Flo had just
flaked out where she stood, bashing her head on the living-room
table as she fell down in a dead faint. Elsie had been left to put
them both to bed, then she'd shot off round to the phone-box
to call Arthur's place of work and, when he came on the phone,
she'd broken down herself trying to think of a way to tell him
Derek was dead.

Jack got back the first time a couple of minutes after Arthur
arrived. The boss at the Annexe had sent him home in his own

521

staff car. Flo was coming round just about then and the minute she opened her eyes it all came back to her and she let out a scream that curdled the blood in their veins. Elsie had got dressed and dashed out to Drummond Street for the doctor and raised him from his bed. He'd given Flo a sedative and she'd gone out like a light.

It was Flo that saved old Arthur from going off the end of the pier himself. He sized up the situation the second he came through the door and realised there was no room for his own tears. He turned his agony into concern for Flo — and for Glad. That bluff, tough Royal Marine mask he'd worn all his life — a mask Jack had often thought of as seventy per cent bull and bombast — had absorbed the blow in a way that made Jack feel ashamed. He bit on the bullet until his teeth met but the pain just came out as simple compassion.

They had all finally got to sleep around half past four but at seven Jack came awake to the sounds of someone stirring in the kitchen. He'd chucked on the old dressing-gown miraculously retrieved from the ruins of Number 14 and went down to investigate — and there was old Flo, bustling around doing last night's washing-up, which had been forgotten in the panic, and preparing Arthur's breakfast as if nothing had happened. She didn't want to talk; her hands were a little shaky and her eyes were red and puffy from a private early-morning cry, but she'd obviously got it fixed in her mind that she had to keep busy and nothing he'd said could change it.

The worst part came just after breakfast when he and Arthur went up to the wardens' hut to telephone Westminster Civil Defence control centre to arrange collection of Derek's body. The Westminster Chief Warden came on halfway through the conversation and he told Arthur straight; there was no body. There wasn't anything at all. Jack had had to argue with his friend to stop him making a futile journey up West to see for himself. He'd convinced him, finally, that their place was with the women; the living. After all, they had a job to do, hadn't they?

Glad was still asleep upstairs when the four of them settled round the table with a pot of tea. Flo was looking a lot better

Funny about people, Jack mused; Arthur saved his sanity because Flo had lost hers; now Flo was getting back on her feet because she could see the strain in Arthur's face.

Jack said, 'You want me and Elsie out of the way for a coupla hours, Arthur? Give you and Flo—'

'No, lad.' Arthur was a rock. He folded his arms across his chest. 'No more to be said. Derek's ... gone.' He drove the nail home, watching Flo, but her face was set. She'd done all the crying she was going to do.

'I was thinking,' said Jack guardedly, looking for a way into it.

' 'S'all right, Jack.' Arthur laid his hands flat on the table in front of him. He looked hard at Flo and then at Elsie. 'Might as well tell you now. Probably for the best. Listen to me. We've stuck it out here because we thought we didn't have anything else to do. We ain't got ... much left. What we have got we ain't going to give away. Not any more.'

Flo's face creased with bewilderment. 'I don't. . . .'

Jack jumped in quickly. 'There's something else, Flo love. The house. We'll *have* to leave.'

'Oh, no-o-o-o!' Flo wailed and Elsie embraced her; she threw a furious glance at Jack.

'How can you say such a thing!' She drew Flo's sad grey head to her shoulder. 'You should be ashamed of yourselves, both of you. At a time like this!'

Jack tried again valiantly. 'The house ain't safe no more, Elsie,' he said, hating himself. 'Civil Defence people told us. Foundations are gone. They'll have to pull it down.'

'Oh, Arthur!' Flo was momentarily on the edge of another collapse. Arthur grabbed her hand and patted it, but there was a look on his face which said he was not going to stop now.

'Ain't up to us no more, love,' he said as gently as he could without letting her think he'd be open to changing his mind. 'We got no choice. The Demolition say it'll have to come down.'

Elsie burst out, 'Well you won't get me shifting from here, not after what we put up with these last few days. *I'm* not—'

Jack really lost his wig then. '*Yes!*' He pounded the table with his fist, so hard Flo sat up in surprise and stopped crying. 'Yes!

Yes! Yes! Can't you get it in your stupid woolly brain, woman? The bloody house is done for. It's a death-trap. You've got to get out. Now don't give me any more bloody argument, all right? That's the top and bottom of it and there ain't nothing we can do about it. For once in your life you'll do as you're told and no messing. Now then — are we straight?'

He glared at them, avoiding Arthur's eyes. Elsie was shocked; she'd never seen Jack in such a state and she could tell at once he was in no mood to be challenged. She looked doubtfully at Flo.

'Flo? You want to?'

Flo conquered a mighty sob. 'Will you come with me, Elsie?'

Elsie put an arm around her shoulders again. 'When've we ever done anything alone?' she whispered.

'It's for the best,' said Arthur, stretching his hands down his back. 'I feel a right tartar, the way it had to be done, but it's for the best.'

'The best,' agreed Jack.

They were standing together in the tiny backyard, looking along the flattened landscape of Baltic Street. After the initial arguments, the women had done what women always do: turned their minds to practical considerations like what they could take with them and how to pack it in three battered suitcases. Arthur had told them they would have to leave on Tuesday morning; the half past twelve train from Paddington. Flo had jibbed about being thrown out of her home without having proper time to make arrangements but Arthur quashed the objection. There'd been another row when he told them he and Jack would be staying behind and Flo had wailed that he was breaking up the family and even Hitler hadn't been able to do that; but Arthur had a touch of the blarney when he wanted something bad enough and he'd explained about Mr Churchill relying on him and Warden Braithwaite relying on Jack and, besides, Barry couldn't toddle off either and that was a fact. So they had settled on a compromise: Elsie and Flo would go on ahead with Glad — no point in sending her down to Eastbourne now — and Janice would complete the advance party. Paul would come down when they let him out of hospital and Edie and the baby would travel as soon as the doctor said it was safe. Jack, Arthur and Barry would find somewhere to muck in together. 'Now you can't call *that* breaking up the family, can you, love?' Arthur had said.

It was only then that it struck Jack that Janice was still staying with that girl-friend of hers over at Blackfriars. They decided to cross that bridge tomorrow, when the women were a little more settled in their minds.

Arthur let his hand drop on to the saddle of Derek's racing bike propped against the scullery wall. Jack winced at the gesture and remembered he had something to say.

'Young Barry came in this morning on his way home,' he ventured delicately. 'Didn't want to say anything till I asked you first. It's about the baby.'

'Baby?' Arthur was still staring at Derek's bike. 'Oh — Edie's, you mean? All right, is it?'

'Bright as a button. But — er — him and Edie had a talk last night, when they heard about . . . what happened. Their little lad — they want to name him after Derek. Barry said they'd be as proud as punch. If you don't mind, that is.'

Arthur Scully cleared his throat with some difficulty. It was a full ten seconds before he trusted himself to speak.

'Tell him. . . . Tell him I don't mind, Jack.' He coughed loudly. 'Tell him it's . . . tell him thanks, eh?'

It was enough for the moment, thought Jack. He'd save the bit about Arthur being godfather till later.

Sunday, 1020

Air Vice Marshal Keith Park led the Prime Minister and Clementine fifty feet down to the Operations Room of Number Eleven Group headquarters, Fighter Command. Winston's call had come an hour earlier. The weather was bright, he'd said; the conditions looked perfect for an enemy assault. Could he drive over from Chequers to watch the action at Uxbridge? He had been over two or three times before but never on a day when anything much had happened.

'I don't know whether anything will happen today, sir,' said Park, leading them to their seats in what Winston liked to call the dress circle, the balcony overlooking the map-table and directly across the room from the giant totalisator board. 'All's quiet at the moment.'

The tote board was divided into six columns representing the six fighter stations of Number Eleven Group, each squadron occupying a sub-column of its own. Each of the rows was lit with an electric bulb of a different colour; the bottom row was aglow at that moment indicating that squadrons were standing by at two minutes' readiness. Above it another line showed those standing by at five minutes' readiness; above that, 'available' at twenty minutes'. Then those squadrons reporting enemy sightings, those in action and, at the top, squadrons turning for home. To the left of the board, imprisoned in a glass box, were five officers linked with Observer Corps H.Q., the co-ordination centre into which fifty thousand men, women and youths fed sighting information as enemy aircraft crossed the coast. Elsewhere in the underground cavern dozens of assessors sorted the incoming messages from the Corps and passed the information to the plotting table. On the right, in another glass case, sat the army officers linked to the two hundred anti-aircraft batteries dotted around the Eleven Group command area of Essex, Kent, Sussex and Hampshire.

Park's forecast ruptured a few minutes after ten-thirty. The Chain Home stations revealed enemy aircraft passing over the Pas de Calais and this time Goering's eagles did not seem to be flying their usual feints along the French coast to confuse the issue. They were massing for a great assault; the first counter showed forty plus raiders from Luftwaffe stations in the Dieppe area.

The electric bulbs on the tote board popped on one after the other in quick succession as squadrons came to stand-by. More enemy counters were raked on to the map-table and Churchill leaned forward expectantly : twenty-plus, forty-plus, sixty-plus, eighty-plus. He switched his gaze to the map-table below; the blue-shirted W.A.A.F.s were ordering the counters along the lines of attack. Back to the board; only five squadrons were left at readiness. Suddenly the line of red bulbs blipped on dramatically as Eleven Group engaged the enemy. Park was talking continuously in a low, precise monotone to a young man at the Prime Minister's side, who translated the instructions into a patchwork detail for individual fighter stations. It would be seven years before Churchill met the young man again and learned his name. By then Lord Willoughby de Broke would be a Steward of the Jockey Club and Winston's host at the 1947 Epsom Derby.

Within minutes the map-table was saturated with winding tails of invading counters as the vast armada wound across the Channel, and the tote board light-bulbs began to change their flickering patterns. All squadrons were aloft; some were heavily engaged and the first line was turning for home to refuel. The Prime Minister looked at the bottom line indicating squadrons standing by at two minutes' readiness. Every bulb was out.

Winston Churchill leaned across de Broke to speak to Keith Park.

'How many fighters do you have in reserve?'

Park's mouth twitched drily. 'None, sir.'

Wave on wave of Dornier 17s and Junkers 88s followed on their leaders' tails, driving the wedge deeper into the trail-woven blue skies over Kent. The first assault waves had broken up in confusion as Park's squadrons bore in for the kill; as the dogfights closed and erupted, the German formations scattered in all directions, dropping their bomb-loads anywhere and throttling up for home.

De Broke caught sight of a movement on the table below and muttered, 'Twelve Group's engaged, sir.' They all looked down.

The five squadrons of Douglas Bader's Duxford Wing had swept their Damoclean sword into the action and Park spoke again to de Broke. Eleven Group and the three Ten Group squadrons were detailed to an ordered withdrawal for return to base, refuelling and rearming.

A messenger clattered up the stairs and bent to whisper in

527

Park's ear. The Air Vice Marshal nodded and Churchill looked at him curiously.

'Bader got his wing off in under three minutes, sir,' Park said coldly. 'They got it right this time.'

The Prime Minister held his tongue and reflected on the memoranda that had crossed his desk in the past few weeks about Leigh-Mallory's Big Wing experiment. He hadn't told Dowding yet of his talk a few days ago with Peter Macdonald, an M.P. for fourteen years and coincidentally adjutant of Bader's squadron. They had met at the House of Commons and Macdonald had harried him for an hour and a half about the necessity of perfecting the Big Wing principle. He had been unreceptive at first but Macdonald's fervour had finally worn him down. The Prime Minister was virtually a disciple by the time Macdonald finished. Park's grudging admission clinched his opinion.

More messages were channelled up from the ops. table below. Bader's wing had met the invaders over London, four thousand feet below the enemy's belly. They had hammered the Dorniers and Junkers mercilessly, according to reports, and with spectacular success. The sky over the capital was a maelstrom of weaving, rolling engagement. Farther south Number Ten Group's three squadrons were playing havoc with enemy formations running for home, leaving the limping bombers lucky enough to escape with bullet-starred windscreens, blood-spattered cockpits and fuselages, smoking engine cowls, dozens of lacerated corpses and hundreds wounded.

Over London itself aircraft and parachuting crews were dropping from the skies like flies in a gas cloud. A Do17 had crashed in the station yard at Victoria; a Hurricane pilot had baled out and landed in a dustbin in Chelsea; another Do17 had locked in a death embrace with a Spitfire and smashed to earth in a tangle of wreckage in Kent.

The map-table configurations suddenly changed; the disposition of the German bombers switched direction. They were heading for home.

Park leaned back in his chair, his spare, unemotional face on line with the tote board. One after another the bulbs were flickering on again on that bottom line as squadron after squadron completed refuelling and rearming and came back to readiness.

Mrs Churchill whispered something to her husband and he nodded enthusiastically. 'You've done for them, Park. Damn good show.'

The commander spared him a brief glance. 'I don't think they're finished yet, sir. The day's only half over.'

Sunday, 1151

The howl of the siren in Hanover Square was so loud Shaffer heard it over the rush of the shower. He ignored it for a while but it seemed to persist longer than usual and his curiosity finally got the better of him. He shrugged on the robe, misty with Janice's cheap scent, and wrapped a towel round his neck. He went out into the corridor and looked out at Brook Street; there was no sign of smoke, no drone of planes, no gunfire. He was about to return to the flat when there was a pounding on the stairs above and Archie Fisk, the party-giving firewatcher, clattered down to join him.

'I say, old boy, I think we're in for a bit of stick.' He looked about him, fixed on a stirrup-pump and a bucket of sand under a far window and ran to them. He lugged them back along the hallway to the foot of the stairs.

'Couldn't give me a hand with these, could you? The bucket, perhaps?'

'Well, I haven't had a chance to dress. I was just in the shower.'

'Don't give it a thought. The boys and girls won't. We're all up there. Looks like a big 'un. Just had a call from Victoria. Everyone's on their toes.'

'Give me two seconds. I'll be with you.' Shaffer turned into the door but poked his head out again. 'Leave the bucket. I'll bring it up.'

He pulled on trousers, a pullover and a windcheater and climbed the stairs to the roof. He planted the bucket to one side of the entry door. 'O.K.?' he called out.

Dorothy Saundersby appeared from around a chimney stack and examined him appreciatively. 'Well, well, well. The Seventh Cavalry, I presume.' She came over and threaded her arm through his. She appeared to have started the party a little early; her pupils were dilated and her mouth slack. 'You come sit with Dot, darling. Archie says the Nasties are—'

'God!' Archie came trotting nimbly from the far end of the roof, one arm waving wildly behind him at the sea of white cloud above the Thames.

'Look at them, old boy! Will you bloody *look* at them!'

Sunday, 1310

Archie Fisk was bouncing like a pin-striped rubber ball. His bow-tie was crushed into the shape of a swatted butterfly under his chin as he crouched, hands on knees, then straightened and crouched again.

'Do-o-own.' He sank until his belt squeaked with the strain. 'Down. Lookatim!' He raised a hand to shield his eyes. 'Another bugger, old boy. *Do-o-own* he goes.' Archie's body tracked the curve of the falling plane. He turned to Shaffer. 'Five of the buggers in what . . . ten minutes?' His face glowed. 'You making a note of this, old son?'

They were still on the roof of the apartment block along with tipsy Dot and the whole retinue of merrymakers. It was, Shaffer had to admit, one time when Archie's insistence hadn't proved to be a pain in the ass. Archie Fisk, ring-master of aerial combat, had, as he might have put it himself, picked a winner.

The sky over London was criss-crossed with vapour trails: a vast ball of white wool unravelling itself above their heads, looping and twisting, sequined with tiny crosses that wavered and tumbled like dropped stitches. Shaffer didn't need a notebook. It was unlike anything he had ever seen. Churchill's Battle of Britain was being played out to the final curtain by what had to be every single member of the cast.

Tommy gave a thumbs-up sign from the far end of the roof

and Archie matched it with a satisfied twitch of the head and two raised fingers in the shape of a victory V-sign. Vera twinkled at Shaffer. He twinkled back.

'Never seen the like of it. Never seen anything like it before!' bawled Archie, bobbing excitedly. 'Look, old lad. They're all over the place. Wetting their knickers!'

It wasn't the phrase Shaffer intended using later but it was graphically accurate. The Luftwaffe was in big trouble. The strict, unwavering patterns the Londoners had grown to associate with aerial attack had shattered.

'Here we go!' said Archie and the ack-ack guns boomed.

Shaffer felt a puff of hot breath in his ear and his heart sank. 'Little old Mel. Well, here we are again!' Dot Saundersby slipped her arm through his with the finality of an anaconda selecting a meal. He tried a feint, but she moved in close. 'Tommy says it's one below the belt.' She let the statement hang in the air suggestively. 'The fighting, I mean. Says we must have been saving it up to wallop them good and proper. Looks like it, wouldn't you say?'

'I'd say so.' Shaffer forced a grin. 'A right old walloping.'

Dot erupted into a giggle. 'Wallhopping? Not Wallhopping, you lovely man! Walloping! After me: walloping!'

Her attempts at coquettishness veered between tragi-comedy and burlesque, but Shaffer was no longer paying her much attention. His mind was wholly occupied with the realisation that any plans he might have had for the day had been wiped out in the face of the battle overhead.

It had to be the final fling; the confrontation that had been so long in coming that no one believed it would happen. A mental picture of invasion barges strung along the Channel coasts flashed across his mind. Invasion? Was this how it started? Someone must know. Not Ashton's crowd; the Gestapo would have to be rapping on their bedroom doors before they admitted to a German invasion. Charles Russell? Yes. Russell would know.

'Love those boys,' Dot was saying. 'So devil-may-care, I always think.' Her hand had begun to traverse Shaffer's armpit. 'Slim. All of them. They have to be, y'know. Such tiny little planes. I

531

admire lean looks in a man.' Her fingers strummed Shaffer's rib cage.

'Oh, bloody hell, will you cop a load of *that*.' Archie's pointing finger trailed down the sky. 'See him? Over there! Like a bloody brick. . . .'

Shaffer watched the spiralling plume of smoke; waited for the puff of silk that signalled the opening of a parachute, but none appeared. He must phone Russell.

A black fleck tumbled from the plummeting Dornier. A fine tail of harness trailed uselessly above the pinpoint of humanity and plunged on to a flat roof somewhere over by Victoria Station.

'Got the sod!' screeched Archie. The ack-ack barrage thundered its agreement and the roof shook.

'What d'you reckon, darling?' Dot glanced back at the stairwell. Her voice descended into glottal seduction.

'I reckon he's dead,' said Shaffer.

'What?'

'The guy who baled out. 'Chute didn't open.'

Dot shook her head. 'No, silly. I meant. . . .' She gave him a playful push. 'You're having me *on*! You know very well what I—'

Shaffer snatched at freedom. 'Dot. I have no idea what you meant. Will you do something for me?'

'Well, I don't know,' she simpered. 'Depends how naughty it is.'

Jesus, she was impossible. Shaffer took her by the shoulders, safe at arm's length. 'Dot, I've got work to do. Now I can't be in two places at once, so I want you to help me out. I'm going to my apartment to write my piece. You stay here like a good girl and tell me all about it when I come back, huh?'

She tore herself away. 'You're trying to get rid of me, aren't you?'

'There's another one!' Archie turned to them. 'That's eight, not counting the one that might have been ours.'

'Oh, push off, you silly old bugger!' Dot flared at him.

'Well, do please excuse me for breathing, old girl,' Archie said with heavy sarcasm. 'I mean, all I said was—'

'Oh, just shut it! Men make me *sick*!'

Shaffer made for the stairs.

'Especially bloody foreigners!'

He sped down the stairs and turned into the corridor to his apartment. Thank you, Mrs Saundersby. Some wars could only be won in retreat.

No reply from Russell. It didn't matter; the details could be filled in later. What he had to do was outline a fast sketch that captured something of the drama going on up there right now. He sat down at the typewriter.

'A city stood still today. . . .'

He got no farther. The unlocked door of the apartment burst open with a crash and he spun in his seat.

'Christ, old boy.' Archie Fisk stood in the frame, his clothes, face and hands dripping blood. His mouth bit on air. 'First aid, old boy!' He slumped down against the wall. 'Help me, will you?'

Shaffer leaped from the chair. 'Where are you hurt? Quick, man! Tell me.'

'Not me, old boy. Out there.' Archie flapped a hand wearily over his shoulder.

Shaffer stepped over him into the corridor. The thing being handed down the stairway was a misshapen chunk of bloodied meat, leaking fluid and viscera. Tommy and the others were bearing it, faces averted. Shaffer's stomach muscles tightened and his throat bobbed.

Archie Fisk came up behind him. 'Bloody shell,' he said. His face twisted. 'Ack-ack shell. Came right down on the roof. Hit her. Didn't stand a chance.'

'Bandages! Get some bandages!' shrilled Tommy hysterically, struggling with the lower end of the mess.

The man handling the upper half of the dead weight suddenly gave up with a whoof of exploding vomit. The mortal remains of Dorothy Saundersby plopped on to the stairs and hurtled downwards, shedding blood.

Sunday, 1540

The second part of the assault had come in from the Channel in three groaning waves at one o'clock; 180 aircraft in all, according to the Observer Corps. Churchill had watched gravely, hunched back in his chair to minimise the relevance of his presence, as Park ordered the twenty-three squadrons of Eleven Group, the three of Ten Group and Bader's five-strong wing back into the air to intercept.

A hundred spinning, reeling battles merged into one. Two of the enemy formations were broken up by Eleven Group squadrons before they reached London and those formations that slipped through to the capital were met head-on by the Duxford Wing. It was not difficult, Churchill had mused theatrically, to imagine the physical and mental stress of those young men at the controls of Spitfires and Hurricanes. The desperate hours that were in reality only minutes; the stuttering cacophony of shells, the burning spears of tracer, the pounding of their own young hearts in the cockpits of their chests. Eyes blinking away the sweat flowing from their helmets, hands slippery with it. Time enlarged and magnified, stained with the enemy's blood. The face of eternity glowering from the reflector that showed yet another Messerschmitt on their tail. Their finest hour; it had been a catch-phrase to rouse a nation as it looked on throughout August; as The Few contained Hitler's thrust to the heart.

They had held the line in the face of hopeless odds and yet, today, those odds had been multiplied a dozen times. Goering's intention had been clear, seen from Uxbridge; one final, overwhelming, overpowering *blitzkrieg*. Saturation bombing by a saturation force. He could almost hear that fat fool's reedy tenor joining in the Luftwaffe's marching song in some appropriate squadron officers' mess last night.

> Listen to the engine singing —
> Get on to the foe !
> Listen; in your ears it's ringing —
> Get on to the foe.

Well, friend Hermann's heart would not be singing this night. One hundred and eighty-five German aircraft had been claimed by the Fighter Command squadrons; Bader's Duxford Wing alone claimed fifty-two destroyed and eight probables. It would take time and much cooler analysis to whittle that number down to a realistic figure but nothing could whittle away the heroism of those young men — the gayest company ever to fire guns in anger, someone had said.

On their way to the surface Park said sombrely, 'I'm glad you saw this, sir. During the last twenty minutes we had so much info coming in we couldn't handle it. That shows you the limitation of our resources. They've been strained far beyond their limits today.' Park was curiously dissatisfied with the interception techniques of his command; he felt that too many German bombers had been allowed to penetrate the screen and reach London.

At the car Churchill shook him by the hand.

He looked the commander squarely in the eye. He knew he was expected to say something memorable, something Park could convey along the ducted grapevine of Fighter Command.

'Details, Park,' he growled pugnaciously. 'It was a triumph and history won't allow you to forget it. You slammed the gates on Hitler's Valhalla today. There will be no heroes in Berlin tonight.'

Sunday, 1545

A wing clipped the disc of the sun and the slate-grey smudge of the city swayed and rose to meet him.

Tom Russell loosened the scarf at his neck and let the Hurricane side-slip until he could make out streets and houses and green gems of parkland.

Brentford. Richmond. Chiswick. Putney. Chelsea. The river keyed the unfolding map. Was it Chelsea? He stretched up in his seat, looking for the wide lawns of the Royal Hospital, but an air pocket rocked the machine, swinging him across the mosaic. He eased back the stick. The big engine vibrated and twin condensation trails flared their streamers from each wing tip. It was down there, somewhere. Not far. Home.

He jerked a thumbs-up in a token gesture to Garfield Court and swung to join the departing wing, voices crackling in his earphones.

One claimed, one definite. The ruin of the Messerschmitt had rained down over the city and he had seen no parachute open. Definite. The blast of its mid-air disintegration had spattered his screen with oil but he had seen it die. The other had been a Dornier, its tail-plane riddled by his eight .303 Brownings. He had seen it whirl away, begin to lose height, but then he'd lost sight of it.

He would claim some credit, though, even if one of the other chaps had finished it off.

So : one and a half. And the sky was clear.

He turned on to the bearing for home. Bader's snappy tone came through the headphones loud and clear. Gathering his flock.

Tom gunned the twelve-cylinder Merlin engine and snatched a final glance down at the sprawling capital. The horseshoe bend of the river stamped itself like a hallmark over the East End, smoke still towering in the sky above it.

Elsie. Old Elsie Warrender's patch. Rotherhithe.

He waggled his wings over the Surrey Docks; caught a blurred glimpse of the open wound through a film of cloud and smoke and oil; began to climb until it fell away no bigger than a scratch on the city.

Sunday, 1550

> I'm in the mood for love,
> Simply because you're near me....

Janice Scully had a naturally earthy voice that could best be described as female-baritone; at the top end of her range she could achieve a mellow tone that was pure Blues, but at the gravelly bottom she was a rasping, burlesque sing-along queen. She had been singing all the way from Cambridge and now, two hours and more after Denzil and Caroline had given up, lost for words and in the advanced state of laryngitis, she was really beginning to warm up.

From Cambridge to Ware she had given them an international cabaret selection, but from Ware onwards she had been Vera Lynn, the 'Sweetheart of the Forces'. Janice fancied herself as the sweetheart of the forces so her addiction to Vera's repertoire was total. Before she began each new song she introduced it as they did on the wireless, except that she announced the details of the number as played on her gramophone in the front parlour at home.

'Now – this one is called "Alone" and you'll have to imagine Primo Scala's Accordion Band in the background. . . .'

'The next one is "A Star fell out of Heaven" with the Casani Club Orchestra directed by Charlie Kunz. Charlie is at the piano, o'course. . . .'

Or, 'This one is a bit seasonal. "The little boy that Santa Claus forgot". Ambrose and his orchestra.'

She sang without fluffing a line. Not only had she memorised the lyrics, she faithfully re-created Vera's style and delivery right down to the last throaty sob. She started with 'The General's Fast Asleep', which was Vera's first record, practically, and which Janice bought as a joke to play for Geoff when he came home. She performed everything Vera'd recorded since 1935, including 'We'll meet again' and 'Goodnight Children Everywhere', which the wireless had been playing constantly since they came out last year, and all the 1940 issues like 'I'll pray for you', 'It's a lovely day tomorrow' and 'Who's taking you home tonight'. But she reserved her best efforts for Vera's latest, which had come out in June: 'A Nightingale sang in Berkeley Square'. That was her favourite. She sang it three times in succession, urged on by Denzil's shouted applause and Caroline's delighted clapping.

> The streets of town were paved with stars,
> It was such a romantic affair....

She loved that bit and her voice sobbed with emotion when she came to it. It made Caroline cry the third time and even Denzil, to whom music was a shapeless blur between the ears, fell silent and serious and thoughtful.

After the third rendering, when the last choking syllable had been snatched away by the light breeze fussing round the open Morris, Janice fell silent too. There didn't seem to be any way of following that. It was ... it was everything she wanted to believe possible about London, about life. Angels dining at the Ritz. A really lovely line, that was. Geoff would never understand in a million years what it meant. He couldn't see the beauty of streets paved with stars because he hadn't got a drop of poetry in him and, anyway, he'd had a job with the Gas Board as a labourer, once, and had dug up too many pavements to see the finer side of them. Geoff wouldn't ever understand love and he wouldn't know a nightingale from a Shitehawk.

Denzil would, though, with training. She ran her eye appraisingly over the back of his head, from the rear seat where she sat with one arm slung lightly around Caroline's shoulders. He wasn't too romantic, sure enough, but that was only because he hadn't been brought out by a woman. Last night had been lovely, though. No nonsense from him when they arrived at the University Arms in Cambridge; two rooms, he asked for, and on different floors so there couldn't be any misunderstandings by the hotel people. That was nice, in a funny sort of way. Never dreamed of taking advantage and he behaved like a gent all through. Like the man in 'A Nightingale sang in Berkeley Square' would; all gentle and painstaking and fluttering round her to make sure she was happy and comfy. They had dinner — she had that fixed firmly in her head now; dinner in proper company was the meal you ate in the evening, not halfway through the day like they did in Nelson's Green — and he'd paid the head waiter to put a rose wrapped in silver paper beside her plate and he'd kissed her hand when she sat down. A polite kiss, though; like it was good manners and breeding to do.

538

He knew all about wine and food and he'd talked about it for
ours in that funny way he had of talking. And afterwards he'd
aken her to her door and bowed as if she was Lady Muck and
he had been so touched she'd forgotten to put on the old
manner. She hadn't slept for a long time after that, what with
thinking about him and making plans. She could do a lot for a
man like Denzil, although she could see clear enough that she'd
ave to do something about improving herself for him and learn
o be a lady and that. Denzil wasn't like old Shaffer; he didn't
ave a clue about women, so the first one to grab him would be
he one he married. Marriage. It was a bit frightening, that. He
vas a toff, all right, no mistake. Got money and land and lots of
riends who had titles and were important, and his dad was a
ir. Denzil would be a Sir too, one day, so his wife would be a
ady.

Lady Janice. Old Geoff would have to be given his marching
rders, of course, and she'd have to play that one very close to
he chest. Mustn't have any hint of scandal, not with a Sir in the
amily. But she knew she could count on Geoff to do the right
hing; it was sort of part of their contract. She'd done right by
im, marrying him and knowing it was only for show, and now
was up to him to do right by her. Keep Nelson's Green out of
completely; that was the best way. She might even ask Denzil
o have old Shaffer as best man. That would look good in the
apers, an important American correspondent as best man.

When they drove out to the hospital to fetch Caroline, Janice
ad had a twinge of nervous apprehension and a shudder or two
f jealousy. She was lovely, was Caroline; that Old English
ovely they always talked about in the Pears' Soap ads. She
alked nice too, and Janice could see Denzil liked her on sight
ecause he got all embarrassed and tongue-tied and his sentences
ot shorter and funnier than ever. That worried her a lot because
he hadn't considered, up to then, that there would be any com-
etition for Denzil; also, and the idea struck home with a nasty
hud, it was pretty obvious she couldn't get Denzil as easy as
he'd got Shaffer and the rest. Dragging Denzil into bed wouldn't
o the trick. He'd just get flummoxed and worry about whether
was the way a gent should behave, and if he came to the con-

clusion it wasn't manners he'd run for the nearest horizon. He had to be brought on slow, old Denzil, and brought on with the kind of things Caroline had been naturally born with. So it was very worrying at the beginning, having her with them, and Janice had insisted they sat in the back seat so Denzil was free to drive without distraction.

The worry hadn't lasted long, though. Janice could deal with women; get them to open up about themselves in ways a man would never have the brain to do. The girl wanted to talk. They had to keep their conversation discreet, of course, but that wasn't difficult with someone like old Denzil up front ... and it all came out. Caroline didn't have to say the actual words because Janice was quick on the uptake. She could see what the trouble was, pretty well straight away. After a quarter of an hour's chat she was promising Caroline she'd take her in hand and the girl was having a little cry and thanking her and telling her she was the kind of girl she'd needed to be friends with all her life. Friends with Janice Scully!

After that Janice just couldn't contain her unbearable joy and she had begun to sing. They all sang at first but Denzil was a croaker and Caroline, who had a sweet little voice, just didn't know the words. So in the end they left it to Janice. She had never been so happy in her life.

They passed through Harringay High Street and Janice came down to earth with a bump. London again. Problems. There had been a raid on, anyone could see that. It wasn't as nice a day in London as it had been in Cambridge but it was made even more dismal by the blanketing smoke clouds that trailed over the city. There were some broken windows in Harringay High Street, probably incendiaries because there didn't seem much other damage, but over to the east the smoke was dense and Jerry had obviously been busy in the City and the West End as well. Caroline got all upset when she saw it and started worrying about her mum and dad but Janice talked her round easy enough. The girl only needed a bit of cheering up to be as right as ninepence. It was a crying shame no one had taken her in hand before.

At the Manor House traffic junction there was a bit of a

shemozzle and a rozzer came over to the car and told Denzil he couldn't turn right for Seven Sisters Road because there was a U.X.B. down there about half a mile and he couldn't turn left for Tottenham because a factory had been blown down across the road. If he was Denzil, said the rozzer, he'd just park the car for a while across the junction in Green Lanes and hold hard for a bit till the smoke cleared because there'd been some bombing down by Clissold Park and they weren't sure how bad it was yet. Denzil said O.K. and they drove over the junction and stopped, but after they had sat there for five minutes and watched a dozen cars and lorries sweep past them into the smoke Denzil said he couldn't see why they shouldn't do the same. So he drove on.

It was slow going but it must have been all right because they didn't come up behind any of the vehicles that had passed them and when he saw the red-brick Victorian castle at the junction of Blackstock Road – it was a waterworks really – Denzil said he thought it was O.K. now and picked up speed a little. Not much; just a comfy thirty miles an hour.

They passed the gates of Clissold Park and the smoke got thicker suddenly but that didn't worry them too much because the smoke had lain in patches all along Green Lanes ever since Manor House.

Caroline was saying she'd like to hear 'A Nightingale sang in Berkeley Square' again when the girls saw Denzil's shoulders strain back into the seat and his body go rigid. The little car's tyres squeaked as the brakes jammed them solid and they all felt it skid over a slick of earth and shale.

Denzil shouted, 'Hold tight!' but it was too late to do anything. The Morris's polished maroon bonnet dipped and dived. The rear wheels clung for a moment on the brink but the impetus was too much for the tyres.

The car slewed sideways into the crater and hit the black water with a mighty splash.

The last thing Janice did was grab at Caroline's hand.

Sunday, 1630

The officer-type in the dark coat and regimental tie doffed his bowler and apologised for the interruption. Eric Warr, across the table on the other side of the microphone, explained curtly that unauthorised persons were not allowed in the studio and, anyway, there was a convention in broadcasting that people stayed on the other side of the door till the red light went out. He might have ruined the whole broadcast. The guy was good at apologies but, as he pointed out, he was also an authorised person in his way. He flashed a Security Police card and hooked Shaffer out into the corridor.

At three-fifty that afternoon, he explained as they walked up to the main floor, Shaffer's car had been involved in an accident in Green Lanes, Clissold Park. The occupants, who were being treated at a hospital in Highbury, were not badly hurt but a man and one of the women involved claimed to be friends of his. In their interests, and in his own, it was essential Shaffer accompany him at once to the hospital and verify the identities of the people concerned and their stories.

Shaffer asked why the Security Police should be involved in a car smash and the guy said that suspected looting of a car now fell within their purview. At the main entrance of Broadcasting House Shaffer suggested they saved time by calling the hospital so he could talk to Denzil and Janice, but the officer said it had to be a formal face-to-face identification and, by the by, could he see Shaffer's own identity card and Press accreditation? A black Wolseley, unmarked, stood at the kerb and they got in.

The officer apologised again. His name was Maconachie; he was a Chief Detective Superintendent and the last thing he wanted at this stage of a long day was to go chasing around London on a fool's errand, but that was his job. He was obviously genuine. Shaffer felt some sympathy for him. They talked about the crash – the Morris was a write-off, it seemed – and Maconachie asked him about Denzil and Janice; particularly Denzil since, as he explained, he was the driver. He didn't mention

Caroline by name and raised no questions about who she was or why she was in the car. Denzil was an easy man to talk about and Maconachie was a good listener. By the time the police car pulled up at the hospital steps the police officer knew as much about Denzil Fletcher-Hale as Shaffer did.

The three of them were sitting together in what their guide, a nursing sister, described as the solarium. Denzil had one arm in a sling; bruised, not broken; Janice had a few cuts and abrasions — 'where it don't show except in bed' — and Caroline had just got wet. Maconachie very decently withdrew to let them talk together and Denzil poured out the whole story.

He was halfway through his yarn when Shaffer switched chairs to a more comfortable, cushioned seat near the window, and in doing so caught a glimpse of Maconachie in a wall mirror. The police officer was seated on a stool just inside the door but hidden from the rest of the room by a partition erected to exclude draughts. He had a notebook open on his knee. He was writing in it.

It was too late then. Whatever he expected to hear had been said. Shaffer let it go but carved a deep notch on his memory never to trust cops again as long as he lived. Anyway, what did it matter? Denzil was clean; so were the girls. There would be a spat with O'Keefe about the car, but he could handle that somehow. There were no charges pending; they didn't charge people for falling into bomb craters. Yet.

The shock of the accident had worn off the victims. Even Caroline was relaxed. She was a beautiful girl; devastating. No doubt about her being Elizabeth's daughter but she had something all her own, too; a pixie-like quality of veiled innocence that was magnified fifty times over by the outsize man's knitted jumper the hospital had found for her and the pyjama trousers and slippers. Her hair was tied in bunches and she had a habit of cupping her chin in long, slim fingers that made her look so. . . .

Forget it!

Janice was snuggled up to Denzil, her arm clamped in his tighter than a pair of Houdini's handcuffs. He didn't seem to mind at all, in fact he had the look of a man who might be enjoying it. Hard to tell with Denzil; if he showed no sign of emotion he had to be feeling good. What that meant in terms of an overnight stay with Janice in Cambridge was beyond human imagination but Janice had greeted Shaffer when he first entered the room with a pout that blew pantomime kisses and she'd winked to indicate to him her proprietorial grip on Denzil's arm.

Shaffer said at last, 'I guess I'd better call the superintendent in, O.K.?' and derived real pleasure from the perceptible scrape of the stool behind the partition as the officer shot to his feet and tiptoed out into the corridor. At least the guy had the decency to look embarrassed when Shaffer strolled out a moment later to fetch him. By then he had been joined by a colleague. Lubbock, the man snapped sourly, introducing himself.

Lubbock turned out to be the blunt instrument because the moment they stepped back into the room he pitched into Denzil. No preliminaries. No apologies.

'Your name is Denzil Whitlock Kentersham Fletcher-Hale?'

'Certainly.' Denzil just didn't have a nose for trouble.

'You have chambers at Number 142 Half Moon Street?'

'Yes.'

'Do you confirm that you have held a card indicating membership of an organisation describing itself as The Link and that you paid into that organisation's account a sum of money formally described as a membership fee and subscription?'

'Good Lord. The Link. Odd you bringing it up like that. Talking with a fellow the other day. Curious about it himself. Couldn't for the life of me remember. Joined at Oxford. You in it?'

Lubbock's mouth snapped shut. He paused, gathering air. 'Are you prepared to make a statement to that effect if requested to—?'

''Ere!' Janice was on her feet at once. She had been as surprised as the others when Lubbock opened fire but she had seen the way the wind was blowing long before they did. 'What d'you mean *statement*? He's got nothing to say that'd interest *you*, old cock. Take it from me.'

'Sit down!' snarled Lubbock. 'This doesn't concern you.'

'Doesn't bloody concern you, either. Who do you think you

are, asking him questions? He's just been in an accident. He isn't feeling right yet. If you think I'm going to let you run all over him with your bloody great jackboots you can think again. He's a gentleman, he is; not some old lag from the Elephant and Castle. You watch your mouth, mate, or I'll have—'

Lubbock had swollen with rage as she spoke, his fists flexing at his sides, and Janice's cheeky bravado pushed him too far. He shot out a hand and forced it down on her shoulder.

'Sit down, damn you, or I'll put you under arrest for obstructing the police in the course of their—'

He got no farther.

Janice squealed dramatically, 'Look what he did! He—'

Denzil was on his feet, his great length unrolling with miraculous speed. Shaffer swore later that he didn't see the blow but Lubbock suddenly rocketed backwards, head rolling, and slammed into the far wall. He banged the back of his head and Maconachie went to him quickly and grabbed his arm. For a few seconds they were all too shocked to say anything; then Denzil spoke.

'Sorry, old chap. Didn't think. Striking a lady, d'you see. Can't have it.'

'I'll give that bastard—' Lubbock began. He nursed his head in his hands, eyes watering profusely.

'That's enough!' Maconachie's tone left no room for argument. 'That was a very silly thing to do, Mr Fletcher-Hale,' he said gravely. 'Striking a police officer.'

'What about *him* striking me then?' flared Janice. 'He laid hand on me first.'

'Look—why don't we all sit down and relax.' Shaffer took Lubbock's elbow and pulled up a chair. They lowered the detective into it. 'I'd say the match was square, wouldn't you, superintendent?' He widened his eyes sharply for Maconachie's benefit.

Lubbock shook his head violently and pushed away the helping hands. He stood up. His fists were still flexing but he had his temper under control.

'No point wasting time, sir,' he said with a glance at his chief. 'No choice in the matter, is there?' He cleared his throat. 'Denzil

Whitlock Kentersham Fletcher-Hale, I have a warrant here for your arrest under Section 18B of the—'

'Arrest!' Shaffer whirled on Maconachie. 'What the hell is this guy talking about?'

'Under Section 18B of the—' Lubbock tried again.

'You ain't bleeding arresting no one,' shrilled Janice. She flung herself in front of Denzil, arms wide, as if screening him from a hail of machine-gun fire.

'Under Section—'

Caroline sat in paralysed disbelief, impossibly frail in her engulfing sweater.

'Maconachie!' Shaffer grabbed the policeman's arm and pulled him round to face him. 'As sure as there's a tomorrow, man, I'm telling you I'll blow this thing higher than kingdom come! If you think you can frame this man for—'

'Quiet! All of you!' Maconachie subsided quickly. 'I'm sorry. I don't like this any more than you do but, as Lubbock says, we have no choice. Mr Fletcher-Hale has confessed his membership of a proscribed organisation and under the terms of Section 18B of the Defence Regulations we have full powers of arrest. We also have a warrant, duly signed by a magistrate. Now be sensible, all of you. You won't achieve anything by obstructing the police. Mr Fletcher-Hale will accompany us to Bow Street where formal charges will be laid.'

'What about a hearing?' Shaffer interrupted.

Maconachie looked uncomfortable.

'I'm afraid that's nothing to do with me, sir. That's up to ... other authorities.'

'I'll want to appear on his behalf—' began Shaffer.

'Me too!' cried Janice. 'Just let me get in that bloody box, mate. I'll tell 'em a thing or two about police bloody brutality.'

'You'll do as you're bloody well told or—' Lubbock shouted.

'*Officer!*' Denzil's raised voice was immense; it cut through Lubbock's anger and bounded around the big room. He lowered it to a conversational drawl. 'Officer. Lubbock, yes? Must insist. Little more circumspect, what? Speaking to a lady, d'you see.'

Janice clamped herself to his good arm with a little cry and buried her face in his chest. Denzil peeled her off gently.

'Mustn't delay. Bound to be an explanation. Must go with them. Have their job to do, what?' He twitched his head at Maconachie and strolled to the partition shielding the door. He produced his tortured scowl of a smile for Shaffer. 'Look after the ladies, Shaffer? Good chap. Get them home. Busy day. Must be tired. Hungry too. Nothing since Cambridge.' He made to go but stopped. 'Ah — Janice?'

Her eyes went round with pleasure at his use of her name. 'Don't you worry, love,' she said proudly, her face aflame. 'If this lot think I'm going to let them keep you in. . . .'

He scowled at her warmly. 'Meant to tell you. Sing like an angel at the Ritz. Lovely voice.'

Lubbock pushed him out.

Janice stared after him, her face blank; then it flickered and creased and tears glistened in her eyes. Shaffer raised his hands, palms up, in a gesture of helplessness, but she was still staring at the point where Denzil had disappeared.

'I liked him ever so much,' she said in a small voice.

Sunday, 1745

He made up the lie on the way to Nelson's Green in the taxicab and repeated it to Janice twice. She nodded but said nothing; the life had gone out of her and there was no way he could replace it It worried him.

The cabbie pulled into Baltic Street and Shaffer helped Janice from the capacious rear seat. The injuries she had so lightly dismissed an hour or so earlier now seemed to weigh on her heavily and she groaned as he levered her out on to the street. He knocked at the door and Arthur Scully opened it. His face dropped.

'Christ al-bloody-mighty, Jan. What you been doing?'

Shaffer moved in fast. 'Hi. Mr Scully? Mel Shaffer. I just chanced on your daughter-in-law in Tooley Street. She was on her way home when the second alert went. Took a bit of blast, I think.'

Arthur's arms encircled the girl and swept her off her feet. He

547

shouldered his way through the door and dropped her on the front parlour bed. Elsie and Flo came to join them, saw Janice's swollen face and pushed Arthur out of the way.

'What happened, Mr Shaffer?' Elsie asked over her shoulder.

He told her the lie.

'Oh, thank Gawd she's alive,' Flo Scully keened on the edge of tears. 'She must've been on her way back from that Maureen's. Oh, Mr Shaffer. . . .'

He said, 'I was on my way to ask if I could see young Paul. I have something for him back at my office.'

Arthur studied him thoughtfully. 'Every time you come to this house, Mr Shaffer, it's to get one of us out of a scrape. Paul's O.K. I'll get Jack to fix up a time when you can go in and see him. Buck him to bits, that would. But there's something else.' He told the American about Gladys's escape, Derek's death and his and Jack Warrender's decision to send the women away to Taunton on Tuesday.

'Can I see her? Gladys?'

'She's asleep, old son. Best not, eh? But I'd take it as a personal favour if you'd come and help us see 'em off down Paddington Station on Tuesday. Half past midday.'

Shaffer had to be content with that.

TUESDAY
17 September

Tuesday, 0845

Maconachie insisted on driving with them to the airport. It was his way of displaying sympathy, decided Shaffer, and maybe of conveying a comradeship with them in suffering. He had shown no hostility when Shaffer presented himself at Bow Street yesterday afternoon with a note authorising him to see Fletcher-Hale off at Croydon. The note was signed by the Cabinet secretary; a fact which did more for Denzil's standing among the Security policemen than it did for Shaffer's. Any man, they reasoned, who could recruit the Cabinet secretary to his side within hours of being frog-marched out of the country was a force to be reckoned with. That kind of string-pulling called for real influence. Shaffer had seen it in their faces. Maconachie's too.

The reality was not that dramatic.

It was true that enormous efforts had been made over the past two days to prise Denzil from the grasp of the Security Police. His father and mother, a formidable pair of medieval battle-axes whom Shaffer had met yesterday morning, had travelled down to London from Scotland to petition, harry and bend every friend, contact and moral debtor they could find. It all proved fruitless, the old man told him. He was a couple of inches shorter than Denzil but a white beard and flowing moustache did wonders for his projection and he had seemed to fill the Stranger's Bar at the House of Commons where they met early to talk with his local Member of Parliament. Sir Torin Fletcher-Hale gave up only when it was pointed out to him that his personal exertions could be interpreted as a strike against his son's interests. For the same reason, he was advised not to accompany Denzil to the airport.

Shaffer had been less bothered by obscure ethical considerations and had called on Charles Russell. Monday morning had turned out to be a good moment at 25 Garfield Court. The family was at one. Caroline had obviously talked at length with Elizabeth and her father and, whatever her problem, it had been dissected and buried or simply waived for the greater mental comfort of all concerned. Russell gave no hint that he might be embarrassed at going to the top on Shaffer's behalf and at two o'clock yesterday afternoon he had phoned the office in Hill Street to say that he'd pulled it off and the note could be collected from him at the Air Ministry. Shaffer would be allowed to see his friend on to the plane.

The drive from town, with Denzil sandwiched between Shaffer and Maconachie, was not the most relaxed journey ever made and conversation was limited to the list Shaffer had compiled for him of friends and business contacts in New York. Security had decided to despatch Denzil to America — deport was not a word in official use in this case — and apart from a requirement imposed on him to report at regular intervals to any British consular office, he was free to make of his life there what he could. Denzil's transparent *naïveté* throughout his cross-examination at Bow Street had done much to influence this decision. But Defence Regulation 18B could not be ignored; just bent a little.

In fact, Denzil was the only member of the trio to appear undismayed by the funereal drive south-westwards from London. For a man who had spent two nights and a day in a cell he was miraculously unscathed. His suit was impeccable, his shoes buffed and his Eton tie perfectly knotted under a stiff white collar. Maconachie had escorted him to his chambers in Half Moon Street last night and allowed him to pack. He confided to Shaffer that he had been appalled at Denzil's idea of bare necessities for travelling — two cabin-trunks and three overweight suitcases — but he didn't have it in him to point out that officially one suitcase was considered sufficient. The cabin-trunks were to be sent by sea. The suitcases bulged in the Wolseley's boot, so fat in their burnished leatherwork that the boot-lid would not close.

Maconachie handed them over to Immigration when they

arrived at Croydon and made his farewells. There was clearly a great deal he wanted to say but his rigid professionalism prevented him giving voice to it. He shook hands with Denzil and told Shaffer he would wait for him outside in the car. The Immigration officer promptly locked them both in his office. Maconachie, Shaffer learned later, became aware of this final insult and minutes later the Immigration man returned. He led them across the departure lounge to an office and, through that, to another.

'You'll want a cup of coffee, I suppose,' he said grudgingly. 'The officer inside'll look after you.' He closed the door on them but this time didn't lock it.

'Well, I'll be buggered! Den, me old mate! Melville!'

Freddie Green was tilted back in a deep chair, his feet on the corner of a desk and a tin mug of coffee steaming at his lips. They couldn't have been more astounded if he had been the King of England.

Freddie swung his feet to the floor, banged down his mug and came across to pump their hands delightedly.

'Well, this is what I call real friends,' he said. There was no doubting his sincerity. 'Bloody hell! Thought they was going to sneak me out of here like a bad smell. Wouldn't let me see no one since—'

'No talking there!' rasped the uniformed police sergeant, moving forward protectively.

'Oh, come orf it!' Freddie expostulated. 'Someone a bleeding sight more important than you must've said it was O.K. them being here.'

The sergeant squared his shoulders. 'The gentleman here' — he nodded briefly at Denzil — 'is on his way out, same as you. He's under guard till he's on the plane.'

Freddie Green's porcelain smile wavered between outright disbelief and dismay. 'He talking about you, Den?'

Fletcher-Hale produced the scowl of a smile and nodded his head. 'Same boat, what?'

'You!'

Shaffer broke in. 'They pinned some crazy rap on him. He didn't even know it was against the law.'

Freddie subsided into his chair, completely deflated. 'But wha
was the charge, for Christ's sake?'

'Belonged to a club ... association they call it. Banned, d'yo
see? Pro-German, they tell me. Dare say they're right. Polic
know their job, what? Can't say I knew, m'self. Joined a
Oxford.'

'Lemme get this straight.' Freddie scuffed at his brow with a
finely gloved hand. 'You telling me they're chucking you out
for joining a bleeding *club*?'

'It's called The Link,' said Shaffer.

'But old Den, here — he ain't political, Melville. I mean, surely
someone told 'em that much?'

'We all told them. It didn't get us anywhere.'

Green reached for his mug and studied the grey-brown liquid.
'Buggers! Wouldn't listen, o'course. Never do when you're on
the up-and-up. Gotta have something on *them* before they'll
listen.'

The officer said smartly, 'You gentlemen want some coffee?
It's getting cold.'

They both declined.

'Where they sending you then, Den?'

'America, actually. New York first stop.'

'Ireland, me.' Freddie made a face but the grin wouldn't stay
under for long. He brightened. 'You and me oughta correspond,
Den.' He dug under his check Ulster for the wallet in his inside
jacket pocket. The sergeant moved forward again. 'All right. All
right. It's only me bloody card, mate. You already frisked me
once.' He slipped a card from the wallet and handed it to Denzil,
who read it thoughtfully.

'Not much for writing,' he drawled. 'Drop you a line, though.
Keep in touch.'

Freddie tapped the side of his nose. 'You make sure you do,
my old son. I got a lot of mates in America. High-ups. Just do
you, some of 'em. Society people, businessmen, bankers, that
kind of thing. Got a job over there, have you?'

'Job?' Denzil looked pained. 'Job, no. Look around. Meet a
few chaps. Shaffer's been jolly decent. Lots of contacts.'

Freddie nodded without enthusiasm. 'Well, you mind what I

told you, eh? You get stuck, drop me a line. Old Freddie sticks by his mates, don't you worry yourself.'

Shaffer said suspiciously, 'What did they get *you* on?'

'That's enough!' snapped their guard. 'This man is bound over under the Official Secrets Acts.'

Freddie winked at them. 'Touch of the old privilege. Trustee, like. Mustn't grumble.'

'Every dog has his day,' Shaffer said sourly.

Green eyed him without animosity.

'Don't get your knickers in a twist, Melville. Fortunes of war, ennit? I mean to say, look at us two here; me and Den. Doing our bit, I'd say, both of us. Old Den getting hisself all teed-up to fight for his country best way he could; and me . . . I was getting on with me war work and, sort of on the side, keeping a few people happy who had the brunt of the bloody fighting. So what do the buggers do? They do *me*—'

'I warned you!' threatened the police sergeant.

'Oh, piss orf!' said Freddie conversationally. 'They do *me* for putting a bit of colour into the lives of the fighting men and they do *Den* for belonging to some bleeding club what was political without him knowing about it. I mean to say — honest, though! — what are decent blokes like him and me supposed to think? I ask you!'

'Don't tell me you think you and Denzil are—'

''Course I don't! I know *Den*. Pure as the driven snow. *I* know that. *You* know that. But they' — he jerked his thumb over his shoulder at the police sergeant — '*they* don't know and it's what *they* think what counts. War, you see. Different rules. That's why I'm saying to you, don't get your knickers in a twist. There ain't no fair and unfair in war. There's winning and there's losing, that's all. Being after winning, you have to close your eyes sometimes, when you're the government, to things what aren't strictly fair, because you can't take a chance on being wrong, see? Don't you worry, Melville. We'll come through this, me and Den.'

The door rattled open from the outside and a grey-faced man of middle age poked his head around into the room.

'Captain Green?' he said politely. Shaffer bridled at the use of the rank.

'Right, old son. On the way, are we?'

'Your plane leaves in two minutes. Perhaps you'll be good enough to come now. All the other passengers are aboard.'

The grey man eyed the sergeant. 'You'll carry Captain Green's bags to the plane, will you, officer?'

Tuesday, 1215

The police driver performed a madman's chase carving through the dense lunchtime traffic like a racetrack ace, but it took nearly an hour and a half to make the trip. He pulled the Wolseley to a tyre-screaming halt under the covered way at the entrance to Paddington Station and Shaffer scrambled out.

Maconachie yelled after him, 'I'll wait for you.'

They stood in a disconsolate little group at the barrier, reluctant refugees in an ocean of frenzied activity. The platforms were crowded; kitbag-carrying soldiers and airmen, R.A.F. officers, gaitered sailors, a whole covey of women in the distinctive grey uniforms and scarlet cowls of Queen Alexandra's Royal Army Nursing Corps; shabby civilians in shapeless, stiff-shouldered dresses and baggy, drooping suits; a crocodile of children collared with parcel labels giving their names and forwarding addresses. There were postmen unloading mail-vans and porters hauling deep-wheeled trolleys, and over all came the boom of loudspeaker announcements in a language that might have been Serbo-Croat.

Their faces lit up as he came towards them and with more than passing surprise he saw that Elizabeth Russell and Caroline were with them. Elizabeth saved him the embarrassment of deciding what his first move, first words, should be. She fluttered across the platform and threw her arms around his neck. The others looked on with varying degrees of discomfort.

'Oh, thank goodness you've come, Mel,' she breathed. She was incapable of embarrassment. 'You don't know what they've been thinking. Come and talk. They haven't got long.'

554

Caroline smiled shyly but Elsie, taking her courage and her shame in both hands, uttered a single blub of remorse and clutched at him possessively. Her husband Jack looked on with an expression finely hung between pleasure and regret; then he peeled her off him and shook hands. Arthur followed suit. Flo stood to one side, shy and afraid and locked up in herself, fearing to show emotion of any kind in case it led to the one emotion she daren't release. Shaffer bent over her and kissed her on both cheeks. He could taste the salt of old spilled tears.

'Wotcher, old Mel.' Janice, he reminded himself, was a survivor; she had the survivor's knack of coming up after a ten-count looking like the newborn day.

'You O.K.?' he asked.

'Right as ninepence,' said Flo, blushing from the kisses. 'Nothing wrong with our Jan. Tough as boots, she is.'

'Telling all my secrets to a strange man, mum! You'll get me a reputation, you will. She managed to blow one of her goldfish pouts without the others seeing her and he came close to a belly laugh.

Then it died cold. Gladys's voice was low. 'I'm glad you could come, Mel. I told them you'd come.'

He walked to her, stopped before his hand made the mistake of reaching for hers.

'I wouldn't have stayed away, you know that.' They stared at each other, unable to pretend for the benefit of the others. 'I just put Denzil on the New York plane.'

'Den?' Janice tugged him round by the sleeve of his jacket. 'Is he...? I mean'—she produced a hard, bright smile—'did he say anything?'

He drooped the lid of his right eye fractionally. 'He said he was going to miss us,' he lied. 'But he'll write, if they give him half a chance.'

The smile softened and withered and her eyes glazed. She turned away and rummaged in her handbag, drew out a handkerchief and blew her nose sharply.

Gladys was the only one to spot the deliberate mistake but she lowered her eyes quickly to conceal her thoughts. She looked up again to find Shaffer's eyes on her.

Could I. . . ?' he began diffidently.

Elsie Warrender came to his rescue. 'Jack, Arthur, Flo — we better check these bags before we go any farther. Madam dear, could you give me a hand for a minute?'

He pulled Gladys away while they scrummed around trying to look unaware.

'Mr Scully told me what happened on Saturday. I wanted to see you Sunday but. . . .'

'It's finished.' His stomach lurched at the way she said it. 'Derek didn't know anything. He died before he knew what was happening.'

'Will you be gone long?' He needed an answer to that.

'I don't know. I sent the club my address in case they want me back.'

'Can I come down to Taunton to see you?'

She shook her head. 'That wouldn't be very clever, would it?' She searched his face. 'Janice is coming too.'

'So?' His throat was tightening. She knew. She knew!

'She wouldn't be satisfied with letters from a man in New York.' Either she was being very clever or he'd missed a chapter somewhere along the line.

'Will you come up to town sometime? On a weekend, say?'

Her eyes were troubling her; flickering to stem the flow. 'You don't really want me to come back, Mel. You just think that's what you ought to say.'

He grabbed both her hands roughly and shook them hard. 'I told you once before. Don't try to tell me what I'm thinking.' His voice had risen involuntarily and he dropped it back to whisper pitch. 'I'll get the address from your father. I'll write. And I don't expect to write to someone I can't see now and again. Now — have you got that fixed in that spaghetti-ball you use for a brain?'

She blinked away the tears. 'Can't stop you writing, can I? Doesn't mean I have to open the letters.' She was smiling now. She'd open the letters.

Arthur Scully cleared his military throat and tugged his beautifully pressed uniform jacket into place.

'Time you were off, mother,' he said loudly, as if there was no one there but Flo. 'Give us a kiss then, old love.'

Flo gave out a little cry and fell into his arms. Elsie straightened up from one of the cases, looked at them, felt her lip tremble and clutched at Jack so hard he nearly lost his balance. The two wives snuffled in their respective husbands' shoulders, then changed places and snuffled some more. The men pecked Janice on the cheek and enfolded Gladys, who immediately lost all control and burst into tears. Elizabeth waited for Elsie to disentangle herself and then hugged her before handing her over to Caroline.

The train for Taunton clanked and clonked busily as the locomotive arrived at the far end and coupled on. The last goodbyes were shouted, the last hugs and tears shed, then Arthur Scully shepherded them firmly through the gate. Shaffer stuck close to Gladys but her father embraced her one last time and Janice grasped the diversion to bring her lips to his ear from behind.

'I'm going to wait for him, old Mel,' she whispered. 'I'll be back and I'll wait for him. Will you. . . ?' He didn't get the rest but he nodded. She really believed it. Lady Janice. He watched her tippy-tap away along the train, looking for an empty carriage, the long, flat backside flaunting its voluptuous roll.

Gladys pulled out of her father's arms and Jack Warrender averted his head as she placed her hands on Shaffer's chest.

'I *will* open the letters, Mel. Honest.'

She stretched up on tiptoes, pressed her mouth hard on his, turned and ran after her mother. Jack and Arthur finally piled them into a carriage and a minute later the whistle sounded and the train pulled out. They waved from the open windows until they were carried out of sight around a bend.

It was Elizabeth's turn to cry but she did it with a flair that made it seem proper without being weak.

'I won't know what to do without her,' she sniffed. 'Fourteen years. . . .'

Caroline put an arm around her mother's shoulders. 'She'll be back, mummy. You'll see.'

'Right you are, young lady,' snarled Arthur, stiffening up to

557

ie proud, unyielding standards of his uniform. 'She'll be
one day. They'll all be back.'

A soft misty look took the sting out of his rock-carved face.
'Mother and Elsie and the girls and my boy Geoff too. All be
back.' He sniffed loudly. 'Right then, Jack. Can't stand around.
I got to get to work and old Braithwaite'll be doing his nut if
you're not back on the beat soon.'

'We'll drive you back,' said Elizabeth.

'Oh, no, ma'am,' said Arthur tactfully. 'That wouldn't do.'

'Mr Scully.' Elizabeth drew herself up. 'We're on the same
side, aren't we? Besides, I've never driven a soldier to war.'

At the station entrance Shaffer said goodbye to them.

'See you again will we, Mr Shaffer?' Jack ventured hopefully.

He looked around their faces – Arthur, Jack, Elizabeth and
Caroline. He grinned.

'As the lady said, we're on the same side, aren't we?'

Ted Willis
The Lions of Judah £1.25

The year is 1939 and war looms. The Nazis, at the peak of their power, hound the Jews with vicious malevolence. Kurt Reiss is Jewish, and determined to fight for his people — whatever the cost. When he is captured, after an assassination attempt on Goering, he knows his hour has come. But he is wrong. Instead, he is offered a deal he dare not refuse, and where the penalty for failure is unthinkable in its consequences...

'Willis is a born storyteller' DAILY MAIL

Alan Scholefield
Point of Honour 95p

It was the perfect subject for a book: Captain Geoffrey Baines Turner VC killed in action on the bloodstained French coast — and who better than his son to write the story of one man's Dunkirk? David Turner begins his research and uncovers a vipers' nest of half-truths, malicious rumour and blackmail. His father, revered by some as a hero, is branded rapist and murderer by others...

'Completely believable' DAILY TELEGRAPH

Matthew Vaughan
Major Stepton's War £1.25

Gervase Stepton, a major in the Confederate army, has seen the brutality and experienced the agony that makes a soldier the killing machine he is. Serving under General Lee and the legendary Stonewall Jackson, he fights at the blood-soaked battle of Bull Run. Captured, Stepton suffers savage torture at Fort Delaware. Sure as hell he'll kill the Yankee bastards who slaughtered his family back home in Virginia. A tale of vengeance wreaked from the whorehouses of Richmond to the battlefields of Manassas and Malvern.

Sharpe
Throwback 95p

'The tale of an illegitimate member of the squirearchy earning his inheritance by increasingly nasty methods – gassing, suing, whipping, blowing up, killing, stuffing – is both inventive and pacy'
NEW STATESMAN

'Black humour and comic anarchy at its best' SUNDAY TIMES

'A savage delight' DAILY MIRROR

Hedger Wallace
End Quiet War 85p

In the green stinking hell of Malaya, jungle warfare was never more brutal. Leading an exhausted army patrol through terrorist-infested country was one hell of a responsibility for young Sergeant Feer – especially when the terrorist leader is the notorious Leu Kim. The possibility of an exchange of prisoners brings hope . . . but are agonizing torture and hideous mutilation the only weapons Leu Kim understands?

Don Bannister
Sam Chard £1.25

'A full-length portrait of a Yorkshire mining village in the thirties . . . children at play or going unwillingly to school, men at work, in the pub, performing the *Messiah* . . . lovers (lots of them) behind hedges . . . the drunkard's closing-time homecoming and an incestuous father battered to the ground by his daughters. An exceptional novel' GUARDIAN

'The pit life is hard and dangerous . . . beer, women, brutality. Moving and absorbing . . . true to the last word' DAILY TELEGRAPH

Leslie Thomas
That Old Gang of Mine £1.25

Meet ODDS — the Ocean Drive Delinquent Society — a band of geriatric drop-outs chasing excitement and danger in their twilight years in the Florida sun. There's Ari the Greek, K-K-K-K-Katy the dancing queen, Molly Mandy who supplies the gang's arms cache (and one and only bullet), and ex-hood Sidewalk Joe.

Hot on their heels comes the baffled Salvatore, local police captain, and bumbling private eye Zaharran. Never was organized crime so disorganized.

'Hilarious' DAILY MIRROR

Patrick Alexander
Show Me a Hero £1.25

nto the 1980s, a tyranny of the Left rules Britain with Saracen troop carriers, while propaganda cloaks the corpses. Backs to the wall, the Resistance plans Operation Volcano, while up at the sharp end of every strike is the man they call the Falcon — a Robin Hood with an Uzi machine-gun and nerves of steel. One of nature's heroes, temporarily useful, ultimately expendable ...

Colin Dexter
Service of all the Dead £1.25

Churchwarden murdered during service the headlines screamed. Inspector Morse found there was more to it than that. After the second death the case was closed ; everyone agreed that the murderer had gone on to commit suicide.

Everyone, that is, except Morse. He sensed that unrest still reigned over the Oxford parish of St Frideswide. He found new evidence and discrepancies ; and then, another body.

He pulls off his tricks with confidence and cunning' GUARDIAN

Wilbur Smith
Wild Justice £1.50

It began in the Seychelles. A seductive, ice-cool blonde slips through customs. Once on the plane, she is revealed as a deadly terrorist, well versed in the art of jet hijacking. At Johannesburg, the stench of death is only a bullet away for the plane's 400 eminent passengers. Anti-terrorist chief Peter Stride sets out to find the sinister power-brain behind a band of ruthless fanatics — a search carrying him across continents towards an explosive climax in the scorched deserts of Galilee.

'Cold-blooded horror' EVENING NEWS

Paula Gosling
The Zero Trap £1.25

After a ruthless skyjack, nine hostages are held in a remote Arctic hideout. Escape can only mean slow, agonizing death in sub-zero temperatures. Amongst them — a beautiful nightclub singer, a seemingly harmless professor, a convicted murderer awaiting trial, an army sergeant with a nasty secret ... Thrown together by fate in a moment of terror, they come to face a reality more terrifying than being held hostage by faceless criminals — will they be found alive?

Jack M. Bickham
The Excalibur Disaster £1.50

Transwestern Flight 161 is a new Excalibur jet, *en route* from St Louis to New York. The 199 passengers will never step from the plane alive. The crash is a mystery. The cause — pilot error? systems failure? — lies hidden in a smoky heap of metal and bodies at Kennedy Airport. One of those bodies was Jason Baines, head of Hempstead Aviation, makers of the Excalibur. The horrible truth begins to dawn on investigator Jace Mattingly. There are other Excaliburs flying, and in each one a tiny, undetected flaw ...

Garson Kanin
Moviola £1.50

The Hollywood novel that tells it all.

Meet 92-year-old B. J. Farber, rich and cantankerous, a movie mogul about to sell his legendary studios. This is his story – the scandals, heartbreaks, passions and mysteries – Fatty Arbuckle's sex disgrace, Chaplin the comic genius, Garbo's tragic romance, the discovery of Monroe and her mysterious death, the trials and backroom feuds behind some of the greatest films ever made.

'More film stars' real secrets than there are footprints in the cement of Hollywood Boulevard' DAILY MAIL

Kahlil Gibran
The Prophet £1.25

Poet, philosopher and artist, Kahlil Gibran's work has been translated into more than twenty languages, and his drawings and paintings have been exhibited in the great capitals of the world. Now, for the first time in paperback, here is his most mystical, most powerful work, illustrated with his enchanting, haunting drawings.

Emma Cave
The Blood Bond £1.25

Eleven years ago, three people sealed a terrible secret in blood. Now, they meet again in London – Esther, the apparently cool career girl, a slave to sexual passion ; Brian, the frivolous Chelsea idler who courts violence by night ; Charles, the smooth social charmer with the pale eyes ... Terror mounts as the past exerts its fearful spell and the games of a summer night merge into a bloody day of reckoning.

'Entirely original, entirely enjoyable ... Emma Cave has mastered the secret of horror story writing' AUBERON WAUGH, EVENING STANDARD

Lord Kilbracken
Bring Back My Stringbag £1.50
a Swordfish pilot at war

Vigorous, honest, at times hilarious, this account by Lord Kilbracken of his five years in the Fleet Air Arm during the last war provides a remarkable picture of the Swordfish aircraft (jokingly known as 'Stringbags'), seemingly 'left in the war by mistake', and the oddball characters who flew them. The author experienced every hazard that could confront a shipborne pilot – torpedo and bomb attacks, mines, flak-filled skies and ditching in mid Atlantic, coming through with his courage and offbeat humour undaunted.

Ian Skidmore
Lifeboat VC £1.00

The heroic story of Coxswain Dick Evans, a man with the special sort of courage needed to step deliberately into danger. For over half a century he has been associated with the Moelfre lifeboat in Anglesey, guarding perilous stretches of British waters and taking part in dramatic rescues. This thrilling account of the only lifeboatman to hold two RNLI gold medals (the equivalent of the Victoria Cross) allows us to share the extraordinary life of a man who has always lived by the sea and whose courage has been an inspiration to many others.